Forever

Also by Pete Hamill

Novels

A Killing for Christ
The Gift
Dirty Laundry
Flesh and Blood
The Deadly Piece
The Guns of Heaven
Loving Women
Snow in August

Short Story Collections

The Invisible City
Tokyo Sketches

Journalism

Irrational Ravings
Tools as Art
Piecework
News Is a Verb

Memoir

A Drinking Life

Biography

Diego Rivera
Why Sinatra Matters

Praise for Pete Hamill's

Forever

"Pete Hamill's entertaining panhistorical fantasy is a paean to New York's immortality."
— *The New Yorker*

"Hamill's knowledgeable love for the city and his writerly exuberance explode here into a New York fantasy: big, extravagant, untrammeled, and as hugely readable as it must have been hugely entertaining to write. . . . *Forever* is old-fashioned storytelling at a gallop."
— Frances Taliaferro, *Washington Post Book World*

"Hamill's inspired descriptions of contemporary Manhattan are as pitch-perfect as only love and understanding, and possibly grief, can engender. . . . A vivid, gratifying, and ultimately uplifting tale about choosing life over death."
— Jodi Daynard, *Boston Globe*

"Pete Hamill conjures a New York that's impossible to leave."
— *Time Out New York*

"While essentially a work of historical fiction, *Forever* is also Hamill's take on lust for life, honor, and vengeance, and how the distinctions between the latter two are sometimes vague."
— Tom Walker, *Denver Post*

"Hamill has constructed a tabloid epic in a folkloric American style. . . . The premise: In the mid-1700s, a young New Yorker receives the gift of immortality on the condition that he never leaves Manhattan." — Troy Patterson, *Entertainment Weekly*

"Cormac O'Connor is able to drink straight from the fountain of epic adventure. . . . Hamill chronicles the ages of Manhattan from its tooth-and-claw infancy and ruthless corruption, through two centuries of pulsing vitality and metamorphosis, to our day's ashen taste of Armageddon — through one man's eyes and memory." — Kai Maristed, *Los Angeles Times*

"This rousing, ambitious work is beautifully woven around historical events and characters, but it is Hamill's passionate pursuit of justice and compassion — Celtic in foundation — that distinguishes this tale of New York City and its myriad peoples."

— *Publishers Weekly*

"*Forever* pays mystical tribute to durable New York."

— Bob Minzesheimer, *USA Today*

"*Forever* is a masterpiece that will warm the hearts of all readers with its sweep of history against the color and backdrop of New York. . . . Hamill is a skilled storyteller with Manhattan in his genes." — John J. Daly, *Waterbury Republican*

"Cunningly written, observant, violent, ribald, profane, coarse. . . . *Forever* is, indeed, full of life."

— Alan Cochrum, *Fort Worth Star-Telegram*

"An epic landscape. . . . A novel about New York that is as challenging and rewarding as the city itself. . . . As Cormac matures, so does the city, and through the lyricism of Mr. Hamill's writing New York itself becomes a character, and whether it's the cholera epidemic of 1832 or the attack on the World Trade Center, the reader feels for the city." — Colin Miner, *New York Sun*

"*Forever* is an impressive primer on how New York came to be the focal city of the world. Its history, splendid and sordid, is rich in anecdote and interest and Hamill — a New York born cheerleader — is just the skilled writer to breathe life into this skyscraper-tall tale. . . . *Forever* is big. . . . A historical novel in the grand tradition with an icing of Irish mystery, Caribbean voodoo, and in-your-face New York brashness."

— G. William Gray, *Tampa Tribune*

"An epic in the classical sense. . . . We watch as New York grows and changes, turning from a provincial outpost into an ethnically and culturally diverse world capital. . . . Cormac O'Connor's final lesson is so stunning in its strength and simplicity that even the most sophisticated and skeptical of readers may find themselves seeing their world in a fresh light, remembering *Forever* for a long time to come." — Jeff Lodge, *Richmond Times-Dispatch*

Forever

a novel

PETE HAMILL

BACK BAY BOOKS
Little, Brown and Company
Boston New York London

Originally published in hardcover by Little, Brown and Company, December 2002
First Back Bay paperback edition, November 2003

The characters and events in this book are fictitious. Any similarity to real persons, living or dead, is coincidental and not intended by the author.

ISBN 0-316-34111-8 (hc) / 0-316-73569-8 (pb)
Library of Congress Control Number 2002114241

10 9 8 7 6 5 4 3 2 1

Q-MART

Printed in the United States of America

This book is for
Fukiko Aoki Hamill,
who let me count the ways

Forever

ONE

Ireland

And what a people loves it will defend.
We took their temples from them and forbade them,
for many years, to worship their strange idols.
They gathered in secret, deep in the dripping glens,
Chanting their prayers before a lichened rock.

— John Hewitt, "The Colony," 1950

1.

There he is, three days after his fifth birthday, standing barefoot upon wet summer grass. He is staring at the house where he lives: the great good Irish place of whitewashed walls, long and low, with a dark slate roof glistening in the morning drizzle. Standing there, he knows it will turn pale blue when the sun appears to work its magic.

The boy named Robert Carson loves gazing at that house, basking in its permanence and comfort. On some days, a wisp of smoke rises from the chimney. On other days, the early-morning sun throws a golden glaze upon its white facade. It is never the same and always the same. He sees the small windows like tiny eyes in the face of the house, the glass reflecting the rising sun. The front door is mahogany, salvaged from some drowned ship along the shores of the Irish Sea, as tightly fitted in that doorway now as any man could make it. There's a low half-door too, placed in front of the full mahogany door like a snug wooden apron. During balmy summer days, the large door is always open, welcoming light and air into the house. The breeze pushes smoke from the fire up through the stone chimney.

Robert Carson goes in, flipping the iron latches made by his father, whose name is John Carson and is called simply Da. The house is as it always is and as the boy thinks it will always be. A sweet odor of burning turf fills the air. He breathes it deeply, inhaling the ancient burned mud of the swamps beside Lough Neagh, where the peat was cut from the bog. Directly facing him is the jamb wall, running from floor to ceiling along the side of the hearth. A diamond-shaped spy hole is cut into its pine boards so that he and his father and mother can observe the approach of strangers. The boy can only do this by standing on the shoulder of the hearth.

The hearth is at the end of a large main room, but it is the center of the house, the holy place that holds the fire. A wide iron canopy rises above the hearth, carrying away the smoke, and on damp, chilly days the boy sits on one of the hand-carved low benches beside the fire. The family has few visitors, but men always sit on the right, facing the fire, so the boy does the same. The women take the bench on the left, and his mother is always there. Her name is Rebecca, but he calls her Ma. He thinks of them as a unit: Ma, Da, and me. The Carsons. To the left of the hearth is the small iron crane his father made in the forge, with its arms of different lengths, and hooks for hanging pots. His mother moves the pots back and forth, in and out of the flame, while the odors of stews and porridges and soups overwhelm the sweetness of the burning turf. There are two low three-legged chairs called "creepies," cousins of milking stools. Built low in the days before chimney flues so that farmers could breathe below the smoke. One day he lifted a creepy, examined the perfect pegs that held the legs so permanently to the seat, and hugged it to his chest, thinking: This is ours, this belongs to the Carsons. Back about five feet from the hearth is his father's own chair, made of woven rush, looking like a throne designed as a beehive. Robert Carson never sits in his father's chair.

Beside his father's chair is one of the many wrought-iron light holders that John Carson made in the forge, long iron poles with four arched feet and hooks that hold lanterns for his reading. They never wobble on the flagstone floor, never lose their dignity.

A wide oaken shelf spreads above the hearth and he can see with his eyes shut the objects that occupy its oiled surface: his father's clay pipes, with their long curved stems, an old thatched horse collar that Da saved from his own youth, a carved wooden cup called a noggin, found in the mud of a bog. Da has told the boy that the noggin is a thousand years old, and Robert Carson is certain that his father is right. To the left, a mound of turf bricks rises off the floor, dried out of dark black bottom mud. The iron tools of the fire, smaller cousins of the light holders, stand as rigid as sentries.

* * *

All are part of the hearth, where the fire burns low but is never allowed to go out. As the center of the house, the hearth gives off warmth and food, and is the place to which the Carsons turn in the evenings for talk and even song. On his birthday, while they faced the hearth, his mother told the boy that his magic number would be nine, for he was born on the ninth of September.

"Do you see, son? You were born on the ninth day of the ninth month," his mother said, "and as you grow up, lad, you'll learn: Nine will be your number."

Sometimes on rainy afternoons, when his father is working in the forge, the boy's mother sits beside the fire to drink tea and eat oat bread while she tells stories. The boy listens silently, the stories entering him in such a way that he later thinks they have happened to him, that he has lived them. Sometimes he drowses, while her voice makes a kind of music. They are the first stories of his life, written on a five-year-old's emptiness. He is awake and asleep at the same time, listening to the magical words, while becoming through his mother's magic the people in the stories. The fire burns steadily in the hearth, and his mother tells him that the fire should never be allowed to go out, because if it does, the soul leaves the house.

Da agrees. There were houses in Ireland, he said once, where the fire had burned day and night for more than a hundred years. In this house, he said, it had burned since John and Rebecca Carson moved in, long ago, before the boy was born. Even as she whispers stories, his mother gazes at the fire, as if seeing people or things unseen by others. Robert Carson later learns that before he was born there were two other children, his brothers, who were born and then died in another house. And when they died, Da poured water into the hearth and moved to this place to begin again. Robert Carson tries (after learning this when he is eight) to imagine those lost brothers, but no faces ever come clear. In bad dreams they have heads with shiny surfaces but no eyes or noses or mouths, and those visions wake him from his sleep. Sometimes he is terrified.

To the left of the hearth is the door to the bedroom where his mother and father sleep each night. A dresser stands outside the door, its drawers holding clothes. On its top there's a wooden tray of knives and forks and spoons, along with a clump of gorse or primrose standing in water in the family's only piece of delft: a tall vase decorated with tulips. Sometimes the boy traces with his fingers the designs on the vase, and caresses its smooth surface. Above the dresser three shelves are cut into the wall, stacked with terra-cotta plates and cups and bowls made by hand in the Mountains of Mourne. To the left is the back door, leading to the West. The room is dominated by the table behind the chairs that face the hearth, its dark planed top burnished by endless cleanings and oilings.

Sometimes he stares at the back door, the one that opens to the West. He knows that no stranger should ever leave through the back door because he would take with him the luck of the house. He knows too that when there's a death in the house, the coffin must leave through that same back door, to be taken to the West, to the setting sun and the blackness that follows.

On the ceiling, great beams cut from bog oak form a huge A, supporting the layers of thatch and sod, tied firmly with fir rods, that lie beneath the slates. His father built this house to last. The roof rests on towers of chiseled stone that form the gable ends, each slab thirty inches thick, cut so fine that they fit together without mortar. The walls are brick, stone, cut rushes that had soured, all bound together and made smooth by river mud and lime wash. They are two feet thick. A house built like a fortress. Even when he is alone, he is safe.

2.

*His father was a blacksmith. John Carson. A tall, silent, clean-*shaven man with fierce cords of muscle in his arms. In his presence, Robert was filled with a sense of the marvelous. His father could lift carriages with those arms and move his mighty anvil without help and swing the heaviest hammer as if it were a fork.

The forge stood about forty yards from the house, at a muddy crossroads beside a stream. A small wooden bridge arched over the stream, part of a post road (the boy soon learned) that carried men and mail on horseback north into Belfast or south toward Dublin. A smaller dirt road moved into the hills behind them or the other way, down to the River Lagan. Sometimes in the night Robert heard horses clattering over the bridge and tried to imagine the places they came from and the places they were going. His father had bought this land because of that bridge and that road. *Those horses need shoes,* he would say. *Those mail carriages need their wheels repaired.*

And so he built his forge first, before he built the house, before Robert came into the world, and put a kind of barn around it, with thin plank walls and a roof above it, not worrying about insulation, since in the heat of the forge and the sweat of his labor he welcomed the wind. There was a corner reserved for fuel: wood at first and then coal or charcoal from England. In another corner he piled a scrap heap with broken shears and ruined horseshoes, pieces of undercarriages, even some lumps of bog iron. All to be melted in the heat ("No metal can resist great heat," he told his son) and then transformed by his marvelous hands into things new and useful and beautiful. In a small room off to the right, he kept his tools: hammers and tongs, chisels and punches, swages and cutters, all hanging on handmade nails. A dozen different hammers: cross peins and straight peins, dressers and chisel makers, round-faced hammers and double-faced hammers, small leaf hammers, soft-faced hammers for cutlery and blunt-faced hammers for making files and rasps, along with hammers that had no names. Five or six sledges leaned against the wall, each head weighing more than five pounds. When he started a new job, he gently caressed each hammer, as if paying his respects, hefting one or two before making his choice. There were tongs too, box tongs and side tongs, straight-lipped tongs and wedge tongs, and a dozen handmade tongs of his own design; sharp-faced chisels, with handles and without; a box full of punches, shaped like hearts or shamrocks, for special decorations; a selection of swage blocks, along with shears and drills and bits. The boy's mother told him that she and his father lived in that tool room until the day the roof was placed on the house, while a fiddler played and men danced with women until the rising of the moon. That day, or rather, that night, they went into the house and set the fire in the hearth they believed would last for the rest of their lives.

The forge was the heart of the shop, as the hearth was the soul of the house. It was the place where metal was made soft in order to be worked, and his father had built it himself, using a combination of cut stone and brick from a kiln in Belfast. In Robert's eyes, the forge resembled a kind of unroofed fort, with the fire burning on a cast-iron grate about a foot below the parapets, all of it about thirty inches above the ground and forty inches square. No marauding army could ever breach that fort. Or so Robert thought. A bellows was plugged into a pipe that entered the forge from the rear and controlled the intensity of the fire.

At some point, without ceremony, his father gave him the gift of work. He was allowed to work the bellows, with its three flat boards, its upper and lower chambers, its leather casing forcing air through the small valve at the end. Man's work thrilled him. His skin pebbled when he saw the fire suddenly brighten from his own efforts, sparks rising in the air, all of them red, racing for the chimney. Then the rough iron slowly turned red, and then white, and when it was white, more sparks danced like fireflies in the heat. The sweat poured off the boy then, from the heat of the fire, from the pumping of the levers of the bellows, from his excitement, and he wanted to stop, all strength gone, and then glanced at his father, working with his tough intensity, and tried even harder to go on.

"I'll finish that now, lad," his father said to him at certain moments.

"No, Da, I can do it."

"Fair enough," his father said, and smiled to himself.

In those hours in the forge, his father would say almost nothing else.

The smoke and sparks rose from the fire into an iron canopy and then through a metal chimney into the empty sky. On cold, clear winter nights, the boy would sometimes gaze at the distant stars and wonder if they were frozen sparks from his father's forge. He asked his father about this one chilly night.

"Aye," he said. "They all go up into the universe, son."

"Do they ever burn out?"

"Never. When you see a shooting star, lad, that's a spark trying to find its way home."

His father's beliefs were as simple as the things of his life. One of those things in the forge was the great tub he called the slake bath, half a wine cask filled with clear, stagnant water. Across its top were two rods that held a smaller tub — a bowl, really — that contained brine. He needed water to adjust the temperature of whatever he was making, cooling the piece swiftly in the water, or more slowly in the salty brine, and sometimes he would return it to the fire if it had cooled too much.

"The first time you do something," he said, "it might not be perfect. But you can't give up. You must try again."

To Robert, such words seemed to be said that day for the first time in the long history of the world. You can't give up. You must try again. Important things to be said by a master for whom the most important of all the things in that shop was the anvil. It stood a few feet to the left of the forge, a mighty workbench that to his boy's eyes was powerful, mysterious, indestructible, and magical. It was the only object in the shop not made by his father, but John Carson loved it with a passion, the way a fine musician loves a grand piano, and he passed that fervor to his son across a thousand different afternoons.

The anvil had come from Scotland and weighed exactly one hundred and seventy-one pounds. The shape was simple and elegant, a kind of small table with a great curved shoulder called the horn. The body was iron, but the face on top was made of steel two inches thick, welded to the body. From the heel to the tip of the horn, it was about two feet long, the face four inches wide. At the heel of the face, slots were punched through to the bottom: the small round pritchel hole, the wider square slot called the hardie hole. With his tongs, the boy's father could insert hot iron bars in the pritchel hole and bend them into any shape. Or slot his many smaller attachments into the hardie hole. The anvil was nailed to a smoothly planed block of bog oak, which had been driven several feet into the earth floor. A leather strap ran around the top of the oaken base from which hung many smaller tools. Robert swiftly learned that the anvil could sing. When his father struck it with a hammer, the ringing sound rose into the air, and sometimes was answered by the calls of birds.

In all years and all seasons, he could see his father working iron with his back to the forge, using tongs to lift the molten iron from the fire and then laying it in a white lump upon the anvil and with his tools transforming it into a sickle or a horseshoe, a lamp holder or a pot. His long-fingered hands were very quick, and in movement he seemed all of a piece: arms, hands, hammer, metal. Everything was fitted together to create rhythm and ease and power. The face of the anvil, for example, was on a level with his knuckles, the best height discovered by the old ironmasters for swinging hammers without tearing up the muscles of the back. Sometimes he dipped the iron in the water of the slack tub, adjusting the temperature as he worked, his brow furrowed and creased, his legs spread to create a fulcrum, his mighty arms bringing either raw power or fluid delicacy to the task. Sweat poured from him in all seasons. Even in dead winter, his gray collarless cotton shirt turned black. In summer, he often sent the boy to the stream with a pot for fresh water and drank it down, letting it splash over his body and neck before returning to hammer and iron and heat.

When the sun began to set in the west and he was finished for the day, he would hang the bellows on a high hook against one wall, to keep it from small dangerous invaders, then sit a while in silence, and then walk to the house. Six days a week, he scrubbed the smell of salt and sweat from himself with cold water and a coarse cloth. On Saturday nights, after the boy was sent to bed, he bathed in a large wooden waterproof tub lashed with iron bands he'd made himself, the joints so tight not a drop ever touched the flagstone floor.

* * *

One Saturday night when Robert was six, he saw his father enter the new room that he was building as an addition to the house, the room where the boy soon would sleep. Da had broken a hole through from the main room and fitted it with a door. Two new walls were already up, draped with canvas to ward off rain, awaiting only their coat of lime wash. But the western wall was not yet finished. Da entered this unfinished room carrying a lumpy burlap package in one hand and a lantern in the other. His tub awaited him about six feet from the hearth, where two huge iron pots of water simmered beside the open fire, but John Carson was not yet ready for his Saturday-night bath. The boy's mother rested in the bedroom. Robert feigned sleep on his rough bed rigged from a base of stools placed near the jamb wall.

When his father entered the unfinished room, the boy slipped off his cot and eased into the shadows to watch him. His father untied the cords of the burlap package and removed the skull of a horse. Robert's heart tripped. On one of their walks to Belfast that summer, his mother had shown the boy a horse's skull off to the side of the road, bone white and sad. The Carsons did not own a horse, and that lonesome skull made Robert whisper a growing desire: to ride a horse. He told his mother that above all he wanted to ride a horse with his father. His mother hugged him that afternoon, and said, "Aye, a horse. I'll talk about it with your father."

And here on this Saturday night was his father with a horse's skull in a burlap sack. Da gazed at the skull for a long moment, holding it in two hands as if it were a chalice, and then in the light of the lantern, he squatted low and began to mix mortar in a tray, thickening it with dry straw. He placed the skull in a hollow place in the wall, and then used the mortar and some kiln bricks to hide it. He was breathing hard. Then he paused, placed his fingertips against the now-blank wall, bowed his head, and spoke for a minute in a strange clotted language.

Robert hurried back to the makeshift cot, and lay awake with his eyes closed and his heart thumping with excitement. A horse's skull! In the western wall! He heard a smooth click as his father shut the door of the unfinished room, hiding the wall with its new and secret resident. Da's boots fell separately to the floor. He walked on bare feet across the flagstones and knocked gently on the bedroom door. The boy's mother whispered words Robert could not understand. Then she was at the hearth, her smell altering the air, and the boy heard her pouring water into the great tub. Water that gurgled. Water that murmured. Eyes shut tight, the boy heard a rustling of clothes, and then Da's voice saying *Ah!* as he eased into the water. Then there was another unbinding of clothes. Silence. Then she said *Oh!*

Robert opened his eyes. Squinting, so they couldn't see that he was seeing. His mother was standing in the tub, facing his father. Her flesh ripe and flushed in the orange light of the hearth. Her breasts full and dark-nippled. Her belly round with a thick black V of hair below. She squatted and slipped into the water with Da, and Robert closed his eyes in shame and fear. He could hear small splashes of water, wordless grunts of approval, a sighing stillness, a chuckle, then a silence again. The slippery sound of water and soap. Of hands on flesh. A long, soaking silence, like peace. Finally the sloshing sound of a body rising from water, and the boy peeked again. His mother was drying herself with a rough cotton towel, smiling, drying under one heavy breast and then the other. His father rose from the water. Robert closed his eyes.

3.

His father was seldom in the house. He had customers in the shop, travelers, wayfarers, men with horses needing shoes, or men awaiting sickles to be carried to harvests, or men with ruined tools to be ground and hammered into second lives. They called him Mister Carson if they were strangers, or John if they'd been there more than once. Sometimes when the moon was high, the boy saw other men emerge from darkness, great burly men with wild orange hair, their shirts cut from animal skins, and Da stopped work and retreated with them into the tool room. They used the language Robert heard when his father buried the horse's skull in the wall and they never called him John. At other times, Da borrowed a horse and packed his tools and kissed Robert's mother on the cheek and then rode off into the hills. He was gone for three or four days, a week. The boy was always afraid that he would never return.

"He has work to do," his mother said. "There's so few like him," she said. "He needs to help people who can't do what he can do."

There were no houses near them and no children his age with whom Robert could play, and yet he was not lonely. He often spoke with Bran, their dog, and the dog understood him. Bran had dark red hair and a setter's long nose, and he understood all of them. In bad weather, Robert was almost always inside with his mother or playing on the leeward side of the cleared open patch that surrounded the slated house. Sometimes, he threw sticks and Bran raced after them, his ears flapping, his legs a blur, snatching the stick with a sudden pounce, then turning, racing back to the boy, dropping the stick precisely at his feet, then demanding that they do it all again. Sometimes, Robert's mother prepared lunch for his father and the boy carried it to the forge and Da thanked him and hugged him with his hard, sweaty arms and then took the food with his handmade forks and knives and sat under the hawthorn tree and ate in silence, gazing into the Irish distance.

In the house, Robert helped his mother as she prepared food or tended the fire. She told him when to add fresh turf. She taught him to count by numbering the remaining bricks of turf, and then she would make notes on rough paper. She called this the List: the names of foods and supplies that she would need for the week, or tasks to be finished. Peddlers came by in horse-drawn carts, one with huge sacks of potatoes and mounds of fresh-picked vegetables, another with turf, a third with butter and eggs, cheese and milk (except on rare days of high heat), and his mother haggled with them in her teasing way, and bought what she needed and crossed the items off the List. Or they would go to town together for beef and fish. They walked to Belfast on Saturday mornings, passing St. Edmund's Anglican Church into lanes gradually more crowded with farmhouses and people: Robert's first glimpses of the world beyond their house. Bran was usually out front, his head high, alert to danger, peeing on stone markers.

On the edge of Belfast, the houses at first were scary to Robert: small, narrow, cramped together, all made of dirty red brick, with wet slate roofs and chimneys poisoning the air with sulphury smoke. From a distance, it was hard for him to believe that human beings lived there, and as they came closer it always felt to him that the clouds had chosen to banish the sun. Robert watched the strange new people: men in dark long coats, collars pulled high under dark cloth hats, women in dark skirts that reached the ground, dark shawls hiding their white wintry faces. Many houses were crowned with English flags, but even they had molted into permanent gray under the steady gray rain and the steady gray smoke from the coal fires. The only flashes of color came from the scarlet jackets of the English soldiers.

One shop sold paper and pencils, tobacco in cans, cigars, and a newspaper called the *News-Letter*. His mother always stopped there first, slipping her purchases into a deep flapped oilskin bag. On the street, she nodded at some women and murmured with others, but she seemed apart from them, even the ones Robert had seen crowded in beside her in the Sunday balconies of St. Edmund's. Sometimes a woman touched his hair and exclaimed that it was black as coal and told him he'd grown bigger. But this chat didn't seem real. In Belfast, the boy never felt part of the people, and, he was sure, neither did his mother. As he waited outside the shops, boys stared at him, at his clothes, at his face. *What are ye?* they'd say. *Papist or Prod?* And the boy learned to answer, *Prod*. Because he thought that was what he was: a Protestant named Robert Carson. The other boys babbled on about Good King Billy and asked him many questions about the glorious Battle of the Boyne, in which some of their grandfathers had been soldiers less than fifty years before, or so they claimed. They demanded from him knowledge of strategy and tactics and the numbers of the dead, the noisy catechism of their triumph. There seemed no use in telling them that he was only six; the knowledge they wanted him to recite was a matter of blood, not age. Bran growled as he sensed their hostility and suspicion: Until the boy's mother left the paper shop and stepped into the gray drizzle and said to them, *Away with ye now, away*.

In spite of the hostile packs of other boys, Robert loved gazing into the windows of the shops, filled with objects small and large, in colors that were dazzling midst all the gray and black; or staring at the sheen on the slates of the sidewalks, where the rain gathered in puddles and color sometimes rose from splotches of oil. But it was never his street, the Carsons' street. It was where his mother went on Saturdays to buy things that she couldn't get from the peddlers on the road outside their house with its hearth that would never die away.

Beef and fish were the main things she carried away from the town. The butcher was a gaunt, pale man who said little. He took his money with a grunt and wrapped the meat. Always the money first. He never spoke Robert's mother's name. No *Thank you, Mrs. Carson*. No *See you about, then, Rebecca*. The fishmonger was thinner and smaller than the butcher but was always laughing and saying, *How are ye, Mrs. Carson?* when she entered. He wrapped the fish before he took the money. Naturally Robert and his mother preferred the company of the fishmonger. Bran, however, much preferred the butcher, although that dour man never once offered him a hunk of stripped bone.

The trip home from Belfast always filled Robert with relief and expectation. Sometimes his mother even skipped along, singing a song, accented by Bran's sharp barks, all of them happy to leave the grim city behind, to make one final stop at the home of Mrs. Benson, who sold spices and salt. Then they rushed together into the greener, leafier, sweeter-smelling countryside. Bran plunged into wet meadows and rolled on his back, growling in pleasure, cleansing himself of the aroma of rotting eggs that had settled upon him from the coal fires of the dark city. Once Bran spied crows gnawing on grass or seeds. He rushed at them barking, then skidded to a stop as they rose in a black flock. The dog froze for that stunned moment, startled by the gathering of crows into a single giant thing that blackened the sky, in awe of a movement he could not make himself.

At home on all days, Robert loved watching his mother transform the raw materials of their journeys into sumptuous meals, singing all the while to herself, for the joy of the song. She cut meat into cubes, tossed trimmed fat to Bran, added spices and vegetables and water, and within hours, all was ready. She then vanished into the bedroom and washed her face and hands, and always donned the silver earrings the boy's father had made for her long before Robert Carson was born. They were each shaped as double spirals, with small clips that attached them to the lobes of her ears. They were simple and beautiful, and sometimes she let Robert handle them, and he tried to understand how they were made. Horseshoes were blunt and simple and powerful; he could see himself making them in the forge; but he could not envision the delicacy of these earrings coming from his father's hard hands.

It was always dark when his father came home, and his routines seldom changed. Each evening, his father washed, and then hugged the boy and whispered words to his mother that the boy could not hear. They ate gloriously tasty stews out of the terra-cotta bowls. Or trout from mountain streams. Or salmon from the sea. His mother broiled the spiced and salted fish on the open fire, basting it with butter, laying the fish out for them with mounds of boiled potatoes upon a plate. All of this done cheerfully, without any apparent effort. Robert loved the way the house filled each night with a new odor, a stirring of the sweet peat fire and the herbs and spices of the food. He would look at his father, see him glancing at his mother. The tall man said very little. But when his plate was wiped clean with an end of bread, he hugged Robert's mother and whispered his thanks to her and then turned to the boy. A nod. Robert understood and thanked her too. Bran always remained still, a prisoner of discipline and ritual, knowing he must wait his turn. When the humans were finished, he could begin. Each of them saved something for Bran, the skins of fish, some lumps of potato, crusts of bread, and he went to his bowl (made by Da from a plumber's flange) and ate with a steady, hungry, well-mannered motion until everything was gone. Then he too went over to the boy's mother and fell to the flagstones before her, thankful and content, licking the last spicy remnants from his chops.

But there was more to Rebecca Carson than cooking, or cleaning, or guarding the life of the fire. Across those endless days when Da was in the shop, she was teaching her son many things. To read, for example, although he could not remember later how she did that. There were few books in Ireland then, but when a new one arrived at the paper shop in town, she would rent it and bring it home and read it very quickly (for each additional day of reading cost more money) and showed Robert the letters and the words and the pictures. They owned a large Bible too, and she read the stories with the boy, or told her own versions of the tales. Robert didn't like the story of Abraham and his son Isaac because he couldn't imagine his father taking him to some lonely hill to sacrifice him to God. He liked other parts of the story better, especially the part about Abraham sending a servant to the land of Haran to find a wife for Isaac and how he found one named Rebecca.

"Are you named for her?" Robert asked his mother.

"Aye," she said, and smiled to herself. "But then there are many people in Ireland named for characters in the Bible. There are Isaacs in Belfast and Jacobs . . ."

"Is there a Robert in the Bible?"

"I don't think so."

And then she shifted back to the story and how Abraham found the land of Canaan and how when his wife Sarah died — there were plenty of Sarahs in Ireland too — he buried her in Hebron and how years later Abraham was buried there too. He was one hundred and seventy-five years old.

"One hundred and seventy-five years old?"

"Aye, and a good man he was, old Abraham."

"Was he the oldest man that ever lived?"

"No, that was Methuselah. He lived to be nine hundred and sixty-nine years old. Or so the Bible says. And when old Noah died, he was nine hundred and fifty."

"Will Da live to be nine hundred and fifty years old?"

She laughed out loud.

"I hope so," she said. "That would be grand."

And then she returned to Abraham, who was the father of his people and took them out of their endless wandering, their living in tents in the desert, and brought them at last to the land of milk and honey, to Israel.

"And where is that?"

She opened her worn paper-covered *Book of the World,* which they also owned and had no need to return to the paper store, and on two of its pages there was an engraved map of the world. She showed Robert where Israel was, although it was now called Palestine. She pointed out some of the other lands where the Hebrews had wandered, way out at the end of the Mediterranean, near the rivers called the Tigris and the Euphrates, before they found the land of Canaan. Even on the small map, it was a long way from Ireland, and on days of thrumming rain Robert dreamed of going there, to the dry, bright deserts and the palm trees, and then to rise like a hawk and keep flying above the lines of the map until he could see the date trees beside the River Jordan. He would ask her to repeat the names of the rivers again and again so that he could remember them always, because it seemed to him wondrous to have rivers with names that twisted and turned like the rivers themselves. How could poor, simple, bald Lagan stand up to Euphrates? And the Tigris: Was it filled with tigers? No, she said, it's a name of a place, I guess, but maybe tigers were named after the river. She sounded very reasonable, but at night, before sleeping, in the room where a horse's skull was lodged in the wall, Robert could see golden rivers filled with writhing tigers.

Over and over again, he asked her to tell him the story of Joseph and his brothers and the coat of many colors. She told it in different ways each time, and later, when he could read, she had him tell it himself, out loud, while she worked at the cooking. Sometimes it was a simple tale of vanity. When he was a boy Joseph had a coat of many colors and was vain about it, flaunting the coat before his brothers, who wore gray clothes like the people in Belfast. Joseph had ten brothers, and they shunned him because of his vanity. Which is why, when his father sent him to find the brothers in the desert where they were tending flocks, they first thought of killing him, and then sold him to some passing men on camels. By this time, Robert knew that he had two brothers who were born before he arrived, and they had died. But suppose they had lived?

"If I'd been as vain as Joseph," he asked his mother, "would they have thought of killing me? Would they have sold me to a circus? Or to some black sailing ship down past Sandy Row, bound from Belfast to Spain or Africa?"

"I should hope *not,*" his mother said. But then she paused and turned her head, as if thinking of those dead boys, her vanished sons, and then went on with the tale.

Sometimes the tale was told as a story of exile. In Egypt, the mightiest country of the time, among its pyramids and glittering houses and its Sphinx staring from the desert, Joseph came to manhood as a slave. *A slave is someone owned by somebody else,* Rebecca Carson explained in a grave voice. *They have to work for that person and don't get paid. They still have them in America, the slaves, I mean. And a few other places, too . . .* But God had given Joseph intelligence and the gift of understanding dreams. Even the Pharaoh, the name the Egyptians gave to their king, called upon him to interpret one special dream. Joseph listened to the Pharaoh and told him that the dream meant there would be seven years of great harvests and then seven years of famine. *When the crops don't come in at harvest, and the people have nothing to eat,* his mother explained, *that's called a famine.* Do we ever have them in Ireland? *Aye,* she said. *Sometimes.*

Joseph convinced the Pharaoh to store one fifth of all the produce of the seven years of great harvests in warehouses, like the ones down by the harbor in Belfast, only larger and brighter, painted white, and gleaming in the sun. That way, when the bad times came, when the famine happened, the people of Egypt would have plenty to eat. And Joseph was right. The famine came, and the people of Egypt ate, while the rest of the area starved, including the Hebrews.

At that time, years had passed since Joseph had been sold into slavery, and now he was tall and strong, no longer a stranger in a strange land, but a man with more power than anyone else except the Pharaoh. And then one day into Egypt came his brothers. They had come to buy grain to feed the starving Hebrews. They were brought before Joseph and did not recognize him, because now he was tall and strong, speaking Egyptian in a deep voice, even using a translator to maintain his disguise. For Robert, this was the best part of the story. For Joseph did not suddenly speak Hebrew, remind them of their plans to kill him and their decision to sell him, and then have their heads lopped off. He was kind to them. He fed them and gave them drink. He listened to them. He inquired about their father and other members of their family, and thus learned that his father still lived. Some details astonished Robert when first he heard the tale. The detail about how Joseph lived to be one hundred and ten years old. Or the way his father passed away at one hundred and fifty. But each time he heard the tale again, such details astonished him less.

4.

When the boy was a week short of six years old, he started school. That meant shoes each day and knicker pants and a white shirt with a short tie and a new coat to keep off the rain. Now he was up each morning at the command of the clock, to wash, dress, and walk twenty minutes to the schoolhouse. It stood to the right of St. Edmund's, Church of Ireland, where his father and mother joined the other proud Protestants each Sunday morning at nine o'clock. The church was neat and handsome, with a spare feeling to it inside and out, and a balcony where the women sat apart from the men. Behind the church, surrounded by a neat garden, was the rectory, where the Reverend Henry Robinson lived, attended by a stout, round-faced, cheerful woman who was his housekeeper.

There were about fifteen of them in the one large schoolroom, of different ages and sizes, all boys (for girls were not allowed to be educated). He was called Robert by some, and Rob or Bobby by others. The teacher was the same Reverend Robinson who thundered on Sundays: tall, wiry, with a large beaked nose always dripping in the Irish chill. Through the mornings, as he gave his lessons, the man would blow into his handkerchief and then examine the product as if it were evidence of sin. He wore the same black jacket each day, shiny at the elbows, and knicker trousers, white shirt, grimy white stockings that vanished into buckled black shoes. He stood on a raised platform beside a desk. Ready at hand was a springy birch cane he called the Punisher.

The Rev. Robinson was never happy. Or rather, he never smiled, at least not in front of the schoolchildren. He did seem happy when whipping the Punisher against the tender bottoms of his charges. And he seemed to single out Robert Carson. From the day of Robert's arrival, he could read without the teacher's help, which seemed to gall the man in black. Whether called Robert, or Rob, or Bobby, he felt the daily condemnation of the Rev. Robinson's beady eyes.

The curriculum was simple: reading, writing, arithmetic, and Protestantism. The Rev. Robinson expressed no reverence for anyone or anything except God, Oliver Cromwell, and William of Orange. His holy trinity. At God's command, and with God's help (he told the boys, his voice quivering, his clogged nostrils flaring), Cromwell drove the treasonous, idol-worshipping, priest-ridden Catholics beyond the Pale of Settlement; they learned no lessons and rose again, and in 1690, William of Orange arrived on our blessed shores to defeat the same Catholics at the glorious Battle of the Boyne. There were still Catholics among us, he intoned, hidden, secret, the spies of Satan, and it is God's demand that we convert them to the freedoms and liberties of Protestantism by any means necessary. Robert's further instruction in theology was of a similar lofty order.

"How can you tell a Catholic from a Protestant?" the Rev. Robinson asked one day.

"By his rotted teeth," someone said.

And someone else shouted, "By the smell, eejit."

"Here, here," the Rev. Robinson commanded. "Don't call a fellow Protestant an idiot."

Robert had never heard any of this at home, and so he said nothing. He saved his religious fervor for Bible class. He could talk about Moses and Abraham and Isaac. And about Aaron's rod, which was a shepherd's staff, and how Aaron could turn it into a snake, or use it to change water into blood, or to bring down upon his enemies great clouds of lice or fleas or hornets or flies. To Robert, that was another amazing tale. He knew about Joshua and his army, blowing their godly rams' horns at the battle of Jericho. He knew about Daniel in the lion's den, and Gideon's fierce army and the wicked Jezebel (although he didn't quite understand what was meant by "wicked"), and how Delilah cut off Samson's hair while he slept, robbing him of his strength. The Rev. Robinson read the line that said "Let my people go," and told his flock that it was the cry of every honest, God-fearing Protestant when confronted by Catholic riches, Catholic corruptions, Catholic vice, and Catholic power. This bored Robert. He wanted to hear more about donkeys that talked, and rocks that gave water, and chariots of fire; he wanted more about all the thrilling murders in the Bible, and the great men who had many wives. A vein in the Rev. Robinson's temple pulsed with fury as he roared about the Whore of Babylon, who lived in Rome and called himself the Pope, but he didn't answer Robert's question about what a whore was (the older boys giggled or whooped at the question, which allowed the Rev. Robinson to avoid the answer and direct his fury at their knowing laughter). The Rev. Robinson insisted on discussing, in order, each of the Ten Commandments. Young Robert Carson wanted to know if it was true that Joseph lived to be one hundred and ten.

He did make some friends. Billy Painter. Sam Longley. Harry Martinson. Boys like those from town, but better dressed, with faces shiny and scrubbed, bursting with mischief. As time passed and one term gave way to another, and then eased into a summer, and then another winter, Robert discovered that he was good at some things in school and poor at others. He had good penmanship (with a reed pen dipped in an inkwell), and that same talent could be used for drawing. He would draw their house and the hearth and the forge, and pictures of Bran and his friends at school. He never drew his parents. His right hand did what he wanted it to do, and when he was bored he could also use his left. The works of his left hand seemed to come from a different boy: the writing blunter, the drawing bolder. The Rev. Robinson always smacked him with the Punisher when he caught him writing left-handed ("A sure sign of Satan's presence," he snarled), so the boy only wrote that way at home. There he had noticed that his father was right-handed, but his mother wrote the List with her left, though completely untouched by Satan and his wiles. He felt proud that he had taken a hand from each of them.

Robert was not as good at arithmetic as he was at reading and writing or even Protestantism. Once he got the hang of Protestantism, it was easy. Catholics were bad, Protestants were good, and the King of England was the greatest man alive in the world. But arithmetic, at first, was more difficult: abstract, without a story.

Seeing this weakness, his mother helped him with his sums, again turning to the turf pile to explain addition and subtraction. But then the boy would cite an example from his father's forge, as if it gave proof of confused logic. If Da put four pieces of metal on the grid and melted them and banded them together into a sickle, didn't that mean that two and two made one?

"Sometimes you think too much for your own good, lad," his mother said, and laughed out loud.

Then one day near the end of the second year at St. Edmund's, it all came together in some mysterious way. Robert was adding a column of about seven double-digit figures. He looked for the first time at the column as if it were a ladder. In his mind, he climbed up the right side, counting as he went. Twelve. Yes: Write down a 2 and carry the 1. Then he climbed down the other side and had 17, wrote it down and ended up with 172. The trick was to make it a journey, not a story with heroes and villains, Hebrews and Egyptians, just a going from one place to another, counting miles, maybe, or trees, or stone markers, or houses; the climbing of a ladder to the top step and then a climb back down. The boy admonished himself for wanting everything to be a story. And now realized that some journeys were not stories. On some journeys, nothing really happened.

You just kept taking steps. Once he had that in his brain, even arithmetic seemed easy. It wasn't the same as a story, because it had no meaning, unless you were counting days and weeks and months and years and, eventually, centuries.

5.

The boy was ten when they saw the strange people coming along the roads. Bran smelled them first and barked in his deepest basso profundo voice, running to the edge of the land to frighten them away from the Carson house. These strangers were not like the burly red-haired men who sometimes appeared in the forge. Bran knew those men and their strange language. These arrivals were ragged and thin and shambling, like trees without leaves, their eyes wide with need. The sight of them filled the boy's mother with fear.

"Come in now, son," she said. *"Come in right now."*

She shouted to her husband down at the forge and then locked the doors and closed the windows. She whispered prayers. She watched the strangers from the window, where Da was shooing them away with a hammer in his hand. If they came near, even the women, even the children, she screamed at them: *"Go away, please, for God's sake, go away."*

Robert had never seen her like this before, she who was ordinarily so kind and generous with everyone who passed, and almost totally without fear. But these people terrified her, and as she held the boy close, she told him some of the story. About how such people had arrived years earlier, when they lived in another house, all of the ragged strangers coming from the west, heading for Belfast, and how they carried with them something called the cholera. And how his lost brothers felt pity for them and ran down with food and water, and these people (or people like them) hugged the boys and thanked them and in three days the boys were dead.

"My poor boys," she said now, fighting tears, her voice a soft croon. "Those poor good boys. It was my fault too, because I didn't know, I was ignorant, *I told them to bring them the food and the drink.* And they did. And they died." She breathed deeply. "They were your brothers, lad."

She hugged Robert tightly.

"Well, by God," she said, "you won't die."

And then Da arrived, his work finished early, bending under the lintel of the door. Grave. His face set.

"Don't worry, Rebecca, " he said. "They'll not get in here."

He held her close to his chest, soothing her, and added. "Well, let's have dinner. And Rebecca, darlin'? Why don't you wear your earrings?"

That night in his bed beside the wall that contained the horse's skull, Robert tried again to imagine the faces of his lost brothers and how they ran down a slope like the slope outside this door, to a road like the road outside this door, and gave food and drink to sickened people. And then died. He tried drawing their faces in his mind. Not the featureless creatures of his night dreams. Faces like his own, or those of his friends at St. Edmund's or the boys he saw on his trips to town. And he thought: That was not fair. How could God let such a thing happen? If he was so powerful, why didn't he stop my brothers before they reached the road? Make a storm or an earthquake or a flight of bees: but stop them while they were running down the slope? Robert began to cry.

Then the door opened and his mother was there, wearing her double-spiraled earrings.

"It's all right, son," she said. "I'm sorry if I upset you. Don't cry anymore."

"I don't like God."

"Ach, son, what a thing to say."

"He let my brothers die. They never did anything bad, I'm sure of that, and he let them die."

"He works in mysterious ways, they say."

"I don't like him."

"Hush, now."

They both went quiet. His mother gazed out the curtainless window, to where the trees stood silvery in the moonlight. She listened, fully alert, but heard no strangers moving on the road. Even Bran was now asleep.

"Did I ever tell you about Noah's granddaughters," she said, "and how the Hebrews came to Ireland?"

"No."

"Well, the story starts just before the Flood. The world was full of wickedness then, and God was disgusted with his creations. So he planned a great flood. He appeared to Noah, who was then an old man, and told him to build an ark, a ship large enough to hold men and women and two of each animal in the world."

"I know that part, Ma. What about his granddaughters?"

"Well, one granddaughter was named Cesara, and she was very smart and very good and kind. But she realized there would not be enough room for her and her woman friends on the ark. So she and her friends began to build smaller boats, seven of them. And sure enough, the rains began to fall, for forty days and forty nights, filling the world to the peaks of the mountaintops. And Cesara and her friends began sailing to the west, because they lost sight of Noah and his giant ark. Only one boat survived the long journey, which took three years, because there was no land anywhere for them to stop. They ate fish. They drank rainwater. Some died. And then finally the waters of the world began to recede. And they saw land. Green and rich and beautiful. There were only three men left and fifty women, including Cesara. And they sailed for the shore, and it was Ireland."

"They were all Hebrews?"

"Aye, every last one of them."

She stared out at the night. The moon was gone. A soft rain was falling.

"They stayed in Ireland, and married and multiplied, and some of them kept the old ways, the old religion, the religion of the Hebrews."

She gripped her son's hand, then turned away. He understood.

"Are you a Hebrew, Ma?"

"Aye."

She held the boy closer.

"Don't be telling all your friends, now," she said with a smile. "Some of them are pure stupid about Hebrews. Or Jews, as they call us. Does it make you feel any differently about me?"

"It feels grand, Ma. Sure, you're related to Cesara. And Rebecca. And Ruth. And Esther too, and all the others. Joshua and Samson and Abraham and Joseph —"

She laughed in a delighted way.

"I don't count that Samson as any relative of mine," she said. "He was a bit of a bollix, wasn't he?"

Now Robert laughed. And then listened to the rain for a moment, spattering the slates.

"This means I'm a Hebrew too, doesn't it?"

"Aye," she said, "and a good one too."

The boy felt as if his mother had handed him a map to a secret treasure. Then she kissed his forehead and whispered: "Sleep now, lad. You've school in the morning."

6.

The cholera passed, and the ragged people vanished from the roads. In school and pulpit the Rev. Robinson intoned against the sins of the victims, and how they must have somehow failed God or he would not have chosen them for death. On the way home from Sunday services, the boy's mother fumed. *The nerve of that bloody-minded, snot-nosed fool,* she said. *How dare he? How dare he say that those poor people died because they were sinners, or Catholics, or people who had fallen away?* Meaning, of course, how could the Rev. Robinson accuse her own two sons, the boy's lost brothers, of some mortal sin that caused their death before he was born?

"Cholera's a disease," she said as they walked together as a family. "It comes from man, not from God."

John Carson listened, saying nothing.

Robert didn't know what his father was thinking, but he now carried within him the secret his mother had given him. The secret of being a descendant of Noah, a hidden, shadowy Hebrew, a private thing that was a gleaming, glittering, *large* secret. When he again read the Bible after receiving his secret, or heard his mother telling the old tales, the book became a kind of biography. Their story, and his story. The Hebrew tale was passed to him across thousands of years, from a world of sand and palms, where murder and betrayal were part of the story, and heroism too. It had been passed to him in the dark, wet northern hardness of Ireland, which itself was a kind of miracle. He held the secret within himself, never mentioning it to his father or his friends. He polished it. He burnished it. "O Noah," he often whispered in the dark. "O Abraham. O Joseph with your coat of many colors. I am you too."

Then, on a day of frail, misty rain, as he sat alone inside the door, Robert heard a tremendous barrage of hoofbeats on the wooden bridge. The sound rushed into his head, to stay forever. He hurried outside, and saw for the first time the black coach of the Earl of Warren. The coach was immense to his young eyes, tall as a house, polished black with silver adornments and a large W emblazoned on its doors above a coat of arms. The metal-rimmed wheels were a blur, the undercarriage bounced violently, and it was heading up the road to Belfast, drawn by four frothing brown horses, whipped by a fierce man with a patch on one eye. Out front were three horsemen in scarlet jackets. Three more followed the coach. Robert ran to look closer. And saw for the first time, peering from the dark interior of the coach, the sallow, fleshy face of the Earl of Warren. Alone. His eyes glittering as he glanced at the boy.

Then the black coach was gone.

And the boy saw his father standing in front of the forge, watching it go.

7.

One Friday evening, his father packed tools in a leather satchel, slung it over his shoulders, said a quick good-bye, and walked up the slope into the hills. Robert felt like weeping. That Sunday, he would be nine. His lucky number. The ninth day of the ninth month. And Da walked off without discussing his return. He could be gone for a night or a week. He could be absent on a birthday made even more important by that number nine. All through Saturday, Robert worked at his lessons and played with Bran near the stream and swept out the forge and helped feed peat to the hearth. He never mentioned the birthday to his mother. On Sunday morning, he went to St. Edmund's with her and saw his friends but didn't mention his birthday to them or explain why his father was not in church. I am nine, he thought, but to say a word would be a sin of vanity.

Through the day, a rain fell upon their part of Ireland, now hard, then suddenly weak. His mother didn't mention the birthday either, acting as if it had completely vanished from her memory. When the rain eased to a steady drizzle, Robert leaned over the half-door, gazing into the dark line of forest.

Then, as the rain began again to drive hard, he saw his father coming from the woods. The boy's heart tripped. His father was riding a beautiful black horse. Robert burst through the door and ran through the rain to greet him.

"Happy birthday, son," Da said, and smiled, sitting high in a rough saddle.

He reached down and scooped up Robert with one hand and jammed him in the front of the saddle, where the boy ran his hands for the first time through the horse's lustrous coat. It was September 9, and his father had come home with a horse. His horse. Their horse. On his birthday.

Together, they trotted to the front door, where Rebecca stood smiling in a delighted, conspiratorial way. Bran barked loudly until he saw John Carson dismount and then swing the boy down, holding him beneath the arms, whirling him and laughing louder than the storm. A rumble of distant thunder came from the south.

"Thunder," Da said. "We'll name him Thunder."

"Yes, yes," Robert said. "Thunder! Yes, Da, thank you, Da, oh Da, oh Da, thank you."

Then all of them stood in the rain and ran their hands over the wet ebony coat of the horse named Thunder, who shuddered in delight. The boy would always remember the feel of muscles rippling in the shoulders of the horse, the grooves of his neck and buttocks and thighs. There were cables of tendon drawn like lines from his knees to his hocks. The horse looked at them with liquid black eyes as the rain pelted them all. Looking as if he knew that he had found his home.

Robert's heart was beating hard. A horse. Here in the gray sheets of Ulster rain. After the beef stew and the slice of apple cobbler and the toasting with icy water; after the hugs and the vows of more and more birthdays and a wonderful year to come at school; after his father hugged him again and again; after he saw tears welling in his mother's eyes; after all of that, they walked Thunder to the tool room of the forge, where he gobbled a huge bucket of oats and then folded his legs and lay down upon the straw.

"He's yours now, lad," Da said.

"No," Robert said. "He's ours. Forever."

In the morning, an hour before Robert left for school, and while the rain eased into mist, Da showed the boy Thunder's hooves, the central cleft, the sole, the wall around it, and explained how the shoe was shaped to fit around each hoof like a sheath. "When you come home," Da said, "we'll make him some fine shoes. The two of us. Now, away with you."

Robert learned very little at school that day. While the Rev. Robinson droned on and on, the boy's head was filled with the beauty and power of the horse. When school ended, he ran all the way home. Da was in the forge. He smiled at Robert and stepped to the anvil, and without a word began shaping new shoes, with the boy's help, adding a fine line of brass as a trim between the hoof and shoe. The new shoes fit perfectly; it was as if John Carson had been preparing for this piece of work for many years, and of course, he had. Then one hoof at a time, gently using nails and calks, he attached the wonderful shoes. The lines of brass looked like gold.

That night they planned the fence that would mark the limits of their land and become the free home of Thunder. Since they had never owned a horse, they never before had need of a fence. Two nights later, some of the burly strangers appeared at dusk, carrying wood and tools, and began hammering and singing and drinking. When they heard the sound of horses in the distance, they went silent and vanished into the darkness until the horses or coaches had passed. Four of them, in fact, were always in the darkness. Robert tried to help with the fence, but was sent off to bed, where his mother told him to dream about lands of milk and honey.

When he awoke at dawn, the strangers were gone and the fence was finished. It now marked the limits of everything that was the Carsons': the house, the forge, the hawthorn tree. Over the following weeks, he and his father made a trough for oats and a one-horse stable in the space between the back of the forge and the hawthorn tree. And every day, in the early morning or after school, Robert rode Thunder. Sometimes his father got up on the horse too, the three of them looking suddenly as if they were one creature, and the man showed his son the tricks of control. Within weeks, Robert could ride with a saddle or without, using the bridle or making the horse stop or turn with the pressure of his knees. Da taught him to talk to Thunder always, because, he said, the horse understands. *It's your tone of voice,* he explained. *The tone of your voice. Just tell him what you want, and he'll know. Be kind to him, be gentle, and when you need him, he'll know how to be fierce.*

Thunder became the happiest of Robert's duties. His father put him to work cleaning and oiling the hard rough leather saddle, doing the work each day until the saddle grew softer. He showed him how to wash Thunder so that his coat glistened without the presence of the sun. He could not leave a trace of soap on the great black coat, for it would irritate Thunder's skin and make him flake. Thunder loved the feel of fresh water, as Robert did, and rain, as the boy did too, and the feel of a coarse towel drying him in the stall. And the horse loved them to talk to him: whispering to him, running fingernails along his long flat brow. Every morning before breakfast, the boy looked into the horse's deep, intelligent eyes and spoke in low, loving tones and the horse answered with the love in his eyes.

8.

One Saturday afternoon, Da took Robert for a ride into Belfast. Down the road past the butcher and the fishmonger, and deeper into places the boy had not seen on trips with his mother. He explained to the boy how they lived in an area called Stranmillis, which ran down to the banks of the River Lagan, which in turn flowed into the Lough, the immense harbor that dug into the land from the east. He told the boy that the name Belfast came from an Irish phrase: *Beal Feirste,* which meant the Mouth of the Sand-Banked River. These were the first words Da spoke directly to him in Irish, but he added no others. He was too busy explaining geography to the boy, pointing out Cave Hill and Divis and the Black Mountain, all rising above the Sand-Banked River, then gesturing across the shimmering water at a distant castle called Carrickfergus.

"That was built before there was a town," Da said. "To guard the entrance to the Lough. And before that, the Vikings were here, the Norsemen, building forts and houses and eating the fish, which were thicker here than in all of Ireland."

His knowledge astonished the boy as they followed a smaller river called the Fearsat, a slow, leaky tributary of the Lagan. Soon the embankment itself was paved and flagged, with Thunder's gold-trimmed shoes making a clacking sound, and they were in Castle Street, the river still moving sluggishly to their left. They passed many shops run by linen merchants. Da named the bank and the post office and the ruin of the original castle of the Lord of Donegal. A large crowd milled about in front of the Market

House, talking and smoking and gesturing, and Da said that much of the town's business took place there, usually out of the rain inside the building. As they moved, Castle Street became Front Street, and his father told Robert the names of smaller streets feeding into it: Ann Street and Rosemary Lane, Pottinger's Entry and Wilson's Court, Crown Entry and Winecellar Entry, with men and women and horses moving steadily in and out of the lanes. Da carefully explained all of this to his son, and to Thunder too, as if wanting to give each of them the essential geography in which they lived.

As they rode, they attracted some attention. Young boys looked up in awe at the black stallion, its massive rider, the boy in front of him, for Thunder had never been seen before in the town. Women paused and widened their eyes. Men nudged one another and whispered.

They arrived finally at the waterfront, where a hundred masts rose beside Donegal Quay. There for the first time Robert saw ships in full many-masted sail, and docks covered with crates and boxes and barrels. Rough men unloaded cargo as they watched: sugar and tobacco from America (his father told him), along with hemp and pitch and tar and timbers, all for the building of new ships. Cotton and silk, spices and dyes from Asia. Salt and wine, silk and fruit from Italy and Spain. The workingmen paid them no heed. They had seen fine horses before, and strangers too. Their hooded, squinting eyes seemed to have already looked at all the strange people and things offered by the world.

Da told Robert where the ships were going, and the names sounded like the words of a fairy tale. Liverpool and London. Cherbourg and Marseilles. Bilbao and Morocco and the Canary Islands. And yes, America. For the first time the boy felt the tug of the world beyond the world he knew, moving in him like a tide.

"Those buildings are full of men who live off the sea," Da said, pointing at the low brick houses that lined the far end of the immense waterfront square. There were chandlers making candles and coopers shaping barrels. There were wheelwrights and sextant makers and stevedores. But he called his son's attention to the second-floor offices above the shops. "Those are the companies that run the ships. They have the power here. Usually," he said, "there's a group of rich men who pool their money and share in the profits of each voyage."

"And the sailors, Da? The men on the ships? Do they get rich too?"

"Never," he said. "They die. Or they live. The voyage begins, the voyage ends. If they come back alive from the sea, they get paid. They never get rich."

Many of the storefronts bore names elegantly lettered on signs above the doors, and through panes of glass Robert could see men in business suits, some wearing wigs, waving paper, sipping tea, writing with quill pens, or talking to clerks. One such business was called the Royal African Company.

"Do they sail to Africa too, Da?"

"Aye," he said. "To our eternal shame."

"And what do they trade for there?" Robert said.

"Men."

"Men?"

"And women and children too."

"What?"

"Slaves," he said. "They go into the Gold Coast and the Gambia River and they hunt men. And then they take them to America and sell them the way some men sell donkeys."

"Do they come to Belfast too?"

"No. They just have their offices here, son. They sign the papers and send the ships to Africa, and they pick up their cargoes and then sail on to America. Then the slaves must work for nothing for the people who buy them. They become property. Like dogs or horses."

He nudged Thunder and they trotted closer to the offices of the Royal African Company. Coming out of the front door, engulfed by six other men, was the Earl of Warren. He was taller than he had seemed in the dim recesses of the black coach, but his body was fleshy, like his face, and soft under his clothes, unlike the lean men of the countryside or the men who worked the ships. He paused for a moment, surrounded by other men, including the man with the eye patch who drove the black coach. He said something, smiled, and they all laughed. Small boys in ragged clothes began to arrive, as if this were a daily ritual, and then from side streets came two women in rags, one of them using a tree limb as a cane.

The earl took from his pocket three small balls, red, white, and blue, and stepped back, an amused look on his face. He planted his feet wide apart and began to juggle the balls. And Robert noticed the change that came into his face. The earl looked younger, like a mischievous boy in a schoolyard, his brow furrowed in concentration, his mouth smiling without showing teeth, and his eyes beginning to sparkle as he moved the balls into a blur. Then, one at a time, he snatched the balls from their flight, smiled broadly, and took an exaggerated bow.

The group around him cheered and Robert wanted to cheer too. He'd never seen a man do such things before, to stand and make people shout in thanks or clap their hands in delight. The scary face of the sneering earl who'd passed their house now vanished. He saw only the smiling man who could juggle. And then another side of him: The small boys crowded around him, and he put a coin into each of their hands, wagging a finger at those who pressed too hard. Then he called the two old women to him and used fingers to pry more coins from a vest pocket and gave one to each woman. The crippled woman bowed in reverence, the other curtsied. The earl said something and looked concerned about the health of the women, while the men nodded in approval.

Then the earl led the way to the corner and went into a public house. Through all of this, Da was silent and still. He explained the function of the public house to Robert in an amused way: "They go to a publican and order courage by the pint." But he said nothing about the skill of the juggling act or the giving of alms. He and Robert looked at the man with the eye patch, waiting outside the front door, arms as thick as thighs folded across his chest.

"That's one of your slavers," Da said as the small crowd dispersed, and he turned Thunder to go back. "Not the boyo with the patch. His commander. The Earl of Warren. The juggler. The man handing out the ha'penny pieces. English, he is, and he doesn't even know that he's insulting Irish people with his public charity." He shook his head. "They say he's full of charm." He humphed. "They say the women love him." He sighed. As they trotted away from the wharves, Da explained that the earl traded in linen and land. "It's said that he's buying choice lots out by the river, knowing Belfast will grow. And the *News-Letter* says he's bought land in America, without ever seeing it. Land in New York, the *News-Letter* says. But mostly it's the African trade that brings in the money. They say he wants to become the richest man in Ireland, and maybe he will. He's done very well for himself. Out past Carrickfergus he's bought a huge demesne, with a mansion and stable and huts for his help. . . ."

"And does he have slaves working for him?"

"Yes, but not from Africa."

9.

They could feel Belfast growing in their direction, even if they could not see it very clearly. Robert imagined the earl as part of that growth, standing on once-wooded hills, juggling, smiling, bowing to applause. On quiet evenings, he heard his father talking to his mother about the people they were seeing more often on the road, with their earthly goods piled in tottering wagons. "They're being driven out of Belfast," Da said, "by the bloody taxes." His voice quivered with anger. By some royal grant, Da said, Belfast was the absolute property of the Lord of Donegal, one of the Chichester family, people who did nothing for Belfast except collect rents while living grandly in London. The taxes were fixed by the local government and then were added to the rents of ordinary people, rising higher and higher year after year.

"Whoremongers," Da called the people who collected rent and taxes. "The whoremonger Chichesters." He gestured toward the people with the carts and said, "They're coming out here to move beyond Chichester's greed." Robert didn't completely understand all of this, such vague words as "rent" and "taxes," although he was pleased to hear from his mother that they owned their land and thus paid no rent. What Robert did know was that month after month, more houses suddenly appeared, scattered around the once-empty fields. Strangers arrived with saws and axes and chopped down the trees and soon a house stood where woods once marched toward the Lagan. There was more traffic on the Dublin road now, wagons, horses, carriages, and new faces. Twice more, he saw the black coach, once racing for Dublin with women inside the cabin, their hair rising like frost off pale faces. A few weeks later, the Earl of Warren returned alone. The boy wondered if the Royal African Company had offices in Dublin too and imagined the earl juggling for the women and bowing to their applause.

With the growth of the town and the heavy traffic on the Dublin-to-Belfast road, his father was busier than ever, sometimes working by the light of lanterns into the night. But there was one consolation after Thunder's arrival: Da could ride now to his appointments beyond their little world, and always returned more quickly. While he worked and traveled, the boy's mother explained in more detail about what it meant to be a Jew, telling tales of angels passing over houses to save the Hebrews from death, and what the commandments meant (as related by Moses, not the Rev. Robinson), and how much they must struggle against the sin of vanity. Robert still hid his secret from his classmates, the private knowledge of being a Hebrew, and in a small way that kept him apart from them. But for a while, he did have more friends. They often walked through rain and drizzle to the Carson house, sometimes gazing in awe at the work in the forge, sometimes bringing little biscuits for the boy's mother, all wanting to ride Thunder. Robert's mother always said that by the rules of the house, nobody else would be allowed to ride Thunder, but then she moved quickly to head off any resentment from the boys.

"Come in now, lads," she always said, "and have a cup of tea by the fire and a nice little sweet."

Then, one frigid Saturday morning while the boy's father was off on Thunder to work on a horse made lame by ill-fitting shoes, Robert and his mother set out on foot for shopping. The rain that January morning was heavy, slanting against them as they walked, driven by a mountain wind. On the streets of Belfast in such foul weather, there were no murmured niceties; on such days, they would quickly make their purchases and hurry home. On this day, which was January 17, 1737, after almost a week of rain, the streets were gluey with mud, rutted by the passage of carriages. Robert and his mother hugged the facades of the buildings. She slipped into the fishmonger's shop, chatting briefly and pleasantly. Robert wandered outside to the street. Across the mud-jammed street, he saw his friend Tommy Hastings and called to him in the driving rain. Tommy waved, then gestured for Robby to come over, pointing at something in a shop window. Robert started across the street, but the mud sucked at his boots. He looked down, and the mud was above his ankles, gripping him like wet mortar. Tommy shouted words that Robert could not hear. Then he heard a noise coming from his left and saw the black coach charging at him from fifty feet away in a blind, slopping, sucking roar, the horses driven wildly, galloping furiously under the lash, the blurred wheels throwing mud everywhere, spattering windows, sending gray brown lumps of muck into the gray slanting rain.

The boy couldn't move. He lifted one foot, trying to turn, and then another, and the roar was coming, coming, coming, *coming*.

Straight at him.

Blindly.

And then the boy's mother was there, grabbing him by the waist, pivoting at once, jerking him free of the mud, and hurling him to safety.

As the horses smashed her into the mud and the steel-cased wheels rolled over her.

Rebecca Carson did not scream.

Her body simply issued a great *whoosh.* As if all the air and all the life and her very soul had been abruptly squashed out of her.

It was Robert who screamed.

He screamed and ran to her, pulling himself through the sucking mud, and screamed and fell face forward into the mud and screamed and rose and screamed and felt hands grabbing his arms while he screamed and felt the rain hammering him and his dead mother and he screamed.

When there were no screams left, and no voice, Robert sat splay-legged in the mud, holding his mother's ruined head, and saw through tears and rain that the black coach was stopped a dozen yards beyond them. The door opened. The Earl of Warren put a tentative foot on the runner below the door, brushing in a distracted way at the rain pelting his black velvet coat. He looked at Robert cradling the broken body of his mother. Then the earl sat back heavily in the coach and closed the door behind him. But the black coach did not move. A murmurous crowd was thickening now, with shopkeepers and Tommy Hastings and other boys and men who looked grim. Patch came slopping through the mud.

"Bloody stupid Irish," he said. "Running in front of a coach like that."

Robert stood up, moved around Patch, and dashed to the coach, slipping and floundering. He jerked at a door handle. When it opened, the earl stared at him with concern on his face.

"I'm sorry, lad," he said in a smooth, sympathetic voice. "I didn't see what happened, but there'll be an investigation, and there'll be some compensation. Of course, I'll pay for the funeral services and —"

Robert leaped at the earl, punching at him, screaming *I'llkillyou, I'llkillyou, I'llkillyou,* up on the runner now, reaching in and grabbing at his neck, trying to hurt him, to give him pain, crazy and snarling: *"You goddamned slaver, you slaver, you cruel rotten slaver."* All of this in a matter of seconds. And then Patch was pulling the boy off the earl, whirling him, heaving him like a sack of potatoes through the rainy air into the mud. Three rain-soaked redcoats were suddenly there. One slapped Robert's muddy face, making his ears ring. Another raised his rifle butt as if to batter the boy. Then the earl emerged again and shouted: "Stop, you brainless bugger, it's his *mother*."

The redcoat obeyed. Robert rose from the mud and saw the earl peering down at Rebecca's body, his face a mixture of fear, pity, and surprise. Robert felt his rage seep out of him like rainwater and he fell into a drawn-up ball beside his mother's body.

Now some of the men came from the side and lifted him, and carried Rebecca out of the mud and laid her in front of the fishmonger's shop. Robert saw the earl wave with a sneer at Patch, ordering him to get up on the coach. Then he slammed the door and leaned out the open window.

"Take her home," he said in a vague way to the crowd. "And the boy too." He paused, then added in a subdued voice: "I'll take care of everything."

10.

Behind the closed door of the bedroom, Da washed the Irish mud off the body of his wife. He dried her. He dressed her in her best cashmere gown. Standing outside the door, Robert heard him murmur one sentence: *"O my Rebecca, O Rebecca, I will see you soon enough."* Da attached her double-spiraled silver earrings. Then he carried her out of the bedroom and placed her upon a pair of planks stretched across the low stools beside the hearth. In the light of the fire and the lanterns, she seemed to the boy to be sleeping. He and his father stared at her for a long while. Outside, Bran began a low, pained, desolated howling.

"Comfort the dog, son," Da said. "We can comfort each other later."

And so he did, lying with Bran in the lee of the house as the drizzle fell from the Irish sky. The dog was on his side, lost, forlorn, empty, his eyes wide, his pink tongue flopping over his teeth, his body trembling with hundreds of small breaths. He was as inconsolable as the boy. They huddled together in the dark for a long time.

Then people started to arrive, trudging through the rain, kicking mud off their shoes at the door, entering in a tentative way, saying what they could say, which was not much. *Sorry for your trouble,* each of them seemed to say. *Sorry for your trouble.* Some of Robert's friends came from school, all but Tommy Hastings, who someone said was beyond consolation, blaming himself. But Robert hid from them in the dark with Bran, and walked with the dog through the black rain to the stable to feed Thunder. There the boy begin to bawl again, and Thunder pawed the straw at his feet and Bran let out a long banshee howl.

From the stable, Robert saw the Rev. Robinson coming up the road, awkward and gaunt. He remained hidden in the dark and was relieved that the preacher didn't stay long. Then everybody was gone. Da called *"Son, son, come home now"* from the door, and Robert walked slowly back with Bran. The boy didn't want to enter the house, but in a hoarse, low voice, his father told him to come in and change into dry clothes. "Him too," he said, nodding at the soaked dog. Bran seemed to understand that they needed him with them that night. He shook off the rain, twice, and followed the boy to his room.

When Robert returned in dry clothes, his father was staring at his wife, at Rebecca, the descendant of Noah. At the boy's mother. He said nothing. The doors were now closed and locked against the world. But the world would not leave them to their grieving.

There was a sudden sharp knock on the door. Bran barked angrily, as if he needed to take out his anger on someone, anyone. Da only looked weary: another mourning visitor, paying respects. He sighed and went to the door. A thin, trembling man stood there, a scarf tied tightly around his head under a tall fur hat. He bowed in a nervous way. Da barred the way to the house, leaving the man in the dripping rain. Bran barked and barked, while the boy tried to calm him.

"Yes?"

"Excuse me, sir. You'd be Mister Carson, sir, am I right? Mr. John Carson?"

"Aye."

"Sorry for your trouble, Mister Carson," the man said. "But I've got something for you."

The man peeled off a kid glove and slid an envelope from inside his coat. He handed it to Da, then bowed, turned, and was gone. Father and son heard the receding gallop of a horse.

The father stared at the envelope, then turned it over. Heavy vellum paper. The deckle-edged flap sealed in red wax, embossed with a W.

He cracked it open with a finger. Inside there was a lone vellum card. He exhaled disdainfully, then showed it to his son. A single word was written with a steel pen: *Sorry.* Clipped to the card was a ten-pound note.

Da held the ten-pound note between thumb and forefinger as if pinching the tail of a rat.

"Ten pounds," he said. And for the first time he sounded bitter instead of grieving. "That's what he thinks an Irish life is worth."

He walked past his son to the hearth and dropped the banknote in the fire.

Then he turned to the boy.

"It's the two of us now, son."

The boy rushed to him, into his enveloping arms, and then all the caged words burst from him, rushing on a river of guilt, *If I'd only stayed by her side, if only I hadn't seen Tommy Hastings, if only I hadn't tried to cross the lane,* words of anger and protest and revenge, *I'm going to find him, I'm going to make him pay, I'm going to get that cruel, slaving pig,* and then no words, just bawling. Then sobbing. Hopeless. Empty. Shuddering. And when Da led him to bed and consoled him with whispered words and told him to sleep, because they were going on a long journey in the morning, Robert didn't want him to leave the room. He wanted him there. He wanted his mother there. He wanted them to tell him stories. He wanted them to sing a song.

But Da closed the door softly and went back to the room where his wife lay cold and broken. Robert heard the sound of turf being dropped upon the fire. And then the doors opened and his father went outside to howl with Bran at the moon.

11.

He was awake before dawn. Robert cracked open his bedroom door and glanced at the hearth, hoping none of this had happened, that he'd moved through a terrible dream, that his mother would be standing there, mixing porridge in a pot. But no: Her body was where he had seen it last, lying on boards beside the hearth. It was wrapped now in a kind of oiled cape, her face barely visible through a tightly drawn green shawl. Da whispered to the boy to dress warmly, for they were going to the West.

In his room, Robert pulled on wool shirts and socks, staring at the wall where the horse's skull was hidden. Tell me *something,* he thought. Tell me what this is all about. . . . When Robert came out, his father lifted Rebecca Carson as if she were a sleeping child and told the boy to open the Western door. They passed through, his father bending under the transom. Thunder was already harnessed to a cart roofed by a small canvas tent. Da laid his wife on rush mats on the floor of the cart. He looked at her for a long moment, as if remembering unfinished conversations, and then went back to place some damp, slow-burning turf on the fire. He emerged with extra blankets, closing the door behind him. Tenderly, he covered her body with the blankets, and then he and his son climbed up on the seat of the cart and started into the bruise-colored darkness, riding to the West. Bran hurried along beside them.

They rode for hours, following narrow paths into dense forest. High trees sheltered them from the rain. They saw no houses, no towns. They climbed and climbed. At one point, they paused and Robert lifted the panting Bran up on the buckboard. It was full daylight now, but still dark among the ancient trees.

Then, from the leafy darkness Robert heard a voice say something in a language he didn't know. A tree was speaking! His father answered back. Using words Robert had never heard him say. The boy trembled with excitement: There in the cold mist, his father was speaking to trees and the trees were talking back. Every fifty feet another tree talked, its branches moving, and his father answered. Bran was alert, his wet nose quivering, his jaws clamped shut, but he didn't bark. He too seemed to know the secret language of the trees.

Finally the path ended. A wall of trees and foliage blocked their way. Da waited and said nothing. Thunder shuddered and pawed the ground as if anxious to go on.

And then the trees parted, and they moved forward into a wide hidden grove.

In the center was an immense flat boulder, like a stone table supported on legs chopped from the face of a mountain. There were carved markings on the boulder that Robert couldn't read. Around the edges of the grove, hidden under the dark spreading branches of alder and oak, he saw tall stone columns rising twelve feet into the air, as if aimed at the stars. Their tops were rounded, their sides finely planed. The hush was eerie, the sound of something that had not yet happened. Thunder shuddered again. Bran growled. A hawk cried from some unseen place high in the sky. Then from the trees came some of the men who had visited Da in the evenings when his mother was alive. Their women were behind them, and some white-bearded men in long dark gowns, all of them speaking that language.

Da eased off the wagon and so did Bran and the boy. The men embraced his father and whispered to him. None of them wept. Four of the women lifted Rebecca Carson from the wagon and carried her to the flat boulder, which Robert now realized was an altar. They laid her out on the altar, applying oils from small jars to her eyelids. Then more men came from the woods with immense torches and jammed them into the ground, one flame at each point of the altar, north and south, east and west. A breeze whipped the flames of the torches, making them look like wild orange hair.

Da took his son's hand and led him to the head of the altar, where they stood together behind the woman they had lost. At the foot of the altar, an old woman (whose name the boy would learn was Mary Morrigan) began to chant. All the others, women and men, followed her lead. Da knew all the words in the strange language. His son didn't know the words, so he stared at the old woman, with her creased, ravined leathery face, her blank milky eyes, high cheekbones, steel gray hair. Her hands were brown, worn, still, as if carved from wood. She finished the chanting and then she began to sing in the voice of a child: pure, sweet, high-pitched, and charged with feeling. A pause. Then more chanting, with her words followed by the deeper responses of the others. At some lines, Da squeezed his son's hand, as if trying to comfort him, responding to the words that the boy didn't understand. And then it was over. For almost five minutes, they stood together with heads bowed, hands gripping arms.

The old woman came to John Carson and took each of his hands and brought him to a clear spot between two of the stone columns. One of the gowned old men handed Da an oak-handled shovel. He turned the first wet clod of black earth, and then three of his friends joined him. They dug until the lip of the long rectangular trench was almost even with John Carson's shoulders. Then they paused, their faces blistered with sweat, hands and furs black with earth. A robed man offered each a hand to climb out of the grave. Robert followed his father as he walked back to the altar where the body of Rebecca Carson lay, and a burly man produced a goatskin bag, translucent and plump with liquid. He handed it to Da, who drank of it, then passed it to the man on his right, who passed it to Robert. The taste was harsh and bitter in the boy's mouth, but he swallowed the liquid and knew to hand the bag to the next man. Robert felt his stomach burning. The old woman was the last to drink.

Then his father lifted his wife's body for the final time and carried her to the grave. There were rush mats now on the bottom of the trench. Da sat on the muddy lip of the grave, holding the body while his son watched, then slid down with her into the grave. He hugged her tight, his face a pained mask, then laid her on her side on the rush matting, with her arms and legs drawn up. The old woman passed an earthenware bowl full of apples to Da, who placed it beside his wife. To Robert it was clear that this moment was about his father's wife, not the boy's mother, but he felt that it could be no other way.

Then one of the old robed men handed John Carson an iron wheel, about eight inches across, with arrows at the cardinal points, and his father rested it against her drawn-up thighs. A sign of the world, Robert supposed, as he inched forward to look down. He realized then that his mother was not wearing her spiraled earrings and he felt better. At least his father would have them as a sign of his loving her. And being loved back.

Finally John Carson grabbed his son's offered hands and climbed out of the grave. There were no signs of obvious grief: no tears, no sniffles, no choking sounds. He took two more rush mats from the old woman and floated them down over Rebecca Carson's body. With the spade, he began to cover her. He threw down seven loads of black earth and then handed the shovel to the boy. "Seven," he said. "Only seven." The soaked dirt was very heavy, and Robert didn't want to do this, but his mother was already covered, and so he added earth to earth. Seven loads. And then John Carson handed the shovel to one of his friends, and he to another, until as many as were needed had taken their turns.

Then she was covered, a black mound rising above her grave. John Carson placed one hand on his son's shoulder and the other on the shoulder of the man next to him, and they all joined together, the men and the women, making a full circle, almost sixty of them, their backs to the stone columns. For Robert, the word *they* had become *we,* and *them* had become *us*. The old woman stood in the center, gazing intensely at the ground beneath her feet, and began again to chant. The rest of them responded, but because the boy didn't know the words, he whispered: *Ma. Ma. Ma. Ma.* And *Rebecca. Rebecca. Rebecca*. Then the old woman began to sing, a reprise of the opening minutes, and everyone was quiet. Her pure, ethereal voice seemed to rise from the bowels of the earth and reach to the roof of the sky. When she was finished, Bran howled once more from his place on the edge of the woods. And then they were finished. Robert knew that a piece of his life was over.

There were some final embraces and whispered good-byes. Then Da and Robert walked to the wagon. Bran refused to sit in the back where Rebecca Carson had lain, cold and alone, on roads where trees talked to men. The dog squirmed between father and son, and they started for home, the talking trees uttering baritone farewells as they descended from the hidden places of the mountain.

After a long silence, Robert found strength to talk to his father.

"So we're not Christians, then, are we?"

"No."

"Are we Jews, then?"

"No."

"Is it Catholics we are?"

"No."

"What are we then, Da?"

"We're Irish, son," he said quietly. "We're Irish."

Two

The Arctic Heart

My comfort and my friend,
Master of the bright sword.
'Tis time you left your sleep;
Yonder hangs your whip.
Your horse is at the door. . . .

— Eibhlin Dhubh
ni Chonaill,
"The Lament for
Art O'Leary," 1745

12.

That night, facing each other before the hearth, the father told his son their true names. They were O'Connors, not Carsons. Da's true name was Fergus O'Connor. His son was Cormac Samuel O'Connor. The O'Connor name went all the way back through history, the father said, back before the settlers arrived from Scotland a century earlier, back before the Normans, back before Saint Patrick arrived with his lonely Christian God and before the Viking invasions, all the way back, in fact, to the arrival of the Celts.

"We've lived a long secret," the father whispered, as they stared at the hearth and sampled the stew that they had made for the first time without the loving touch of Rebecca. Bran was out by the dark barn, in the company of the sleeping Thunder. To the boy, the stew had a strange, alien taste.

"Is it still a secret?" he said. "Our own true names?"

"Aye, among us it is. And will remain a secret, lad."

"Why?"

"Because this is a country where religion can be dangerous. They will kill you for having one. Or for having the Old Religion, which to some is like having no religion at all."

"You mean . . ."

"I mean that the name Carson was taken by my father to keep us alive. It was a mask, lad. A way to live, to work, to eat, to get educated. It will remain that way, perhaps for a long time, but I believe you must know all this, and say nothing to anyone but me."

The boy tried to think of himself as Cormac but he still felt as if he were Robert. His legs and hands trembled. This was the most his father had ever said to him at one time, aside from talk of horses and iron. Cormac or Robert, he felt as if he had suddenly grown up.

"And where does the Samuel come from in my true name?"

"From your mother. Her true name was Rebecca Samuels. She wanted the name to live in you."

"Do we have a religion?"

"Aye," he whispered. "We call it the Old Religion."

He was about to explain when they heard Bran barking. Then there was a knock on the door. Da looked at it warily and signaled with an open palm that the boy should be quiet. He stood up and went to the door. Bran was barking more fiercely.

"Who is it?"

They heard the muffled voice of the Rev. Robinson. Da opened the door.

"Yes?"

"May we come in?"

Behind Robinson stood three other men, their faces familiar from Sunday services. All wore dripping coats and fur hats. Bran still barked, making feints and passes at them, unnerving them.

"Of course," Da said. "Do you want some tea?"

They stepped in, smelling of rain and the waxy sulphur of chapels. Da hushed Bran, telling him to remain outside. The dog growled with hostility and suspicion.

"No, thank you, Mister Carson. No time for tea. We'll be brief."

The boy thought, in a secretly excited way: *My father's name is not Carson. His name is O'Connor. Fergus O'Connor. And I'm Cormac Samuel O'Connor. Not Robert Carson.* He watched as the man he knew was Fergus O'Connor placed himself between his son and the visitors.

"Well?"

"We're quite sorry about your wife, Mister Carson."

"Thank you."

"But we have a question for you," Robinson said.

The boy's father — *His name is Fergus O'Connor* — looked at the preacher in a blank way. He seemed to know the question before it was uttered.

"It's about her burial, I suppose."

Silence for a long moment. *Her name was Rebecca Samuels. She was a Jew.*

Robinson said: "She was not buried in our churchyard."

Fergus O'Connor folded his arms across his chest.

"True?" the Rev. Robinson said.

"You know that's true."

"Where *is* she buried?"

"In the West," Da said. "According to her wishes."

The visitors looked at one another, as if the blacksmith had confirmed something for them.

"That leads to another question, Mister Carson."

"Ask it," he said, the muscles in his bare forearms moving.

"Are you Catholics?"

"No."

"You're sure? Because it's very suspicious that —"

"I told you that we're not Catholics. You see us every Sunday at your chapel. You —"

"There are many hidden papists here," one of the other men interrupted. "Full of treason, the lot of them."

Cormac Samuel O'Connor moved around to the side, watching his father.

"I've answered your questions."

"But I'd like —"

"Good night, Reverend Robinson."

Fergus O'Connor unfolded his arms and opened the door. Then he bowed slightly, making Robinson's face twitch. The faces of the other three knitted themselves into angry furrows.

"Try to stay dry," Da said. "And don't fear: I'll control the dog."

13.

Cormac Samuel O'Connor learned that he and his father were not unique. Everywhere, men and women changed their names and embraced strange gods in order to live. The Spanish did it, and the Muslims did it, and the Jews did it. In Spain, the Jews became *conversos*. Christians became Muslims and later, after the fall of Granada, Christians again. And so in Ireland, where Christians killed Christians during the wars of religion, Fergus O'Connor's father changed his name, and the name of his children. And, many centuries earlier, so did the family of Rebecca Samuels. But such a conversion was always a lie told in order to live. It was the making of a mask. And sometimes, in order to survive, a mask was not enough. Sometimes a man must have a weapon.

14.

Late on the afternoon after the visit from the Rev. Robinson and his posse, Fergus O'Connor began to make the sword. He did this with Cormac's help, describing each step in detail. While rain fell steadily from a dark sky, Bran sprawled on his belly, his eyes alert to danger or absorbed in watching the process. Thunder was led in from his stable to watch. The boy had seen John Carson make hundreds of sickles, and many knives, but he had never before made a sword. Now Fergus O'Connor was making a sword.

He went to work as if he had made hundreds. He began with three old iron horseshoes, laying them on the fired grate of the forge until they turned white, then lifting them with wide-mouthed tongs to the anvil. There he straightened them, lengthened them, braided them together. They formed the core of the sword. "They'll make it light in weight," Fergus O'Connor explained, "and easier to swing many times without tiring." Then he melted the steel, flecked with iron, and applied it smoothly in three heats to the core, folding it over three times, welding again, dressing it with glancing hammer blows, molding it, packing the steel around the core, adding a groove down each side, forming a perfect point.

Between each welding heat he scoured the blade with a paste made of charcoal, the ashes of straw, and fine Lagan riverbank clay. He held it up with the clamps, examined it in a piercing way. "The danger," he said, "is oxidation and scaling." Then he covered it with a thicker paste, adding polishing-stone powder and salt. He stripped this off the edge, exactly one sixteenth of an inch, and returned the emerging sword to the fire. When it was cherry red, he withdrew it, wiped away the coating, and drowned it in oil so sizzling that Bran barked.

While the blade cooled, he made a sword guard from rolled-up bars of iron and steel, welding the roll together and then flattening it so that it would protect the hand. He used shears and chisel to shape it into an elegant metal flower.

All of this was done in a day, Fergus O'Connor working with a sense of urgency, glancing out at the road as if wary of being seen. When the sword had cooled but was not cold, he used a needle-pointed burin to etch two figures into the broadest part of the sword, just below the handle.

Two spirals, thin at the top, curling around, then widening at the bottom. Like sea serpents. One on each side. Matching the spiral earrings of Fergus O'Connor's wife.

There was little traffic that day; the weather was too fierce. Da delicately sanded the etched markings, then passed the rough paper to his son for more sanding while showing him a hunk of white bone he had long saved, part of a wolf killed in the mountains.

"This will be the handle," he said. "The grip. We'll be finished by tonight."

"It's very beautiful, Da."

"Aye," he said, "but it's not meant to do beautiful things."

He told Cormac to go home and lay out the makings of dinner. He'd be home soon. Bran followed the boy back to the house and watched as he chopped onions and potatoes, and peered into jars of unlabeled spices, trying to remember what his mother had done on all those days when the two of them were here together. At one point, as he dropped the vegetables into a pot of water, Cormac Samuel O'Connor begin to shake.

Thinking: She's gone.

Thinking: Da needs her. I need her. As do Bran and Thunder. The O'Connors need her. But she's never coming back. She'll never turn her head suddenly from this hearth, with her spiral earrings flashing.

And then he forced himself to stop.

Thinking: Not now, not ever. No tears. No sobbing. Now you've got to be a man.

Thinking: You are no longer little Robert Carson. Not Robby or Bobby or Rob. You are Cormac Samuel O'Connor, from the days before Saint Patrick. You're the son of Fergus, not John.

When his father came home, he had the sword in his hand and smiled in a proud way. He whipped it in the air, making five or six cutting movements in a few seconds, and then smiled again, as if at himself. Cormac thought: *He has a wonderful smile.*

"We're not done," Fergus said. "But it's what I wanted. Light and hard and tempered."

They took turns polishing the blade, using a file crosswise on its flat sides, emery cloth for the fine edges. The boy could see his face in the polished steel and thought: *You are Cormac*. The cutting edge was like a razor. He glanced at his father, staring into the fire. *And he is Fergus.*

"Let's eat," Da said.

15.

Over the next few years, Cormac received three separate educations. All were happening at the same time, but in separate places. As young Robert Carson, he heard one version of the tale of the world at St. Edmund's, the one about the civilizing glories of the British Empire. Jesus, of course, came first, the Redeemer of sinful Man, the son of God whose gospel of love was tempered by the vehemence of the Old Testament. But the mission of Jesus also explained the mission of Britain. With God's blessing, he and his schoolmates were told, the British were expanding all over the earth. To America. To the Caribbean. To distant India. Taming barbarians. Bringing law to the lawless. Saving savages from the idol worship inflicted by the Whore of Babylon who ruled in Rome. They heard about brave Sir Francis Drake and his daring battles against the corrupt Spanish and treacherous French and even Cormac O'Connor, safe behind his Robert Carson mask, found those tales thrilling. He kept his questions about the moral point of the story to himself. Clearly, said the Rev. Robinson, God had chosen Britain to civilize and pacify the world, creating both a national duty and a personal mission for every God-fearing Protestant. And God had truly smiled on his blessed people. Hadn't God created a monstrous storm to defeat the Spanish Armada? Hadn't God helped the British build the greatest fleet of naval vessels in the world? This was all clear to the Rev. Robinson, although not quite so clear to the boy. The Rev. Robinson insisted that in Ireland, and particularly in the valiant North, fearless English armies (with help from the Dutch) had waged a righteous struggle to break the papal yoke, the tyranny of Rome, the Whore of Babylon, and in the process rescued Christianity itself.

"And the battle might never be fully won," he said, turning to blow loudly into his soiled, pebbly handkerchief. "We each have the obligation of eternal vigilance! Watch the man next door!"

Cormac was certain that Robinson glanced at him while speaking these words, but he absorbed the glance in his newly chosen role of spy. This was a secret personal performance that transformed many of his days into exciting patrols of enemy territory. He covered himself so well that to all his schoolmates he remained young Robert Carson, gifted at writing and drawing, a poor fellow whose mother had died, but who was, like each of them, an heir to the grandeur of English civilization. There were no questions from his friends, no suspicions (uttered or suggested) that he might actually be Cormac O'Connor, son of Fergus. The Rev. Robinson might have had his suspicions about John Carson, but he never transferred them to the blacksmith's son. If anything, after that first taming year when he used the Punisher so freely, Rev. Robinson seemed to approve Robert's growing mastery of ritual speeches about the moral missions of English monarchs and the debased perfidy of the Catholic Spanish and French. Cormac had a good memory and as Robert Carson he had the ability to infuse his speeches with emotion. Without a plan, the boy was serving a partial apprenticeship as an actor.

This personal form of espionage required much discipline, because unlike his schoolmates, Cormac O'Connor was learning other histories. To begin with, Irish history. "Our present," his father said, "is also our past." They talked much about the Penal Laws, which still existed today, in their Ireland; the O'Connors were saved from their brutality by the success of their disguises, by being Carsons. But the vicious Penal Laws were destroying thousands of innocent Catholic men, women, and children, those without disguises, those too full of defiance and pride, and were rooted in the immediate past.

"They were imposed," Fergus O'Connor explained, "only thirty years before your birth, Cormac, and are one reason why you're called Robert and I'm called John. They are the creation of the kind of men who take, sell, and keep slaves."

Under these laws (which Robert heard recited at St. Edmund's too, as the rules of eternal vigilance), no Catholic could vote or hold public office. No Catholic could study science or go to a foreign university. Only Protestants could do such things. No Catholic could buy land or even lease it. No Catholic could take a land dispute to court. If a Catholic owned land from the time before the Penal Laws, he couldn't leave it as in olden times to his oldest son; he must divide it among all his children, so that each plot would become smaller and smaller, and poverty would be guaranteed within three generations.

The most absurd of the Penal Laws stated that no Catholic could own a horse worth more than five pounds. Any Protestant could look at a Catholic's horse, say it was worth six pounds, or thirty pounds, or a thousand pounds, and take it from him on the spot. The Catholic had no right to protest in court. In a country of great horses and fine horsemen, the intention was clear: to humiliate Catholic men, to break their hearts.

"If you can break a man's heart," Da said, "you can destroy his will."

That was why they must remain Carsons to everyone they ever met. When they rode Thunder through country lanes or city streets, they must be Protestants. "Even poor Thunder must be a Protestant horse," his father said, and laughed in a dark way. But he'd told his son that they were not Catholics either, so what did they have to fear? "Sick bastards," Fergus O'Connor said. "In this country, they think that if you're not Protestant then you must be Catholic, even if you're not. It's a sickness, a poison of the brain."

And so Fergus began telling his son the longer story too, the one not told in school. They were part of that story, as the hidden grove was a defiant remnant of unconquered Ireland. Unconquered by either Rome or London. In the schoolroom at St. Edmund's, the boy learned the names of English kings and English heroes. He read the Magna Carta. He recited English ideals. But as his father told him the story of Ireland, his mind also teemed with Celts and Vikings, informers and traitors, and murder after murder after murder.

As Fergus O'Connor ate greedily each evening (his manners grown coarser after the death of his wife), he sketched the history, relating the brutal story of Oliver Cromwell and the vast slaughters of unarmed Catholics, and then leaped backward in time to the arrival of Strongbow on May 1, 1170, as the result of the treachery of Irish nobles. He told his son about how "that bitch" Elizabeth I was really a heartless killer, and how her father, Henry VIII, encased in fat and pearls, was even worse, killing two of his six wives, along with thousands of Irishmen, while imposing his own version of Christianity on the islands. Such words always came from Fergus with a sense of growing outrage, as if each new telling of the tale drove fury through his blood. For Cormac, the Irish tales were like those in the Bible, full of heroism and cowardice and martyrdom — and, too often, exile. And in the Irish story, the result was always the same: the English stealing Ireland for themselves, acre by acre, for its wood and its crops and its cheap labor, and for its fine horses too, while insisting that this grand robbery was something noble.

Cormac heard his father explain how the unarmed Ulster Irish were beaten back off the good land into the rocky hills and the stony mountains, the good land handed to the likes of the whoremaster Chichesters, while poor Protestant settlers were brought from Scotland to work the land and pay rents to the English. "They were made into slaves," Da said, "and thought they were free." After a while, when the British perfected the use of religion as an excuse for cruelty and theft, the Irish began to think that being Catholic was the same as being Irish, which of course it wasn't.

"The Irish were here before Jesus Christ was even born," he said. "So were their gods."

The evening monologues of Fergus O'Connor were in startling contrast to his silence when he was playing John Carson. The words came in streams, rising and falling, emphasized with his long fingers, or by hands balled into fists. Still, in all that he said to his son, he insisted there were men in Ireland who cared for true justice.

"There's a fellow in Dublin, the Dean, they call him," he said one night. "Jonathan Swift. You must read his *Drapier's Letters,* son. I have them in a bound book, hidden out in the stable. He's a man with justice in his heart. A Protestant, but an Irishman first. And you must begin reading the newspapers. The *News-Letter* here is run by fair men. The Dean writes for the *Dublin Journal,* and I have some of those hidden here too."

"Why do you hide them, Da?"

"Because of the bloody injustice here, lad. Some writers expose the injustice, and just reading about it will make you a suspect. And whenever there's trouble in Ulster, every suspect dies."

"Are we suspects, Da?"

The older man paused for a long moment.

"I think we are," he said.

16.

On Sundays, father and son trudged to St. Edmund's to inhale the odors of an orderly piety. Each wore his mask. For a solemn hour, Fergus and Cormac O'Connor played John and Robert Carson. An hour later, all sermons absorbed, all visions of Hell behind them, they mounted Thunder and trotted into the glens behind the Black Mountain. There, beyond observation, Sunday after Sunday, with a kind of religious intensity, the father showed his son the power of the sword.

In one lesson he cut off a tree limb that was eight inches thick. Not chopping it or hacking at it like a butcher. Cutting it in a single stroke with his blacksmith's arm and his perfect sword, like a knife cuts butter. More important than the sword's strength and power, he said to his son, was the way it was used. He taught through example and drill how to unsheathe the sword in one whiplike motion. How to slash with it or stab with it. How to avoid the other man's sword, his thrusts and swings. In their first lessons they used simple wooden poles, father making son repeat the motions over and over again until all his movements became swift and fluid. Then he handed his son the sword itself. The feel of it always awed the young man, at times even cowed him. Its power seemed to surge up his right arm in a liquid way. Sometimes the younger man's exhausted arm would ache, but at such moments the father urged him to try even harder. Or to switch to his left hand.

"You don't ever want to die," he said, "because you're tired. Or because you've been wounded in your fighting arm. Each arm must have equal strength. And one other thing: If you *think* you'll get tired, then you *will* get tired. If you *think* you'll lose, you *will* lose."

Fergus showed Cormac the principles of balance, and the way to shift weight, sliding forward on one leg, not leaping but pushing on the back leg. He urged him to move side to side, never to stand straight in front of an opponent, chopping at him, but to use quickness and surprise to fool him, and then to finish him. He knew everything about sword fighting, and one Sunday Cormac asked his father where he learned what he knew.

"I was a soldier," he said.

"You were?"

"Aye. When I was your age."

"And where did you soldier?"

His eyebrows rose. "Why, in Ireland, of course."

"Tell me about it."

"No."

"Why not, Da?"

"I did nothing more than did better men than I. 'Tis nothing to brag upon."

"Did you fight the English?"

"Aye."

"Did you . . . kill men?"

"Aye."

"Many men?"

"Too many."

Fergus turned the sword over in his hand, retreating into himself, then said: "We'd best be going. It's almost dark."

Back at the forge, they never displayed the sword in the open air, afraid that some spy might be watching. If they were indeed suspected of being Catholic, then a spy could be peering at them from the woods, and it was forbidden for a Catholic to possess a weapon of any kind. For a while, Fergus hid the sword behind a false panel in the tool shed, then he moved it to a slot he built into the rush matting of the roof. On days of hammering rain, when the woods were empty of curious strangers, they practiced reaching for it by standing on one of the three-legged stools, making a swift, fluid movement that ended with a slash of the air. One late night, Fergus designed a map case for the sword, with a wide fluted bell for the handle, equipped with a leather loop that could be slung upon a saddle horn. That was the way they carried it while traveling. Cormac O'Connor was learning that people and things were not always what they seemed to be.

In the forge, when Cormac was not sharing the work, his father made him lift hunks of iron and steel, working his biceps and shoulders and back, doing curls and thrusts, then lifting pig iron over his head, the weight always increasing. Cormac's muscles grew harder and tauter, and in the dark Sunday forests the sword felt lighter. His father had him skip rope too, explaining that a swordsman needed legs with spring and power. And he established codes. Never use a sword on someone who can't fight back. Don't drink, ever, because drink makes the wits rust, and you can die without a fight. If you draw your sword, prepare to kill with it or to die.

"And tell none of these to any man," he said. "He must never know what you're thinking. That's the business of yourself, lad."

17.

Across two summers, Cormac became a Celt.

He was taken by his father to the sacred grove, passing through the talking trees, and placed in the care of Mary Morrigan. She was assisted by the men and the younger women. Each time his father left, Cormac hated the moment of separation, and so did Thunder and Bran, who were going back with Fergus. That first time (Cormac later thought of it as a first semester), the dog refused to move and Thunder tossed his head in protest. But Fergus growled his orders, and they obeyed in a sulking way, and off they went through the trees. When they were gone, the old woman took Cormac by the hand led him through the woods to the mouth of a cave on the slope of a hill. Here the young man slept on furs while becoming an Irishman.

Mary Morrigan taught him the Irish language, with its eighteen letters, starting with the words for man, *fear,* and woman, *bean,* and bread, *aran,* and water, *uisce*. She taught him how to say "I want." And then she began talking in Irish to him, even though Cormac didn't yet understand. Cormac was angered by this new stage. He thought: Why does she insist on speaking this language? It's gone, destroyed. He thought: Why not just use English? But she calmed and fed him, and named the food in Irish, and the pots and the fire, and told him to sleep and then, in the morning, started over again. As he moved around the forest that surrounded the grove he understood that it was actually a village with trees separating and hiding the houses. About six hundred people were hiding there from the world. Beside one house there was a huge well, and all drew from it, using hand-carved wooden buckets. In another house were supplies of oats, available to all. Cormac didn't see anyone using money. About a dozen horses, small and lean, were tied to trees with straw ropes (he never once hear them whinny). Pigs and chickens roamed freely. At a tanner's, animals were skinned, their pelts hung on ropes to dry, while sweet, sickening odors rose from boiling pots. A metalsmith gave shape and beauty to shields and jewelry, and Cormac chatted in his broken Irish with a blacksmith who knew Fergus. Mary Morrigan introduced Cormac to the men and the women and the young people, and all of them spoke to him in Irish. He listened and nodded shyly and remained mute.

Then one morning Mary Morrigan asked him in Irish whether he had slept well and he answered her in Irish, "Yes, I've slept well." The key had turned in the lock, the way he had climbed a magic ladder into arithmetic. By the end of summer, he was not simply speaking Irish, he was thinking in Irish. And, yes: dreaming.

"Good," Mary Morrigan said that first morning after the key turned. "There's much for you to know."

She instructed him about the seasons, and the great feasts. Imbalc, with its sacred flame, and the white stones that were marked with your own sign and thrown in the fire, and how if your stone wasn't there when the fire cooled then it had been consumed like food by the flames and you'd been blessed by the gods of fire. Beltane, on the first of May, when Cormac saw cattle driven between walls of flame, and a maypole dance, and then men and women falling down together in the woods. And though this had not happened to him, although he had lain down on the earth with no girl, he wanted to dance around the maypole with all of them, red-haired women and golden-haired girls, dark-haired and black (while rough-skinned Mary Morrigan whispered to him in Irish: *"No, not you, not here, not yet"*). Lughnasa in August: a great gathering of horses and cattle, to be traded and sold, with beef roasted for the tribe, and fires lighting up the night sky, mad dancing and much music and Mary Morrigan telling him that Ireland is a woman, is called by some the Dark Rosaleen, is always deep in the dark heart of the dance. Samhain in November: the harvest gathered, fruits and grains and great soups simmering in immense kettles while the music drifted through hills and over mountains and into caves and down into the Otherworld. They used that word a lot, as if it named a specific place. Cormac would hear more from Mary Morrigan about the Otherworld.

Across those years, he attended all of the feasts except Imbalc, because if he disappeared from St. Edmund's in February, he might attract hard attention. In summer, many people scattered around Ireland, including the English and the Protestants; none went off in winter. Across those years, a new calendar was being added to his sense of time. The calendar of Ireland. Before Samhain, he and his father cleaned every speck of dust from the house, as was the custom, and followed another custom by leaving food for Cormac's mother. When they returned to the house from their journeys to the forests or the town, the food was always gone.

All those great feasts revolved about the land and the sun and the marvelous gifts they granted to mortals. If the sun was not a god, what was? *Who* was? In the old days, Mary Morrigan said (and his father confirmed), the feasts were held under sun and moon on free, unfenced land, drawing men and women from all over Ireland. They were held now in the last unconquered forests of Ireland (the timber along the edges departing each month to build mansions in London or to be turned into ships for pirates and buccaneers who stole and looted for the English crown). The boy, becoming a man, becoming a Celt, saw that guile was essential to all his summer Irishmen. They needed the gift of deception as they traveled to the feasts on roads patrolled by British redcoats. Guile and deception, along with the ability to see and to hear and to connect their facts, because informers could be among them. The feasts were now held behind hidden pickets of men armed with swords and pikes, disguised as trees, allies of birds and deer and wolves, watching always for the English with their guns.

Cormac was never clear about his exact location, because none of the Irish made maps that could be found by their enemies (later he was certain that the grove was on the inland side of the Mountains of Mourne). What he did know was simple: He was in pure, untouched Ireland. They all spoke Irish. The jokes were Irish and the laughter was Irish and the gods were Irish, and so was the story, the legend, the binding tale. Along with one other immense thing. Beside the fire in the cave, on rainy summer nights, Mary Morrigan explained to him about the Otherworld.

"The Otherworld is beneath us," she said, gesturing with a leathery hand, her palms flat with the ground beneath them.

The Otherworld was a *place,* as she described it, not a mere story or an abstract idea, and it was reachable through raised mounds called *shees*. Down there lived people called the Tuatha de Danaan, who had been in Ireland before the Celts, a race of poets and warriors who fought to maintain their place and then, after one final defeat, had retreated beneath the surface of the earth. Ever since, the Irish, when they died, had been following them into the earth. Hearing her descriptions, Cormac understood that the Otherworld was not like the ferocious Hell described by the Rev. Robinson, filled with flames, torture, screams, and horror. There was enchanted music down there, she said, and endless games, and eternal feasting. Nobody ever got ill in the Otherworld, and nobody fought, except for fun. There was no such thing as old age or even time. The future was the same as the past, and the present contained both. Or so said Mary Morrigan, as Cormac struggled to understand, and to imagine.

"Who gets in and who's kept out?" he asked.

"The just are admitted, the unjust barred," she said. "The Christians borrowed all that from us."

"So my mother is there?"

"Aye." She paused. "If you live a just life, you'll see her there. Of that, there is no doubt. Sure, didn't we help her into the Otherworld from this very spot?"

"Who else is barred?"

"Those who fail to avenge injustice," she said. "For want of courage. For want of passion. If an unjust act is done in the family of a man or woman, it must be avenged. That is the rule."

Another pause.

"And suicides," she said. "Those who cannot live with the pain of the world and kill themselves are barred forever."

On many smoky evenings, she told him tales of the Otherworld. There was a very special, beautiful light down there too, she said, invented by the Tuatha de Danaan. A light never seen in this world. A light created by millions of emeralds embedded in the walls, a green, watery light that was both alluring and welcoming. The just people who came to the Otherworld were cared for by the Other People, which was what some called the

Tuatha de Danaan. Sometimes the Other People emerged into our world from the emerald caves, disguised as fawns or birds or beautiful women, and lured our heroes back down into their secret world. Wasn't the great Finn MacCool himself tempted? And the great Celtic warrior Cuchulain?

"Are the Other People angry with us?" Cormac asked.

"Never. They've come to accept everything. They understand human weakness. But they can be rogues themselves. There are so many old people down there — those who've lived long lives — that they miss certain beautiful sounds and faces. That's why they sometimes steal children. Once in a great while, for a joke, they'll steal your food."

"Do they marry and have their own children, the way we do?"

"Never. They can't have children. That was part of the bargain with the gods. That's one thing they gave up when they chose to live forever."

"And do they live only in the *shee?*"

"No, Cormac. The *shee* is the entrance. That would be like trying to live in a doorway."

The Otherworld, she explained, stretched everywhere. There was an entrance in the Cave of Cruachain, where it was possible during the feast of Samhain to enter the Otherworld. But no human should go before it was time. That was one reason for the rule against suicide. And there was a dark part of the Otherworld too, she said, ruled over by Donn, the lord of the bad Irish dead, full of immense serpents, red horsemen, the walls hung with severed heads. She didn't dwell on this, and Cormac was pleased; it sounded too much like the Rev. Robinson's Christian Hell.

"When your time arrives," she said, "and you have lived your full portion, and added to decency in this world, then you too can live in the Otherworld. You can unite with all those you once loved here in the world. You can share the music, the feasting, and the emerald light. But," she went on, "if you add to evil, if you defy time, you'll find yourself in the land of Donn."

Hearing these tales, Cormac looked differently at the land, imagining those who lived beneath him, including his mother and his two lost brothers, and he often ached to be with them. He also woke sometimes at night in a sweat and trembling, in the slippery grip of the enraged and punishing Donn. He wanted then to pray, to find the strength that Joseph found in the land of the Pharaohs, but he felt there was no god who would hear his prayers. He said his mother's name and his father's, Thunder's name and Bran's, and swore to whoever might hear him that he would avenge all injustices, starting with what had happened to his mother.

Most of the time he was free of nightmares. And in his waking hours, his head was full of other visions, exuberantly brimming with drama and magic. From leathery Mary Morrigan, he heard wondrous tales of Cuchulain and his great warrior rages. And of Finn MacCool and how he assumed the leadership of the Fianna by getting rid of the killer of his father. This wasn't easy to do, for his father's killer was smart and hard and vicious. But Finn was special. A druid gave him a crane bag containing a shield, a sword, a helmet, and a pigskin belt. A great bard allowed him to eat the Salmon of Knowledge, which gave him wisdom and the gift of poetry. With armor and poetry, Finn became the man who saved Tara. He was the man who married Sava, who had been magically transformed into a fawn and became human again at the sight of Finn, and who gave birth to their child, Usheen (which Cormac later learned was spelled Oisin). But Finn was not perfect. No god was perfect. No warrior or poet was perfect. And as he grew older, imperfect Finn made a terrible mistake: He fell in love with a woman named Grainne while he was still married to Sava. But there was a younger, shrewder rival for the love of Grainne, a man named Diarmuid. At this time, Finn's wife prophesied that if Finn ever drank from a horn, he would die. After treacherously arranging for the death of Diarmuid, Finn went off, bursting with vanity and dishonor, to leap the River Boyne in one bound. But first, in his defiant arrogance, he sipped liquor from a horn. And then fell into the river and drowned.

"A fool," said Mary Morrigan, telling him the story for the first time. "A great man was Finn MacCool, a hero. But also a bloody fool. You see the point? Love can do that to any one of us."

"Has it done it to you?" Cormac asked.

She looked at him for a long time, then stared into the fire.

"Of course," she said, but offered no details.

Cormac loved the story of the stupid end of Finn MacCool and believed it completely, and sometimes laughed out loud at the ending. He wished there were books in Irish so he could read these tales, but all were spoken by Mary Morrigan. More than all other tales, he was entranced by the story of Usheen. As told by Mary Morrigan, Usheen was the son of Finn and Sava, but he never knew his mother. She had come as a fawn from the Otherworld and was reclaimed after the birth of Usheen. But the boy was brought up among the Fianna and became one if its bravest warriors. Then he met a beautiful woman: Niave of the Golden Hair. She was the daughter of the king of Tir-na-Nog, the Land of the Ever Young. Usheen was entranced by her and followed her across distant seas to this magical land in the West. For a very long time, he was blissfully happy. There was an abundance of food and flowers, and weather that was an eternal springtime. But after several hundred years, during which he didn't age a single day, Usheen got homesick, wanting desperately to see Ireland. Once again, stupidity played its part. Usheen had been warned upon arrival in Tir-na-Nog that if he ever again set foot upon the soil of Ireland, he would die. He ignored the warning, or deceived himself about its terms, thinking that if he went on horseback, and remained on his horse, he could avoid touching Irish soil and thus remain alive. He was prepared to live forever with Niave in Tir-na-Nog, but first he must rid himself of the aching longing for his first home, for his comrades in the Fianna, for the place where he once was a great warrior. So he set off on horseback for Ireland. And when he arrived, everything had changed.

The great old houses had crumbled into rubble. His comrades were dead. Tara was gone with the wind. The warriors, poets, and women he knew had vanished. He learned from strangers that almost three hundred years had passed since he left with Niave of the Golden Hair. He sobbed for all that was gone and turned his horse to return to his much-loved woman in Tir-na-Nog. Then he saw a famished woman on the road, apparently dying of thirst. Touched by pity, distracted by his sense of loss, he leaned over awkwardly to give her a drink, slipped from the horse, and landed hard on the earth of Ireland. Before the old woman's horrified eyes, Usheen instantly withered into bone and skin, giving off the sweet, sickening odor of death and decay.

Cormac asked Mary Morrigan to tell him that story over and over again. Where was Tir-na-Nog? To the West. Was it an island? Yes, she said, it's an island. But sometimes it's under the sea, she said, and sometimes it's in a far part of the Otherworld.

"Can it be in America?" Cormac asked.

She looked at him in a dubious way.

"Why do you ask that?"

"So many people are leaving Belfast for America," he said. "Maybe —"

"No," she said, her voice as old as tombs. "I don't think it's in America."

18.

Then came the night near the end of his second summer in the Irish grove. Cormac noticed Mary Morrigan staring long and hard at the fire in a kind of absolute solitude. Her shawl was pulled tight against her lean, hard frame. He asked what was the matter. She didn't answer. He waited. Over two years, she had taught him to wait. Finally her voice rose whispery and distant from someplace deep within her.

"A bad time is coming," she said in Irish.

Her eyes remained fixed on the low orange flame spurting liquidly in and around the burning logs.

"There'll be starving and wailing and killing," she said. "You'll hear the banshee cry in the night."

She poked the fire with a blackened oak stick. The flame stirred. Sparks danced into the air but had no way to reach the stars through the roof of the cave.

"You'd best get ready," she said. "It's coming."

Later, her words made him toss and shift beneath the thin muslin blanket in his place in the darker recesses of the cave. He kept thinking of Joseph and his brothers, the warning to the Pharaoh, the horrors of the bad time: the tale coming to him in his mother's voice. The cave felt damper, colder. He knew Mary Morrigan's prophecy was true; she didn't lie. And that meant he must warn his father. Mary Morrigan would speak her truth to the tribe, but Cormac must tell his father. He was coming in the morning, to bring his son back to his life as Robert Carson, son of John. He knew his father would come for him, because whenever he said he would do something, he did it. He wondered whether Mary Morrigan would tell the tribe the tale of Joseph and his brothers. There were no Christians in this holy grove, and no Jews other than Cormac, and he was only half Jewish. These were the Irish. And Cormac was Irish, and a Jew, and he knew the tale. He thought: Shall I tell the tale of Joseph to Mary Morrigan? Shall I tell the Irish tribe? And what, after all, did she mean by her prophecy? Will plagues come first, arriving tonight as I fight against sleep? Will they start in the city of Belfast and follow John Carson into the forest? And will plagues be followed by locusts and boils and hunger?

All those calamities from the Christian Bible, spoken softly and carefully by his mother or bellowed by the Rev. Robinson: They were coming. They *must* have been what Mary Morrigan called the bad time. They must. But although Cormac knew the words of calamity, they didn't put pictures in his head. What, after all, was a boil? What did a locust look like? His mother had tried to explain them to him. A boil, Rebecca Carson said, was a great shiny swelling on the body, pale yellow, bursting with disease. And a locust was an insect like a grasshopper that came in great clouds of its fellow creatures to eat the green off the face of the earth. Turning now in the damp, peat-smelling darkness of the cave, trying to convert words into vivid pictures, he wished his mother were there to describe them better to him. He wished she could rise from the place where she was buried, only a few hundred feet from this cave, emerge from the emerald light of the Otherworld, and explain to him what she knew and the truth of what she'd seen and whether it was like the truth of

Mary Morrigan. And if the plagues and the boils and the locusts were real, if they were part of that bad time coming, he wanted his father to be safe from all the badness. And, yes, he thought: I want to be safe myself. I want to live a long time, to see what happens to everyone, to discover what happens to people I don't yet know. Thinking, as he remembered the rules set by Mary Morrigan: I need to earn my way to the Otherworld. I need to build my courage. I need to forge my passion. I need to avenge all unjust acts committed against family and tribe. I must learn to live with the pain of the world until my time comes. Then I will see my mother. Then I will see my lost brothers. He fell asleep trying to imagine the sound of the banshee.

Then he was awake. An hour later, or three hours, he could not tell. The fire dozed, and in its light he saw the leathery face of Mary Morrigan very close to his own. Her grainy fingertips touched his cheek. She was kneeling beside him.

"You're a good lad," she whispered.

And then leaned down and kissed him.

She shuddered. So did he.

Then, with a wind rising beyond the cave mouth, rustling the trees before it, her hard, granular skin fell away, vanishing into the dark orangey air, and Cormac O'Connor was afraid. Looking down at him was a woman with an oval face framed by thick ringlets of black hair, eyes lustrous and hungry. He smelled pale roses. Her full lips widened into a serene smile. He touched her face. To see if it was real. And to still his trembling hand. Her skin remained the color of leather but was now smooth and pliant. Dark-skinned woman. Dark Rosaleen of the old, sad Celtic song. She moved his blanket aside and played with the bone buttons of his coarse blue shirt.

No words were spoken. She eased out of the ragged clothes of Mary Morrigan, naked now in the firelight, shifted above him and his tense, sweating body, and held in her dark smooth-skinned hand her smooth full dark-nippled breast, and offered it to his mouth. He took it. Hard-nippled brown-nippled dark-skinned woman. Suckling him. Dark-skinned woman with hair falling like a black flower from her head, as he tried to suck all she knew, all she was offering, all she could give him. Her soft smooth kneading hand, damp and cool as the dark air, found his bursting cock and slowly smoothly moistly firmly she began then to move him out of himself, out of that place, out of time, into the future.

19.

He told his father none of this, of course, when he came for Cormac in the morning. Nothing about the wetness and the tightness and the milky taste of Mary Morrigan, nothing about the scent of pale roses seeping from her flesh, nothing about the rising midnight wind and the whipping sound of trees and the long, deep stranger's roar that had come from within him and the caress of hands and the taste of tongue and lips and hair: and nothing either about the dark, emptied sleep that followed.

From his place in the morning trees, he saw Fergus O'Connor, his fierce-limbed father, drive the cart into the grove, and the men of his Irish tribe rushing to greet him while Bran leaped from the seat and bounded forward to greet Cormac. The dog was jumping and leaping and licking his hands, his tail whipping the air, then gestured with his head for Cormac to follow him to Thunder. His father waved, signaling with his hands for Cormac to stay back for now, follow the dog, his face saying, Wait, son, I must do something first. Cormac understood. Following Bran to the horse, he looked around, but Mary Morrigan was nowhere in sight. He wondered if she'd told the men what had happened in the night (for in the time of feasts they spoke of all things) and then thought that she had not. And then wondered if it had happened at all, if it had only been a dream. Then, thinking: No, it was not a dream. I can smell her on me. The scent of pale roses.

Bran and Thunder broke his thoughts. The great horse was slick from the journey, his black coat streaked with white foam. Cormac loosened the harness, hugged Thunder's massive head, and led him to the hidden stream, where all three drank together from the silky current. The water was the color of the sky.

Through the trees he could see the men now unloading crates from beneath a false bottom Fergus O'Connor had added to the cart, using one of his father's tools to open each in an almost reverential way. Suddenly they were all holding new muskets. Then Fergus was showing them how the guns were used. This was what he needed to do first, Cormac thought, and he didn't want me to be part of it. Men use muskets. And I'm not yet a man. Da must know that a bad time is coming.

The men moved into the forest with the guns, and Fergus came to fetch his son, to hug him, to drink sky-colored water with the boy and the horse and the dog. Then they all gathered with the others for a small feast of eggs and bread, bacon and vegetables, washed down with icy water from earthenware mugs. The other women brought the food, young women, golden-haired, long-gowned, their bodies hidden. In his mind, Cormac could see their breasts and bellies and hidden hair. But none were made of the stained dark skin of Mary Morrigan, who was still nowhere in sight. The men grew flushed and excited, skin reddening, nostrils flaring, but not because of the women. *"Let them come now,"* one said. *"Let them come, and we'll be ready for them."* Another said, *"Aye, let them come, and we'll fight them with their own weapons."* All talking abruptly, breathily in Irish, while Fergus said nothing. He had done his work, kept a promise to deliver the weapons; what was to happen with the guns was in the future. Cormac asked him where he'd gotten the guns. He answered that it didn't matter. He said he hoped they'd never be used, that they would rust in their hiding places, because he hated the guns, which were mere machines.

"But we must be ready," he said, "if the English come for us."

Then they were leaving, Fergus exchanging somber embraces with the men and polite, grave nods with the women. Thunder was harnessed to the empty wagon. Cormac still could not see Mary Morrigan, and he ran through the trees to the cave, but she was not there. He felt that this was not right. Not right, after what had happened in the cave. Not right, to just go away without a word. All summer she'd been his teacher, of language and music and stories. And in the cave . . . He returned, breathless from running, to the cart. Bran hopped up between them and his father uttered a word in Irish and Thunder stepped off.

Then at last Cormac saw Mary Morrigan. She was high on the slope of the hill at the mouth of the cave. He stood up in the wagon and waved. She made a small, sad, finger-curling signal with her ancient hand, and then was lost behind a screen of trees. As he sat down, his mind filled with images of dark and pliant skin, the flesh of roses.

"It's all right, son. She'll be here when you come back."

"I hope. Because she says that a bad time is coming."

All the way home, they talked about what Mary Morrigan had told Cormac. "We must be ready, Da, " Cormac said, and his father answered, "Aye." The boy reminded him of his mother's story, the tale of Joseph and his brothers and how the Pharaoh listened while the Hebrews did not. "Aye," he said, "I remember it well." Nodding, listening, his face heavy with memory. Rebecca seemed to be with them on those roads: Rebecca to the father, Ma to the son. Dark hair and sweet voice and still dead in the rain and mud of Belfast.

"Well," Fergus O'Connor said, "if bad times are coming, we must prepare."

"Would *she* know all this?" Cormac said. "Our Mary Morrigan?"

"Yes."

"Suppose she's wrong?"

"About such things, she's never wrong."

20.

A*t home that night, they began to prepare. Fergus made a list (as if* dictated by his mother) of the tasks they'd share and the things they must store. Food most of all: potatoes, oats, corn, salted bacon, cooked beef, limes against the scurvy. And turf to keep the hearth alive.

"We'll get through it," Fergus said. "No matter what form it takes. Now, get ye to bed, for we have much to do on the morrow."

In the dark room where the horse's skull was buried in the mortar, Cormac thought of plagues and locusts and his mother, imagining Joseph's face and the Pharaoh's voice, and then saw in the blackness Mary Morrigan beside him, with her damp hands, her voice whispering Irish words in the light of a fire, her tight, fleshy cave enclosing him and her smooth skin pressed against him.

In the morning they began their tasks. Cormac rode Thunder to town on the first of many trips to buy candles, bacon, lime, biscuits. A produce wagon arrived late in the day with a special order of turf and another wagon brought sacks of oats. Together, father and son moved furniture to make room for the turf and the oat sacks against the inside walls of the house, and then ordered more. Every day, Da worked furiously in the forge, making horseshoes and sickles to earn money and handing some of the work to his son. At school, Robert Carson said nothing, as always; reticence had become his way, the truth of his thinking and of himself, buried in restrained talk of games or discussions of the stories in their schoolbooks.

One afternoon he did remind his friends about Joseph and his brothers, hoping they'd understand what he meant; but they discussed it only as a good story. The Rev. Robinson was teaching more quietly now, with fewer rants about Moloch and the Whore of Babylon (for he was older too), but Robert Carson said nothing to him about the bad time either. In truth, if boils and plagues did arrive, he would feel little sorrow if they went at the preacher. Perhaps he would emerge a humbler man, one who questioned his brutal God. The warning was Irish; the Irish would do what they must to survive.

Each evening now, after a hard and exhausting day in the forge, John Carson stood outside the house, looking for signs in the sky and the sea and the movement of birds. Inside, when they became Fergus and Cormac O'Connor, they talked beside the hearth. Fergus gave his son any news that might be connected to Mary Morrigan's prophecy. Hints of bad times came from customers in the forge, from travelers with damaged axles, facts decoded from the oblique reports in newspapers. In Belfast and Derry, groups of men had been making midnight raids on certain houses, searching for disguised Catholics. The incidents seemed isolated. Fergus said he thought they were not. "They are signs," he said, "and must be read correctly, like the tracks of wild animals." He explained that these actions were caused by a kind of fever that would lie dormant for years and then suddenly erupt. A fever in the brain. A black fever in the heart. "Good men are taken away," he said, "never to return." Cormac asked if these raids were the bad time coming. His father nodded at that possibility.

"We must be very careful," Fergus said. "Whatever you do, don't speak Irish in public. Not a word. Give them no excuse. Create no suspicion. They are worse than fools. They are murderous fools."

Sometimes they spoke of life and death, and how death came to every man. And how some forms of death were unacceptable. He didn't mean the death of Rebecca. That was, when all was said and done, an accident. It was carelessness made deadly. But it was not murder.

"And murder?" Cormac asked. "What is to be done about murder?"

The older man gazed into the fire, his eyes smoky.

"In our tribe," he said, "the murderer must be pursued to the ends of the earth. And his male children too. They must be brought to the end of the line."

A pause.

"That's very harsh, isn't it, Da?"

"Aye," he said. "But murder is harsh too."

In the blue black hour before dawn one morning, Fergus woke his son, telling him to dress and follow him. He was carrying the map case and a small leather pouch tied with a leather thong. In the forge, Cormac watched as his father stuffed the matted sword into the case. He handed the boy a spade and took one for himself. They eased outside and flattened themselves against the shadowed side of the house, wary of being watched. Bran was with them, silent, so dark they could see only the whites of his eyes. They all paused, sorting the sounds of awakening birds and small animals in the darkness. Bran growled but didn't bark. Then, as an inky cloud veiled the moon, they hurried across the open space to the hawthorn tree. Together, they removed a rectangle of sod and then dug a narrow, shallow trench. Fergus laid the leather bag down first and it made a dull clunking sound, so that Cormac knew it contained coins. Then Fergus placed the encased sword on top of the bag. The clouds passed, and in the sudden moonlight the leather bag was darker than Mary Morrigan's skin. To Cormac, it looked, in fact, like a lumpy leather pillow for the sword, and for a moment he saw his mother again, lying in her piece of the Irish grove with the things beside her that she would take to the Otherworld.

But he also knew that this was not a burial; it was a preparation for this world. As they covered the bag and sword with heavy earth, Cormac longed for the sweet earth of Mary Morrigan's cave and the taste of her earth-colored breasts and the scent of pale roses.

"If anything happens to me," Fergus whispered, "come here and retrieve these, son, and take them on your journey."

"I understand."

Fergus didn't say where that journey might take him, but it would surely be away from their small piece of Ireland. In silence, they fitted the sod perfectly upon the trench, tamped it down, returned the spades to the forge, and went to prepare breakfast. They were sure they hadn't been seen. If they had, Bran would have warned them. As they reached the house, a morning wind blew hard off the sea.

One evening a week later, with the days edging toward Christmas, Bran began barking loudly in his deepest baritone, and there was a fierce hammering at their door. Bran told them: This is danger. Fergus dropped his newspaper and pointed at his son.

"Get ye in your room," he ordered, "and stay there."

"Da, I'm sixteen, I —"

"Now," he said.

Cormac did as he was told, leaving the bedroom door open a few inches so that he could see what was happening. The main room was illuminated by only one candle and the low, dull fire of the hearth. Cormac's heart was fluttery. Bran kept barking.

Fergus placed one stool on top of another, leaving three blunt legs facing the roof. Those legs were now the height of his anvil, within reach of his hand. The knocking on the door was harder, muffled voices louder. Carefully, Fergus opened the door, holding Bran by his leather collar. Cormac glimpsed gaunt, pale faces and the flickering of torches.

"What do you want?" Fergus said.

"We want to search this house," said a hard, burred voice. The speaker moved closer to Fergus, and Cormac could see the man: short, bull-necked, the apparent leader.

"Why?" Fergus said.

"We've reason to believe you're a papist. A hidden Catholic. A Catholic with a Protestant mask."

"You're wrong," Fergus said, and chuckled.

"You're lying, mister," the bull-necked man said.

"That, I'm not," Fergus said, his voice darkening.

"We'll see to that. We're going to search this papist hole. Step aside."

Cormac saw his father's fingers curl around a leg of the stool.

"If you take one step into this house," Fergus said, "I'll break your bloody head."

The bull-necked man stared at Fergus for a long moment. Cormac knew what he was seeing: eyes as cold and gray as steel. Squatting in the darkness, Cormac reached under his bed for the length of iron he used for his exercises, and remembered the horse's skull buried in the wall of this room long ago. He thought: Give me what I need, horse.

"We'll see about that," the bull-necked man said, as if by talking tough he could ease his own doubts. He turned slightly, eyes on Fergus but speaking into the torches. He said dramatically: "Billy?"

A taller man, younger, with a hat pulled tight over his eyebrows, stepped into the doorway to the side of the bull-necked man. He was nervously holding a pistol in his left hand, pointing the long silvered barrel at Fergus. Cormac's father didn't move.

"You're breaking the law," Fergus said calmly. "Just pointing that pistol at me is a crime."

"'Tis a far worse crime to be a secret papist," the bull-necked man said. "Your crime is treason."

Now Cormac could see the pistol and the forearm but not the face. The man was stepping back to take aim. Cormac slipped out of the bedroom, gripping the iron bar, moving quietly along the wall toward the door. His father's attention was focused on the men, and on controlling the angry Bran.

"You're all very brave and sure," Fergus said, "when you're holding that gun on a man."

"We're following God's orders, papist."

"Sure, God wouldn't have the likes of you pathetic bastards doing his work," Fergus said.

Cormac thought: He must sense that I'm approaching the door, out of the sight of the men, but he won't move his eyes my way. I'm sure he isn't blinking.

"If you've naught to fear, let us in," the bull-necked man said, a tremor of uncertainty in his voice. "We'll know in two minutes if this house is fouled by the Whore of Babylon."

"Now I understand," Fergus said. "You're an expert on whores."

"Stand aside," the man said angrily, "or you're a dead man."

"Ach, go home, will ye? Go home and hammer your wives — if you're tough enough."

"Billy!"

The unseen Billy cocked the hammer, and then Cormac swung the iron bar, pivoting on his left foot, hurling all his weight into the blow. Billy's hand must have splintered into many pieces (Cormac thought) because he screamed and screamed, the way an injured baby screams, over and over, his voice fading into the darkness. The gun fell with a clattering sound, and Fergus placed a foot on it, gesturing to his son with an open hand without ever taking his eyes off the group of gaunt Christians. Cormac tossed him the iron bar. He squatted and with one blow smashed the pistol. Then he stood and kicked the pieces across the threshold. The men looked whiter and gaunter now, their eyes as tentative as the flames of their torches. The bull-necked man was wide-eyed. Out behind the others, Billy the gunman was whimpering.

"You can pick up those pieces, you bloody idiots," Fergus O'Connor said. "They'll fit right well now up your arses."

Then he slammed the door shut, flipped the latch, released the furious Bran, winked at his son, and smiled.

"Thank you, lad," he said.

As the enraged Bran barked and leaped and scraped paws against the door, they could hear God's messengers murmuring and talking outside, their voices rising and falling like jangled music. They must have known (Cormac thought) that the house with its stone and plaster and slate roof was immune to fire from outside. But they didn't sound interested in storming the doors to charge into the house with their torches. The sound of Billy's voice moved above and through the other voices, a whimpering and groaning thread of pain. And then they went away.

Fergus O'Connor exhaled. So did his son.

"They'll be back," the father said.

21.

But on this, Fergus O'Connor was wrong. The gaunt men didn't come back. What came instead was the killer wind.

It arrived on the evening of December 27, 1739, while all the good Ulster Christians were still exulting over the birth of their various Christs. Father and son were reading by the light of candles. Fergus was again absorbed in *The Drapier's Letters,* by the Dean. Cormac was reading the poems of Alexander Pope, borrowed from school before it closed for Christmas. He was copying some of Pope's verses into a folio book, using a new reed pen and ink his father gave him as the season's gift. In the margins of his precious green notebook, Cormac doodled faces he remembered (Robinson, or the gaunt night visitors) and images provoked by the poetry (hills and streams and ruined castles). From time to time, his father told him to listen to a few sentences from the Dean. Or asked his son to show him the sketches or recite some lines from Pope.

"If some of our more neighborly eejits ever saw that book of yours," he said with a laugh, "they'd be sure it was written by the Pope in Rome." He smiled. "And there was a Pope Alexander, you know. A right bastard he was, at that."

Then, in the pause after talking, they could hear a whine, distant at first, thin, then widening and growing louder, and Bran was up and alert, growling in baritone counterpoint to the whine, baffled because there was not yet anything to smell. Fergus laid the Dean on the floor beside him, went to the top door, cracked it an inch, and then was shoved back two feet by the wind. He braced himself and slammed the door shut. They latched the shutters on the windows and gazed at the roof, which had begun to tremble.

"A gale," Fergus said, trying to hide his alarm. "From the east. The worst I've ever heard."

For an hour, Cormac imagined the wind coming all the way from Russia, across Germany and France, gathering ice in the Alps, adding more force over chilly England, driving with all its arctic strength to Ireland. Nothing could stop it. No king could demand it to halt, no soldier could shoot it. They heard Thunder whinnying in the stable, the high-pitched panic of a trapped animal. At first they did nothing, waiting for the wind to die. But the wind did not die. And then Fergus could stand it no more. He donned his heaviest coat and pulled a wool cap down tight upon his brow.

"Stay here," he ordered.

"I'll go with you."

"No, you've got to be ready to find me if —"

And he was gone, with Cormac's weight shoved against the double doors, pushing hard to latch them shut behind him. Cormac heard huge branches being torn from trees, thumping as they landed, and the deep, throaty sound of the wind under the high-pitched whine, and something clattering off the roof: branches, slates, bricks. The wind drove down the chimney, forcing smoke into the room, and the windows shook and rattled and made cracking sounds as the punishing wind shifted and whipsawed and turned upon itself. Cormac no longer heard Thunder's anguished voice. Bran paced, prowled, made nervous circles. Head up. Alert. Pausing to smell and listen at both the east door and the west.

Finally there was a hammering at the doors, and Cormac opened the inner one. His father's face was raw and scraped. His hat was gone, his eyes wide. But he had Thunder by the harness. He unlatched the bottom door and tried pulling the horse into the house, urging him: *"Come in, Thunder. Come with us. Come in."* In the roar and the whine, the great horse refused to cross the threshold. Cormac thought: This is not his world. His world is the barn and the fields and the forest. The horse backed up. Cormac joined his father, hauling on the reins. Useless. The wind roared past them into the house, extinguishing candles, knocking over pots and chairs and rattling the dishes on the sideboard.

"Hold him," Fergus said, and while Cormac held the taut reins, his father rushed into the darkness past the whinnying, frantic Thunder.

Thunder winced, his eyes widened in pain, he made a twisting sound in his chest and rose with hooves pawing at the air, and then Cormac pulled hard on the reins, forcing the horse's head down low, and with an iron stomping of hooves, a shuddering churning movement, the horse entered the dark human house. Father and son dropped the reins and hurled their weight against the doors until they closed. Fergus jammed the latches shut. Cormac could see dimly in the light of the hearth; he found a candle and lit it from an ember. An aura of light rose from the flame, and Cormac could see his father still at the door, his butt pressed against it, legs stiff, facing his muddied boots, until he straightened up, flattened his shoulders against the door, and slid to the floor.

"Glory be to God," he said in Irish.

And then he laughed and switched to English.

"Glory be to bloody God."

Cormac squatted to face him.

"Can I get you something, Da?"

"A spot of tea, Your Worship," Fergus said, in an English accent.

"Righto, Your Lordship. But shall I first show the king to his bed?"

Fergus looked past his son at Thunder, stood up slowly, and they both laughed.

"How *did* you get him to come in?"

"Squeezed his balls until my hands hurt."

He guffawed and so did his son. Thunder whinnied, as if demanding an explanation, or lamenting the condition of his balls. Bran looked baffled; the rules of the world had abruptly changed. The two humans bent over laughing until the tears came. All the while the wind was howling as it arrived from Siberia.

The wind howled all that night and through the next day. And when the wind began its retreat, the cold remained. For seven weeks, the temperatures stayed below zero. On the first day, father and son stepped outside and their eyes flooded and Cormac's lashes stuck together. They found the stream frozen and the well a deep block of ice. They took Thunder with them, the two of them riding him, great clouds of steam rising from his nose and mouth. Everywhere, trees were uprooted. At least a dozen houses were smashed flat. The steeple of St. Edmund's was jammed like a spear into an iced thicket twenty feet from the church, and there was no sign of the Rev. Robinson or anyone else. On the bald, distant hills they saw three frozen horses lying on their sides. When they returned home, Thunder bent easily under the doorframe.

The cold went on and on, and they set some routines: the dog and horse released each morning to relieve themselves, to be followed by Fergus and Cormac. The outhouse blew over on the first night of wind, so Da fashioned a harness to go around Cormac's waist, to be strapped around an alder tree if the wind blew too fiercely. When Fergus gripped a tree, nothing could blow him over. They made jokes about shite freezing into cordwood before it left your arse and the miracle of pissing icicles.

They learned from a passing coach that the ink had frozen on the presses of the *News-Letter*. All schools were closed. Churches had locked their doors. In Belfast, ships were frozen to the quays. You could ride a horse across the iced surface of the River

Lagan. When the weather warmed slightly in the third week, snow fell for eighteen hours, and began to melt the next day, and then the Siberian wind came howling more angrily than ever, as if showing its contempt for all of them, and the wet snow froze into giant hard-packed drifts. Six weeks into 1740, the odd traveler told them of destroyed crops and dead cattle and horses all over the north of Ireland. Within a week, food had begun to run out, because people had not been warned, had not heard Mary Morrigan speak about the bad times that were coming, had not understood the story of Joseph and his brothers. Fergus and Cormac O'Connor were among the lucky ones, for they had food. But as more reports of starvation came to them, Cormac began to feel guilty about having what might save the lives of others, and he told his father so.

"There's nothing to be done," Fergus said. "If we give out all we have, it'd be gone in two days. Then there'd be nobody left to bury the dead. Or tell their story."

"But who *will* feed them?"

"When there's this many starvin', only a government can feed them. But they won't. Not this lot. The whoremonger Chichesters are happy and warm in London, burning Irish logs in their fires and eating Irish beef. They know how great — for them — is the news from Ireland. The more Irishmen that die, son, the more land for the landlords when it's over."

He was right (Cormac thought), but his son was still angry, and struggling with guilt, and trying to bury both feelings in hard labor. They took axes to the stream and broke off large splinters of ice and filled pots with them and boiled them at the hearth for water. They rationed their food and the oats. Thunder gave off much heat, so they could be stingy with the turf, and at night the horse settled against the western wall, and Bran huddled beside him. As the stack of turf lowered and the merciless cold continued, they embraced Bran's intelligence and soon all four of them huddled together in the nights, covered with coats and blankets.

Cormac used the green notebook as a diary and made sketches of what he saw when he rode Thunder through the cold. The notebook filled (his script now smaller to save space and often cruder because he was forced to write and draw with gloved hands) as more and more reports arrived about the general calamity and the indifference of London. Soon there was talk of famine. Just as there had been in Egypt and Israel. Corn stalks had been burned black by the great wind. Grass died everywhere, turning pastures the color of blood. Many shops in Belfast were closed because there was nothing to sell. Cormac wondered in his green notebook about the fate of the fishmonger and the butcher and about his friends and even the Rev. Robinson. The mud of Belfast must be like brick now. He was careful about some of his thoughts, since he did not want the notebook to turn into evidence. He did not, for example, record his feelings about the Rev. Robinson. Would the good reverend find a way to blame the Vatican for the Irish disaster? Of course. It was God's will, wasn't it? God's harsh lesson about sin. Cormac wished God, if he did exist, would just show up and speak plainly.

One February day, it was warm again, and the snow melted away. But still, it did not end. That night the cold returned, driven by a brutal wind, freezing the earth into iron. Two mornings later, Cormac was riding west alone on Thunder, in search of wood to feed the forge and food to feed himself and his father, because at last they were running out of both. The frozen trees resisted his ax, and he settled for stray fallen branches that he lashed to the saddle. There was no food. Anywhere. Fields and woods were littered with the corpses of cows, wolves, sheep, and horses, some of them stripped of flesh, many of them wedged beneath fallen trees that had provided no true shelter. Some villages were blocked by red-coated soldiers who warned Cormac that everyone left alive was dying of fever and dysentery.

"There's no water since the snow melted," a soldier told him. "At least they could melt the bloody snow. Now the wells are frozen like fecking rocks and the fecking streams are dry. 'Tis a pity. They're even drinking piss."

On the way home, Cormac saw the body of a coatless young girl in a stiff blue dress. She was about nine. Her face was black. A dark blue hand was bent across her brow. She was shoeless. He tried to imagine what had driven her into the cold without coat or shoes, and then imagined both being ripped from her corpse by foragers among the dead. And what had driven her into the cold at all? He imagined a brutal father or a dead family or the fear of ghosts in some ruined cottage. He wondered too where the Other People were and whether they were huddled together in the Otherworld for warmth the way he and his father and Thunder and Bran huddled each night in their house. That dead girl might have been looking desperately for the door to the Otherworld, where she would be warm in the place of emerald light.

Suddenly Cormac wanted the warmth of a woman. Tight and wet and warm in a cave that smelled of peat. There before him was a girl who would never be a woman, and the earth was so frozen that he couldn't even bury her. He rode hard for home.

22.

Then, early one blue morning, Cormac came awake beside Thunder. He felt a dampness on his brow and he could see light through the cracks of the door and his breath didn't make steam when he exhaled. Bran sensed the change too and started shaking himself, and then they were all up. Fergus said nothing, as if afraid this was an illusion. He opened the door, and Bran dashed outside, leaping and rolling, with Thunder after him, bumping the doorjamb like some large younger brother, shaking his great black body, testing the earth with his hooves. Fergus stood with a blanket draped over his shoulder. An immense brightness was coming from the sea. They heard a bird sing.

"We've come through it," Fergus said.

And so they had.

In late morning, with the doors and windows open to air out the horse-smelling house, Fergus hitched Thunder to the cart and told Cormac to join him and explained to Bran that he must stay behind. "There's smoke coming from the chimney," he told the dog, "and that's good. We don't want strangers believing there's nobody at home. So you must stay inside, Bran, and bark your head off if anyone comes." The dog listened unhappily but accepted his duty. He went inside, and Fergus locked the door behind him. Then they started west.

"We need a wagonload of wood," Fergus told his son. "We need food. There's only one place to find both."

For hours they traveled to the secret country of the Irish. Death was everywhere: more dead cattle, more dead humans, more dead wolves. They crossed a stream and saw a dead swan wedged in ice against boulders. They arrived at the grove before dark. Whistles and howls echoed through the cold-stripped forest, and then words in Irish and Fergus answered and then the guards appeared, wrapped in thick furs, thinner, grimier. They nodded and smiled and moved father and son forward into the sacred grove. They saw a huge cauldron on a mound of burning logs, with smoke and steam and sparks rising into the dark air.

"You see, Cormac," Fergus said. "It's a time to rejoice."

And so it was.

The women were smiling in their furs and woolen shawls, and dogs barked, as if demanding news of Bran, and someone was playing pipes in the darkness beyond the fire, and Cormac could hear the steady beat of a drum. Then Mary Morrigan appeared, her eyes welling with tears. She had been right; a terrible time had come. As predicted. But she said nothing now about her prophecy, took no vain comfort in the proofs offered by so much desolation. It was enough that her own part of the Irish tribe had been warned, and had survived. She was thinner now in Cormac's eyes, frailer, as if the seven arctic weeks had reduced her to bone and gristle. She gripped Cormac's hands in her callused fingers and he wondered where that other woman had gone, the woman who was also Mary Morrigan, the woman with the soft flesh and gripping wetness. He thought: Perhaps this Mary Morrigan, withered and dark, was only a mask for the other, her face and body and clothes worn the way he and his father wore their Protestant masks in the world beyond the grove.

But Cormac could not ask those questions, and they might never be answered if he did. Mary Morrigan slipped away, to preside over the chanting and the drum and the thin bird voice of the flute moving through the darkness as if trying to be joyful. They sat at the fire and ate boiled beef while Fergus listened to the terrible accounting. Seventeen Irish men dead, twenty-six women, thirteen children, along with nine horses, eleven cows, fifteen sheep, and twenty-one dogs. All pigs had survived. At least two of the women had died from some English disease they picked up in Belfast while foraging for food. After their deaths, it was decided that nobody could go again to the city until the terrible time had passed. The bodies of the dead had all been burned to protect the living. Fergus and Cormac listened to all of this in silence. Cormac wondered which of the Irish he'd known in his Celtic summers were now dead, and thought that it was unfair that he was alive and they were dead.

"Perhaps now the dying is over for a while," Fergus said in Irish.

"Perhaps," said Mary Morrigan, staring into the fire.

That night Fergus and Cormac slept with some of the other men in a hut made of rough logs. Cormac longed for the cave of Mary Morrigan but remained beside his father and the other men, more than a dozen of them, along with some dogs and a cow, while distant singing, full of lament and mourning, drifted through the midnight grove.

They rose early to a damp, fog-bound morning. The air was warmer, the earth still spiky with ice. Their cart was already piled with firewood and sacks of oats. They embraced each of the Irish who were not already out foraging. Mary Morrigan, one of a group of women, waved a small farewell. And then they started back. For a long time, Fergus was silent.

"Too much death," he said after a while. "Too much death. Too much death . . ."

Cormac wanted to console him, but he knew it wouldn't help to say that he was alive and Thunder was alive and Bran was alive and Mary Morrigan was alive.

"Well," Cormac did say, "maybe they've all gone to the Otherworld. Where it's warm, Da, where they want for naught."

"Maybe," he said, without conviction. "I hope . . ."

They rode for hours, saying little, with Thunder's hooves clip-clopping on the frozen path, his hot breath making white clouds and his breathing as steady as a clock. Fergus had wrapped his face in a dark blue scarf, and Cormac buried his own face in the collars of his coat. His mind, thrummed by the rhythm of horse and loaded cart, eased into a dark, private cave with a fire burning low and his face hot with flesh and hair.

Then Thunder slowed.

Cormac was alert, his heart moving faster. Thinking: Something is not right. Thinking: Thunder should not be moving slower. Not yet. He knows the way. And we're at least six miles from home.

But the clip-clop, clip-clop became something else.

Clip.

Clop.

Fergus was fully alert, his eyes wide, pulling the scarf down to his chin. He glanced back. There was nothing behind them. But the road ahead curved to the left and then vanished behind a hill. Cormac thought: Whatever danger Thunder senses, it lies beyond that curve.

"Get ready to run," Fergus said.

They moved slowly around the curve.

Clip.

Clop.

Clip.

And there in front of them were six men on horses, one holding the gathered reins of two horses without riders. They were stretched across the road, blocking the way, as still as death. Each of the men was armed with a pistol. Fergus and Cormac knew two of them. One was Patch, his bald head covered with a fur hat. The other was the Earl of Warren.

Fergus tugged on the reins, and Thunder stopped about thirty feet from the fence of men on horseback. Nobody moved.

There were dense brown thickets on each side of the road, and a drainage ditch to Cormac's right, its surface frozen.

"Are you looking for the road to Rome?" the earl said, smiling in an amused way while the others laughed. His abrupt English accent was sharp and hurting, with an odd feminine pitch to its tone, as if squeezed by the cold. Cormac remembered the day of his mother's death in the mud of Belfast, when the earl's voice was uncertain and trembling. That voice was gone. After the brutal Siberian winter, he seemed harder now, dressed for command in a long black coat, heavy wool scarf, broad-brimmed hat, high polished boots. He did not seem to remember Cormac. The boy who had once flailed at him so bitterly was now a young man of sixteen.

Fergus whispered again to Cormac that he must prepare to run. The young man's heart thumped in fear and anger.

"I won't run," he said.

"You'll run if I say so," Fergus insisted, not moving his lips.

The earl nudged his gray stallion with his knees, and the horse moved forward. Thunder shuddered and tensed, as if challenged. Cormac saw Patch jam his pistol into his belt and slide a musket from his saddlebag.

"You must run," Fergus whispered in Irish. "If you don't, there will be no witness, and nobody to avenge what might happen."

"Is that Latin you're speaking, my proud blacksmith?" the earl said. "Listen, Patch, listen to them talk Latin. Can't manage the King's English, but listen to them spout the old Latin."

Fergus said nothing. Cormac could feel tension coming off him like bristles.

"That's a lovely horse you've got there," the earl said. As he came closer, Cormac noticed for the first time that the earl had a diamond cemented into his right bicuspid, worn like a badge of fashion.

Fergus stared at the earl.

"I'd say he's worth about eight pounds," the earl said. He turned to Patch. "Don't you think, Patch? About eight pounds' worth?"

"At least, milord," Patch said, grinning. "P'raps more, sir."

The earl looked at Fergus for a long, calculating moment. His doughy face was very still.

"I want the horse," the earl said.

"The horse is not for sale," Fergus said.

"Is that so?" the earl said.

"Yes."

"My good man, I don't think you under*stand* me. I want that horse."

The diamond glittered when he smiled.

"You see, this blasted famine has killed a lot of horses. Including many of *my* horses. So we're buying horses. And *that* horse, dear fellow, looks to be worth at least eight pounds."

He gestured with the pistol in a weary manner while he talked, his gun hand flopping loosely. Then, with a sigh, he slipped the pistol into his belt, as if deciding that even two Irishmen must understand that they had no way to resist. He took some coins from his coat pocket and slapped them together. Cormac wondered if he was about to do his juggling act. Patch and the others seemed impatient. Then, coming closer, the earl adopted a harder tone.

"And since it's well known that you're a papist, and since the law of this land clearly states that no papist can own a horse worth more than five pounds, and since —"

"I know the law," Fergus said. "It does not apply to me. I'm not a Catholic."

"Of course, what else would you say? But we have reason to believe otherwise, don't we, Patch?" Cormac heard the coins slapping. "And, of course, sir, you can always go to argue your case in the assizes." He turned to his men. "You lot, unhitch the horse, and Patch, you —"

And then Fergus shoved Cormac off the seat and said, *"Run!"*

Cormac hit the frozen ground and rolled into the iced ditch and what he saw, rolling and hurting and flopping on the brown drainage ice, were a series of jagged moments: Patch's horse bucking in fear, and his father's face in fierce resistance, and the earl moving to the right, and Thunder rearing: huge; enraged, striking at the earl, at his horse's gray head, blood suddenly spouting from the horse's split brow, and the earl wide-eyed, and a last glance at Cormac from his father.

And then Patch fired the musket.

"No, you fecking idiot!" the earl screamed. "Don't —"

The noise of the shot echoed in the emptiness. Birds rose and cawed and beat their wings. Horses whinnied.

Then Cormac glimpsed his father sprawled back awkwardly in the seat of the cart. His eyes were wide, staring at the sky. His body made the effort to rise, but a great crimson stain seeped from his chest. His scarf was slippery with blood. All of this glimpsed in seconds. And punctuated by the thin, panicky voice of the earl.

"God *damn* it all!"

"He's twitching, milord," Patch said.

"Then finish him off, you bloody fool! And find his son! He's a fecking witness. And we can't —"

Then, as Cormac rolled into the thicket, frantic, panicky, terrified, enraged, pushing belly-flat under the needles of the briar, as Bran always did, he looked back, and saw the earl's extended arm, his finger pointing, and then Patch gripping a pistol, and heard a smaller explosion as another ball was buried in his father's body. And the earl's voice: "The horse, Patch, calm the bloody horse! And take the oats and the firewood too, and — where's that *other* one? The young one. Find him!"

Cormac had rolled into a frozen creek, screened from the road by dense walls of trees, and was up now and running.

23.

The following hours assumed the feeling of a dream. He was running and falling and wailing in rage and running again. Avoiding all roads, hamlets, and farmhouses. At one point, he bent over in pain as if a knife had been shoved into his side. And when the pain was gone, and the world was silent, he rolled his body into a ball and cried. In the cold silence of the bruised Irish twilight, he saw his father at the forge, muscles like cables in his arms, and heard his laugh when he was happy, and remembered the way he struggled for control when Rebecca died. Thinking: *They've killed him.* Shot him down on a road to get his horse. The bastards. The dirty, cowardly bastards. Now only I am left. And he heard his father talking: *In our tribe, the murderer must be pursued to the ends of the earth. And his male children too. . . .* He listened for the sounds of horses, for Patch and the other men, for the thin, panicky voice of the earl. Nothing. And heard Mary Morrigan speaking to him: *If an unjust act is done in the family of a man or woman, it must be avenged. That is the rule. . . .* He rose then in a crouch, sheltered now by the seeping darkness. Thinking: I have my tasks now. Things I must do, or live, and die, in shame.

It was dark when he reached the O'Connor part of the world. He huddled under the bridge that the carriages crossed on the road to Dublin. Now his grief and rage were replaced by fear. He trembled with that fear, afraid the earl and his men were waiting for him. His bowels loosened. He dropped his trousers, hoping he would shit out all his fear. Then was newly afraid that the stench would betray him by drifting to the nostrils of ambushers. But as he paused in the silence, Cormac felt better. Colder. In something like control, with the clarity of emptiness.

His fear didn't vanish. But the mixture of overlapping fears worked within him like fuel. Fear, and its brother, rage. He was sure they would try to get away with everything. The killing itself. The theft of Thunder. And if the horse appeared in the earl's stable, he could merely say that he bought it from a passing Irishman. How was he to know the passing Irishman was a bandit and a horse thief?

Except that a witness was still alive: Cormac himself. They would try to find him and kill him too. Then nobody would be left to tell the tale. Or to settle the account. He thought: I need to kill them first. And there was something else: He must stay alive to make certain there was a proper end to this story. The rules of the tribe moved through him in the voices of his father and Mary Morrigan. But now it was Cormac's story. He was a Celt. He must honor the code of his tribe. To do so, he must live. For as long as it would take. He told himself: I must use my fear to stay alive. If I die now, in these cold woods and dark fields, then this long day will be only another brief chapter in the story of the Earl of Warren. And I will never be allowed to pass into the Otherworld, to join again with my people.

Away off he heard dogs barking, but none of the voices belonged to Bran. Cormac was afraid to call to him, afraid of revealing his presence to anyone who might be watching. He fought down an image of the dog with his throat cut. There was no moon. And although a wind was blowing from the sea, there were no leaves to rustle on the nude trees. He listened. He heard no human voices. Before him was an emptiness. He waited, trying not to breathe. But as his eyes adjusted to the dark, he could see the house better. The doors were open. The half door. The full door. Crouching low, he scurried toward the house that had been their home.

His father's legs were jutting across the threshold.

Now he didn't care who might be watching. He rushed toward his father in the darkness and fell across his bloodied chest and wept as he had never wept before. The blood of Fergus was wet, but his body was like ice. His blood was on Cormac now, on his shirt and fingers, and he sucked the blood off his hands, his father's blood, his own blood: and again heard him say *Run!* And again heard him say, *We're Irish*.

And then, his mouth slippery with his father's blood and his hands sticky, there in the moonless soundless dogless motherless fatherless night, Cormac knew what he must do.

He stepped past the body into the dark house. There was no light, no ember or spark from the hearth, and he could feel in every bone one more bitter truth: The soul was gone from the house. The Earl of Warren had killed it. In the darkness, nothing was where it was supposed to be, where it had been since the beginning of Cormac's remembering. He moved now like a thief in a stranger's house. Then, rolling on the floor under his foot, he felt a candle. He found matches scattered on the floor like twigs and lit the candle.

The house had been savaged. Chairs, crockery, pots: All were smashed into bits. Curtains and clothes had been sliced with knives. The beds were slashed, the floor littered with straw and goose-down stuffing. He smelled urine and saw a puddle against the western wall. The secret house of the O'Connors, that masked house of the Carsons, was mutilated and dead.

He didn't care now if the house was being watched. Let them come, he thought. I'll die fighting. He placed the candle in an iron bucket and then started dragging ruined furniture to the center of the room. He stuffed the mound with newspapers and the slashed pages of books. With the disemboweled Alexander Pope. With the assassinated Jonathan Swift. He found loose pages ripped from his green notebook and then the gutted book itself and added them to the pile. When the pile was two feet off the floor, he returned to the corpse of Fergus O'Connor.

Cormac reached under his father's armpits and dragged him into the house. Grunting and heaving, breaking pieces of wood beneath his feet, afraid now of time and the arrival of strangers, he hauled the corpse to the top of the pile. His father's icy muscled arms flopped to the sides. His wide, startled eyes faced the ceiling he had made with so much skill and love. Cormac folded his arms across his chest and closed his cold eyelids.

Then he blew out the candle and hurried into the night. There was still no moon. No sounds. No Bran. In the barn, where the anvil lay toppled on its side, Cormac piled mounds of wood against the walls and throughout the tool room. His father's tools were scattered and some were gone, plunder for the true bandits who worked for the earl. But Cormac found what he was looking for: a spade. At the base of the hawthorn tree, he began to dig in the icy earth until his spade bumped against the lumpy leather bag and the case that held the sword. He slung both over his shoulder and ran to the house. Above him, clouds were moving more swiftly. He could see the dangerous shimmer of the emerging moon. On the doorstep, lying like a small animal, was his father's fur hat. He lifted it. Then pulled it onto his head.

In the dark interior, he faced the pyre.

"Good-bye, my father," he said out loud. "I shall not forget the man you were and what they did to you. And I will see you in the Otherworld."

He scratched a match against stone and smelled sulphur. Then he lit the newspapers and the torn, crumpled pages of the books. Flames exploded from the dry wood. His father lay dark and still upon the orange mound, and Cormac backed out through the Western door. In the barn, he ignited the bundles of wood and paper, thinking: Nobody else will ever live or work in these two buildings. They will vanish from this earth, as my mother vanished, as my father does now. I will go away, but I will not vanish. He felt the last of his fear rising out of the fire, the sparks scattering into the sky. He ran toward the dark, distant hills.

From the slope of the first hill, he could see the buildings burning like torches. He was certain that the torches were gripped by those who were escorting his father to the Otherworld.

24.

He awoke in the stale, dry straw of an abandoned barn. From the barn's murky interior, he saw a small farmhouse, its chimney toppled, one shutter banging in the breeze, the sagging carcass of a cow propped against a stone wall. In the dim light before dawn, there were no signs of human beings. He stripped the rush matting from the sword and clenched the wolf-bone grip, turning it over, running a finger over the smooth finish of the blade. He could feel it speaking to him: *Go,* it said. *Go and do what must be done.*

Then Cormac opened the leather satchel, loosening its long thongs. The interior smelled of earth. He removed sixteen gold pieces, his mother's spiral earrings, and a new leather-bound copy of *The Drapier's Letters*. Nothing more. He thought: This is my inheritance. My father is speaking to me. He is saying that all I might need in the fearful world is money, a memory of my mother, and the Dean. Oh, my father . . .

Cormac opened his shirt and used the bag's leather thongs to tie the satchel across his stomach. Then he pulled his father's fur hat tightly onto his head, gripped the sword, and took a deep breath.

For a few minutes, his stomach gnawed by hunger, he foraged in the barn. He found some stray oats for the vanished cows and horses, and gobbled them down. They were not enough. His stomach growled and contracted, but there was no other food. He thought of boiling straw but saw no water. He stared out the door at the farmhouse. Nothing stirred. No smoke drifted from the chimney. Holding the sword, he sprinted to the house. He used the sword to gently prod the door. It was open. He slipped inside.

Three bodies were lying in one another's arms on the bricks in front of the hearth. A man, a woman, and a child. The flesh of their faces and hands was white as snow and falling away like paper exposed to wind and rain. The child looked a hundred years old. The man's skeletal hand gripped a Bible. The woman's eyes were shut tight against the certain darkness. The shutter banged: *ka-tock, ka-tock-tock.* Something scurried in the darkness, unseen, tiny, with nails like hooks. Cormac backed out, his skin pebbling, and turned in flight to the woods.

He walked in a wide arc around Belfast. By late afternoon, he was exhausted, his legs heavy, his stomach screaming, his throat parched. He saw patches of virgin snow in the blackened woods and chopped off pieces and ate them. He sucked bark torn from a tree. Then he saw a long, low building, once white but grayed now by weather and famine, with two farmers going in and out and tendrils of blue smoke rising from a chimney. From behind a low stone wall, he watched for a long time. Then the smoke disappeared, and the men came out of the main door and trudged together to a road that would take them home. Cormac could hear their voices for a while after they were out of sight, and then heard nothing except the wind in the trees. When the sky darkened, he sprinted to the door. It was locked. He kicked at it in fury, once, twice, paused, then again, harder, and the door burst open.

A dairy.

With butter churns and cheese vats and four cows in stalls, mooing and swishing their tails.

A vision of heaven. The air was heavy with the aroma of food and animals. Two scrawny cows stared at him from a stall, and he found a small kitchen area, with a counter and a cold teapot and a wooden box that held two loaves of bread. They were hard as rocks, food for animals now. But he sliced them with the sword and shoved the pieces into the fresh butter and chomped them, gobbled them, his hands trembling. He could not risk a fire to make tea, but he grabbed hunks of cheese and shoved them into his mouth. He grunted. He felt the food make a move, rising, demanding escape, but held it down. He made sounds that were neither Irish nor English. No meal had ever tasted better.

When he was gorged, he stood there for a long while, holding the edge of a table, belching, panting, feeling the great wads of food filling his emptiness. He went outside and relieved himself as a fine rain started to fall, cold and laced with sleet. Inside again, he ate one final wedge of cheese and then fell upon one of the rough tables and went to sleep in the mooing, tail-swishing darkness.

Hours later, he was wakened by the sound of rain hammering on the roof. A blanket of rough burlap hung on a peg beside the stalls. The cows didn't seem to mind that Cormac took it for himself; he thought they looked pleased to have his company. He cut a hole in the center of the burlap and pulled it over his father's fur hat so that it hung across his shoulders. It hid the lump of his leather satchel. It concealed the sword. He thought: I have donned my cow shit–smelling burlap armor.

Then he closed the door behind him and ran into the driving rain.

25.

Around midnight, out past Carrickfergus, Cormac reached the edge of the estate of the Earl of Warren. He was about six miles from Belfast. The cold rain was falling steadily as he moved through the trees, peering at the property. Two white-brick gateposts marked the entrance; a freshly painted golden arch above them was marked with the same W that was emblazoned on the black coach. But there was no fence to the sides of the gateposts and no guards. The estate was not finished, the gate new. Through the rain, in the distance, he could see a big house, painted white, two stories high. The windows on the ground floor were a dim orange from candles or gas lamps burning on the inside. Off to the left was a large stable with a fenced corral behind it and cleared fields moving to the horizon. Cormac angled through the woods and then trudged across a soaked field toward the stable. Watching, remembering. He had arrived at his destination; he must know how to leave.

Thunder picked up his scent through the rain and whinnied in greeting. Once, twice. Like a signal. The whinnying stopped as Cormac came closer to the barn. Thinking: I would know that voice anywhere (for it is a voice). Thunder is alive. Here. My father's horse. My horse now.

The barn door was unlocked and he slipped inside, leaving the door ajar behind him. A way in, a way out. A lamp burned dimly to the right, and in the light he saw Thunder. There were a dozen stalls, filled with horses and piles of hay, but Thunder was alone in his own small jail. Some of its slats were hanging loose from his resistance. Cormac turned down the wick of the lamp and went to his horse. He opened the stall's gate, and the horse nuzzled him in a wet, frantic way while he ran a hand over his coat and felt the welts from a whip. More than a dozen small ridges of flayed horseflesh, some of them open. Thunder didn't care. He bounced. He shuddered in joy. He shook his great mane. Other horses made soft pleading sounds.

Then Cormac heard a voice behind him.

"I say, what's this?"

The man was small and wiry, holding a whale-oil lantern. Cormac recognized his face from the road where his father was killed. He gripped the sword.

"I've come for my horse," Cormac said. "And for the Earl of Warren. You understand why. You were there, you bastard."

The small man shook his head and smiled a toothless grin and gazed out through the open door. Thunder stomped at the earth, warning of danger.

"Ach, sure, you're too late, lad," the small man said in a soft, reasonable way. "Sure, the earl's gone off. To America, they say. I suspect —"

He suddenly whirled with a pistol in his hand. Cormac swung at him with the sword. The way his father had taught him: short, quick.

The small man's pistol hand came off with the pistol in it.

Blood spurted, and he tried to scream in a shocked way. The lantern fell. Cormac picked up the pistol and smashed the butt into the small man's nose. He fell to his knees, blood streaming now from his nose, staring wide-eyed at the pumping blood from his wrist, gripping his forearm to try to stop the flow, gazing at his lost hand, at the door, at Cormac. Stunned. Wordless. Cormac kicked him in the face, and he fell over on his side, with the blood still pumping. Thunder whinnied again, ready to leave, but Cormac wasn't finished. He jammed the pistol into his belt, beneath the shit-smelling poncho, and then moved from stall to stall, releasing the other horses from the Earl of Warren's wooden cells. Cormac thought: Maybe they're each worth more than five pounds. Maybe each will find its way home.

Finally he picked up the lantern and went to the door. Horses raced past him into the rainy night, clumping and breathing hard. Thunder waited. Cormac hurled the lantern into a pile of straw. It burst into flames.

Then he mounted Thunder, without a saddle, and they raced around the corral with the frantic horses, who were plunging now through a gap in the corral fence into the Irish night. They rode to the big house. When Cormac glanced back, he saw the handless man crawling out of the burning stable.

The big house was built in the style of many others in Ireland: to create an image of power. About twenty marble steps rose from the earth to a gallery framed by Doric columns. Cormac raced toward the house, urging Thunder up the rain-slick stairs, his steel shoes clattering.

The front doors burst open, and four alarmed men came out. They were led by Patch, who was barefoot in a long gray nightshirt and carrying a shotgun. He was the only man with a weapon. And he wasn't wearing his patch. One eye socket was a black hole; the other glittered. Patchless Patch.

He started to say something.

Cormac cut off his head.

Which bounced and rolled down the marble stairs. For a moment the headless body stood upright. Then it fell chest down. Without urging, Thunder pounced upon the body, stomping at it, while the other men scattered into the rain. Cormac took the pistol from his belt and fired a shot after them. Thinking: That will bring out the earl. The men ran into the rain-drowned darkness.

For a long, blurry moment, the world seemed red. Red house, not white. Red blood mixing with lashing red rain. Then the red was gone, and Cormac urged Thunder into the house, through the open doors, to find the earl.

The rooms on the first floor were empty of furniture or paintings. The fireplaces were cold. Piles of lumber were stacked against walls. The earl clearly had not yet furnished his grand mansion. An uncarpeted staircase rose to the second floor, with a chandelier hanging in the stairwell. None of the candles were lit, but the device glittered with crystal and cut glass. Up they went. Horse and rider.

Before them were a dozen doors, some of them open. In one, a table was covered with whiskey bottles and jugs and fancy glasses, obviously the lounge where Patch and his men had been drinking earlier in the night. Cormac dismounted and kicked open the other doors. Empty. He arrived at one near the end of the hall where an oil lamp was burning on a side table. He flipped the latch and entered a kind of suite. Dressers and an armoire and dozens of mirrors. A second door leading to a bedroom. Someone was under the covers of the canopied bed.

"Come out of there," Cormac said, gripping the sword.

There was no movement.

"Come out or I'll chop you to pieces."

The covers came down. A woman's face appeared. Red-haired, pale, trembling, about fifteen. Irish.

"Who the hell are you?" he said.

"M'name's Bridget."

"Are you the earl's whore?"

She turned her head, her eyes wet.

"Aye," she said.

She turned to gaze at Cormac.

"I had no choice, sir. Didn't me own father sell me to him during the great cold?"

She buried her face in the pillow, a picture of shame. Cormac didn't trust the image he was given. And he knew the earl was gone, headed for other parts until any talk of murder had drifted away, or until Patch and his men had hunted down the only witness.

"And where is the great earl?"

She turned to him again.

"Away," she said. "Left for America for a while, says he. Two days ago. A boat out of Galway, he said to me. That's what he says, of course. That's what he told me. He could be in Dublin, for all I know. He could be in London. But I think maybe 'tis America."

There were plates beside her bed and an empty wineglass and a piece of bread. Cormac came closer and took the piece of bread.

"I should kill you," he said. "Whorin' for that English bastard."

"Then you'd better kill me father too," she said angrily. "He put me in this bed."

She looked weepy again. He lifted a half-eaten chop from a plate and gnawed at the bone.

"Would you like to have me?" she whispered.

She rose like an offering to a sitting position, showing him one full, rosy breast above the line of her nightgown. Yes, he thought, I'd like to have you. Yes, I'd like to slide into those smooth sheets and enter your body. Nipples. Hair. Wetness. Sleep.

"I can't," Cormac said. "I must go. And you should too. Now. Get dressed, pack, and go home. Before they come back."

"You mean Patch?"

"Patch is dead."

"I don't believe it. Not Patch."

"His head is out there on the steps," Cormac said. "I put it there."

She moaned. Cormac started to leave but then felt pity for the girl. If the men came back with a platoon of redcoats, they'd probably kill her too.

"Get ready now, woman," he said, "and I'll take you into the forest. You've got ten minutes. Then I'm burning this place to the ground."

He took the reins and led Thunder to the staircase and then down to the door. Awkwardly, delicately, the horse afraid of slipping on the stairs made by men. Cormac told the horse to wait. Then he took the stairs two at a time, reached over, and cut the four chains that held the chandelier to the ceiling. It fell with a ferocious crash, scattering glass and crystal over the oak steps. Thunder pawed the wooden floor, as if saying to Cormac: You're taking too much time. Outside, the rain was still falling. Cormac saw Patch's legs jutting awkwardly and naked above the marble steps, aimed at the front doors. He found dry matches in one dead fireplace and went through the main floor, making small piles of wood, chopping planks into kindling with the sword. Thinking: Our house is gone, the home of the O'Connors, and now it's your turn. Thinking: Patch's men must be nearing Belfast now, or at a guard post, alerting the militia. Thinking: *Hurry*.

Suddenly Bridget was coming down the stairs, leathery boots clicking on oak, dodging around the smashed chandelier. She was dressed in a long, fancy dark blue coat, a fur hat, leather boots and gloves, and carrying a velvet bag about three feet long. The wages of sin. She looked smaller than she had in bed. Her eyes were jittery with fear, made worse when she glimpsed the headless body of Patch. Cormac boosted her onto Thunder's back and handed up her bag, which was light and must have contained clothes.

Then Cormac went back inside to the piles of wood. If the Earl of Warren did come back to his grand mansion, he would find only ashes.

26.

They rode and rode into the gray morning light, into rain, into hills; finally, as the rain faded off, into forest again. They were heading west. He thought: There is blood on my sword, from the small man in the stable, from the severed neck of Patch. I'm now a different man. I am sixteen and I have killed. What's more, killing Patch was too easy, too final, too personal. And too *savage*.

Cormac barely knew Patch and had killed him as easily as Patch had killed his father, and with about as much feeling. Thinking: No, that's not true, I did have feeling. Before I cut off his head, there was true rage. Rage is a feeling. But when it was over and his bald, one-eyed head was rolling down those marble steps like a fruit that had fallen off a wagon, I didn't feel what I wanted to feel. I wanted to feel clean. I wanted to feel that I'd closed a small circle. Now, riding to the West, to where the dead go, to where the sun sets into the ocean sea, I don't feel either emotion. I've closed no circle. I'm not clean.

And what of this young woman, the earl's whore, who said her name was Bridget Riley? She was behind him on Thunder's bare back, gripping Cormac's waist with her small pale hands. Her bag was strapped across her shoulders, her weight thus disproportionate to her size. He could feel her hands on his stomach. He could feel through all the layers of wool and shit-smelling burlap her hard breasts upon his back. He felt her breath on his neck. While they rode on, pressed together, he listened to her whispered tale, her story entering him like the warm breath from her mouth.

She told of how her father was widowed when her sixth sister was born and how there wasn't ever enough to eat and how the Siberian cold came and how the father (tearful, gruff, almost wordless) sold her to the earl for two sacks of oats and three bushels of potatoes. The price of one young Irish woman. She talked about a boy she had loved when she was thirteen (long ago, for she was sixteen now), Richard, his name was, Richard Murphy, and how she had let him have his way (her voice trailing into forest cold) and how he had gone to America and how he promised he would send for her and never did. She told Cormac that she had lost all faith in the Christian God and his commandments (for how could he love us if he sent away the people we loved and let so many others die?) and then had begun to go with other young men (not many of them in that forlorn region) and some older men too (with their wives at home and she in the woods or a wagon with the poteen-smelling farmers) and finally some Englishmen from the barracks (challenging even the old Irish gods with her blasphemy) and how after all of that (and all of them) she had never found one who was like the one who went away to America. Richard, his name was. Richard Murphy.

That was when Bridget Riley began to feel like a whore. Not from opening her thighs. From opening her heart and having nothing enter. And so she didn't even mind when the earl bought her for oats and potatoes, because (she thought) maybe her sisters would survive the long starvation and maybe one of the horses would live and maybe her father too. And after all, she'd be warm and she'd be fed.

"I didn't love him, and most of the time didn't even like him," she said. "But sometimes he made me laugh. Sometimes he made wicked remarks. Sometimes he would sing some music-hall song, and act it out. Sometimes he juggled with dinner rolls."

He felt anger make a move, remembering the earl as he juggled outside the public house in Belfast, then tried to picture him juggling for Bridget Riley. He heard his father's voice: *They say he has charm. . . .* He said nothing and the anger seeped away. They paused beside a frozen stream and he chopped a hole in the ice and they knelt down to drink. Together above the water, they smelled of perfume and cow shit and fresh sweat, soap and pine and dirt. Her face was flushed, her hands raw from the cold.

She opened the wide bag and lifted out a small bundle of men's clothes and told him to get rid of what he was wearing since the English soldiers would be looking for someone dressed in burlap and smelling of cow shit. She giggled when she said these things and laughed out loud when he replied that he could never wear clothes that were worn by the Earl of

Warren. Her voice turned angry and she told him that he had no choice, if he wanted to live.

"You've murdered one man, and possibly two," she said. "Surely to God, the earl's men want you dead. And just as sure, they've told the soldiers. They'll all be after you and happy to hang your Irish bones from a tree limb. If they don't burn you instead, nice and slow. Don't make it easy for them."

She paused then and added in a solemn voice: "Besides, they didn't belong to the earl. He was a bigger man than you."

Cormac surrendered to her logic (and his growing fear), stripped off his own clothes, and donned the new ones, including a long black overcoat. She smiled up at him and told him he was now a fine figure of a man. And while he shoved aside some rocks and hid his old clothes, she dug deeper into the bag and brought out two small loaves of bread and some salted pork and a few figs, and said that she wished they could have a spot of tea, but that was, of course, impossible.

They ate in silence, while Thunder took long drafts of water from the hole gouged in the icy stream. Bridget Riley seemed lost in her own thoughts, her eyes unfocused, chewing steadily. For a moment, he felt that he must protect her, that he must first help her get back to her home place before he went off on his own journey. Then he saw himself taking her with him. If the earl had gone to America, they could go to America. There he would keep his vows to the Irish tribe. And free Bridget Riley from the man who had bought her for two sacks of oats and three bushels of potatoes.

It was almost dark in the empty world, and they watched the sky change and black clouds race and the moon begin its climb. She touched his cheek. He touched her hair. Then she was standing above him, her body blocking the moon, looking around their little thicket (as if trying to remember each naked tree). She shook her head. "We'd best go," she said. "Before it's too late."

He could not tell what she was thinking as they resumed the ride through the empty land, heading for the West. Is she afraid of feeling anything for me? Are some other feelings moving in her? She seems much older now than when I saw her in the silky bed in Carrickfergus. Older than I am. Old as caves. She shows a hard face to me, and then feeds me and warms me and clothes me. The earl's possession. The earl's woman. And she seemed able to read his thoughts.

"Sure, he's already gone," Bridget said.

As if she knew that he was seething with the unseen presence of the earl.

"Then I'll find another ship," he said.

Her voice was weary.

"For God's sake, get off it," she said. "Stay where you belong. Find yourself a woman and a house and — Jaysus, why do you care for him anyways?"

And so, moving under the arc of the moon, he told Bridget Riley the bare bones of his story, and how the earl and Patch had taken the horse, *this* horse, and killed his father, and how he must avenge that act, no matter what it took. She listened and then breathed out heavily, making a small puff of steam.

"You're terribly bloody young," she said. "Aren't you?"

He didn't reply. But she talked then in a casual way, as if discussing someone she had read about in the *News-Letter*. The earl had long spoken of going to New York, but surely not to stay forever. Just to open a branch of his business. "Which is, of course, the slave business," she said. "Aye," Cormac said. "I know." The earl would rave sometimes about the fortunes to be made in America, she said, and how foolish it was to pay strangers a commission to handle his New York business when he could make money at both ends of the trade. "He needs New York," she said. "It's a growing market, after all." He could feel her nodding behind him, bumping against his shoulder. "Now I understand better why he left so quickly," she said, and then told him even more.

"I was home — if you can call it home — the night he killed your father," she said. "I just didn't know it at the time."

She told him how the earl came back to his unfinished mansion that night (Thunder whipped and shoved by eight men into his stall), his eyes jittery, ignoring her for the brandy snifter, running his hands through his hair. He slept only three hours and then rose in a colder mood. He had his manservant pack some bags and load the black coach. He told Patch to guard the house and say nothing to anyone who came calling. Then he and the manservant (a Londoner named Marley) took the coach to Belfast.

"He never said good-bye, the cold bastard," she said. "He told me I'd be taken care of, to stay where I was, and if he was delayed in New York, he'd send for me. Bloody liar that he is." She paused. "The last thing I heard him say was to Patch: 'Get rid of that bloody horse.' "

He might have been telling her a tale, she said, when he mentioned New York. He could have gone to London or France. But he was probably on his way to America.

"If you want him badly," she said, "you'll have to cross an ocean."

They arrived at last at a crossroads. Off to the left, back from the road a hundred yards, there was a collapsed church. The stone walls remained standing, but the roof was gone, another victim of the long winter.

"I know the way from here," Bridget Riley said abruptly, backing away from Cormac, prepared to slide to the ground. She was ready to walk miles to what might only be a place of death. Dead father. Dead hearth. He thought: I've just begun to know her.

"Please stay with me," he said.

"I can't," she said. "You have something in your head, Cormac, that's more important to you than I am. You've got America. You've got murder."

"I can manage both," he said.

"Sure, you'd just lie with me and leave me," she said, and laughed. "Another Irish bastard." She smiled. "Better I leave you when it's me doin' the leavin'."

She eased herself down off the horse and gazed at the road that hooked back north. A few streaks of reddish dawn appeared to the east.

"Let's rest a bit before you go," Cormac said. "I can build a fire."

Her face went blank, then tight.

"I'd best be going," she said.

She ran her fingers along Thunder's mane, slung her bag over a shoulder, looked at Cormac, and smiled. Then she turned. He slipped off the horse and grabbed her hand. She pulled it away from him and walked off. He watched her get smaller as she climbed a rise. She waved a hand in farewell but did not turn her head. Then she was gone.

27.

In the grove, fed and warmed by a fire, Cormac told his story to the men. There was much fury about the killing of Fergus, but no tears. Their huge hands clenched spears and muskets, eyes first blazing and then going dead, cursing the earl, cursing the English. They told Cormac that he'd done the right thing, laying his father on a blazing pyre, properly helping his passage to the Otherworld, where they'd be certain to meet again. And he should not worry: They would track down the men who worked for Patch (for they had their own men in Belfast and every other town) and kill them. They asked Cormac to describe those men again and again, and at his urging brought forth paper and charcoal for him to draw their faces from memory. They knew at least two of the faces; the men with those faces would surely not survive.

He told them too about the gold coins his father had buried for him, and the earrings and the copy of the Dean's book. He told them about the sword and showed it to them, and they examined it with almost religious reverence. They listened as Cormac spoke and murmured in Irish and spit out bitter words, and then they stood and sipped from goblets and shook themselves loose in the night air, and then once more admired Cormac's sword, hefting it and saying that Fergus of the Connor was a great maker of swords, like his father and his father before him and the many Connor fathers all the way back to the years before the conquest. As Cormac finished eating and talking around the fire, one man began to croon a sad tune and the others joined him, and when they were done it had become a song of resistance and defiance and ultimate triumph.

While they talked and sang, the women worked on Thunder's wounds, rubbing them with an oily unguent that smelled of spring mint. They promised Cormac (when he strolled away from the fire, looking for Mary Morrigan and not seeing her, and afraid to ask after her) that if Bran was alive (they were sure he was) and made his way here to the grove (he knew the way), they would care for him for the rest of his life and then make certain that he eventually joined Fergus O'Connor in the Otherworld. They giggled at Cormac's new clothes, which were baggy and wrinkled but at least (one woman said) not hairy with the skins of wolves. Then the women retreated. The men sat with Cormac in silence, and then one of them, burly and red-haired and named Fintan of the Hills, said: "You must go to find the earl."

"Aye."

"You must hunt him to the ends of the earth."

"Aye."

"You must erase all of the men of his line."

Another said, "Until no man lives that carries his seed."

"Aye."

"And, of course," said Fintan of the Hills, "you will have to go to America."

The question was how and when. Not all were sure about the location of America, except that it was over the sea to the west. A grizzled older man just back from the western coast said that a ship was leaving from Galway in two days' time, bound for America and specifically for New York. Not Canada. Not Jamaica (he said, as if reciting a litany). Not Charleston or Philadelphia. Saying the names of places in a language that was as foreign as the places. This ship's bound for New York, he said. The voyage took eight weeks (he'd heard this from one of his men in Galway City, but the others couldn't believe a voyage could last for eight weeks, unless it was a voyage to the moon). The grizzled man said that if Cormac left on Thunder before the morning light, he might arrive in Galway in time to board the ship. All agreed he must try. So did Cormac.

They explained the roads and the hazards. None, not even the grizzled man, knew the price of the passage. They did know Galway. They described a city with white houses and Spanish women (for Galway traded with Catholic Spain even if Belfast did not) and a wide road through the town leading directly to the quays. He was warned: There was some risk. English soldiers could be waiting to arrest him at the ship if word had spread to the ports about the killing of Patch. The earl's own men could be waiting too. Cormac must pause and look hard at what stood before his eyes, and read the signs of danger. But there might be greater risk in staying, both for Cormac and for the tribe. All these possibilities were minor. There was one dominant reason for departure: the debt of honor that could only be satisfied in New York. Cormac Samuel O'Connor must satisfy his father's spirit by killing the man who had killed him.

And so it was agreed that Cormac should sleep a few hours and then hurry to Galway. In the town, he could release Thunder and someone (one of their men) would make certain that the horse found his way back. The horse, they said (as his father always said), knows the way.

Excited, sad, angry, feeling very young and very old, anxious to leave and desperate to stay, Cormac went off to sleep in Mary Morrigan's cave. He hoped she would be there. He heard a lone horse move off through the forest, vanishing into the west. In the cave, as his eyes adjusted, he saw Mary Morrigan huddled under her mound of furs, her head turned away from the smoldering fire. He undressed in silence, feeling awkward, strange, altered: and finally curled beside her. Her body was cold as stone. Her eyes were closed. He thought: She's dead. He touched her face and then kissed her withered lips. This time there was no change. Tears leaked from her shut eyes.

"Don't," she whispered. "You smell of a whore."

The scent of Bridget Riley was on his skin, put there by their long ride together, intensified by the heat of the cave. She must have also smelled the remnants of his desire. He rose, shivering in the cold, and retreated to a mound of pelts and burrowed into them and tried to sleep. Behind him was the blank wall of the back of the cave, furry with damp. He could see the mound near the fire that he knew was Mary Morrigan. Sleep was broken by jagged images of the past three days: his father taking the steel ball in the chest; fire rising from a pyre; the head of Patch bouncing on steps; Bridget Riley's red lips and white teeth and one bared breast; his father again (laughing); Mary Morrigan's cold neck; his father (urging him to run); the horses galloping for freedom; his father staring at black clouds; icy rain; barns; the smell of shit; Da.

Then nothing.

He wakened to a fluttering noise and a thin, high-pitched wail and reached for the sword. In the dim light above the guttering fire, he saw a shiny crow beating its wings. Darting forward. Darting back. Beating glossy black wings against the smoke-tinged air. While the high-pitched wail filled the cave, louder and louder. It was not the wind, because nothing stirred except the crow. He didn't move. It was surely the banshee.

Then, from the bundle, the other Mary Morrigan rose in her nakedness, full-breasted, round-bellied, hair falling in the dim rosy light. She started walking toward Cormac, but her eyes didn't see him. She was smiling. Following the crow. His heart froze. He could say no words. She walked past him, her hips swiveling, going to the blank back wall of the cave.

The crow vanished first.

Into and through the rock.

And then Mary Morrigan turned, gave him a small mute wave, walked straight at the wall, and vanished.

Cormac lay very still in the emptiness. The high-pitched wail was gone too, leaving a loud silence. Her clothes made a formless pile beside the fire. He knew where she had gone, and now it was time for him to begin his own journey. He dressed quickly.

28.

The world was windless and thick with fog. Thunder bent into the task of taking Cormac to Galway, head lowered, great muscles straining on the rising slopes, then relaxing as they descended into depressions in the land. The horse seemed to know that an irreversible choice had been made. For Cormac. For him. A decision based on blood. And though Cormac whispered to him in Irish and English, he seemed to know that he had no say in the matter. They kept moving west and south to Galway City.

Sometimes they heard men talking in the fog, the sound amplified by the stillness. The words were never distinct. Each time, Thunder paused, alert and silent, until the loud blurred voices faded. The fog thickened. Cormac felt them climbing, then descending, but saw nothing through the fog. Away off: the sound of rushing water. A stream coursing over rocks. But Thunder stopped and wouldn't move. Cormac nudged him, ordered him to go ahead now, we have little time, horse. He did so carefully, his ears alert, not so much showing fear as an immense reluctance. Finally they pushed through tattered fog and saw the stream and Cormac knew why Thunder wanted to avoid this crossing.

The stream was thick with corpses. Almost two dozen of them. Jammed against boulders to form a human weir. The glistening current had ripped flesh from exposed hands and arms and faces and washed bones to an ivory white. A dozen fleshless skulls grinned up at them, the scoured heads jutting from shredded clothes. The arms of one corpse were wrapped around the remains of a child whose body still carried strips of blue flesh. Like the family in the farmhouse. Cormac thought: When was that? Two weeks ago? A month? Five years?

A dozen yards downstream, the smashed timbers of a raft were jammed against rocks. He thought: They must have been fleeing to the sea, to a town, to houses, to fish, to a place, another place, someplace better than the place they'd left. He thought: They were full of prayers and fear. And then came the heart-stopping moment, the careening raft turning the bend and ramming against those boulders. Destroying heads and bodies and drowning the rest. He thought: Here they are before us: nameless and lifeless, from no place anymore, arrived at a final place whose name they never learned. The weather is surely warmer now than on the day they died. Smell them. Smell the sweet, corrupt stench that can't be cleaned by the rushing stream. Not now. Not for a hundred years.

Thunder abruptly became his own navigator, jerking to his left, moving upstream a few hundred yards from the bodies and their rotting odor. He crossed at a broad, shallow place where boulders had been ground by the years into pebbles. On the far side, Cormac dismounted and they drank from the icy water. Cormac paused at first, afraid, wondering if there were other corpses upstream, poisoning the rushing waters. But Thunder took deep drafts, and he trusted the horse's judgment and his knowledge and followed his example. Slaked, exhausted, he opened a coarse canvas bag and fed Thunder some oats.

Then he untied the thongs of the leathery sack his father had hidden for him. He fingered his mother's spiral earrings, remembering her voice and her smile. He hefted *The Drapier's Letters,* thinking it would be fitting, a kind of prayer, to read some lines of Swift as a way of remembering his father. He pushed open the clasp. And stopped. Folded in the pages were sixteen one-pound notes, ornate with the printing of the Bank of England, and a folded letter. The letter was addressed to Cormac and was written in his father's careful hand.

> My Son,
>
> If you should read this Letter, then I shall be gone to the Otherworld. I have left here for you these Objects that I hope will be of assistance in your own Journey. I can give you Money and Gold but cannot give you what you will need most. That is, a belief in Justice and Work. I think you have a Love for both and will not let that Love die. I think you know that the Tyranny of those who stole Ireland will eventually be defeated no matter how many of the Irish they kill. As long as one Irishman remains alive, singing in Irish, they have lost. In your life, I hope you will never

oppress the Weak, that you will oppose Human Bondage in all its guises, that you will bend your Knee to no man. Be kind. Find a good Woman and love her. And thank you, my Son. You have made my life a great Happiness.

Your Father

Struggling for control, Cormac pressed his father's words to his trembling heart. Read them again. Saw his face, his sinewy arms; heard his voice; pictured him sitting alone at night to write these words (as if knowing he might never get to speak them); saw him hammering iron; saw him gently taking Rebecca's elbow as they left a church that was not their own. Cormac wanted to speak one final time to him.

Then he and Thunder were on the move again, the letter and the banknotes folded into Cormac's shirt, the heavy coins in his pocket, the Dean and the earrings back in their satchel, the forest dark, a road below them to the left (the wheels of a coach making a far-off screeching sound), and he kept whispering to Thunder. *"On to Galway, great heart. On to the town of white houses and Spanish women. On to the sea, Thunder. To the ships."* On horseback, he drowsed into a jagged sleep. Hours passed. Mary Morrigan took his hand and led him to the blank wall. His mother stood on the road to Belfast, dressed in a coat of many colors. His father laughed and shaped red iron.

He snapped awake to the barking of a dog. Once, twice. Far off. Perhaps miles away in the smothering fog. The barking stopped as quickly as it started. They were on a true road now, not a forest trail, in a thick yellow fog, all signs of the wider world erased. He could see the ground, with its gashed ruts and a few white-painted stones on the sides, and it was going to the west.

A hint of a breeze. The road rose. The fog lightened. Farmhouses emerged silently in the distance, and he could hear the lowing of unseen cows. Then again, suddenly, from somewhere behind them, much closer this time, the barking. Thunder stopped, turned his head. Cormac followed his glance.

And then, racing from the fog, came Bran.

He barked and yipped and ran in a mad circle around them until Cormac leaped down beside him and hugged him and growled to him, saying his name again and again, *Bran, Bran, Bran,* and rolled with him on the lumpy earth of the frozen road. Finally the dog was exhausted and flopped on his back while Cormac scraped the caked mud off his filthy belly with his fingernails. Bran was thin. He was scratched from thorns and bramble. But he was delirious with joy. He ate greedily from the oats in Cormac's palm while Thunder nuzzled them, breathing warm air upon them, until Cormac gave the horse some oats too.

Then, in the distance, coming fast but still unseen, they heard galloping hooves and squealing wheels. Cormac stood, leaped onto Thunder's back, and unsheathed the sword. Thinking: It's too late to turn and run. He angled Thunder so that his sword hand couldn't be seen. He hoped, for a moment, that the hoofbeats and wheels belonged to the Earl of Warren. In his black coach. With his diamond tooth and emblazoned W. Thinking: Then I'll have no need to reach Galway and sail to America. I'll kill him here. On this Irish road. In this Irish fog.

But it was not the Earl of Warren. Visible, as if plowing through the fog, was a royal mail coach pulled by two bony horses. A teamster sat high on the seat. A bearded fat man was beside him, cradling a musket. They seemed startled to see Cormac, Thunder, and Bran (who was barking fiercely), but they were not afraid (for there were two of them and one had that musket). They slowed and stopped. The man with the musket raised it in an agitated way and then lowered it again. Cormac thought: He must recognize that if I were a highwayman, I would have to be a very strange one indeed. Even the great Dick Turpin, hero of schoolyard songs, did not bring a dog with him to rob mail coaches. Still, the two men peered anxiously about them, as if looking for possible accomplices.

"Is this the road to Galway City, sir?" Cormac said, trying his best to sound as innocent and needy as a lost boy.

"'Tis."

"How far would it be now?"

"Dunno, in this fog. Maybe six hours?"

"Are the ships sailing? For America, I mean."

"There's one at dawn. If you hurry, you might make it, lad."

The driver abruptly whipped his team and they rolled on, taking no chances on Cormac's apparent innocence. Cormac sheathed the sword and nudged Thunder toward Galway, with Bran moving beside them on the gullied road, the horse careful not to move quicker than the dog could run. They rode for miles, the fog relentless, but the world growing warmer. They came to a bridge over a small running stream and Bran darted down the bank and plunged in, twisting and shaking as he cleaned the dirt from his coat. They all took long drinks and then returned to the road, going up a steep incline. At the top of a ridge, they could smell the sea.

29.

They couldn't actually see the ocean, but its immense, full presence was somewhere before them. Cormac worried about the hour (for it remained dark), and the day, and whether the ship had already hauled its anchor and unfurled its sails. *Hurry, Thunder. Hurry.* The sky slowly brightened beyond the fog. Cormac took dried beef from the pouch and ripped a piece off with his teeth and tossed some bits to Bran, who leaped and took them before they hit the ground. Through the fog, he heard a breeze combing unseen trees, and they were climbing again on the empty road, and the breeze was louder, smelling now of salt and the dark Atlantic. The road twisted and climbed and then peaked, and suddenly the fog was gone and below them they could see the great wide bay and the city of Galway.

They paused and gazed down upon it, at red tile rooftops and a few steeples and the battlements of a castle and all the houses white as salt. Limestone houses. Mortar houses. Smoke rose from chimneys, and here the morning breeze was a wind, the smoke streaming horizontally, the fog blown south. Away off, Cormac could see the masts of ships.

"We'd best hurry," he said, and Thunder set off, moving downhill on dirt roads and then into streets covered with mashed straw mixed with mud and then onto cobblestones. Bran was anxious now: in a strange place with strange odors and (Cormac was sure) detecting the odor of farewell. They found a main street whose name kept changing — from Williamsgate to Williams Street to High Middle Street — and he saw buildings bearing coats of arms, and morning shops beginning to open, and gargoyles grinning from the sides of one gloomy church. Three wagons moved slowly toward them, the first drover yawning. The wagons were empty, their dawn business already done.

"The ship for America?" Cormac shouted. "Has it sailed?"

"Not yet. It's the *Fury* you want. But if you're needin' her, you'd best hurry."

He urged Thunder on with his knees, but the street traffic was thicker now: horses with riders, carts and wagons and a few coaches, and people hurrying from narrow lanes toward the shops.

More traffic blocked their way, carts, horses, wagons, and Thunder picked up Cormac's anxiety *(the* Fury, *we need the* Fury, *get to the* Fury*)* and tried to go around and was shouted at *(fecking horse, big bloody horse, get back, fecker)*, and then a burly red-haired teamster tried to grab his reins and Thunder shook him off and another wagon came from a side lane and up that lane Cormac saw a flash of scarlet. Jesus. Brit soldiers. A toothless old man placed himself in front of Thunder.

"Ye feckin' eejit, ye can't go this way!"

"I'm going anyway," Cormac shouted.

One wagon moved and there was a narrow space and Thunder plunged toward it and passed through and then began to gallop. Free of the jam, free to run. And he ran. It was two long blocks to the quays, and he ran the run of his life, hooves clattering on stone, Bran barking, women jumping to the side, and Thunder dodging carts and carriages and panicky horses, running for the water, for the ship, for America: and then they were out on the pier.

At the far end a three-masted ship was easing away from the pier. An English flag. Sails unfurling. Ropes cast off. The *Fury*.

"Run," Cormac screamed. *"Run, Thunder, run, run, run."*

And Thunder kept running, his hooves hammering the timbers of the pier, running full out, head low, running for the *Fury*.

Men looked up at them with alarmed faces.

And Cormac's heart began to wither.

The *Fury* was now about fifteen feet away from the pier head.

Thunder didn't care.

At the end of the pier, at the end of his frantic gallop, at the end of Ireland, Thunder leaped.

Rose.

Soared.

They were suspended high above water.

Flying.

There was a human roar.

And then Thunder came down hard and splay-legged on the planked deck, skidding in a sliding, scattering rush, then pivoting somehow to avoid going off on the far side. Cormac spilled out of the saddle to the deck. The passengers shouted like an audience at a circus. Cormac got to his feet, grabbing the sword case from the saddle. Thunder snorted and shuddered, at once defiant and afraid, his ankles intact, his eyes blazing, backing up, prepared to fight.

"What in the name of Sweet Jesus is *this?"*

Cormac turned to the face of an enraged man, his skin and red beard merging into a kind of hairy fire. He had pushed through the astonished passengers.

Cormac said, "You're going to New York and —"

"We board at the bloody *quay!* Not after we've hauled anchor and not on bloody *horseback!* Who in the hell *are* you, anyway?"

"Martin O'Donovan's my name," Cormac said, making up the name on the spot, not knowing if his own name was on some list for immediate arrest.

"Well, I'm Tom Clark and I'm the first mate, and I never bloody well heard of you."

He glanced at Thunder, then back at Cormac.

"My father's dying in New York," Cormac said, compounding his lies. "I need to get there, please, Mr. Clark. I've got the fare."

"Not with this bloody horse on board you're not — as fine a bloody horse as he is. We've got enough trouble carryin' our fourteen niggers without adding a *horse*."

He ran rough, covetous fingers along the side of Thunder's head, but the horse jerked away as if touched with hot pokers. Clark came closer. Thunder backed up, pawed the deck, snorted at the first mate, then dashed for the railing and leaped into the sea.

Another roar, shouts from crew members, and Clark was astonished.

"Jesus bloody Christ!" he said, peering down at Thunder, who was moving in the sea. "Are yiz part of some circus?"

"No, sir," Cormac said. "I just have to get to America and I'm told the fare is three pounds."

"I should let you keep your money and drop you in the bloody bay," Clark said.

Then his attention shifted as the ship itself seemed to pause, water sloshing at its hull, reluctant to depart. Tom Clark barked orders to men in the rigging and marched aft. Cormac thought: I've made it. I'm on the *Fury*. I'm about to sail the ocean sea.

Down at the aft end of the ship, passengers were shouting across the harbor water at the shore. Cormac pushed in among them as the ship suddenly began moving with purpose. People were waving from the receding shore. Men, women, and children in long, dark clothes formed small, shrinking, wedgelike silhouettes against the gray morning sky. Beside Cormac, men were weeping and calling names. *Good-bye, Ma. Good-bye, Eileen. So long, son.* Then he saw Thunder's head bobbing in the water, slick and black as a seal, swimming relentlessly for the shore. And off to the right of those who were waving their farewells, he saw Bran. He was on a spit of sand, among scattered rocks, barking and pacing and darting into the water. Thunder was aimed at him like a black spear, until he seemed to stop, his legs finding land below the water, and he hauled himself up in a bent, exhausted way. Bran danced around the horse, and then, as the ship moved out of the bay, they turned together to face the strange, cold, receding sea creature with its billowing sails, and to face Cormac. They were still as statues and watched him go until he could see them no longer.

Good-bye, Thunder. Good-bye, Bran. And good-bye, Ireland.

30.

Cormac searched for order in the shouting and tumult of the open deck. Clark directed him in an annoyed way to a man called Blifil. He was the purser. A pale, dusty man with dandruff on the shoulders of his crumpled serge jacket. He explained in a mournful, dubious voice that for a late arrival, there were, hum, only two choices: a cabin berth, which was of course too expensive for the likes of an Irish lad in his teens, and, hum, a plank belowdecks with the indentured Irish. He was shocked when Cormac (or Martin O'Donovan) presented him with three one-pound notes for the cabin berth. "I've saved for three years, sir," Cormac said shyly. "I might as well splurge." Blifil shrugged, pocketed the money, made a check mark and a scribble in a book, and led Martin O'Donovan to his cabin. It was on the main deck, to the right of a passageway leading to the captain's quarters, and Blifil said he must share it, hum, with a Mister, hum, Partridge, yes, Partridge, about whom he told Cormac nothing. Blifil opened the door with a key, told him to, hum, guard it with his, hum, life, since there were thieves everywhere, see, and then hurried away in a bent shuffle.

When Cormac entered the gloom of the cabin, a heavy middle-aged man was sleeping deeply on his cot (to the left), fully dressed, one booted leg trailing on the floor. This must be Mr. Partridge. A second cot was to the right. Cormac stared at the sleeping man. His round belly rose and fell slowly, as if tied to the slow roll and fall of the *Fury*. His breath was phlegmy. His hair was thinning. His double chin needed a scrape with a razor. The leg on the floor seemed to be guarding a worn leather bag that was jammed under the cot.

The sight of Partridge (exhausted, collapsed, a huge breathing softness) made Cormac drowsy. He fell upon the empty cot, turned his back to the bulkhead, hugged his few possessions, and, while the ship rocked as gently as an immense cradle, fell into a deep sleep.

He awoke in the dark. Mr. Partridge was gone. In the dim light from a porthole Cormac found an oil lantern on a small table, but he had nothing to light it with. Beside the lantern there was a bowl of water. He sniffed, to be sure it wasn't urine, then splashed his face. He hid the sword case and his small bag under the cot and went out, locking the door behind him, shoving the key deep into a trouser pocket. He still felt the presence of Ireland, although he could no longer see its shores. From all sides of the open deck there was a hum of conversation, lamps moving and bobbing, men laughing. In the center of the deck stood a kind of caged barnyard holding chickens and pigs, and past it dozens of sailors were smoking from clay pipes, while a few passengers lolled against bulkheads. None were distinguishable; they were simply figures in the darkness. The sea made a swishing sound as the *Fury* cut its path west.

Suddenly they entered a bank of fog. And through the fog Cormac could see the sheer cliffs of a small mountain rising at least three hundred feet out of the sea. It was covered with a golden mesh.

A voice beside him said, "Jesus Christ, what's that?"

It was his cabinmate, Mr. Partridge, his jaw slack as he stared in awe. Plummy English accent. Intense stance as he gazed at the sea. First Mate Clark appeared at his side, and all three stared at a gold-meshed mountain rising from the sea.

"It's on no map," Clark said in a hushed voice. "*They* live inside it." His voice softened. "You know, the Other People. Sometimes it's here, and sometimes it's not. . . ."

The Englishman looked at him, then laughed out loud.

"*What* other people?"

Cormac stepped away from them because he knew what Clark meant. He peered at the gold mesh, the small black sea mountain. High on the summit there was a woman. Completely alone. Waving farewell. When the ship came closer on a hard angle in order to pass to the vast ocean, he could see the woman more clearly.

Mary Morrigan.

THREE

The Ocean Sea

Without a sigh he left, to cross the brine,
And traverse Paynim shores, and pass earth's central line.

— LORD BYRON, "CHILDE HAROLD'S PILGRIMAGE," 1812

31.

Ireland had vanished. Cormac and Mr. Partridge were lodged in one of two cramped cabins built under the raised platform of the poop deck, on the starboard side of the *Fury*. A gloomy passageway separated the cabins and led down six steps to the captain's own cabin. When his door was open, Cormac could glimpse a polished table and windows opening to the foamy wash behind the *Fury*. A clergyman and his wife occupied the port cabin. Cormac saw them the first day out to sea: he tall and grim, she small and pale. They were dressed in mourning black. The clergyman's wife soon disappeared into the cabin. The clergyman, whose name was Andrew Clifford, carried meals to her on a small board. Cormac couldn't tell if she was seasick, or being guarded from the heathen roughness of the crew. Sometimes, late at night, he could hear her weeping.

Mr. Partridge told Cormac (or, as he knew him, Martin O'Donovan) that he was himself a Londoner and that this was his third voyage to New York. *With any luck, I'll make my fortune this time,* he said. *And if I do, I'll have to decide. Do I stay and get even richer? Or do I go home to London?* The source of his potential fortune, he explained, was crated and wrapped and buried in the hold: a printing press. *They have something unique in the colony,* he said. *Freedom to print what they want, thanks to this legal case — have you read about it? — this case of John Peter Zenger.* He told Cormac how Zenger, a printer, had been charged by the authorities with using a press to subversive ends, and how he fought the charges in court in 1735, and won. *The problem is they have much to say but too few presses upon which to say those things. I intend to help them speak.* At the moment, he said, there were only two printing presses for eleven thousand people! *Incredible!* He laughed a deep belly-growling laugh. *So it's missionary work, lad. Bringing the modern world to the barbarians!*

His enthusiasm seemed to press against the walls of the cabin. He showed Cormac the books he planned to print in his own New York editions, volumes that would give the barbarians some instruction and pleasure. Like an excited schoolboy (he was at least thirty-five) Partridge rummaged in his cloth bag, dropping items on the bunk, and when Cormac saw the titles of the older man's books, his heart beat more quickly. There were four by Alexander Pope: his translations of the *Odyssey* and the *Iliad,* his own *Rape of the Lock* and *Dunciad.* Partridge seemed startled when Cormac quoted a few lines from Pope's poem on Heloise and Abelard. And when he showed the young man his copies of Swift's *Tale of a Tub* and *Gulliver's Travels,* Cormac took from his satchel *The Drapier's Letters,* and Mr. Partridge's eyes widened and his lower lip trembled.

"Well, at least *you* will not add to the barbarism of New York, lad."

Then he saw the banknotes folded into Swift's pages and looked surprised.

"You have a lot of money for a young man," he said.

"My father died and left it to me," Cormac said, telling the truth. Or a truth.

Mr. Partridge looked at Cormac in a dubious way and handed back the book with its folded notes.

"How old are you anyway?"

Cormac told him.

"Sixteen? And do you have a trade?"

"I can blacksmith a bit, Mr. Partridge, sir."

"Well, you can learn to print then too," he said, his jolliness returning. "Everybody should have more than one trade. I've got more than one myself."

He handed Cormac a copy of John Milton's *Paradise Lost* and a Milton pamphlet called *Areopagitica.* He caressed the pamphlet in a loving way.

"Read that, lad. It's the best argument ever made for freedom of the press. Perhaps we can personally hand it to this Mister Zenger."

He talked of Milton and Pope and Swift as if he knew them (and, of course, he knew the best of them) while they walked the decks and ate their meals. His tone was enthusiastic and always personal and very serious. Cormac thought: O Father, I wish you could have met this Englishman.

Hour after hour, when he was not reading or dozing, Mr. Partridge explained what the sailors were doing in the rigging, which they climbed like athletes, and why there were so many objects lashed to the deck. All had to do with the voyage. The rough wooden cage was called the barnyard, with its four segregated pigs and many chickens, and that grave, solemn man peering through the slats was Jeffries, the cook. Other bundles contained provisions for the voyage: kegs of water, salted beef, limes for scurvy. The rest were the luggage of sailors and passengers alike. Mr. Partridge said that among his several trades (barber and knife sharpener, along with printer), he was a tailor, and one of the lashed bundles contained cloth for suits he planned to make in New York, or even during the voyage. He eyed Cormac's ill-fitting clothes when he said this.

"You'd best get a suit yourself, lad, or they'll think you're a fugitive. That thing you're wearing looks pulled off a dead man. And, yes, we'd better trim your hair before you land."

Cormac's nerves trembled then; if Mr. Partridge believed he looked like a fugitive, perhaps some of the ship's officers would too, and they might wonder about the money he was carrying and hold him for arrival in New York. On general suspicion of felony. He vowed silently to get himself a new suit, quickly cut to fit by Mr. Partridge. But he said nothing, because at this point Mr. Partridge was serving as a guide to the world called Belowdecks.

32.

Down there, Cormac began to see what he had never seen before. The crew's quarters, Mr. Partridge explained, were all in the bow, on the first deck below the main deck. Holding a lantern, he showed Cormac the next deck, and for the first time the young man saw the deck of the emigrants. They lived in four rows of bunks hammered together from rough plank, with no bedding supplied by the ship, jackets serving as pillows, coats as blankets. All slept in their clothes. The only natural light came dripping down from the fore and aft hatchways, but in the orange light of Mr. Partridge's lantern, faces peered at them in a wide-eyed way. A few old men stared at the deck, blinking, ignoring the light. Strapping young men tried to stretch, smoking from short earth-colored clay pipes, nodding, smiling, or throwing hostile glances at the visitors. Children scampered about, up one aisle, down another. Many women were seasick, their faces ghastly with the loss of control, and the air was stained by a mixture of vomit and shit. On that deck, they were all Irish.

A moment of silence greeted Cormac and Mr. Partridge and was broken by a man crooning in Irish from the shadows, a melody Cormac knew, a melancholy tale of a lover's journey. Then dozens of them joined in, and someone produced a fiddle and began to play in counterpoint, and all of them were shaking heads about the loveless land that was vanishing behind them and then smiling about the magic land to which they were going. The land ahead, of course, was Tir-na-Nog. The land of eternal youth.

"They have no idea how far it is," Mr. Partridge whispered. "They think crossing the Atlantic is like crossing the River Shannon. The educated ones know but won't explain to the others. Afraid of what might happen, I suppose, afraid of despair, or riot. They're almost all Presbyterians, the educated ones, fleeing the Church of Ireland and its endless bloody cruelties. But the ones singing in Irish, they're real Irish, out of the hills and the bogs and the hungry towns. Most of them don't speak English. And they've signed on as indentured servants. Poor buggers."

He explained what an indentured servant was (for Cormac had never heard the words), and how these hungry Irish people, listening to the siren call of America, signed on. They pledged five to seven years of their lives, without pay, without schools, five years of labor for English planters in America, in exchange for their passage. They would be free of heartbreaking Ireland and the terrible hunger. The English were, of course, happy to see them go, particularly the Presbyterians, who were gifted at making trouble. In America, they'd work in the earthly paradise, and when the passage was worked off, they'd be free to live their lives.

"But except for knowing they'll someday be free, they're no different from the poor, bloody Africans. They're owned, lad. D'ye understand me? *Other men own them.* And in America, the men who own them, who have them under contract, those men sell them, just the way they sell the Africans. Although on this ship, the Africans are in even worse shape than the Irish."

"What Africans?"

"Come."

With the fiddle playing behind them, and the Irish joining in their sad, hopeful song about Tir-na-Nog, Mr. Partridge moved down still another ladder, with Cormac behind him, descending into the bottom level of the ship. He told Cormac to mind his head, since the space was cramped, only four feet of room. In the lantern light Cormac saw the grillwork of a jail and beyond the timbered grille, the glistening forms of men. Black as coal. Black as midnight. Eyes stared at him and at Mr. Partridge. Eyes yellow in the light. Eyes sullen. Eyes angry. Mr. Partridge raised the lantern, said a polite hello (to no reply), and told Cormac that there were thirteen men in this fetid place, with its smell of swamp (as Cormac remembered the rotting Irish corpses in the river that made Thunder change his course). And there was one woman, he added (citing the captain himself as his authority), a woman who claimed to be a princess. In the far corner of this small prison, there were lumpy shapes covered with rough blankets. Cormac thought: One of them must be the woman.

"It's a dirty business," Mr. Partridge said. "But it's England's favorite business because it's so easy. They buy Africans for three pounds from the Arab traders and sell them in New York for fifty pounds. So you're looking at, what? Seven hundred pounds' worth of living, breathing merchandise, lad."

The pieces of living merchandise looked at Cormac, breathing lightly but saying nothing, asking nothing, expressing nothing except some muted, wordless, seething anger. In his mind, Cormac saw the shop on the Belfast quays, the shop of the slave trading company, and the earl's face, and wondered if these human beings could be his property.

"Let's get some air, lad," Mr. Partridge said in a desperate way, holding a handkerchief to his nose.

They retraced their steps to the main deck. A clean wind was blowing, filling the sails, and the swishing sound of the ship was louder as it cleaved through the Atlantic waters. But the clean wind couldn't scour from Cormac's mind the images of the Africans and the Irish, jammed on their separate levels below his feet. The words of his father's letter rose in him: *I hope you will never oppress the Weak, that you will oppose Human Bondage in all its guises, that you will bend your Knee to no man. . . .*

33.

The captain's name was James Thompson. Tall, with a gimpy right leg. Face fleshy, his long nose veined from weather or whiskey or both, his mouth held in a tight slash. He had kind eyes, brown and liquid. The captain found time to explain his charts and instruments to Cormac, and how the prevailing Atlantic winds blew from west to east. All ships bound for America in these cold months were forced to sail south into warmer waters, where their sails could take the winds at an angle. Even this route had its perils. On the ninth day out, when they were hit by a roaring, terrifying two-day gale, Captain Thompson was in full command, sharing the deck with his sailors. When they ran into the region of windless calm called the Doldrums, he wore a worried look and tried to be just in doling out the shrinking rations. As the Irish began to die, he was dignified as he presided over their burials in the ocean sea.

The old died first, and then some taut, frail women, and at least six infants. Cormac soon stopped counting. He nursed Mr. Partridge through the delirium of fever, and each day took his uneaten food and a jug of water to the Africans on the bottom deck. They never said thanks. They never spoke at all. On one of those furtive trips, while a fiddle played from the deck above his head, he saw at last in the light of his lantern the face of the African princess, who, he later learned, was named Tomora. She had gleaming ebony skin, black wiry hair, high cheekbones, full lips. She glanced at him with contempt and then vanished behind a blanket that hung from the low ceiling like a wall.

That night, another African stepped forward: tall, bare-waisted, with powerful shoulders and a hard body. Cormac pushed a loaf of bread through the grillwork that formed their jail. The African took it, his eyes wary.

Cormac pointed at himself and said his true name: *Cormac.* Then: *Cor-mac.* Then more slowly. *Cor. Mac.* The African gazed at him for a long moment and then shifted his eyes to the bread, then back to Cormac. His eyes glittered with lantern light as he passed the bread behind him. The woman said something else. The African scrutinized Cormac's face and eyes. Then he nodded.

"Cor-mac," he said.

The young white man smiled and nodded yes.

The African pointed at his own chest.

"Kon-go," he said.

"Hello, Kon-go."

"Hel-lo, Cor-mac," the African said without smiling.

Cormac tossed him a small salute and went back to the ladder leading to the sky.

34.

One night during the second smothering week of the calm, Cormac awoke to a long, deep scream. Mr. Partridge tumbled in the dark to the floor as Cormac jerked open the door. There was the minister, Andrew Clifford, bent to the side in agony, and beyond him in the cabin was his wife. She was hanging from a beam, a scarf knotted tightly around her broken neck. Her eyes were wide open, staring at the ceiling. Clifford sobbed and lifted her at the thighs, as if to ease her out of the noose, sobbing, *"God forgive me, God forgive me, oh my Martha. God forgive me."*

Mr. Blifil arrived, officious and annoyed, bringing a lantern, making marks in a book, and then, with Martha Clifford laid out upon a cot, her neck dark purple, the captain appeared in the cabin door. His face was drained, his eyes red from too many days struggling with the sea and the vanished wind. He gazed at Martha Clifford, shook his head sadly, whispered some condolence to her husband, and went back to commanding his immobilized ship.

Four hours later, in the first light of morning, Martha Clifford was sewn into a canvas shroud and buried at sea. At the edge of the small crowd, Mr. Clark whispered to Cormac about the minister's wife. She and her husband had lost all four of their children during the famine in Armagh (or so the minister had told him). She was desolated by the loss, mute for weeks, and her husband believed that in America they could begin all over again, in a land blessed by God and free from famine, free from memory. She came with him reluctantly, wanting to remain in Ireland near the bodies of her children. Clifford forced her to leave. Each night on the *Fury,* in turbulent seas or prolonged calm, she called for her children, as if demanding the reunion of death. The captain, on his solitary midnight watches, heard her more clearly than Cormac or Mr. Partridge. She had chosen to hang herself while her husband was far forward, ministering to feverish sailors.

"It appears that if God wouldn't give her what she wanted," Mr. Partridge said, "that is, reunion with her children — then she'd take it herself. May God forgive her, poor injured soul."

The Rev. Clifford didn't preside at his wife's watery burial. Captain Thompson assumed the duty. They placed the shroud on a greased plank, and the captain read from a Bible. Then the plank was lifted at one end and tipped over the side, and the packed shroud disappeared in the motionless sea. Clifford didn't watch it go. He was staring at the silent sky.

35.

The rations were shorter now. The captain (or the company that had hired him) had laid in enough food and water for eight weeks at sea. But the voyage of the *Fury* had been slowed by the storm, pushed out of its path through the ocean and pushed back in time, and now in the Doldrums they didn't know how long the voyage would last or how it would end. Not even the captain knew. They could be there forever. The pigs not washed overboard had now been eaten. The peas had run out. The chocolate was gone. The slabs of salt meat first became smaller and then vanished. Days passed. Nights passed. Early in the voyage, each meal was three potatoes and two sea biscuits. Now it was two potatoes and one sea biscuit. Water casks rattled emptily around the deck at night. Cormac almost never saw the Rev. Clifford, but from behind his door, his wounded voice kept up an endless punishing conversation with the invisible. Prayers and laments, the rhythms of a baffled love. For his wife. For God. Rejected by both.

Sometimes, to rid himself of Clifford's unseen presence, Cormac read Swift or Pope in the half dark of the cabin floor. Searching for words he might whisper to the wind. Or the sea gods. Mr. Partridge slipped into and out of fever. He mumbled, or ranted, and Cormac thought that perhaps he'd gone mad. Or was always mad and had simply disguised his madness with a civilized mask. The older man mumbled: *Face it now, milord. Face your death. Face Africa.*

During the days when they were becalmed, Cormac went around without jacket or shirt, following the example of the crew, with his money pouch tied across his groin. Each day, he sipped his rationed water and brought what he could to the Africans. Small portions. Not enough for anyone. Just what he could cadge, or hoard, or steal. On each visit, Kongo looked at him and nodded and spoke the young white man's name. Cormac's beard began to grow. Wispy and scraggly at first, like pubic hair, then more full, shaping a rich black mask. Three times a day, emigrants were brought on deck to bathe in seawater. Most were naked men and small children, and their bones had begun to push forward, pressing from within against blotched, yellowing skin. The women were too shy to wash naked in front of strangers, and of course the women began to die more quickly. Sometimes in the evenings, the smothering silence was broken by a fiddler, Mr. Makem from Armagh, but slowly, after days and days, his music became more mournful. A lament. An acceptance of death. From belowdecks Cormac heard less weeping and fewer groans and almost no prayers.

The figurehead of the *Fury* was an angel, nameless, carved by some forgotten boatwright, and someone in the crew whispered that they needed that angel now, that they desperately needed a guardian angel, and Mr. Clark growled that what they needed was a fecking wind. One night, while Mr. Partridge dozed and mumbled and whispered in conversation with himself, Cormac walked out on deck. The air was thick and still, and the ship seemed to be anchored to the bottom. He stared down at the carved angel on the prow.

The head turned to look at him.

It was Tomora.

She smiled at him, her black skin glistening in the moonlight. He reached for her, wanting to touch her flesh, caress her breasts, to whisper to her in the hot sea air. But when he touched her ebony face, she turned back to pale painted wood.

Tomora.

Later, he saw her in many of his dozing hours. Above him. Below him. Beside him. Her dark body glistening with sweat, his vision made up of fragments actually glimpsed in the darkness of the slave deck and brought together by his own feverish longings. On his visits below, bringing scraps of bread and drops of water, Tomora looked at him from the darkness, flanked by the men, her eyes still refusing any expression of gratitude. In fever, she took him to her dark interior.

36.

Did he see the things he thought he saw in the days that followed? Perhaps not. Perhaps they were only part of the fever that had touched all of them, made intense and vivid by the hard blue sheen of the cloudless sky. They seemed as real as the masts and the decks and the rigging. As Cormac gazed at the sea one still morning, a figure erupted, part woman, part fish, then submerged, then rose again, breaking from the surface. Triumphantly rising. Teasingly rising. Her breasts were pale sea blue. Her dark, wet, golden hair was streaming. Each leg was covered with silvery scales and ended with the twin tails of a fish. A mermaid. Or a dolphin. Una sirena. O una delfina. Cormac thought the vision was his alone, an invented creature leaping from cool water to calm his blistered mind. But there soon were other men at the rail, gazing slack-jawed at the sea or speaking softly, personally, to the sea creature and not to one another. Voices full of need. Wanting to believe. Until she burst again from the sea, rising high, sea-cold breasts glistening, a smile sea-chilly, hair wet and whipping the air. She turned like a marlin. Spread her scaled legs to allow one glimpse of the place between. Golden-haired. Salmon-colored. She smiled in a pitying way.

And then dove hard into the sea, leaving behind only an immense stillness.

The men looked at one another, uneasy, afraid to be labeled fools or idiots. They knew they had seen her. Knew what had appeared before their eyes. But they said nothing. They were like witnesses to something wondrous or shameful, unable to admit what they had seen. In the cabin Cormac said nothing to Mr. Partridge, who was engulfed in his own visions.

More people died. They buried seven tiny children on one windless morning, tipping them into the sea as if they were bags of onions. They gave the sea one old man and four young women. Then they buried in the still water two men who were Cormac's age. All emigrants. And then one of the crew was found facedown on deck, and they sent his body after the others to the bottom.

The next day, after assuring himself that Mr. Partridge still lived, after forcing pulpy potato past his cracked lips, Cormac descended to the slave deck. The stench from the emigrant deck was thicker now than air, touchable, chewable, a substance, some fine compost of sweat and shit and decaying flesh. He struggled to keep from vomiting, helped by the fact that he had so little in his stomach to vomit. Then he heard the voice of Kongo calling desperately in his language, his voice cutting through the fevered wailing and mumbling of the emigrants between them. Cor-mac. Cor-mac. When he saw Cormac, he gestured wildly, pointing at Tomora, who was lying on the planked floor against the bulkhead. Her body was covered to her chin with rough cloth. Her eyes were open. But she was not moving.

37.

They prepared to bury Tomora. The captain didn't want the crew to see her nakedness and ordered up some last piece of canvas to serve as a shroud. Cormac helped Kongo raise her body for the sail maker to make his coarse sheath. Her flesh was still warm. The captain said sadly that Kongo and three other Africans could accompany her body to the deck, to say their private farewells. Four men. No more. They protested in their own language. The captain held up four fingers and then made a slashing gesture that said: *No more.*

In the bright, sultry haze of the main deck, Kongo and the three others looked even angrier than they did in their dark cage on the bottom deck. The crew gazed silently at the Africans as they stretched their bony bodies for the first time in many weeks. But the white men didn't come forward to join the ceremony. Cormac seethed with a mixture of rage and a jumbled emotion he could not name. Thinking: Tomora, you are so beautiful. Thinking: And now you'll be dropped into the sea far from home on a voyage that you did not want to take. Thinking: A voyage forced upon you by men with swords or guns or whips or branding irons. Thinking: By men like the Earl of Warren. From a world that allowed one group of human beings to own another group of human beings.

When Kongo bent with the other Africans to lift the lumpy shroud, Cormac stepped forward and took a corner. Kongo threw him a suspicious look but didn't shove him away. Together, four Africans and an Irishman, they carried Tomora's shrouded body to the plank. They laid her flat. Her shrouded feet faced the immobile sea.

The captain, holding his Bible, uttered words in English, the same words they had heard uttered over other bodies, and then nodded to Kongo. The African began speaking in his *click-clocking* language. Short bursts of words that snapped like whips. The other Africans bowed their heads. Kongo's deep voice was grave and strong. He finished and nodded at the captain.

Finally the lumpy shroud was slipped over the side. They all stared at the motionless sea that had now swallowed Tomora, the princess from Africa. A full minute went by in silence. And then, a hundred yards away, something small and black burst from the sea. A bird. Fluttering its wings. And then rising into the sky, making a turn, and heading finally toward the west. A raven.

They all seemed to exhale at once.

A breeze stirred.

A sail flapped lazily. And then another. And then one sail made a sharp, cracking, explosive sound.

The captain spun on the deck, shouting orders, exuberant, released, alive, and the men began climbing into the rigging. The captain peered through his spyglass at the point where last he had seen the raven. They were under way. To America.

Four

The New York Morning

We do not worry about being respected in the towns through which we pass. But if we are going to remain in one for a certain time, we do worry. How long does this time have to be?

— Pascal

38.

They smelled the land before they saw it. A rich, dark odor of sweet earth, coming at them through a misty rain. Then seabirds appeared, crying and screeing. Cormac was on deck, his hair and beard trimmed, his new brown suit and long blue coat fashioned by Mr. Partridge, who had refused his money. He had a new sling for the sword too, strapped down his back, clipped across his chest, the weapon in a flat leather sheath. When he donned the long coat, the sword could not be seen by any police inspectors who might peer in suspicion at the bearded face of someone named Martin O'Donovan. Even Mr. Partridge, with his high standards of craft, admired the handiwork of the crew member who had fashioned the sling, a dour saddle maker from Mayo. Mr. Partridge was now a smaller version of himself. Almost thirty pounds had melted away in the cauldron of his fever. Now his flesh hung off him as loosely as his clothes (which he insisted must wait to be tailored after a few weeks in New York). Under his smart beaver hat, his eyes were clear and bright with anticipation.

"Almost there, lad," he said, inhaling deeply.

Then a dark line spread across the horizon, and there was a huge cheer and waving of hats. Haggard Irish faces peered up through open hatches, still barred from the deck by Mr. Clark. "Stay below!" he bellowed. "Stay below, you lot! Yiz'll get kilt up here." Mr. Partridge explained that because of tides and currents and prevailing winds they had come around in a wide arc to their destination. The land on the right was the Long Island. Dutch farmers were scattered over much of it, he said, along with their slaves. But all were intelligently huddled far from the sea with its summer hurricanes and fierce winter winds. All Cormac saw were long strands of beach, white in the rain, and thick forests so dark they seemed black. And then up ahead, rising from the sea, there was a small mountain. Like the small meshed mountain he had seen in the Irish fog on the day, long ago, when they had set out upon the ocean. The island where Mary Morrigan had waved good-bye.

"Staten Island," Mr. Partridge said. "It'll be to port as we turn into the Narrows."

For a long moment, he was quiet on the bustling deck.

"Now remember all I told you, lad," he said.

"Yes, sir."

"We have much to do together."

"We do."

He had given Cormac the address on Stone Street of a place called Hughson's, where he might rent a room while Mr. Partridge looked for a place for his print shop. He himself would be staying at the Black Horse Tavern. Run by friends. Booked long ago. Cormac should call on him once a day, that was the plan, and Mr. Partridge would tell him of his progress. He had given Cormac a crudely printed map of the town, along with a litany of dire warnings. Don't let anyone carry your bag, or you'll never see it again. *(The fastest thieves in the world live here.)* Don't get drunk and lose control, or you'll lose even your shoes. *(Lock your door, button your coat, strap your hat, tie your laces.)* Don't sleep with any woman who offers her services *(It's a city of whores)*, or you'll end up with a pox that will swell your tongue to the width of a plank. New York was a dangerous place, Mr. Partridge said. Full of thieves from many nations. *(They speak seventeen different tongues, not counting the African languages.)* The English were the worst. Lazy buggers. Rather steal than work. *(As an Englishman, they fill me with shame.)* There were hundreds of Englishmen transported to America for crimes committed in English cities. *(They start by cutting their mothers' throats and then go downhill.)* And they weren't even the worst.

"The most dangerous of the lot are the ones who now think they're respectable," he had said when they were a week away from America. "They go to church. They wear fine clothes. They use snuff. And they'd steal the eyeballs out of your head."

He paused, staring at his journeyman's hands.

"Still and all, they'll give us much to print."

And he laughed out loud.

They had agreed to work together in New York. Or rather, Cormac would work for him. As soon as Mr. Partridge found a place for his press and his shop, he would teach Cormac the printing trade. The prospect thrilled Cormac. He could always work as a blacksmith, but to learn to set type and print Jonathan Swift and Alexander Pope and who knew what other great writers: that made his skin tingle and his blood rush. To be sure, he had a mission in New York, one he did not mention to the older man. But if the Earl of Warren was not there, or otherwise eluded him, then (Cormac thought) he could master a trade that would give his life a purpose.

Now the *Fury* moved steadily toward New York, passing the small mountain rising in Staten Island, and Cormac thought that he might never come this way again and so should remember the thrill of arrival. He might die in prison. He might be pursued into the blank interior. Indeed, in his pursuit of the earl, he might lose his own life. He might not even get past the pier, if someone recognized him. Some policeman or redcoat who knew that in Ireland he had killed a man. Or even two (for Cormac did not know the fate of the man who had crawled without a hand from the earl's stable). If they had a list, an alert, a warrant, they'd be looking for a young man named Robert Carson. Not Cormac O'Connor. Not Martin O'Donovan. They could be looking for him without need of a name.

But as the new land surrounded him, as a new breeze ruffled his hair, as he swerved into this port in the New World, this New York, another feeling blossomed within him, nurtured by the frail, almost tender rain and the smell of American earth: a yearning to live beyond the end of his mission. In some odd way, he wanted to kill the earl in order to live on. To live with all blood obligations honored and all blood debts paid. To end one part of his life and begin another. Here, in Tir-na-Nog.

Such thoughts vanished among shouts and cheers, the creaking of timbers and the swishing of water against the hull, as they turned into the great harbor. That was Brooklyn to the right now (Mr. Partridge said), named for a town in Holland, covered with woods that climbed in a long slope to a ridge of hills. Its scattered houses faced the harbor, with plumes of smoke rising from chimneys like pennants. Small boats were tied along the Brooklyn shore, and fishing boats, in from sea and river, were aimed at wharves. A few figures moved on a morning wharf and one of them waved in welcome and the crew cheered and waved back. Sails flapped. Flags streamed in the breeze. Captain Thompson watched in melancholy silence as his ship moved steadily to Manhattan.

At last the emigrants were released to the freedom of the deck. Blinking and trembling. They were now a ghastly remnant of those who had embarked so hopefully from Galway: red-eyed and wretched, their hair matted and greasy, pallid skins grimy with thirteen weeks of filth and fever and death. All were silent. Tears streaked the grime on some women's faces, but they could not even manage a sob. They gazed at Brooklyn as if it were the seacoast of the moon.

Manhattan grew larger and more clear. A fort at the tip. Four squat cannon aimed at the bay. Or at the *Fury*. Low houses behind the fort, and the steeple of a church, and away off to the north, ridged green forests. Small boats crossed before them. Sloops and skiffs. To the right the East River moved sluggishly between Manhattan and the Long Island, its marshy shore thick with masts. As they drew closer, the seabirds were braver, more aggressive, yipping and snarling around the masts. Cormac glimpsed scarlet uniforms near the fort and remembered them on the roads of Ireland. Along with the one British redcoat who had shown him the body of the dead girl after the Great Cold, his stricken face, his small lament for people who had died drinking piss.

Captain Thompson guided them into the East River. The *Fury* slowed, idled for a time, then turned with its stern toward what Mr. Partridge told him was Wallabout Bay. The seamen worked expertly, shouting curtly to one another, all engaged in the docking of the ship. Then they were pointed directly at the foot of Wall Street (although Cormac didn't yet know its name, and Mr. Partridge, his guide to geography, had retreated to his cabin to retrieve his precious personal cargo). Creaking timbers. Seabirds. A billowing of sail. A collective holding of breath. They saw other ships tied up at timbered piers. And parts of the shoreline dwindling into mud.

Mr. Partridge returned. Directly before them on shore was a large, empty, tin-roofed shed. Beneath the roof, an elevated stage. A large, still-faceless crowd watching the *Fury*'s approach. "That tin-roofed building," Mr. Partridge said, "is the Slave Market." Cormac thought: This is where Kongo will be sold. This place. Kongo and his men. But not Tomora. She has escaped this disgusting stage.

They entered the slip. The crew worked at mooring the *Fury*. Now Cormac could read the signs on the three-story buildings behind the Slave Market. Coopers. Meat sellers and victualers. Cordwainers and fishmongers and shipping agents. A pyramid of empty barrels climbed to the left, and beside them stood great piles of wooden crates awaiting shipment. Black men moved among the whites on shore, dressed in the same coarse clothes. Lifting, hauling, watching the ship as it docked. Behind the Slave Market, Wall Street cut through row houses up a long slope, and in the distance was the steeple they'd glimpsed from the harbor.

Ropes were thrown. Knots tied to stanchions. Mr. Partridge and Cormac were there, lashed to the American shore. The Rev. Clifford was now on deck. He was dressed in black, his eyes dead, standing behind them as Captain Thompson offered the top-deck passengers his thanks and his apologies for the rigors of the journey. The captain wished them good luck and gestured toward the wide plank leading to the wharf. Clifford's skin was dusty with seclusion, his eyes beyond all offers of luck or thanks. He went down the plank first, into the waiting crowd, in his salt-stained black suit, carrying his black bags and his black Bible. Mr. Partridge and Cormac in turn embraced the captain, shook hands with Mr. Clark, waved to the crew (which paid them little attention), and walked down to the land. There were no policemen or soldiers waiting with lists, and Cormac took a deep breath and exhaled slowly.

Then, to Cormac, it was as if the land were tilting and shifting, and some in the crowd laughed as they wobbled and lurched and tried to turn sea legs into land legs. Mr. Partridge laughed back, and so did Cormac. Someone shouted, "Welcome to America!" They mumbled their thanks and drifted to the side of the crowd. "Carry your bag, sir?" came one voice. "Food and lodging, gentlemen?" said another. "A nice warm woman after a long cold voyage?" whispered a third with a knowing giggle. "Absolutely *not,*" said Mr. Partridge, speaking for the two of them, his face wearing an expression that said: *We're not idiots.*

They were waiting at the quayside because Mr. Partridge couldn't take possession of his printing press until all passengers had cleared the ship. He told Cormac to go on to Hughson's on Stone Street and have a bath and breakfast. Cormac insisted on waiting with him. The older man went off to find help, while Cormac stood with his own bag on top of Mr. Partridge's suitcase and his foot on top of both. The sword felt heavy in its hiding place between his shoulder blades. A few minutes later Partridge returned in the company of a stevedore with a large cart who promised to deliver the press to Van Zandt's warehouse, three blocks south. But Mr. Partridge didn't trust its safe portage without being with it every minute. They waited together, with the stevedore off to the side.

The rain was falling harder now, drumming on the peaked tin roof of the Slave Market. They found dry refuge under a lean-to used by the stevedores, and while Mr. Partridge went for a look at the warehouse, someone offered Cormac a cup of coffee. His first in America. He ignored the dark warnings of Mr. Partridge and accepted. It was thick, sweet, dark, delicious, and if it contained some drug, Cormac didn't care. His bones began to warm.

Now the emigrants were tottering down the wide plank, looking like the risen crew of a death ship. A few of them were freemen, not prisoners of an indentured contract. They responded to a name shouted from the crowd — *Here, Billy! Right here, Robert* — and rushed to collapse into the arms of some relative. The rest were herded toward a brawny man in a leather vest who waited at the bottom of the plank, with an African holding an umbrella over his head. He was clearly a boss. Or *the* boss. Four men stood to the side, watching him the way lieutenants always look at a captain, the way the earl's men had looked at him before the killing of Cormac's father. They tensely gripped muskets, as if ready for battle — not for England or America or even themselves, but for the boss.

Each emigrant gave a name, and the burly man checked them off a list and pointed to a space in the rain to the left of the Slave Market where they must wait. The lieutenants took up positions at each corner of an imaginary square enclosing these indentured servants. The message was clear: If one of the Irish runs, he (or she) will be shot. Other men (in fancier clothes, with their own Africans holding umbrellas) began to bargain over their fate, pointing and choosing, and pinning small colored ribbons on the emigrants' soaked clothes. These were badges that made each emigrant the property of specific American agents. Some would remain in New York. A few were sent to New England. Most were bound for South Carolina or Virginia to work with the African slaves. Now some of the indentured servants found their tongues. This woman needs to go with that man and not be separated from him (for they'd fallen in love in the purgatory of the crossing). Or that woman is carrying my child, for the love of God (in pleading Irish and clumsy English). Or I'll not move a bloody inch until my child is fed!

A huge black man suddenly detached himself from a group of agents. He was about six-foot-two with muscles rippling under his denim vest. A leather whip was curled in his huge hand. Cormac heard some of the stevedores call his name. Quaco.

He stood alone in front of the unruly Irish. He didn't say a word but simply glared, and they hushed. Cormac knew why. They were cowed, beaten, beyond humiliation, with the rain falling steadily on their heads and shoulders and hopes.

Then a man on horseback arrived at the edge of the crowd and leaped down. He tethered the horse to a rough-hewn post in front of a meat shop. Quaco looked hard at him. He was about forty, his gray hair pasted to his skull by the rain, his broad shoulders pushing from beneath a coarse mechanic's shirt. His eyes were wide and frantic as he pushed through the crowd to the huddled emigrants. He was calling a name. *Caroline Heaney? Caroline Heaney? Has any of yiz seen Caroline*

Heaney? Heads shook slowly, as if concealing a secret. *Heaney? Caroline Heaney?* He turned to the *Fury,* peered at wet faces, and then walked hard to the man under the umbrella, the man checking off names. Quaco eased around to the side, as the new arrival whispered to the man with the Irish list. He was given a negative shake of the head and a jerk of a hand in the direction of the ship. There Mr. Blifil stood alone at the foot of the gang-plank, holding a sheaf of his own papers in one hand, an umbrella in the other. The man went to him. *Caroline Heaney.* Mr. Blifil flipped a few pages, paused, said something, and looked away. The man fell to the flagstones, writhing, weeping, cursing. His fists hammered at the earth. *Oh, my God; God damn you: Oh, my Caroline, oh, my sweet Caroline, I never should have wrote you, oh, Caroline, oh, oh, oh, oh.*

Some of the women broke past Quaco and bent over the man and held him and whispered to him (no doubt about the fate of Caroline and how she was now in Heaven, or the Otherworld), while the rain drummed harder on the roof of the Slave Market. Quaco did not intervene, even when an agent barked something at him and pointed at the disturbance of the grieving man. Quaco waited and watched until the grief ebbed and the man stood up and walked off to the place where his horse was teth-ered. Two English soldiers in rain-stained scarlet jackets were watching from their place in front of a cooper's shop. One of them laughed. Cormac wished he could unsheathe his sword.

39.

At last nine Africans were brought up on deck, with Kongo in the lead, all that was left of the original thirteen men and one woman. For a few defiant minutes, they stood shoulder to shoulder in a line, facing the American shore. The place of the enemy. The place of their captors. Behind them, Captain Thompson slipped into his cabin, presumably to wash his hands. The Africans wore only breechclouts. Their bodies were thin but not frail, and in the rain their skin was as glossy as wet coal. Their hands and feet were shackled, the hands tightly, the feet more loosely. With gestures and scowls, the boss beckoned them forward, his lieutenants tensed, as if ready to drag them ashore. Quaco watched from a distance. Kongo obviously calculated the odds of escape, and they were too long. Then he led the way down the plank, walking with small hobbled steps, but somehow managing to look like a victor.

The Africans stood very still on the flagstones along the edge of the pier. The boss agent said something and pointed to the stage of the Slave Market. The slave with the umbrella translated for his boss. But Kongo didn't move. Quaco watched more intently. The biggest of the private guards nudged Kongo sharply with the musket. Still Kongo refused to move. Then the guard hammered him on the back with the butt of the long gun. Kongo bent from the blow but did not go down.

Cormac rushed in.

"Wait," he shouted. "Don't do that!"

"And who are you?" the boss snarled, examining Cormac's young face and new clothes.

"I know this man. He's a good man and proud. Treat him well. Treat him like a man."

"I'll bust 'is fecking head, I will. If that suits *you,* sir."

"And *then* what? Can a man with a broken head be sold?"

One of the laughing English soldiers suddenly appeared, no longer laughing. His lip curled and he was annoyed by the rain that was soaking his scarlet coat to the color of old blood.

"What's all this?"

"Nothing," Cormac said, afraid now of an arrest, a request for papers. "Just trying to protect someone's property."

"Well, get on with it. We need no trouble here."

With a shrug and a turn of the head, Cormac urged Kongo to go along. The African looked at Cormac with that familiar mixture of anger and suspicion, then glanced around at the crowd. Quaco was staring at both of them. He was detached from the Africans, charged only with controlling the Irish. But he nodded at Kongo. A moment of contact, with something else built into it: a promise, a hope for a better moment. Kongo took a deep breath and led the way to the stage of the market. Walking like a captured king.

Then Mr. Partridge returned from his tasks, his face wet, his eyes angry. From a distance, he had seen Cormac's small intervention. He pulled his beaver hat lower on his brow.

"Are you mad?" he whispered, taking Cormac's elbow and leading him away.

Cormac looked back at Kongo as he moved up the steps leading to the tin-roofed stage. He was branded, as they all were, as Tomora had been, with a flared cross on the shoulder blades. A consignment of merchandise.

"They could have arrested you, you young fool," Mr. Partridge said.

"I suppose."

"Suppose? Sup-*pose?* That's their business. Their merchandise! They are shameless monsters, the lot of them. But that's why they're here. To peddle humans for money. Confronting them *physically* is foolish bravado."

A clipped English voice started announcing the imminent auction. The words were tossed and fractured by the rain. Cormac saw nobody who resembled the Earl of Warren. But when he gazed at the gray turbulent sky, a lone raven was making wide, slow circles above the town of New York.

40.

Then it was all settled on the quay at the foot of Wall Street. The huge crate was safely stored in Van Zandt's warehouse. Mr. Partridge shouldered his heavy bag, refused Cormac's offer to carry it for him, grabbed two smaller satchels in each hand, and they set off together into the town.

They walked up the slope of Wall Street, heading west, and the crowds filled Cormac with a sense of the marvelous. Here were all the nations of the earth, their languages drifting through the soggy air, or cleaving passages between the nouns and verbs of English. He didn't yet know French from German or Spanish from Dutch, but Mr. Partridge kept saying, *Listen, listen to them, lad* while telling him the names of the languages. The faces seemed to fit the words themselves, and their smooth or jarring rhythms: lean or fat, dark or fair. Cormac felt that he had entered the main street of Babel.

New York was an English town, of course, and had been one since 1673, the second time the English took it from the Dutch at gunpoint (Mr. Partridge said), the way they'd taken Ireland from the Irish. As they moved past the meat market, where great slabs of beef were loosely covered with burlap and tradesmen in blood-stained aprons shouted in London accents, the words on the walls were all in English. The signs above shops spoke English too. As did the quick, furtive men in rain-soaked coats and beaver hats calling to them from doorways: *Room to let, sir? Place to stay? Good big meal after a long journey? A nice entertaining bit of fluff?*

"Don't talk to any of that lot," Mr. Partridge said. "It wouldn't suit you to get a clap the first day in America."

He waved them away as if they were flies, and they passed through the lower part of Wall Street. Women revealed themselves among the milling crowds. Hatlesss women with rain-slick hair. Swaggering women and big-hipped women, coarse and fleshy women. And a few younger women flashing eyes at them, wearing paint on their faces. Cormac looked at one of them and she smiled in an available way. He averted his gaze (certain his face was flushed) and saw women pale as ghosts in upstairs windows, and women moving down the jammed side streets, stepping out of small houses made of yellow bricks, or backing out of shops. Their high-heeled shoes lifted the rims of their skirts above the mud.

Mr. Partridge grunted and paused, short of breath, but still refused Cormac's offer to carry his heavy bag, with its books and papers and secrets. And while he paused, Cormac now noticed how many Africans there were in the streets. "They're a fifth of the population, lad," Mr. Partridge explained. "A fifth, out of eleven thousand souls." Most of the Africans were young, like those on the ship and those who worked around the stage of the Slave Market, but some were older, shouting in good English, and a few were very old, squatting against walls, their hands open for alms. They were dressed like all the other workingmen, in rough muslin shirts, some with vests over the shirts, most with caps or hats because of the rain, all in heavy work boots. Two Africans maneuvered a load of cut lumber, removing it from a cart, while a horse shuddered and a white man gave orders in English. The Africans might have been a fifth of the people, but after you grew used to them (their like did not work in Belfast) they didn't stand out; they seemed part of the hurly-burly of the street. Cormac wondered if Kongo would become just another one of them.

There were black women too. They didn't resemble Tomora. Most were in the company of white women, carrying their bundles from the shops, or packages of meat from the market. The African women held umbrellas over the heads of their white mistresses, unless their hands were filled with packages, and then the white women gripped their own umbrellas, shifting to keep the packages dry. White or black, there were fewer women than men. At least on Wall Street. But the African women seemed more casual in their movements than the black men, as if they had settled for living out their lives here on this continent far from home. Cormac wondered what they were thinking on this jammed New York street, and in what language they dreamed.

As they walked, Mr. Partridge tried to fill Cormac with the lore of the place, but the younger man was too busy seeing it before him to listen to what it was. They stopped again, at the corner of Broad Street and Wall. Mr. Partridge leaned his bag on a stone marker, holding it in place with his body. He struggled for breath. That immense steeple up ahead, he told Cormac, is Trinity Church. It rises one hundred and seventy-five feet into the air. Cormac was astonished. This was the tallest structure he'd ever seen. Mr. Partridge didn't see it as architecture, and hissed: "It's just another attempt by the bloody Church of England to impose itself on people who're not in the least bit interested."

Across the street, that three-story building was the City Hall. "Look quickly," he said. "It's sure to get bigger and grander in the blink of an eye." He told Cormac that the Dutch had governed themselves from a tavern, but the Crown, in its majesty, preferred arcaded bricks. "Security!" Mr. Partridge said. "Order!" He laughed. "That's what they mean by God and King!" Gazing at the City Hall, Cormac remembered the plain weathered bricks of Belfast.

On their side of the street, a small crowd of men was gathered in the rain, cupping lit cigars or smoking clay pipes, talking in low tones, observing each new arrival at the City Hall. The arrivals were tall, well-dressed men with cold faces and the manners of command. A few emerged from horse-drawn carriages. Most arrived from side streets to the north. Cormac thought: If the Earl of Warren is in this town, he's certain to come here.

"Look at those faces," Mr. Partridge said. "Enough to make you a revolutionist."

Then he sighed and so did Cormac. They were now too exhausted to do almost anything at all beyond finding the solace of a land-bound bed. They turned into Broad Street. Mr. Partridge paused at the entrance to the Black Horse, where he would stay until he found a shop for his press. They agreed to meet the next morning (after a good night's sleep) and every day after that (if necessary), and then he pointed Cormac down the wide, crowded avenue toward Stone Street.

"And don't eat anything sold in the street," he shouted in farewell. "That'll kill you faster than the voyage."

41.

Broad Street was unpaved, widening out as it moved away from Wall Street, with a shimmer of harbor light at its distant end. It was filled with even more human beings than Wall Street. As the rain eased into a fine mist, dozens of motionless carts and wagons were engulfed by customers, shouting and bargaining with the peddlers. Many peddlers were women with coarse, thick, plain faces, selling eels and venison, oysters and fowl, limes from the Caribbean and vegetables from Brooklyn. Cormac's stomach coiled with hunger. Two soldiers on horseback rode by at a trot, splashing gluey mud around them, and some of the women yelled insults at their scarlet backs. Then there was a great surge and shouts, and Cormac was pushed aside, and suddenly a giant sow thumped in among them in a whirl of mud and fury, followed by six piglets and a large man shouting in what Cormac learned later was Dutch, and more men coming behind him. It was the biggest pig Cormac had ever seen, and probably the smartest, for it dodged and slithered and ran, eluding the men. It would not easily become bacon. The women shouted and cursed the pursuing men, clearly rooting for the sow. Cormac looked up the sloping street from which the sow had charged and saw more pigs, calmer, burying their snouts in mounds of garbage while a few young boys watched over them. He was too hungry to watch the end of the pursuit race, but like the peddler women, he was surely on the side of the pigs.

His new clothes were soaked now, as he searched for Stone Street. No street was marked with a sign. Three Africans were coming up Broad Street, one after the other, with poles braced across their backs, carrying immense pails of fresh water.

"Excuse me," Cormac said. "I'm looking for Stone Street."

"Two block," one of the black men said in a breathless voice. "Can't miss."

"Thank you," Cormac said. The African nodded in a surprised way and they moved on. Cormac passed more shops, a bank, a tobacconist, a button maker, and more carts, and finally reached Stone Street. The cobblestoned street sloped down toward the wooden stockade walls of Fort George. On the ramparts, he could see the shiny peaked caps of soldiers, slashes of scarlet, the points of bayonets, and a British flag dripping and limp from the rain. It was as Mr. Partridge had described it to him, the place where the governor lived, the center of colonial power in the province, cut off from the people as if its inhabitants feared them. But it told Cormac that he was truly here. He had crossed the fierce Atlantic and was here in New York.

At the bottom of the street on the left stood an old Dutch brewery converted into a warehouse, and across the street was the tavern run by John Hughson.

The house was three stories high with sloping eaves and a chimney at the back. There was a careless quality to it. Dark blue paint was peeling on the front door, showing a coat of pale blue underneath. The window frames were crooked. One wall sagged, as if it had been built before the earth below it had settled. A half-dozen loose slates were askew on the roof. On each side of the doorstep, patches of earth made for flowers were slick and bald and muddy. Pausing there, facing the tarnished brass knocker, Cormac remembered the straight true lines of their house in Ireland and flowers bursting from spring earth. All now ash.

He knocked on the door. Waited a long while. Then knocked again.

The door was jerked open, and he was startled by the woman who stood before him. Sharp, beaked nose. A slash of mouth. Gray, suspicious, disappointed eyes. There was a hint of rouge on her cheeks and a silver stud glistening in each earlobe. Her hair was pulled straight back. Her bosom was large and pillowy.

"Is it a room you want?" she said.

"Aye."

"Are you Irish?"

"Aye."

"Are you Catholic?"

"No."

"Three shillings a week, meals included. In advance. Do y' have money?"

"Aye."

"Come in," she said, "and don't be clompin' them boots on our nice dry floors."

They were in a tight hallway, with coat hooks on the wall, a bench, a chipped porcelain umbrella stand, stairs leading to the next floor, and a closed blue door at the rear of the hall. She turned her back on him, and he noticed that she had wide hips and was wearing a scent.

"Mary?" she called up the stairs. "*Mary*? Come down here, girl."

Then she turned to Cormac and scowled.

"Take off the boots," she said, "and the socks too, if you're wearing any."

He sat on the bench, unlaced the boots, peeled off the socks. The odor of rain and feet and wet wool filled the tight hallway.

The stairs creaked, and he looked up and saw a young woman's bare calves first, and then the rest of her: dark brown hair, sullen eyes, full lips, small waist. She was wearing a loose blue sweater over a white blouse and a long dark blue skirt. She inspected him in a chilly way.

"This is Mary Burton," the older woman said to Cormac. "Your name is . . . ?"

"O'Donovan," Cormac said. "Martin O'Donovan. From Galway."

"Good," she said. "I'm Sarah Hughson. I run this place, with my husband, John."

"Nice to meet you," Cormac said.

"Mary, take Mr. O'Donovan to room three, would you, dearie?" the woman said in a flat voice.

"Yes'm."

He lifted his shoes and socks in one hand and his bag in the other. At the sight of him, Mary Burton laughed out loud.

"Don't you be laughin' at a guest, y' young flit!" Sarah said sharply.

"I don't mind," Cormac said. "I must look a right idiot."

"It's not for you to excuse her, young man," Sarah said. "We live with rules here. The first rule is the three shillings is paid in advance."

He dug the shillings from his pocket and handed them to her.

"Try to get some sleep," she said. "You look fit for bein' buried."

"Aye," he said, and followed Mary Burton up the stairs, eyes fixed on her bare calves. She led him to a small room under the eaves, furnished with a narrow cot and a battered bureau. A small window faced south to Fort George. He dropped the bag on the floor. There was a piss pot against the wall.

"Well, you're certainly not from Galway," she said. "Not with that accent. I'm from Galway, and I know. So I assume your name's not Martin O'Donovan."

"Are you a policeman in disguise?"

"Not in this bloody house," she said, chuckling in a private, knowing way.

"Call me Martin anyway," Cormac said.

"All right," she said. "In this bloody town, nobody is who they say they are anyway."

She stared out the rain-dripping window toward the harbor.

"Is there a way to get a bit of breakfast?"

"First take off your clothes," she said.

He laughed. "Is this the way you welcome people to America?"

"No," she said. "It's just that I can't stand the feckin' sight of that lovely feckin' suit turning into a feckin' coal bag."

She stared at him. "And besides," she said, "I want to know what it is you've got strapped to your back."

He removed his jacket and hung it on the bedpost.

"It's a sword," Cormac said, unbuckling the straps across his chest and then holding the sword's handle in its scabbard and showing her. There was a glitter of fascination in her eyes.

"A fecking sword it is," she said. "I thought so."

"Actually, it's my father's sword."

"Was he thinkin' of New York when he gave it to you?"

"No," he said, and paused, as an image of his father's corded arms scribbled through him, hammering the sword in his forge. "No, he was dead when it passed to my hands. He left it to me."

She looked at him with another kind of disbelief. He sensed that there were few stories that Mary Burton truly believed.

"I see," she said.

She lifted his jacket off the bedpost. A sour odor filled the room. Cormac was sure it was from him: sweat and rain and the stench of the ship.

"The trousers too."

"Uh, I don't know you that well, miss. I don't —"

"I told you: The name's Mary Burton. I owe the feckin' Hughsons six more feckin' years on me feckin' indenture. Let me have the feckin' trousers."

"Why don't you fetch me some breakfast and I'll take them off while you're gone."

"Jaysus, another tightnutter from Ireland."

She hustled out with the jacket, closing the door behind her. A key was slotted in the keyhole and Cormac turned it, locking the door. He was not really shy of Mary Burton seeing him naked, but he didn't want her seeing the money belt. He stripped off the trousers, unbuckled the money belt, and shoved it under the mattress. He pulled off his long, soaked underwear and hung it with the trousers on the bedpost. Then he unlocked the door and eased under the coverlet, his hunger fighting with his exhaustion, and both in combat with images of Mary Burton's body. Little squalls of rain spattered the windowpane. He smelled bacon frying. His body drowsed, but he remained awake, the sword on the floor, his hand on its hilt. Then Mary Burton returned with a tray. She laid it across his covered thighs: three fried eggs, slabs of greasy bacon, brown buttered bread, and a pot of tea.

"Sit up," she said.

He did, leaning closer to her.

"Do you think I could have me a bath?" he said.

She snickered. "The rule is one bath a week. There's seven feckin' rooms in this hole, and your room doesn't get its bath for two more feckin' days. Don't feckin' complain to me. I don't make the rules."

He laughed. "How many times a day do you say 'feck'?"

"As many as I feckin' can."

She paused at the door.

"I suppose you'd like me to join you?" she said.

"Well, I —"

She humphed in a dismissive way.

"Just leave the feckin' tray outside the feckin' door," she said, picking up the rest of his clothes and closing the door hard.

He ate desperately, jamming the bread into his mouth, taking bacon in his fingers. Thinking: Mary Burton. Thinking: Who are you, girl? Thinking: Why do you talk worse than a sailor? Mary Morrigan moved in his mind, smelling of the forest, whispering the old tales. He saw the perfumed breast of Bridget Riley in the Earl of Warren's bed. Then Tomora, gazing with her liquid black eyes from the blackness of her jail. Then the door opened again and Mary Burton came in, holding a steaming bowl of water. She placed it on the bureau.

"If you wait two days to feckin' wash," she said, "we'll be dead of the stink." She put a piece of gray muslin and a sliver of soap beside the bowl. "And don't tell that bitch Sarah I took you some soap. She'll add thruppence to the feckin' account."

With that, she was gone again. Cormac finished eating and then stood up naked, using the soap and the muslin cloth to wash his face and neck, armpits and balls and feet. He felt at once filled and purged, his stomach full, his flesh scoured. He then put the dirty dishes on the tray and laid them outside the door. The corridor was empty. He heard smothered female voices from below. Then male growls. He locked the door. He shoved his bag between bed and wall, with the small leather pouch inside containing his mother's spiral earrings. He laid the sword under the thin mattress and strapped the money belt to the small of his back. Thirteen pounds. His mother's spiral earrings. His father's sword. They were all that he truly possessed, which was a lot more than most. All of them with him now in this room in America. The rain whipped the windowpanes, and he fell asleep.

42.

In the dark, Cormac heard the muffled sound of a fiddle and thought he was still on the ship. But nothing rocked or creaked, no seaborne timber cleaved water. He was in a room. On land. With dim light leaking through crooked shutters. He rubbed his eyes, and the room emerged dimly, in dark gray tones. He stretched, felt the sword through the mattress and the straps of the money belt digging into his flesh. He unbuckled the money belt and rubbed his skin. Then he sat up naked. And stepped into the chill, and felt for the candle and wooden matches on top of the bureau. He snapped a sulphur head with a thumbnail, lit the wick. Almost reluctantly, yellow light revealed the room. From beyond the door, the unseen fiddler played a melancholy tune.

His suit was not in the room. He cracked open the door and peered into the darkened hallway. The sound of the fiddle was louder now, but no less melancholy. And there was the suit, neatly hanging on a rough hanger hooked upon a wall peg opposite the door. He took it in behind him. Again, he washed his face and armpits with the chilly water and dried himself with the coarse, damp cloth, dressed quickly, buckling the money belt under his trousers, and went out, locking the door behind him and pocketing the key.

He followed the sound of the fiddle down two flights of stairs to the blue door in the back of the entrance hall. The melancholy tune ended, and the music shifted into an up-tempo reel, which was greeted by a loud, growling, masculine roar of approval.

He opened the door and stepped into another world: a low-ceilinged, smoky room crowded with white men and Africans, some of them up and jigging madly to the music, the floor shaking, laughter pealing, some of the black men doing wild parodies of the white men's dances. One white woman was dancing with two black men, laughing and taunting them. And from the side came Mary Burton, all rosy in the light of lanterns. She grabbed Cormac's forearm.

"The feckin' suit looks better now," she said.

"It does. Thanks very much." He smiled. "And thanks for the water and soap."

"You must smell a lot better," she said. "Can you jig?"

"No."

"Well, try anyway."

She jerked him into the center of the dancing men, her back straight, her arms rigidly hanging at her side, her breasts bouncing to the music and the movements. The room roared. *Dance it, Marymouth. Do it, do it . . .* She glowered at Cormac until he stepped in and tried to match her moves, feeling clumsy and oafish, his legs like lumber. Until one of the Africans shouted at him.

"Don't *think,* boy. *Move.*"

And so he did, surrendering to the music, and the packed heat, and the smoke, and the open mouth of Mary Burton, her lips shifting as he stared, and the music pulsing, and her breasts pushing against the cotton blouse, and she was Mary Morrigan and she was Bridget Riley, and his head started seething and he felt himself hardening and her hand brushed his hardness while other dancers bumped against him, closing the tight space around Mary Burton, and she ran a tongue over her mouth in a teasing way. And then it was over. Everyone cheered. And then Mary Burton embraced him, pressing into him, pushing her small breasts hard against his chest.

"Ah, that was feckin' grand," she growled, suddenly turning and shoving her way through the crowd to the bar. He followed her. From the jumble of excited talk he kept hearing *Marymouth, Marymouth,* at once affectionate and charged with lust. She pushed an African aside and reached for a plate. The bar was covered with jugs and glasses and mugs, and platters of ham and venison and bleeding beef, potatoes, turnips, and cabbage, bread loaves and a butter tub, and a kind of porridge called *sappaan*. She heaped food on a plate. Behind the bar stood a tall, unsmiling, fleshy man with skin cratered by smallpox. His body was still, but his hands moved quickly: uncorking bottles, pouring drinks, gathering coins, and dropping them into the pockets of his greasy apron. His eyes were as soft in their own way as his body. But to be sure, Cormac thought, I've spent so many weeks with men made lean and hard by hunger that almost everybody else in the room looks soft.

"John," Mary Burton said, "this is your new boarder, Mister O'Donovan, he says his name is." Then to Cormac: "John Hughson. He owns this feckin' dive."

Hughson's mouth smiled, but his eyes remained soft and disappointed.

"Welcome," he said. "Have a drink, lad."

He glanced at Mary Burton.

"Maybe you'll be the one to land Miss Mouth," he said, opening a bottle of porter.

"Oh, shush, John. Let the man eat."

"That's sixpence," Hughson said, as Cormac fumbled for change. "You must be just in from the sea. You've got that ship hunger on you. Ah, well, you're not alone. Some of 'em come in here ready to eat the bloody furniture."

"The feckin' furniture might taste better than some of your food, John," Mary Burton said.

"Don't give the lad a bad impression, wench."

He turned to a foot-wide opening in the wall behind him, beyond which was the kitchen, and shouted something Cormac couldn't hear under the sound of another kind of music. The fiddler bowed a few bars, and then the Africans joined him, using rattles and gourds and polished wooden bars that made a *klawk-klawk-klawk* sound. Some chanted together and were answered by others. The voices were taunting, bragging, laughing, sharing the close, dense, happy air of the place to which they'd been taken at gunpoint. Cormac understood only one large thing: He was hearing Africa.

"Come on," Mary Burton said, grabbing Cormac's plate and pushing him along through the chanting crowd to a table near the far wall. Three black men were seated on a bench, drinking rum. In the corner, the white fiddler played in solitude, overwhelmed by the African rhythms but trying to play into and through them.

"Move over, you lot," Mary Burton said to the three Africans, and they did, smiling and polite. "We've got us a new feckin' inmate."

Cormac had already seen one of them: Quaco, the tall man who had behaved well at the Wall Street quay that morning. He said nothing, but gave Cormac a look of recognition, perhaps remembering that he had tried to protect Kongo from the hard men. The others were named Sandy and Diamond. Sandy was Cormac's age, the other two older. They were all dressed in clean shirts and rough trousers. Mary Burton turned her back to them and picked at some of the food on Cormac's plate.

"Why do they call you Marymouth?"

"Because of my dirty feckin' mouth. Or — no, that's it." She smiled in an almost proud way. "John Hughson says I've got the dirtiest feckin' mouth in America."

Cormac squeezed her hand.

"Well, there's a lot worse things, I suppose."

"Aye, like being a feckin' slave," she said. "They call us indentured servants, but that's the fancy way to say it. The true feckin' word is slave. Just like all these black fellas from Africa. There's no bloody difference. I did two years up in Poughkeepsie with a fat feckin' Dutchman that bought me from some feckin' English poof. The Dutchman tried to get up into me, but I fought him off, and then his fat feckin' wife was sure he was gettin' me anyway, and she it was that had me sold again. John Hughson's brother bought me for John, and I told John, You might own me, but you won't have me body and don't expect me to act like a feckin' lady while I do the slave work." She smiled. "Drives him feckin' wicked, it does."

She got up and went to the bar, and carried plates to another table, and sat down again with Cormac, talking and moving to the music, and then was up again. She was always in movement, cracking wise with customers, dancing variations on the jig with Africans, clearing plates, then sitting with Cormac again. Across the night she explained in bits and pieces this small part of the world into which he had arrived, turning for confirmation to Quaco, Sandy, and Diamond. "Isn't that right, Quaco?" "Yes ma'am." "Tell the man I'm not feckin' lying, Sandy." "Oh, you don't lie, Miz Mary." Among other things, Cormac learned that Hughson's was one of only four taverns where blacks and whites mixed freely.

"There's two hundred taverns and only four of them is like this. Isn't that right, Diamond?"

"Right, Mary."

The British authorities didn't like it, Sandy said, but they took Hughson's little bribes and left him alone. Mary laughed. "John says the English captain is really his partner." Sunday was the slaves' day off, and because there were so many of them, the white people tried hard to avoid direct confrontations. Yes, it was against the law to serve strong drink to a slave, but this was New York. Yes, it was against the law for slaves to assemble in groups larger than three, but this was New York. After dark, no slave could move through the city without a lantern and a pass from his master; the law meant little because this was New York.

"They're not a bad lot, the Africans," Mary Burton said. "I pity them, kidnapped by those English feckheads and brought to this feckin' sewer."

There were some free Africans, she said, most of them too old to work anymore, cast into the streets by their masters, who were then spared the task of feeding them. "They're up in the Out Ward, just above the Common," Mary Burton said. "They've got their own burial ground there. They won't let them be buried with the feckin' whites. That's the bloody English for you. The Jews are in their own wee bit of turf too, along the Chatham Road. The bloody English, always on their own, even when they're feckin' dead."

Cormac heard that first night from Mary, from Quaco (with nods and mutterings from Diamond and sad remarks from Sandy) what he would hear for many weeks to come. For the Africans, New York was getting worse, not better.

"They see too many of us now," Quaco said quietly. "They needs us. But they don't want us too." A flash of something dangerous washed through his composed, intelligent face. "They fears us too," he said, and started to say something else, and then cut himself off.

Quaco told Cormac that he was twenty-two and had been in New York since he was twelve, working most days in the meat market for Wallace the victualer. Now that he was older and taller and stronger, and showed a gift for African languages as well as English, he was often rented to the dockmaster when ships came in. There were so many languages among the Africans, but the ones he heard most were Ashanti and Yoruba, which was the language of his part of Africa.

"I try don't to be mean," he said. "Try don't to hurt a man or woman. They be scared, them from the ships. They don't know if they still in the world. I talks to them in Ibo or Yoruba or Ashanti, calm 'em down, tell 'em they be fed soon, get them clo's to be warm. I gets milk to some chile his mother's dead from the ship. Cawse, a man get crazy, want to kill somebody, I have to stop him. Man he runs, I catch him. But I helps more than I harms people."

"Ain't always be such a way," said Diamond. "Ain't all times you be down there helpin', Quaco. Just proves: Africaman got to help his own self."

"Don't talk no foolish words, boy," Quaco said in warning.

"They sure to be a day," Diamond said, staring at his small hands, and his rum. "They sure to be a day. Our day."

"Shut down, fool," Quaco said, and playfully squeezed Diamond's head and sipped his own porter. But as the night lengthened, and Mary Burton worked other tables, and Quaco's tongue was loosened by drink, he told Cormac what it was like to be a slave in New York. Slaves couldn't ever confront a master. If they did, they got the lash. Sometimes they got the lash for no reason. "Master don't like the way you look at him, here come the lash. Master don't like the cookin'? Here come the lash. Silverware missin'? The lash. Africaman can't go to school to learn to read, 'cause they might read newspapers and see stories 'bout slaves who murder they masters. Or slave rebellions in Jamaica or Georgia." Silence. "Like we don't know," Quaco said, shaking his head. "Like we don't hear."

Slaves couldn't work as coopers or coachmen, they told Cormac (while the music pounded and the porter flowed), because the white coopers and white coachmen couldn't compete with them for wages. "Nobody competes with us," said Sandy, "'cause we get *no* wages, sir." This in an English accent (he was born in New York, and then his mother died and his father was sold to a man in Canada while he was sold to a brickmaker). "They see us as mules, sir, or horses," Sandy said, waving a thin hand. "Sell us, trade us, rent us." Diamond murmured, "They sure to be a day."

Mary Burton heard this fragment of talk and said, "Explain about the great God-fearin' dog-feckin' shite-eating Bible-thumpin' piss-drinkin' Christian churches!" The three Africans laughed and so did Cormac. "We can't be Christians," said Sandy, "because that would mean we had souls, sir. Mules don't have souls, sir, horses don't have souls —"

"And if you don't have a feckin' soul, then they can give yiz the feckin' lash!" said Mary Burton.

Slaves couldn't get married in any Christian church, so they had their own ceremonies.

"I marry my wife here in Hughson's," said Quaco, and for the first time, his eyes looked bitter in the yellow light of Hughson's lanterns. "My wife, she work in the fort. Cookin', cleanin'. They won't let me see her on Sunday, won't let me see her at night; she have to sneak out and go with me in the trees, like the white whores by the fort. My wife! And they own her!"

Mary Burton put a calming hand on Quaco's forearm, sipped furtively from Cormac's glass of porter, glancing through the crowd at the bar to be sure Hughson didn't see her.

"In other words," she said, turning to Cormac, "these poor buggers're treated like we was treated in the feckin' Old Country." She shook her head. "They don't even have a Catholic church here. Just like the Old Country. It's against the feckin' law. So if you're a Catholic, keep your mouth shut, boy. It's a Godawful feckin' crime to be a Catholic priest, and if they find one, they'll strip him and whip the feckin' life out of him. God help you if you're a Catholic *African*. That's a double feckin' crime."

She was laughing bitterly through this discourse, and so were the Africans. Then she glanced at the bar and her mood suddenly altered. Sarah Hughson had come around from behind the bar and her swagger made clear that she was the real boss of the tavern. Quaco looked uneasy. Other Africans nodded politely to her, not wishing to trigger her wrath and find themselves barred from Hughson's. The fiddler played a lament, full of Irish sadness, and Sarah came over to the table.

"Ach, it's the mud man," she said to Cormac, hands on hips. "You look much better than you did when you arrived. And whatever you do, don't believe a word from Mary the Mouth." She smiled, showing her crooked teeth. "Bring the new lad a drink, will you, Mary?"

Mary Burton went to the bar, and Sarah sat down beside Cormac. Quaco, Sandy, and Diamond smiled in welcome but eased away, keeping a respectful distance.

"So what brings you to New York?"

"I want to be a printer."

"A good trade," she said. "But you might not find labor. The town's full of illiterates. Starting with the people that run it." She turned to Quaco. "How's your wife, Quaco?"

He shrugged. "Reg'lar, Miz Hughson."

"She's still over in the fort?"

"Yes, ma'am," Quaco said, seething again.

"A beautiful woman she is," Sarah said to Cormac. "A bosom'd make most women weep in envy." Then, to Quaco: "Better keep an eye out on her. Those soldier boys can't be trusted."

"Yes, ma'am."

Mary Burton returned with a porter for Cormac and a small whiskey for Sarah Hughson. Sarah downed hers and got up. So did Quaco. His brow was knitted into a grid.

"Don't you go anywhere, Quaco," Sarah said.

"I go where I want," he said, grunting.

"Don't go to the fort."

"I go where I want."

"That's nothing but trouble," Sarah Hughson said. "She's surely fast asleep."

Sandy grabbed his arm to hold him back, but Quaco jerked his arm free and headed to the back door. Diamond and Sandy hurried after him (the music pounding now) and the three of them passed into the New York darkness.

"Jaysus feckin' Christ," Mary Burton said.

"I shouldn't've mentioned his wife," Sarah said.

"He thinks the governor and the feckin' officers and all the men are getting it from his wife," Mary Burton whispered to Cormac. "And he might be right about the governor."

43.

Sarah moved quickly to the back door, and Mary sat down beside Cormac. She was weary now, her hair loose and tangled from the heat of the room and the long hours of the day. An African fiddler was playing his own instrument, plucking the strings in a percussive way instead of bowing them. The gourds and rattles were out. Africans drummed with fingernails on tabletops, while Mary Burton explained one other truth about the tavern (whispering, covering her mouth, looking at her glass). The Africans didn't just come here for the drink and the freedom. They were there every night of the week because John Hughson was a fence.

"If you're a slave," she said, "the law is a feckin' joke. And so most of them are thieves."

After dark, she said, they came to Hughson's with those things they had foraged. Things that could be turned into a form of payment for labor. Pieces of cheap silverware, bearing no engraved stamps. Stray tools. Casks of nails. Leather whips. Stolen liquor, meat, potatoes, and fruit. They stole while their masters were sleeping, or away on business, or assembled in the Christian churches, full of piety and breakfast. "It's a way to keep some kind of feckin' pride," Mary Burton said. "There's not too many ways to do that under the English flag."

Hughson didn't often give cash to the Africans. And it was not easy for an African to spend money, since he was not supposed to have any. What Hughson gave them was credit in his own tavern.

"I'd steal meself," said Mary Burton, and laughed. "But I could hardly fence Hughson's own things to Hughson himself."

Her rebellion, what she did for pride, was a simpler matter. Hughson owned her but could not have her. "As simple as that." He could not go between her legs or invite anyone else to do the same. "And that's fine with Sarah." In the end it was really Sarah's place, not John's. She it was who forced poor slow John to sell his house up in Westchester and come down to New York. She it was who had him rent the first small tavern, and then to lease this one, and then to spread the word that the blacks would be welcome. She it was who made certain that at least one white whore lived on the premises, and this year's whore was Peggy, who arrived one snowy midnight from Newfoundland and never left.

"That's Peggy there, Peggy the house whore," Mary Burton said, and motioned toward a young woman across the room, red-haired, thick-breasted, broad-shouldered, and large. She was smiling and flirting in a mannered way. "A nice woman, in her way, but dumber than feckin' whale shite."

Peggy slept with the Africans too, if they had the money in cash.

"Sure, the English preachers give off lots of blather about how the blacks and the whites are meant to be separate," Mary Burton said. "But there's no holdin' men from drink. And when there's drink taken, their feckin' rods always lead them to women. Every man in this place has offered me good money for a look at me quim. They've offered me everything except what they can't feckin' give me. Me freedom."

The back door opened. Quaco, Sandy, and Diamond returned, herded inside by the shepherdess Sarah. She stood them drinks at the bar. The music was steady and full of rhythms Cormac had never heard before, like the beat of a heart. The back door opened again. "Here's the African feckin' Lucifer himself," Mary Burton said. A large black man bent his head under the door frame. The room hushed, and even the fiddler stopped for a few beats. "That's Caesar. The one I'm sure's put a child in poor, dumb Peggy." Sarah smiled in welcome. Hughson looked nervous. Peggy averted her eyes shyly and removed a hand from inside a black man's shirt. Caesar moved slowly and theatrically, performing an image of latent violence. He smiled at Sarah in a thin way and then the talk resumed, muffled, murmurous.

"He's a dangerous fecker," Mary Burton whispered.

Quaco, Sandy, and Diamond reclaimed their seats. Quaco glanced across the room at Caesar, then looked down at Mary Burton.

"I think I'll dance with you, Mary," he said.

"You will not, Quaco. You're a married man." She laughed. "Besides, I'm working."

She went off to retrieve glasses and plates (Quaco shrugging away the rebuff), and Cormac realized how thin her body was, and how long her neck. As she moved, her eyes assumed a distracted look, as if she were seeing something that was not in the room. In spite of her foul, bitter mouth, he thought she was beautiful. He noticed Caesar's glance at her, and Hughson watching her too, and then Sarah identifying desire in Hughson's eyes and turning to examine Mary Burton, as if wondering what her husband wanted from this thin, common Irish girl. Or knowing what he wanted but finding it hard to believe. Caesar's back was to them now, but when Peggy eased beside him at the bar, his large ebony hand wandered casually to her buttocks and caressed them in a possessive way. A sign to all the others. Including the whites.

For while he was watching the Africans, Cormac's attention had been diverted from the dozen white men in the place. They were scattered around the long, low room, six of them together in a bunch, others mixing with the Africans. At one point, two African women came in and joined two white men at a table. The women were tall, dressed in American clothes, with bonnets on their heads. One of them had neat scars on both cheeks, arranged in rows, and wore gold hoops in her ears. Tomora's face moved in Cormac. Full lips. Liquid eyes. Lush body in a shroud on a windless sea.

"You've got lust in your face," Mary Burton said, sliding down beside him. "Do you want one of them?"

"No," Cormac lied.

"You can have either one for a few shillings," she said. "Or both. God knows they need the money."

The women were drinking rum paid for by the white men. One nodded at Caesar: the obvious ponce. "Whatever they get, he gets half," Mary Burton said. "He's got women in some of the other feckin' taverns too." Cormac noticed Quaco staring at the African women and mumbling in English to Diamond and Sandy. Cormac couldn't hear everything he said, but he did hear words about his wife and the fort. The woman with the scars turned and looked at the blue door leading into the house and then at Sarah Hughson, who nodded her approval. "Here she goes," Mary Burton said. "There's one room on the top floor that's always free." The African woman whispered something to the white man, then went to the blue door. Quaco started getting up, as if to intercept her, but Diamond pulled him back. "Caesar cut your throat, Quaco," he said. "Beside, the woman got two girl children she need to feed." Indeed, Caesar was glowering at Quaco through the smoke and music. The scarred woman vanished. Within seconds, one of the two white men (paunchy, mustached) followed her.

"She's feeding her children," Mary Burton said. "Poor soul."

She gazed blearily around the room, and Cormac asked her about the other whites. The six men bunched at one small table were soldiers from Fort George, all of them Irish. "Serving His fecking Majesty," she said with contempt. "Shameless bastards." The small, precise man at the other table was a dancing master named Holt, who claimed that the Africans were the greatest dancers he'd ever seen. "He won't even dance with the likes of us," she said. "But then, he doesn't like women much." When Holt bowed before the remaining African woman and took her hand to dance, even Quaco didn't mind, and Caesar patiently sipped a drink. "The African men think Mister Holt wants to dance with *them*. In bed."

With an African woman on the floor, the music shifted. African rhythms drowned the room. Holt the dancing master tried valiantly to adapt a minuet to the grinding music. The black woman (long-necked, large-breasted, hair piled above her brow) towered over the small white man and caricatured his steps. He smiled, knowing what she was doing, trying to be a good sport. She turned in one quick move and her right breast bumped against Holt's face. The room exploded in applause. She turned the other way and did it again, with her left breast. That became her dance. Bumping the small white man's face with her left breast and then her right breast, as he flushed and perspired. She moved in loose steps, her belly thrust forward, using her breasts like weapons. She stared down at Holt with an ambiguous smile. The blacks roared.

"Whip the man!" Quaco shouted, laughing now. "Whip him *down*, woman!"

"Do you want *her?*" Mary Burton whispered.

"I want you."

She squeezed his thigh in a playful way and got up.

"I'm too old for you," she said.

44.

In Cormac's three weeks at Hughson's, the routine was always the same. Breakfast at half-seven, eggs and rashers and buttered bread, along with coffee that looked (and tasted) like pitch. Dinner at half-five. A nap. A visit to the bar at night. A bath on Friday evening, poured from jugs into a sealed cask by Mary Burton. Each day, he'd pay a visit to Mr. Partridge at the Black Horse, to hear about his search for a shop or to join him in some new examination of a place for the press. The other hours were Cormac's, and he used them to search for the Earl of Warren. He had learned that a man could walk all of the New York streets in a single day.

Most of the time he was on his own, wandering in the mornings down to the Battery, where four squat cannon were aimed at the harbor, fearful of the Pope's imminent arrival on board a Spanish warship. Redcoats drilled in Fort George. Lone women gazed out to sea, where their men had gone but had never come back. The breeze at the island's tip was heavy with salt, and he could see the green humps of New Jersey and Staten Island and boats in full sail passing through the Narrows. Not once did he see the earl.

But still he peered at faces, gazed at strangers, and walked. On some days, he wandered up Broadway, past Trinity, to the Common, where boys played games and old men sat on the grass smoking seegars or clay pipes, lost in themselves. If they'd been raised on Mars they could not be farther from home. Cormac felt disconnected from all of them. His own history was of no interest to those he passed. New York, he was learning, was a city of the present tense, an eternal now. Except for a few old Dutchmen, it was not a city of the past. Today ruled.

Tomorrow might be richer and fatter, the Christian evangelists told them, but tomorrow also brought certain death, followed by the rewards of Heaven or the punishments of Hell. The various Christian rivers flowed through the streets of New York. Quakers quaking. Congregationalists congregating, Baptists baptizing, Dutch Reformers reforming; Episcopalians pissing on the lot. All asked for money to support the war against evil. Only the proud, haughty Anglicans of Trinity were not present on the street, since they were supported by taxpayer money and had no need to panhandle for God. All other messengers of the Lord were forced to pay taxes to support the Anglicans, just as they did in Ireland. All preachers were dressed in shades of black. From deep, fresh black to gray, faded, disappointed black. All used the same nouns: death, punishment, corruption, Hell, suffering, papist. All proclaimed that they were opposed to (or part of) something called the Great Awakening, a religious revival spreading south from dark, witch-haunted New England. They spoke, as always, of a vengeful Puritanical God, a God of brutal whims and divine ego, quick to suffer insult and explode in wrath. Cormac thought of him as the God of bad temper. The Celtic gods would laugh him out of the room.

A few preachers were capable of surprise. One Welshman was a marvelous singer. One Cornishman had a sense of humor. One or two even agreed (under questioning) that black people might have souls. Such an admission didn't lead in their logic to any utopian notion that the enslaved souls might be freed. Africans would have to await freedom and redemption after death, when God would sort them out in his Eternal Kingdom.

Most New Yorkers paid the preachers little heed; they were too busy rushing from one appointment to another, chasing the whims of Mammon. Blacks were not welcome among the small knots of fevered religiosos in the Common, but when each pulverizing sermon ended and the hat was passed, the few Indians who had paused to listen, dressed in wild combinations of buckskin and English jackets, usually broke into laughter. They simply could not be convinced that God was a dead carpenter. During any given lunch hour, there were more preachers than auditors, all demanding that New Yorkers be born again, give up their filthy corruptions, beg for forgiveness, endure punishment, dwell on the certainties of death and the afflictions of Hell. Although Cormac used them as cover, an excuse to stand around watching, he didn't tarry with them very long. He was certain that the listeners would never include the Earl of Warren.

Then, on the second Sunday after his arrival, he saw a familiar face among the preachers on the Common. He was gaunt, his clothes dirty and crumpled, his boots muddy. He was holding the Old Testament. Mumbling to those who passed.

"She's dead," said the Rev. Clifford. "She's dead. She's dead. She's dead. She's dead. She's dead. . . ."

Cormac backed away in horror and slipped into a side street.

45.

Twice, Cormac pushed beyond the city's northern border. He found his way to the Collect Pond and walked around its edges. The Collect was no small body of water. It was sixty feet deep, more spring-fed lake than simple pond. At dawn, men scraped its bottom for oysters. At dusk they trolled in rowboats for bass. It was the primary source of the city's water. A creek emptied to the west of the pond, meandering down through the farmlands of Lispenard Meadows. Another creek emptied to the south, into the Little Collect and on to the East River. The creeks were sluggish and dark. Each day, cartmen hired by the city heaved unburned garbage into the pond. The shore was littered with broken bottles and battered pails, the gnawed cores of apples and the shells of oysters glittering in the mud. A hill rose abruptly at the southern edge, bald and craggy and vaguely sinister. On this hill (Cormac was told) the hangman plied his trade. After dark in its thickets, young men tried to enter the bodies of young girls. He heard (from a raving preacher) that many succeeded. From the peak of the hill, he could see the island rolling north into thick forests, sliced with the silver lines of streams. Beyond the northern shore of the pond, he smelled grass and rich, loamy earth and a sweetness that helped erase the growing odor of rot from the side of the Collect closest to the city.

He knew that he would never find the earl in the fields and forests above the town, but they pulled at him in some mysterious way, filling him with memories of Ireland. In turn, the emptiness of that forest, and the longings it provoked, drove him back to the streets of the city. Thinking of Ireland made him think of his father, and then he wanted to find the earl again. There were images he could not shed.

In the city, he was often in the company of Mr. Partridge, as he searched for a place where he could house his printing press, himself, and Cormac, his apprentice. Along the way, Cormac got to know him better, and liked him even more. Partridge had had very little formal education in England, since schools were generally closed to the children of farmers. "They thought if a farm lad could read and write, he'd leave for the city, and then who'd feed the rich?" he said one bright morning on Pearl Street. "Or the pigs, for that matter! And they were right, of course!" Pausing. "Stupid, but right, from their point of view." But he'd found his way to the printing trade, apprenticing to a cranky man named Steele, and in the setting of type, and the printing of books, he had learned many things. On their New York walks, he spoke with passion about cloves, elephants, the best way to make paper, the translations of Alexander Pope, the many varieties of sugarcane, and the art of weaving carpets. He knew the history of garbage, and all about the making of aqueducts in ancient Rome, the development of graveyards, and the sexual habits of the Arawak Indians in the Caribbean at the moment of the arrival of the Europeans. He owned several copies of *Don Quixote*.

In short, he was as English as roast beef, but an Englishman open to the whole wide world. He was outraged by English cruelties in Ireland and Scotland. He hated kings. In his view, all kings were gangsters. Not just English kings, but kings in every country where they presumed to rule over ordinary people. Their pretensions to nobility made him laugh when he was in a benevolent and ironical mood, or slam walls and tabletops when he was soaring into high democratic rage. Nobody was better suited to being an American.

"How do they get *away* with it?" he said to Cormac as they walked down Broad Street one hot and sticky July afternoon. "How do they get armies to carry their stupid flags and march off to die? That's the mystery. How do they get to sit on a throne in court, dressed in silks and lace and powdered wigs, and get intelligent men to kneel before them? In *awe!* In bloody suppli*cation!*" Such words would have been treasonous to most of His Majesty's loyal subjects in New York. But Mr. Partridge was also a careful man. He only spoke his republican thoughts to Cormac when there was not another soul in earshot.

"Noble!" he said on another day, his voice lathered with sarcasm, the words flowing from him in paragraphs. "Aye, they are noble. Noble bastards, they are. How did it begin? And how will it end? I'll tell you how. The story's in the history books, if you know how to read them." He gestured with his hands in the general direction of England, out beyond the Battery. "There were a few of these swine long ago, readier to kill than decent folk, their mouths full of a line of velvety tripe to turn the ears of the dumber sort. Tripe about Noble England, and the Noble King. All they needed was a handful who believed them, or saw a chance to get rich without work. Together, they stole from weaker people and then used the money to create *armed theater*. That's what it was, lad. That's what it is! *Armed theater!* Castles and music and fine robes and crowns and jewels — it's all theater. Acting! Performing! And all of it made possible by the use of swords and muskets and cannon, and driven by jealousy and theft! First they rob the other dukes. Then, out of the stolen money, they give small rewards to the footpads and killers who are not so powerful, those minor actors who are not able to fill the air with flowery rubbish. Then they go on to robbery of the poor, stealing the fruits of their labor — for all kings are determined never to do an honest day's work! They use the Christian message to convince the poor that they are not meant to be truly happy until they are dead and go on to Heaven. To see the Lord. Who is, of course, English, not Jewish. The farmer, the tradesman, all are willing victims. They bow down before the Great Actor, the King Himself, and work the soil and feed these bastards and then they die, and their sons turn to the same task, while not one of these so-called nobles ever turns a spade in the earth. The poor are robbed by rack rents and taxes. They pay tribute. They even pay for churches so the useless, lazy clergy can tell them how unworthy they are. The kings sneer at them for being fools, and with all that stolen money, they build armies and fleets and export their skills at robbery to the entire world! That's how it all began, lad. A few cynical actors who fooled entire nations!"

"And how will it end?"

"If there's a God in Heaven," he said, "it will end at the gallows."

He sighed.

"Any civilized man must be against homicide," he said. "But *regicide* seems a most admirable crime."

46.

And so it went as they wandered the town. Mr. Partridge didn't always rant about cabbages and kings. He fed Cormac's mind with geography and history, occasionally referring to a map of New York he'd bought in London. He knew exactly where they were on the maps of the world: at 73 degrees and 58 seconds west of the prime meridian, 40 degrees and 47 seconds north latitude, about halfway between the North Pole and the equator, and on a line with Madrid.

When he pointed across the East River at Brooklyn, he knew that the other island was 118 miles long. "That's why they call it the *long* island," he said. "Brilliant bit of naming, isn't it?" The East River itself wasn't a river at all; it was an estuary, with one side running north, the other side south, and a great dangerous place at the top of the estuary called Hell Gate. "Don't ever try sailing it," he said. "The water flows in from the Long Island Sound, through a narrow little channel. It tears apart every ship whose captain dares to confront it. Stay away. It's a true gate to Hell." And yet there was a simple reason for docking ships here on the East River, instead of the North River. The island protected them from the western winds.

"The winters are brutal here," Mr. Partridge said, "and the summers are worse. Spring is very short because the water coming down the North River is still very cold. October is the best month, but the air is never dry — not even in October — because of the rivers and the blessed harbor. Still, it's a perfect place to build a town, because of that harbor. Mark my words: New York will end up bigger than Boston and Philadelphia combined."

This was not easy for Cormac to believe as they wandered through the low, cramped town. The town of shitting horses and rooting pigs. But Mr. Partridge loved it, and saw a city that Cormac didn't see, the city that was coming. He pointed out the gabled rooftops and yellow-brick facades of the old Dutch houses, and the arrogant new Georgian houses of the English rich. The names of old families rolled from his lips: Roosevelts and Beekmans, Phillipses and Verplancks, De Peysters and De Lanceys, and, above all, Livingstons. The town was still too small for a district of the rich, as there was now in London, an area made fashionable or aristocratic through guns and money. The homes of the rich shared streets with taverns and shops and markets. "That can't last," Mr. Partridge said. "It never does. The rich build private fortresses. That's part of their triumph." The old Dutch town, he said, was huddled together, like a primitive castle, behind several pathetic wooden walls (meant to keep out marauding Indians, who no longer existed), and water came from a single well on Broadway because the Collect was too far out into the wilderness.

"Water is the big problem now," he said, "and the town can't grow until it's solved. How? With aqueducts, the way the Romans solved their problem. The sooner the better. Have you ever smelled such stinking people? They use incense in the churches because the people in a crowd smell like they've been dead for nine days. And breakfast: How is it possible, without a major effort, to eat one's eggs when the room smells like *feet?*"

Cormac started smelling feet everywhere. For two days, he could not eat eggs. Meanwhile, they looked at shops too small, and shops too large, shops that resembled prison cells, and shops made for rallies, and along the way, Mr. Partridge tried to explain the great New York political rivalry between the Livingstons and the De Lanceys. Cormac couldn't follow its intricacies. He was too busy drinking in the variety of the town, its faces, its languages, its hand-lettered walls. Seeing it with the same joy — in spite of the stench — that filled Mr. Partridge.

"Look at all these signs, lad," the older man said. "They're going to feed the two of us!"

Posters adorned many walls, advertising dentists and writing teachers, elocutionists and dancing masters, goods freshly arrived from England or taken by some privateer. Shops sold cutlery, pewter, glassware, tobacco, watches, coffee, boots, trunks, tools. Sometimes their owners stood outside, shouting the virtues of their wares to those who could not read the signs. More often, posters did the shouting. Some offered rewards for runaway slaves, or runaway apprentices, or runaway indentured servants. Each of these was written in a mixture of surprise and rage. This trusted slave had stolen a horse. That Irish wench had absconded with clothing. This apprentice had lifted a master's tools. Cormac thought the physical descriptions sounded like the Sunday customers at Hughson's. Some probably were.

In the shops or on the streets, Cormac began seeing Africans who'd passed through Hughson's, working as tinners and carpenters, butchers and handlers of horses, and they exchanged subtle nods of recognition. Cormac kept seeing them as runaways. Moving through the green forests to the north of the island. Heading for wilderness. And freedom. In his mind, he saw Kongo too. Wherever he was. Getting ready to run.

On days when Mr. Partridge was following his own trails, Cormac sometimes wandered down to the Slave Market at the foot of Wall Street, hoping for news of Kongo and the others. One morning he watched the landing of seventeen new Africans. Quaco was there, helping to keep them calm, but Cormac didn't approach him. The Africans were sold at an average of fifty pounds each and then led away to a holding pen to wait for a ship that would carry them to Carolina. Forty-seven Irish men and women were also sold, their indentures assumed by speculators, and sent to separate cages. Then he saw the guard who had hit Kongo on the back with his rifle butt. He went over to him.

"Excuse me."

"What is it?"

"Do you remember?" Cormac said. "Two weeks ago, I was here and you hit an African with a rifle butt and I asked you to stop."

"Yes, you Oirish bastard. I remember you."

"I want to apologize."

"You do?"

"I know that you were just doing your work. But you see, we'd all just come off the ship after thirteen terrible weeks together and I was just —"

"Forget it."

Cormac thought: He must know I'm feigning the apology, but he's English. He accepts the formal hypocrisy; it always makes life easier.

"Let me ask you," Cormac said. "Did you ever see those Africans again?"

The guard's face tightened as he tried to recall.

"Well, I don't know, we see a lot of them here. And they're all blacker than fecking pitch. This is the season, before the winter. They —"

"The ones from that day, were they shipped off? To the Carolinas? Or Virginia?"

"Well, I believe — I think they were divided, actually. Most of them shipped, three or four bought here. Yes. I'm sure at least three of them stayed in New York. Including that surly bastard you were so anxious to protect."

Kongo was somewhere in the city.

"Thanks, uh . . ."

Cormac offered his hand and the guard shook it.

"Adams. Francis Adams. From Liverpool."

"You're a long way from home."

"Aren't we all," he said. "Aren't we all."

On his second Friday evening at Hughson's, Cormac dined on ham and roasted potatoes at the bar, sipped a porter, and then passed through the blue door and climbed the stairs to his room. The door was unlocked. When he stepped inside, Mary

Burton was pouring hot water into the tub. The curtains were drawn. She nodded a hello. He noticed that her features had softened in the muted yellow light of the lamp. The tub was almost full.

"Get in," she said, "while it's hot."

"Thanks."

She paused, looking at him.

"Tonight, I'll join you," she said. "If you don't mind."

"That'd be grand."

Neither of them moved.

"I want you to take off me clothes," she whispered. "And then squeeze the loneliness out of me."

They made love in the hot, cleansing water and then again on the flat, open bed. She dressed and went down to work. In the nights that followed, they tried squeezing away loneliness on the floor and again on the bed and standing by the window in the darkness with the night sky of America spreading away to the south and west. They almost never spoke. They never once mentioned love. She never once said "feck."

47.

On the Friday morning of his third week in New York, everything changed. Cormac was finishing breakfast in the quiet bar at Hughson's, reading the *New York Gazette*. At separate tables, two commercial travelers did the same, preparing for the rigors of the day with bread, butter, and tea. The knocker banged, the front door opened. Cormac heard a few murmured words. Mary Burton appeared, mop in one hand, a sheet of paper in the other.

"It's for you," she said. Her blank stare told Cormac that she'd read the unsealed note. He took it from her and saw Mr. Partridge's handwriting.

PACK YOUR BAGS AND COME AT ONCE. I'VE FOUND A PLACE. P

Cormac thought: *At last!* At last, I can leave Hughson's and be in my own small piece of New York, doing work, learning a trade. He glanced up, and Mary Burton's eyes were drilling holes in his skull.

"So you're leaving," she said.

"Leaving here. But not leaving New York, Mary. I'll be back."

"No, you won't."

"I will," Cormac said, waving the slip of paper. "But this is what I've been waiting for. You know that. I told you."

"Oh, just go, without the feckin' blather."

"All right."

He packed his things quickly and strapped the sword to his hip, letting it show. When he came down the stairs carrying his bag, Sarah Hughson blocked the front door. The blue door to the bar was closed, and Mary Burton was out of sight.

"You owe us ten shillings," Sarah Hughson said.

"I do not," Cormac said. "I paid for my room in advance. And I'm leaving two days early. You should be returning me —"

"You owe us ten shillings," she repeated. "For the use of Mary Burton."

The blue door opened, and Mary Burton burst in, gripping her mop.

"How feckin' well dare you!" she shouted at Sarah.

"Stay out of this, girl."

"I never missed a feckin' minute of labor for you, Mrs. Hughson! I've been a perfect wee slave!"

"Shut up!" Sarah Hughson said.

"I will not."

"This is my place, you dirty wee thing. I make the rules!"

John Hughson emerged from the bar, large and slow, holding the *Gazette*.

"What's all this?"

Mary Burton whirled on him. "Your bloody wife wants to charge this boy for the use of me quim."

Hughson laughed out loud, and Cormac smiled in relief.

"You've got some mouth on you, Mary," Hughson said.

"He *owes* us, John," Sarah insisted, her back splayed against the front door.

Hughson sighed and put a hand on Cormac's shoulder.

"Run along now, lad," he said, "before this gets worse." Then to Sarah: "Get out of his way, Sarah."

There was a kind of fed-up menace in his voice, and Sarah retreated from it, easing away from the door.

"You're a bloody softhearted fool, John Hughson," she said. She pushed past Cormac and Mary and John through the blue door into the bar, slamming it behind her.

"Thank you," Cormac said to Hughson. "You're a very sensible man."

"No, I'm not. I'm just soft. Go. Please go."

Cormac lifted his bag and opened the door to the New York morning. He turned to say good-bye, but Mary Burton was climbing the stairs.

48.

And so he entered the printing trade. Mr. Partridge had found an unused former stable on Cortlandt Street, over by the North River, a place so forlorn and anonymous that they had passed it at least three times on their walks without actually seeing it. When Cormac first walked through the chipped, flaked double doors, his heart sank. The space was dark and cobwebbed, reeking of ancient shit and rotting vegetable matter. The windows were so caked with grime that no light entered. He followed Mr. Partridge across the lumpy brown mat of the floor. High up in the back he saw the trace of a ladder rising to a second-floor loft. Behind them, the double doors on the Cortlandt Street side were immense, built for carriages, but so thick with crusted paint, dampness, and bad care that only one of them moved on its runners. A smaller door opened into the muddy backyard.

Cormac was appalled. But Mr. Partridge saw the place with other eyes, the same eyes that gazed at New York. Seeing it for what it could become, not for what it was.

"You see," he gushed, "it *must* have been a stable — attached to the Dutch house next door. That's why the ceiling's so high, to make room for hay. . . . The rooms upstairs must have been added later," he said, noting a ridge in the high wall where the stone of the ground-floor walls give way to gray planed pine. "The Dutchman next door must have got prosperous at something, become a patroon instead of a horse-handler, and sold the stable. Then . . ."

He jumped around, too excited and full of youthful joy to finish his thoughts, and together, without much ado, they began to prepare the space for the Monday arrival of the printing press.

"Those front windows," he said. "We'll have to scrape away the crusty dirt so a person can see in at us, see what we do, feel like *entering*. I'll attack *that* problem, and you can . . ."

Cormac went to work scrubbing the flagstones: pulling stringy tufts of weed from the spaces between the stones, raking mushrooms from the narrow trenches where the stones had once abutted the walls (before the house had settled). He scattered beetles and worms from around the dead, ashen fireplace. He used wire brushes on the floor, removing years of impacted dirt and coats of ancient horseshit. His breath quickened when he saw the first blue gray quarried stone beneath the brown fibrous carpet, and he worked almost frantically to uncover each of its buried brothers. All day Friday, until the light was gone, he washed stones, his pouring sweat mixing with the precious water (carried in heavy buckets from the Tea Pump by the same black men he'd seen on Broad Street). In the center of the room, he discovered the rim of a blocked and rusted drain, packed with a cement formed of dirt and horse piss. He jammed a stick into it and moved nothing. Then he picked up his sword and cored out a passage, breaking open some unseen blockage underneath. Abruptly, the spilled water from his bucket flowed in a gurgling way into the unseen earth. He shouted in happiness — "The drain works!" — and Mr. Partridge turned from his glistening windowpanes and exulted at the sight.

"A bloody drain!" he shouted. "Without which no print shop can exist!"

Then Mr. Partridge vanished for a few hours, returning with bread and beef and water, and a large pink-faced Dutchman and two Africans, who carried in a pair of cots that he'd bought in the Dutchman's shop behind Trinity. One cot was for Cormac, and they parked it beside the fireplace. The Africans carried the second cot up the ladder to the loft where Mr. Partridge would live, while the Dutchman, looking dubious, waited for his money.

After midnight Cormac took off his shoes and fell upon the cot. He thought for a while of the hard, taut body of Mary Burton and her small, hard breasts and rosy nipples. He thought: I must be done with her. I did not say a proper good-bye, and that was rude of me, but I must be done with her. I have things to do here that come first. Before a woman. Before anyone. Still, I had no intentions of hurting her, and I have. She gave me her body. She washed me and fed me and made me laugh. And I've put one more hurt upon her. Ah, Mary: I'll try to make it up. I will. Then he eased into a dreamless sleep.

On Saturday morning, he was back again at the stones, scraping, washing, polishing with emery, until by early afternoon they were gleaming. Meanwhile, two Norwegian ship's carpenters arrived, carrying planed lumber and leather sacks of hammers and tools. After discussing measurements and placement with Mr. Partridge, they went immediately to work building a platform upon which the press would stand. Rectangular, rising about a foot off the flagstones, with a base beneath it. Almost like an altar. The Norwegians spoke little English, and said very little in Norwegian. They simply worked. With care and speed, using spirit levels for adjustments, fitting each joint with uncanny precision and exactitude. Mr. Partridge had them add a door to the platform, to provide storage space beneath the press, and they designed it so that it was flush to the sides. No locks were needed. Simple hand pressure popped it open. The smell of fresh-cut lumber helped drive out the odor of shit and time. And after Mr. Partridge peeled away the last of the gray film that clouded the windows and polished them with soap and rags, bright bars of summer light streamed in upon the fresh boards and polished stones. Cormac and Mr. Partridge smiled in delight. So did the Norwegians.

The town was shut down on Sunday, but the Norwegians didn't observe any religion except work. As Cormac and Mr. Partridge filled chinks in the stone walls with cement and erected rope lines from which paper could be hung by pegs, the Norwegians swiftly fashioned shelves for paper and ink and type, glancing at diagrams and old woodcuts for guidance. They adjusted the legs of an old table to make it balance on the uneven flagstones. They used a wood plane on the back door until it opened and closed as if buttered. They placed a bookcase beside the fireplace. They grunted. They muttered in Norwegian. And in the scalding summer heat they worked and worked. They worked without shirts and then without trousers. They paused to smoke seegars. They took long drafts of water. And they worked.

By Monday morning, all was ready for the arrival of the press. At a few minutes after eight, it appeared on the back of a horse-drawn wagon from Van Zandt's warehouse, still in its huge crate. Two black men eased the crate on rollers into the backyard, then opened it carefully with chisels, then snapped the wires and cables that had kept the press suspended in the crate during the long journey. On the floor of the crate beneath the press was a long smaller crate. "Type!" Mr. Partridge said. "Without type, we print nothing!" He asked the Africans to carry the box of type inside and lay it in a corner against the wall. Then they lifted the printing press itself, an African at either end, with Mr. Partridge on the left side and Cormac on the right. Hauling and muttering and gasping for breath, they carried it around to Cortlandt Street and in through the open double doors. A small crowd had gathered to stare at them, to observe the new tenants, the beginning of a new shop. They positioned the press on its fresh new altar, moving it and shifting it until it stood exactly where Mr. Partridge wanted it to be, with space on the platform to walk around it on all sides.

As they finished, one of the Africans looked at Cormac with recognition in his eyes. They moved together out the back door, where Cormac began collecting the remains of the crate to use as firewood.

"Hughson's?" Cormac said.

"Yah."

"I'll not be there for a while."

"Yah."

"Can you do me a favor?"

He stared at the young white man.

"I'm looking for a man. An African. A . . . friend. His name is Kongo."

He looked at Cormac in a blank way that said more than he intended; the name Kongo carried weight with him.

"If you see him, tell him Cor-mac is looking for him."

"Yah," he said, and walked off toward the waterfront.

Back inside, Mr. Partridge sat on the lip of the fireplace, staring at his wonderful machine. He wiped his sweat-blistered brow. Cormac sat beside him and gazed at the press. It looked to him like some strange, godlike giant insect. An immense grasshopper. Or a praying mantis. They stared at it together, then stood up, exhausted by heat and toil, and bolted the creature's feet to the platform. When they were finished, Cormac felt like singing a hymn.

"By God," Mr. Partridge whispered, shaking a fist, "we've done it, lad. We're in business."

Not quite.

That evening, as they sat on the edge of the platform eating fish and chips from a tavern in the light of candles, Mr. Partridge grew silent. His exuberance ebbed. His body slumped. It was as if the past three days had drained him of some invincible spark.

"Are you feeling all right, Mister Partridge?"

"Yes. Of course."

"You . . . don't seem all right."

"Well . . ." He sighed. "The truth is, lad, I'm almost out of money. And we still need many things here. . . . Paper, above all. And ink, of course. And other things. This has been *so* bloody expensive. The storage fees at Van Zandt's —"

Cormac unbuckled his money belt. Along with the paper money, there were eleven gold crowns left from those passed to him by his father. He pocketed one for himself and handed ten crowns to Mr. Partridge.

"Here," Cormac said.

The older man looked embarrassed. He wouldn't accept the money, and Cormac laid it upon the edge of the platform. He sat down with the heavy coins between them.

"No, absolutely not!" Mr. Partridge said. "You're a boy, an apprentice —"

"I'm not a boy, Mr. Partridge. I've already killed a man."

He looked at Cormac with eyes wide and steady.

"You have?"

"Yes," he said. "Maybe two."

49.

He sketched his story for Mr. Partridge. He revealed his true name and told him everything he could remember about the Earl of Warren and what had happened in Ireland. He explained the oath of blood and tribe that had sent him here, to New York. He left out many details. But the words flowed from him like water breaking through a weir, and he felt his rage rising again as he told of the day his mother died and the day his father was murdered for a horse. While Cormac talked, the eyes of Mr. Partridge never left him. And when the young man finished, the older man stared at him for a long moment.

"How sad," he said finally. "How infuriating. And how very sad."

Cormac stared at his hands, which had already wielded a sword, and must wield one again (soon, he hoped, soon), relieved now that one lie had been removed between himself and Mr. Partridge: the lie of his name. Martin O'Donovan was, for the moment, dead. Cormac Samuel O'Connor was now living here on Cortlandt Street. He looked up from his hands. Mr. Partridge was staring out through the polished windows in the double doors to the unlit street.

"Have you ever killed anyone?" Cormac said.

A pause.

"Not directly."

In the confessional intimacy of the large warm room, Mr. Partridge began to speak.

"This was eleven years ago," he said, his voice containing a kind of echo, enforced by the emptiness of the workshop. "In a terrible London winter. I was married then to my Esther. My beloved, thin, sweet Esther. We had four children. Robert. Michael. James. And the baby girl, Catherine. I was then certain that I wanted to move us all to America, to this new land, to a place far from kings and princes, dukes and earls, a place where the children could grow up strong and prosperous. A country that was new, where men and women could correct all the mistakes of the Old World."

He cleared his throat, turned to Cormac. The money Cormac had offered was still lying on the lip of the platform made for the press.

"I had made one trip," Mr. Partridge said. "Bringing printing supplies to Mister Bradford, and that journey convinced me. When I told her all about it, Esther shared the vision." He turned uneasily on the edge of the platform. "Such a move would take money." His eyes moved toward Cormac's money for a moment. "So I was working then at two printing establishments, day and night and Sundays too. Saving money. Saving for a press and the passage and some money to begin again in America." He exhaled strongly. "To save money, *to save bloody money,* we lived in a filthy slum. You don't know London, do you, lad? Of course not. Well, the neighborhood was vile, criminal, evil. But the rent was low, which is why we were there, and my Esther somehow fortified our little piece of it while I worked, and we both saved. She was following my vision, my belief that one must sacrifice in the short run so as to have an amazing future."

He stood up, touching the press, walking around it with a heavy tread.

"Well, one night I came home from Sorby the Printer's, very late, after midnight. There were constables blocking the street. What's this? Hello, what's this? And they told me the cholera had taken the street, that it was quarantined. Nobody in, nobody out. No, but I *live* here, I said, my *wife* is here, I said, my *children* are here! Sorry, nobody in, nobody out. There were others like me, of course, those of us who worked in the watches of the night. And when we tried to push through, to see wives, children, they beat us with clubs and charged us with horses and arrested some of us. Starting with me."

His hand involuntarily touched his head and he ruffled his graying hair.

"I woke up in an alley by the Thames, where I'd been tossed. My face was bloody, and my clothes too, and my shoulder wouldn't work." He made a grinding movement with his right shoulder. "And when I reached our street, long after dawn, with the rain falling, they were all dead. My Esther. The children. Along with twenty-seven others. All dead. Dead of bloody disease. Dead of bloody filth. Dead because of me."

His eyes were brimming, but he didn't cry. He sat down again, talking as much for himself as for Cormac.

"After I buried them, I took the America money and got drunk for seven months," he said. "I spent it all. Every shilling. On rum and spirits. I slept in filthy rooms, praying for the cholera to take me too. I slept in alleys by the river. I was crawly with lice. I was as thin as a bird. I howled at easy ladies and their ponces, at constables and doctors. I raved outside Westminster. I was moved on, moved on, beaten, pummeled, laughed at, as I wandered in my frayed and filthy rags."

He looked at Cormac in a steady way. The younger man was holding back his own tears.

"And then one morning, I woke up in a brickyard, huddled for warmth against the side of a kiln. I stared at the sky, and the clouds, and heard the whistle of some bird, defying the city: and got up. I was scabbed, hurt, scarred, broken. But I said then: enough. Just that word. *Enough.* And I stood up. I went to a shelter run by some upper-class ladies. I had a bath. I donned some old clothes that didn't quite fit. And I said: Esther, I am sorry. My children, I am sorry. But now I will do something that will give this all some value. I'll begin again. I will go to America. In your name." A long pause. "And I'm here."

Cormac embraced him.

"Well," he said, "we have work to do."

"Yes," Mr. Partridge said. "Work."

He took the coins now, hefting them, and walked to the doors and stared into the street.

"There are some dreadful people in the world," he said, slipping the coins into his pocket, where they made a bulge. "They must be fought. They must be beaten back, caged, prevented from spreading their misery. Your Earl of Warren is one of them. There are many others."

"And what can be done about them?"

"Plenty."

"Such as?"

"Such as destroying them."

He turned to the printing press.

"With *that.*"

50.

Mr. Partridge lived in a blur of movement. He set type, pulled proofs, handed them to Cormac to dry. He'd be gone for two hours and return with jobs: tax notices, wedding invitations, advertisements for shoes and medicines and coffee, for dance instruction and English tutoring and lessons in French. He printed anything and everything, except posters about escaped slaves.

Cormac had no time for Hughson's, but even if he had a few rare empty hours, he stayed away. He thought: What can I tell her? How can I tell her that I have these other things I must do, that I'm searching for a man from Ireland? And yet he began to yearn for her. To hear her dirty mouth, to feel her rebellious spirit. One humid Sunday night in late August, he walked to Stone Street. He stood outside the back door in the darkness. Africans passed him in the dark, entering, departing, and a few nodded and went on. Then a familiar face appeared. Quaco.

"What you standin' here for?" he said.

"Just getting the night air."

"You a bad liar, mon."

"I miss some people, I suppose."

"What people?"

"You. Some of the others."

"You mean that little girl Mary, ain't that it?"

Cormac shook his head.

"Wait here."

Quaco slipped inside the tavern. Cormac could hear water sloshing against pier heads, and sails flopping on the dark river, and somewhere the squeal of a lone pig. From inside, the music of a fiddle and the instruments of Africa were joining. He heard a muffled roar. Then the door cracked open, and Mary Burton stepped into the hot night air, closing the door behind her.

"Hello," she said.

"Hello, Mary," he said.

"What is it ye want?"

"To be sayin' I'm sorry, Mary. For going off so quick that morning. For not saying a proper good-bye. For not comin' back to see you."

"Feck off."

She turned to go, and he grabbed her arm. In the dim light he could see her eyes glistening with anger and tears.

"Mary, listen, please listen. I've been workin' eighteen hours a day, I've been grinding and hauling and pulling in the print shop on Cortlandt Street and . . ."

"Ah, you poor wee lad," she said, voice heavy with sarcasm. He was holding her rough-skinned hand now, which was warm in his grip.

"And there's more. I'm looking for a man, a man I'm sworn to find, a man I must kill. I have to find him. And if he's not here in New York, then I must know that too."

She said nothing.

"I don't want you mixed up in any of this," he said. "It'd not be fair to you, Mary, if I do what I must do and the constables came looking, or the bloody redcoats."

She pulled her hand away and folded her arms across her breasts.

"I don't believe you," she said. "I think you just wanted to be up in me quim, and have your fun, and be done with it. I think you see me as some low, common trollop. You with your fancy accent from some fecking school somewhere, and your books, and your fecking poetry spoutin'. I think you look at me and think, She's just another feckin' slave. And one that can't read or write and has only one thing to offer, and that's between her legs."

"Not true, Mary," he said in a soothing way, pulling her close. "Not true."

Her arms dropped, and he could feel her soften. She pressed her hard breasts against his chest. He wanted to take her down to the river edge. And then he heard a voice. The door cracking open. Sarah.

"Mary? Are you out there, Mary? Come in at once, the tables are filthy with plates!"

Mary kissed him and touched him and then hurried back into Hughson's, where Africa drummed steadily on gourds and tabletops.

The weather turned. He saw his first October in New York: the harbor sparkling, the air crisp and bright. He met Mary Burton one Monday evening and they made love on the slopes above the Collect. That night he told her his true name. She was not surprised. Early one Sunday morning two weeks later, when the sky was just brightening in Brooklyn, they met at the Battery and held hands while seated on a large stone and she talked about how she'd like to go to a right school and learn to read, even if it meant putting up with the preachers at Trinity.

"Tell me I can do it," she said, as the breeze shook leaves from the trees above them and a four-masted ship turned in the harbor, bound for the East River quays.

"Of course you can do it, Mary," he said. "I'll loan you a book for starting. Just march into Trinity and say, 'I want to read this book.' Just don't say 'feck' when you ask."

"Feck off," she said, then turned her head and laughed at herself.

Cormac was working with Mr. Partridge one Saturday noon on fifty large copies of legal advisories when he glanced out the windows. Mary Burton was standing in a doorway, staring into the shop. The light was so hard and bright (Cormac thought) that she must have been unable to see through the glass. She waited, as people teemed around her. Then a horse-drawn wagon came by, loaded with crates of dry goods, and when it passed, she was gone. She was trying to send him a message. He was sure of that. But she could not write a simple note. That night, he went back to Hughson's on Stone Street.

The bar was packed, every table filled, and Mary Burton was moving around in the blue tobacco fog, taking orders, grim. She didn't see him come in. The fiddler was fatter and playing more joyfully. Sarah came to Cormac.

"Are you here with the ten shillin's?" she said.

"I can leave now if you like, Mrs. Hughson."

"No, we'll take your money one way or another."

He eased past her, trying to move among three large Africans who were joking at the bar. The sound of singing and clomping feet grew louder. Suddenly Mary Burton grabbed his hand.

"I must talk wit' you," she said. "Tuesday night, on the north end of the Common."

She turned away, gathering empty glasses, forcing passage to the bar. John Hughson started filling the glasses. He didn't notice Cormac. Against the far wall, British soldiers were on their feet, arms on shoulders, loudly singing a marching song, as if challenging the Irish to fight. Mary threw them an ugly look, then grabbed a half-dozen full glasses and whirled back into the stomping crowd. John Hughson saw Cormac now. His face was different, more furrowed with care and seriousness.

"You're back," he said.

"Aye — in want of a glass of porter."

"But it's not the porter, is it? It's not the porter that's pulled you back at all."

"I don't know what you mean."

He leaned forward.

"It's a priest you're after, isn't it, lad?"

Cormac laughed.

"A priest?"

"An R.C.," he said.

"You mean a Catholic priest?"

"Aye."

He was so serious that Cormac didn't want to disappoint him. He shrugged. Although he was curious about the presence of a secret Catholic priest. After all, if such a person did exist, and the British found him, he'd be hanged.

"No, I'm not looking for a priest, Mister Hughson. I'm not really what people would call a religious man."

Hughson looked unconvinced.

"It's all right to tell *me,* lad. If I've guessed correctly."

"You've guessed wrong, Mister Hughson. With all due respect, sir. All I want is a glass of porter."

Hughson filled a fresh glass and placed it before him. Cormac laid a piece of eight on the bar.

"Well," Hughson said, smiling, "if you do remember what you came for, let me know."

Cormac gave Hughson his back, sipping his porter while watching the hollering and dancing, the drunken British soldiers, the Africans pouring sweat and shouting secret words in their own languages, while Mary Burton moved among them all. Her breasts rose and fell as she breathed. Her hips seemed to churn beneath her muslin skirt. Her eyes flirted. She has something to tell me, he thought; when will she tell?

Then he heard the back door open and turned to see the new arrivals.

There stood Kongo.

51.

Behind him were two other Africans, both larger than Kongo, but it was clear that he was in charge. He was wearing a high-collared blue jacket, a coarse pale-blue workshirt, clean baggy trousers, and scuffed boots. It was the first time Cormac had seen him without manacles. Without being obvious, his eyes took in the entire room, the black faces and white, the fiddler, the smoke and food, Hughson and Sarah and Mary Burton. And, of course, Cormac O'Connor.

In his glance he told Cormac that he knew him, all right, but he didn't know whether Cormac wanted that known. His nod was almost imperceptible. There was a still, frozen moment, everyone in the room sensing the possibility of danger. The Africans froze. The soldiers froze. The music paused and the only sound was an icy breathing. It was as if they expected constables or redcoats to barge in behind Kongo and his men. Then Kongo stepped forward, the sense of danger eased, and he moved to the bar, next to where Cormac was sipping his porter. The music resumed with a relieved burst, along with the stomping of the dancers.

"Cor-mac," he whispered.

"Kon-go."

He tapped a balled fist to his heart and then to Cormac's chest. His friends nodded. Other blacks watched. The whites tried to look casual. Cormac laid some pieces of eight on the bar.

"No," Kongo said, his voice insistent. "No."

He pointed subtly at an African seated against the wall. Quaco. He came over. They talked softly, heads against ears. Quaco then spoke to Cormac in English, his voice very low.

"Kongo says you gave him drink when he thirsted," Quaco said. "Now he must give you water in return."

"All right."

Hughson looked annoyed because Kongo asked for water.

"How can I get rich if he drinks water — and you join him?"

"He'll probably pay you for it."

"Aye, and then tell all these other buggers what a cheap bastard I am."

He drew three porters and filled two glasses from a water jug. Kongo took one glass, Cormac the other. The African lifted his glass as if in a toast, then drained it. Cormac did the same. Kongo said a word. Cormac repeated it, without knowing its meaning. He could feel Hughson watching them, and others too. Kongo handed mugs of porter to Quaco and his men, one of whom now seemed familiar to Cormac from the dark hold of the ship. They sipped. Kongo gazed around the room again.

"Where do you know him from?" Hughson said. "You serve in Parliament together?"

"No," Cormac said. "We shipped together."

Then another black man came over and bowed his head to Kongo, who squeezed his hand. Then another, and still one more. They all said words that Kongo accepted as if they were gifts. Quaco saw Cormac watching.

"They know he has come for them," he said. "They have wait a long time."

"They waited for him? How could they know he was on the *Fury*?"

"They just know he is to come. It is foretold."

"Who is he?"

Quaco sipped his porter.

"Babalawo."

A word Cormac didn't know. An African word.

Babalawo.

52.

That Tuesday, Cormac waited for Mary Burton on a bench at the north end of the Common. She was more than an hour late, her eyes jittery, the ends of her hair unkempt and loose. She was carrying an Old Testament.

"Can you read me some of these words?" she said abruptly. "I'm stuck with this 'begat.' And someone begat someone who begat someone else, all of these begatters."

"Who gave you this?"

"Nobody," she said. "I stole it from one of the preachers. He was lyin' on the ground, shakin' and rollin', looking like a mad dog, his eyes up in his head. So I lifted it and watched him rollin' for a while, figuring he was more in want of a doctor than a book, and then I went off with it. The next day I took it to Trinity, and they didn't want me, certain they were that I was a papist, but I said no, I was no papist, I was a fine Protestant from the Church of Ireland and wanted to worship God and the King of England, but I couldn't do it 'less I learnt to read. So the preacher, fella name of Wrightson, he starts to read it, and that's when I start hearing 'begat' until it was coming out of his arse."

Cormac laughed. "Did you say 'feck' to him?"

"No, but I came close."

"And he let you into the classes."

"Aye, after paying a visit to the Hughsons, and shamin' both of them. I get an hour each mornin' now. I learnt the letters first, and then on to the fecking begatters. . . ."

"It gets better," Cormac said, holding the book, riffling its pages. "You'll love the story of Joseph and his brothers and the coat of many colors."

"Will you read it to me?" she said, taking the book back into her hands.

"No, I want *you* to read it to *me*."

She was quiet then for a long while as they watched passing couples, and occasional teams of redcoats, and carriages carrying rich people to the houses down beyond Wall Street. She held the book in her hands as if it were made of gold.

"I have to tell you something," she said.

He waited, suddenly afraid that she would inform him that she was going to beget their child.

"There's something going on at Hughson's," she said. "The Africans and the Irish together. They're talkin' about a risin'. About strikin' at the English. About killing people . . ."

She stared at the ground. A cool wind blew in from the North River.

"Stay away from them," she said. "Stay away from Hughson's. They're all a-headin' for the gallows."

She turned to the hill above the Common, where dead leaves were swirling in the fresh river wind.

"Stay away," she said. "Stay away."

Kongo was working in the Fly Market, a few blocks south of the Slave Market. He was the property of a housepainter named Wilson. But Cormac was so busy that autumn that he didn't see much of the man Quaco had called a *babalawo*. He was just pleased to know that Kongo was alive. He stayed away from Hughson's and the rumors of revolt, hoping that Kongo was not involved but knowing that no rising could go forward without him. He did run into Kongo in the streets as the African carried a stepladder and paint jars to a job, wearing a canvas girdle round his waist, from which hung his brushes. If Wilson, his owner, was with him (thin, solemn, red-faced, lonesome), they exchanged only nods. If Kongo was alone, they embraced and talked, for Kongo was adding new English words every day.

"Don't go Hughson's," he whispered during one chance encounter. "Danger thar."

The warning didn't surprise Cormac. Once a week now, he met Mary Burton in the fields and woods to the north of the Common, to listen to her faltering attempts to read (each week they were better), to make love in a desperate way among the leaves and the grass, until it grew too cold and they could be too easily observed among the skeletal black trees. Then they would simply talk, flattened against a tree, warming each other against winter, and sometimes she talked about what she wanted more than anything else.

"I want to walk out the door," she said. "At any hour of the day or night, and without making up a lie or askin' permission from no one, and just walk around the town. Without sayin' I'm a-runnin' an errand. Just free. Free. To be free to live with a free man, maybe you. To have him come in the door and put the rod to me, 'cause he loves me, and loves me juicy quim. No sneakin' around. Just close the door and have it, on the floor, on a table, in a bed." She turned her wounded eyes to him. "Do you see, Cormac? Do you see why I can't do six more years at Hughson's as a slave? I don't want to have Sarah making me scrub sheets all sticky with spend or boarders' drawers stained with shite. I don't want to end up like poor Peggy, taking the Africans' money to give them two minutes up me cunt."

"Yes, I see."

She looked at him for a long moment.

"I want to have us in a bath again," she said.

"As do I."

"But not at Hughson's," she said in a cold voice. "They're talking a lot of fecking trouble."

53.

At home in the shop on Cortlandt Street, Cormac's mind was jittery with warnings about the coming trouble. Something was surely in the air, some kind of trouble, as ominous as the warning of Mary Morrigan, and those issued long ago to the Hebrews, and Mr. Partridge began providing the American context. He was talking almost without cease about a new war and how it was wrecking the economy of New York. Britain was fighting Spain again, this time over Jenkins's ear. Who was Jenkins? And why (Cormac asked) should anyone care about his ear? The story was splendid. The Spaniards had stopped a British ship in Spanish waters, one of those royal ships whose sole business was hijacking Spanish gold from the Americas. One of the English officers gave the Spanish captain some lip and they cut off his ear. War!

"But it's hurting New York, lad!" he said. "You can see it everywhere around us!"

He reminded Cormac that the fort was emptying, the redcoats marching to the ships each day, bound for the West Indies and Florida to do battle with the Spaniards. That was why the waterfront was such a lonesome place these past weeks. Mr. Partridge insisted that the war wasn't about poor Jenkins's ear at all; it was about sugar, tobacco, and Florida.

"The English have Jamaica, and they want Cuba and Hispaniola and Florida so they can bring in another two hundred thousand slaves to make themselves even richer!" he shouted. "They can't imagine the Spanish will come this far north. They are idiots!"

But as Mr. Partridge ranted, Cormac understood the warnings. The soldiers were going. Now was the time for revolt.

In the following days, the outrage of Mr. Partridge was mixed with a kind of joy. He sizzled with happiness. Together, they worked all one night making broadsides at their own expense, headlined "We will win!" All sorts of patriotic nonsense (as Mr. Partridge described it), expressing immense anger over the fate of Mr. Jenkins's ear, using a medical engraving of an ear repeated fifty times as a border. He attacked the Spanish affront to justice and the law, and urged all the King's loyal subjects to support the noble British war, wherever it might go. Mr. Partridge was merry as he set type. But he had motives other than patriotism.

"We'll put the Partridge name here at the bottom," he said, "and the address, and no matter what happens in bloody Barbados, or on the streets of Kingston, we shall win, lad."

He was swiftly proven right. Cormac slapped the broadsides up on the blank walls of the town as soon as the ink was dry. By noon the next day, the name Partridge was clearly synonymous with patriot. And printing jobs flowed into the shop: wedding announcements and rallies for the troops, advertising for shoes and jewelry, special rates for travel to England and news of the arrival of a shipment of wool. The money flowed in too. Mr. Partridge put all the profits into the shop, buying supplies of paper and ink, adding cabinets and type racks. They were so busy, Cormac didn't notice the winds howling from the northwest.

Only at night, when he was alone, did he imagine the revolt, did he add together the odd look from black man to black man, and from the Irish to the Irish. He heard again the warnings from Kongo and from Mary Burton. Only at night did he imagine what would happen if they all rose together.

In the frigid winter nights, when Stone Street seemed an immense distance from Cortlandt Street and it was impossible to meet Mary Burton out of doors, Cormac began to draw again. He used the reverse side of overinked proofs, odd scraps of board, diluted printer's ink, and reed pens. He made drawings of Mr. Partridge, of people he saw in the streets, of soldiers in uniform, of the fort, of certain houses, and of Mary Burton: all from memory. Mr. Partridge was delighted.

"You've a gift, lad," he said one night, examining a drawing of his own marvelous head. "You captured something there, the mouth, a kind of sadness. Very good. Very good."

He tacked the drawing to a beam. Others would follow, although Cormac kept his drawing of Mary Burton in a private folio fashioned from thick brown board and tied with cord. Cormac was now so deep into the world of the print shop that other things receded. The images of bloody revolt were threaded in a minor way through his days, but for all the whispered warnings, nothing, after all, had happened. Perhaps it was the drink talking in the smoke of Hughson's. He also brooded in a confused way about Mary Burton. What was it he truly felt for her? Was it simply lust? Or was it something more like that immense word *love?* That word issued from many people's lips, from preachers to whores, and he read it in even more books. But what did it mean, really? He wanted Mary Burton to be happy, but that wasn't love as described in the poems, some rapture that carried you into realms of bliss. And was he leading her somewhere that she could not go? Into reading and trying to find the education that had eluded her in Ireland and in her American servitude? He hoped she was not imagining a future with him. For he had no true vision of that future, or whether he would live long enough to have one.

The reason for this uncertainty was the power of the past. And his duty to old vows, to the tribe, to the rules, to the memories of his father and mother. The truth, however, was that he was thinking less about the Earl of Warren now too. Sometimes three or four days passed and the earl never forced himself into Cormac's mind. But then he would see months-old newspapers from London in the print shop and begin scanning them for the earl's name, to see if he had appeared at some event in London or Paris, or in dispatches from other parts of the colonies from Canada to Kingston. Always in vain. In the newspapers, the earl did not exist. Then Cormac would lie awake in the dark, picturing the earl as he must look now: perhaps bearded, as was Cormac; perhaps dressed in common clothes; perhaps lolling in the slave markets of Charleston or Savannah. He imagined himself wandering the continent on an endless search. And then thought it would be better to stay where he was. If the earl was in America, eventually he would come to New York. Better to work, better to learn the craft of the printer, better to prepare for a future, even if that future would be denied him in a moment of violence.

On some nights, he wondered exactly what Quaco meant when he called Kongo a *babalawo*. One slow day, he asked Mr. Partridge about the word, and the older man riffled through a fat volume, then shrugged. "It's not in the dictionary," he said, "but it could mean a shaman, you know, a kind of witch doctor. The parish priest, so to speak, in a tribe." He pondered this. "Though a shaman — if that's what it means — is also a kind of magician. So maybe your friend Kongo is an African Merlin."

For Cormac, this image was exciting: Kongo in Camelot, searching for a black grail. He tried to draw the image but gave up in disgust and tossed the paper into the fireplace. The truth was that all images, including the possibility of riot and fire, were always erased by work. The printing life consumed them. All their type was set by hand, and Cormac was amazed at how swiftly Mr. Partridge laid out the metal letters, since all of them were in reverse. Cormac's first job was inking the type, using wool-packed sheepskin balls with hickory handles. The fresh ink was laid on a slab beside the press. At first, Mr. Partridge did the crucial final task of pressing down on the lever, throwing his weight joyfully into the task of pulling an impression off the inked type. Then he acknowledged that Cormac was physically stronger than he was, and Cormac, within a week, got their rate up to two hundred pulls an hour. While doing this work, Cormac felt himself become part of the machine, his mind counting the sheets while the words of the posters came to vivid life: war, sale, arrival, ship, brass, shoes, instruction, now.

Sometimes Mr. Partridge delivered an aria on the beauties of type. "We're a Caslon shop," he said. "Look at the beauty of that *T*," he said, "the elegance of that flick of a serif!" The names of fonts rolled from him like liturgy: Roman and italic and boldface, caps that were swashed and caps that were sloped. Picas and points and em quads, and the beauty of white space. Caslon wasn't the only great type. There were other glorious typefaces, he said, his voice swelling, their names coming from him like the names of artists or generals: Bembo and Petrarca, Palatino and Griffo, Fraber and Garamond. But above all of them, close to God, was Caslon.

"Look at those letters, lad, and *listen* to them! Can you hear them singing? Look at those lines and those curves, and then close your eyes, and what you hear is William Caslon *singing!*"

Sometimes, in mid-aria, he vanished into the frozen morning, bouncing up the three steps into the street, off to do business. And Cormac worked on, cleaning and oiling the press, using stone slabs to flatten wet paper, hanging samples on the unpainted pine-board walls, cleaning the pieces of type and placing each in one of the 152 compartments of their cases. Sometimes he set type himself, slower than Mr. Partridge but loving the order and beauty of a page. Or he cleaned ink balls. Or trimmed sheets. Ink rimmed his fingernails, resisting soap and brush. He washed his hands in the same sink where he cleaned the punches. There was no running water (not there and not anywhere in New York), just two buckets, soap, and the coarse cloths he used for cleaning type. After his daily ablutions, Cormac would heave the inky water into the backyard, a blackening rectangle of frozen mud where nothing grew.

In the afternoons, Mr. Partridge returned, bursting with news and gossip and jobs for the shop. Terrible fighting in Jamaica.

Dreadful cold, the worst winter in New York memory. A shortage of cordwood. Trees like iron, blunting the woodsmen's axes. Water frozen in the Collect. Dutchmen skating. Taverns empty. Only two ships on the waterfront. A Mrs. Robbins left her husband for a notary and they've sailed for England while Mr. Robbins has become a sot. More soldiers departing.

Finally the night arrived. Sometimes Mr. Partridge carried home a joint or a rib, and cooked it on an upstairs stove (for he wanted no grease anywhere near his precious stores of paper). They dined together, and at such times he was calmer, and often spoke obliquely about subjects that never appeared in a newspaper. As he did one night a few days from Christmas.

"There's something happening in the town, and I can't put my finger on it," he said. "Not just poor sales in the shops. Something else. An unease . . ."

The cold got colder and didn't relent. For Cormac, it was as if the Irish storm that killed so many people and crops and horses had made its way across the Atlantic. The North River was frozen solid all the way to Poughkeepsie, almost eighty miles distant. He worked in heavy clothes and slept in his overcoat and remembered the tale of Joseph and his brothers. Sometimes he saw himself huddling in the house with his father and Bran and Thunder, all of them together, refusing to give in to weather or fate. Thinking: Only one winter ago, but so long ago too. Would they both survive better if he and Mary Burton could huddle together through the frigid American nights? If he returned to his room on Stone Street, would that become more possible? But it couldn't happen. The Hughsons would never allow her out at night, for she might end up on a runaway poster on the city's walls. And he had no money now to pay for a room.

But in some way, the brutal New York cold and his memories of Ireland combined to revive his own search for the man who had brought him here. If the earl's own horses had survived the Irish winter better, surely he wouldn't have gone hunting for the horses of strangers. He could have stood on the pier and juggled while Africans eased out to sea in the wooden dungeons of the slave ships. The arctic wind had changed the earl's life too.

In Cormac's free time, or when running errands or delivering printing jobs, he looked with renewed passion for the Earl of Warren. Snow fell through one long night. Then fell again two days later. The piles of snow and hillocks of black ice made walking difficult, and if there were fewer people on the streets, they were revealed in greater clarity. But he felt more often now that he'd made some terrible mistake in coming to New York. He began to think that he had followed the earl to a place where he had not gone.

And then, on the day before Christmas, after dropping some printed notices at the Lutheran Church, which stood then a block south of Trinity, he turned into Wall Street and there he was.

The earl.

Getting into a cream-colored carriage in front of City Hall.

Cormac's heart jumped. His chapped hands begin to sweat in the cold. The carriage started moving east toward the waterfront. Cormac thought: Is he leaving on a ship? In this cold? No, the river is frozen, with great slabs of ice crunching against one another and bending the pilings, and it's almost Christmas. No ship will sail.

He went after the cream-colored carriage, walking cautiously at first through the most crowded, snow-packed blocks (for business had not paused yet to celebrate the birth of Christ). He steadied his pace, afraid of attracting attention, wishing he had the sword. Thinking: I could catch him and kill him. But not without a sword. Thinking: I must know where he goes. Must know where he lives.

And then the carriage picked up speed. Cormac hurried, skipping faster, shoving aside small knots of men, sliding on glossy sheets of ice, thumping through crusted snow. The carriage turned left into Water Street, heading north, and Cormac began to run. He fell once, then again.

The carriage was too fast. It didn't pause at any of the wharves, and rolled north. Cormac watched it vanish over the ridge and the frozen stream that spilled from the Common.

He stood there, his heart skipping beats, gasping for frigid air. His elbow ached from a fall. He bent it and gazed at the blank white haze to the north.

Thinking: He's here.

The earl is here.

54.

Early Christmas morning, while the sky remained blue with night, Cormac rose early, dressed warmly, and hurried down to the Fly Market to find Kongo. The streets were icy, snow-packed, and empty. Windows were rimed with ice. He found Kongo in the backyard of Guilfoyle the builder, where he and Quaco were feeding a fire with scrap wood. Both wore fur hats, cloth gloves, and heavy coats, and reminded him of the Celts in their hidden grove. Quaco bid Cormac good morning, uttered an ironical "Merry Christmas," and smiled as they shook hands.

"How is it you're not in the big church with all the other wonderful Christians?" Quaco said.

"I'd rather be here," Cormac said. "I need to talk to . . . the babalawo."

He gestured for Kongo to step aside and speak to him alone. Kongo excused himself to Quaco and walked with Cormac to the dark side of a shed.

"Yes?" he said.

"I need your help."

"What for?" he said, his accent slightly Irish.

"I have to find a man named the Earl of Warren," he said. "Last year in Ireland, he caused my father to be shot dead, and in our tribe, the son must avenge the father."

"In my tribe too."

"I came here to find him," Cormac said. "That's why I was on the *Fury*. I've looked for him for many months, and yesterday, at last, I saw him. On the street. He went north in a coach, but I couldn't follow in the snow and ice."

"You want him dead?"

"Yes, but I'm the only one who can do it. I've already killed one of his men, and perhaps a second, whose hand I chopped off. It's my responsibility, Kongo. But I hope that, somehow, you and your friends can find him for me."

He showed Kongo a folded drawing he'd made of the earl, and the African peered at it, his brow tightening. Perhaps Kongo could spread the word among the Africans (Cormac said), to look for the cream-colored carriage and the Englishman who looked like the man in the sketch. The diamond tooth, Cormac said, pointing, and then pulling a face to show his own bicuspid. The tooth. If they find him, he said, tell me. I'll do the rest. He reminded Kongo that the earl had made much of his fortune in the slave trade. The African glanced again at the drawing and slipped it inside his coat.

"I'll look," he said. "If he on this island, we find him."

Cormac hugged him, then smiled and stepped back.

"Your English is much better."

Kongo shrugged. "I have no, uh, *choice,* yes? To eat, I must speak."

But Cormac thought: His English is now too good to have been merely lifted in passing. He has been studying. Or receiving help more mysterious than studying. *Babalawo.* He wanted to ask Kongo more. Instead, Kongo explained that for the next week Wilson the painter had rented him out to Guilfoyle the builder. Right here. This building. No work today. No work on Christmas. But he shook his head at the shame of being as rentable as a dray horse. Then, after a long silence (one that silenced Cormac's questions too), he took the young man's elbow and walked him toward the shore.

"There is something . . . coming?" he said. "Yes, the word is 'coming.' To come."

"What do you mean?"

"I mean there is something big to happen, as soon as winter ends."

"What kind of something?"

"I let you know," he said. "It's about us. The Africans and the Irish. And the fleets of Spain."

He glanced at the wan winter sun rising slowly across the river in Brooklyn.

"Say nothing," he said. "Ask nothing." He gestured toward the sun. "But know that . . . the gods know. The gods say yes."

He turned and hurried back to Quaco and the fire. Cormac thought: I'll have to wait to ask the meaning of the word *babalawo*.

55.

Something big was indeed happening. Part of it Cormac saw. Part of it was told to him. But all the bits and pieces, the muted warnings, the whispered gossip came to the same thing: a rising. In the first weeks of 1741, the town was almost empty of redcoats, their main force now down in the Indies, defending the sanctity of Jenkins's ear. In their absence, New York Africans and New York Irishmen were meeting in Hughson's tavern to talk about guns and death and freedom.

"You're very . . . *distracted* these past days, Cormac," said Mr. Partridge one afternoon. He looked at Cormac in a worried way. "Are you homesick?"

Cormac smiled. "Sometimes."

"What is it that you miss?"

"Oh, just . . ."

He paused in the process of pulling sheets for a wine seller.

"Small things, I s'pose," he said. "The house we had, made by my father's hands and the help of his friends. The wet grass on a summer morning. We had a dog named Bran and a horse named Thunder. I miss them. I miss my mother telling stories. I miss my father in all ways. I miss the woods and the fields and the hearth in the house. . . ."

Mr. Partridge stared at him.

"Well, all of us here feel the same things, in one way or another," he said. "I feel them and the soldiers feel them and the Africans too."

"I know that."

"It's why some go back," Mr. Partridge said. "They can't bear it. We're like colonists on the bloody moon. And yet . . ." He sighed. "And yet, we might have something in our hands that's not been seen in hundreds of years, maybe never, lad. For the King and his hired hands can't forever impose their will on us here, can they? Not with an ocean between them and us. We might have the chance to build a country. Not a colony. A country! Imagine that! And not just a country, a republic!"

Cormac realized that Mr. Partridge saw a blankness in his face. A republic? What was a republic?

"You must read Machiavelli!" Mr. Partridge said. "I think I have a copy upstairs, and if not, I'll find one. Not *The Prince*. That's the book Machiavelli wrote to get a job, full of blatherskite. No, you must read the *Discourses on Livy*! Best argument ever made for a republic. Old Machiavelli knew you couldn't have a country — or an army — or collect taxes — unless the people gave their consent. That meant, *no kings!*"

He had begun to sweat, and tamped his brow with the clean side of a printer's rag. Then turned again to Cormac.

"There's another reason for your . . . preoccupation, isn't there, lad?"

"Well, I don't know . . ."

"What's her name?"

Cormac feigned a grin, the response that he thought Mr. Partridge expected. He didn't answer.

"I suspected so," Mr. Partridge said. He smiled in a dubious way and turned to the press. "Well, let's get on with it. . . ."

In the solitude of the night, Cormac tried to sort out the separate boxes of his life. He told himself that he must arrange them as if his mind were a type case. The largest letters were in the top drawer: they spelled out the name of the earl, and his presence in New York, and Cormac's hope that Kongo's men would find him. His Irish vows were in that box, and the rules of his tribe, and there were mornings when he awoke on Cortlandt Street and thought he was still five years old in Ireland, about to run barefoot on wet grass.

In the drawer below was Mary Burton. She scared him in some ways, because she lived most completely in the future, in some glorious place where she was free. At the same time, she threatened his own freedom. He wanted a woman's body, a woman's voice, a woman's voice in the dark. But he could not yet imagine a life with children, in a house where he would live and die, far from home. He couldn't imagine building a hearth that would put a soul into a house shared with Mary Burton. Not now. Not yet. He could imagine no future until he had rid himself of the pursuit of the earl.

And he felt too the thrilling pressure of the conspiracy that was building in the town. He wanted Mary Burton to be free. But he wanted Kongo to be free too, and Quaco, and Quaco's wife, serving in the fort, and all the others: Diamond and Sandy and even the wretched Caesar, and the child of his making that would soon burst from poor Peggy. They should be free. How could he even imagine putting a child into a world where men owned other men? How could he do that and be his father's son?

And so he volunteered his name to the conspiracy. He didn't tell this to Mary Burton, but offered himself to Kongo, who was the leader. They met briefly one Sunday morning, and Kongo accepted him, with a dubious look in his eyes. "You help with words," he said. "With printed words. Not with gun or torch."

Cormac learned that Kongo had found instant allies in six Spanish blacks. The young man knew their story. They were free men under the flag of Spain, working for pay on a ship captured by an English privateer named John Lush. An apt name, said Mr. Partridge, for a man who'd been seen staggering around the taverns of New York, spending his stolen Spanish pieces of eight. "He's a terrible fellow," Mr. Partridge said, leaning over his trays of Caslon. "The world would be better rid of him." Lush had plenty of other money, he explained, because the English crown insisted that anyone black was automatically a slave, a thing to be sold. It didn't matter if they'd already been freed of their bondage by other nations; if captured, they were slaves. Lush could sell them as if they were captured horses. "Human merchandise!" Mr. Partridge roared. The six captured Spanish seamen were taken to New York, protesting in vain that they were not slaves, they were prisoners of war, men who had long since earned their freedom. The British sneered. "The laws of Spain," Partridge said, "don't apply to Englishmen with guns." The black Spaniards were sold at the market at the foot of Wall Street. Mr. Partridge knew this. But so did Quaco.

"Quaco helped me know them," Kongo said. "They will be of great help."

Cormac didn't mention the contact between Kongo and the Spanish blacks to Mr. Partridge, who would have understood that the Spanish blacks could serve as messengers to the fleets of Spain. Any Englishman involved in such a conspiracy could be hanged for treason. The Africans were not Englishmen, and in his heart, neither was Cormac, in spite of the English flags that billowed over Belfast. He would take his own risks. But he didn't want to draw Mr. Partridge into the conspiracy. What Mr. Partridge did not know would protect him if the conspiracy failed.

But as he passed brief outings in Hughson's, whispering with Mary Burton, wary of spies among the Africans and redcoats, and as he wandered in his free time down by the markets, Cormac understood that the Spanish blacks were to play a major part in the larger plan. Their leader was named Juan Alvarado. Lean, intelligent, with greenish highlights in his angry eyes. He was fluent in Spanish and could read and write that language, but he spoke Yoruba to Kongo. Cormac had heard them talking, sensed the hardness behind the words, even though he did not know their exact meaning.

He also learned that the arrival of Kongo had made the Africans believe that a rising could be victorious. Quaco told him all of this, a revelation confirmed by the attitudes of the other Africans. Now Cormac finally understood the meaning of *babalawo*.

"Prince of spirits," Quaco said one freezing Sunday morning near the Fly Market. "Kongo have magic. White magic and black magic. He speak to gods and they speak through him. They give him gift of tongues too, so he can speak many African language, and now English."

After a few weeks with Juan Alvarado, Kongo spoke Spanish too.

"Kongo can lead us all to freedom," Quaco said. "My people. You people, Irish people. Not alone. Kongo can no say magic words and English go away. Men have to do that. And men can no win if bad people too big. Men need help." He paused, glancing around the empty streets. "That why we try to reach the Spaniards," Quaco went on. "With English, you need big guns."

In one quick meeting on the street, Kongo told Cormac almost nothing, as if trying to keep Cormac out of the conspiracy.

"Wait," he said. "You have your own task. The man who killed your father."

But the plan was emerging. If the African and Irish rebels could wound the English forces in New York, if they could seize arms, if they could panic the civilian population, then Spain could take the city with a handful of ships. Timing was everything. And it was not just talk. One Saturday night, a Spanish-speaking slave named Morales disappeared. His name appeared Monday morning on a poster offering a reward. But the gossip of revolt provided a motive: Morales was already heading south, to find the Spanish in Savannah or Florida.

For Cormac, the conspiracy was like a novel read in glimpses, with many chapters missing. The falling snow provided the continuity. And one February night he went to Hughson's at the invitation of Quaco. Irishmen and Africans arrived with snow melting on their hats and shoulders, their faces glistening as they stamped their feet and accepted hot tea or strong coffee. On this night, at Kongo's order, there would be neither porter nor strong liquor. Mary Burton, Sarah Hughson, and Peggy were absent, and off-duty soldiers were kept out by the posting of a sign that said "Private Party." In the street, lounging in doorways out of the snow, lone men watched for redcoats or constables. Finally Hughson tapped a spoon on the side of a metal tankard and the room hushed.

"Hear ye, hear ye," Hughson said, and laughed in an ironical way. Cormac was deep in the crowd. Kongo stood before the blue door, while Alvarado lolled with folded arms against the back door. Quaco was at the bar, his face tense. There was an odd glint in Hughson's eyes. Cormac noted that his face trembled, as if he were trying to decide which mask to wear.

"We've met here often as friends," he said. "Tonight, we meet as allies. All here share a common condition: the lack of freedom. Many of you are slaves. Many are indentured servants. You are both — Irish and African — the property of others. That situation has become intolerable. Sinful. Criminal. We believe it's time to do something about it."

"Like what?" someone shouted. Cormac thought: Like freeing Mary Burton.

"This is neither the time nor the place to discuss details," Hughson said. "The bloody British are masters of bribery, of informing, of spies. Some here might indeed be spies, and they have our warning: Betray us and you will be sorry." Cormac glanced at Kongo. His face was skeptical, as if he too sensed that Hughson might be a prince of horseshit. "But the worry is real," Hughson went on. "And so before we proceed, there must first be a swearing. An oath, binding us all to silence."

"Good," came a shout, and a murmured chorus of approval.

Hughson continued, "If any of yiz can't swear such an oath, please leave now."

Nobody moved. Cormac's flesh tingled.

"Then, gentlemen, the oath."

He cleared a space on the hard earthen floor, gesturing for men to move backward. Then, with a long-bladed knife, he cut a wide circle into the packed dirt. The men closest to the circle placed feet inside the line, then grasped hands, pushing deeper inside, while Hughson extended the border to make room for others. Cormac hesitated, thinking: What am I about to do? My only oath was sworn above the body of my father. . . .

But he shared the feelings of these men, African and Irish, even if he felt no confidence about Hughson. He loved that thrilling word *freedom*. And he felt too that in some small way he was being admitted to the secret world of men. This was an American version of the men bound together in the Sacred Grove of Ireland.

He grasped the hands of a Spanish black named Torres and the young African named Sandy. He saw Quaco, his head bowed, holding the hands of two other Africans. Three men watched the full group: Kongo, Hughson, and Alvarado.

Hughson bowed his head and began speaking in a solemn voice, the others echoing his phrases.

"We swear (we swear) to hold secret (to hold secret) all that is spoken of here (all that is spoken of here) and to maintain (and to maintain) our faith in each other (our faith in each other) under punishment in Heaven or Hell (under punishment in Heaven or Hell) or here on the earth (or here on the earth), so help me God (so help me God)."

Kongo stepped into the center of the circle (with Cormac seeing him now as a prince of spirits) and spoke the oath in Yoruba, and the blacks responded. Alvarado did it in Spanish, and his men answered. There was a small cheer. Then Kongo assumed command of the room. He spoke in English and Yoruba, choosing words in a careful, direct way, and made the case for revolt. "Men are not horses," he said in English. "Men have souls." Now Cormac saw uncertainty in Hughson's eyes. If he thought of himself an hour earlier as the leader of the revolt, that role had now been lost to Kongo. He did not look happy as Kongo used his fingers to enumerate his points. He separated the men into units of three. He reiterated the need for secrecy. Near the end, repeating this in Yoruba, he pulled one long finger across his throat, and about half the Africans laughed. Then he stepped out of the circle.

Hughson stepped forward, trying to assert again his own role. Cormac felt oddly isolated. Kongo had not assigned him to a three-man unit.

"As far as you Irish are concerned, the word is wait," Hughson said. "Wait for word from us, from the high command. We'll be in touch as the hour draws near. We'll know our roles, what must be done. I'll coordinate with the Africans. But the purpose is clear: to end these intolerable conditions." Then he smiled. "As for now, gentlemen, the bar is open."

A murmur. Scattered calls of "Hear, hear." A pushing toward the bar. Some faces were flushed, as if the saying were as good as the doing. Kongo nodded at Cormac, placed fingers to his mouth, indicating they would speak later, and then went with his men out the back door into the falling snow.

Then Sarah came in from the kitchen, and the talk became politer, more guarded, less flushed with the possibility of rebellion. She laid plates on the bar piled with herrings, potatoes, hard-boiled eggs. Peggy showed up too, bursting with Caesar's child. Cormac realized that Caesar had not been part of the group of oath-takers. And Mary Burton was nowhere in sight.

After a while, Cormac went out the back door to piss against a wall. The snow was falling more heavily, whipped by a wind. Cormac finished. Then heard his name. Mary Burton was at a top-floor window, her hair wild, a shawl upon her shoulders and neck.

"Be careful of that lot inside," she said. "They're going to cause a lot of trouble."

"How are you, Mary?"

"Still in prison."

"It can't last."

"Wait there."

In a few minutes, she arrived at his side, in the deep shadows beside the building. She was bundled against the cold. They embraced and he could feel the warmth coming from her body.

"You must be wary," she said. "I've heard John Hughson talking to his brother, that thieving lecher from Poughkeepsie. And what he's saying here is not what he's sayin' to his brother."

"What is it they're saying?"

"It depends on how much drink is taken," she said. "Sometimes he brags that he'll soon be king of New York, the ruler of all he surveys, so to speak. Then he's to be a viceroy for the Spanish crown, with the Spanish fleet in the harbor to fight off the bloody English. Then he's to search the whole town, while the British get organized, and take everything of value, ship it off to the south somewhere, to bloody Cuba or Mexico or some such, with him and his brother in the ship. Or he'll make a separate peace with the British, betray everybody, have them all hanged or burned, and then get the British to make him a lord, for services rendered to the Crown, and become governor."

"He sounds as if he doesn't know what he wants to do."

"Whatever the feck it is, it'll be for to serve John Hughson, not the Africans or the Irish or anyone else, includin' his wife."

With that, she brushed his face with her lips and went to the back door and was gone. Through the falling snow Cormac could see a red smear of torches on the ramparts of the fort.

56.

For two days, Cormac searched for Kongo. He must be warned. They all must be warned about the slippery secrets of John Hughson. Kongo seemed to have vanished. Finally he saw Quaco near the Slave Market and learned that Kongo had gone with his master to someplace in New Jersey. At night, Cormac tried to sort out the boxes in his type case, opening and shutting the drawers until he fell into sleep.

Then, early one Sunday morning, after another heavy snowfall, he saw Kongo in the yard behind the print shop. He was holding the reins of a horse. Cormac dressed and went out. Kongo explained that he'd been ordered north to pick up messages for his owner, Wilson the painter. He showed Cormac a signed pass allowing him to travel on horseback. Both men smiled.

"But I want to show you something," Kongo said. "Come."

Cormac climbed on the horse's back directly behind Kongo and began telling him what he had heard about John Hughson. He never mentioned Mary Burton, but he outlined all of Hughson's possible ambitions.

"Thank you," Kongo said.

"Don't trust him," Cormac said.

"We don't."

He waited a bit.

"He thinks he is using us, all of us," Kongo said. "But we are using him."

They rode north for hours, avoiding the few churchgoers out in the snow. That is, avoiding anyone who might be alarmed by an African and a white man sharing a horse. They went beyond those parts of the lower island that Cormac already knew. They rode beyond rocky promontories, frozen streams, open fields dotted with snug Dutch farmhouses with smoke rising from chimneys. Some land was cleared and fenced. Most remained wild. Kongo pulled his fur hat down over his face to hide his black skin. He said almost nothing, and never mentioned the rebellion or his reasons for keeping Cormac out of a three-man unit. He did nod in a conspiratorial way at a group of six Indians walking south, dressed in English clothes and heavy English boots. He pointed out two redcoats lounging outside a tavern, smoking seegars, and seeing them, he nudged the horse into dense forest, moving west across the spine of the island. The wind off the North River assaulted them, icy and hard.

They came to a small road cutting away to the west through the Bloomingdale properties, a section where virgin forests stood like walls protecting cleared land, now brilliant with snow. Kongo was cautious, alert. Animal tracks were cut all over the snow, but the animals were hidden. Kongo slowed the horse and moved into a hilly forest of dark evergreens. And then stopped and pointed. Off in the distance, on a cliff above the river, was the house of the Earl of Warren.

Cormac knew it belonged to the earl because from that distance it was an exact duplicate of the ruined house in Ireland. They moved closer, the horse snorting, steam billowing from his mouth. They saw black men off to the right taking their ease at the entrance to a stable. Just inside the stable doors was the cream-colored carriage. On the great porch of the house, facing inland, its back to the river, two white men moved back and forth on the steps. One held a musket. Over the main doorway there was an elaborate W emblazoned in gold leaf that glittered in the hard noon sun. They moved again, very quietly, maintaining a safe distance, and saw well-tramped paths through the snow from the front stairs to a kind of deck on the river side of the house. Three men were talking on the deck. Each had a musket. Cormac longed for his sword but saw that the earl had defended himself against any sort of direct assault. What had happened in Ireland would not happen here. Only a fool would charge this small fortress alone.

"This is the place you were looking for?" Kongo said.

"This is the place."

"Good. We come back."

57.

For months, the earl had existed for the young man as a kind of ghost, a specter made of anger and memory, and now he was everywhere. Cormac saw the earl walking through the empty square of the Slave Market, glancing at the vacant piers and surely cursing the War of Jenkins's Ear. He saw him on another day leaving the expensive shop of Edwards the bootmaker, the usual fence of bodyguards behind him, to be engulfed swiftly by the Pearl Street crowd. His body was thicker, face fleshier, but he was the same man who had traveled the wet roads of Ireland.

The following afternoon, he passed the earl in a crowd near Hanover Square. The earl glanced at Cormac's bearded face but saw nothing. He was comforted by the simple fact that the earl was in New York. Perhaps he had been away while his fine new mansion was being built. The Carolinas. Distant Georgia. Boston or Philadelphia, those larger, grander towns. But here he was. Cormac thought about carrying his sword, to hurl himself at the earl when next he saw him. But he discarded such a plan as foolish. He would be hanged in an hour and never find out what happened to the other stories unfolding in his life. The story of

Mary Burton. The story of Kongo and John Hughson and the whispers of revolt. No, he must wait until the moment was right.

A week later, while making an evening delivery of posters, Cormac saw the earl again, entering one of the storehouses on Beaver Street, leaving his bodyguards at the door. Cormac dawdled, brushing dust from his coat, ambling toward the river. Other men arrived, alone or in pairs. Not a woman among them. No wife. No mistress. They walked in with masculine swagger. They didn't come out. A frail snow was falling on the town.

An hour later, behind the locked front door of the print shop, Cormac related news of his sightings to Mr. Partridge. His hands were busy cleaning punches and sorting type, but his mind was jumbled. Mr. Partridge urged the young man to be careful, to avoid being obvious. "This earl . . . such men have power," he said. "The power of money, of a willingness to hurt others. Which means they have the ability to do great harm. Once they get power, they'll do anything to preserve it. Watch yourself, lad." He seemed exhausted. "Whatever you do, no matter how strong the motive, do nothing rash."

Mr. Partridge retired early, hauling his weary bones to the second floor. Cormac removed his shoes, hearing boards squeaking above his head for a while, and then silence. As he lay down to sleep, glancing out at the falling snow, his head was swimming with words he was learning from Mr. Partridge, including the word *republic,* and what Niccolò Machiavelli had written about it two hundred years earlier. Then he heard a soft knock on the back door. Could he have been spotted by the earl? Seen as a threat? Followed to the shop? No, such men would knock much harder, if they knocked at all. He took a candle in one hand and the sword in the other and opened the door an inch.

Mary Burton stood there, shivering in the cold. Snow had gathered on the shawl she wore over her head.

"I've come to warn you, Cormac," she said.

He blew out the candle. "Of what?"

"It's about to happen."

"Come in."

She shook the snow off her shawl and sat on the edge of the fireplace while Cormac planted himself on a stool. In strings of nervous whispers, leaning forward with her hands clenched, she told him what she knew: The rising would begin on Saint Patrick's Night. Five days hence. The fort would be set afire, Quaco's wife liberated, the armory looted of guns, which would then be dispersed to the rebels. Others would rob the major shops and haul away all valuables and weapons from private homes. There was a list of good masters and bad. The loot would be taken to the brewery building at the foot of Stone Street. Then John Hughson's brother would cart everything away in a sloop to exchange it upstate for more guns. While the fort was burning, certain whites would be attacked and, if necessary, killed. All bad masters. All arrogant whites, including women. Many buildings would be torched. And the Spanish fleet would then sweep into the town.

"We've got to leave this place," she said. "It will be like the fires of Hell."

"What are you saying, Mary?"

"I'm sayin' we've got to run, you an' me. I'm sayin' that if you love me, we've got to pack a bag and be gone. To Philadelphia, or the bloody west, to somewhere. Maybe we could find a way to Ireland. Get out of this place, some way. We've got to feckin' go. . . ."

Her eyes were frantic and afraid.

"I can't do that, Mary."

She went very still then, her eyes slivering with ice.

"You can't *do* that?"

"I'm obliged in other ways, Mary. To this shop and Mr. Partridge. And to something else, something that goes back to the old country."

"You're *obliged?*" Her voice was now a knife blade. "You're fecking *obliged?*"

"Aye."

"And are you not obliged to me?"

He looked at her hardening face, her disheveled hair, thinking: Am I? She saw the question on his face.

"You low bastard," she said.

She stood up, looking around the darkened shop. A lone horse and rider trotted by in the night. The snow fell steadily.

"I'll be goin' then," she said. "What happens to you will be none of my business." There was bitterness in her voice now. "I have to fecking laugh. I actually thought you loved me. What a fecking fool I was."

She jerked open the door.

"Don't be looking for me in Hughson's," she said. "For I'll be gone. With me child."

She closed the door softly and hurried into the snow. Cormac grabbed a coat to go after her, but she was gone.

He stood there, his body trembling, but not from the cold. She says she's carrying a child. Her child. But my child too. This is a girl, only sixteen, who sleeps with no men save me. A hard girl, lean and stringy and tough, but a decent girl too. And now she is enraged. She is enraged at being an indenture, a slave, caged in a city she didn't choose. She is enraged at me. And in her rage, she might become what everyone in the Irish tribe hated above all living creatures: an informer. Able with words to create peril and havoc, flame and death. Like Samson toppling the temple upon himself. If she can't have freedom, if she can't have me, then feck it, bring everything down. Create ruins. Hurt everyone in sight. If Mary Burton went to the fort and told the English what she knew, Kongo and Quaco and all the Africans would be in danger of death. So would John Hughson. And so would he, whether called O'Donovan or Carson or Cormac Samuel O'Connor.

He should warn Kongo, tell him of the danger, explain his own stupidity, and take responsibility, no matter what the consequences. But if he did run through the snow and find Kongo, the Africans would almost certainly cut the throat of Mary Burton and slide her into the river. Before morning. They had too much to lose and would easily sacrifice one life to free hundreds. But (Cormac thought) if Mary Burton vanishes, so will my child. If there is a child. If she hasn't built a lie to trap me. To make me flee with her across the North River and into New Jersey and keep going until they found a place where she would be free. Some lost, hidden grove in the back of beyond.

He glimpsed himself in a wall mirror and hurled unspoken accusations: How could you have done this? How could you have been so weak? Why didn't you see the trouble coming? Why after sliding into that water with her didn't you simply go away? Why did you keep going back? Again and again. Drawn to the softness within her hardness. His answers to his own questions were shapeless. Nouns without verbs. Lust. Desire. Connection. Weakness.

And then he felt a great pity for Mary Burton, seeing her moving tearfully through the snow, slapped down by his words, infuriated by his coldness, a victim in some way of that Irish story, the story of his father, the story he could not tell her. He addressed explanations to her, ones he should have made, and still might make this snowy night. You see, he told the absent Mary Burton, there's something I must do first. Something that comes before my own life and your life and the life of any unborn child. Something I must do, because if I don't do it, if I don't first avenge the murder of my father, I can never be free. My vow comes before Kongo too, and before the rising. It comes before everything.

Then, just past the door, he could see a lean, coarse-skinned man peering through the glass. He wore a crumpled suit, a scarf, a wool hat. Little puffs of steam pushed from his nose. He gestured to be admitted. As if relieved to be free of his anguish, Cormac unlatched the door.

"I need a broadside," he said. Clipped English accent, accustomed to giving orders. "Quickly."

"We're closed, sir."

"Is your master here?"

"Asleep, sir."

The man exhaled in an exasperated way.

"Make an exception. This is for a ship arriving in a week's time. We need two hundred posters no later than Saint Patrick's Day. We intend to fill the hoardings of the town. First ship in —"

He fumbled in his jacket for a sheet bearing the copy, explaining that the bark was named the *Valiant,* carrying a consignment of raw sugar, rum, and thirty-six seasoned slaves. The first ship in two and a half months, since this bloody war over a bloody ear got serious. Politely, Cormac tried to explain that the Partridge shop didn't do slaving business, but they could handle the sugar and the rum.

"Well, in that case . . . I'll have to discuss it with the earl."

Cormac's heart skipped several beats. "Which earl is that, sir?"

"The Earl of Warren, young man. That's why I've arrived so late. He lives way up in the bloody Bloomingdale."

"I see. In that case, sir, I'm certain we can make an exception."

The man smiled, showing crooked teeth, and handed Cormac the sheet of paper.

"Wonderful, wonderful. You can deliver them, of course? Here are the words, in the earl's own hand. And —"

"I'll need directions, of course."

"Of course."

They briefly discussed price and paper size and type fonts, then the directions to the earl's mansion, and off the man went.

Cormac stared for a long while at the earl's cursive writing. In the street, the snow was turning to a cold rain. He dressed in warm clothes and slipped into the night. He moved through the rain-pelted streets all the way to Hughson's. Slivers of light leaked from the back door, and music strummed in a muted way. He went in and ordered a porter from John Hughson.

"Bloody wet night," Hughson said. Then leaned forward and whispered: "Meeting tomorrow night."

"I won't be here," Cormac said, glancing around the crowded room, searching for Mary Burton, who wasn't there. Nor was Kongo or Quaco, Sandy or Diamond. "The master wants me to go to New Rochelle."

"It's important," Hughson said. "Do we have your vote?"

"Whatever Kongo says."

Then he saw Mary Burton coming in the blue door from the house, her eyes swollen, her mouth loose. She gathered empty glasses from a table. Then came toward the bar, muscles taut in her jaw. Cormac stepped aside, his back to Hughson, and whispered in her ear.

"Give me three days, Mary. I've business to clear up. Then we can talk."

"Feck off."

"Please," he said. "I didn't mean to be so cold back at the shop. I was just, well, shocked." A pause. "And I've been thinking. . . ."

She was listening but wouldn't look at him. She ordered three porters and a rum flip from Hughson.

"Just, for God's sake, don't do anything rash," he said.

She struggled for control.

"Three days . . ."

"Go away, Cormac," she said. "For three days or three hundred."

She turned and plunged into the noise of the room, where three redcoats were singing songs about the King in one corner and six Africans were trying to push rhythm behind the tune.

Mr. Partridge was hesitant about breaking the rule against advertising for slaves. And he knew Cormac's story. He knew the young man had carried a sword from Ireland to kill the Earl of Warren.

"I suppose you think the posters will gain you access to his house?" he said.

"Aye."

"And then you'll lop off his head."

The way he said this made Cormac laugh. Partridge smiled too.

"I suppose —"

"You don't *suppose*. That's what you want to *do*."

Cormac's voice went cold. "I have no choice."

Mr. Partridge looked at him for a long moment.

"I suppose you don't."

He gazed at the copy and then walked to the type tray.

"He should be killed just for what he does to the English language."

They both laughed.

"But if you must do this dreadful thing," Partridge said, "you must be smart. If you go directly to the house and send the wretch to perdition, they'll have you with the hangman three days later. And I'll lose the best apprentice I ever had — and the primary investor in this shop. So please: Use your head for something other than parking your hat."

Cormac thought: He's right.

That night, after most of the type was set (for there were two jobs even more urgent), Cormac wandered the town for an hour, the weather chilly but no longer wet or arctic cold. Near the Common, he gazed at the town's two fire engines: side-stroked, goose-necked tub machines, with pump handles and foot treadles. If more than one blaze started at the same time, the town could burn to rubble. He'd seen the volunteers at one small fire, wearing old leather helmets slung low on the back of the neck to protect hair and skin, designed to be whipped around to cover the face. Remembering their foolish looks and clumsy efforts, he understood why the conspirators might believe in triumph. And yet he felt he could not join the rebellion without first killing the earl. Thinking: That's why I'm here. That must happen first.

Either way, if the rebellion then succeeded or if it failed in a chaos of gunpowder and death, he could escape with Mary Burton. He could lead her across the river. He could try to find some refuge for both of them, and let all notions of permanence wait for the future. As he tried to imagine the future, he strolled through dark streets past the fort, where three prostitutes laughed together in the shadows. Zenger's *Journal* called them "courtezans," but there was nothing courtly about them. In daylight, their flesh was coarse, teeth missing. Better to work their sad trade in the dark. They called to Cormac, offering various services. He strolled on, ignoring them, looking at the high walls of the fort, thinking: This can't work. New York could be taken without firing a shot; the English, after all, had taken it twice; but only if many-masted ships were in the harbor, loaded with cannon and soldiers. In New York, fear was more powerful than loyalty. But you created fear only with a show of force. The tutorials from Mr. Partridge were alive in his head. Wasn't the older man right? The English were accustomed to cheap victories in their endless search for loot. But (thinking then in the face of the harbor wind) the Africans and the Irish of New York shared one terrible fact: In their own lands, they were defeated. Thinking: That's why they're here. Thinking: Defeat is a habit too.

He circled around through dark streets, where gorged pigs slept in doorways and dogs barked and rats slithered toward garbage. He turned through unlit streets toward Cortlandt Street, planning to enter the shop through the alley. A hand gripped his biceps in the blackness. Like a vise.

"Cor-mac."

Kongo pulled him close. Cormac could see his eyes and teeth, smell Africa and the sea and hard work rising together from his skin.

"Come with me."

He released his grip and began to walk, making no sound as he moved. They headed toward the North River. Streets vanished in rising mist, the river water now colder than the air. At the river's edge, Kongo paused, as if waiting for a scent. Finally he relaxed.

"You need to kill that man?"

"Yes."

"Before the big trouble?"

"I hope. And I now have a way in, to his big house."

He explained about the proofs of the posters.

"Good," Kongo said. "My friends, they have watch the house. And we have a man in the stable, he is with us."

Cormac felt his blood streaming through his arms and legs.

"Here is what we do," Kongo said.

58.

Quaco waited on the driveway in a borrowed phaeton while Cormac stood at the door of the mansion. The late-afternoon light was rosy, the wind soft. Three armed men watched him as he waited for payment for the posters. Cormac remarked on the end of winter and the beauty of the house. The men grunted. Cormac hoped they would not search him, for his long coat covered the sword. And nothing could cover the beating of his heart. The door opened. The lean man with the coarse skin, now dressed in the more formal clothes of a butler, handed him an envelope. Payment for the posters.

"The master says good work indeed," he muttered. "And there's a bit extra for delivery."

Cormac thanked him and turned away, glancing at the stable, where three of the earl's Africans were watching and smoking. He climbed back in the phaeton, and Quaco flicked a whip. They trotted back down the road to the south. When they were out of sight, Cormac thanked Quaco, asked him to hold the envelope until he saw him next, and dropped into the forest. He moved toward the river, along the Indian trail marked by Kongo on a rough map. The trail wandered past mounds of ancient oyster shells to another path that zigzagged down the cliff to the river's edge. He waited in the shrubbery until the sun slipped down behind New Jersey and the sky turned mauve. He searched for the large boulder from Kongo's map. Saw it twenty feet down the muddy river edge. On the near side of the huge rock, out of sight of the earl's house, was Kongo's boat. He was poised at the oars.

"Good," he whispered as Cormac climbed in. The African began rowing back upriver, until they saw the glow of the earl's house against the darkening sky. Cormac could make out the earl's dock, and the stairs leading up the cliff, and then the house itself, the balconied facade facing south, rosy near the roof from the final light of the vanishing sun. The March wind turned colder.

"Until later," Cormac said. Kongo tapped his shoulder with a fist.

Now Cormac was driven only by the quest for the earl. He removed the long coat, and the sling for the sword, and dropped both on the bottom of the boat. He held the sword, feeling its weight and power. Then jammed it into his belt and waded ashore. Kongo said nothing. There was a plan. Now Cormac must make it work.

He knew the house from another sketch, made by Kongo's man in the stable. And as he moved through dense woods, approaching the southern side of the house, Cormac saw the huge oak tree, its branches leading toward a second-floor balcony. He began to climb the trunk, but his shoes were wet from the riverbank. He removed them and gained traction with his bare feet, rising on the trunk into the branches. Through the sparse leaves of the tree, he saw an armed man dozing on the deck behind the first floor, and the line of the railing leading down to the river. He climbed higher. Lantern light burned beyond the doors of the second-floor balcony. That was the goal. The earl's study.

Cormac paused, now feeling oddly calm, gathering strength, and then crawled out upon the thick oak limb leading to the balcony. The limb held his weight well but was three feet short of the balcony. He must leap. Silently. And grab the rail. Hoping that nobody saw him. Hoping he didn't fall twenty feet to the ground. He looked down. A wide path of gray gravel surrounded the house. He saw nobody on patrol. Inside the room, a shadow moved. Bulky and male. The earl was home.

Cormac stood now, legs bent, on the thinnest end of the tree limb, balanced precariously, about to leap, when he heard footsteps below on the gravel. A man walked around the corner. A face familiar from the earl's company in town. He carried a musket and whistled in the dark. If he looks up (Cormac thought), I'm dead.

He gripped the branch above him for balance. He stopped breathing. He held himself as still as the tree itself. The man below continued walking around to the deck in back, his whistling fading away.

Cormac thought: Now.

I must go now.

And he did.

He leaped. Fell short. Grasped the balcony railing. Held hard, his naked feet splaying for traction but finding only air. He saw himself falling. Imagined being impaled on his own sword. Imagined the earl opening the door, pistol in hand.

Silence.

Then he swung himself, his body twisting, and felt one bare foot catching the lip of the balcony. Now, he thought. I can do it now. He heaved, holding his breath, and then he was up, weightless, safe. He stepped over the rail and inhaled deeply. Once, twice, three times. Exhaling as silently as possible. Hoping there was no dog.

Cormac looked in at the room. The earl was at a desk with curved legs made of polished wood. French, like the goods sold on Hanover Square. Empty bookshelves rose behind him. There was a door in the wall past the desk. Closed, with a key in the lock. There was a pistol on the desk beside his ink pot. And he could see the three porcelain balls, red, white, and blue, that the earl had used to entertain his men outside a building in Belfast. He was wearing a white ruffled shirt, open at the neck, and his coat was folded carelessly on the desk where he'd dropped it. His brow was furrowed. The posters were stacked to the side of his writing space. He finished writing, blotted the paper, began addressing an envelope. Some vagrant thought passed through him and he smiled. Cormac turned the door handle gently. And stepped inside with his sword drawn. He moved quickly to the desk.

The earl looked up with alarmed eyes and reached for the pistol. Cormac placed the blade of the sword across his wrist, took the pistol and shoved it in his own belt.

"What is this?" the earl said.

"I'm the past, sir."

"You're a lunatic is what you are."

"Perhaps."

"There's no gold here, no specie, nothing for you to peddle in town. I have a dozen men guarding this house. I —"

"I don't want gold," Cormac said. "I want an explanation."

The earl chuckled in a dry-mouthed way, the diamond flashing in his mouth. Cormac saw a woman's portrait on the wall behind the earl. Dark hair, long, aristocratic neck, rosy skin.

"An explanation of *what*? The laws of gravity? The Magna Carta?"

"I want to know why you killed my father."

Now the earl studied Cormac's bearded face in the muted light. Searching time, searching memory. He glanced at a wall clock, then at the door, and smiled in a nervous way.

"I'll tell you what killed my own father," he said, his voice suddenly blithe and light. "Whiskey. Or whiskey and rum and too much wine. Don't let anyone tell you that the gout can't kill a man. You could have asked my mother." He gestured at the portrait. "She died of *him,* of *living* with him, *suf*fering with him." He shook his head. "Sad. I never did get to know either of them."

He reached for the three balls and stood up and slowly began juggling them. "I was raised by . . . an uncle," he said, spitting the words through jaws tightening in concentration. "He was a wonderful . . . man . . . who had been orphaned himself . . . and went off with a troupe of buskers instead of going . . . to school. . . . He taught me how — to do *this.*"

The balls moved more swiftly now, and Cormac thought: I've come to kill you, you idiot, and you're making an entertainment. He felt a twinge of sympathy, imagining the earl when he was twelve. "I loved . . . that man," the earl said. "Loved . . . him." And Cormac told himself: *Stop!* Remember the day! Remember the diamond glinting in the light, the dead eyes, the man urging Patch forward. Remember the shot, and the shouts that followed: *Finish him off!* Sweat blistered the older man's brow. His mouth tightened in concentration.

"You haven't answered my question," Cormac said. "Try to remember, please. It was a bit more than a year ago. On a road in Ireland. You and your men stopped an Irishman and told him to surrender his horse. He refused. And you killed him."

Now the earl understood. The balls slowed in the air, and one at a time he snatched them into his right hand. He gazed at Cormac, as if considering using them as weapons, then laid them on the desk beside the posters.

"You're talking about that fool. Patch."

"No: You made it happen, sir. I was there."

"The man refused to obey a *law.*"

"A law that didn't apply to him. My father wasn't Catholic."

"He was Irish, wasn't he?"

"But not Catholic."

"Yes, but —"

A feathery sound on the balcony. And now Kongo was there, eyes alert, silent in Indian moccasins. Carrying a canvas shroud. The earl's eyes widened and he backed up under his mother's portrait, hunching like a small boy trapped.

"Do you recognize this African, sir?" Cormac said.

"I don't know any Africans, except those who work on the grounds here."

"You should meet this one. Your company kidnapped him and brought him here in manacles."

The earl began speaking more quickly, the words bunching. "You're talking outofa *profound* stupidity. Forwhat you've already-done, *you'llsurelyhang,* unless I plead for your wretched life!"

Thank you, Cormac thought. I was beginning to pity you, and you've shown me your true face. Thank you. Thank you. The earl saw Kongo spreading the shroud upon the carpeted floor, as if preparing a ceremony. "Sit down," Cormac said, pointing at the earl with the sword. The earl obeyed, searching for a posture, for an attitude that might save him, then sagging into the chair. Cormac placed a bare foot upon the earl's polished desk and leaned closer, the sword a thrust away from his ruffled chest. For the first time, the earl had doom in his eyes. He glanced at the door as if expecting rescue, but there was no sound from the hallway. Kongo picked up the sign, eased around to the door, and listened. He shook his head. No sound. Not even breathing. Cormac took his foot off the desk and came around closer to the earl. Kongo approached a second door, leading to what they knew from the house map was a bedroom.

"What do you want?" the earl whispered. "What in God's name do you *want?*"

"I want you to take that pen and a sheet of paper and confess that you had my father killed for a horse."

"Of course," the earl said. "Gladly."

Nerves twitched in his face, which was runny with calculation. He picked up a goose quill, pulled a sheet of paper closer, dipped for ink, and began to write. He finished. Signed it with a flourish. Cormac leaned forward to lift it from the desk, and the earl lunged for the pistol. He gripped the barrel, then forced open the lock, prepared to shoot. Cormac slammed the flat of the sword across his brow, and his grip loosened. Cormac pried the gun loose of the earl's grip and tossed it to Kongo.

"That was stupid," Cormac said.

"I'm sorry," the earl said in a beaten voice. A thin line of blood lay open on his brow.

"No, you're not."

"Go ahead and shoot me," the earl said. "But remember: one shot from that gun and I'll have ten men in this room."

"Yes, and they'll find you with a hole in your head."

The earl's eyes were now brimming, moving to the ceiling, to the doors, to the portrait, and back to Cormac.

"Please, just leave," he said, while Cormac read the note. "I won't pursue this if you just leave now. Here, I'll give you some money." He played with a key in a locked desk drawer. "Not enough for the terrible thing that happened to your father. But —"

"Nothing changes with you, ever," Cormac said. "You tried to pay for my mother's death too. Do you remember that? She died under the wheels of your coach. In the mud."

The earl looked doomed. He opened the drawer as if fumbling for money, mumbling broken words, sweating harder, and then there was another pistol in his hand.

Cormac rammed the sword into his heart.

The earl's surprised eyes opened wider, and so did his mouth. Cormac jerked the sword free, blood spread across the ruffled shirt, and the earl's face hit hard upon the desk. Jesus God, Cormac thought: I've done it. I've done what I came to America to do. I've completed the terms of the vow. Jesus God: I'm free.

Then Kongo touched his arm. "Quick," he said. "We go." Together, they laid the earl's body in the shroud (his face whitening, his eyes wide). The blood was flowing now, slopping on Cormac's hands, puddling and staining the shroud. They closed the open end around his head, tied the lumpy bundle with ropes, and lifted it together. "Quick," Kongo said again. Cormac could feel the leaking blood as it sloshed within the shroud. He and Kongo moved its dead weight to the outside stairs that would take them to the deck and the river. Cormac heard himself panting, and for an instant he saw images of shrouded bodies on greased planks falling into the sea.

From the distance, he heard muffled shouts. As in Kongo's plan, a fire had begun in the barn. To distract the earl's men. To cover their flight. "Quick," Kongo said. "Quick." Cormac turned for a final look at the earl's study, at the desk, the posters, the juggler's polished balls: and saw the room's second door open.

A woman stood there, horror on her face.

She was big with child.

Bridget Riley.

All the way here from across an ocean, from the damp earth of Ireland, from the smoke of a lost, gutted mansion: Bridget Riley herself. Cormac stepped toward her and she backed up. Kongo had his back to the doors, listening to the muffled sounds of alarm. He raised the pistol and aimed it at her. *"No,"* Cormac said. "Don't kill her." Kongo's eyes were cold and impatient. Bridget took in the bloody sword, the pistol, the lumpy shroud, and understood what had happened.

"Don't scream, Bridget," Cormac said.

"Who *are* you?" she said, a trill of terror in her throat.

"You know me. We rode together through Ireland. And here you are, Bridget, still the earl's whore, living in another Big House."

"Good God," she whispered.

"And now carrying the earl's bastard," Cormac said.

The noise from outside smothered her sudden wracked and hopeless weeping. Horses were whinnying. Men shouted. A distant bell was ringing.

"Don't kill me."

He could hear Mary Burton, another soul far from home, pleading in the same way: to him, or to Kongo, or to others who had the power to let her live or make her die. For a fraction of a moment, Mary and Bridget merged, their faces, bodies, masks, wombs. As if they were sisters. His contempt for Bridget, for the earl's whore, for the woman who had told him her sorrowful story in Ireland, smashed against his pity. Pity for her. For the child she carried. Then he thought: If she's carrying the earl's child, I must kill it, and her too. To make certain that I've gone to the end of the line. But suppose it was a girl child? Suppose . . .

Kongo could no longer wait. He untied one of the cords in the shroud, went to Bridget Riley, grabbed her blouse, pulled it up over her head, exposing a laced garment covering her swelling breasts. He tied the blouse like a hood, the rope tight around her eyes. Then he stepped to the side and punched her hard. She fell without a word.

"Quick," he said.

59.

In the black river, the skiff was pulled by the current. The earl's body lay on the bottom of the boat, tied into its shroud, which was now heavy with rocks. Kongo stood guard at the stern, armed with the pistol and an ax, his eyes searching the river. They were passing the palisades that thrust up from the New Jersey shore. Cormac rowed desperately, trying to move them out of the grip of the current, closer to the Manhattan side, to a place of escape, but the skiff was being pulled by the black water toward the open harbor. Upriver, coming fast, they could see the bob and flicker of lights. A boat, with at least two lanterns. Coming after them. The earl's men.

This was not in Kongo's plan. There was no time to feel what he'd done, taking one life, sparing two. Sparing Bridget. Sparing a child. Almost surely the earl's child. Did it matter? It might. The tribe ordered pursuit "to the end of the line." Where was the end of the earl's line? Not now, Cormac thought. No time to think. Time only to row, adding my own feeble power to the force of the river.

Until Kongo told him to stop rowing. Then he grabbed the upper part of the wrapped shroud and Cormac the bottom. The boat wobbled as they heaved. And the shroud sank into the black waters.

Upriver, the light was now larger. Yellow lantern light. The lamp of vengeance and punishment. Coming so fast that it must have five or six men rowing together.

Kongo glanced around, and then gripped the ax.

"We swim," he said.

Cormac remembered swimming in rock pools in Ireland, in wide streams over hot summers, but he was afraid of the northern waters of the river. I can't die. Not now, when I'm free.

But Kongo left no room for argument. He smashed at the keel with the ax. Sharp splitting sounds. Water erupted from one hole like a geyser. Followed by another, and a third. The boat slowed, the black water rose, and they were in the river.

The winter river shocked Cormac. He felt absolutely alone now, sinking and sinking, water filling nose and mouth, as he plunged into a black, shapeless, bone-freezing world. The sword was hooked into the back of his belt and seemed to weigh a hundred pounds. He beat hard with his hands and arms and kicked with his legs, but he seemed not to move. And then he started rising. He saw the smeared roof of the sky. He felt his long coat swollen with water, the sword digging into his flesh. He tried to wriggle an arm free of the coat, but water filled his nose and mouth. He now felt nothing in his hands. Or his feet. Down he plunged, down and down, ripped by the current. Thinking: I am dead. Thinking: I now join the earl. Thinking: I have done what I came to do. But now I die. Far from home. Thinking: Revenge drowns.

Then he felt a bumping beneath him.

A roundness.

Cold and sleek and bumping him, pushing him up and up and up, forcing him away from the dark, drowned river bottom. It was as if he were being pushed by some enormous fish. Some round, cold-fleshed dolphin lost in the icy north. Up. And up.

Until he burst free and saw the sky.

He gasped as air and life flowed back into him. Went under again. Then was bumped. Almost gently now. Like a series of cold caresses.

He surrendered to the creature.

And then the world swirled and the watery sky was full of black clouds and the cold gauzy moon and the bumping caresses turned him, shoved him, moved him into endless blackness.

He awoke to a cold pink dawn, lying in sand and scrubby weeds. A pale moon lingered in the sky. He ached in every joint and felt a throbbing pain in his back. He sat up. Felt a pressure. The sword. I still have the sword. The pain ceased as he stood on aching legs. Then the river and his fear erupted from him in bile and vomit. Finally, after another five minutes, he felt empty of everything. He stood with his head bowed, vacant, boneless, exhausted, freezing, and whispered hoarsely, "I'm alive."

Seabirds cried and screeched above him, as if angered by his intrusion, circling, diving, swooping, but not attacking. Across the harbor, he could see the island of Manhattan and knew he was on the wild empty shore of New Jersey. Pushed here. Bumped here. Saved. When he looked again at the seabirds he saw among them one that was black and knew that it was a raven.

60.

When Cormac arrived that afternoon, after the ferry ride to the Manhattan dock, still barefoot in his soggy coat, Mr. Partridge looked relieved. Cormac didn't show him the blurred, water-swollen letter signed by the earl.

"Have you been swimming?"

"Yes."

"They say it's good for the health."

"It's better in August."

"Well, have a sleep, and we'll work tonight."

He surely must have suspected something terrible (Cormac thought), but he didn't ask another question. Cormac removed his coat and trousers, brushed away the mud and nettles, hung them on a peg, then hid the earl's letter and the sword. He fell into an aching, dreamless sleep.

When he awoke, Mr. Partridge was setting type by lantern light. He mentioned casually that an African had delivered the money for the posters.

"And by the way," he said, "happy Saint Patrick's Day."

The night of the rising.

The date that had fueled Kongo's urgency.

Cormac listened for street sounds but heard no clamor or alarm. He opened the door, and the night was very still, without wind. Of course. That was it: the wind. Or the lack of it. They had spoken about the need for wind before firing the fort. On this night, there was no wind. He closed the door, feeling reprieved.

"Expecting someone?" Mr. Partridge said.

"No, just a breath of air is what I needed."

Mr. Partridge was silent for a while, type clicking in his swift hands. Cormac could hear his shallow breathing. Finally the older man spoke, in a grave voice.

"You've killed him, haven't you?"

"Aye."

He sighed. "And now what will you do?"

"I'll finish learning my trade."

Mr. Partridge looked at Cormac carefully, then handed him a sheet of foolscap.

"You can set this. I've work to do up above."

"Good night, Mr. Partridge."

And up he went on the ladder. No judgments. No expressions of a regret he did not feel. Cormac set type that night until he could no longer see.

When Cormac lay down to sleep at last, he was filled again with the events that had brought him there. He still felt almost nothing. It was as if the black river waters had purged remorse, and guilt, and even conscience. He hoped he would not be traced and arrested for murder most foul. He hoped Mr. Partridge was not drawn into any of it. And he feared Bridget Riley. As she must fear him. She was the only witness. She could call the constables, tell them about Cormac, and about Kongo, and that could be the end of them.

But he did not think she would give names or descriptions. If she had married the earl, then she was the widow. That possibility must have drawn her to America. To assail the earl with guilt, or threats of exposure, to force him to marry her in some chapel, anywhere from Boston to Charlotte. That would be her triumph. She'd been sold for oats and corn, and now she'd be a lady. She could make him juggle before admitting him to her bed. There must have been some risk: The earl could have had her killed. But perhaps there was something else. Perhaps he loved her. Perhaps he sent for her. Perhaps he felt an aching loneliness on the shore of this empty continent, this outpost on the moon.

Either way, she might choose silence. If she was truly married, or could persuade others that she was, she would now own everything that the earl had owned when mysterious robbers broke in and committed murder. She would own the property in New York and the property in Carrickfergus. She would own his shares in the trading company. Better to vanish. Go home to Ireland or England instead of standing as witness in a trial that would make her name known from here to London and certainly provoke scrutiny.

He got out of bed and found a newspaper to see what ships might be sailing on the morrow. The war had cut the number to two, when there would normally be ten. But neither ship was bound to cross the Atlantic. One was going to Charleston. The other to Nova Scotia. Cormac thought: It must be the war with Spain. But if Bridget Riley couldn't leave, performing her grief for a small audience, then why would she not talk? The constables might suspect that she had a hand in the killing. Particularly if she had married the earl, if there was a certificate, a will. After all, the constables were faced with a mystery. There was much blood in the earl's study, but why was there no body? What mere thief would steal a body? If they suspected Bridget Riley, she would surely save her own skin. She would describe the African and the Irishman. Cormac's breath quickened in fear. And then another face appeared in his jangled reverie, another woman who might be carrying a child. Where was Mary Burton?

What was she doing with her rage? What could be brewing through this long night that would come for him in the day?

And then at last he slept.

In the morning, the wind was making flags curl and pushing dust and paper down Cortlandt Street. A gathering wind. A wind certain to stiffen. And when he moved through the streets to deliver posters to Jameson the vintner, he felt a strangeness in the air. He searched for Kongo on the waterfront but didn't see him, didn't see Quaco either, or any of the other Africans he knew, and didn't even know if Kongo still lived. He wanted to go to Hughson's, to try one final time to get them to call off the rising. And to speak with Mary Burton. But he was afraid that if he spoke too strongly they would turn on him, accuse him of weakness, leave him out of the struggle that he wanted now to join. Mary Burton might hear his words the wrong way and turn on all of them in her bitter anger. And another form of strangeness gripped him. There were no alarms over the death of the earl, no posters, nothing in the day's edition of Peter Zenger's newspaper. It was as if nothing at all had happened. He thought about writing a crude letter to Bridget Riley, addressed to Lady Warren, demanding a cash payment for delivery of her late husband's body. Write it with his left hand. To explain somehow to the constables the mystery of the vanished body. But that might only lead to a harder hunt, with rewards and informers. . . .

And besides, the tension in the streets told Cormac another story. Something was coming that was much larger than the Earl of Warren.

Around three o'clock he hurried down to the waterfront to look for Kongo. He lolled behind the empty Slave Market, trying to look casual, and watched the two ships that would depart at four. The *Carolina* and the *Arcadia*. All cargo had been loaded, and the stevedores on the piers were smoking and laughing, waiting for the ships to sail. A few passengers appeared on the deck of each ship, but the flags showed the stiffening of the wind, blowing north from the harbor. Most passengers were in cabins or the cheap bunks belowdecks. Captains and company men chatted, examined documents, smoked seegars. Cormac stretched, as if tired after a hard day of work, gazed into the windows of a ship chandler, hoping for the sight of Kongo. One lonely redcoat leaned against the side of the deserted Slave Market, huddling out of the wind.

Then a black unmarked coach, with trunks lashed to its roof, galloped up in front of the *Carolina*. An African in livery, his face familiar from the earl's stable, leaped down, called to some stevedores for help in unloading the trunks. He opened the door and offered a hand to Bridget Riley.

She gazed around, near and far, her face still marked by fear, and then saw Cormac.

She stopped. The African followed her gaze. It was too late for Cormac to back away. Bridget's head turned toward the lone redcoat. Cormac thought: I must want to be caught, to be hanged for the death of the earl. Then the African whispered to Bridget Riley, and she threw Cormac a chilling glance and turned to board the ship.

The gangplank was raised an instant after she stepped on deck. She turned one final time, looking directly at Cormac, and then vanished into a cabin on the poop. The *Carolina* eased into the river, bound for Charleston. Officers barked orders. Seamen scrambled in rigging. The African watched for a while, then turned and walked toward Cormac, taking his hat from his graying head. Cormac glanced at the redcoat, saw him stretching his arms over his bored head, and moved to meet the African.

"She ask me to tell you some words," the man said.

"Yes?"

"She ask me to tell you: Thank you very much."

He glanced out at the departing ship, and then at some flags on the rooftops of warehouses. "She tell the constables someone hit her," he said, "and she saw nothing that happen to her husband."

"Much obliged," Cormac said.

The African looked at Cormac now. "Tell Kongo," he said. "We are with him."

He moved to the carriage, climbed to his seat, and flicked his whip as if punctuating his brief conversation, and the horses started off, heading north.

61.

They worked across the day into the night. Around seven, Mr. Partridge was joking about the contents of a marital document asking for a legal separation, and musing on the folly of man. Then from the street they heard a shout followed by an excited response. Someone ran past the front of the shop. They went out together, locking the shop door behind them, and turned the corner. There was a red glow in the sky above Fort George. The wind was now blowing hard off the harbor. The rising had begun.

They were hurrying now, Mr. Partridge huffing with his exertions but alert to his surroundings. Citizens were running toward the fort, and they heard the word "fire" over and over again: shouted, called, bellowed. They neared the fort and then there was a surge of people, and scattered redcoats, and the sound of bells ringing. Mr. Partridge went one way, Cormac another.

Great orange tongues of flame roared and twisted angrily against the inky sky. The air was grainy with the odor of burning wood. Firemen arrived with their two new engines, but the water came in useless dribbles. The fire roared and Cormac could see now that it was also consuming the mansion of the governor, beyond the burning ramparts. Redcoats watched with muskets pointed toward the fort but with nobody to shoot. Tongues of fire were aimed at the houses on lower Broadway, and the crowd backed away. Sparks scattered into the sky, and Cormac's mind flashed on sparks from a lost forge scattering across the Irish sky, aspiring to be stars.

He cut into an alley behind the Lutheran church, trying to see the fort from the river side. The alley was piled high with barrels and crates, and reeked of garbage. Then two other people rushed into the alley. Cormac flattened himself against the wall and saw Quaco running, holding the hand of his wife. An African woman, hair piled high, struggling to run in long skirts, panting. Behind them were two redcoats. Quaco's eyes were alarmed and furious. He saw Cormac. Started to say something. But pulled his wife's hand and kept running. Cormac saw a redcoat drop to a knee and take aim. And he stepped away from the wall, placing himself between the aimed musket and the fleeing African couple.

An enraged British voice: What are. Who is. Stop now.

Then Cormac jerked at the barrels and they came tumbling down with a great bumping clatter, filling the width of the alley, and Cormac ran too.

He made a wide circle to the north, crossing Broadway, and found Mr. Partridge in the crowd.

"Where did you go?" he said. "I've been worried sick."

"First I was looking for you. Then I wanted a better view."

Mr. Partridge gestured toward the burning fort.

"This could be a right disaster."

Buckets were being passed from man to man. A portly constable named Michaels burst into the crowd, announcing another fire to the east, on the near end of Pearl Street. He asked for help and men followed him away from the glow of the burning fort. Suddenly four ferocious detonations split the air and rocked the ground, one immediately followed by the next, as the ammunition in the fort exploded. Cormac was knocked to his back. Mr. Partridge hit the wall of a house and slid down to a sitting position. Behind them, splintered windowpanes fell upon the streets. Missiles of stone and broken timber hurtled through the air. Cormac got up and hauled Mr. Partridge to his feet. Women were screaming and men shouting, and everybody was running, including Cormac and Mr. Partridge. They ran directly into Peter Zenger. He was thin, harried, trembling with excitement.

"Is zis your boy, Partridge?" Zenger said, his reedy voice thick with a German accent.

"My man, sir."

"Can he zet type?"

"Yes."

"Can I borrow him tonight? I have a man out zick und —"

"It's up to him."

"I'd be glad to help, Mister Zenger."

"Gut. Go to my zhop now. I'll be along in a vile."

All night, Cormac worked for Peter Zenger. His first newspaper job. Setting type for the *Weekly Journal*. Correcting Zenger's mangled English copy. Writing two brief stories himself. The reports kept coming in, gathered by Zenger himself or delivered by citizens exploding with gossip and outrage. Reports of Irishmen laughing, Africans running away from the fires (for there were four fires now, including the fort and the mansion). Quaco and his wife were among those who ran, but Cormac wrote nothing about them. As the night went on and on, there were scarier reports: Some of the Irish and the Africans were seen with guns. *Did you see zem mit guns? No, but I heard — Zank you very much.* Cormac knew it was a rising, and he wanted to be part of it. But they had not asked him to join, had not assigned him a part to play. He set type. He absorbed information.

Around five in the morning, there was good news for the English, if bad for the rebels. The wind had shifted. It began blowing out toward the harbor, away from the houses of Broadway and the larger town. The third fire, nine blocks away from the fort, had destroyed a warehouse. The owner was dead. Rumor said that an African had caved in his head with a frying pan. Through the night, Zenger understood what was happening.

"Zey vant to burn New York to the ground!" he said. "It's der Irishers und der blacks against der vites!"

Cormac forced himself not to laugh, and kept working without comment until all the forms were locked up. Zenger thanked him and paid him two shillings. His eyes were sore and bleary, but he did not go home. He walked through the ash-gritty air to Hughson's. No lights were burning. He knocked at the back door. Nobody came to open it. He knocked again. An upstairs window opened a few inches.

"Yes, what is it?"

"I need to talk to Mary."

"Good luck."

"Is she asleep?"

"No," Sarah Hughson said. "She's flown."

And closed the window hard.

He stood there for a long moment, then moved toward the waterfront, hoping to come around far from the fire and make his way down Broadway to Cortlandt Street. He could see a boat moving north on the river, with masked men lying low on the deck, but there were no ships of the Spanish fleet. His mind filled with dark possibilities.

She's flown.

She's flown.

62.

When he woke up, the city had changed forever. Until that night, the well-fed, respectable whites had convinced themselves that slaves loved being slaves. That they were happy and secure and accepted their inferiority. The Africans and the Irish both knew they were nothing (or so the theory went) and therefore were happy to have food to eat and a roof above their humble, worthless heads. Now, on the morning after, the English knew better.

The fire was out at last, the king's fort a settling, smoking pile of glistening charcoal. Only one wall of the governor's mansion remained standing. Cormac moved through the crowd gazing at the ruins, hoping to see Mary Burton staring in satisfaction or anger. She wasn't among the gathering audience. But as he moved, he heard the same words dripping from angry tongues: Africans, Irish, Catholics, traitors. There were more questions than answers. Is the Spanish fleet coming? Will New York be taken and the papists installed in Trinity? Will all the whites be murdered? Someone suggested in a reasonable way that an African laborer using solder on a pipe might have accidentally set off the blaze in Fort George. He was laughed at by some and lacerated with words by others. *You bloody fool, can't you see what this is?* Even a few women shook fists at him, calling him a traitor to God, King, Anglicanism, and the white race. The man backed away and then drifted out of the crowd.

In the shop on Cortlandt Street, Mr. Partridge had other news: Two Africans were under arrest for stealing silverware. Caesar and Prince. They'd buried it under floorboards in Hughson's Tavern on Stone Street. "A true pair of master criminals!" Mr. Partridge exclaimed. "And Hughson no better! Idiots! Fools!" And that discovery of the stolen goods led to a fresh theory, one with its own banal logic: The fire at the fort was set to cover the crime. That was all. "Not a revolt, but a burglary!" said Mr. Partridge. And it seemed certain that one of the thieves, Caesar, had fathered a child with a white woman. "It's a fever out there, lad!" More seriously, he whispered, a much wider conspiracy was being exposed.

"They have an informer," he said. "Some Irish wench. They've promised her money and freedom, and she can't stop talking."

Cormac's stomach flopped.

Mary Burton.

Turned informer.

Talking her way to freedom.

That afternoon the reaction began. A grand jury was convened, complete (Mr. Partridge observed) with a Grand Inquisitor named Daniel Horsmanden. The eminent jurors now had a secret list of names. And the authorities vowed to quash this treasonous revolt as swiftly as possible. Working in the print shop, often alone, Cormac tried to absorb the rush of news. The Hughsons were arrested and swiftly condemned, with Mary Burton the chief witness against them. Hughson blubbered, said a man who'd been inside the jury room, while Sarah shouted her innocence. Three more fires broke out, and the hysteria increased. Within hours, Caesar and Prince were hanged on the ridge overlooking the Collect Pond, their bodies dumped in unmarked graves in the African cemetery on Duane Street. Cormac didn't see this happen; the event was carried into the shop by Mr. Partridge. "Stay away from these insane crowds," Mr. Partridge warned Cormac. "They'll be searching every face for proof of allegiance."

English flags blossomed on many buildings, some of them sewn together overnight, serving now as declarations of loyalty to the Crown. Another fire broke out. Then Hughson was hanged, sobbing, protesting, claiming his innocence, demanding a fair hearing. As soon as his neck was snapped by the rope, young Sandy was placed above the drop. He showed no emotion. His last word before death was "Freedom!" The authorities left the two corpses dangling for days, as a warning to Africans and Irishmen. Cormac came around two days later. Hughson's body had turned black, while the African's body had turned white. Some of the more fanatical citizens saw this as a dark omen.

Mary Burton was hidden away somewhere, protected by agents of the grand jury, but she must not have given them Cormac's name. His proof of this theory was simple: Nobody came knocking on the print shop door at midnight. Cormac could not find Kongo, but he was sure he was alive because even the reaction didn't stop the fires. Flames destroyed the sumptuous home of Captain Peter Warren, no relative of the earl but the brother-in-law of James De Lancey, who was the most powerful politician in town and chief justice of the New York colony. De Lancey was enraged and as a member of the grand jury swore brutal reprisals. "He's making this personal now," Mr. Partridge said, "and that means more deaths, more hangings." Then Van Zandt's warehouse erupted in flame. Cormac sensed Kongo's plan: to create fear and uncertainty while the rebels waited for the arrival of the Spanish frigates.

From the first day after the fire at the fort, the constables and redcoats started rounding up the Africans and the Irish and packing them into the new Bridewell prison. After three days, it was bursting. An abandoned warehouse on Water Street was seized by the army and used for more prisoners. Then several run-down private houses were filled with Africans. Shopkeepers complained that they could not operate their businesses because so many slaves and Irishmen had been imprisoned. De Lancey snarled, "You'll have no businesses at all if we don't smash this rabble now."

A few men were released because, as Mr. Partridge explained, they were not on Mary's lists. But many prisoners were threatened and beaten, and dozens were tortured. "If you torture a man badly enough," Mr. Partridge said, "he'll say whatever is necessary to stop the torture, even if it means lying." Mr. Partridge refused to allow Cormac to go out on the streets — "Every young Irishman is a suspect" — and now delivered his work himself, shuffling along, trying to look old. Cormac slept with the sword in his hands.

But they didn't come for him. Mary Burton, the great accuser, was also his guardian. He tried to imagine her at that moment, and how she felt after giving names, and what she thought about before sleep came. Was she truly carrying a child? Was it his child? Had she arranged with the grand jury to be allowed to vanish, with a new name and new papers and some money to give her a start? Did she understand that now she would never be free? Dark avengers would track her down. If she had a child, its name would be stained by her betrayal. Perhaps she didn't care. Perhaps she wanted to die. Perhaps she was not with child at all. Perhaps she simply wanted to erase every humiliation she had ever endured. Perhaps. Mary Burton was a perhaps.

On a Friday in April, Quaco's friend Diamond was led to a spot of ground on the Common, sentenced to die for starting the fire at the fort. Cormac insisted to Mr. Partridge that he must be there, saying, "I know this man," and Mr. Partridge argued, cautioned, sighed, and wished him Godspeed. The Grand Inquisitor had made his ruling: Fire must be repaid with fire. Almost every white person in town came to watch this burning at the stake, except the haughty merchants and the grand jurors who had passed the sentence. And in the crowd, Cormac saw a familiar face, now hollow-eyed, grizzled, filthy, his clothes grafted together from various shades and textures of black. The Rev. Clifford.

"The Lord giveth, the Lord taketh away," he chanted in a singsong voice. "What comes, goes. What goes, comes. All ends in death and fire. All ends in the flames of Hell. All sinners must burn . . . and we are all sinners."

Cormac eased away from him, as if he carried some terrible contamination. So did others in the crowd. Cormac stared at the scene, trying to record every detail without being seen to write notes. A rough, freshly skinned post had been driven into the earth, with a pile of dry kindling and split logs at its foot. A man wearing a hood and a black woolen suit watched patiently while a clean-shaven clergyman in black read from a Bible. He was a more grave, more solemn echo of the Rev. Clifford, clean, clear-eyed, well-dressed, but delivering a more hopeful version of the same message. We are all sinners. Repent, all of ye, repent.

But on this late morning, his last on earth, Diamond was impenitent. He walked to the stake with his head high, his face composed, and a look of contempt in his eyes. Some turned away from his scalding look as he was tied to the post. Others cheered when the hooded man ignited the kindling. *"Off to hell, you savage!"* a plummy voice bellowed, while others laughed. Cormac saw the Rev. Clifford speaking directly to the sky, his words lost in the general chatter.

But then there was silence, even from the Rev. Clifford, as the flames gathered strength, and Diamond writhed and his mouth opened against his will and they could smell a sickening odor and the flames rose around the African's head. Then Diamond screamed. He screamed and he screamed and he screamed. A woman fainted. And the screaming went on. The flames crackled and sparked and roared. And finally Diamond was burned into silence. His smoking body didn't move. The flames kept burning, poisoning the air with the odor of ruined flesh. Some black flakes of his charred skin floated above the pyre.

And then the Rev. Clifford began to laugh. A wild, high-pitched cackle of a laugh. Laced with pleasure. With satisfaction. With death. A heavyset man shoved him rudely, as if to force him into solemnity, but Clifford fell to his knees, laughing and laughing, and rolled to his side and drew up his legs and plunged his clenched hands between his thighs until the laughter turned to tears.

Cormac felt nauseated. At what was done to Diamond. At the sight of the Rev. Clifford. He turned away, fighting off a surge of vomit. He needed clean air and there was no clean air. Others trudged away in silence, stained by the odor of burning human flesh and burning human fat and burning human blood. But as he walked south toward Cortlandt Street, Cormac noticed that some men had not had enough. Their nostrils flared, their eyes glittered, they formed angry clusters on the Common and shouted for more hangings, more burnings, more death. That night, they gathered together as the first of the mobs.

63.

Mr. Partridge was alarmed, for he had been moving among the fearful men who ran the town and were prepared to unleash the mobs. "You're in mortal danger, lad," he whispered. "They want every African, except the ones they own. They want every Irishman." Cormac offered to leave, to keep Mr. Partridge out of danger. He could go to Boston or Philadelphia, or find refuge for a while in the northern forests. When this had settled down, he could return. Mr. Partridge shook his head in a vehement no.

"It might come to that, and soon," he said, "but we've got work to do first."

Together they began packing the best books and most important documents. His precious books made by William Caslon. Swift and Pope, a copy of *Don Quixote* in Spanish, books by Plato and Machiavelli on forming republics, sheaves of slave trading invoices. "These must be saved first," he said. "We must hide them, in case the mobs come here." Some went into a wide worn leather bag. He opened the storage space beneath the printing press and shoved the bag into the darkness. "Let me think about where they'll be safe for a year or two."

As they packed, mobs were sweeping the town. For three nights, Cormac searched for Kongo and saw white mobs beating blacks with clubs or kicking them into meat. One African, accused of stealing, had both hands chopped off at the wrist without charges being presented to the grand jury. An African woman suspected of sympathy for the rebels had her clothes torn from her body on Beaver Street and was tossed from man to man until she was sent raving through the streets, naked and alone and wailing. The decent whites closed their shutters and locked their doors: seeing nothing, hearing nothing. Cormac saw that the white men in the mobs were crazy now: muscles and faces distorted, tendons stretched like cables in their necks, hair wild. They were armed with pistols, muskets, and certainty. All of them were drinking something: rum, gin, whiskey. "Instant courage," Mr. Partridge sneered. "To keep the shite from their trousers." At night, their torches lurched through the streets, and there weren't enough redcoats to control them. They shouted back and forth, one mob to another, claiming the right to certain streets, reporting on their quarries, their instant trials, instant judgments, and instant punishments. "One Irishman tarred and feathered, one nigger with his balls cut off!" When a black man was spotted, they roared like valiant warriors, although there were four of them for each black man, and they ran in pursuit like hounds after a fox.

That Saturday night, the mobs were larger, moving everywhere in their purging fury, and searching homes and shops and workplaces. Cormac suggested to Mr. Partridge that they rent a horse and move books and documents somewhere north, out of the city, to hide them, wait a few weeks, and then return when the mobs had gone quiet.

"I'm afraid you're right," he said. "I'll go for a horse."

Off he went, and then Cormac heard a mob coming down Cortlandt Street, and looked out and saw Kongo. Stones and bottles were smashing around him. He saw Cormac but kept running. Cormac grabbed the sword and stepped outside as the mob rushed by the shop.

Kongo was down, his skull bloodied. He was bent into a small target, hands covering his head, while the whites kicked at him, cursed him, jammed the blunt ends of poles into his ribs, trying to get at his balls. They were screaming *fecking cannibal* and *goddamned savage* and *black bastard*.

Cormac broke through, holding the sword.

"Enough," he said. "Let him be. If you kill him, you'll all be charged with murder. I'll make certain of that."

They backed up, wary of the sword, scrutinizing Cormac's bearded face. One jittery-eyed man with glossy black hair shoved a hand inside his coat.

"You Oirish bastard," he said. "You're one of them, ain't you?"

Another rushed from the side holding a club, and when he raised it Cormac knocked him down with a punch. Then they started poking at him with the poles and bats. Cormac ducked and bobbed, and glimpsed Kongo's eyes in the light of a torch, angry and cold, in a sitting position now, thinking of what could be done. One man lunged with a pole and Cormac cut it in half. Another made a thrust with his own crude lance and Cormac sliced it clean an inch from the man's hand. Then Michaels, the old constable, pushed through the crazed men, his lantern held high.

Not another kick, you lot. Away with ye.

His severe tone was enough to stop them. Cormac stood back a few feet, the sword hanging loose behind him, out of sight. The whites consoled themselves with a simple fact: They'd captured an African. The constable told four of them to remain, to help him bring Kongo to a holding pen, and the rest turned and went off toward the waterfront, chanting words Cormac couldn't fully hear, brave as any mob. The constable reached down, bringing thick twine from a pocket, and lashed Kongo's hands behind his back. Kongo stood up. He said something in Yoruba, and the constable clubbed him across the brow.

"He was thanking you, Mr. Michaels," Cormac said.

"For what? I wish they'd killed him."

Kongo was bleeding from a deep gash in the back of his head and from a rip above his right brow. The sight of blood encouraged one of the four men. He stepped forward and kicked Kongo in the groin. And then smiled as Kongo doubled over, refusing to utter a sound.

"You must have balls of iron, nigger."

Kongo spat some blood.

"Let's try it again," the man said.

Cormac stepped forward, now holding the sword for all to see. They looked at him in amazement. Michaels paused. Kongo stared.

"Release him," Cormac said.

Nobody moved.

"I said, let him go."

"You'll be hanged for this," the constable said.

"Perhaps. But you'll be dead."

The constable looked anxious. Then one of the whites rushed from the left side, a club raised high. Cormac cut the club in half and then smashed the man's face with the wolf-bone handle of the sword. But he didn't see the man on the right. The man who fired the pistol. The sound was very loud. Pain cut through Cormac's left shoulder. Above the heart. He thought: *I've been shot in the back.* Cormac turned, bleeding from chest and back. He pivoted. Swung the sword down, cut into a meaty thigh, and a fat man holding a pistol fell in a gush of blood and high-pitched wailing. The pistol clattered on cobblestones. Another man drew a sword. Cormac wobbled, losing blood front and back, a red film falling across his eyes, but even a feeble swing severed the swordsman's hand from its wrist. The man yelped in shock, gripping his forearm, fell to one knee, rose in panic. The constable ran after him, and so did the others. They only wanted to fight if they were winning.

Cormac sliced through Kongo's ropes. The walls of shuttered houses seemed to bend forward, then back, tottering like drunks. He saw three moons in the sky. From the distance, he heard an unseen chanting mob. The voices getting louder. Thinking: Get the bag of documents. Thinking: Get the horse. As he heard shouts for blood and death.

And then he was on a horse. Lashed to Kongo. His blood seeping: into Kongo's body. As Kongo's blood seeped: into his own. He felt the sword lashed to his bleeding back. There was a worn saddlebag behind him. Slippery with blood. He was up on a great horse. Under a red moon. The horse knew the way. This sleek black horse. A horse called Thunder.

They galloped through farms and forests.

64.

He was a long way away, drifting in silent seas. The air was wet. But the wetness had no form, no edge, no shore. He went out and returned, went farther, soaring through wet, empty galaxies, and returned through watery voids where all was the color of emeralds. And then went out again on the dark, cold tides. He had no body. No bones or flesh and no warming blood. He saw nothing but the emerald water, and dreamed no dreams, and longed for nothing. He did not want food or flesh, and no part of him moved, and yet he was moved through the silent seas.

And then came awake on a bed of hay and thatch on the floor of a cave with a high granite roof. Pain gave him back his body. He was pierced in back and chest, and when he tried to rise it was as if a spear were lodged in his flesh. His mouth felt as if he had eaten sand. The wetness had been replaced by the parched, coarse touch of his tongue upon the roof of his mouth. I'm so dry (Cormac thought) that my blood must all have drained away.

He moved his fingers against one another and then into the sandy earth upon which he lay. His fingers felt swollen, as if his hands were made of thumbs, but they could touch and feel. His eyes moved from roof to side. He saw the worn leather satchel of Mr. Partridge a dozen feet away. He saw his sword lying upon a thatch mat that made it seem almost sacramental. He tried again to rise, but his body refused the command. He could smell a fire burning somewhere, but his teeth clacked against one another in the cold.

Then he heard footsteps, bare feet on sandy earth.

And from some dark place, Kongo appeared above him. He was wearing a white robe. White horizontal bars were painted on his cheeks. He squatted and took Cormac's hand and stared into his eyes.

"Good," he said.

"Hello, Kongo," Cormac said, thinking: My voice is coming across a very long distance.

The African smiled without showing teeth.

"W-where are we?" Cormac said, his teeth still fluttery with cold.

"You've been dead for nine days," Kongo said in Yoruba. Cormac thought: He speaks Yoruba to me and I understand each word.

Kongo went somewhere out of Cormac's vision and returned with a cup.

"Drink," Kongo said. "All of it."

The African held the cup to Cormac's mouth, and he sipped a cold, bitter liquid. Cleansing. Cooling. It seemed to flow through all of his body, and although he could not yet move without pain, his senses were returning. One thing he sensed was the presence of someone else in the cave. When he finished the drink his mouth tasted of lime. The juice of emerald fruit. He tried again to sit up, rose a few inches, and saw a brown gullied scab above his heart. His back felt tightened by another scab. He turned to his side, and pain surged through him, making him gasp.

"Lie back," Kongo ordered.

Cormac asked again where they were, and in an almost diffident way Kongo told him they were in a cave at the very top of the island of Manhattan. In a wild place. Just below the smaller river that cut across the top of the island. The trees were very tall and there were wolves in the forest. As he spoke, Cormac heard breathing from somewhere else in the cave.

"Will you bury me here?" Cormac asked, trying weakly to grin.

"You will not die. Not here. Not yet. Not for a very long time."

Then a figure emerged from the darkness behind Kongo. Tall in her flowing white cotton gown. Her face as beautiful as Cormac remembered.

"Hello, Tomora," he said in Yoruba.

She gave him a pitying smile in reply but said no words. Kongo moved out of the way. Tomora stretched out her brown arms, the sleeves of the gown falling aside. She closed her eyes and began to chant in Yoruba. Cormac knew that she was offering a prayer. To the wind god and the moon god, the river god and the forest god. Kongo bowed his head, closed his eyes, and responded to each call with a blurted word that meant "So be it." She prayed to all the inhabitants of the Otherworld. She begged them to reject Cormac. She implored them to keep him here on earth. She urged them to heal the young man. To give him life.

"Here is a man who did not abandon me," she said.

"A man who did not abandon any of us," Kongo replied.

"Here is a man who gave his life to save another, one of us."

"Gave his life for another, O mighty gods. I am the one."

"Here is a man destined for more time on the earth."

"This earth, this island."

"We must reward him."

"Reward him, O mighty gods of wind and moon, of rivers and forests. Give him life."

Then they bowed their heads in silence, standing together at the feet of Cormac. Tomora turned to Kongo.

"Go," she ordered. And he padded on bare feet into the darkness.

Tomora knelt beside Cormac's head, her legs tucked under her. He could smell musk and forest, rain and the sea.

"O gods of earth and sky, heal him," she whispered in Yoruba. "O gods of wind and rain and sun, give him life. Give him this place between rivers. Let wind and rain and sun fall forever upon his face."

Then she ran her tongue over the scabs on his chest, licking their pebbly brown surface. She lifted him with strong hands and ran her tongue over his scabbed back. He felt his flesh shudder and curl like a flower at sunrise.

"Give him the gift," she whispered, eyes tightly shut. "The reward of the just. The long-lasting gift of women and meadows and water. Give him your eternal gift and do not make it a curse."

Then she was silent. Her eyes opened, liquid and dark. She kissed Cormac on the lips, and he felt her warm breath mingling with his own. She pressed her fingertips to each of his temples and then kissed each of his eyes until they closed into sleep.

* * *

When he woke, Tomora was gone and Kongo was dressed in the clothes of the American world.

"I must go soon," the African said.

"Wait. Not yet."

Cormac sat up without pain. His scabs were gone, the skin of his chest marked only by a thin white line. He was naked.

"How long have I been here?" he asked in Yoruba.

"In your time, almost three weeks, including the nine days when you were dead."

"I understand your language."

"Of course," Kongo said, smiling. "My blood is mixed with yours and yours with mine. We always say that words are a kind of blood."

Cormac began to say that he had dreamed a long strange dream.

"That wasn't a dream. Tomora was here."

Cormac stared at Kongo's face as the African seemed to search for precise words.

"She gave you a gift," he said at last. "A rare gift. More precious than diamonds." He paused. "You must take it."

And then, in careful language, turning his head to gaze at the walls of the cave, he explained.

The gift was life.

Long life.

Perhaps eternal life.

"You can live as long as the world lives," he said. "When the gods are finished with the world, when they decide that they have seen enough, then all will die, and you with them. But even then . . ."

He waved a hand as Cormac rose, his joints stiff, hunger gnawing at him.

"You must understand," Kongo said, his voice now solemn. "Even the gift of life has its terms. Its rules."

Cormac lifted a blanket, covered himself against the chill.

"Otherwise," Kongo said, "a man would be a god. Only gods have no limits."

"I understand."

"No, you don't. Not yet, for you are a boy, too young. But you will. You will learn."

"And how old are you, Kongo?"

He shrugged. "Old."

Then he laid out the rules, the terms, the limits.

"Your life," he said, "will be lived here, on this granite island, this Manhattan. If you leave, if you cross the waters, you will die, and be forever barred from entering the Otherworld." He paused, letting Cormac absorb the words. "Choosing to leave would be choosing to kill yourself, and that would keep you from crossing over to the true place. The place where your father waits, your mother, the people you will love."

Cormac thought: The Otherworld is always the Otherworld, no matter who tells of its existence. And in Africa or Ireland, suicide bars the way.

"You can be shot or stabbed, your bones can be broken, your blood can flow, you can sicken with disease and suffer its agonies. Life will not free you from pain. But you will not die."

He was speaking without emotion, while Cormac listened.

"But in order to live," Kongo said, "you must truly live. You cannot simply exist, Cor-mac, like a cow or a tree. You must *live*."

"I don't know what that means. To truly live."

Kongo paused again, his eyes wandering to the walls of the cave, to the blackness at the far end.

"To find work that you love, and work harder than other men. To learn the languages of the earth, and love the sounds of the words and the things they describe. To love food and music and drink. Fully love them. To love weather, and storms, and the smell of rain. To love heat. To love cold. To love sleep and dreams. To love the newness of each day."

He stared at his hands.

"To love women. To pleasure them. To make them laugh. To be foolish for them. To protect them. To respect them. To listen to them." He paused. "They are the lifegivers. To live is to love them. . . ."

He picked up some doubt in Cormac's eyes, a kind of smiling uncertainty.

"You will see," he said. "The proof will be in your living."

Cormac hesitated, intimidated by Kongo's seriousness.

"There are only two ways to find release," he said, and sighed.

"How?"

He closed his eyes and his brow tightened, as if he were receiving a message.

"I told you the first. If you leave this island, then you will die, and be forever banished from the Otherworld." He smiled in a thin way. "But someday, if you choose, there can be an end, after all your living."

He folded his arms across his chest, gazed at the walls of the cave.

"You will meet a dark-skinned woman," he said. "Her body will be adorned with spirals. You will love her. She will love you. You will lie down with her here, in this place, you will enter her in this deep part of the granite island, and then, only then, if you wish, will you be able to pass to the Otherworld."

A dark-skinned woman marked by spirals. So said the babalawo. The prince of spirits. The shaman. He gestured to a pile of Cormac's clothes, dry and clean of blood. Cormac began to dress. Remembering their flight from death, the mingled blood, the sensation of riding Thunder through the night.

"The great horse is gone," Kongo said, as if reading the younger man's mind. "I sent him back. Now you must go on foot. As must I."

"We can go together, Kongo."

"No, I must go home now. There's a ship that will take me to Africa. Leaving from Boston, and I must go there. A privateer." He smiled. "It's all arranged. In this country, money makes everything possible."

Cormac said, trying to sound casual, "What is happening in the city?"

Kongo breathed deeply.

"The rebellion is crushed. The Spaniards didn't come to the harbor. The English burned or hanged eighteen Africans and four Irish. They enjoy killing when they think their God has given a blessing. . . . But it was not a failure, just a defeat." He said this in a tone edged with doubt but empty of bitterness. "It will live in the minds of all who saw it, and victory will come later." He stared directly at Cormac. "Here. In all places."

"Was Mary Burton the informer?"

"Yes." He sighed. "The major one, but not the only one."

"Where is she?"

"Gone. But she is being tracked."

"Don't kill her," Cormac said.

Kongo shook his head as if the trackers had no choice.

"She wanted to be free," Cormac said. "Like you and all your people. She might be carrying a child and wanted the child to be free too."

"Yah, and she caused much death."

With that, he embraced Cormac and kissed his brow.

"Remember: To live — you must live," he said. "I will see you again. That I promise."

He turned and walked quickly into the darkness, to follow the forest trails to the sea trails that would take him home.

Five

Revolutions

Those cart loads of old charnel ashes, scales and splints of
mouldy bones,
Once living men — once resolute courage, aspiration, strength,
The stepping stones to thee to-day and here, America.

— Walt Whitman, "Leaves of Grass," 1891–92

65.

They waited in the dark with the ridge of forest at their backs and Kip's Bay before them. Cormac moved among them, his own face as black as theirs, skin stained with ink. He nodded at Bantu, who was stocky and muscled and cradling a smoothbore musket.

"Maybe they don't come," Bantu said, speaking English with an Ashanti accent.

"They'll come," Cormac said.

"Good," Bantu said. "I kill them and be happy."

They squatted together for a while, listening for sounds, staring at the dull waters of the East River. All around them in the cool September night there were other soldiers, thousands of them, it was said, being very still, not smoking, all waiting. But here they only cared for one another: the black patrol. Six of them including Cormac, who had recruited them in the months before the beginning of the war. Here beside him was Bantu. Over to the right were Silver and Aaron, lean and black as night, deadly with short swords and long-bore rifles. Below him on the slope, screened by dense shrubs, were Big Michael and Carlito. Cormac went from man to man, whispering the words that had brought them there, the most important of which was "freedom."

"We have to smash them here," he whispered to Carlito. "After Brooklyn, we have to hurt them, let them know they will pay a terrible price."

"Donde están?" Carlito said in Spanish that had been driven into him like nails on the sugar plantations of Cuba. "Where are they?"

"Out there," Cormac said. "Brooklyn."

The disaster in Brooklyn haunted all of them. Cormac hadn't fought in Brooklyn; he could not leave Manhattan, even for a cause greater than himself. So while the armies faced each other on the fields of Brooklyn, the black patrol had moved through the lower city, setting small fires as diversions, hoping to panic the English, to draw redcoats away from the field of battle. Their work did Washington no good. The battle of Brooklyn was, by all reports, a rout. Soldiers broke and ran. Fifteen hundred Americans were killed, blown apart by artillery, shredded by rifle fire and bayonets, and more than two thousand captured. The redcoats swept the field, and Washington led the survivors down to the river and into boats to fight again on another day in Manhattan.

"We will beat them here," Carlito said. "Then we go back to Brooklyn."

"First we must beat them here, *'mano."*

Silver and Aaron dozed against the trunk of a giant oak tree, swords in hand, rifles on their laps. They smiled when they saw Cormac. All glanced at the river.

"They must be praying," Silver said in Yoruba.

"Or toasting the King," Cormac said.

Aaron smiled. "Foog the King."

"And all his foogin' court," Silver said, and laughed.

Alone, alert to sounds in the forest and echoes from the river, Cormac closed his eyes and leaned back against a tree. They had been waiting now for two days for the force that Washington was certain would come to this cove along the river. He remembered the first time he saw Washington, bending under a lintel to enter a smoky room on Beaver Street, full of conspirators. He was even larger than Cormac had imagined from the descriptions of others; in every room he ever entered, Washington was the tallest man. Six-foot-four at least, with broad shoulders, the large ass of a horseman, huge hands, large booted feet. His skin was pockmarked. His cold blue eyes had an odd Oriental cast, the eyelids slanting upward. His nose was hawked, long, the taut skin rosy from the sun, the nostrils quivering as if trying to sniff out the person who would betray him, betray them all. While Cormac picked up that thought, asking himself: Which of them, in this room packed with men, was Mary Burton?

Now, remembering that first sight of Washington on the eve of the war, hearing again his laconic words about the coming struggle, the need for all of them to take arms and if necessary sacrifice their lives in order to be free, he wondered if Mary Burton was still alive. In those months in 1741, she had given her names to the inquisitors, adding new ones as she went along, and then had vanished. He had never heard from her again. She would now be fifty-one, ancient in these colonies of the young. Across the decades, as he had eased back into New York and returned to the print shop, he hoped he would find one morning a crudely written note from her, telling him she was alive, telling him about the child. He placed several blind advertisements in newspapers. *Mary, please write, C.* But immediately thought the effort was useless, since she could barely read and almost surely didn't care about anyone in New York. There were no replies. She was gone. As Kongo was gone. As Quaco and his woman were gone.

And I am here, he thought, obeying the command to live by taking lives, killing strangers. He looked like the same seventeen-year-old who had learned the printing trade in a shop on Cortlandt Street. The same young man who had buried Mr. Partridge after the cholera took him in 1753, while he raved about the coming republic of America. The same young man who had sold the print shop to a competitor and gone to work at the John Street Theater to be instructed in the use of masks and dyes and the postures of disguise. In the mirror he was that same young man. The one who last saw Kongo in a cave in Inwood, and learned across the years that the words he spoke to Cormac there were true. He was alive and young while everyone else his age was old or dead.

"They come," Bantu said.

They arrived at dawn in eighty-four six-oared longboats, each carrying a dozen men. The English wore red and the Hessians wore blue. The guns of the frigates roared. All around them, the earth exploded with fire and metal. Cormac heard a young voice screaming in the dark: *"Oh, Ma, oh, Ma, help me, Ma."*

The black patrol waited, saving ball and shot. They could hear scrambling in the woods behind them, men panting. A bony farm boy came up from the river's edge, his gun as useless as a reed, yelling, *"Run, run, there's thousands of them."* Bantu shot him and picked up his rifle.

The naval barrage was ferocious. Cormac didn't need to tell the black patrol to lie flat, to use tree trunks as shields. Now trees were falling, splintered by cannon shot, and more young men were running past them in the dark.

"Don't shoot them!" Cormac shouted. "Let them assemble in the rear!"

Now they saw four Hessians lumbering up the hill from the river's edge. They waited. Then killed them all. Cormac felt nothing. They come to kill us, he thought, and so we kill them.

As the sun struggled to rise in Brooklyn, they could see Kip's Bay more clearly, and the steady movement of empty longboats returning for more soldiers and packed longboats rowing toward the shore. To the left, Cormac glimpsed a long blur of scarlet. He gestured to Bantu, pointing to the rear, then went down and told the others. Big Michael didn't want to retreat.

"I come to kill these bastards," he said. "Let me kill them."

"We will," Cormac said. "Come."

"Where we go, man?"

"The rock pile."

They eased around in the darkness in a single file, glancing behind them at the blue-and-scarlet lines. The cannon kept exploding the earth and felling trees, and new troops of the Crown chose to pause until the fierce barrage had ended. The six men of the black patrol found their way to a cluster of jagged boulders at the crest of a hill. Now they could see the Americans in flight: farm boys and city lads, brave while marching, panicky in the face of cannon and bayonets. It was one thing to wave *Common Sense* on the streets or join the mob that toppled the statue of George III in the Bowling Green; it was another thing to face English guns. The young Americans dropped their ancient flintlocks and old fowling guns, their dragoon pistols and close-bore rifles. They abandoned a few pieces of cannon. They left tents for the invaders. They were in full flight.

"Don't show yourselves!" Cormac told the others. "And don't shoot our own lads. Hold as long as you can."

They knew that the six of them would have to cover the retreat of thousands. Cormac thought: It's absurd. The amateurs are running, and the professionals are coming. But we have to stop them, for at least an hour. And so they waited, huddled down, peering at the assembled scarlet-and-blue masses below them. Off to the left, smoke had begun to rise from a fire on the forest floor. Cormac thought: Good. That will give us some cover, a dark screen.

Then two columns began climbing the slope, about twenty yards apart.

"Wait," Cormac said.

The climbing men were heavy with packs and rifles.

"Wait," Cormac said.

A lanky Hessian paused, looked behind him, then squinted at the drifting smoke. He took a deep breath, said something to the men behind him, and resumed the climb.

"Wait," Cormac whispered.

A fat, sweaty Englishman led his column into their view on the right. He mopped his brow with the sleeve of his free hand. In the other hand he held a rifle.

"Now," Cormac said.

The air exploded as they poured fire on the troops below. Men fell like broken dolls, face forward or whipped to the side. A few knelt to fire and were knocked over. Cormac aimed at one Englishman but then saw his face explode from a shot by Big Michael.

"Gone down," Big Michael exulted, starting to rise. "He gone down."

Then Big Michael was dead. A ball tore open his chest, and he sagged and went down with one leg twisted under him. The black patrol kept firing, and saw the blue and scarlet uniforms turning to find cover. Cormac saw a beplumed officer and shot him between the shoulder blades. Then he turned to the others.

"Toward the smoke," Cormac said.

They fired another volley and then ran, one at a time, squatting low, spaced apart, toward the screen of smoke, leaving Big Michael where he'd fallen. Bullets and balls whizzed around them and pinged off stone. Then they were in the smoke.

So were hundreds of the retreating Americans, coughing, gasping, climbing, falling, desperate to reach the crest of the hill and the plain beyond, all of them beaten without firing a shot. Cormac and Bantu, Silver and Aaron and Carlito aligned themselves in a picket, ten feet apart, and raised hands to break up the panic.

"Stop running!" Cormac shouted. "Stop or we'll shoot you for desertion!"

One brawny blond-haired man lowered his rifle to shoot his way out. Carlito killed him.

"Hold this ground," Cormac yelled at the deserters. "Face them and fight them!"

They ignored him and ran to the side or plunged back down the slope, hands in the air, to surrender. He heard shots crackling below and knew the Crown forces were killing those who wanted to surrender.

And then through the smoke and noise, they saw Washington.

He was high on a sorrel horse, waving a sword in his right hand, his eyes ablaze, his mouth a tight slash.

"Are you soldiers or mice?" he shouted. "What do you call yourselves?"

He swung the sword at one fleeing man and missed, and then glanced at Cormac and the blacks and then peered down the slope at the advancing blue and red uniforms. He paused, and then started forward. Into the guns. It was as if he wanted to be shot down to end his shame.

Cormac grabbed the reins of Washington's horse and wrenched with all his strength and turned the horse.

"Stop, you stupid bastard!" Cormac screamed.

"Unhand this horse!"

"We need you alive, God damn you," Cormac said, and hauled the horse around and pointed him west. Bantu ran up and slapped the horse hard on the haunch, and away he went, carrying the general through the trees.

Silver and Aaron and Carlito stood laughing, bumping one another's shoulders. Then they turned, backing up, and killed more men.

66.

*In the vast camp in Harlem Heights, Cormac was escorted to Wash*ington's tent. Almost five thousand men were sprawled around the camp, cleaning guns under a dim moon, soothing horses, eating at campfires. A few were singing. Many were sleeping. Two lieutenants flanked Cormac as if he were a prisoner.

The general was seated in a camp chair, examining his gleaming fingernails. An empty chair faced him. His cocked hat was on a table, with gloves folded neatly on its crest, and the buttonholes of his frock coat were embroidered. The man took care about the way he dressed. Too much care, Cormac thought. Behind Washington was the famous six-and-a-half-foot-long cot that was carried with him everywhere. A coal fire burned in a stove. Maps were spread on a table, along with a few plates and a bottle of wine. He didn't look up.

"You can leave, gentlemen," he said to the officers. They stepped outside.

Washington turned over his large hands and looked at his knuckles.

"You're the man who jerked my horse?"

"Yes, sir."

"You know that I'm the commanding officer of this army?"

"Yes, sir."

Washington stood up as if stabbed, the hands turning into fists, the eyes blazing.

"Why did you *do* such a goddamned thing?"

"To keep you from being killed, sir."

"That's for *me* to decide, God damn it. And how could you be sure I would die? How could you be sure that they would not run?"

"You're one man, General. One ball could kill you. One of my men —"

"They can't kill me!"

"They can kill anyone they can shoot, General."

Washington snorted. He turned, flexing his hands, rolling his shoulders. He was breathing hard, struggling for control.

"What's your name?"

"Cormac O'Connor."

"Irish, of course."

"Yes, sir."

"Catholic?"

"No."

He paused, breathing more normally now.

"How many men did you kill today?"

"Our patrol killed about thirty."

"Your patrol? What patrol?"

"The black patrol, sir. There's me and five blacks. One of them was killed today. We'd like to go in tomorrow, sir, and bring out his body."

Now he was staring at Cormac.

"Are they all slaves?"

"They were, sir. They're soldiers now. American soldiers."

"Have they been fed?"

"Yes, sir. They're looking for ammunition now. They used all they had."

"And they're good soldiers?"

"You saw them. They didn't run."

He sat down again in his camp chair and offered the empty chair to Cormac.

"Why did they fight while so many ran?"

"They want to be free, General. That's why they're with us. That's why they listened to me when I recruited them. That's why they won't disappear when times get hard. They want to be free, sir. Free."

Washington looked at him for a long moment and there was something moving in his eyes that Cormac couldn't identify.

"Would you like a glass of wine?" Washington said.

The cannon screamed through the night, exploding around them, scattering soldiers, collapsing tents. Cormac knew what was happening: The English and their hired Hessian soldiers wanted to smash the Americans here in Harlem Heights, splinter and ruin their five thousand troops, capture or kill Washington. If they could do that, the revolution would be over. They could all sing songs, get drunk, sleep with whores, and get ready to go home.

Washington that night would not let them do any of that. He was everywhere, sword in hand, his face filled with furies, shouting, commanding, calling on pride. "Your children will remember you for this night! Don't fail them!" And, "Die on your knees, you crazy American bastards!" And, "Send them all to Hell, boys!"

And they held. They held the lines, Cormac and Bantu, Aaron and Silver and Carlito among them, pouring fire into the moving lines in the dense wooded hollow below the heights. Still the cannon roared, the balls tore through young bodies. An old man rose in fury, his white hair spiky against the dark sky, and cried: "Come and fight, you feckers! Come and die!" And then was smashed by a cannonball, knocked over into death like a bowling pin.

Cormac looked up and there was Washington on his horse, right above them.

"Their cannon are killing us!" he shouted. "Get your niggers and destroy the cannon."

Cormac thought: They are not niggers, they're Americans.

But Washington was gone, and there was no time for debate. Cormac and the black patrol slipped down the western side of the ridge, seeing the distant shimmer of the river, trying to estimate the location of the cannon from the arc of the balls. Then they saw the first scouts of an English flank, coming up the west side of the forest on a dirt road. Bantu gestured at a stone Dutch barn, its doors open, its animals gone. From its weed-sprouting walls, the path was a pale line under the moon. They hurried to the barn, spread themselves from the loft to the doors, waited, and then started killing soldiers. They shot the first two men who came up the rise, then the next three, then two more, all of them falling upon one another, forming a mound. All were redcoats. All kept coming as if they were toys, and the Americans kept firing and reloading and firing again, hands moving in a blur, fingers squeezing triggers. Redcoats fell to the forest floor.

Then the first cannonball tore through the roof of the barn, caroming wildly off the flagstone floor, and then another, and Cormac and the others slipped out the back and into the woods between the road and the river. Cormac thought: I killed the earl somewhere up here. Long ago. In another life.

They made a wide arc, moving the way wolves would move, drawn to the sound of the cannon. The moon did not penetrate the forest. Cormac strapped his rifle to his shoulder and drew the sword. So did the others. They did not need to explain to one another that here in the darkness they would fight silently. They came upon two Hessians, who turned in fear at the sight of four black faces. Too late. Bantu and Silver cut their throats.

Then they saw the clearing. Five cannon on wheels, a dozen redcoats loading balls, pouring powder. Cormac and the others hunkered low in the shrubs. They spread out, each charged with attacking the crew of one piece. Bantu was to shoot as many as possible while the others pounced with sword and knife. They watched as all five cannon were fired at once, the crews jamming fingers in their ears, some of them grinning. Then the Americans charged. Bantu had two rifles now, one lifted from a dead soldier, and he fired one, then the other, rolled on the ground to reload, and fired twice more. Three redcoats went down. Others turned in horror, reaching for rifles as their throats were slit. Cormac beheaded two men, then chopped another man's arm at the shoulder.

They became a single creature made for killing. There was nothing else now. Just the killing. No fear, no choice, no thought. They stabbed and slashed and ripped. They chopped at necks. They drove swords through hearts. Few words were spoken as men grunted, or gagged on blood, or groaned, and then died.

Then it was over.

Cormac sat down hard on the thick leafy floor of the clearing. His hands were slippery with blood. It coated his sword and his clothes and his boots. He looked at the others. Silver leaned on a cannon, Bantu lay back against a tree. Aaron seemed dazed and drained, standing with short sword in hand, while Carlito draped a hand on his shoulders. All glistened with blood. They didn't even look at the men they had slaughtered.

"We should take the heads," Bantu said.

"Yah," said Aaron.

Take the heads, Cormac told himself. The way the Irish always took the heads, the way the Fianna took the heads. Sever them. Hang them on poles. No. Don't take the heads. Please don't take the heads.

"They weigh too foogin' much," Silver said.

They laughed, and then went silent.

Now they could hear the trees riffling and sighing in the wind, and away off the crackle of rifle fire. A lot of rifle fire. But they still didn't move. The air was thick with the odor of powder, of burning trees and smoldering leaves, of ripped-out guts, of leaking shit.

Finally Bantu stirred. Suddenly alert. He gripped his short sword, and turned to peer behind him into the darkness. The others tensed. He went on hands and knees, and then moved into some shrubbery. He came out grinning, holding a wolf cub.

"Yah!" he said. "Look."

The cub was small and gray with a white face and yellow eyes. Bantu held it close, cradling it, and the animal began licking blood from his neck and face. Bantu smiled.

"American!" he said. "American!"

Each of them came to touch the cub, playing knobby fists against its small sharp teeth, stroking its fine new hair. Cormac felt a surge of emotion, as if he were again the boy on the fields of Ireland, with Bran barking beside him. They kept saying in the city that all the wolves were dead, and here was one of them, alive, separated, like every member of the black patrol, from the pack.

And then, as time stretched and compressed, an hour later or three minutes later, they heard another sound: a distant roar. They stood still, listening, hands clenching weapons. The roar was louder, coming to them through the trees and across boulders and above the bodies of the dead. Louder and louder. Louder than any sound he'd ever heard, punctuated by rifle shots.

It was the Americans.

A dozen of them, dressed in the uniforms of the Continental Army, bursting among them, seeing the dead redcoats and the four men with black faces. One shouted: "We've broken their lines! They're running!"

And rushed past them, raising weapons, leaping into forest, crashing forward, shooting. Cormac realized that they were in the midst of the first victory of the Revolution.

But still the black patrol did not move. The wolf cub made a crying sound. Somewhere in the woods were other cubs, a mother, perhaps all of them dead, killed by fearful men.

"We go now," Aaron said. "We fetch Big Michael."

They moved toward Kip's Bay through the morning. Along the way, they saw scattered corpses in Hessian blue or English scarlet, providing a harvest for flies and worms. At a small river, they entered the cold waters and scrubbed at the blood on their bodies and clothes, Bantu holding the cub over his head, its jaws now shut by gold braid torn from an English corpse.

A hard gray rain began falling. When they came to an abandoned farmhouse, they entered and bolted the doors behind them. The farmers must have been gone for only a few days, fleeing the war. Carlito started a fire in the hearth and they boiled potatoes and carrots and fried strips of bacon and slathered butter on hard bread. "Better it does not spoil," Silver said, and smiled, his mouth full of wobbly wooden teeth. "Better we eat." There were apples too, and grapes, and they ate quietly, peering out at the falling rain and the rolling forests. Bantu fed bread and bacon to the cub and put water in a dish for him to drink. With his back to a wall, staring at the fire, Cormac remembered his hunger in the arctic winter in Ireland, devouring cheese in a dairy, more hungry than he'd ever been before or since. He told the others to sleep while he stood the first watch. They would go for Big Michael in the dark.

They slept, the wolf cub curled into Bantu's armpit, and Cormac surveyed the house. It was more than a house, he thought: It was a home. He and the others were sleeping within its walls, but it was not their home. Men like us, he thought, have no homes.

He entered the next room, where there were two hard, narrow beds covered with quilts. The closets held women's clothes.

Shifts and dresses for a large woman, broad-beamed, large-bosomed. The others were for a smaller, thinner woman. Mother and daughter, perhaps. Or sisters. Mother and cub.

The clothes and bodies and faces of women flooded through him as he moved on bare feet around the room and then back into the place where the men were sleeping. It was thirty-five years since he'd seen Bridget Riley sail out of New York, thirty-five years since he'd last looked upon the hard, confused face of Mary Burton. There had been many women since then. Which was to say, he'd had no women.

He knew enough about himself now to understand his habits of holding back, of refusing. He had read much poetry and a few novels, and had listened to many women, to their questions, to their tears. He knew that the combination of Bridget Riley and Mary Burton had put fear in his heart in the place where love demanded fearlessness. He knew that not all women were like those women of 1741, that no woman was exactly like any other woman. But their presence remained alive, full of the potential for betrayal, for illusion, for inexplicable loyalties. Bridget was loyal to the earl; Mary had been, in her way, loyal to Cormac. How could he think all women were alike?

And more important, there was this other thing, this gift granted to him in a cave in Inwood. There was no way, at first, to know if this was a dream, a wish born in his own brain. He could only know its truth by living. Now he knew it was true. He had continued to live while others died, he had remained young, in all obvious ways, while others withered and turned gray and walked Broadway in feeble, palsied steps. That affected him with women. How could he remain with one woman who would gaze at him and then gaze in the mirror? She would know he was different. She would know that he was beyond the normal cycles of a life.

Better to let each woman know that he was a passing fancy, that they could enjoy the pleasures of each other's body, but that each could be alone in the morning. Many women welcomed such an understanding. Widows, the wives of seagoing men, women locked in loveless unions, older women whose children had gone off. They welcomed the excitement of aroused flesh.

They welcomed whispered words. They welcomed the gift of a rose or a locket. As years passed, more of them thought he was a handsome young man, when he was actually older than any of them. All were excellent teachers, and he thought of some of them as if they were books he had taken down from shelves.

"There's something I've always wanted to do," they would say, and then do what he had done many times with women in his rented rooms. The town was filling up with strangers, with women who did not know one another, and were thus free of the intimacies of gossip. The village he'd come to as a boy was becoming a town and was certain to become a city. And in the anonymous crowds, all was possible.

Bantu stirred, without benefit of a clock. He would now take the watch. Cormac nodded and went into the bedroom, to lie down and inhale the odor of a woman's body.

At some hour before midnight, they found Big Michael where he had fallen, facedown in the earth. Animals had gnawed the flesh on his neck and arms. Aaron started digging with a spade stolen from the farmhouse, and the others gazed toward Kip's Bay, visible under the moon, with lanterns blazing on the English frigates and men still crossing to the shore in longboats. They must be quick. Silver took the spade, followed by Bantu and Cormac and Carlito. Grunting and digging, until the trench was deep enough to keep Big Michael from the paws of foraging animals. They lifted Big Michael's body together, the wolf cub yipping and excited, and then lowered him gently. His bones would be part of this island, Cormac thought, for as long as there was an island.

Bantu spoke in Yoruba, consigning Big Michael to the care of the gods.

"We will see you in the Otherworld, O brother," he said.

And then they started the long journey to the north, to meet with Washington's triumphant army. They passed small groups of redcoats sullenly guarding campfires. They forded streams. They saw bodies of Americans and Englishmen and Hessians. They paused to rest, then began again. At last they saw the escarpment of Harlem Heights, outlined against the dawn.

It was empty. Washington's army was gone.

"They've marched to White Plains," an American scout told them. "The whole lot of them."

"And will fight in White Plains?" Cormac said.

"I suppose. They don't tell the likes of me such things. But I guess they'll fight a bit, then cross the river. The English are now between us and White Plains, they came in the morning, so the only place for Washington to go is New Jersey. . . ."

The black patrol was silent, staring at one another's stunned faces. They'd been left behind. Abandoned. God damn it. Silver asked if there were any other boats that could take them across the river.

"Not that I know," the scout said. "My orders are to go home in another day."

"Where is home?" Carlito asked.

"Westport."

"So Washington is handing New York to the Crown?" Cormac said.

"I don't know. I just don't know. I know I go home tomorrow."

Cormac looked south. The sun was seeping into the sky above Brooklyn.

"Let's go," he said to the others.

"Where?"

"New York," he said.

Bantu took the braid from the muzzle of the wolf cub and walked him into the woods and set him free.

67.

They fought their own war now. They sawed through the beams of bridges at midnight, spilling carriages and caissons into streams. They broke into warehouses and killed guards and stole rifles and sent them on boats across the river to New Jersey. They spread posters on the walls of buildings, advising English soldiers to save their lives by going home. Most of all, they burned houses.

"They keep taking houses for their soldiers and their officers," Cormac said. "We have to force them to sleep in the rain."

He explained what had been done in 1741, and how the conspirators had waited a day for the wind. They must set up everything carefully, straw, paper, oil, kindling. So they did, with Bantu and Silver posing as water carriers, lamp oils suspended at each end of poles. Aaron was a carpenter, with papers stating that he was a freeman, manumitted by a dying owner (printed at night by Cormac in the shop of one of the Sons of Liberty). He went from door to door, offering his services, peering around storerooms and workshops. Carlito met with the Spanish slaves, learning the vulnerabilities of the homes and workplaces of their masters. Cormac marked maps. In the afternoons, one at a time, they wandered past the places where the fire pumps were stored and punctured the bottoms of water buckets and sliced holes in the hoses. At night, Cormac dreamed of fire and destruction.

The rest of life seemed almost normal. As the English officers arrived in New York, the Tories welcomed them, throwing elegant parties, hosting nights of song and loyalty at the John Street Theater. They called down God's blessings on the Sovereign while clavichord music tinkled from the mansions near the Bowling Green. Tory mothers presented their daughters like offerings. Whores began ringing the fort. One or two at a time, and then in larger numbers, the Americans had been slipping away, some carrying their valuables to country places, others boarding ships for the South. Some were loyal to Washington. Others wanted to avoid what was certain to come to the streets of New York. The English did not interfere with their flight. They wanted the abandoned American homes.

Cormac, dressed as a mechanic, was watching part of this sad American exodus one evening on Broadway when a large red-haired man came up beside him. He was wearing a cape, his hands hidden.

"They'll be back," the red-haired man said. The accent Irish.

"Aye," Cormac said.

"Don't ye think?" the man said.

Cormac shrugged. It was impossible to know the sides that each man had chosen in this town; this Irishman could be just another English spy. "Where do you come from?" Cormac asked in Irish. The man seemed startled, and answered, "Armagh." Another voyager from Ulster. They stood together, and as the last carriage passed on its way north, Cormac heard the sound of uilleann pipes. He was surprised. The sound was mournful, sad, angry, all at once, and seemed to come from the chest of the red-haired man from Armagh. Cormac stepped back and realized the man was playing his pipes under the cape, using his right elbow for power.

"Good day, sir," Cormac said, and walked quickly away as the man gave voice through his pipes to the ghosts mixed with the higher-pitched howl of the banshee.

Then one night, as a hard wind blew toward the west, the fire began. Cormac set it off in the empty upstairs rooms of a tavern called the Fighting Cocks, down by the waterfront off Whitehall. The barroom was full of Hessians, singing in German, and Cormac left through a window. He moved languidly through the streets toward the East River, then cut north and back west toward the Common. When he turned, the sky was red. Bells replaced the tinkling of clavichords. Soldiers ran in a dozen directions and then backed away from the roaring flames. Water once more dribbled from hoses as small geysers arose from punctures. The buckets were like sieves. Horses whinnied and bucked and pounded at stable doors. There were screams and lamentations.

Cormac and the patrol moved separately north. Then, at the bottom of the Common, he stood very still and saw flames rising in the immense steeple of Trinity Church. The tallest building in New York. The symbol of English domination. The flames burned on the surface. They burned inside the church. The tongues of the fire were pointed toward New Jersey, blowing hard, and were jumping roof to roof all the way to Barclay Street, somehow missing St. Paul's Chapel. But he could not stop himself from gazing at Trinity. That was not one of their targets. And now the flames were eating at it. The steeple wobbled, then gave off a noise like an immense complaint and fell straight down in a giant roar. The burning pinnacle of the steeple lay on its side in the graveyard, like a corpse. Screams of awe filled the air. He remembered the way, on an afternoon thirty-five years earlier, Diamond had been burned on the edge of this Common, and the way John Hughson's corpse had turned black and Sandy's turned white, and the way the Rev. Clifford had grasped at his crotch in a delirium of death.

It was time to go. He hurried to the hill above the Collect, where the Africans waited. The sky to the south was as bright now as at noon, and they could see tongues of flame rising from many houses below Wall Street.

"Let them sleep in snow," Bantu said.

When the long night was over, 407 houses had been reduced to smoking rubble. Now it was the Tories' turn to trudge north to their estates or to board ships for England. And the redcoats came down upon the Americans with all of their fury. Every young man was a suspect. Men with histories in the Sons of Liberty were arrested and questioned and executed by firing squads. Others were crammed into the Bridewell prison, built upon the grass of the Common. Six men were hanged from the ancient gibbets on the hill above the Collect. Others were rounded up and press-ganged into dousing water on the smoldering rubble of the 407 ruined houses. All events were canceled at the John Street Theater. There were no more tinkling dinner parties. Soldiers, hard Tories, and Americans settled in for a long occupation.

Cormac and the black patrol found shelter in the swamp beyond the Collect, in an old cabin shrouded by tangled vines and dense thickets. Each day, one of them would slip into the town, to find food, to pick up news and gather information about future targets. They learned that the English were making concessions to the Africans now. They didn't call them concessions. They called them pledges. But the message was simple: If the Africans swore loyalty to the Crown, if they defended their masters, they would be freed at the end of the war.

"Do you believe them?" Cormac asked Bantu one cold night in the swamp.

"No."

"Why not?"

"You take freedom. Nobody give it to you."

Silver said: "But some Africa people listen. They want to believe. You tell them, this is a trick. They say nothing. But they thinkin' 'bout it, all sure."

"They think Washington is finish," Carlito said. "They think it be over soon, so they listen, they listen."

"What do you think?"

"I think we keep fighting," Bantu said.

On another early morning, after a night spent cutting ditches through a main road to harass coach traffic, Cormac asked them what they would do when they were free.

"Farm," said Aaron. "With my woman, my children. Farm up in the island. Grow potato and yam. Have chickens to sell. Milk . . . Send my boys to school. And girls too, ef I have girls."

"Open a shop down by Wall Street," said Silver. "Make all kinds of leather stuff, belts and shoes and cases, all leather things. Live upstairs. Drink rum on Saturday night. Eat turkey on Sunday."

Carlito said nothing. He shrugged as if the idea were too far in the remote future.

"Go home," Bantu said. "Go find my family. See who lives, who died."

He told about how he'd been captured with a net when he was fifteen by a search party from another tribe, how he was turned over to Arabs and herded in shackles to a fort on the coast, how English traders came to change cowrie shells and rum and guns for the Africans penned in the fort.

"I don't want to kill people," he said. "Just find my sisters, my boy brother, and say prayers for my father, and then bring them here, all the people that's alive."

None of them wanted to return forever to Africa. They didn't want to live in a land where human beings were trapped like animals and then sold to others. Africa was a bitter memory. They wanted to live out their lives in America.

"This, my country," Bantu said, digging hands into the loamy earth that made the floor of the shack. "This."

One night, Cormac asked the men to vote for their leader. He had recruited them, but that didn't make him their leader for all the days of their lives. In this army, this revolutionary army, they should choose. After all, they called themselves the black patrol and Cormac was white. The blacks should make the choice. They seemed surprised at this suggestion from Cormac, and asked for time to discuss it. He felt certain they would choose Bantu. Instead, after huddling together outside the shack for about ten minutes, they returned to face Cormac.

"We all the leader," Silver said. "You die, Bantu the leader. Bantu die, Aaron the leader. Aaron die, Carlito the leader. Carlito die —"

"Then we fucked," Bantu said, and laughed. "Then some god the leader."

They all laughed then and hugged one another. But Bantu slowly grew somber.

"We better die together," he said.

For weeks, scavengers worked the mounds of ruined houses. Redcoats did the work for the first few weeks, finding pewter and scorched paintings and clothes for men and women and saddles and bottles of wine in cellars. All were taken to Fort George, where they could be awarded to friends, or passed through merchants to the empty slavers that were still heading for Africa. The later scavengers were Americans, including some loyal to the Crown, searching for remnants of their lives, or secret rebels looking for hunks of old iron, gnarled candelabra, anything that could be melted down to make ammunition. Sometimes at night, as scavengers worked the cold piles, they could hear the uilleann pipes, mournful and defiant.

The English authorities did not clear the site of the most destructive fire in the history of their colonies. They left the steeple of Trinity lying on its side. They did not replace the ruined houses. They left the rubble as a kind of monument. One that said, Here is what your Revolution brings you: destruction and rubble. Choose sides now.

The rich were gone, but the poor now gathered on the fringes of the ruined streets in tents made of old sailcloth, the place soon named Canvastown. They killed off the pigs and ate them. They stole apples and potatoes from abandoned farms and kept pots simmering on fires through the cold nights. On his forays into town, sometimes dressed as a peddler, sometimes hobbled by age, Cormac saw that the town was filling with predators. Sharpers from London bargained for goods that could be sold in Jamaica or Charleston or even back in England. Slavers offered good prices for Swedish ingots, chintz, Italian glass, brass kettles, knives and axes and guns. There was no money in Africa, other than cowrie shells; things were the currency of slavery. Men and women from Canvastown stole to supply the market, while the better-off families, their fortunes shrinking, sold off their own small treasures to the slavers, who could turn things into purchased humans.

The gray weather added to the sullen sense of corruption. Snow fell, blanketing the town, then melted, turned black, then fell again. The tents of Canvastown sagged under the weight of snow, and sometimes collapsed, and people were found frozen on the streets. Lone chimneys rose toward Heaven from the white mounds of the ruined town like the masts of ghost ships.

They received news in whispered conversations, in messages delivered by old men and Africans and a few women. Washington was losing every battle, off in New Jersey and in Pennsylvania, but he was not defeated. As long as he remained alive, the Revolution lived. The English were working hard to control Manhattan, which was the headquarters of the entire enterprise. They were mapping the island. In the spring, when the frost went out of the trees, they would begin clearing the island of its ambush lanes. The Americans continued refining their own operations. They had a system of couriers now, taking information to Washington's small and battered army. They exercised their own rough justice against informers. A dirk in the heart. A rope tied around a neck.

The black patrol destroyed seventeen bridges. It fired two more warehouses. One night, Bantu and Aaron waited patiently in the darkness on South Street and killed a London slave merchant who was to leave at dawn for Newport. Bantu placed a cowrie shell in the dead man's mouth.

They moved when instinct told them to move. One night, while Cormac and Bantu, Aaron and Silver packed their things for a shift to a new place, the English arrived, passing through the tangled paths of the swamp as if they had a map. A soldier from Leeds cut Carlito's throat where he stood watch. Then an officer bellowed at the shack.

"Hallo, in there," he said. "We know you're there, and it's best you surrender."

Bantu snuffed the candle with his fingers. They listened tensely to the officer's voice.

"You're to walk out with your hands above your heads. You are to lie facedown on the ground. Any sign of a weapon will be a sign of hostility, and you'll be killed."

Cormac and Bantu glanced at each other, Aaron and Silver inhaled and then sighed.

Then they rushed out the door, firing guns, Cormac wielding the sword. The redcoats were surprised. Two fell dead. Then another, and the black patrol drove a wedge into their line. For a long moment, men screamed and cursed and shouted. Jesus Christ, Cormac thought, there must be a hundred of them. He slashed and swung and pivoted and slashed again. Men cried in pain.

He saw Bantu's chest explode. He saw the front of Aaron's face vanish. He turned for Silver, and then his own head exploded in high white pain. His face fell into the wet earth. He could hear the howl of a wolf. Then he was gone.

68.

He woke up in a windowless cell in the Bridewell prison. Packed tightly with other men, who told him that almost eight hundred of them were now jailed on three floors. His head was splitting with pain, the back of his skull soft to his touch. The sword, he thought. They have my father's sword. He wanted to cry for its loss but didn't. He told himself: You will live through this. He told himself: Someday you will find the sword again. Now, he told himself, you must live.

He gazed around at faces filthy and faces haggard, then sat very still with his back against the rough wall. Oh, Bantu, you American warrior. Oh, Silver. Oh, Aaron. I will see you in the Otherworld. Carlito: If you have escaped, I will see you in New York.

He began to examine his cage, taught by some of the others. The Bridewell stood beside the four-story poorhouse, which was flanked on its other side by the old town jail. All windows were barred but were open to the cold. Down below street level was a basement used as a dungeon for torture or executions. But men died on all the other floors of the Bridewell, stinking of shit and sickness, hunger and fever and British corruption. Smallpox took many of them, and cholera too (for nobody there was allowed to wash), and many starved. The rations were meager, bits of gristly pork, pieces of biscuit, some rice, peas, butter, a day's normal food stretched over three, and some days no food at all. There were no blacks in this jail; they were being kept in a place called the Old Sugar Factory. But Cormac saw men laid here upon the floor at night, crushed against one another, trying to keep warm; and in the morning they counted the corpses, always one, but sometimes two or three, which were hauled away and dumped in the Negroes Burial Ground, four or five to a single grave, a burial intended to be an insult. And Cormac thought: Mr. Partridge, in his own sad grave, has plenty of republican company now.

Cormac was always hungry, always mildly sick, but while others died, he lived on. Month after punishing month. And thought himself lucky. At least they had not moved him beyond Manhattan to the prison ships in Wallabout Bay, for he would surely have died before being slammed in the fetid holds. I must stay here, he thought, stay in this Manhattan, this piece of the world defined for me by Kongo when he passed me the gift. Manhattan is my jail.

And in the jail, time was suspended. There were no calendars, no newspapers, as days turned into weeks and then into months. Men scratched lines into the walls with nails, trying to keep count, but lost the sums to fever and injury. They asked new arrivals what month it was, what day, what year.

The Bridewell was soon called by the prisoners the Bribewell. Every guard was corrupt. Everything forbidden was available for a price, except weapons. The guards looked the other way when relatives smuggled food, tobacco, or cash to prisoners. They knew the contraband was the currency of the prison, which was to say it helped them to earn a living. But Cormac had no relatives. And all his friends were dead.

On the western side of Broadway, trailing away to the Hudson, there were rows of shabby two-story houses, and from a few high windows of the Bridewell, the prisoners could see the Holy Ground, where the whores worked at their bitter trade. One chubby woman would emerge at dusk and fondle her naked breasts and place a hand between her chubby thighs while dying men masturbated in their cells; it was a whore's version of charity. Or of a sweet American solidarity. Cormac too longed for a woman, and then erased that possibility with images of the dead and the dying. Of Bantu caressing a cub. Of Aaron longing for a home.

The whores' numbers were swollen by the arrival of two thousand Liverpool women sent to provide comfort to the British soldiery. They were housed in the older homes of Tories who had fled. But Cormac knew, from watching, from words spoken by agents before his capture, from other prisoners, that the whores were, in fact, neutral. They serviced English soldiers and secret American patriots, gathering money for themselves and intelligence for both sides. Whores, Cormac knew, were always citizens of the country of money. But even in the Bridewell, with his skin scabbed by sores, his bones protruding from his eroded flesh, his hair crawling with lice, he soon discovered that he could not escape his past.

One morning a new prisoner passed him a sheet from a smuggled newspaper, and Cormac began to read every line. If there was a report about the war, it must have been on another page. On this page, there were items about shipping, and a disease without a name that was infecting North African ports, and then some social notes. Down at the bottom of the social notes, a name caught his eyes.

LADY WARREN SAILS

It said:

Lady Warren of Carrickfergus has sailed for Charleston on the Intrepid. *She was in New York visiting her son, who is serving with the Crown forces. From Charleston, she will return to her estate in Ireland.*

Lady Warren of Carrickfergus.

Bridget Riley.

Visiting her son.

It never ends, Cormac thought.

It never fecking ends.

The commander of the Bridewell was a major named William Cunningham. The older prisoners included a victualer named Anderson, who knew how Cunningham worked.

"He pockets half the money allowed for food and sends it home by courier," Anderson said. "He doesn't give a fiddler's feck if we starve to death on half rations, and they are starvin' right now on them ships in the Wallabout. He wants the war to last forever, so he can bank enough to join the gentry."

Cunningham didn't come often to see the victims of his corruption. But eight months into Cormac's stay in the Bridewell, he looked up to see Cunningham's new second-in-command. He was walking beyond the bars down a safe corridor beside Cunningham.

The son of the Earl of Warren and Bridget Riley. His hair was lighter, with highlights of red, but otherwise he could have been a twin of the earl in that year when he stepped from the black coach to look upon the broken body of Rebecca Carson lying in the mud.

69.

They called him Tony Warren. He worked under Cunningham, but in all the small ways, Cunningham deferred to his noble blood. Together, they helped men die. The prisoners died of typhus. Died of floggings. Died of hunger. Died of tuberculosis. Died of cholera. Died because William Cunningham, the provost marshal, stole half the ration money while Tony Warren shrugged and cocked an eyebrow and chuckled.

All the prisoners knew the system and how it worked. They heard from new arrivals how Cunningham's men starved and flogged and tortured the prisoners on the ships across the river on the Brooklyn side, over in Wallabout Bay. Eleven thousand of them were packed in those ships that never sailed. The soldiers tossed the bodies into the tides or shoved them into the mudflats, where the shrouds soon rotted and American bones could be seen at low tide. His men tortured the Africans who paid for their revolt in the Old Sugar Factory. In the Bridewell, Cunningham executed those he thought were Obnoxious Persons and those who were Cormac's old comrades in the Sons of Liberty, their activities revealed by men who took the King's shilling. A man could die for refusing to bow or defer to some red-coated dandy. A man could die for reading Thomas Paine or the secret newspapers of the Revolution. Trials were not necessary. Suspicion was enough. The killing took place at night, against the walls of the army barracks, all doors ordered shut in the neighboring houses of the Holy Ground, all windows sealed, all lights extinguished, and the prisoners were brought, blindfolded and gagged, and walked up the steps of the scaffold. The rope was attached. And then they were dropped into permanent darkness.

Cormac vowed to remember the names of the dead: Guinness and Sterling, Hewitt and Roberts, Arundel and Dubois, Frankie Hannigan and Sammy Payne. Good men and true, he thought, even with (or because of) the flesh hanging loose and gray on their brave bones, wrapped in flea-ridden blankets, and to the end refusing everything: refusing collaboration, refusing deferential manners, refusing to bow to any king. On the night of the Fourth of July in 1780, the prisoners roared defiance in the Bridewell, and sang the liberty songs, and cursed the King. Cunningham came himself that night, with Tony Warren behind him, their faces dark with fury, their leather boots clacking on the stone floors. They chose the men they wanted, Guinness and Sterling, Hewitt and Roberts, Arundel and Dubois among them, and then called on the services of Bloodstone, the army blacksmith. He was carrying a twenty-pound hammer. They laid each man flat upon the floor for all to see and then Bloodstone smashed their knees and elbows. They screamed and screamed and screamed.

"Fecking rabble," Warren said, as he followed Cunningham out of the row of cells.

And as he whirled, his coat opened, and Cormac saw that he was wearing the sword. Saw the spirals etched in steel. Thinking: *My father's sword.* Telling himself: I must get out of the Bridewell. I must find Tony Warren on the streets of New York. I must get to the end of the line. I must return my father's sword to the blood of his blood.

Whores were the agents of salvation.

One of them was named Kitty Nevins: red-haired, full-breasted, with the guts (Cormac thought) of nine burglars. She devised the code and smuggled it into the prison and then chalked the first coded messages on slate that they could read from the cell windows. She it was, with two of her sisters in the life, who seduced the guards with perfumed flesh and smuggled in the guns. Who had horses waiting. Who waited in the hammering midnight rain while the prisoners used keys wrenched from drained guards and then smashed and threatened their way out, unlocking as many cells as possible. Suddenly more than twenty of the prisoners were running free, mad and desperate, filthy as sewers, manacled and bony. Cormac was with them, running into Broadway, a pistol in his waistband, a musket in a manacled hand. Hobbled, weak, fierce with life. In the break for the street, the shooting started. Cormac shot two redcoats, one with the pistol, the second with the musket. He dropped the musket, jammed the pistol in his waistband, lunged for one horse-drawn carriage, and fell short into mud, and watched the carriage gallop toward the North River. Heard shouts. Curses. More gunfire. And ran north through the black rain.

Then saw torches ahead. Veered left. More torches.

And then from the ebony darkness he heard the whinny of a horse. Familiar. A song. And here he came, black as the night, there when Cormac needed him.

Thunder.

They galloped together into the blind watches of the night. Moved like ghosts through blank spaces, across creeks and streams, heading to what was left of the Manhattan wild. Cormac gripping Thunder's mane with manacled hands. As the rain pounded down, making a great drumming, ceaseless sound on the trees, obliterating all voices and the sound of gunfire and even the pounding of Cormac's heart.

Until Thunder slowed, then stopped, then shook, as if telling Cormac to slide off here. He did. And could see a low, dark house, and some shacks beyond, and hear the lowing of cattle and the shuddering of other horses. Thunder galloped into the darkness. Cormac felt boneless from fatigue and could see nothing clearly through the curtains of rain. He bent forward, gripped his knees, breathing deeply and freely, gulping air as if it were food, then stood up and lifted his face to the cleansing rain. He whispered, in Irish: "Wash away the filth, please." He whispered, in English: "Heal the rawness where the manacles bit my flesh." He begged, in French: "Wash away typhus and cholera and fleas. Please." He asked in Yoruba: "Save me."

Then an arm gripped his neck, and he felt the tip of a knife against his back. "Who *are* you?" a deep voice growled.

Cormac said his true name. It was too late and too dark for deception.

The arm relaxed, and he was spun around. And there, soaked and grizzled, white hairs driving like tacks from inside his black cheeks, was Quaco.

"God damn," he said, "if it ain't you for true, Mister Cormac."

Quaco saved him. He snapped the manacles with wire cutters, and his wife, now white-haired, fed Cormac lentil soup and meat and bread. He handed Cormac a blanket and fresh clothes and a bowl of warm water, and then shredded the prison clothes and fed them, piece by piece, into the fire. Roger, the oldest son, then opened a trapdoor leading by ladder to a room chopped out of stone beneath the house. Actually two rooms. The first room was loaded with coal and firewood. The second room was behind a door covered with thin layers of stone. A secret room with a bed, several muskets, trunks, a sacred African drum, and jugs of water. Refuge.

On the first night Cormac slept for many hours. He woke to the sound of heavy boots on the floor. Heard indistinct British voices. The trapdoor opened, and a grunting man came down the ladder and was very still. Cormac held his breath. The man saw only coal and firewood and then climbed the ladder and left as Cormac exhaled. He did not come upstairs until it was dark.

"You not the first Irisher been down there," Quaco said, laughing. "Passed a few of you along, sure enough."

Quaco's four sons moved in and out, curious about this latest white man, and wary too. They lived in an area of free blacks, with Quaco carrying faked papers dating his own freedom to 1738, before the revolt. He and Cormac talked about the night when Cormac helped Quaco to escape with his wife, telling the story more for the sons than for each other. They talked into the night about those who were burned and hanged and mutilated, and those who disappeared and what might have happened to all the inquisitors and the mysterious fate of poor Mary Burton. They laughed. They mourned. One night, in the second week, Quaco looked at Cormac in an inquisitive way.

"You ain't aged but a day," he said.

"I don't feel the way I look."

"I ain't even goneta ask how come."

"Good."

"But you was close to Kongo."

"Yes."

"The babalawo."

"Very close."

Quaco didn't go beyond this, and Cormac just stared at the fire. Then they talked about the Revolution, and the future.

"I keep dreamin' of home," Quaco said on another night. "I keep dreamin' of the village where I was a boy. I keep wantin' to go home."

"Maybe you can."

"Yeah. Maybe."

But he didn't seem to believe it. And he had little faith in the Revolution.

"You notice somethin'?" he asked one night. "The English, they promisin' freedom to their slaves, *after* everything's finished. But the Americans? They ain't promisin' nothin'."

Cormac said to himself, You're right, Quaco. You're right.

When the snows melted, Cormac found work as a blacksmith with a man named Tingle, whose love of metals had driven him into the madness of alchemy. His forge in a dark forest glen was empty when Cormac arrived, calling himself Alfred Defoe and faking a Liverpool accent. Tingle was locked in a windowless shack trying to turn lead into gold and muttering about the philosopher's stone. He said very little while Cormac built a new fire in the forge and took over the blacksmithing and moved from Quaco's cellar to a heatless room above the barn. Each week, more British soldiers moved north carrying axes and saws to attack the forests. On a few summer days, Cormac serviced Tingle's gaunt, forlorn, and childless wife, Juliet.

"Thank you," she would say, "and you know that I would not do this if my husband wasn't mad."

Tingle didn't seem to know that his wife offered herself to Cormac in the woods while he was chanting cabalistic numbers in his locked shack. But if he did know, he didn't care. Their couplings were always in late afternoon, after the horses were shod or the scythes repaired. At night, Cormac was always moving, his face sometimes stained black with berry juice, visiting the scattered Africans. He made speeches in Yoruba and English, trying to persuade the Africans and their American children that their best hope for freedom lay with the Revolution. This was not easy. The Africans heard the news too, and it seemed almost certain that the military power of the professional British Army would defeat the amateurs commanded by Washington.

"If the British wanted to free you, they would do it right now," Cormac would say. "They were the people who enslaved you. How can you trust the word of slavemasters?"

About a dozen Africans and their children believed Cormac. Most important was Quaco's son Roger, now almost thirty years old, intelligent, literate, careful. He put together a new version of the black patrol and made certain that Cormac was a member, but not the leader. Together, they set fires. They stole ammunition. They released rats into food warehouses.

At the same time, disguised as a lame peddler or a hunched old man and even once as an Indian, Cormac tracked the movements of young Tony Warren. The son of the earl moved from barracks to confiscated house and back to the barracks, to the reopened John Street Theater to the whorehouses of the Holy Ground. He had the sword. Cormac wanted it back.

70.

In his pursuit of Tony Warren, Cormac moved alone. This was a private affair, after all, not the business of the Revolution. So he walked through the dark, sour, occupied city like a ghost. The gaunt skeletons of the lower town, with their cold chimneys and formless mounds, looked at midnight like a zone in the Christian purgatory: black, glistening, a place where lost men moved with the rats. On moon-bright nights, all was as clear as a drawing. Cormac seldom went out without clouds to smother the moon.

Then, almost a year after his escape from the Bridewell, he picked up the trail. Warren now lived in a house on Beaver Street. A house taken from Americans and shared with three other officers. But the Englishman was never alone there, and a redcoat stood on permanent guard at the door. There were rumors (brought to Cormac by Roger and Quaco, and whispered by another in a grog shop) that young Warren was building a new house on his father's land, high in the Bloomingdale. That he had a young family in England. That he planned to settle in New York, once the rebels were destroyed. All rumors. All noted. Cormac knew he could not go to the Bloomingdale in hopes of somehow repeating what he and Kongo had done in 1741. There were soldiers all over the area now, making a show of their presence so that Washington would not be tempted to make a sudden assault on Manhattan, thinking he could cut it in half. If the soldiers felt safe in the denuded upper island, so, surely, did Tony Warren.

During his walks through the lower town, Cormac saw Tony Warren four times, but he was never alone. The city remained ruled by martial law, but it was more relaxed now, as social life returned. Cormac could even hear the music of string quartets drifting from a few of the mansions. The English had created routine to make their duty both safe and pleasant, and a guard on the doorsteps of officers' quarters was part of that routine.

Then, one rain-drowned night, easing out of Canvastown into Cortlandt Street, Cormac started toward Broadway. Across the street, Warren stepped out of a bordello. He was alone. He began walking toward his billet on Beaver Street, ignoring the rain, taking small, precise steps, like a man who had sipped too much wine. Cormac moved past him, then turned and placed himself in front of the man. Warren was suddenly tense. He squinted at Cormac and drew his sword. *The* sword.

"Clear the way," he said in a slurry voice.

"Sorry," Cormac said. "I can't do that."

"I'm ordering you to do that."

"I respectfully decline the order, Mister Warren."

Warren's eyes widened.

"What is this? Who are you and what do you want?"

"I want that sword," Cormac said. "It belonged to my father."

Warren squinted, his face puzzled, and raised the sword. Cormac took a dirk from his belt.

"This is my sword," Warren said. "I paid for it. I own it. And if you don't leave, you'll taste it quick."

He smiled then in a cold way and stepped forward.

"I want that sword," Cormac said.

Warren took another step, put his weight on his left foot, and swung. Cormac stepped inside the arc and deflected the sword with the dirk. Warren smiled, shifted to another angle, grunted, and swung the sword in a wider arc. Cormac backed away almost daintily. A third swing knocked the dirk from Cormac's hand. Then Warren charged, lifted the sword to finish the fight, and Cormac stepped inside the arc of his swing, grabbed Warren's right arm, and spun him, slamming him against a wall. Before Warren could again cock the sword, Cormac grabbed his sword hand in both of his own and drove his thumbs into the cleft between his first and second knuckles. Drove them with splitting force. Until Warren made a whimpering sound, dropped the sword.

"You'll be hanged for this," Warren said.

"Perhaps."

Cormac picked up the dirk, then started for the sword. Warren jerked a pistol from inside his coat. Cormac didn't wait. He rushed Warren, pushed the gun hand aside, and drove the knife into his chest.

Warren's eyes widened. His lips moved, but no words emerged. The rain pelted him. Then an arm jerked and a leg moved and he fell to his side on the wet street with the knife handle jutting from his heart.

Cormac picked up the sword and walked quickly into the rainy wilderness of burned houses.

Something went out of Cormac after he killed Tony Warren and recovered the sword. He could feel it in his bones, and in the odd lack of feeling about killing another man, another Warren. It was something he was bound to do, by the terms of an old contract. And Tony Warren was a mean man. The earl without the smile or the juggling. But he felt no satisfaction. The earl sometimes appeared in his dreams, floating in black rivers, but there was no trace of his son. It was as if he had never existed. Or that the killing on Beaver Street had been an affair between two strangers.

There was, of course, no notice of the death in the newspapers; the censors would not permit such dreadful news. So Cormac didn't know where Tony Warren had been buried, and whether his mother would come to visit his grave. He had killed him. That was that. Now he'd go back to the war. Except that in New York, there was no war. The war was elsewhere. Upstate. In Pennsylvania and New Jersey and in the South. Cormac continued gathering bits and pieces of intelligence and passing them to couriers. He continued walking the streets of the sullen town, looking for vulnerabilities, for targets. He worked with the Africans on small acts of sabotage and carried his sword with him, strapped again across his back. But after Tony Warren, he never killed another British soldier.

"You lost something, Cormac," said Quaco one evening.

"I did," said Cormac. "And I don't know what it is."

The news came about Yorktown and the end of the war, and Cormac celebrated with Quaco and his wife and three of their children. There was little talk of the future. "We see what they do," Quaco said, "not what they say." The peace conference was held in Paris, lasting for months while Washington sheltered with his army up the Hudson in Windsor Forest. The war was finally settled, the treaty signed, a date set for the departure of the British armies. Cormac wandered among exuberant Americans who gathered around the Common, and greeted the few men he still knew from the Bridewell, as they were released a dozen at a time. Nobody talked about the Africans, and he saw them in small, cautious clusters, quiet in the celebrations, watching, pondering.

Now the Tories were leaving by the many thousands, boarding boats for Canada and England, carrying with them huge trunks and crates of goods and their slaves. On the ships, many of the Africans were smiling. They were going, they truly believed, to freedom.

A few Tories wept as they left the town they had come to love too well. Many turned sullen and withdrawn. Families from Canvastown began moving into the abandoned Tory houses, chopping furniture into pieces to make fires under the carved mantels. Bands of small boys threw stones and horseshit at redcoats and were smashed with rifle butts or chased down alleys. But the commander didn't respond with great force; to avoid clashes, he ordered the redcoats confined to their barracks. The rented Hessians had been gone since Yorktown. Now English officers were forced out of the houses they had taken from Americans, and Cormac watched as officers loaded wagons outside the house on Beaver Street where Tony Warren had lived his last days. He felt no sense of victory.

In late summer, many Americans who had supported the Revolution began to return, to see what was left of their lives. They filled the taverns. They sampled the Shakespeare at the John Street Theater. They combed the flea markets in search of their stolen furniture, the portraits of their Dutch and English ancestors, engravings made of their now-ruined houses. Most of their businesses had been destroyed by fire, but they began to sketch out plans for what would rise from the ashes. They would drain the swamps and level the hills. They would build stone buildings. They would dig deep wells for water. Cormac asked some of them what they wanted in a constitution. They had clear ideas about individual liberties. With one major exception. Slavery would continue. "It must," one of them said, "or we'll have no country."

They began searching for their own slaves, forming small posses of armed men to gather them as if they were stray horses. Many Africans fled into what was left of the woods above the town. Cormac and Quaco assembled a dozen armed Africans, divided into groups of four, all wearing the badges of the Revolution. They followed the slave-gathering posses, placed themselves between the Americans and their African quarries, and liberated them at gunpoint. But the Americans were relentless. They placed bounties on their former slaves, posted their names on the town's walls. In one encounter, two of the bounty hunters were killed by Quaco's sons. One enraged American pursued a slave in a longboat to one of the ships anchored in the East River. Cormac watched from the shore as the blacks rowed hard in a longboat of their own, came alongside the American boat, fought briefly, and then tipped the Americans into the river.

On many nights, Cormac went sleepless with rage.

71.

On Evacuation Day, the victorious army of George Washington came into New York through McGowan's Pass. They moved down the east side of the island, and Cormac, Quaco, and the others joined the ragged troops near the grave of Big Michael in Kip's Bay. At the head of the long line of soldiers, Washington sat high on a pale gray horse, shoulders squared, head held as erect as a Roman statue, his uniform pressed and clean and sparkling. Other officers trailed behind him on horseback and his soldiers came on foot. Their uniforms were tattered and patched, their shoes held together with rope. Some of the men limped along, swinging on crude crutches. Some wore bandages across foreheads. Some were hunched and weary. All carried rifles. There was a small band of musicians, but no music. Hundreds of people came out to see them, most of them women and children, some of them cheering, many just peering at this rabble in arms, as a British general had called them. The children tagged along with the soldiers. The grown women stared with arms folded across chests, as if wondering what would happen on the morrow.

Cormac said good-bye to Quaco and slowly moved toward the head of the long column as it entered the Bowery. Then they all stopped. Washington dismounted, ran a fond hand on his horse's brow, and walked into the Bull's Head Tavern at Bayard and Pump. Here they would wait until the last English soldier had boarded the last English ship and moved out toward the Narrows. The general turned to his army and waved. He did not smile. The soldiers cheered him, and cheered themselves too. A cool November wind blew from the east.

"General Washington!" Cormac shouted from the crowd at the foot of the tavern's wooden deck.

The general turned, smiled slightly, showing his caried yellow teeth. His nose was puffier, his hair whiter. He looked straight at Cormac.

"I'm the man who saved your life at Kip's Bay!"

Washington squinted. Two guards flanked him, bayonets at the ready. The general seemed to be searching his memory for one dangerous night out of two thousand. Then he nodded.

"Of course. . . . Do come in."

He waited for Cormac to join him and then led the way into the crowded tavern. Everybody hushed. Washington was taken to a small table against the far wall. The air smelled of beer and sweat. They sat down while attendants created a small human fence around them. His officers remained standing against the wall to his right.

"I'm glad you're alive," Washington said.

"And I'm glad to see you too, sir."

A fat man brought a pitcher of water and two glasses. Washington poured. The exhaustion seeped from him like fog.

"You grabbed the bridle of my horse," he said.

"I did. Cormac O'Connor is my name."

"You slapped the haunch and sent me flying."

"That actually was done by a man named Bantu, one of the Africans."

"A brazen lot," Washington said, an amused smile on his mouth. "But you have my thanks."

"We needed you alive, General."

"Not everyone agreed with you — including some of my officers."

"The men knew," Cormac said. "Including my fellow soldiers."

Washington sipped the cold water. "You were commanding coloreds, if my memory serves me."

"I served with five African soldiers, sir. We were irregulars. There was no commander."

Washington's nostrils widened and twitched, the old hunter detecting hostility.

"And where are those soldiers now, Mister O'Connor?"

"Dead, sir."

Cormac quickly told him about the deaths of Big Michael and Bantu, of Aaron, Silver, and Carlito. He mentioned the great fire, and the Bridewell, and the escape, and the long campaign within the city.

"God . . ."

"But those soldiers had children, sir, three of them had children. They had wives. They talked sometimes about the future. About going to free schools. About working their own farms as free men, about opening shops . . ."

Washington drummed the fingers of his right hand on the tabletop. His mouth tightened.

"Yes?" he said, as if knowing what was coming.

"I hope, sir, that you will do all in your power to honor the promises made by our Revolution." Hating the self-righteousness of his own words. "I told my men of those promises. I read them the Declaration of Independence, one that you read to us here in 1776." Appealing now to Washington's vanity. "They fought for those words, for 'inalienable rights,' for 'all men are created equal . . .' And right now, General, Americans are roaming New York, chasing their former slaves as if they were dogs gone astray. . . ."

Washington sighed.

"All of that will be debated, I assure you," he said. "But not in a tavern."

He took a longer sip of the water. Cormac leaned forward, his anger rising.

"Debate will not be enough, sir," Cormac said. "There can be only one decision. Slavery must end. Or all those men will have died for a lie."

Washington was now annoyed. He was waiting for a ceremony of triumph, waiting to mount his horse and ride majestically into New York. He was waiting for the British flags to be lowered and the American flags raised. He was waiting for a moment of immortality.

"For now, all of that is in the future, Mister O'Connor."

"This *is* the future, General Washington."

The general stood up, his chair scraping on flagstones. He offered a hand to be shaken. Cormac gripped his large hand but didn't shake it.

"If you don't give the slaves their freedom," he said, "this country will die in its crib."

"Thank you," Washington said in an icy way, withdrawing his hand and motioning with his head to his officers. "I have much to do now."

Washington turned his back and moved to his waiting men. The guards stepped between him and Cormac. He had been dismissed. Cormac turned and walked through the crowded tavern into the American morning, hoping he'd live long enough to heal his aching heart.

He wandered alone to South Street to watch the last British ship leave. There were American flags waving now on some buildings, looking tentative and modest. Many Americans were moving toward the river and the Battery, some joking and laughing, others solemn. There were no Africans among them.

Around noon, they saw the ship easing from its pier above Wall Street, its decks crowded, its flags and pennants waving as if in triumph. Cormac could not read the name of the ship as it floated slowly downriver and he felt nothing. The crowd cheered and blew whistles and small horns, and then grew quiet and started moving toward Broadway to wait for the procession of Washington.

Six

The Time of the Countess

What is the worst of woes that wait on age?
What stamps the wrinkle deeper on the brow?
To view each loved one blotted from life's page,
And be alone on earth as I am now.

— Lord Byron, "Childe Harold's Pilgrimage," 1812

72.

Cormac eased to his left outside the doorway of the basement room at 7 Cedar Street, trying for a better view of the slaughtered woman on the bed. A tall mustached policeman barred his way. Floorboards creaked above his head, the heavy tread of a detective named Ford, who was speaking to the owner of the bordello. Cormac put a hand on the stone wall beside the door, trying to steady himself. The wall was scummy with a decade's worth of damp. He felt as if some dark yellow fluid were beginning to drip through his veins.

He made notes, using pencil on a small cut pad, forcing himself to concentrate on what lay before him. About twenty-five, perhaps younger. Dark brown hair, thickened by blood. Rouged cheeks beneath the drying blood. A red dent above the brow. Her throat cut from the left ear to the right clavicle bone. Her tongue jutting from her mouth. One ear severed. Puncture wounds in her small left breast.

"Do you have a name yet, officer?" Cormac said.

"Dubious," the policeman said.

"That's her name?"

"Yeah. Dubious Jones. No wonder he killed her."

He laughed a cop's dark laugh.

"Who's the he?" Cormac said. "The one who killed her."

"Fucked if I know," the cop said.

Cormac kept making notes. A single thick candle burned down to a saucer, the wax glazing the table. A wick like a thin stump of charcoal. Her left leg bent at the edge of the bed, one bare foot on the greasy stone floor. A laced black boot on the other foot, caked mud on the heel. Dark blood soaking the bed beneath her buttocks. The dress jerked up. Cut there too.

A rat with a leathery tail appeared under the bed, licking the drying blood.

Cormac turned away, the yellow fluid thickening in his veins. He heard footsteps coming down the stairs behind him. Inspector Ford. And Jennings from the *Journal-Advertiser,* notebook in hand.

"What's it we've got here?" Jennings said.

"What's it look like we've got here?" said Inspector Ford. His reddish mustaches looked fierce, his nostrils flared. "We've got a fucking murder."

"Can I quote you on that?" Jennings said, smiling. He flashed his rabbity front teeth, touched the brim of his bowler hat. Thin, young, a British edge to his accent. "Jesus," he said, "it smells like a bear's ass down here."

"It would smell like that if you filled it with flowers," Cormac said.

"Ah, an aesthetic observation from the aging veteran of the *Evening Post,*" Jennings said.

"Why don't you interview the rat under the bed, Jennings?" Cormac said. "He must've been an eyewitness."

"Totally unreliable."

"Perfect for you," Cormac said.

"Will you two goddamned shite-for-brains shut up, please?" Inspector Ford said. "I'm trying to work."

Cormac turned, the bile rising, the yellow fluid surging, and hurried up the stairs. He walked through the barroom, with its watercolors of the Hudson and its worried owner, and made it to Cedar Street. He held on to a tree and then vomited into the gutter.

A fine way to spend a birthday, he thought, walking toward the *Evening Post* on Pine Street. A fine way to celebrate another ninth of September. Puking my guts out on Cedar Street. Happy birthday, in the year of the Lord 1834. And even now, I don't feel much better. The air is the same as it was before I got sick. And it's filling me and rotting my guts.

Who killed Dubious Jones? he asked himself.

I don't care, he answered.

The morning had been cool and quiet, and as always on his birthday, he walked to the edge of the North River and dropped a white rose into the flowing waters. As always, he wished for it to sail out past the many-masted ships and through the Narrows and into the Atlantic. With any luck, it would float all the way to Ireland. He sent that rose each year to his mother. She, after all, had done all the work on the day he was born. She was the one who should be celebrated. As always at the edge of the river, he thought about the coat of many colors and the magical pots simmering on the fire and her dark hair and wonderful smile. Then he went to work.

That morning, as on most weekday mornings for the past twelve years, he left the river's edge and went to the office of the *Evening Post* on Pine Street. The morning was hot, with steamy August lingering into sweet September. The odor was beginning to rise from the streets, the buildings, the people.

He spent the morning scanning month-old newspapers from London, Edinburgh, Dublin, and Paris, freshly arrived on the Liverpool packet. On slow days, he would cobble together stories from those newspapers, including the dailies in French. In a way, such work was like painting, which he did in the rooms on Cortlandt Street that he'd rented now for sixteen years. You took various elements, you were precise about each one of them, but you made them fresh by the way you arranged them. The process kept his brain alert and alive. Or so he thought, as the months became years, and the years became decades.

He liked the work of journalism from the day he started at the old *Commercial-Advertiser* just before the century turned. He'd been urged into the craft by a printer who had employed him for night work when his business was heavy. For the first ten years Cormac used the name Ridley Rattigan, but it never mattered what name he used in his new life since no article was ever signed. The same was true at the *Evening Post*. The skills of the acting craft helped him in several ways. He could make himself gradually look older, so that when he announced his retirement from the *Commercial-Advertiser*, he could go off, paint for a year on his savings, and then apply for work at the *Evening Post* as a new young man, eager to work on a newspaper. The other skill of the actor's trade was technical: He could write in whatever voice was required. He could be a Hamiltonian conservative or a Tom Paine radical. He could be lyrical and melancholy or sarcastic and scathing. And he could supply what his editors most frequently demanded: a tone of numbing banality. Cormac worked at this craft ten hours a day, six days a week, which left him about twenty hours a week for his painting. He soon discovered that he needed both: the journalism to eat time, help it pass swiftly, to give him a sense of human proportion; the painting to slow it down, to allow him to meditate on sky and weather and the endless varieties of the human body.

He had a talent for newspaper work, delighting in the discovery of stories and then writing them in units of five hundred or a thousand words. He became quick and accurate. He enjoyed the company of other journalists, even the unspeakable Jennings. He liked the way the day's routine could always be interrupted. He'd be assembling a tedious story about the fate of the Bonapartes, a story that would be read by about seventy-five people in New York, and someone would rush in the door, breathless and urgent. As had happened this morning. "Bloody murder! Woman killed at seven Cedar Street." And out the door he'd go. There were more and more homicides in the town these past ten years, because of the opening of the Erie Canal and the flooding of the town with strangers. The newspaper had to record them. But Cormac knew that the gory details would never make it into the sanitized columns of the *Evening Post*. Such details, said his editors, Mr. Bryant and Mr. Leggett, were low and common. But still, someone had to go. Someone had to ask a policeman: Who killed Dubious Jones? Even if the answer never appeared in the newspaper.

There was one other part of newspaper writing that he came to need more than all the others, including the regularity of a paycheck.

It was about other people, not himself.

He walked to the office of the *Post* and paused at a stall on the crowded Broadway corner to buy a cup of mocha coffee and a piece of plain bread from a heavy black woman named Beatriz Machado. She was also selling corn and oysters, but he needed something plain in his trembling stomach.

"You look like you swallered a boiled ferret, Mist' Co'mac," she said.

"I feel worse than I look, Beatriz."

She leaned in and whispered, "You need somethin' special?"

"No," he said, "just a hot bath."

"Now, that's harder for to get you," Beatriz said. "Easier for to get a hot woman than a hot bath in this dirty ol' town."

In addition to corn, oysters, and mocha coffee (introduced the year before by seamen from Jamaica), Beatriz sold other things, secret things, ranging from magical roots, fried insects, and herbs to opium. These were not displayed in her stall, but she had them for her special customers. Adding and subtracting, Cormac tried to remember how long he'd known her. It was now fifty-seven years since Bantu died, and Big Michael died, and Aaron died and Silver died and Carlito died. Beatriz had been born a slave, up by Albany, but came with her parents to New York when she was seven, right after the Revolution, and had lived to see the final end of slavery in New York. That was just seven years ago. Forty-four years after the Revolution. Cormac had met her with Quaco at the African Bookshop on Lispenard Street when she was seventeen. She had just given birth to her first child. Cormac couldn't recall the name of her husband but remembered him as a grave, humorless young man who forbade her to talk with white men. He was soon gone, but Cormac didn't see Beatriz again until Quaco died at ninety-eight years old in 1816. They met at the burial ground. She was then heavier, the mother of four boys, living with her third husband.

"You some strange white man," she said, "talkin' that old Africa talk, that Y'ruba talk."

"I speak French too," he said. "And Irish. And a little English."

She laughed. "You some strange white man."

Now she handed him the bread and mocha, and as always refused his money. He sipped in silence as she poured coffee and handed sweets to other customers and dropped their money in an apron pocket. Most took their coffee in cups from Beatriz, but some brought their own cups and carried their coffee away to their offices. Cormac's coffee was sweet and the bread fresh, but his body was still in a state of runny rebellion.

Other people, he told himself. Think of other people, look at other people; you're a journalist and other people are your business. Who killed Dubious Jones? Who gave her the name?

Down Greenwich Street he could see old black men sleeping in doorways or standing on corners, waiting for work that did not come. Their masters had held them to the end and then were happy to see them go. They no longer had to care for these old men. No longer feed them and clothe them. They'd simply cast them out. Like old dogs. Now the white-haired Africans begged for alms, and Cormac wondered which of them had fought for the Revolution when they were young, which of them had believed all the shiny words from the likes of Cormac O'Connor. He could not look at them without feeling shame. He had trouble listening to them too. Like almost everybody in the city, they asked about a place to wash. They were too old for the treacheries of the summer rivers and there were no baths in the winter churches. They had no homes. After every blizzard, two or three were found dead in alleys, sometimes hugging each other for warmth that finally vanished. All had lost or outlived their children and their women. Sometimes Cormac gave them a few pence and offered his apologies in Yoruba. He could do nothing about the water.

"You can't do nothin' for them folk, Mist' Co'mac," Beatriz said, following the direction of his gaze.

"I could do more than I do," he said, finishing the coffee.

"Mist' Quaco tol' me long time ago jes' what you done, Mist' Co'mac. You done plenty."

He smiled, took a deep breath, stopped himself, exhaled.

"When are you going to pose for me, Beatriz?"

She giggled. "I'm too old to get naked for *no* man, Mist' Co'mac. Not even you. And you the man never gets old."

73.

For months now, starting in the unseasonably hot days of late April and through the scalding summer, Cormac was like the abandoned Africans on the streets: He longed for water. He did not mind the heat; some secret part of him, chilled by the arctic winter of his Irish youth, would always be cold. He did mind the filth. The aroma that came from his own filthy body. The itching dirtiness of his hair. He wanted to be hot and clean, and wanted the same for all the others in the town: the ancient Africans, the children, the women. In dreams he turned and rolled among dolphins in the ocean sea. He was scoured by salt. He was perfumed by the sun. Upon waking, he washed from the tepid water that waited for him in a bowl. The ritual did not help. There were more and more people in the city and the same small amount of water.

"It's like money, Mist' Co'mac," Beatriz said one morning. "They jus' ain't enough to go around."

At the *Evening Post,* Cormac could not convince the editors to make New York water as important a cause as independence for Greece or the compromise in Missouri over slavery. Still, Cormac made notes about the scandal of water. He wrote articles that were not published. "Everybody knows that," said one white-haired editor. "It's not news." But no water yet ran from the taps of New York. There were, in fact, very few taps, and they were in the homes of the rich, fed by water tanks erected on the roofs of their private fortresses. For all others, water was still drawn from parched wells and did not run into bathtubs or sinks or toilets; it was dipped, splashed, heated on hearths. It did not run as the rivers ran. And in the articles he wrote, and held in a desk drawer when they were not published, he made clear that the reason was corruption.

The major agent of the corruption was called the Manhattan Company. For decades after the redcoats sailed away, it had controlled all water supply in New York through a corrupt charter. Even Burr and Hamilton had been allies in the swindle, and its outline was simple. The spring of 1800, the turn of the new American century, the newspapers full of Napoleon in Europe . . . that year, the Manhattan Company was awarded two million American dollars by Albany for this water project. A generous arrangement, said the Federalist newspapers. An intelligent act of faith in the future of the fine little town at the mouth of the Hudson. Blah, they said, blah, they repeated, blah blah blah. But the deal had a nasty clause: It allowed the directors to use all unspent moneys for whatever purpose they desired. Before supplying a drop of water to citizens, they founded a bank. The aim was to make money. Or *more* money. For themselves, of course, not for the citizens. So they spent one hundred thousand dollars on water and used the rest of the two million to start their bank. The Manhattan Bank.

All of this Cormac wrote in his unpublished articles. All of it he urged upon his editors. All of it he spoke about to friends in taverns and women in bed. Water, he kept saying. Water is a problem of money. And he was laughed at.

"This is New York," one editor said. "This is the way it is. If people are so desperate for a bath, let them move to Boston. And besides, the Manhattan Bank advertises in this newspaper."

That was the key to the silence: advertising. The new El Dorado for the twenty-three newspapers struggling for profits. In the years after the charter, nobody would have cared too much about the Manhattan Bank if the Manhattan Company had only supplied the water. But they gave the growing city only a trickle. They hammered together some wooden pipes, which rotted and collapsed. They dug deeper into the existing wells. They used slaves to carry water from the slimy depths of the Collect Pond, right up to the day when the pond was filled with the dirt and gravel of the hangman's hill.

The result was the stinking city through which Cormac still moved each day. Many thousands of human beings were shitting and pissing in privies, emptying slops into the streets. Garbage was piled in the streets to be gathered later, and the mounds served as wormy meals for pigs and dogs and goats and rats. Rain turned the mounds to a vile gray paste; cold froze the mounds; snow buried them. And the animals burrowed noses and snouts and teeth into the mounds, and in summer Cormac saw flies the size of butterflies buzzing above them. While the directors of the Manhattan Bank kept counting money.

Alone in the flat on Cortlandt Street, Cormac was sometimes overwhelmed by rage. Rage against the men who had betrayed the Revolution. Rage against those who had turned all that sacrifice of the brave into empty rhetoric. Rage against the Manhattan Bank. Rage against private deals made in secret clubs. The stinking odor of the town felt moral, a sign of its spreading corruption. And it was personal too, for his own body carried a stench that he could not bring to even a casual coupling with a woman. For months at a time, he was celibate. He made drawings of women from memory, for the drawings did not send out an odor. And he brooded about the impossibility of forging a connection with any woman. They came and went in his life, temporary presences, as fleeting as the seasons. They told him their stories. They revealed their bodies to his pencils and brushes. But how could he truly promise to live with a woman for the rest of his life? That was a ghastly joke. A woman would want children, as he would himself. But how could he bring a child into this world so densely stained by human excretions, solid and moral? And besides: He had learned across the decades that he might never be a father. The way other men were fathers. He entered a woman's body as any man did; he erupted in ecstasies of the flesh, as any man did; but his seed did not flourish. He did not know if this would always be true. Perhaps it was a curse conferred on him by Bridget Riley or Mary Burton or both. An Irish form of *voudon*. They still came to him in dreams, smiling in knowing ways, stoking his fears, beckoning, retreating, betraying. The two-headed Irish hydra. Awake, he shrugged them away. But when he met a new woman, when he began to calculate the risks of love and the temptations of hope, they came to him again in the night, whispering of vengeance. Time did not erase them. Sometimes, trying to make himself believe in happiness, Cormac thought that if he did finally trust a woman's love, he might tell her the story of the gift he was granted in a northern cave. The secret of his life. The guarantee that he would love her for the rest of her life, if not the rest of his own. But he never reached that moment. He could not be certain about the way the woman would react. She could pack up, as so many humans now did in the exploding city, and abruptly vanish. Or she might laugh, mocking him, questioning his sanity, offering to volunteer him as a performer at Mr. Barnum's museum of freaks on Ann Street.

Sometimes he even stopped drawing and painting. In those times, the longing for beauty seemed trivial in a city drowning in shit. Most of the time, he found refuge in journalism. He took his notebook in hand and moved among other people, merging his odor with theirs, recording their lives and their deaths. He was sure, on this day of smothering heat and rising stench, that Inspector Ford would eventually tell him that Dubious Jones was named by her father, a mechanic in Troy who did not trust his wife's fidelity, and that her killer was an unemployed Hungarian whose name had more consonants than vowels and who had a wife and four children in Budapest. He killed her, as usual, because he loved her. The details were always different, in the lives of other people. The stories were always the same.

Today, as his body felt sickened in every waking hour, he became obsessed with water. Today, he wanted to be clean. Today, he wanted to taste clean female flesh. Today. The rich had water, of course, bringing hogsheads in by cart from country wells to fill those rooftop tanks. But ordinary folk had no water for washing clothes or sheets or themselves. No water for scrubbing floors or sidewalks or the windows of stores. The little water they could find was used for boiling potatoes. They had that trickle, measured by the bucket, some still drawn from the ancient Tea Water Pump on Chatham Street, and little else. And in winter there was often less than a trickle, as the pond froze and the pumps froze and women melted ice and snow in pails. At all hours in all seasons, the city gave off this rotting stench.

The miasma, they called it.

The hod carrier emerging from a house on Hudson Street: "Sure the miasma's not bad today, is it, Mick?"

Or Beatriz, presiding over mocha and biscuits: "Damn miasma eat your heart out today, Mist' Co'mac."

Women tried to erase the miasma with perfume. Self-proclaimed gentlemen carried perfumed handkerchiefs in their sleeves. When theaters were allowed to flourish after the Revolution, the longer plays were shortened, there were many intervals to allow a breeze to cleanse the rancid air, and there were no plays at all in summer. As the town filled up, and then doubled and tripled in population after the opening of the Erie Canal, the stench grew worse. Crowded Sunday churches used lots of incense to overwhelm the stink of the faithful, and when August broiled the city, sea captains claimed that they could smell New York six miles out to sea.

Some young New Yorkers didn't care, for they'd been born into the smell of shit. It stained their days and nights, and unless they traveled into the wild country to the north, those patches that had escaped ax and saw during the war, they could not imagine a world that did not smell of shit. The hoariest New York joke (Cormac must have heard it thirty times in two weeks) was about the New Yorker who wandered into the open country, collapsed of some infirmity, and revived only when a handful of shit was held under his nose. New Yorkers told the joke on themselves. It always got a laugh. But Cormac had known the sweet smell of grass in Ireland and the salt air of the sea. And so he never got used to the miasma. It began to feel like the walls of an unseen jail, a trap, a punishment, a purgatory.

Nobody mentioned this in the churches, which Cormac sometimes visited as a reporter on the state of the New York soul. Filth, after all, enforced celibacy. The fanatics on the Common, assembled near the new City Hall, preached that man was in essence filthy and the only hope of true cleanliness depended upon a Christian death and the eventual embrace of pristine angels. They were all offspring of the Rev. Clifford, whose days had ended in the old lunatic asylum on Chambers Street. Their visions brought some small relief. Apparently the angels greeted all new arrivals with tubs, soap, and clean towels. Cormac laughed to himself at the notion that the only way to get a bath was to die. All the while, in spite of the stench, babies kept being conceived and born. They all entered the world of the miasma.

Meanwhile, men and women shit in pots. They shit in boxes. And Cormac was one of them. What they did, he did. There was no choice. He shit in bags and carried them to the privy in the yard behind the house in Cortlandt Street. The landlord finally built a privy, four feet deep, a lined tub. Once a week, teams of filthy men came around to collect the tubs of shit and dump the contents into the rivers. But after the canal opened, the number of shit collectors did not increase. The businessmen who ruled the town through the Common Council didn't want to spend the money, and the people could do nothing because in this glorious democratic city; they were not allowed to choose the mayor. The overwhelmed shit collectors worked more and more slowly. They dumped their cargoes into the East River too late for the tides to flush them out to sea. The stench then rose from the sluggish river. Indians stopped coming to town. The last of the deer and wolves retreated to the forests of the Catskills and Adirondacks, appalled by the odor of humans. Fish and oysters died. The otters died. Whales remained out past the Narrows now. Ships that had been scoured by the harsh Atlantic came to the New York docks for a few days, unloaded, loaded, and departed coated with shit and slime.

"I hate coming to this town," one sea captain told Cormac. "I end up puking for a week after I've left it and can't get the stink out of me skin."

"Try living in it," Cormac said.

"I'd cut me feckin' t'roat first."

The corrupted water made New York a hard-drinking town. Taverns opened everywhere, two or three on the same block. Cormac entered them with other newspapermen, but he didn't drink, because the taste of alcohol now sickened him. His companions drank his share. They drank beer and rum and flip. They loaded drinks with molasses and brandy and plunged hot pokers into the mess on bitter winter nights. This added the odor of vomit to the miasma. Many drunkards brawled in streets and gutters, and on public holidays such as the Fourth of July or Evacuation Day they celebrated with swords and pistols and increased the number of widows in the town. Others went home to fearful wives and fucked them brutally and passed out, while some went off to the brothels, where even the most forlorn whores backed away from them and their stinking flesh.

The shit and the piss and the rot brought infection and death. The old Africans had carried immunities with them across the Atlantic, and Cormac was certain those immunities had been passed to him through Kongo's blood, for he never was infected. But his rage was fed by that too. For decades, the Africans saved many white lives during yellow fever seasons, but were seldom honored, and until 1827 in New York, were not given freedom. The old, immune Africans were almost gone from New York, dying in frozen winter streets, begging for alms on stinking summer afternoons. Death huddled in the city's shit, and in 1832, it had risen in full fury.

Omens preceded the dying. For nine straight mornings in June, old Africans showed Cormac two black spots, like angry eyes, in the scarlet face of the rising sun. "This is very bad," one said in Yoruba. "Many will die." There was a report of red water churning from the depths of Hell Gate. A thousand dead fish rose one afternoon from the bottom of the harbor, and the seagulls would not touch them. At the Battery one morning, anxious for a cleansing breeze, Cormac saw a raven.

For months in the offices of the *Evening Post,* he read ominous reports from abroad. They told of Asiatic cholera in France and then in England, killing thousands, then leaping the Atlantic to Canada. The Common Council read short versions of the same newspaper reports and did nothing. When Cormac approached them for comment, they shrugged and moved away from him as if he were infected. They didn't even clear away the filth on the streets, for that would have cost money. "They don't want to hurt business in the city," said William Cullen Bryant, a dry young poet who was the new editor, "and, of course, they're correct." Normalcy was the byword, even when it was a lie.

Then, on a Tuesday morning in June, Cormac heard a tale from a Nassau Street barber. He lived on Cherry Street. The night before, a neighbor named Fitzgerald came home from work as a tailor, and within an hour was simultaneously puking and shitting and bending over with cramps. He went quiet for a while, then groaned with headache, laughed in a giddy way, then drowsed in a jittery slumber. He jerked awake and vomited, heaving hunks of undigested food upon the floor, and then hacked up phlegm that was sticky and glistening in the candlelight. He screamed in thirst: *"Water, give me cold water."* His eyes went dull as lead, and his face turned pale blue and his eyes and mouth and skin pinched in tightly and the skin of his hands and feet grew as dark and wrinkled as a prune. And then the body shuddered and the man was very still and quite dead. Five hours after the first symptoms.

Hearing this account, Cormac reached for his copy of Boccaccio. In *The Decameron,* the good doctor had wondered in the fourteenth century as the Black Death raged in Florence how many gallant gentlemen, fair ladies, and sprightly youths, "having breakfasted in the morning with their kinsfolk, acquaintances and friends, supped that same evening with their ancestors in the next world!"

Cormac rushed to see Bryant, waited an hour while the editor chatted with some visiting politician, and, after citing Boccaccio as a way to get Bryant's attention, explained what he'd been told by the barber. Bryant then was in his early thirties, with a sharp nose and piercing eyes, and was not yet encased in the pomposity that all would remember later. Bryant listened, his eyes narrowing, and whispered, *"Good God, it's the cholera."*

Bryant sent Cormac to the City Hall for more information, but nobody would confirm or deny what had clearly happened on Cherry Street. Back in the office, Bryant told him to wait. To write nothing. To wait for more facts. Above all, to avoid spreading panic. That night Cormac's friend the barber died, along with his mother, aunt, and oldest child.

They became numbers, as first two died each day, and then twenty, and then the epidemic could no longer be hidden. Too late, the

Council began to clear the pestilential mounds of infested garbage. Too late, the slum buildings were emptied and scoured and whitewashed. Old women awoke one stinking morning and then fell back dead. Infants died. Children died. One of Cormac's friends died, a fine African musician named Michael George; he might have become one of the first great American composers and became instead a corpse at twenty-nine.

As in all plagues, as in Boccaccio, as in Daniel Defoe, all manner of quack and charlatan appeared with cures they were happy to sell. Opium was peddled openly as a curative, along with laudanum, and cayenne pepper, and camphor and calomel. Doctors offered bleedings. People drank salt or mustard, hot punch and hartshorn, or enveloped themselves in tobacco smoke. They still died. The God Cure revived for a week or so, with bellowed pious demands for prayer and fasting and repentance. But then the preachers joined the rich in the flight to the countryside, leaving the souls of the poor to the personal judgment of God. As always, the dead and the dying were blamed for their own fate. Many were Irish, and Cormac heard them condemned by the rich as their carriages trotted away to safety. *A filthy lot, the Irish* (said one perfumed auctioneer). *Papists too. Animals as low as the pigs and rats.* In the empty streets at night, Cormac could hear wailing songs in Irish (for many could not speak English) and garbled prayers and the jerking sounds of horror at still another death. Many must have imagined the consolations of the Otherworld or the Christian Heaven. Hundreds died.

Sales of all newspapers fell as their rich readers departed and the illiterate immigrants were left behind. Advertising ceased, for few shops were open. The South Street waterfront was deserted, the streets empty day and night, crews and captains refusing to enter the infected port. There were theories for a few days in the *Evening Post* about diet being the cause of the deaths. But meat-eaters died in the same streets as vegetarians. Cranks who ate only nuts and grains (while chanting Iroquois prayers) fell as if axed. A week later, the drastic New York weather was blamed. But they died on dry days and damp, in the hammering heat of noon and at the black midnight hour, calling at all hours for water, cold water. The poor died most of all, but so did the favorite daughter of John Jacob Astor in flight to Europe. Shit collectors died and so did insurance peddlers. Some of the infected grew mad after the first symptoms struck and lurched into the streets and reached for strangers to give them the infection, as if insisting they would not go alone on the swift journey to Heaven or Hell. There were many brave doctors who obeyed their oaths, but even they were hampered by much ignorance and not enough hospitals. *The cholera is,* said one, *and that is all we know*. New York Hospital slammed its doors to the dying and the new Bellevue, a combination of hospital and almshouse, was transformed into a vast filthy limbo. Nurses died. Doctors died. Too many churches slammed shut their doors too, the clergymen bolting them before departing. Policemen were assigned to the abandoned churches and the empty houses of the rich to prevent looting, but soon they too were gone, fleeing the city or buried in its crowded trenches.

As he had been in the yellow fever epidemics, Cormac discovered he was immune. An immunity to yellow fever could be traced to African blood, to Kongo. Cholera was another matter. But as he roamed among the dead and dying, gathering facts that were written with haste and anger on foolscap but never appeared in the newspaper, or trying to comfort the afflicted with useless words, part of him longed to be taken by the cholera. If this was life, he did not want it. Until that summer, he had never thought such things. Now they came to him almost every day. Life, in this season, was about shit and death.

To keep from thinking, he wrote many stories for the *Evening Post* while Bryant and his most favored editor, William Leggett, gathered their families together across the Hudson in Hoboken and found shelter from the storm. At last, some stories made their way into the newspaper. Stories about water and corruption. Stories that told people where to go for help but offered no easy hope. Cormac hoped that a person who could read would tell ten persons who could not. He hoped thousands would demand water.

Cormac was ignorant of the causes of the cholera but knew that it wasn't the Irish (blamed as the Jews were blamed for the Black Death) and knew it wasn't something as vague as the miasma. Whatever it was, science would discover the cause. He was convinced that the cure would come from water, cold water.

Finally it ended. After nine terrifying weeks. And three thousand five hundred and twenty-six known deaths. The rich slowly returned, sending in their African or Irish servants as the advance patrols, like canaries into a coal mine. Bryant and Leggett returned too, and Cormac urged them to start a crusade in the *Evening Post,* demanding that the city obtain a big, strong, muscular supply of clean water. They nodded, they listened, they thanked him, they published a few polite editorials.

New York got no clean water.

The miasma returned with the people.

The cholera returned in 1833.

Shit and filth got worse.

The cholera returned in 1834.

All that dying passed through him again as he went home after sundown on his birthday, September 9, 1834. The flat was an oven. He opened the windows, removed his tie and shirt, pulled off his shoes. He sat in a chair, very still, gazing at his books and paintings, at the pots of color and the clean brushes. But his skin was crawling. The room filled with the stink of his feet and his armpits and his balls. He scratched at his skin, which felt as if millions of insects were crawling under the surface. He scratched at his hair. He dipped a cloth into the bowl of water and scrubbed his armpits, feet, and balls. The stench did not leave.

He heard a window breaking somewhere in the night and the barking of dogs and a woman wailing. Tomorrow's murder. Dubious Jones had named herself, said Inspector Ford in time for the morning edition. Her true name was Mildred Vandeventer, and she was from Rochester. She was nineteen and had been a whore for four years. She was killed by a man named Collins, from Philadelphia, who went back to his boardinghouse on Pearl Street, wrote a note saying how much he loved her, and then hanged himself. Case closed.

But Cormac told himself, There's no such thing as a closed case. Who will bury Dubious Jones? Why did she choose the name? And when they bury her as Mildred Vandeventer, who will tell her family how she died, and how she lived? She and Collins will be together forever now in the democracy of Potter's Field. And at least they're free of the miasma.

He was not.

He scratched and shook and rubbed his back against the wall. His body hair felt as if it were growing inward, follicles fed by the fertilizer of the shit-stained air. He pulled at the curtains. He yanked his hair. Then he dressed again and went into the night. Near Broadway he saw a woman come out of tavern with a basket of wilting geraniums. He bought four of them and a length of string and tied them to his face, the petals tight against his nose.

He walked toward the water, hoping for a breeze, one fresh zephyr of air. But then the smell of shit overwhelmed the flowers. He began to weep. He imagined leaping into the river and swimming away. An act of suicide. Motive: shit.

And instead turned right into Duane Street. His eyes searched the rooftops, looking for a water tower. There, he said. There. Up there. On the roof of the bordello near Chapel Street. There.

74.

She greeted him at the front door.

"Do come in," she said. "I'm the Countess de Chardon."

"Cormac O'Connor," he said.

"I've seen you in town," she said, "but never, alas, in this place."

She was dressed as if married to one of the richest merchants in the city, with a swelling high-necked bodice that suggested (but did not display) full breasts, her waist impossibly tightened, and a dark maroon crescent-shaped bustle that rose airily behind her when she moved, hinting at layered crinolines and plump hidden cheeks and thighs. Her lustrous brown hair was piled in plaited coils held tight with a bone tiara. Diamond earrings glittered in her ears, matched by a diamond ring on each finger. Her skin was tawny in the shifting light of oil lamps, her cheeks lightly rouged, her full lips painted a muted crimson. They exchanged platitudes in French, hers polished, his as crude as any self-taught language. She closed the door behind him. She was certainly no ordinary madam of a bawdy house.

"Do have a drink, monsieur," she said, reverting to English to help Cormac out of his clumsy French. As he passed, she gave off a scent of lavender. He told her he didn't drink. She smiled in relief. She said she had a perfect young woman for him, just recently arrived only months before from the upstate town of Waterloo, and she made a small joke about the fate of Napoleon. "Do not," she said, "be *too* daring."

Cormac paused, and then said he'd much prefer a bath to anything else.

"Yes, it's been a smothering day," she said. "I'll arrange a bath. Can you wait for . . ."

"I've learned to wait for everything," he said.

She led him to a sitting room where mustached businessmen sat with some of the nine women who worked in the nine upstairs rooms. One young woman played Mozart badly on a stand-up piano. Gilt-framed paintings of ruined castles and the Roman Colosseum adorned the pale papered walls. The lights were muted here too. The men made bad jokes. The women giggled. Cormac sipped water. The countess returned and motioned with her head for him to follow her.

She led him up a back stairway to her suite on the top floor. The music ended when she closed the perfectly carpentered door, and Cormac relaxed. Thick drapes warded off the city, and the smell of shit was replaced by the scent of lavender. The main room of the suite was dominated by a four-poster bed, high off the floor, covered in bridal white, trimmed with purple, and plump with silken cushions. The walls were covered with patterned red plush. The countess pointed out three small landscapes by Asher B. Durand, who was the best American painter so far, she said, and would surely produce even more impressive work. "He needs to paint some human beings," she said. "If he can." A tall glass-fronted bookcase was crammed with books in democratic disarray, the sign of a true reader. She was enthusiastic about Mary Shelley's *Frankenstein* ("Only a woman could have written such a book") and was reading George Sand's *Indiana,* which had arrived from France just before the epidemic struck. She loved Boccaccio too, she said, opening the case to bring out a worn volume in French, delighted that Cormac could name four of the seven traveling women: Pampinea, Fiammetta, Filomena, and Emilia.

"They all work here," she said in an excited voice, "or at least that is what I've named them. For everybody in New York must have a public name that is not their own. I'm waiting for the remaining three to arrive on my doorstep, women of the life who can also tell tales: Lauretta, Neifile, and Elissa."

As she riffled the pages of the book, Cormac noticed that the nails on her slim fingers were long and painted white. Except for the nail on her right forefinger. That nail was severely trimmed.

She casually opened a side door, and in the light of a candle he saw the bathtub. Seven feet long, up on golden lion's feet, with a drain leading somewhere, and a tap that she explained was attached to an immense tank on the roof. The tub was porcelain, the taps and soap dish gold.

"Would you like your bath now?" she said.

"Yes. I'd like that very much."

She smiled in an enigmatic way and then pulled a cord. A tall white-haired African man came in and she told him to prepare coffee and the bath. He nodded and slipped away. The countess and Cormac sat near a bay window in facing chairs, and when she heard that he was a newspaperman, a journalist, she asked what he thought about Lord Byron and Coleridge and her own favorite, Shelley, whose death was such an abomination. He gave glib answers. The African came in with coffee on a silver plate and then retreated to the bathroom, closing the door behind him. She asked Cormac about William Cullen Bryant.

"His poetry is dreadful, no?"

"Yes."

"I have one of his books here," she said, shaking her head slowly. And then laughed out loud and squeezed his hand.

"Let's wash him out of our hair," she murmured.

And led him to the bath. The clear, scented water was heated elsewhere and kept hot by a tray of coals beneath the steel-bottomed porcelain tub. The countess opened his shirt. He opened her bodice, with its eyelets and hooks. She then backed away while he completed his undressing. He hung his trousers on a peg. Then she was back, wearing a thin white gown.

"Get in," she said.

He slipped into the healing water. The gown fell. She stepped in behind him, uttering a small squeal at the hot water, then squatted and wrapped her hands around his chest. Fingers caressed the ridge of dead flesh on his shoulder.

"I love a man with a scar," she said. "He's lived at least some small life."

In the months that followed, the bath was always the prelude. By day, he worked at the *Evening Post*. He went home now to the Countess de Chardon, where he lived in a small room down the hall from her suite. She had insisted that he give up his flat, and the promise of water and the scent of lavender convinced him she was right. He paid off his rent and arrived back on Duane Street with his books and clothes and the traveling bag filled with his father's letter, his mother's earrings, and the sword.

"You're a perfect companion," she said one morning, with a flicker of irony on her face and a taste of France in her accent. "Busy and quiet. Literate, funny, strange, and free of disease. You're what I need and I hope I'm what you need too."

"You'll never know how much I need you," he said, trying to match the lightness of her tone.

"For God's sake," she said, "don't tell me."

He certainly didn't tell the countess that at first he thought of her as an escape. In her company, or alone in his room on the top floor, he escaped the miasma. His flesh had revived with water and the aroma of soap and lavender, and so he also escaped into her body. As he savored her ironies, her private codes, he also understood that with the Countess de Chardon he would be free of any delusion of domesticity. He suspected that she knew what he was thinking, and accepted it, even welcomed it. They just never spoke about the details.

"Human beings want to know too much about each other," she said. "And that's why there are so many lies."

She did tell him some of her own story. She was then thirty-two years old. Or so she said. She was born in Port-au-Prince and was a creole refugee from the uprising on Hispaniola that had driven so many of her class to the United States. Or so she said. If her tale was true, she must have come from the side of the island called Haiti, ruled for so long by the French. But Cormac didn't know if any part of the Chardon story was true. And it didn't matter. Many people came to New York with a script, one that allowed them to begin again, to be other than the unhappy persons they'd been in the places they'd left behind. In his own way, Cormac himself was one of them. But Cormac did sense that the countess had seen much horror. Only those who had lived with appalling horror could fully understand the consolations of living flesh. And she did speak excellent French.

When she first saw him unpack his drawings, she was joyful. At Christmas, she bought him a new easel, brushes, paint, and paper. And so that he would not feel like a kept man, she commissioned him to do some drawings that she would use as decoration in the nine rooms of her nine young women. These were nine views of her own vulva, and one view each of the vulvae of the other women. They were drawn in black and red chalk in a Renaissance style on tinted paper and designed in such a way that a casual viewer would not instantly recognize the subjects. They could have been flowers. The countess posed gladly, her knees drawn up, her rosy buttocks high on silken cushions. She had Cormac draw her before the bath and after, before sex and later. The first four drawings were framed by her dark brown silky pubic hair. Then she shaved off all of her hair, and the final five were as bald and naked as drawings of fruit or orchids. Once she was overcome by the sound of chalk on paper and could wait no longer and reached deliriously for the focus of his attention.

The other women were not so enthusiastic about the project but did what the countess ordered, and in the closed space of his studio room often lost their reluctance. Pampinea was universally plump. Fiammetta was shy and lean, lying back with her eyes closed, and kept asking Cormac to tell her it was pretty. Filomena was ashamed of her thick beardlike hair and squirmed to hide it from his sight. Emilia was a large girl with a small buried vulva and an almost invisible button. It always hurts, she whispered. Every man hurts me. Every one of them. In Cormac's drawing, her lips seemed to whimper. All stared at the finished drawings as if trying to understand something about themselves.

For Cormac, those were the months when there was no water anywhere in New York except in that house, the secret garden of the Countess de Chardon. And water became part of life itself. It was prelude. It was culmination. It was a reward for concentrated work. Or it made work possible. Clear, warm water was a source of entertainment and luxury and sex. In a way, Cormac told himself, I'm a kind of novel for the countess, as she is for me, and water is the connecting device of the tale. The heat departed in cool October, and then, shuddering with winter cold, they would leave the bath and dry themselves and then lie upon the vast white bed. She was lover, mother, teacher.

She taught him, among other things, the joy of fasting. She would stop all sexual play on a certain date and remain aloofly celibate for ten days or two weeks. She would let her desire build slowly, deny it, welcome it, deny it again, until there was some enormous need that always started in her imagination, in some dark cave of denial. He matched her fasting and then erupted with her in a shared paroxysm of flesh and water.

She never once used the word *love* and said nothing about the two of them forging a private pact. He didn't even sleep with her through the nights. "Nothing," she said, "is more horrible than seeing each other after a night of sleep." She didn't have any form of conventional jealousy, certainly not about the flesh. And definitely not his flesh. As long as they began each evening with the bath, just she and Cormac, she didn't even mind if he made love to the other women. It was simply understood, without being said, that he would not develop any emotions for them beyond the simple needs of the flesh. And shared talk. And the details of food and books and music.

"You're always humming tunes," she said. "You should learn to play an instrument."

"Such as?"

"Such as the piano. We have one downstairs, you know."

He laughed. "If I play it, the customers will revolt, and so will you."

"The rooms are sealed," she said. "There's no one here until the lunch hour. And nobody can hear if you close the door."

"And who would teach me?"

"I would," she said.

And so she began teaching him the fundamentals, explaining the keys and the correct position of his hands, and then scales and the mysterious notations of music sheets. You need three fingers to make a chord, she said. Your fingers have specific targets, she said, those keys, and you must hit the keys cleanly. He kept hitting between keys, clanging them too hard, and she cried out in mock horror, laughed, and made him try again. She explained about flats and sharps, and how chords were major, minor, or dominant. She showed him the language of music too, and he realized that he had first heard Irish and Yoruba and French as sounds without meaning and then slowly broken them down into individual words, which were here called notes. He told himself that music was a language like any other, and he would learn it.

"Time is everything in music," she said, demonstrating with a booted foot the way to maintain tempo.

"In life too."

"Please, *cheri,* it's too early for philosophy."

The tempo of his days was also shifting. He could not always appear beside her at the piano at eleven in the morning. His duties to the *Evening Post* often had him running from one event to another, and the work had greater urgency now because a Scotsman named James Gordon Bennett was bringing something new to the newspaper trade. He had founded the *Herald* and, after some false starts, was beginning to find readers. He published the sort of details that Cormac put in his notes and failed to get into the *Evening Post.* Instead of burying tales of mayhem and horror in the back of the paper, Bennett put them on the front page, which all other journals devoted to advertising. He used crude woodcuts as illustrations. He broke the neutral tone of the writing. As his sales increased, particularly after his accounts of the murder of a prostitute named Helen Jewett, the other editors dismissed him as a cheap vulgarian. But the *Evening Post* was now selling eight thousand copies each day, delivered to the desks of businessmen, while Bennett was selling thirty-five thousand, peddled on the streets by boys. The *Evening Post* began to run more tales of murders than before, discreetly, of course, and still buried in the rear of the newspaper. That meant more work for Cormac O'Connor. He moved around the town with a mask pulled across his lower face to reduce the miasma, checking with policemen and lowlifes for stories, humming the tunes that he was taught by the Countess de Chardon.

On slow days, or Sunday mornings, he sat beside her on the piano bench and ran his fingers over the keys, savoring each chord, astonished at the way music brought something from deep inside him. A choppy Celtic anger. A longing for a world already lost.

"You have very good hands," she said one morning. "But then I already knew that."

"They're not good enough for music," he said.

"They will be."

She showed him what to do with her own long-fingered hands, telling him to watch the way those fingers moved. Sometimes she lost herself in the music, doing a concert for an audience of one, her eyes closed, her head tilted slightly backward, listening as if the rest of the world were a vast silence. Her music was lyrical and romantic, and he saw her as a girl in some stately white mansion in Port-au-Prince, alone in a vast room, or with some French exile serving as her musical overseer. In his imagination, her instructor looked like the dancing master from John Hughson's tavern, small, a dandy, and then he wondered: Where did the dancing master go? Where did all of those people go who were in my life for a month or a year and then moved off the stage?

And so music merged with water as he meshed more closely with the Countess de Chardon. A set of rules was being formed between them, unwritten, unposted, but part of their shared time. He understood, as he painted the women of the house in his studio down the hall, that he might finish the night with a token of mutual gratitude. With shrugs, or phrases, the countess encouraged it, for she insisted that jealousy of the flesh was an absurd form of human weakness.

"Jealousy kills," she said. "It kills love. It kills people. You know that. You see the results at least once a week in your job. The cemeteries are filled with people who thought jealousy was love."

"But it's there; it's part of human nature."

"No, it's part of the idea of property. Read Mary Shelley, Cormac. I mean, *truly* read her. Men think women are their personal property. When women decide that they own their own bodies and will use them as they please, men kill them."

"Women kill men too," he said. "Jealous women."

"To protect themselves. To kill before they are killed. They don't really care if men go off with other women, as long as they come home, as long as they don't pick up a disease and carry it into their beds and their bodies. I know. I see certain men here all the time, and then see them with their wives going down to Trinity or St. Paul's on Sunday mornings. Then I see a notice in a newspaper that poor Missus So-and-so has died after a long illness, and I know she's died from what he brought home. Not from this place, because I have the doctor to check each woman every week. But from a hundred dives on South Street. My point is simple: More women are murdered by men's pricks than by gunshots, Cormac."

"Can I quote you in the *Post*?" he said, and laughed.

"You can translate me into Latin and chisel it over the courthouse door."

She implied that when he was alone while she traveled to Philadelphia or Boston on business, she would not care if he sampled the other women of the house. They were there for many men, even Cormac. He was entitled to small pleasures, and so was she.

"I just don't want your personal report," she said. "I don't want you to tell me that Fiammetta is wonderful. If she is, I want to be there myself, with the two of you." She smiled. "The only way to prevent jealousy is to share one's flesh. To be generous. To break down the notion of permanent ownership."

"I don't want to know what you might do in Philadelphia or Boston, either."

"Fair enough," she said. "But I won't do anything. That's not a promise to you. That's a promise to me."

Together, they often engaged in what the countess called "research." The suite and the bed and the bath were all part of the laboratory. She wanted to do with her body (and Cormac's) everything she could imagine as a woman. She guided him on some nights the way she guided him at the piano. There were chords in bed too, and solos, and glissandos. She tried to do things so impossible they both fell laughing into uselessness. But some worked. And then, as a businesswoman, she would offer such services, after the proper training of her young ladies, to all of the customers. Every house in New York had its specialties, and she wanted to keep changing the menu in hers.

"Think of this place as a restaurant," she said one midnight, after dining with Cormac in the suite. "We have to satisfy certain . . . basic appetites. Every house must have a fat woman, of course. Every house must have a negress. Every house must have its ugly woman. And its girl dressed as a nun. The menu must contain the basics." She laughed. "Livened up, of course, with a few . . . specialties."

Some of her competitors had their own restricted menus. In one house, the customers would not be admitted if they were older than eighteen, a shameless play for the Columbia College trade. The older women, said the countess, loved working there, in spite of the low wages. Another house provided a silk-lined coffin for necrophiliac men. A dozen catered to those who wanted lashings. *We can't offer everything here,* said the Countess de Chardon. *But we* can *give them the odd surprise.* Variety was good for business, and all these bored men, bored with wives, bored with life, needed those surprises. But there was a personal motive too for her own experiments. *"I don't want to die without trying everything, at least once,"* she whispered to Cormac one night. *"I don't know anything about the soul, but I want to know everything about flesh. Everything that I can possibly know. To see it. To feel it. To do it. For I could die tomorrow."*

So Cormac realized that he was also living with a woman who knew something about mortality. In a room on the top floor of a building on Duane Street. The palace of water and flesh and music.

One Tuesday morning, she moved a new piano into the suite, and across the long evenings, while the countess mingled with the customers, flirting, teasing, confiding, Cormac played. He learned to read music without much of a struggle; it was, as he'd thought, another language, and if he could think in Yoruba and Irish, if he could teach himself French, if he could decode Latin, then these notations, which were a kind of drawing too, did not intimidate him. Execution was another matter. Sometimes his hands felt encased in wool. He hit the wrong keys, smashed chords, lost the tempo. And started over.

On some solitary nights, he ignored the music sheets and allowed his hands to drift, to caress each key, to discover music he had never heard and could not imagine. It was as if he were bringing forth some hidden spirit from the secret caves within the piano, revealing its desperate yearning for pleasure. He could feel Ireland in the music. And Africa. And the ocean sea.

On other nights, he felt music as a form of landscape, with rolling hills and a placid river and trees with rustling leaves. He could feel it in his painter's hands, which were not yet the hands of a musician. The terrain was not made of earth, or paint, but sound. He would try to find paths through the hills of sound, he would try to find a way to the river. He always failed. His hands were too crude. The paths were not marked. Then he would try again. He did not feel frustrated. Frustration, after all, was an impatience with the ticking of clocks. He had all the time in the world.

On some nights in early spring, after their bath, the countess would sit naked at the piano, commanding him to lie on the bed. Teaching him had brought back the passion she felt, long ago, for music. Or so she said. A passion she'd erased through an act of will. Now it rose from her again, like a ghost. Here is Vivaldi, she said. Here is Scarlatti. Here is something without a composer. Here is France. Here is Haiti. She would play then as if the notes were licking his flesh and entering his body. The music of such nights always made him hard.

The countess was one of his best sources. She knew stockbrokers and real estate speculators, police spies and politicians. She knew who was planning the newest financial scheme that would reward those who knew before others did. She sometimes invested her own money and made even more than the men in the know. She knew too which marriages were disasters, which rich young men were bound for personal calamities. She discreetly fed private information to Cormac, who put some of it in the newspaper and held some of it for himself. She knew, above all, how New York worked.

"Nothing is as it seems," she said. "Not here and not in France. Not anywhere. And everything is driven by money. The thing you must do is find out what is truly happening, not what seems to be happening. Understand the lie, and you'll see the truth. Start off by believing that everything is a lie."

She paused. "The God story is a lie, told by archbishops to enrich themselves. Democracy is a lie. The police are a lie."

"And us?"

"We're a lie too," she said with a smile. "A good lie."

75.

Cormac didn't hear them come in. It was after midnight on a frigid January night, and he was putting final touches on a somber portrait of a woman named Millicent. She was from Poughkeepsie and the other women called her Millie the Weeper. She cried the way other people laughed. That was her specialty. She cried when she heard a sad song. She cried reading a sad tale in the newspaper. She cried when the weather was beautiful and cried when the weather was ugly. If a customer performed with unusual vigor, she wept torrents. If a customer failed to perform at all, she wept as if the apocalypse were due in an hour.

On this night, she was off in her own room, and Cormac was alone, adding highlights to her painted raw sienna hair, humming Scarlatti. Then he heard a door slam down below. Then voices raised. Then something shattering. He went to the landing and looked down.

Three men wearing rough cloth caps were confronting the countess. One growling voice came up the stairwell.

"We'll close ye down, ye bloody whore, if you don't do what we say."

"Get out of here now," she shouted back. "Go now, and I'll do nothing. Stay, and keep this up, and there'll be hell to pay."

The heaviest man, his face still hidden to Cormac's view, shoved her hard against a banister.

Cormac went into his room and took the sword off its hook on the wall. Then he moved silently down the stairs.

"It's a hundred a month," the big man was saying. "If you don't pay the hundred, we'll close ye shut."

Cormac saw him clearly now. Most reporters were coming to know him. Hughie Mulligan from the Five Points. One of the gang of young men called the Dead Rabbits. As a reporter, Cormac had witnessed him a year ago, standing before a judge in the courthouse, charged with gouging a man's eyes out in a brawl. His mother sat weeping without conviction. "My son, my son," she moaned, "my poor wee boy." But the judge was fixed and Hughie Mulligan walked free, while his fellow Dead Rabbits cheered.

His face was veined and red now, his eyes glittery with danger, his arms hanging from his shoulders as if prepared to punch. Two others, smaller and younger, stood behind him. Most of the women were on the stairs, peering down, while the night's last customers huddled in the rooms. Mulligan glanced at Cormac as he came down the final flight of stairs. And saw the sword.

"Look, lads, this poof's got him a sword."

The two smaller men grinned and each drew a new English-style revolver, made to fire five bullets without reloading. The countess backed up, eyes wide. The women on the staircase made a sighing sound. Millie the Weeper was weeping.

"You're in the wrong house, aren't you, Hughie?" Cormac said. "If you want a woman, you should be at thirteen Baxter Street, isn't that the case, Hughie?" He smiled and moved around, turning his shoulder toward the three men to make himself a smaller target. "That *is* where your mother lives, isn't it?"

Mulligan howled *Youdirtybastardofawhoringponce* and charged, and Cormac turned into the charge and put the tip of the sword under the larger man's chin. Everything stopped. Mulligan seemed to stop breathing.

"Oh, poor Hughie Mulligan!" Cormac said. "What's that red stuff coming from your neck?"

Mulligan's face went pale. He started moving a hand to his neck, and Cormac jabbed with the tip of the sword and then blood actually did trickle down the man's neck.

"Now, tell these two midgets of yours to hand those pistols to the countess. If you don't, this sword will come out the back of your fucking head."

Mulligan made a gesture with his hands, directing the two smaller men to hand over the guns.

"Hold the barrel with your thumb and forefinger, boys. You know which fingers they are? That's it. Nice and easy, now. Real dainty-like."

The countess took the guns, gazing at them with a curious respect.

"Countess, you can now shoot these three idiots for breaking into your establishment."

"What a marvelous idea," she said. "Look what they've done. Those three vases are worth, oh, a hundred dollars. And the door . . ." She shouted up the stairs. "Ladies, you saw what happened, didn't you?"

A chorus of yeses.

"Should I shoot them?"

The words came rolling down from above: *Right now, of course, between the eyes, why not?*

Cormac took the tip of the sword away from Mulligan's chin, and the big man swiped at his neck and saw blood on his fingertips. His nostrils widened in rage.

"You've got some nerve," he said.

Cormac laughed out loud.

"You come in here to break the place up and try to extort money, and *we've* got some nerve?"

"You're foolin' wit' the wrong people."

"In that case, we should kill you. To make sure you never come back."

Mulligan turned as if to leave, then charged. He shoved Cormac against the banister of the stairwell, and Cormac fell, rolled, came up with the sword in both hands, and put its point against Mulligan's heart.

"That was stupid."

He turned to the countess, who was holding both revolvers. He nodded. She aimed.

"Take off your shoes," Cormac said to Mulligan. Then turned to the other two. "And you two idiots: shoes, jackets, and trousers."

The two smaller men were alarmed. They looked at Mulligan's back, at Cormac, and the guns in the hands of the countess. They started undressing.

"You too, big boy," Cormac said to Mulligan.

"I'll not do that."

"Let me help."

He sliced Mulligan's belt and the man's trousers fell. He wasn't wearing drawers. From the stairs came giggles and titters and one woman's loud sob.

"The rest," Cormac said.

Within minutes, all three men were naked, using hands to cover themselves, and the chorus on the stairs erupted in applause. Even the countess was grinning.

"Now go home."

"It's ten bloody degrees out there!" one of the younger men said. His teeth were already clacking.

"If you run hard, you'll be warm enough, boys."

They went out, and Cormac saw that it was snowing.

The next afternoon, with a foot of snow upon the ground, a mob showed up at the door of the brothel of the Countess de Chardon. It was led by clergymen, who declared themselves firmly against sin. One Methodist, one Anglican, one Presbyterian. They prayed. They hurled anathemas. They chanted. They sang. A few policemen watched carefully but did nothing. There were no laws against prostitution, since, as the countess observed, the laws were written by men. The age of consent in New York was ten. Watching with the countess from a high window, Cormac saw Hughie Mulligan and a dozen other Dead Rabbits on the edge of the crowd.

"I hope I haven't caused more trouble than it's worth," he said.

"It was worth it," she said, and giggled.

"What will you do?"

"Pay a few visits."

While the mob still chanted, the countess slipped out the back door, dressed warmly against the cold. When she returned three hours later, the mob was gone.

"They won't be back," she said.

"Who did you visit?"

"Certain gentlemen who would rather not have their private tastes made public."

The mob showed up over the following months at other places run by women but did not return to Duane Street. Hughie Mulligan and his boys had created one of the first true New York rackets: They would protect the houses from themselves. That is, if they were paid a fee, nobody would bother the madams, their women, or their business establishments. And through connections at Tammany Hall, they'd make certain that no fool of a politician would try to pass a law in Albany that would close the houses. They did not try again to move against the countess.

"But be careful, Cormac. Hughie Mulligan won't forget what you did."

"I know."

Then one night, after a mild summer when only 213 New Yorkers died of cholera, the countess came to wake up Cormac in his room. The clock said 1:20. He sat up.

"What is it?"

"They have a plan," she said, her voice breathless. "They're going to burn out some blocks downtown, get rid of the old wooden houses, and . . ."

"Wait, slow down."

She calmed herself and explained how she had learned from a favored customer that a certain group was planning to burn out some of the old streets, because the land titles and squatting rights were now too complicated to deal with. Later, they would help move the rich up to the new districts in Greenwich Village, where they could come to work on the new horse-drawn omnibuses. The speculators among them already owned the land up in Greenwich and were investing in the omnibuses. The mechanics, the apprentices, and the poor would be forced into the houses off Chapel Street, where many other poor now lived (including the children of Africans). Others would be directed to the houses of the Five Points. Everything below Wall Street would be rebuilt and devoted to business.

"And who is this favored customer?"

"I can't speak his name. I call him the Wax Man. He likes, well . . ."

"And the name of his group?"

She sighed. "They don't have a name. But they are real."

"And why would the Wax Man tell you?"

"He was drinking wine, a lot of wine, he was getting . . . I suppose the word is sentimental. He wanted me to know — so that I could buy land *now,* in Greenwich Village, or along Bond Street, or even farther into the country. He was offering me a favor. A piece of the information. It's not the first time."

Cormac wrapped a blanket around himself against the seeping September cold.

"I should put this in the newspaper," he said, knowing that Bryant would surely find some excuse to refuse its publication.

"Never," she said. "They'll kill you, and worse . . ." (smiling broadly) "they'll kill *me.*"

They both laughed. She took Cormac's hand and led him across the hall to her room, closing the door behind them. She talked a lot about how real estate was the most important of all businesses in the town whose true god was Mammon. That was why she thought the Wax Man's raving was more than raving. She rang for a maid and ordered two omelettes, fresh bread, and a bottle of water. She swore Cormac to secrecy. "This is not about some stupid thugee like Hughie Mulligan," she said. "This is about the big boys." And then mentioned names. Ruggles, Hewett, Vandermeer, Astor. "They're not thinking about Saturday night," she said. "They're thinking about the future. A future we can't imagine, and they can."

Months passed. There was no fire. There was at least serious talk now about building a reservoir in Croton, high in Westchester, and digging a system of pipes to carry fresh water to the city. That was still the distant future, and it was still merely talk, but the newspapers were finally behind it, in the name of the expanding metropolis. In the present, Cormac was more grateful than ever for water and the aroma of lavender and clean flesh. His hands grew a bit looser on the keys of the piano. The playing of the countess, in contrast, was richer and more supple.

He understood better the theory of half notes, quarter notes, eighth notes, and sixteenth notes, of semiquavers and time stops, but his execution of the theory remained mechanical and crude. The countess was kind and patient.

Cormac worked hard at the newspaper, mentioned the rumors of an impending fire to Bryant, asked discreet questions of Beatriz and other friends on the streets, but he heard nothing more that was concrete. Neither did the countess, although the Wax Man continued making his Thursday night visits to the various rooms of the house. Sometimes he brought his own candles.

Cormac was careful in his movements, his eyes searching Duane Street before leaving the house. He avoided the frontiers of the Five Points at night, when the friends and associates of Hughie Mulligan might be watching from ambush. On most days, the sword was too bulky to strap to hip or back, but he did start carrying one of the revolvers he'd taken from Hughie's boys. He kept this hidden from editors and other reporters, and did not even tell the countess. On several Sundays he went off to the north on a rented horse to practice shooting at targets in the woods.

The stranger arrived in November. It was just after midnight, and Cormac was sitting back, deep in a plush chair, while the countess played an aching tune, full of longing. His eyes were closed, and he saw rain-washed streets and gabled rooftops and a river. The music was full of the river, the water flowing through time.

Then, from beyond the door, he heard the music of a violin.

Playing in counterpoint to the music of the piano.

The countess stopped playing, and he saw shock in her eyes. She did not move. The violin continued, picking up the melody of aching loss and an unseen river.

She got up without looking at Cormac and walked to the door. She paused while the music played, then turned the knob and opened the door.

A man in a cape was standing there, playing the violin. He didn't look at her, for his eyes were closed, his square jaw pressed into the chin rest, his brow crumpled into concentrated creases. His left hand moved subtly on the strings, there seemed no movement at all with the bow, yet he was pulling music from his instrument that was charged with enormous delicacy and power. The countess touched her mouth. The stranger kept playing and then glided deftly into a diminishing passage of farewell.

He finished and stood there, his brow still furrowed.

"Hello, Monsieur Breton," she said. "Come in."

He stepped across the threshold, his hazel eyes taking in the room and falling upon Cormac, who was now standing. The countess closed the door. The stranger did not move and neither did Cormac. For the first time, he saw the countess appear awkward.

"Cormac, this is Yves Breton," she said in French. "Yves, Cormac O'Connor."

Cormac stepped forward and offered a hand. M. Breton ignored it, busying his hands with bow and violin. His cape was dirty, his shoes slippery with black city mud.

"Can I get you a drink?" Cormac said.

"Yes," M. Breton said. "Cognac."

His tone was dismissive, and he turned to the countess.

"You're playing again," he said.

"Yes. I tried to give it up, but —"

She shrugged and gestured toward a chair. M. Breton looked in an inquisitive way at Cormac, who was returning with a small glass of cognac. He did not take the offered chair. In a sacramental way, he placed the bow and violin on a table, then sipped the cognac, thrust a hand in a trousers pocket, and stared at the countess. Cormac thought: Too theatrical by far.

"You look well," M. Breton said to the countess. "Better than I expected after, what? More than five years."

"Thank you," she said, but did not return the compliment. M. Breton stared at her.

"How did you find me?" she said.

"I looked. I asked. Someone told me you were in New York, and I thought, She could only be a whore."

Cormac's stomach churned. He felt something new: that he was an intruder in the suite of the Countess de Chardon. Who denied the past, and now clearly had one.

"And how was prison?" she said.

"I survived. I'm here. It doesn't matter."

Now he turned on Cormac.

"Bring me another cognac," he said.

Cormac gestured toward the bar. "The bottle's over there. Help yourself, Monsieur Breton."

The Frenchman turned to the countess. "Is he the butler?'

"No, he's my lover," she said.

Cormac could hear himself breathing now. And the countess breathing. And M. Breton too.

Then M. Breton stared into his drink, laughed, and shook his head.

"Well," he said, "every cunt must have its servant."

Cormac stepped before him, anger quickening his pulse.

"You can leave now, my fiddling friend. There's the door."

"I don't think so," M. Breton said.

The countess stepped between them.

"Cormac, this is my husband."

76.

That night, as on every night, he retreated to his room down the hall. But now everything was different. No word had passed to him from the countess, but it was clear from her posture, her silence, and her eyes that he must stay away from the suite. This was a complete change. Before the arrival of M. Breton, after food and music and water and bed, they had always kissed good-night and retired to their separate beds for the replenishments of sleep. She wanted it that way, and he came to luxuriate in his own solitude. Alone in his room before sleep, he could read, he could imagine, he could paint, he could hum vagrant melodies. He could think, too, about the strangeness of his life, the long years, the old vows that were printed on him, the names and brief lives of the dead. He could indulge in the secret pleasures of philosophy. He could exercise blankness, wiping away all imagery and all regret.

On the second night, the countess stopped him in the hall and kissed his cheek.

"He'll stay with me," she said. "I hope you don't mind."

He said, "Fine, no, no, I understand. I don't mind."

But, of course, he did mind. Part of it was the impression made upon him by Yves Breton. He was arrogant and vain, convinced, it seemed, of his genius as a violinist and the superior rights that must be granted to him as a result. Who the hell was he to show up after many years and move back into his wife's bed? Cormac lay in his own bed thinking these things, and felt his anger growing in spite of his attempts to control it with his will. How could she take such a man to her bed? She had never told him everything about her past, and that was all right with Cormac. The past was the past. It could not be changed. If she did not tell him everything about her past, then he had no obligation to reveal his own, even if what he told her was an elaborate lie concocted to hide the truth. She would have laughed at the truth and suggested he take a room in the madhouse. But the past never completely passed, and here came her past, embodied in M. Breton, walking into their present.

He told himself that the countess might only be testing him, creating through this surprise a way to see whether Cormac was indeed free of jealousy. If so, she was playing a silly and dangerous game. Too French by far. He told himself he was not jealous but angry over a breach of manners. And then realized that he was indeed suffering from a slippery attack of jealousy. To his own complete surprise.

His ruminations were interrupted by a knock on the door. He got up quickly and cracked it open.

Fiammetta was there, in a sheer nightgown, holding a candle.

"Madame says you need me," the girl said.

"Thank you, Fiammetta," he said. "But I don't."

Her face was trembling.

"I can help you sleep," she said.

"I'll be all right."

"Okay, Mister O'Connor. Sleep tight."

"I'll try."

He did not sleep well that night or the next night or the night after that. He plunged into reporting, moving from hearings into the Croton water project to the murder of an apprentice boy on Baxter Street to the burning of a ship at the dock on Coenties Slip. He was cut off from the piano in the closed suite of the Countess de Chardon and put his energies into painting. He did not see M. Breton. He saw the countess on the fourth day after her husband's arrival in their lives.

"I can explain," she said. "But not now."

Jennings was in the doorway of the house on Hudson Street when Cormac arrived. His face looked pale and wasted, his eyes rheumy with horror. He was smoking a thin rum-soaked cigarillo.

"Even *you* don't want to see this one, Cormac," he said, a tremble in his voice. His eyes wandered to the small crowd on the sidewalk, and the horse-drawn carts beyond, and the old black men huddled in the doorways. Jennings clearly wanted to see something banal and comforting and familiar on this morning gray with the threat of rain.

"How bad is it?" Cormac asked.

"Two babies, their brains beaten out of their skulls. A woman shot three times in the face. A man with a bullet in his brow. They think he's the woman's son, and the babies belong to him."

"Oh, God . . ."

"The babies . . ." Jennings had lost all his mannerisms. His mouth trembled. "Oh, Jesus, Cormac . . ."

He seemed about to cry, then clamped the cigarillo in his teeth and slipped a whiskey flask from his jacket pocket.

"Who's on it?" Cormac said.

"Ford. Who else?"

"I don't envy his dreams."

Jennings took a swig from the flask, offered it to Cormac, who declined.

"How do you handle *your* dreams — without drink?" Jennings said.

"I don't."

Cormac patted Jennings on the back and entered the house of the newly dead. A young doctor pushed past him, climbing the stairs to the third floor. Children and adults peered from the partly opened doors, white faces and black. The odors of soup and shit and sewage filled the air. On the second landing a thin mustached cop blocked his way.

"Who are you?" the policeman said.

Cormac showed a press identity card. The cop squinted at it and handed it back.

"It's pretty bad up there," he said.

"So I've heard."

"All niggers," the cop said. "And a lot of opium too."

Cormac moved past him up the stairs. The egglike odor of soft coal now mixed with the stench of shit and blood. Another policeman blocked his way.

"Not now," he said. "They're still working."

"Ask the inspector if he can give his friend Cormac some names."

They were not friends, but he wanted the names.

"Ask him yourself," the cop said.

Cormac leaned past him, glimpsing blood on polished plank floors. "Inspector Ford, it's Cormac O'Connor. . . . I need some names."

Ford emerged from another room. His face was pale too, as if the crime were draining blood from the living.

"Come in, Cormac," he said softly. "I think you know this woman."

That night, his story written coldly and set in type, his stomach empty to fight off the nausea, he made drawings of Beatriz Machado. He drew her as she was in life. He drew her as a young woman in the bookstore in Lispenard Street. He drew her as she was at Quaco's funeral, an American in the presence of the oldest Africans. He drew her rich with fat, as she sold corn and oysters and opium from her stall on Broadway. He drew her with charcoal and sepia chalk, pulling her into life from memory, from the river of time. He hummed music as he used line and shadow and volume to make her as she was in life. He hummed the melodies that came from the hands of the countess. He hummed music that had never been written on paper, music that came from gourds and fiddles in a lost year in a vanished century. He worked in a kind of anguished frenzy, sweat pouring from his body.

Then, his hands black with chalk, he fell on the narrow bed, pulled a pillow over his face, and wept. He was sick of the things human beings did to one another. He was angry too. Too many people were chopped out of the world before you had a chance to say good-bye.

He did not hear the door open. But he felt the bed sag as she sat on its edge, felt her hands in his hair.

"Poor Cormac," the countess said.

He looked at her, expecting some gloss of irony. All he saw was care.

"You're hurting," she said.

"I am."

"And I'm one of the reasons you're hurting."

He sighed in a reluctant way.

"Yes," he said.

"But she — the woman in these drawings — she's a reason too."

"She is," he said. He sat up now on the edge of the bed and stared at his blackened hands.

"Tell me the story."

He stood up and went to the sink and began washing his hands.

"I knew her for many years," he said. "She sold oysters and other things from a stall on Broadway. She was warm and human and funny. At some point last night, she was murdered."

"My God."

The black would not come off his fingers. He pulled at it with a towel.

"Her own son killed her, along with two of his own children, and then shot himself in the brow." He heard his voice as if the voice alone were the cold teller of a tale. "He beat out the brains of the children. He shot off his mother's face." Then he took a deep breath, not looking at the countess for the effect of his words. "He told a woman on the first floor that he hated his mother because she laughed at him. That was probably true. She laughed at everyone and everything. She laughed at me, as well she should. She laughed at life." He paused, turned to look at the countess, whose face was lost in imagining. "The same woman on the first floor saw the son yesterday, in the morning. He told her he had been out of work for eleven months. He was tired of depending on his mother. He was tired of being black."

He glanced at the black lines dug into his fingertips, and the sanguine chalk red as blood. The countess looked up at him.

"Sit down," she said.

Then she told him some of her story: how she'd met Yves Breton in Paris, where her mother had taken her to study at the Conservatory. They were living then in New Orleans, which was still French, the place to which she and her mother had fled in 1802 when the slave revolt had come upon them. She remembered the cemeteries above ground because of the high level of the water, the porous soil full of writhing stone monuments, and how the one of her father was a kind of boast, because there was nothing of her father inside the tomb. His body had been hacked to pieces in Haiti. She was eight years old when her father was murdered, and her mother rose out of a cellar hide-out a day later, packed up jewels and cash and some paintings and pastels, and left for Louisiana, dry-eyed and angry. She was angry in some obscure way at the countess (who was not, of course, a countess) and angry with her dead husband, for failing to take the black revolutionists seriously until they walked into his drawing room; she was angry with Napoleon Bonaparte, the consul for life, for failing to protect them; she was angry at leaving the life they had made in the Caribbean.

"She never stopped being angry," the countess said. "And when Napoleon sold Louisiana to the Americans, she was angrier than ever. Anger kept her alive. It was her food."

They had a small house with a garden on Royal Street and a piano in the front parlor. They had two slaves, both women: a cook and a woman who cleaned. When the Americans arrived after 1804, all wild and bearded and wearing the skins of animals, drunk and mean-eyed men, as they said, from the back of beyond, whooping and raising rifles in the air, her mother had added a male slave to guard the doors, armed with an ax. His name was Jacques. The piano teacher stayed on, and the countess played every day, escaping from the anger of her mother, and the growing disorder of the town. And finally, when she was sixteen, after pleading and sobbing and many tantrums, she convinced her mother that they must go to Paris.

"She sold the women slaves," she said, "and freed Jacques, closed the house, and we sailed away."

She met M. Breton at the Conservatory, where he was teaching harmonics and violin. She tried to explain to Cormac how handsome M. Breton was then, in spite of the way he limped (from a wound at the Battle of Wagram), how reckless he was, how charged with passion. He talked without pause, about Goethe and Schiller and Madame de Staël, names she'd never heard in New Orleans, about the endless possibilities of music, about painters, about the way Napoleon was changing all of Europe and all of history. He became the first man she ever slept with.

"It was like a summer storm," she said, "without warning, without time for escape, and I have never regretted it. Everyone should fall in love in such a way, at least once."

M. Breton was eleven years older than she was, twenty-eight to her seventeen, a brilliant violinist, his music brooding with regret or exploding into exaltation. He had been too young to savor the enormous excitements of the Revolution, but he remained, in that year before Moscow, a passionate follower of Bonaparte, who had repaired all the errors and excesses of the Jacobins and restored the nation to glory. Or so he said. The loss of three toes on his right foot and part of his right femur at Wagram kept him out of the Grand Armée. But as he limped along the marble halls of the Conservatory, and through the streets of Paris, he kept telling her that all French honor, all *European* honor, was now derived from Bonaparte. M. Breton played his violin for soldiers in hospitals and at the funerals of the fallen. He cheered at parades.

"That was the only thing he did without sarcasm: cheer," the countess said. "And I cheered too."

Then came Moscow, and the end of the myth of invincibility, and the long, slow, violent fall that followed. When M. Breton looked up with clear eyes, the streets were filling with cripples and widows, and Napoleon Bonaparte was on Elba.

"By then, my mother and I were gone," the countess said. "We were back in New Orleans. We arrived three weeks after Andrew Jackson defeated the British, and my mother found her two women, and Jacques too, paid them for their services this time, and we tried to make the house a home. Now I gave lessons too, for there was not enough money, and my mother was still angry."

Nine months later, M. Breton arrived like a corsair. He courted her again, courted her mother too, charmed their friends, who were enchanted by his music. And so they married. A year later, a child died stillborn. One rainy summer night, M. Breton sat down and wrote a letter to his wife, explaining that he could not look at her without thinking of death, and then he vanished. There were a few letters over the next few years, from Mexico, from Havana, from Italy. A few lines here, a few lines there. She did not see him again. Until now.

"All true stories are unhappy ones," she said, once more protected by irony. "That's the essence of the romantic."

When she was gone, he fell into bed in the dark, thinking of the Countess de Chardon, and remembered where he was living when she was in Paris: that small sweaty room on Reade Street, and a woman whose face was now dim in memory and whose name was gone. Those were the years when he began thinking about women in categories that he knew were unfair: episodes, chapters, events, stories. As if each woman were a mere book taken down from a shelf, to be examined, pondered, and closed. He had no more women than other unmarried men, just more time. Year after year after year. All the time in the world. Everything could wait, including the possibilities of love. He learned in those years to avoid learning too much about a woman, because knowledge would make parting more wrenching, for her and for him. It was unfair, and in some cases cruel, but that came with the strangeness of his life.

Now he knew much more about the countess than he had learned in all the months that came before, but the knowledge gave him no comfort. His stomach churned. He wanted to go down the hall and lie with her. He wanted to confront M. Breton. He lay there until night melted into dawn.

77.

He paid for the burial of Beatriz Machado and her son and the girls. The adult coffins cost two dollars each and the children's seventy-five cents. A preacher from the African Methodist Church spoke over the coffins, and they were placed in the earth of a small cemetery near the Bowery. Some of the neighbors were there, and when it was over they hugged, whispered words of regret, and went their separate ways. Cormac thought: I have gone to too many funerals.

For four days he worked harder than ever at the newspaper. On one of the days, he talked to three politicians about the way New Yorkers were at last able to elect a mayor, and what that would mean to the future. He covered the suicide of a stockbroker, caught embezzling, and wrote a story that was not printed. "I know the poor lad's family," said Bryant, waving the story away. "They've suffered enough." On the following day, he visited a house overrun by rats, where women were beating at them with shovels while policemen laughed and small boys took target practice with rocks. He wrote a story about the American settlers in Texas and their revolt against Mexico, which refused to let them own slaves. He interviewed Samuel Colt, visiting from Hartford, who was showing off his new invention, the six-shooter. He did an article about the men who were paving lower Broadway, all of them Irish. He wrote for the *Evening Post*. He read the *New York Herald*.

He left the house on Duane Street early each day and returned late. He dined one night with Jennings, who was still sickened by the slaughter of Beatriz and her grandchildren, and did his best to console the man. He found an inn where the steak was tender. On the third night, he bathed alone in the room where the women of the house washed away the aromas of their work. He saw little of the countess. Then, on a rainy Saturday night, he was at his pad of paper again, working up finished drawings from tiny sketches made on the street. His fingers ached for the piano, wanting to bring music out of his head and into the air. The door burst open and M. Breton stood in the frame. His hair was unruly. His shirt was open to his chest. His mustache needed trimming.

"You, Irishman," he said in English. He had been drinking.

"Come in," Cormac said.

"I am in."

"Then close the fucking door."

M. Breton closed the door and gazed around the small studio. He glanced at the books and studied the drawings.

"Laurence Sterne?" he said. "Jonathan Swift. Théophile *Gautier*? Goethe . . . You're a reader."

"When there's time."

"I'm a musician," he said with a shrug. "Musicians don't read. They feel. They play."

"I've heard you play," Cormac said.

M. Breton waited as if expecting a blow.

"You're very good," Cormac said.

M. Breton sighed. "Not as good as I once dreamed of being."

"But very good, nevertheless."

"*Merci*. Do you have anything —"

"I don't drink. But I can pull that cord near the door and —"

"Cognac," he said, and sat down on the edge of the bed.

Cormac ordered cognac from the black servant who answered the pull of the cord.

"I came to apologize," M. Breton said, and asked if Cormac understood French, and switched with Cormac's affirmative nod. "I've come here, Irishman, to apologize." There was a scatter of rain on the windowpanes. "I have disrupted your life. My wife has told me the story, and of your . . . arrangement, and of how you have comforted her."

The hall porter arrived with a bottle of cognac and two glasses. M. Breton poured a glass for himself, offered the bottle to Cormac, who declined, then inhaled the aroma of the drink. His features seemed to loosen.

"I loved her from the day I met her," he said, staring into the glass. "She was the most beautiful creature I'd ever seen."

"She's beautiful now."

"Of course. But then she was still innocent. Then she was still flowering in music. I would see her, and sing. I would think of her, and play."

Cormac thought: Please don't say "We were meant for each other."

"We were certain to destroy each other," M. Breton said. "Music made her innocent. It made me corrupt. And corruption is always stronger than innocence."

He drained the cognac and poured another. The rain spattered the windowpanes now, and from away off to the west, Cormac heard thunder.

"So, Monsieur Breton, why did you come here?"

He looked at Cormac for a long beat.

"To die."

He didn't know where he had picked up syphilis. He was sure it was after he abandoned his wife in New Orleans. It could have been in Mexico City, where he played violin in a bordello on the Calle de la Esperanza; or in Vera Cruz, among the Africans and Indians and mestizos of the waterfront; or in Havana, where he lived for three years in a house on the Malecón facing the sea. He wanted the sun, not the cold drizzle of Paris. He wanted bodies warmed with the sun. He wanted to coarsen his talent with drink and women and the smothering stupor of heat. He found his way to Martinique, so that he could speak in French, and cursed Bonaparte for a fool, with his dreams of conquering arctic Russia while he had Louisiana and New Orleans and the islands of the southern sea.

"He could have ended his days glazed by the sun, a free man," he said. "But his vanity was too strong. He ruined himself. He ruined France. He ruined Europe."

He was happiest in Italy, where he landed in 1829, playing in Frenchified Milano, wandering on foot south to Tuscany, to Florence, listening to madrigals in cathedrals, on to Rome, then back again, instructing the children of the Italian rich. He was already sick, although the first stage had faded, and cognac was the only consolation. Until suddenly some guttering ember of his youth burst into flame. Charles X in France decided to bring back the hard old authority of the hard old regime, smashing freedom of the press and dissolving parliament, and M. Breton knew what would happen next. He took a coach to Paris in time for the July Revolution.

"I wanted to die on the barricades," he said. "A properly romantic death. One that would absolve all my sins."

He was wounded in the taking of the Hôtel de Ville, with a bullet through his side that just missed his kidneys, and did not see the celebrations after the August abdication. A woman nursed him back to health, a woman who loved him, who took him to the countryside near Lyons, who fed him, who dressed him and bathed him. When he could walk again, he fled.

"I could not give such a woman what I had," he said. "Could not kill her with my prick."

He shrugged again, shook his head. He was quiet for a long time. The storm rumbled around the New York streets. The windows trembled.

"I don't sleep with her," he said, motioning at the door and the apartment of the Countess de Chardon. "You should not worry."

He stood up heavily.

"I wish you'd play something," Cormac said. "There's some melody of yours that I've never heard before. . . ."

"Berlioz," he said. "It's from the *Symphonie Fantastique*. . . ."

"It's beautiful."

M. Breton sighed. "Yes." He gazed around the room. "But not tonight."

Three nights later, M. Breton insisted on a dinner for three in the suite of the countess. The service was handsomely laid out, with golden light from gas lamps and candles and the silver gleaming. There were oysters, and cheeses, and chilled wines, and veal and asparagus and small roasted potatoes. He had bathed and was crisply dressed, his shoes polished, his cravat precise, his fingernails scrubbed. The countess looked at him in a cautious way, laughing at his jokes, accepting his pouring of the wine, nodding at his ruminations on the fevers of politics.

"I must play," he said, and then took his violin and limped a few feet to the side, and gave them the aching, then soaring melodies of the *Symphonie Fantastique.*

Cormac saw tears welling in the eyes of the countess and held her hand. She placed her other hand on top of his. When M. Breton finished, he took a mock bow, and they applauded him.

Around three-thirty that morning, M. Breton hanged himself.

She buried him in St. Mark's-in-the-Bouwerie. Cormac did not attend. She returned with her face dry, and he sensed her anger struggling with her pity, as it must have struggled within her mother after Haiti. But she said nothing and he asked no questions. She had his own old custom of closing a book and leaving it closed. With his door open, he heard her tell the maids to air out the rooms and cast out the clothing of M. Breton, and place his violin in its case on a high shelf of a closet. That night, they resumed the habits of their lives together. In the morning, he sat down again to run his fingers on the keys of the piano.

And yet it was not the same. A shadow had fallen upon them, as indefinite as any shadow. On a primitive level, it was simple: He knew too much about her now and she knew nothing of consequence about him. The old symmetry of unknowability had been upset. But he'd learned something about himself too. After so many years, he could be jealous. He could tremble with anger and weakness and need. As old as he was, that tangle of nerves still lived within him. And he knew a larger truth: He loved this woman.

Just after dark on December 16, the countess came to his room.

"They've done it," she said. "Pearl Street is burning."

Cormac dressed quickly in warm clothes, with beaver hat and lined gloves, for it was a frigid night, pocketed a sketchbook and pencils, and went out. High up on Duane Street, he could smell smoke, carried by the north-blowing wind, and peering down Broadway he saw a glow in the skies above the First Ward. He heard the *dong-dong*ing of warning bells and shouts of alarm and the strangled din of human voices. He turned his back to the wind, which blew more fiercely as he came closer to the harbor, clogging his eyes with cold tears. Thinking: Fire again. Like the fire that took my father's body to the Otherworld. Like the fire that destroyed the earl's mansion in Ireland. Like the fire that leveled the fort in 1741. Or the fires from the start of the Revolution, those great blazing, wind-driven fires that even toppled Trinity Church. Earth, air, fire, and water: the elements of the world.

When he arrived at Pearl Street, the firemen were already wild with panic. The icy wind whipped the flames, shifting, turning, creating immense orange flames and whirlpools of fire, as if playing some evil game with the puny structures made by men. The pumps didn't deliver the water that was needed. The water itself was frozen beneath the ground, in the shallow wells, in the rotting wooden pipes of the Manhattan Company. The water that did flow quickly froze in the canvas hoses. In the orange light of the flames, Cormac saw cobblers and coopers backing away from their burning homes, blankets draped across their shoulders, their children wailing, their wives mad with loss. A woman in a shawl raced toward the flames, screaming, *"Our silver, our wedding silver!"* A fireman tried to stop her, but she plunged through the great orange wall and didn't come back.

"Fucked," a fireman said. "Too much wind and too little water. We're absolutely fucked."

And so they were.

For hours, with his fingers freezing in their gloves, Cormac moved through the crowds, swollen now by other New Yorkers who had come to witness the calamity (or to bring blankets and soup to the dispossessed). There was no control, nobody in charge. Sparks and embers rose into the purple sky, and to Cormac looked oddly beautiful, like very slow fireworks. Those sparks and embers fell upon the shingled rooftops of other buildings. Beams crackled, bottles exploded and popped, and then there was a great *whoosh*ing sound as a roof came down upon an upper floor. Followed by the sound of an immense coal chute as the roof brought down everything with it: beds and books and nightgowns, silverware and tools, crockery and etchings, boots and crinolines and andirons. Some people wailed as the artifacts of their lives vanished. Some looked too stunned for human feeling. The smoke made all of them choke and cough, and Cormac tied a handkerchief across his mouth and nose. Men were leading horses to safety up Broadway, but he could smell burned horseflesh from the midst of burning buildings. Dogs howled. Men cursed. Carts arrived to help evacuate houses in the path of the flames, the cartmen tripling their prices for the night. Cormac the painter made sketches. Cormac the newspaperman made notes. One fireman told him that the fire had started at 88 Pearl Street, near the corner of Exchange, and was discovered by a watchman named Hayes. Another said that fifty buildings had been burned in the first fifteen minutes. Some citizens blamed the volunteer firemen for the chaos, saying they were nothing but amateurs, if not criminal gangs. And what was more, some were looting the burning homes, stuffing their pockets with silver and tools and pistols.

"We shouldn't pay them," one outraged citizen shouted. "We should hang them!"

This had some truth to it. Around two in the morning, he saw Hughie Mulligan and his boys moving out of buildings on the far side of the densest fire. All wore the leather helmets of the volunteer fire departments. All wore heavy coats with bulging pockets. They moved quickly, darting in and out of smoke, then vanishing toward their carts.

About four in the morning, Cormac hurried to the *Post* on Pine Street and wrote a story (one of three that made the newspaper that morning), left some broad-brushed sketches for the engraver Fasanella, and then returned to the fire. It burned for two days, and firemen came to help from as far away as Philadelphia. When it was over, twenty square blocks and 697 buildings had been destroyed. It wasn't known how many died, because no bodies were found in the ashes. Twenty-two of the city's twenty-four insurance companies went bankrupt. The stench of the fire lay over the downtown streets for months, and one thing was absolutely certain: The old wooden town was gone forever.

"I warned you," said the Countess de Chardon as Cormac stretched in her bath on the afternoon of the seventeenth and tried to scrub the soot and grime out of his hair and off his exhausted body.

"And I kept my word and kept my silence."

"So you did."

"But you're in danger, Countess. You must understand that."

"Why am I in danger?" she said in an amused way.

"Because *they* know that *you* know."

She pondered this, her face darkening. "I know more than just this, alas. The Wax Man loves to babble."

"That's the problem."

That night she decided that it was time for a vacation in Paris. She would place a friend in charge of the house and vanish for a year. Would Cormac come with her? She could show him all the secret places that she saw when she was sixteen. They could try to meet this writer named Balzac whose name was in all the gazettes. He wanted her to stay but knew she had to leave. Cormac told her that he couldn't go to Paris. But he would be waiting for her in New York when she returned.

"It's nice of you to say that," she said in a melancholy way.

"I'll be here. I swear it."

She shrugged. And began the rituals of departure. She packed trunks. She went alone to purchase a ticket on the Black Flag packet that went south to the Caribbean before crossing the winter sea to Le Havre. She said that a heavy, sweet-voiced woman named Sara Long would run the house, and introduced her to Cormac. "She's a delight," the countess said, while the woman blushed. "Particularly in bed." Then she wrote out a long letter filled with what she knew about the conspiracy to set the fires and sealed it, appropriately, with wax.

"Before I leave, I'll let the Wax Man's friends know that this exists," she said. "And that it will be made public if anything happens to me. If anything does happen, I want you to put this in your newspaper."

"I'll do my best. It's never up to me."

"Yes. I understand. I know, better than most, who decides what goes into newspapers. . . ." She sighed. "Just do your best."

She then opened a panel above the bed, slipped the letter into a small safe, and handed Cormac the key. Then she sat down hard on one of her chairs, while snow fell steadily beyond the windowpanes behind her.

"I don't want you to go," he said.

"But for us, the timing might be right, no?"

"What do you mean?"

He sat beside her and she huddled against him while he played his fingers in her hair.

"I mean something has happened to us," she said. "When Monsieur Breton arrived, it meant that each of us had a past, and that was too much to carry. The fire was just . . . a kind of way to end things."

"I can't accept that."

"You didn't think we would grow old together, did you? Sitting in chairs somewhere, gray and full of years, looking at the sea?"

"No."

"Nor did I."

"But you could move with me somewhere else for a while. Say you're going to Paris and actually live in a house up on top of the island until they forget you. They'll know you've said nothing because there'll be nothing in the newspapers."

"Yes, and one night, some fool is passing by, lost and needing directions. And he sees my face, and they come for both of us."

She eased away from him, poured a glass of white wine.

"And you? In such an arrangement, you'd be a prisoner. You'd be living my life, protecting me, my Irish knight, and slowly going crazy. No, that won't work. And if I'm quiet, you'll think I'm remembering Monsieur Breton. And if I play piano, you'll think of him with his violin. And you might be correct."

She stood up and stared out at the snow.

"Sooner or later, you would go."

"I don't think so."

She turned to him and smiled a radiant smile.

"If you wouldn't go, then I would," she said.

He returned her smile.

"Who will teach me to play piano?" he said.

"You will."

Later that night, they made love while snow fell upon the wounded city. She left for South Street before dawn.

For three days and three nights, he never left the house on Duane Street. He told the *Evening Post* that he was exhausted, sick from the smoke of the Great Fire, and needed some time to recover. They gave it to him graciously. The women came to offer him flesh and biscuits. He accepted the biscuits. All day, he played the piano, caressing the keys, trying to remember the melody of Berlioz while failing to club it out of the piano. At night, he lay alone, his mind full of death.

They all danced for him in the flickering light of a single gas lamp. His father waltzed with his mother. Bridget Riley danced with Mary Burton. The Earl of Warren danced alone, juggling three balls in three-quarter time. Here came all the black women, dancing with Bantu and Silver and Aaron, Big Michael and Carlito, all young and free. There was Quaco dancing with his wife, safe from the fires of the fort. And Dubious Jones with Beatriz Machado. While Kongo watched in the shadows. Cormac hummed as the dance unfolded in the gaslit room and the snow fell steadily and he ached with loneliness.

It's time to go, he told himself. It's time to move on. I have lived too long in this refuge, with its water and scent of lavender. I have lived in a parenthesis of time, and now it has come to an end. The countess is gone, and I must go too. I can't live in a haunted house.

He found new lodgings on Mott Street, avoiding the pillowy consolations of Sara Long. Four days later, a mob of puritanical zealots, including Hughie Mulligan, newly converted to the banners of God, stormed the house on Duane Street, beating the women, rousting the customers, carting away the art and the candelabra and the furnishing, and then set the building on fire. When Cormac arrived the next day, scavengers were poking in the rubble. He looked for the safe for hours and in late afternoon found it under some glistening timbers. The metal was still hot. He wrapped it in burlap, cooled it in some blackened snow, carried it to Mott Street, and opened it with a key (using oil to lubricate the lock). The last note of the Countess de Chardon had been baked into ashes.

Two weeks after that, he was in the office at the *Post* when news arrived that the Black Flag packet to Le Havre had been lost at sea. There were 216 passengers on board. Cormac scanned the list. The name of the Countess de Chardon did not appear, but he knew she was among them.

That same week, the clearing of the ruined houses was well under way. The work was done quickly, efficiently, almost ruthlessly. New buildings made of granite blocks and Corinthian pillars began to rise from the rubble. The most important of them looked like temples, dedicated, of course, to Mammon.

Seven

Boss

How strange it seems, with so much gone
Of life and love, to still live on.

— John Greenleaf Whittier, 1866

What are you gonna do about it?

— William M. Tweed, 1871

78.

The bells of the Essex Market Tower were tolling six times when Cormac went up the steps of the Ludlow Street Jail. It was a mellow April evening, and he could hear a piano playing from the open doors of Erchberg's Saloon across the street. He pulled a bell. A slot opened in the thick iron doors.

"Who do you want?"

"Mr. Tweed."

"You on the list?"

"I should be."

"Name."

"Devlin."

A pause. The slot slammed shut and the door squeaked open. A ruddy man in a pale gray uniform sat on a stool, holding a book. He was in a wide gray room with gray women and a few gray lawyers sitting on benches. There was a gray photographic print of the mayor on one wall, and a sad American flag nailed to another.

"Sign here," the guard said, offering the book.

Cormac signed in as Devlin.

"What's in the pail?"

"Ice cream," Cormac said, lifting the lid.

"You been here before?"

"Yes."

"Then you know the way."

"I do."

He walked through the gray room and down a corridor to a door at the rear. He knocked twice. The door opened and a young black man was there. He smiled at Cormac.

"Evenin', sah."

"Hello, Luke. How is he?"

"Not so good. The doctor bin here, and it don't look none too good." He smiled. "But he lookin' forward to you comin'."

Cormac entered the bedroom, where there was a narrow bed beside a curtained window, steel bars outlined by the streetlights beyond. A mattress was beside the bed, where Luke slept at night, watching over his boss. A pot of geraniums sat on a small night table, which also held a single candle.

"Jes' go on through," Luke said.

He opened a door and walked into the larger room. Tweed was sitting in a Windsor chair, a colorful quilt over his shoulders. The chair had been built wider than most such chairs, with special orders from Tweed, who was particular about his chairs, since he'd spent his youth making them.

"Well, you're the first decent face I've seen since the last time you were here," he said. The voice was lower, but had the old gravelly texture.

"How are you, Bill?"

"Not worth a fiddler's fuck, if the truth be known. The doctors tell me I've got bronchitis, cystitis, some other fuckin-itis. My feet are numb with the diabetes. My head hurts. I feel like a bag of bonemeal." He laughed. "But I've still got a heartbeat. Pull up a chair."

Cormac set down the pail of ice cream and crossed the room for a chair. There was a boxy grand piano against one wall, a table for meals, flowers everywhere. Cretonne curtains. Bands of thick rubber attached to a casement for exercise. Two of Cormac's own paintings hung on the walls, one of the Great Fire, and a view of Cherry Street toward the river, along with pictures of yachts outside the Americus Club in Connecticut and a daguerreotype of Tweed's wife and children. Cormac took a chair from the table, twirled it so that the back faced Tweed, and sat with his arms draped over the curve.

"I'm worn out," Tweed said. "Luke has some woman mad for him, that right, Luke?"

"Yeah, she crazy for me."

"And she writes him these letters, very fancy handwriting. Mister Luke Grant, Ludlow Street Prison, on the envelope. Like *he* was the prisoner, not me. And so I help him with the writing. I mean, I talk, and he writes. He likes those big words."

"She do too, boss. She likes that 'extraordinary.' She likes that 'mellifluous.' She likes 'magnificent.'"

"She's after your magnificent fortune, Luke."

Luke laughed, and Cormac lifted the pail toward him.

"We'd better eat this before it melts," he said. "There's enough for the three of us."

"Yes, sir, Mist' Cormac."

"You know how to spoil a man," Tweed said.

"It's from Braren, the German."

"To hell with what the doctor says."

Luke came back with two dishes and spoons, and Tweed started to eat.

"I hope they've got ice cream in Hell," he said.

"I'm sure they don't, so you'd better have all you want while you're here."

"Luke," Tweed said, "fill this again."

He wasn't really old, only fifty-five on this night, but Bill Tweed looked ancient now. His beard was white without seeming patriarchal, his hair thin on his skull, gray and lank. But it was the eyes that looked a thousand years old. They were looking at last like the black sunken eyes in the Nast cartoons, with small stars of yellow light reflected from the gas lamps. He had never been a drinker, and smoked only a rare cigar, but the face looked dissipated, and there was a wheezing sound from his lungs. The great body was shrinking too, the shoulders somehow narrower inside the blanket.

"There's less of me every time you show up," Tweed said.

"There was a *lot* less of you when we met," Cormac said.

"Aye, wasn't there . . ."

"You were tough as a mule that night."

"What the hell year was that?"

"It was 1844. . . ."

"Jesus Christ."

A summer night. On Grand Street, on the Seventh Ward side of the Bowery. I was still living on Mott Street, Cormac remembered.

Painting. Writing the first of the dime novels. Laying cobblestones for a living. In early July, American nativists rioted against Catholics, killing two, beating hundreds, most of them Irish who thought they'd left all that behind.

"That scoundrel Ned Buntline was stirring them up that summer," Tweed said. "Another goddamned writer that liked trouble."

"And Morse."

"That bastard," Tweed said, taking a fresh dish of ice cream from Luke. "Samuel F. B. Morse. Always insisting on the F. B."

"Which the Irish said stood for Fucking Bigot."

"Which he was," Tweed wheezed. "Him and his goddamned telegraph. An invention he thought gave him the right to judge people. If there was any justice, he'd have ended his days here, instead of me."

"He certainly helped put those Know-Nothing idiots on the street that night."

"The poor bastards."

On that summer night in '44, Tweed was walking west on Grand Street, while Cormac walked toward him from the east. They were a block apart when Cormac noticed him. Nobody else was in the street. Tweed was then twenty-one years old, and in the obscure light of Grand Street he walked with a big man's casual confidence. If he was Catholic, that rolling gait would have infuriated the men who came upon him from the safety of their carriage.

"They thought I was a Catholic," Tweed said. "Me, who believed in nothing, even then. Me, the child of Presbyterians from the River Tweed in Scotland."

He laughed.

"The theory was simple: if they didn't know you, you were a Catholic."

On that night in '44, the three men in black followed that theory. They leaped from the carriage, hefting clubs that were two feet long. From a distance, Cormac saw them approach Tweed but couldn't hear their words.

"They said, 'Hey, papist!'" Tweed said, "and I said, 'Fuckest thee off!' Which they thought was Latin. They started swinging the cudgels."

Cormac saw Tweed knock down one of them with a punch, but he couldn't dodge the clubs of the other two.

"Then you got into it," Tweed said. "What the hell for?"

"I was like them," Cormac said. "I thought you were a Catholic and I didn't want you killed over some horseshit from the seventeenth century."

Cormac picked up the club of the fallen man and stepped in, swinging. He gripped the club horizontally, kicked one of the young men in the ass to get his attention, then slashed left-right, then right-left with the club, driving the man's jaw off its hinges.

"I remember the scream from the fucker even now," Tweed said, laying the ice cream dish on a table beside a Bible.

"I didn't need to hit the third idiot," Cormac said.

"That's for true. I was givin' him a good hammerin'."

His head rose now, remembering that night, and there was more light in his eyes.

"A terrible hammering," Cormac said, remembering Tweed smashing the man against a stoop, wrenching the club from the man's hand and tossing it behind him into the street. The carriage suddenly galloped away toward the East River. The last man was spread on the stoop, unable to rise because of the angle, and every time he tried to get up, Tweed hit him. The man pleaded that he was done. "Well, I'm not," said Tweed, and hammered him again. Without his cap, the man on the stoop looked to be sixteen or so, with a hairless face, blood gushing from his nose and leaking from a cut over his right eye.

"Who are you, you rotten little shit?" Tweed said.

"Johnson, sir, I'm sorry. Bill Johnson, sir, sorry, a mistake —"

Tweed stepped back, paused, then hit the man again, driving his head to the side. Blood now covered his teeth.

"Easy now, mister," Cormac said. "You don't want to kill him."

"No, I don't," he said, and chuckled, then went fierce again, grabbing the frightened boy by the neck. "Who sent you after me?"

"I don't know, sir, I —"

Tweed was laughing now in his room in the Ludlow Street Jail.

"I did get the fucker to tell me who'd sent him out to beat up people, including me," Tweed said. "I remember that."

Cormac again saw young Bill Tweed driving a hand between the man's legs, grabbing his testicles, and squeezing. The man's eyes bulged and a gargling cry rose from his throat. Then the first man who'd been knocked down by Tweed rose on wobbly legs. His bleary eyes gazed around for his club. He patted his jacket as if looking for a pistol. Cormac walked to him, again gripping the club with two hands, and jerked it hard to the man's chin. The young man fell in a shambling pile. Two of them were groaning on the street now, while Tweed squeezed the third man's balls.

"A name," he said.

"Martinson, sir. Yes, that's it. Martinson. Frankie Martinson, sir . . ."

"Of course. Frankie Martinson. That hopeless Know-Nothing idiot."

Tweed called to Luke for a glass of water.

"Frankie Martinson," he said. "Wasn't that the man?"

"That was the man, all right," Cormac said. "And I remember how you thanked the fella for his cooperation."

"Oh, sweet Jesus . . ."

Cormac saw young Tweed step back, gaze down at the man for a moment, then grab his ankles and drag him roughly down the steps and out into the street. Tweed was laughing a deep, excited laugh. Holding each ankle, he swung the boy around, once, twice, three times, and then let him go. The young man sailed a few feet and then skidded through mud and horseshit and was still.

"Now," Tweed said, turning to Cormac. "I believe I owe you a drink."

He draped a large hand on Cormac's shoulder (he was taller than Cormac by at least two inches) and they began moving toward the Bowery. Tweed laughed and said he knew Martinson from the endless arguments between the fire companies. Tweed was with the Big Six on Gouverneur Street. Martinson was a big shot with Engine Company 40, who called themselves the Lady Washingtons after the wife of the first president. Tweed had infuriated the man for arguing against the lunatics among the nativists and then laughing at his stupidity. He laughed harder that night at the memory of the three men laid out in the mud and fog of Grand Street; laughed, and said they should have delivered the wrecked trio to Engine Company 40; laughed, and then asked Cormac for his name. He told him his true name and Tweed said his.

"You're a good man," Bill Tweed said. "I think I've found a friend."

Now that Tweed's life was in ruins, Cormac could trace that friendship through all its labyrinthine ways; through the rise from the firehouse on Cherry Street that gave Tweed life and a sense of power, into politics as it was, not as he wished it could be. Tweed was like all the others in that New York who lived in the worst places or had the wrong names. They wanted some taste of power, to level out the rules of the game, and Cormac felt what they felt, and so did Bill Tweed. You have the banks, they said together, and you have the churches, and you have the mighty sailing fleets, and you have the deeds to land and the finest houses and servants and water; fair enough: But we have the votes.

"I can count," said Bill Tweed when Cormac asked him one night why he supported the Irish against the Know-Nothings. Then laughed. Then looked down Orange Street and said, "Somebody better fight for the poor bastards."

Cormac learned a few days after meeting Bill Tweed that the big man was also quite serious about fighting other enemies. The proof was in a brief note in the *Herald:* the saloon owned by one Francis Martinson, a volunteer fire captain of Little Water Street, had burned to the ground. The cause of the fire was being investigated. After that, Frankie Martinson was said to have moved to Albany. He was never again seen in the Five Points.

"Don't get mad," Tweed said one night, in a philosophical mood. "Get even."

In the years that followed, Cormac often roamed the night town with Tweed, stopping in saloons, listening to the gossip and the jokes, hearing the tales of faction fights and endless schism. Almost always, Tweed was the man who suggested compromise, conciliation, the smooth solution of a decent job. He was big; the most violent men were all small. On these pilgrimages, Cormac tried to remain a shadow, someone who helped watch Bill Tweed's back but who never stepped forward to insist on his own importance. And he never asked for anything. Not a job. Not a payday. And when Tweed rose and started consolidating his contacts and powers, when he sold the chair-making shop on Cherry Street to become a full-time politician (heavier now, craftier, measuring every uttered word), when he was elected to Congress for a term, Cormac continued asking for nothing.

"Where, for Christ's sake, do you live?" Tweed asked one night. "I've known you for three years and don't have a clue."

He insisted on being taken to the flat on Mott Street. Cormac did not say that this was the room where he had tried to write a true novel, and failed, and where he had begun to write dime novels while working days as a laborer. Tweed stepped into the room in a clumsy way, glanced at the stacked books and clothes hanging from pegs, and a trapped look darted through his eyes.

"It's like a cell," he said.

Cormac laughed. "Just what I deserve."

Tweed picked up a sheaf of Cormac's drawings.

"These are yours?"

"What I do to keep out of a real cell, Bill."

"They're very, very good."

"Thank you."

"Why don't you paint? You'd be a bloody good painter."

"I couldn't get a chair into this room," Cormac said, "never mind an easel."

"Well, get the hell out of here. I can find you a place. We can find one where you don't even pay rent. Where —"

"Thanks, Bill. This'll do me fine. Let's take a walk. Get something to eat. It's a lovely night."

"I'm buying," Tweed said.

Now Luke went to the door in the bedroom, and two more men arrived. Both were dressed in well-cut worsted suits, and they lifted their derbies as they entered. Cormac had met them both.

One was a small precise Madison Avenue doctor named Frank Cahill. The other was Billy Edelstein, one of the first of Tweed's lawyers after the fall, and now surely the last. Edelstein was plumper than Cahill and had a weary sardonic voice.

"A doctor, a lawyer, and me," Tweed said. "The last living Indian chief."

They laughed, since both were Tammany loyalists, members of the Society of Saint Tamenend, an Indian chief who had never existed. The Tammany headquarters in Fourteenth Street was known by friends and foes as the Wigwam.

"No law talk tonight, boys," Tweed said, his face brightening. "No talk about my ailing heart. Just food, boys, and fun."

"Fair enough," Cahill said. "But not too much food, Bill."

They all knew that for Bill Tweed food was fuel, pleasure, and even the producer of meaning. An extravagant meal told Tweed that he existed. He didn't drink much, except for iced light Rhinelander wine. But in the glory days, he would have six eggs for breakfast with a slab of ham; three steaks for lunch; bowls of soup, loaves of bread, and buckets of butter with every meal. As he grew older and the power came, the appetite did not vanish. He could never name the void that he could not fill and neither could Cormac. He had one wife, eight children, two mistresses, three houses. Enough wasn't ever enough.

"Sometimes I think this is all there is," he said with a smile, twelve years after they met, as they settled into an immense platter of chilled oysters. "All the rest might be bullshit."

Cormac heard that glorious word for the first time in the 1850s, and it came to epitomize for him all of New York's rough skepticism. It had much greater weight than the word *horseshit*. Horseshit was flaky and without substance; it dried in the sun and was blown away in a high wind. Preachers were the masters of horseshit. But bullshit was heavier, filled with crude truth, a kind of black cement. The voters knew the difference and they appreciated bullshit when practiced by a master. Any politician who used God in a speech was practicing horseshit. When he talked about building schools, getting water into Chatham Square, or lighting the darkest streets, Bill Tweed was practicing bullshit. If a third of the bullshit actually came into existence, their lives were made better. Tweed, as he moved up in the system, was a master of bullshit.

The world in which he worked his public arts and his private craft had been formed years earlier by a political enemy named Fernando Wood, who would serve as mayor three times. Wood was a genius, the creator of alliances and secret agendas, his system's machinery based on the understanding that politics was just another profession and the men who practiced it were entitled to rewards. The hard truth was known by all; to think otherwise was horseshit. Wood just didn't have an idea in his head and made nothing happen.

When Tweed took power as head of Tammany Hall, he presented plans for water, for housing, for schools, for decent wages, for the right to form unions among tradesmen and mechanics; in some way, those ambitions were shared by all of the Tammany professionals, so much so that the principles were seldom mentioned. To talk too much about them would be bullshit. Cormac sometimes drew up the plans, making them at once precise and vague, and gave them to Bill Tweed and stood in the shadows as Tweed tried to make at least parts of them real. Tweed's friends and associates listened, calculated, made swollen budgets and phony invoices to include their personal shares, and then sighed. They would need money to pay off the upstate Republicans. They would need money to pay off those who lived in the way of the street that must be widened. And of course they needed money for themselves and their boys. To Cormac, the Tammany sachems were like worldly archbishops who no longer believed in God.

In private, or over oysters, Cormac argued the issues of slavery with Tweed but was greeted with a shrug. "It's an injustice, the whole goddamned thing," Tweed said. "No doubt about it. But there's nothing to be done. It's the way things are." They would walk along South Street at lunch hour, and Tweed would point at the endless rows of masts and the small armies of stevedores and say: "All from the South, brother. Cotton, sugar, all of it . . . If we lose that trade, we'll be a cemetery." And Cormac said, "If you keep it, we'll be a cemetery." And Tweed said nothing, as they walked among the Irish and the Africans on a day when

Cormac did not hear a single word in Irish or Yoruba, in the city whose past was swiftly sliding away.

All of that seemed long ago, in this room in the Ludlow Street Jail. The table was set for five, and when Luke Grant went to pick up the food, the fifth man arrived: Charlie Butts, former head-breaker from the Cherry Street days of Tweed's youth, now the owner of a livery business with 109 carriages. Butts had a thick neck, broad shoulders, fierce mustaches dyed black, hard gray eyes, and short legs. He was carrying a cardboard box, which held the birthday cake.

"Charlie, you know everybody here?"

"I do."

"Could you do us a favor and fix some drinks for them that's drinking? Luke's gone for the chops."

Butts lifted a bottle of Rhinelander wine from the glass ice bucket (no silver allowed in Ludlow Street) and gave Cormac a squinty look. They'd been seeing each other for twenty years in the company of Bill Tweed.

"You still a newspaperman, Cormac?"

"No, not for a long time."

"Good. What's said here is between us."

Tweed said: "He doesn't have to be reminded of the rules, Charlie. We've been friends longer than I've known you."

"He looks too young for that."

"He's a freak of nature," Tweed said, sipping his water.

Cahill, the doctor, leaned forward, trying to lighten the moment.

"He's not a freak of nature," he said. "He's Irish. When they don't drink, they look good forever. In Mayo, there's a guy a hundred and nine years old, and not a white hair on his head."

"Is he still fucking?" said Billy Edelstein.

"Only nuns," Cahill said, and Tweed laughed and wheezed and grabbed at his chest until the doctor's face went pale. He held Tweed's wrist, he patted his back.

"For Chrissakes, Bill, we don't want you dying over a hundred-and-nine-year-old Mick fucking nuns."

That set Tweed going again, his eyes dancing with laughter, but the huge body wracked and hurting. He coughed a wad of phlegm into a handkerchief. Cormac saw a few spots of blood.

"Will somebody please talk about the fucking water problem?" Butts said.

"Or that rat Dick Connolly?" said Edelstein. "Blabbing away and living free in Paris."

"Not till after dinner, for Jaysus' sake," Butts said.

The mention of Connolly calmed them all down. They knew that everyone else in the Ring was free, and only Tweed was in jail. Connolly was indeed in Paris, carrying with him six million dollars. Elegant Oakey Hall, the former mayor, supreme horseshit artist (as the Boss called him), was off in London, charming the British. Brains Sweeny had paid a fat fine and was dozing in the country. Tweed was the only one of them in jail. And the attorney general, Charles S. Fairchild, had double-crossed the Boss, promising him freedom in exchange for some sort of confession. Tweed had confessed, and stayed in jail. There was a minute of somber silence as the faces of their old friends passed among them.

Then Luke returned with the food.

"Salvation, gentlemen," Tweed said.

Luke laid out the veal chops, corn, asparagus, and roasted potatoes. He put a basket of bread on the small table, and a small tub of butter and slabs of cheese. Everybody got up, except Tweed. He tried, but fell back, and Cormac took one elbow, and Butts the other and they lifted him out of the Windsor chair. He shuffled to the head of the table. Cormac noticed that he gave off a moldy odor, as if something had exuded through his pores and dried on his skin.

"Jesus Christ," he said in a feeble way. "Jesus Christ . . ."

They all carved away at the chops, remarking on their tenderness, while Tweed grunted and chewed. Cahill tried to guide the talk away from anything upsetting. They chatted about this fellow Edison who had invented a sealed light bulb, with some kind of filament inside that made fire impossible. "He'll get rich on that one," Edelstein said, "as long as he got it copyrighted." Butts said they'd never get enough electric lights in New York to light a single avenue, and Tweed whispered, "You're wrong, Charlie, you're wrong. They're gonna light up the whole city. There'll be no such thing as night."

"There'll be subways too, Charlie," Cahill said. "You'll be out of business with the carriages if you don't get a piece of them."

"People won't ride under the fucking ground."

"They're doing it in England."

"New Yorkers will never do it. It's like being in a tomb."

"Or the Tombs," Tweed said, and smiled.

"What do you hear from the wife, Bill?" Cahill said.

"She's fine, she's fine. You know, I just wanted her to be away from all the flying shit here if, if . . . She's taken care of no matter what happens."

He paused, the knife and fork in his hands.

"But listen to this," he said. "She's in Paris, right, with the young children? And she goes to the opera with some friend of hers. And who's sitting in the twelfth row? Connolly. Slippery Dick himself."

"Jaysus."

"So at the interval, she goes right to him. He looks shocked to see her, but she says to him, 'You, sir, are a cur.' And walks out."

"Good woman."

"Bravo."

A pause.

"I hope to join her there soon," Tweed said. "If I get sprung."

"We're working on it," said Edelstein. "And we've got some chance. The public is outraged over Fairchild's double-cross. They want the state to spring you."

"I should have built this goddamned jail on Spring Street," Tweed said, and they all laughed.

"Let's talk about something else, Bill," Cahill said. "I don't want your blood pressure to go through the roof."

"I wish *I* could go through the roof!"

Then he led them again into the food, like a commander set against a foe, eating with a kind of frenzy. Once Cahill placed a hand on his wrist, as if to slow him down, and he waited, inhaled, sipped some water, gave Cahill a filthy look, and went on. Edelstein said the corn was delicious. Tweed said, "I don't have the teeth for it anymore." He cleaned his plate with buttered bread. Then turned to Cormac.

"Where is that ice cream store, anyway?"

"Two blocks from here, Delancey and Essex."

"Luke!"

They cleaned their own plates in the sink while Luke went for the ice cream. Then they helped Tweed back to his Windsor chair and sat facing him. He looked at Butts, and then at Cahill and Edelstein, and turned his face toward the barred window with the flowered cretonne curtains moving languidly in a breeze. Cormac noted their grave faces. Finally Tweed whispered, "I'm never getting out of here alive, am I?"

Ah, Bill, Cormac thought. Ah, you goddamned fool. God damn it all to Hell.

Tweed had helped him more than once, had helped them all, the way he'd helped thousands of people in the bad parts of town. He had paid for medical school for Cahill and law school for Edelstein. He'd arranged a place for Cahill on the staff of St. Luke's and got Edelstein into a good law firm. Neither man was part of the Ring. They didn't vote early and often. They didn't line up with the shoulder hitters to intimidate voters on election days. They gave Tweed something in return that he needed more than cash or votes. They gave him unconditional loyalty, which was another way of saying that they loved him. In a way, that was all he truly wanted.

"I'd take a bullet for the man," Cahill said one night after Tweed had been through a day of agony in a courtroom. "I mean it. I'd take the bullet."

"He's the only true Christian I've ever met," Edelstein said on another night, silent with snow. "Jews don't meet many of them."

They knew, and Cormac knew, that Tweed was presiding over the most corrupt system in New York history. He didn't tell them this, never brought them into the system. But they all read the newspapers, and particularly the *New York Times,* which had all the documents, and saw the Startling Revelations after 1871 about how Tweed took 25 percent of all city contracts, which were inflated by the contractors to cover the bribes (while Slippery Dick Connolly, as controller, took down his own 10 percent). Money was flowing everywhere in New York after the Civil War, and the Ring took its piece. The newspapers seldom mentioned that the system was invented in the 1840s by Fernando Wood, who was thinner than Tweed and slicker and knew as much about loyalty as an oyster. Tweed was in the business of politics and he would end up convicted of standard business practices. The newspapers didn't mention that most of the swag, about twenty million dollars of it, went to the Republicans in Albany, because Tweed could get nothing done without their approval. New York was the only city in the state that could not levy taxes without the permission of Albany, and the upstaters would never give up such a cash cow. If Tweed wanted money for New York City schools, he had to bribe the Republicans. If he wanted Croton water to flow into the streets where the poor lived, he had to pay off Republicans. One night before it all went bad, Tweed paused over a meal at the Astor House and said, "It's cheaper to buy the legislature than to elect it." And laughed and laughed.

A lot of the money stuck to him, of course, and Cormac knew it. So did Cahill and Edelstein. Tweed owned the building on Duane Street where he ran his office on the third floor and accepted the bundles of cash. He owned property on both sides of the new Central Park. He moved from one large Uptown house to another as his family grew bigger, and each house was grander than the last, with three carriages always waiting at the curb. He had a seven-room suite at the Delevan Hotel in Albany and a more luxurious one at the Broadway Central, a hotel he loved because it had a back door. The Americus Club on the Connecticut shore had started as a fishing club where his friends could smoke cigars and drink brandy. But it became grander too, with formal clothes on Saturday night and testimonial dinners instead of clambakes. The old modest skiffs were replaced by yachts, and a separate cottage was built out in the woods for his mistress of the moment. Tweed hid almost nothing, which was why the voters loved him. He bought that diamond stickpin, which Cormac urged him to hide at once in a coal bin. It was the size of a nose and glittered in every room he entered. Tweed laughed and laughed, and flaunted the stickpin on every possible occasion. This added still another symbol to the sunken eyes, the swollen belly, the polished shoes, and the Tammany Tiger that flowed from the pen and brush of Thomas Nast.

They knew all that. They didn't care. They lived in the real world, where bullshit warred with horseshit and sin was part of the deal. And besides, they were his friends.

Luke brought the ice cream, and Edelstein asked the Boss to tell Cahill about the great fights between the Dead Rabbits and the Bowery B'hoys in the 1840s, and Tweed smiled and wolfed down ice cream and started telling the old stories. Cormac had heard them all before, and surely so had Cahill, and even Charlie Butts. But they made Tweed happy in the telling, and in the remembering. Cahill and Edelstein lit up cigars. Luke brought brandy and took away the ice cream dishes.

"The thing you learn in a street fight," Tweed said, "is that it's not how big you are, but how smart you are. So . . ."

As Luke laid slices of birthday cake before them, Tweed talked about those days when he was a big lean street fighter, one of the Cherry Hillers, long before he joined the Big Six fire company on Gouverneur Street. They first fought two dozen Dead Rabbits on Bayard Street, and beat them badly, and then joined forces with the Bowery B'hoys to beat them again, and then the Rabbits came with guns and they dropped bricks on them from the Bayard Street rooftops and the police came and they shoved a chimney down on one of them too. And then . . .

"It was a rough old school," Tweed said.

"I'm sorry I missed it," Cahill said.

"Don't be," Tweed said. "Many's the lad didn't escape it." He glanced away. "Or was broken by it."

He looked tired again, staring at his hands. Then something in memory turned him to Cormac.

"Play the piano, Cormac," he said. "Play that thing that the little blond girl loved."

Cormac flexed his fingers, remembering the little blond girl named Rachel who had intoxicated Tweed for one long winter in the Broadway Central. There was a nocturne that she loved hearing.

"I hope I can remember it," Cormac said.

"Give it a try."

He went to the piano, gazed at the keys, saw — as he did each time he sat on a bench like this — the face of the Countess de Chardon, and began to play. The music of a nocturne filled the room in the Ludlow Street Jail. Full of night, with clouds scudding across the moon and a distant sound of the sea pulling on the shore. Cormac's technique had been acquired the hard way, at the keyboards of tuneless pianos jammed against walls in saloons, in the studios of teachers, and, after moving to Leonard Street, at the piano he bought with the money from his first cheap novel. He played to the end, and then the four men clapped.

"Just beautiful," Tweed said, his voice lower. "Just beautiful."

Cormac started to get up.

"No. Nononono, Cormac. You know what you've got to play now. All of us need it. Me most of all."

Cormac smiled. He'd learned the song in Tweed's company, at clambakes and Fourth of July celebrations, at rowdy election night parties at Tammany, in oyster bars and a hundred saloons. Tweed called it the Fight Song.

Cormac started to play, plunking the keys as if the piano were a percussion instrument, the song a march of some kind, an American tune. He began singing in a light voice. Cahill and Edelstein knew the words too, and the three of them were singing together, with Butts finally joining too, and the music pounding, and then, without help, Tweed got up. He just stood there, the backs of his knees jammed against the seat of the chair. Then his arms were moving, his face was grinning, his eyes were sparkling, and he swung his arms like a bandmaster and joined in the final words:

Then pull off the old coat!
And roll up the sleeve!
Bayard is a hard street to travel.
Pull off the old coat!

And roll up the sleeve!
The Bloody Sixth is a hard ward to travel . . .
I BELIEVE!

They roared at the end, and Cormac hammered the keys in punctuation.

Then Tweed sighed in a wheezy way and collapsed slowly into his chair, everything gone out of him, even the fight.

The bells in the Essex Market tolled eleven. Luke appeared from the bedroom, to signal with looks and hands that the warden wanted them all out, except, of course, Tweed.

"Happy birthday, Bill," Cahill said.

"We'll keep fighting for you," said Edelstein.

"Thank you, fellas," Tweed said without conviction. "Thank you, it was a grand night, thank you . . ."

When he looked behind him through the doorway, Cormac thought Tweed was the loneliest man in the world.

79.

Cormac, Cahill, and Edelstein stood for an awkward moment on the sidewalk in front of the jail. Butts was already on his way home. Music drifted from the saloon across the street. A few women chatted on the corner, gazing up at the dark windows of the prison. A drunk staggered across the street, heading south.

"Can I give you a ride home, Cormac?" Cahill said.

"Thank you, no. I'll walk. It's a lovely night."

"It's a lovely night in a bad part of town," Edelstein said.

Cormac laughed. "I know the way. I'll be all right."

They shook hands, and Edelstein climbed into a carriage behind Cahill and the driver flicked a whip and they trotted away.

Cormac glanced once more at the jail and began to walk south. Into the past.

He told himself, Be careful now, you'll be up all night. Be careful, you'll be trapped again in memory.

He did know the way, walking down the Bowery until it became Chatham Street, and then turning west into the Five Points. That was the fastest way to Broadway and Leonard. He still knew every street and most of the houses but no longer knew the people who now lived in the houses. The name Five Points, after all, came from the meeting of five streets: Mulberry, Anthony, Cross, Orange, and Little Water, the noisy heart of the district. The streets were still there, although some of the names had changed since he moved among them after the countess went away. Anthony had become Worth, in honor of some blowhard general in the Mexican War. Cross had become Park, after a sour little park created from a lot left by a burned-out house, and Orange turned into Baxter Street, after another man who died in Mexico, but primarily to ease the sensibilities of Irish Catholics.

And he remembered now, as he seldom did anymore, the second night of the Draft Riots. For two days, sometimes with Tweed, he had moved through the anarchic city as men were shot down and women picked up guns and buildings were torched. Tweed pleaded with many of them, trying to save lives, and he did change some minds. But each day, the fighting got worse. When Cormac went out on Tuesday night, he strapped on the sword.

He had not carried the sword in years. It was part of the past, more an artifact than a weapon, reduced to an elegantly made relic of his father. He knew it was useless against guns. But when he hefted it in the smoky night, he was sure he felt again the sword's old power. He strapped on the flaking leather scabbard in his room, tried a few of the old moves (which were so like the moves of boxers), and then took a long drink of water and went out. He had no aim, except to find Tweed and offer his help. Tweed had been threatened again and again, sometimes by decent men, sometimes by the Mozart Hall remnant led by Hughie Mulligan. Perhaps the sword could do its old work and save someone he wanted to save.

At the corner of Cortlandt Street, he saw a bonfire throwing flames into the night, came closer, saw a mob, came even closer, saw a noose attached to a lamppost with a pile of kindling and lumber stacked at its foot, and then saw a smaller mob coming from Broadway, carrying a black man above their heads. His arms and legs were bound. He was shouting for help. Cormac drew his sword.

"Stop, you fucking idiots!" he shouted.

And stepped into their path.

They paused. Most of them young. Many of them Irish.

"Put that man down!"

Remembering the odor of charred flesh in 1741. Remembering the screams.

"Feck off!" one man said.

He drew a pistol, and Cormac sliced off his hand. Saw the man's astonished face and then heard his scream. Heard pistol shots, a furious roar, felt a forearm close on his neck, felt a sharp, sudden crack, and fell into a blinding whiteness.

Three days later, he woke up in a strange bed to see Bill Tweed peering down at him. His hands went to his head and felt wads of bandage.

"You're lucky you're alive," Tweed said. "You're lucky you've got a thick Irish skull."

He put a brandy bottle to Cormac's lips. The room dimmed and brightened, and he saw another man behind Tweed, saw Tweed nod, and the man slipped out. The young Frank Cahill. He saw flowers on a windowsill, and thick, high foliage beyond the glass. He heard canaries chirping from another room

"Welcome to the Tweed home," said Bill Tweed. "Do you want some eggs?"

They sat together for a long time, as Tweed explained that the riots were over. Nobody knew the numbers of the dead: between two hundred and two thousand. There were no numbers at all for the wounded. The Colored Orphan Asylum had been burned to the ground. Many blacks had been lynched. Many had been saved, including a black man they'd wanted to hang and burn on the street where Cormac was found.

"The Five Points held," he said. "And the Fourth Ward. Not a shot was fired, not a black man harmed, not a building burned. I suppose we should be proud of that."

He turned away and gazed into the yard.

"But there's nothing to be proud about in the bloody city. It was . . . terrible. We might never get over it."

"You did what you could," Cormac said.

"It wasn't enough."

Luke came in with a platter of fruit. Younger then, without gray hair. He laid the platter on Cormac's lap.

"Thank you, sir," he said to Cormac. "I heerd what you did."

Then went out.

"It's all right, Cormac," Tweed said, and laughed. "It didn't get into the newspapers, so you don't have to worry about the gangs coming for your hard Irish head. . . ."

"The way I feel, they could take it and make me happy."

"Not on your life." Tweed sighed. "I've got to go out now and visit the ruins."

"One thing, Bill."

"Yes?"

"When . . . when they found me, did they find a sword?"

"A sword?"

"A sword with spirals etched in the blade, and a grip made of wolf bone. My father's sword."

Tweed gazed at him.

"I'll ask around," he said. "But I suspect it's hanging on some lout's wall."

From Tweed's casual tone, Cormac knew, as he peeled an orange, that the sword was gone and might never again be held in his hand.

He saw Transfiguration Church in the distance, and other scenes merged in his mind: murders and suicides, in his days as a reporter, and deaths from cholera and smallpox and yellow fever. He remembered when the Collect Pond was still there, with the tanneries and garbage dumps at its edge. He watched as the Collect was drained (writing about it for a newspaper in 1804) and filled in (with the rocks and mud of the hill), and saw the new houses going up in 1811 before the land settled, and the way they leaned and tottered toward each other a year later, so that nobody would ever live there except the most desperately poor. They were still the only people living there.

And here came two of them, silhouetted against the distant shimmer of a gaslight.

"Evenin', mister," the first one said. Runty and belligerent and drunk. The other taller and gawky. Both with derby hats.

"Is it somethin' you're lookin' for?" the gawky one said, his rhythm Irish, but the words hardened by New York.

Cormac tensed. "Just walking home."

"Is it far ye have to walk?" the short one said.

"Not far."

He started to go around them and they moved with him, blocking his way.

Aw, shit.

"You must be carryin' stuff that's weighin' ye down," the short one said. "I mean, tryin' to get home alive."

"Like money," the tall one said.

Where are you now that I need you, Bill? When you were young and tough?

"Listen to me carefully," Cormac said, as if addressing children. "You will get out of my way right now. And if you don't, you'll be very, very sorry. Fair warning, all right?"

The two men looked at each other. Cormac saw himself doing what he'd done a few times before. Two punches. Fast and vicious. Like cutting with a sword. One left hand, one right. Each to the neck. The men gagging, reeling backward, panting for air, each strangling in pain and shock.

He didn't have to do it. They stepped aside, and he walked between them, thinking: It must have been the tone of my voice. Or the way I stood with my feet apart, ready to punch. Or maybe it was their own woozy weakness. No matter. He walked on, thinking: The city fathers change the names of the streets. They bring water pumps to the thirsty. The preachers open mission schools to teach trades. Tough, hard, determined people move on, Uptown, to the West Side, to Brooklyn. There are always idiots left behind. And sometimes the idiots get rich for a while, and then disappear. Like Hughie Mulligan disappeared.

One night, after leaving the Five Points for the larger rooms on Leonard Street (driven there by Bill Tweed's scorn), Cormac found a note under his door from Hughie Mulligan.

MEET ME AT THE PIER FOOT OF CANAL AND NORTH RIVER. THURSDAY NITE EIGHT O'CLOCK. NEED TO TALK TO YOU. HUGH M.

This was on a night in '68, when Bill Tweed was in the fullness of his power, and Hugh Mulligan was the boss of the opposition Democrats who had failed to get that power themselves. Cormac studied the note. Then he went to Duane Street and showed it to Tweed.

"Go," he said. "See what the treacherous fucker wants."

"It might have nothing to do with you," Cormac said, and told Tweed what he'd done to Mulligan years before in the front parlor of the house of the Countess de Chardon. Tweed laughed.

"Jesus, you've got some terrible history in you, Cormac," he said.

"I was young."

"But he must've seen you around the Sixth Ward," Tweed said, alert to a possible ambush.

"He saw me all right, over the years," Cormac said. "At events I covered. At rallies. A few times in the street. But I don't think he made the connection."

"Don't be so sure," Tweed said. "Hughie looks dumb and slow, but he's got something dangerous inside that brain too. He's like a cunning old warthog."

Cormac laughed.

"The only way to find out is to go to see him," he said.

He turned to go.

"Wait," Tweed said, turning to a wall closet. "I'll give you a gun."

"I don't want a gun."

"Why, for Chrissakes?"

"I might use it," Cormac said. "That's why."

Two nights later, he went to the pier at the end of Canal Street. Mulligan was alone, holding a lantern. Cormac looked into the darkness behind him but couldn't see anyone else. Water sloshed at the timbers. Boats moved on the river. The air was thick with the threat of rain.

"Hello, Cormac," Mulligan said.

"What do you want with me?"

"I've got a job for you."

"I've got a job, Hughie," Cormac said.

"I mean a *job*."

There was a pause, the water sloshing louder, sails flapping in the darkness. Mulligan led the way farther out onto the pier, until the river was beneath them.

"Why me?"

"'Cause you're a nobody. You got no wife. You got no kids. You make crappy paintings. You work on a newspaper and nobody ever fucking heard of you."

"You've got that right."

"But you're a nobody that's close to Bill Tweed."

"Bill knows ten thousand people like me," Cormac said. "He even remembers their names."

"But nobody like you. Nobody that goes up to his apartment in the Broadway Central when everybody else is leavin'. Nobody that sits around laughin' wit' him. Nobody that plays the piano and gets him singin'."

"You've been watching, all right."

"For a long time, pallie."

He laid the lantern on the planks at his feet and lit a cigar, turning to gaze at the river with its black glossy sheen. A few drops of rain started falling. Cormac thought: Jesus, he's big. And his cheekbones look like walnuts now.

"What's the job?"

"Kill Tweed."

Cormac laughed.

"Why the laugh, pallie?"

"I was thinking about a philosopher I once met. He said there were three categories of belief. Plain old belief, disbelief, and beyond fucking belief. This is beyond fucking belief, Hughie."

"We don't think so."

Cormac looked toward the dark stacks of packing cases at the land end of the pier. He still saw nobody.

"What's the deal?"

Mulligan took a drag on the cigar and let the smoke drift from his mouth.

"A hundred thousand," he said. "Half up front, half when the job is done. You'll get a whole new identity. You'll get a first-class passage from Boston to France. You'll get a place to stay in Paris, where you can make your fucking paintings to your heart's content. You could just vanish."

"Why Paris? Why not Mexico or Russia or County Mayo?"

"Go wherever the fuck you want to go, pallie. I don't care. Why are you breaking my stones?"

"Details, Hughie. It's all in the details. For example, how do you propose I do this . . . job?"

"Up to you. You can shoot him. You can stab him. You can strangle him. You can poison him. We don't give a fiddler's fuck. As long as he's dead."

A lone bell *ding-ding*ed as a dark skiff moved downriver toward the harbor.

"A simple question, Hughie. Why do you want to kill Bill Tweed?"

Mulligan laughed.

"What kind of stupid question is that? He's got the Ring."

"And you want it."

"Of course. He's got the mayor, he's got the controller, he's got the aldermen, he's got —"

"Wouldn't you have to kill them all?"

"They'll work with us if Tweed's gone." Mulligan paused. "There's nobody else."

"So the deal is simple. I kill Bill Tweed so you and your friends can get the swag."

Mulligan shrugged. Why even discuss it?

"But Hughie, I'll never get to spend the down payment. I'll never get the rest of the money either, isn't that right? I'll never even make it to France. Because you couldn't afford to have me around. If I'm alive, you'd have to pay me off forever. And you'd never do that. You'd kill the killer, isn't that the way it's usually done, Hughie?"

In the light of the lamp, Mulligan looked angry, his eyes sinking under his brows, his nostrils flaring. He wiped in an annoyed way at the falling rain.

"You put it that way, I might have to kill you now," he said, "and get someone else for the job."

"You're welcome to try, Hughie."

Mulligan stared at him, and then Cormac turned to go. Hughie grabbed his arm.

"I know you, pallie," he said. "I know you from the whorehouse. The one the countess ran. Where you made a fool of me."

"It was a long time ago, Hughie."

"And you never got what you deserved, pallie."

"You've seen me around," Cormac said. "You could have tried a hundred times."

"Maybe I thought I could use you one day."

"To humiliate somebody?"

"No. To get you in a jam and see how you wiggle out."

"That's the real reason I'm here tonight, isn't it?"

"Yeah."

"You've got the wrong man, Hughie."

He pulled away.

"Where are you going?"

"Away from you."

Now Cormac could see the rage, the tight mouth, the flickering eyes. And then there was a pistol in Hughie's hand. Cormac kicked the lantern over the edge of the pier, heard it sizzle as it hit the water, then dropped to the deck as a shot rang out. He rolled toward Mulligan. A second shot ripped through his thigh. But he reached the bigger man and kicked at a kneecap from the ground, then got up and lunged for the pistol hand. The pain was searing his leg.

"Fucker, fucker . . ."

He grabbed Mulligan's coat with both hands and butted him in the face with his head, then grabbed the arm, again in both hands, and jerked it backward as if breaking a tree limb. The pistol fell to the dark deck. Still nobody came from the darkness. Mulligan made thin, frantic sounds, full of pain, and went to his knees, searching desperately for the gun. Cormac stood over him, planted his feet, and bent him sideways with a punch. Then he reached around until he found the pistol.

"I've got the gun, Hughie."

He cocked it so that Mulligan could hear.

"Don't shoot," Mulligan said.

"Get up."

"Just don't shoot me. I want to take care of you."

"I'll bet."

"You can get very rich."

"Don't horseshit me, Hughie."

Mulligan got up, his silhouette hulking and black.

"The one thing I'll give you, Hughie. You came alone. But I think I know why. This is a private deal. It's about you and me. You've been pissed off for thirty years at me. You're getting old. You don't want to die knowing I watched your funeral." He laughed. "Your boys want nothing to do with killing Tweed. This was one of those great ideas that came to you at two in the morning. You get me to kill Tweed, and then you get me killed, and you have everything you want. You try to take the Ring, and I'm dead and gone."

He could feel the blood leaking from his thigh down into his boot.

"You got it all wrong, old pal."

"I don't think so."

Cormac hefted the pistol, put it to Mulligan's chin, cocked it, heard a whimper, then turned and heaved it into the river.

"I'll see you, tough guy."

He started to walk away, and then Mulligan rushed him. It was like being hit by a cart. He bent away, let Hughie slide off him, then stood up and punched him in the temple. The big man staggered but did not go down. Cormac hit him again and felt the pulpy nose splay, and heard a whimper from his chest, and then he bent low and hit him with all his strength in the balls.

Mulligan staggered backward as if his immense body had been broken. His hands flailed. He gasped for breath. And then he went off the pier into the swift water.

The tide carried him out toward the watery boneyard that held the Earl of Warren.

The rain fell harder.

He told all of this to Tweed later that night, dressed in bathrobe and slippers while his clothes were being cleaned by Luke in the valet quarters of the Broadway Central. At first Tweed was serious, then amused, and then, as he pried the full tale from Cormac, he grew more and more merry. Finally he fell back laughing.

"It's as funny as a Saturday night on the Bowery," he said.

"Except that Hughie's dead," Cormac said. "That's not so funny."

Tweed grew serious.

"I suspect someone will find a suicide note before dawn," he said.

He looked at his nails, an expression of admiration on his face.

"And we were here together," Tweed said. "If anyone asks." A pause. "And nobody will."

That morning, a housekeeper came to Hughie Mulligan's suite at the Metropolitan Hotel, where he lived alone. She found a note on his desk.

CAN'T STAND LIVING IN THIS TERRIBLE WORLD. HUGH MULLIGAN

Four days later, his body was found floating off Sheep's Head Bay. It was bloated and partially eaten by fish. His boys threw him a grand funeral, and Tweed sent flowers and a few well-chosen words of respect.

80.

As he walked west, hurrying home on this night in April 1878, he remembered coming to the Five Points when for him it was an undiscovered country. He didn't move to Mott Street, on the district's eastern border, in a spirit of contrition, although some of that was alive in his tired bones. He didn't move there to give himself a sense of proportion over the loss of the countess, and her bath, and the scent of lavender, although that was one of the things he received from the move.

The truth was that when Cormac crossed Broadway that first day, with a cartman behind him carrying his things, his mind felt like sludge. The countess was gone, and something he needed had gone with her: a current, an uncertainty, a set of undecoded codes that had kept his mind alert. When she left, it was as if a switch had been thrown. His body felt young, and looked young, but his brain felt ancient. That was when he remembered the German lesson.

The sludge had entered his brain before, early in the century, when he had been in New York longer than any other inhabitant. It was made up of age, memory, repetition, banality. Then, while trying to learn German in order to read Goethe, he discovered something about himself. When he entered another language, when he tried to absorb its rules, its nouns and verbs, and above all, its rhythms, the sludge in his brain began breaking up. He sought out Germans who could correct his pronunciation, who could explain subtleties of usage, and he could feel a small bright place opening in his brain. It touched everything else. He wrote better in English for the newspaper. He saw more sharply, absorbing details that had been sinking in the sludge. His mind became swifter, his visions more glittering, as if he were three years old again, learning English, or thirteen and learning Irish on the wrong side of the Mountains of Mourne.

He learned then, as Kongo had told him in the cave in Inwood, that in order to live, he must live. And living was a long learning. Learning to paint was a way to break up the sludge.

The same was true of the piano. He learned in different ways: by trying to read everything by an author so that he truly entered the writer's world; by distinguishing between one composer and another so that he could see immense landscapes while hearing a mere eight bars drifting from an open window; or by knowing without thinking the difference between an accent and an umlaut. And it wasn't all in books or sheets of music. Truly knowing a woman was a way of smashing into the sludge. Knowing a place was another.

And to learn a neighborhood was like learning a language. That was what the Five Points taught him. You needed to recognize the subtle differences in accent, clothing, gesture. You learned to know if a certain blind pig was selling the illusion of menace, for a Saturday night thrill, or was truly a place of danger. Every newcomer had to learn that world in his or her own way. All of it was measured against the past. The Famine Irish measured their present against the horror left behind. From his monastic room on Mott Street, Cormac too looked back at Ireland, and the crossing of the ocean sea, the first years in New York and the years of the Revolution, and thought of them as part of his youth, that strange youth prolonged by a gift from African gods. That youth filled with miracles and magic. But a youth that was, he thought, only sporadically real.

In the Bloody Ould Sixth, he also learned that observing — as a painter or newspaperman — was not the only way of living. So he walked away from both, for a dozen years, and plunged into other ways of living, laying stones on Broadway, laying track for the omnibuses, working as a drover, and then selling groceries, and then unloading ships. Three of those years were lost to drink, which he at first forced himself to do, to see what it was about, to try to understand why it pulled at so many people, and made them so happy, and wrecked them. It wrecked him too. Led him into brawls in sawdust bars, into ferocious arguments, into foolish performances, into strange and dangerous women. That created a different kind of sludge: briny, eradicating, filled with shame and guilt. But it had its rewards too: In almost every place he entered, there was a piano, and the owners let him play.

And look, here I am tonight on Mott Street.

Here I am, and the building is still there, lived in now by others, all lost in sleep.

He remembered clearly the L shape of the tiny flat. He saw again the pegs where he hung his clothes, felt himself swivel again to stand and turn in the two feet between the edge of the bed and the wall. He could see the shallow oak cabinet he built under the narrow bed, locked on each end, the secret place in which he placed the sword, the earrings, the letters he had saved; remembered that secret place, and the cloudy window opening toward the tottering walls and sloping rooftops of the streets that descended from the height of Mott Street into the Five Points, the streets swirling with corner boys and oyster sellers, whores and dock wallopers, lurching drunks and proud abstainers, church bells ringing, glass breaking at midnight, much laughter, many tears.

Across Mott Street in those first years stood the Presbyterian church, locked and abandoned, the building that would later open its doors to the injured and humiliated believers as the Church of the Transfiguration under the command of a Cuban priest named Varela. That Catholic church right there now, across the street. Closed for the night. But seeming to give off its odor of candles, incense, and piety. In its shadows, Cormac had studied the texts of the great religions. Judaism and Catholicism and the infinite variations of Protestantism. He had read among the limited texts of Buddhism. He had found a foxed copy of the Koran, stained by its journey from Turkey to London to New York. He tried to approach them all with an accepting mind. He found in each some small thing of value that might help a human being to be more human. In the end, none dislodged him from his belief in what they all called the pagan. The gods of Ireland and Africa. The gods whose powers were proved by the absurdity of his life.

81.

Edelstein came calling just before noon.

"Get dressed and we'll go," the lawyer said. "Cahill's there already."

"How bad is it?"

"Very bad."

They rode through streets where Tweed had worked day and night during the Draft Riots.

"You're thinking too hard about him," Edelstein said. "Let's wait until we see him."

"I was thinking of some good things he did," Cormac said as they crossed Grand Street.

"He did a lot of them."

"And nobody will remember any of them."

"Except us."

They were quiet for a while, the horse clip-clopping on cobblestones that Cormac had helped lay years before. They bumped over the rails of the tramlines, and he had worked on them for a year too: sanding them in icy winter, watering them in summer.

"The worst things he did, he did to himself." Edelstein said. "Like the escape."

"Definitely the dumbest."

"That's why three million in bail. That's why twelve different trials. That's why he's not home now in bed." He looked out into the street. "You were in on that, weren't you?"

"I tried to talk him out of it," Cormac said. "He said he wanted to see the ocean and flowers and his kids. He asked, so I helped."

That was during Tweed's first stay in the Ludlow Street Jail back in 1875. He had stayed in New York while the others fled, so he was allowed monthly trips around the city in the company of the warden and a policeman, and visits with his wife. On December 4, a Saturday, he went for a long ride. The last stop that day was his own house on Madison and Sixty-seventh Street, where he'd have dinner. Cormac was waiting around the corner in a landau carriage with a leather roof. He lolled on the seat as Tweed stayed until after dark. Then he saw him, dark felt hat pulled over his face, the huge body swathed in a cloak. He said nothing and climbed into the carriage. Cormac then took Tweed north along the river roads, to the cove where he had once waited with Kongo in sight of the mansion of the Earl of Warren. A rowboat was waiting. They embraced, and Tweed went off to a waiting sloop and the long journey that would take him to Key West and Havana and finally to Spain. Cormac was sure that night that he would never see Tweed again.

"He always said later that you were a stand-up fellow," Edelstein said. They were at the jail now.

"I still wish I'd told him to fuck off."

Here they were in the suite again, with Luke serving tea and biscuits, and Tweed dozing in his bed. His eyes were closed and his breathing was shallow. His body smelled like swamp. Cahill motioned to them to follow him to the living room.

"His daughter's gone out for ice cream," Cahill said quietly. "Her husband's with her. She might be gone a while, since she doesn't know the neighborhood."

"I should have brought some from the German," Cormac said.

Cahill shrugged as if it wouldn't make a difference.

"What is it, exactly, Frank?" Edelstein said.

"It's everything. It's his heart and his kidneys and his lungs. It's his blood pressure. And now he's got a mild pneumonia."

Cahill inhaled deeply, pursed his lips and exhaled, then patted his jacket pocket for a cigar. He decided against it, as if the smoke would hurt Tweed.

"Why don't you play the piano, Cormac?" Edelstein said. "You always make him feel better."

Cormac sat down and noodled the keys, playing a nocturne. Tweed didn't move. Then, slowly, Cormac began to play the Fight Song. Played it as a soft, distant march. But in some odd way, as a soft tune full of defiance. Cormac glanced through the connecting door at the heavy man on the bed.

Tweed's eyes opened.

"God damn it, I was hoping it was you," Tweed said. He smiled. His teeth seemed darker.

"Sing, Bill." Cormac said. "Sing the song."

"I'll sing if you all sing."

So they began to sing, the tempo slower than it was written, the march turned into a ballad.

So pull off the old coat!
And roll up the sleeve!
Bayard is a hard street to travel.
Pull off the old coat!
And roll up the sleeve!
The Bloody Sixth is a hard ward to travel . . .
I BELIEVE!

Then it was quiet.

"Come here, Cormac," Tweed said.

Cormac went over, his back to the others. Tweed reached under the covers and came up with an envelope.

"You've been a good friend," Tweed whispered, his voice thin, the skin of his face slack, the fat no longer shiny. "The only one who never asked me for a fucking penny." He handed Cormac the envelope. "So this is for you. . . ."

"I don't want anything, Bill."

"Fine, you can throw it away if you want, or piss it away on a woman, or give it to the poor."

He smiled, then laughed. "Just don't give it to the fucking government," he said. "It's full of thieves."

Cormac didn't ask what was in the envelope, although he could feel the outline of a key. Tweed murmured that his wife and the family would be all right. "I took care of them long ago," he said. "Before I went to Spain." His lawyers had all been paid too, although that goddamned Hebe out there, that Edelstein, he wouldn't take a dime.

"There were a few laughs, though, weren't there?"

"Enough for five lifetimes," Cormac said.

Tweed was quiet, and then he was gone. Cahill hurried over, took his pulse, and said, "Shit." Tweed's fingernails turned black.

The door opened and his daughter Josephine came in with the ice cream. She looked at them, looked at her father, and fell to the floor of the Ludlow Street Jail. The lid came off the pail and the ice cream made a cold white scab on the planked floor.

82.

The envelope contained a bank draft for five thousand dollars and the key to a safe-deposit box at the Bank of New York. And there was a note in Bill Tweed's hand: "I wish this was more, but it's something. So long, old friend."

When Cormac opened the box on the following morning, he found the deed to a house on Duane Street next door to the building where Tweed did business while he was the Boss. He walked down there for a look and realized that he'd passed it many times without ever noticing it. Four stories of red brick on the northeast corner of Church Street. From across the street, he could see a studio on the top floor with windows facing south toward the harbor. A studio. With windows glistening in the sun. While newsboys shouted the story of the death of the Boss.

"Bill Tweed is dead, readallabout it!"

"Get it all in the Herald. . . ."

Cormac's hands trembled as he gazed at another note in Bill Tweed's hand. "Fill in the blanks with whatever name you want to use," the note said. "Then take it to Edelstein." But that day, and part of the next, he couldn't move. He lay on the bed in the Leonard Street flat, the newspapers scattered around him, images of Tweed in life gliding into the cartoons of Thomas Nast.

He didn't go to the wake at the Tweed home on Madison Avenue and couldn't leave Manhattan for the burial in Greenwood Cemetery in Brooklyn. But he waited under gray skies at Broadway near City Hall and watched the procession of eighteen carriages move south toward State Street and the Hamilton Ferry. Two mounted policemen led the way. Cormac joined those who walked behind the carriages, and then moved away at the ferry. He threw the Boss a salute and started for home. In the sky, a flock of seagulls cried a farewell.

The day after the burial, he went first to his own bank and added the draft to the one hundred and six dollars he had in his account. Then he walked to Hanover Square to see Edelstein.

"I hated yesterday," Edelstein said.

"Yes."

"That mayor wouldn't even lower the flags to half-mast."

"He'll be forgotten when Bill is still remembered."

"You've got something for me, right?" Edelstein said.

"I do."

He handed the paper to Edelstein, the deed to the house on Duane Street.

"What name do you want to use?"

"I haven't thought about it."

"I have," Edelstein said. "There was a man was killed in Antietam, no family, no relatives. I went to school with him. Francis Aloysius Kavanagh. No *U* in Kavanagh."

"Sounds good to me."

"In a year or two, we can change it to some company. We'll make one up."

"Even better."

He started filling in the blanks on the deed, then took a stamp and some wax and a notary's seal and thumped on the paper.

"Just sign here, Mister Kavanagh."

Cormac signed his latest name.

"Done."

"That's all?"

"That's all, Mister Kavanagh."

Edelstein smiled and lit a cigar.

"It's a fine house, Cormac," Edelstein said. "You could live there forever."

Eight

Now

I live, which is the main point.

— Heinrich Heine, 1826

83.

Cormac waits for the dark young lady on an evening of steady rain. Not just rain, but an unruly New York rain, pushed by river winds. He is in the backyard of a restaurant called East of Eighth, on Twenty-third Street, next to a movie multiplex. It's a few minutes after seven on an evening in March. A huge Cinzano umbrella spreads above the table, but the wet breeze toys with it, lifting it along an edge, filling it like a parachute, then dropping it, spraying him with rain. A young bright-blond waiter comes over, shielding his hair with a large menu, and says that he can move Cormac inside to the upstairs room. Cormac smiles and shakes his head.

"I like the rain," he says. "And I'm meeting someone here."

"Suit yourself," the waiter says in an irritated way, and goes back to his place inside the back door that opens to this garden. Cormac does like the rain. Across all the years, it has felt like a gift, a cleansing refreshment of air and skin. And it always puts him, if only for a few seconds, in Ireland long ago. The New York rain is drumming now on the umbrellas of the empty tables the way it long ago drummed upon the roof of a blacksmith's forge. The way it hammered then on the snug slate roof of the vanished old house. His first house in the world. His truest home. Now, in this fleeting present tense, he watches the rain racing down the brick walls of the adjoining buildings, making a million little glistening rivers. Rain released by the March sky. Falling upon this street where once he lived many days and nights, long ago, in a world now vanished.

The wall he now faces is the wall of an office building. The wall behind him rumbles with explosions from a movie being shown in the multiplex. Images of other Twenty-third Street theaters race through him, quick as rain. The tail end of the nineteenth century, the years after Tweed died, and New York changed again as everything moved uptown. Gaslight and fog. Streetcars and horses. Golden footlights. An orchestra leader in a tux with his back to the audience. The odor of forgotten perfumes. Women in the lobbies of hotels. Rouged faces. Eyes defined by kohl. And there: a wife, now long dead, laughing when she sees him enter the foyer. Betrayal in her laugh. He tries to remember her full name. Catherine something Underwood. The middle name will not come. The rain drums on the umbrella. A fire engine screams through the evening.

When Tweed died, time flowed on, of course, and so did life. Slicker bandits arrived in New York, with even greater appetites than anyone in the Ring. The pigs were gone from the street. Another kind of swine took over the elegant Victorian sties. Electricity killed the darkness of midnight and drove elevators into the high floors of new buildings. Great armies of immigrants arrived at Castle Garden, speaking Yiddish and Sicilian and the English of Ireland. They were coming to the New Jerusalem, and the population soared to more than a million. Tenements rose to house them, while the Brooklyn Bridge soared majestically over the East River. Sailing ships became more and more rare as steam power brought liners to the new piers along the North River.

Cormac fought brain sludge writing dozens of preposterous novels for Beadle & Adams and the other fiction factories, into which he sneaked sympathies for unions, and the poor, and the despised Irish, along with his astonished love for the city itself. He did not exactly think of himself as an American, but he was definitely a New Yorker. That meant that he embraced the city's culture of work, even though the bounty of Bill Tweed had freed him from the need to earn money to eat. He wrote one dime novel in three days, a nine-part serial in two weeks. To flush his brain, he wrote another entirely in German, and then did it all over again in English. He moved from one newspaper to another, the rhythm of his life falling into a year of work, a year of disappearance. In New York, nobody expected constancy anymore. On newspapers, he welcomed the anonymity of the copy desk, where he corrected the style and grammar of younger men, but he was still thrilled by the chance to go out to the streets as a reporter. He saw the arrival of Pulitzer from St. Louis and worked for him at *The World* in three different years under three different names, without ever meeting him. He saw the arrival of Hearst too, young and brash and full of the romantic excitements driven into him by the West, convinced that the coming century would belong to him. While Hearst and Pulitzer fought it out along Park Row, the halftone changed the look of newspapers, allowing reproduction of photographs on high-speed presses, and the old pen-and-ink sketch artists were soon gone, to make illustrations for magazines or to draw comic strips or to create paintings that evoked the streets where they had worked for newspapers, instead of some lost European Arcadia full of nymphs and princes. Some of them lived here on Twenty-third Street, others drifted to the small houses west of Greenwich Village.

The subjects of Cormac's scrutiny as a reporter had not changed from the early years of the century: the usual murders, the usual suicides, the usual robberies, the usual schemes for instant wealth. Only the details were different. There were big stories too, from the astonishing beauty of the Blizzard of 1888, when the Battery was turned into a blinding white pasture and the only sound for three days was the rasping of shovels, to the horrors that followed the Panic of 1893 (brokers diving from windows, children found starved in tenements, undertakers working triple time), and, as the century wound down, the jingo fever of the Spanish-American War.

All of this was impersonal, which was the way Cormac wanted it. But in the years after Tweed died, he began to see stories in the newspapers that entered him like knife thrusts. They were all small: social notes, really, in diaries from London, and in the society gossip that flowed from Gramercy Park and Madison Square. They were not the stuff of page-one headlines. But there was a story of a woman at a party in London, and a young man who appeared at an opera opening in Paris. Another was found dead in Australia of heart failure. A fourth was living out West, beyond the Rockies, operating a mine. All were Warrens.

All traced their descent to the Earl of Warren. He could not leave Manhattan to pursue them, but he feared their arrival on his granite island.

"Please don't come to New York," he said out loud one night in his studio in Duane Street. "Please don't come here. . . ."

One of them did, Michael Warren, a handsome young fellow (the newspapers said), with a reddish tinge to his dark brown hair, tall, broad-shouldered, witty. He was on his way to London and was staying with friends in Gramercy Park. Cormac read these stories with a weary sense of responsibility. The Warrens were appearing in his life now like the terms of an old curse. From the distant past, he heard Mary Morrigan repeat the rules of the tribe. He remembered the way his father had died. He heard his father speaking: "In our tribe, the murderer must be pursued to the ends of the earth. And his male children too. They must be brought to the end of the line. . . ."

And then Cormac was relieved. One newspaper explained that this Michael Warren was leaving for London on the morning Cormac read the newspapers. That is, he was already gone. There was no need to travel to Gramercy Park, to stand in leafy shadows, to observe, to plan an ambush. No need to replace the lost sword with another weapon. It was a kind of reprieve. But he knew it was not permanent. For certain Americans, all roads led to New York.

Meanwhile, he could only try to live his life. He told himself that change was everything, that it was essential to any life, long or short. One year, he drew and painted with his left hand only, which took the slickness out of his drawing and even made him stand and sit in new ways. In another year, he learned to sign, so that he could speak to deaf-mutes, and wrote an article about them for the *Century*. He bought a camera too, which used 4 × 5 glass plates, and wandered the streets photographing buildings, later pasting them together along one wall of the top-floor studio. He thought of this as a way of seeing more deeply what he had known too familiarly. When he had photographed every house on three blocks, he stopped using the camera and buried himself in the Hall of Records, examining documents and deeds for each building, writing the information on small cards that served as captions for the photographs. His brain sparkled.

Across those years, he had love affairs. He made cautious friendships. He helped bury Cahill in 1894 and a year later did the same for Edelstein. He read many books and listened to much music. He walked each year to the river on his birthday and dropped a flower in the flowing waters, hoping it would sail to Ireland. He sometimes longed for the Countess de Chardon. About once a week, he'd remember Bill Tweed and his marvelous laugh.

Now, as the March rain falls on Twenty-third Street, he rises up again from the past.

"Hello," a voice says.

He looks up, and she is standing above him, Delfina Cintron. Smiling, her teeth very white in her dark face. She is wearing a wet tan trench coat, the collar up, and her hair is a wild mass of sprouting black curls. She carries no umbrella, for the day had begun with sun. Cormac rises, takes her elbow in greeting.

"We can go inside," he says. "They have a table upstairs."

She glances around the yard, with its empty tables and steady drumming of raindrops, and a look of satisfaction crosses her face. It's as if she accepted the feeling of an intimate fortress, walling off the world.

"This is fine," she says. "I like the rain."

He uses a white cloth napkin to wipe a puddle off a chair, and she sits down.

"I'm sorry I'm late," she says. She pronounces the word "sawry." The long soft vowel of the Caribbean.

"You're not all that late," Cormac says. She glances at her watch, with its red plastic wristband.

"Nine minutes," she says and smiles again. "People used to say Latinos were always late, so I made a big deal out of being on time. My friends called me En Punto Cintron. On-the-dot Cintron. But at the store, the customers never leave on time, so we can't leave either."

"Inconsiderate swine," Cormac says, and they both laugh in a way that is not quite comfortable. Cormac thinks: I don't know how to do this anymore. I don't know what to say or how to begin. I don't know the music or the movies or the slang. Every woman in the world is too young for me. The Queen Mother of England, aged one hundred, is too young for me. This girl: She's an undiscovered country. And beautiful too.

Delfina Cintron wears no makeup, but her dark ochre skin is reddish with youth. Cinnamon skin. Redolent of Africa and the sun of the Caribbean. An airplane passes overhead, flying very low.

"That guy must be trying to land on Ninety-sixth Street," she says.

"Or Central Park."

"If we hear a boom, he missed something."

The sound of engines roars away into nothing, and they hear only the rain drumming on umbrellas. The waiter arrives, now protecting his yellow hair with a fuchsia umbrella bearing the name of the restaurant. He hands them two menus. He is gym thin, his hair combed into quills. Delfina smiles at him in an amused way.

"Something to drink?" he says. Cormac turns to her. "Delfina? A drink?"

She nibbles the inside of her full lower lip. Actually choosing. The pause of someone who does not drink.

"A rum an' tonic," she says. Her voice is hoarse and furry.

"Pellegrino for me," Cormac says.

The waiter nods and goes away.

The curls of her hair are tiny and fine and very black. For the first time in years, he wants to plunge his hands through hair until he can feel the curved bone of a female skull. Delfina reads the menu as if it were a sacred text. Delfina Cintron. Her body hidden under the raincoat the way her skull is hidden under her exploding hair.

And Cormac remembers seeing her for the first time, walking on Fourteenth Street, on a day thick with August. Last year. Last summer. The year of Our Lord 2000, when all the predictions about the millennium came up empty on the first day of the year. There was no universal computer crash. There were no arrivals of long-dead gods. He had never felt more tired, more thickened by sludge. A sludge made of boring televised repetitions. A sludge of journalistic alarums and diversions that turned out to be nothing. A sludge dominated, day after day, by the tyrannies of clocks and calendars.

And here she came: wearing low-cut jeans and a black halter with part of her smooth brown belly showing. Then he glanced up at her face. She wore her face that day like a mask of defiance. The makeup severe. The eyes dead. The combination of smooth flesh and hardened eyes saying: Go ahead and try, *pendejo*.

"How is the food here?"

"Okay," Cormac says. "But don't try anything fancy."

"Maybe pasta, no?"

"Sí."

"Tu español está mejorando, Señor O'Connor."

"Ojalá, Señorita Cintron."

Remembering how he had stopped that August day as she went by. Stunned. Short of breath. His heart pounding. Fourteenth Street jammed with shoppers and junkies, cops and schoolboys, telephone repairmen, cable installers, women with kids in strollers, delivery boys, homeless men in winter coats. Her hair bobbing as she cut a path through the crowd. Then there was a surge of pedestrians, and he lost her. Cursing himself for a goddamned fool. Cursing his slowness, his caution. Looking and looking and looking, then cursing the gods for playing with him. He came again to Fourteenth Street, at the same time, the same corner, arrived day after day for three weeks: hoping to see her in the crowd. To approach her. To try to know if this dark lady was *the* dark lady, sketched for him long ago in a cave in Inwood. And then thought: Perhaps she was an illusion, a specter created by August heat, by lack of water, or by my own need. She might have been just another ghost in the haunted city.

In September he saw her again at last, coming out of the New School on Fifth Avenue, cutting across Fourteenth Street to the north side of the street, then moving west. He followed her like a detective on the trail of a murder suspect, watching the bobbing hair, the rhythmic walk, the long tawny legs (for this time she wore a skirt and blouse), while car horns blared at a double-parked sanitation truck and an ambulance screamed for passage. She hurried into a drugstore, pushing the door sharply before her. A Rite Aid. On the corner. She vanished through that front door. And didn't come out.

"So I'll have the fettucine," she says, as the rain pounds down. "And a green salad."

The waiter returns with a small green pad, exposed to the rain. Cormac orders the pasta and salad for Delfina and a medium burger for himself. The waiter is irritated in a thin, blond way. Imagine: reduced to *this*. Serving philistine food to *philistines*. He hurries off.

"Poor baby," Delfina says as the waiter vanishes.

"Life is hard."

"Claro que sí," says Delfina Cintron, her voice almost a whisper.

And Cormac sees himself staring at the front door of Rite Aid that day, wondering why she has not emerged. Ten minutes went by. Twenty minutes. And then he entered the drugstore in search of her. He glanced down each aisle, as if searching for shampoo or pretzels or mouthwash. She was not there. He saw a fat woman pushing a fat child in a stroller. A grizzled homeless guy was spraying Mitchum deodorant on his neck and wrists. A middle-aged man examined the label on a bottle of Advil.

He looked toward the front door, and there she was, behind the counter at the cash register. Her brow furrowed as she punched computer keys to ring up a sale. She was wearing a green smock over her street clothes. He drifted closer, paused before candies and chewing gums, and saw her name tag. Delfina. The dolphin. A line of customers waited their turn for her attention. Cormac left, knowing he would return. In search of the dolphin.

Now she is here before him, under the Cinzano umbrella, in a public place as private as a cave without a ceiling. The wind briefly rises. There's a spray of rain. They hunch forward to avoid the raindrops, closer than they have yet been. He can smell her hair. Soap and rain. And look upon her unmarked skin. Skin of Arabs and Andalusians, Tainos and Africans. Shiny with dampness and rain. He gazes at her. Thick black eyebrows. Eyes set widely, lined only with her own black eyelashes, not mascara. In Spanish, it would be two words: mas cara. More face. Another face. Like that Mexican wrestler on channel 47: Mil Mascaras. A thousand faces. And beneath the brows, set in their black rims, are eyes so black and liquid it is impossible to penetrate them. Opal eyes. Her nose slopes in a clean curve, tilting abruptly upward at the tip. Wide nostrils. O Africa. Her lips are plump with Africa too, and she has a habit of wetting them with the tip of her tongue. The bone of her chin is firm and hard, with a thin strap of flesh beneath it, either baby fat that has not departed or the beginning of age. She is twenty-eight years old.

"Why are you alone?" he asks.

"I'm not alone," she says, raising an eyebrow. "I'm sitting here with you in the rain."

"You know what I mean," he says. "Why don't you have a man?"

"I've had men," she says, and shrugs. "Lots of them. I've even had a husband."

There is more in her eyes, more words struggling for expression, more images undescribed. They exist in the way she looks down at the table, in the way one hand kneads another on her lap. But she doesn't go on. The waiter arrives with the food. Cormac doesn't press her. He didn't press her when he started going to the drugstore. Once a week. Saying hello. Ordering cigarettes. Or buying toothpaste. Thanking her and calling her by name. Seeing her smile. Watching like a teenager from across the street at closing time, screened by the crowd, discovering that no young man waited for her. In this part of her life, she was alone. He saw her hurrying into the subway. Trudging through piled snow. Bending into bitter winter winds driving hard from the North River. Always alone, bundled in a dark-blue knee-length down-lumpy coat and high-heeled black boots. Until finally he brought her a brightly wrapped book at

Christmas and saw astonishment in her eyes. Pablo Neruda. In English and Spanish.

"Mil gracias," she said that day.

"A usted," he said.

The day before New Year's Eve, he asked her to go to a movie. She accepted in a confused way, curious, wanting a diversion, resisting his approach, resisting contact or connection, perhaps men themselves. But accepting. She sat beside him in the dark, very still, very formal. Afterward, she thanked him, refused dinner, shook hands, and went off to the subway. A week later, he waited for her again where no young man yet waited. On that corner on Fourteenth Street. Once more they went to a movie. Then again, and after the third movie, they exchanged telephone numbers. On the phone, she was restrained, and he noticed how she spoke English with a very precise accent, hitting every *d* and *t* in words like "damned" and "Connecticut," and pronouncing the *g* at the end of words like "talking," "laughing," and "eating."

Now tonight they are having dinner. On each date, she has been guarded, careful, saying nothing of importance. She won't tell him where she lives and doesn't ask where he lives. They see a movie and then discuss it over coffee and then she says goodbye at the entrance to the subway. She treats him like an older man, but one in whom she has only marginal interest. And he urges patience upon himself, thinking: Don't scare her off. Beneath the toughness, she's capable of being easily scared.

"I feel funny when you stare at me that way," she says, twirling fettucine on a fork. Her mouth is open, her hand poised with a pasta-laden fork.

"I can't help it," Cormac says, smiling casually. "You're beautiful."

"No, I'm not. "

"Liar."

"I mean, I'm okay, I guess. But beautiful, hey, come on. Models, they're beautiful. Cindy Crawford, yeah, or Naomi Campbell. Or that blond one, Gwyneth Paltrow. Movie stars are beautiful. Not me. I'm too short. I'm too fat. Those girls . . ."

She finally delivers the pasta to her mouth and eats hungrily, greedily. The rain begins to ease and so does she. At last. She's from Queens, she says. She has been here since she was ten, when her mother brought her from Santo Domingo, along with a broken heart, forty-four dollars, and one suitcase of clothes. Her father was a piano player. Delfina remembers his dazzling smile and his aroma of Old Spice and little more. She has been told that he married another woman. He was small and skinny, though very handsome. The woman he lives with weighs three hundred pounds and is very ugly. Or so the story was told, on evenings in the kitchens of Queens.

"Do you want to talk about the husband?" Cormac says. "Your husband?"

"No," she says, chewing the fettucine. "Not really . . ."

"*Ni modo.* It doesn't matter."

She finishes the pasta, pokes at the salad. Cormac is still only halfway through his burger. She stares at her plate, then rests her chin on her thumbs, her elbows on the edge of the table. The rain has ended. The backyard is alive with dripping sounds. She looks at him in a frank, deliberate way, then turns away.

"He was a junkie," she says. She sips the rum drink without enthusiasm, as he lays aside the rest of the burger.

"I didn't know that when I met him, of course. I was nineteen. He was thirty. I was a student at Hunter, thinking about teaching history."

She pronounces it "heestory."

"Then mad for physics . . ."

She chews the inside of her lip again, as if arranging the words.

"He . . . he saw me in the street, just like you did. And he followed me, just like you. And he hung around and waited for me. . . ."

"Just like me."

"Just like you."

She smiles in a sad way and turns to watch the raindrops dripping down the wall, and when she turns back, her eyes are brimming.

"I went out with him, okay? To discos and parties, because it was exciting, because I had been studying since I was ten, because I was bored, because I wanted something that I didn't even know I wanted. I went out with him because I was tired of being En Punto Cintron. Because I wanted to sleep late. All the usual stupid reasons. And then I got pregnant. My mother was hysterical. She thought I would lose my chance, you know? My big American chance. To graduate from college, to have a life. And she was right, of course. I mean, look where I'm working. Selling Bufferin and condoms to kids who think they can make me blush. Anyway, we got married. His name was Enrique, but his street name was Block, like he owned the block. The block was 117th Street, near Second Avenue, in El Barrio. His block. He was a Puerto Rican and made a lot of jokes about Dominicans. Most of them dirty. About Dominican women, and the special way they were supposed to like sex. He tried that a few times and got mad when I wouldn't let him do it that way, and he would yell at me: 'You're Dominican!' Like I was betraying my country!" She smiles. "A real schmuck." The smile fades. "Me too. But he was nice for a few months. Then he started coming home late and then not at all and then he stopped working and you know, it was the same old story, the same old New York shit."

The waiter arrives again, his irritation gone as he performs for a tip. He turns on an acting-class smile and tries being gracious. They order coffee. Delfina says she's finished with her drink too. The ice cubes have melted. A second waiter leads a party of six to another table, wielding a large towel. They are laughing and loud.

"You don't want to hear all this, do you?" Delfina says.

"Only if you want to tell it."

She is quiet for a long time. The other table settles down. Mozart begins to play from the restaurant's sound system. The Sonata No. 1 in C Major. But through the dripping wall behind them they can hear the bass line of another movie soundtrack and the muffled sound of explosions. Buildings blowing up. Shouts. The combination triggers something in her, releases a flood of words.

"I had a daughter," Delfina says, talking as much to herself as to Cormac. "She was so beautiful. Carolina, her name was, same as my mother. My mother came to take care of me while I was pregnant because Enrique now, he was on the streets all the time, selling crack, shooting smack. I would see him, with the baby in my arms, and he would laugh and walk away. As thin as a fucking nail, he was now. Pardon my language. Hanging with all the crack zombies. My mother wanted me to come home to the house in Queens. But I couldn't. I couldn't face my friends again. All those kids I knew. The ones I left behind when I went to college. The problem was, when I got into Hunter, I acted like I was hot shit. And here I was two years later, another welfare mother. It was so . . . I don't know — shameful? So I stayed on 117th Street. The more the goddamned zombies hit on me, the hotter I made myself look. And then I beat them off. If a friend of Enrique's hit on me, I would say stuff like, 'Your dick's smaller than Block's, *cabrón,* and his is a peanut.' Hoping it got back to Enrique. Finally I got a job in a record store on Columbus Avenue, Tower Records, and my mother would baby-sit for me, coming all the way on the train, two trains, from Queens. All the time telling me, 'Come home, *m'hija,* come home.' All the time telling me, 'We can go back to the D.R., we can go someplace else. You can go back to school. Get your degree. Start over.' While I hugged the baby and went downtown to work in the record store."

The coffee arrives, steaming in the chill spring air.

"It went on like that," Delfina says. "Almost a year," she says. "Until the fire."

Cormac's heart trembles. He knows what is coming, all the way from the dark streets of the past, all the way from the Five Points. He touches her hand and her flesh is cold as sorrow. She eases her hand away.

"They both died," she says in a remote tone. "My mother and my daughter. And two other people on the floor upstairs. It was in the *Daily News,* on New York One. I always thought Enrique set it, and so did the cops, but they couldn't prove it, and it didn't matter anymore because by then he had the virus. The motherfucker was gonna die. I prayed it wouldn't be quick."

She sips her coffee, part tough slum kid, part grieving adult. She makes a face as if the coffee were bitter.

"I don't remember much after the fire," she says. "I was crazy for a long time. I made love to a lot of guys one year and then shut down like a nun."

Neither speaks for several minutes, as the rain drips. He can think of no words that will not sound like horseshit. Laughter skitters around the backyard. More customers arrive, fresh from the movie house. Chairs scrape on brick. Tables fill. Cormac's coffee is cold when he sips it and he signals for fresh cups. She looks directly at him now.

"Does it bother you when I say I slept with a lot of guys?"

"No. It's a kind of consolation sometimes."

"I don't want you to think I'm some kind of a whore."

"I could never think that."

"It was part of the craziness," she says. "Every day was different. On Monday, I wanted to die, to get the virus too, and just fucking die. Sometimes I saw myself on the Brooklyn Bridge, going over the side, or jumping out of the fucking Twin Towers. On Tuesday, I wanted to make another baby, get another Carolina, and start all over, and do it right this time, and watch her crawl and watch her walk and hear her talk and —"

"Stop," Cormac says, remembering another woman, long ago, who longed for the same repaired life and spoke about it in French. "You don't need to justify anything, Delfina. Not to me. Not to anyone. You got through it. You're here. You're eating food. You look beautiful."

Now Cormac can hear the Sonata No. 9 in D Major. Filling the air, melding together the chatter of other tables. The music throws a wisp of another room and another century into his mind, and he forces himself to look at Delfina and hold her hand. Here. Now.

"I'm sorry to put all this in your head," she says, her hand warming in the hand of Cormac. "I should go home."

"Not yet. Please."

She nestles against him, her fine wiry African hair unspooling against his face. He can feel one of her breasts against his arm. With one hand, he touches her hair, his fingers plunging into its springy fineness until he briefly feels the curve of the back of her skull, her skin as warm as blood.

And then she pulls away.

"I have to go," she says.

"Wait. Let me pay and I'll walk you to a cab."

She touches her napkin to her eyes, quickly, so nobody can see the gesture. Cormac makes a scribbling sign to the waiter, who smiles and nods. Delfina inhales deeply, as if forcing a shift in memory, and then exhales slowly. She turns to Cormac and tries a smile.

"Okay, what about you?"

"What about me?"

"I told you about me. Now you have to tell me about you."

He stares at the check, peeling off bills and adding the tip for which the waiter has performed so erratically.

"It's a long story," he says.

"Try," she says.

"Where do you want me to start?"

"I don't know. I know your name. I know you're some kind of a writer and — did you say you were an artist too? A painter, right?" She pauses. "I know you're very kind to me, even when I'm a pain in the ass. I know you speak Spanish and French and Italian."

"And Yiddish. And German. And a little Latin too, *mi vida*."

"But the rest of it, I don't know anything," she says. "Like how old are you?"

"Old enough to be your ancestor."

She laughs.

Cormac doesn't.

84.

Out on the wet sidewalk, he offers to take her home in a taxi. She thanks him and says she'll find her way. An invisible shield is forming. Delfina Cintron is backing away.

"And listen," she says, "I'm sorry I told you all that in there, you know, about myself." Her face turns tougher. "I don't know what that was all about."

Flawless bands of red light from the Krispy Kreme store scribble across the wide street and are then ruined by passing taxis. Scarlet bubbles rise from the gutter like blood.

"I'm actually a little ashamed of myself," she says. "It's not like me."

"Enough, Delfina. I'm flattered you said anything, so forget it."

She smiles a thin smile. Cormac wants to lean over and kiss her cheek and starts to put a hand on her shoulder. She turns stiffly, offers her hand instead, and he shakes it.

"I'll call you," Cormac says.

She nods in a casual way.

"See you," she says. "Thanks for dinner."

Then, looking cool and detached, Delfina Cintron adjusts the strap of her shoulder bag, thrusts her hands in the pockets of her raincoat, and starts walking quickly to the east.

Cormac watches her go, feels the impulse to follow, to shout her name, to take her arm, to feel her warmth: and does nothing. He lights a cigarette, as about fifty customers line up for the late movie. He inhales deeply. All of his life he has switched from smoking to not smoking. Cigars, pipes, and then cigarettes when they arrived, always for nine years at a time, followed by nine years of not smoking at all. Nicotine was the basic drug of the solitary. He loved the aroma when he started again, and hated it when he was finished. Now he's in the final year of nine years of Marlboro Lights. He'll be glad when they're gone. Sometimes he thinks he'd be gladder if he were gone first.

He watches the young people as he smokes, the giggling girls, the macho boys. All Delfina's age. They seem decent enough, doing what boys and girls have always done, some of them right here on this street. Flirting, lying, inventing themselves and each other. He wishes he could caution them: Listen, young man, that girl you are inventing does not exist; or, Listen, blissed-out girl, that perfect boy is not the one you're gazing at. *Cuidate, jovenes. . . .* A siren splits the air, and he looks left, toward where Jay Gould's Opera House once stood on the corner of Eighth Avenue and where, in a different time, Fred Astaire took his first dance lessons. Gone now too. Replaced by an ugly white-brick building that had something to do with a union. The ambulance pushes through traffic, siren screaming its useless tantrum, moving up Eighth Avenue. The last of the young people file into the lobby of the multiplex. Not one of them, he thinks, has ever heard of Jay Gould. Was he related to Jay-Z or something? And who was Fred Astaire? Cormac turns and walks east.

He pauses near the Flatiron Building, driven to a sheltering wall by a squall of rain, looking north over the expanse of Madison Square. Once the great boisterous laughing heart of the city, now a placid remainder of a heart bypass. On this night, flattened against the cowcatcher of the Flatiron, he sees again what nobody else can see. Bill Tweed laughing with his friends in the restaurant of the Hoffman House. The old Madison Square Garden, the first one, rickety and frail, rises across the north wall of the square, with its tentlike rooftops like a vision of Samarkand, and then coming down, after Commodore Vanderbilt, its ruthless owner, added a story and a wall collapsed and killed five people. Cormac stood there, making notes for the *Herald* as the Commodore's pleasure palace was smashed into splinters and rubble and hauled away; stood there watching the new Garden rising, and Stanford White gazing at it in wonder, for the second Garden was his, his child, his masterwork, his personal pleasure palace too (in the rooms of the seven floors he occupied in the bell tower), and it was the one that would kill him. As always in the city of memory of which Cormac was the only citizen, Stanny is laughing in a triumphant pleasured way. The architect of desire. If only he had met Bill Tweed. What laughter they'd have shared.

Another siren in the night. A car horn blares.

"Move dat ding! Willya move dat goddam cah?"

That voice. That lovely hard demanding urgent New York accent. An accent like a fist. He wants to embrace the shouting man. To hear him talk. To hear that accent born in the Five Points, with Africans and Irishmen working as collaborators, the accent now almost gone, replaced by some weird (to Cormac) rhythm where every declarative sentence ends with a question mark. I was twenty years old? I need a newspaper? He looks for the faceless old New Yorker, but traffic is moving and the man is gone.

The rain eases now. Cormac crosses Broadway. Almost surely Delfina lives in East Harlem and has taken the Lexington Avenue subway uptown. He will take the same line downtown because he always takes the Lex if it's possible. He loves it more than all the other lines. It was, after all, the first to cut through the city. And besides, he helped build it. And most important, it always makes him think about his father. On this night, his body trembles slightly. Perhaps soon he will see them all again in the Otherworld.

On the platform, a Chinese woman holds shopping bags in each hand. A man dozes on a bench. Three kids with portfolios talk solemnly about the use of encaustic and how you could get the effect on a Mac. Cormac gazes into the darkness of the tunnel.

He whistles a fragment of "Body and Soul" and remembers working with two dozen other men on the final section of the subway. The job was his own choice. Earth, air, fire, water: Who had urged him toward embracing them all? He'd seen too much fire. He'd helped build the aqueducts that brought the Croton water, and worked on the masonry of the reservoir where the Public Library now stands. He'd worked in the air high above the city. It was earth that was missing, deep earth, earth that was dirt, but earth that was granite.

And so he enlisted and came to 195th Street at St. Nicholas Avenue to work with a team of dynamiters, work that almost nobody else wanted. Most of the railroad had been driven through Manhattan using the technique of cut-and-cover. Up the East Side to Forty-second Street and then west to Longacre

Square and north again. A trench was dug, the track laid, and then covered with steel grids, dirt, pulverized rock. Simple. A job where you could always see the sky. But at 195th Street they faced a granite ridge that could not be done that way. Here they must cut through rock sixty feet below the surface, mining a tunnel that was fifteen feet high and fifty feet wide. Deep bore, the technique was called. As was done in London.

That morning, as on other mornings, a foreman named Sullivan packed dynamite against the virgin face of the tunnel. He set the dynamite, then shouted for the men to clear the tunnel, and they retreated as far as they could go, to stand among the bobbing lanterns. Sullivan signaled for the blast, and they all plugged their ears with fingers. Even then the great *ka-boom* knocked some men down and a *whoosh* of sandy air sprayed all of them. Cormac heard falling rock, then silence, and all rose, to move forward to shovel the broken rock into mule-drawn carts.

Then came the second explosion.

The world blackened, and Cormac heard screams and the panicky bleats of the mules and rock falling in great heavy slabs and then silence.

When he looked up, there was a high jagged gash in the mine face. And from beyond the gash, he saw the emerald light.

And the figure of a man silhouetted against the light.

Behind him, there was almost no passage back to the tunnel, but a man was groaning under one of the slabs. Cormac could hear muffled shouting too.

But he turned and moved forward, toward the dark figure. The light brightened, glowing, luminous, a radiating light that bathed all in its color.

It was his father.

Smiling.

"My son," he said.

Cormac tried to hurry to him, but his legs felt encased in water.

"I'll fetch your mother," he said. "Wait . . ."

And then there was a rumble, and more slabs fell from the ceiling, and the emerald light vanished, and Cormac felt a thump, sharp cutting pain, and fell into a darkness.

In the hospital, his leg in a cast, his cuts and abrasions bandaged, he met the man who had been trapped. "Did you see it?" Cormac whispered. "Did you see the light? And the man standing in the light?"

"What light?" the man said.

85.

At the building on Duane Street, he uses the elevator key that will let him out on the top floor. He passes the two first floors, occupied by his most recent tenants, two separate groups of young dot-commers who labor above a stationery store. He passes the first of his own two floors and steps out into what he calls the Studio. He doesn't switch on the lights, for he could walk blindfolded through this space and never knock over a lamp. But more important, the long dark loft shimmers with the illumination of the city. He closes the door behind him and stands for a moment in the magical glow. This is where he always comes to sit on the leather couch and listen to music in the dark or to drowse into skittering images of the past. He knows every inch of the place, the chairs and the tables, the file cabinets, the stacks of art books, and the closets full of drawings. Even when he's alone, the room is crowded with the faces and names of the past.

He takes off his coat and jacket and loosens his tie, drops all on a brocade armchair, and then goes to a small refrigerator for an icy bottle of Evian water. His back is to the skylight. He twists open the cap, takes a long sip, sloshing his mouth with the cold, clear water. To his left, he can see the silhouette of the easel, holding a canvas completed forty-three years earlier. A painting done from memory. The face of the Countess de Chardon, parts of it lifted from old drawings, but her clothes all different. She is wearing clothes that could have been worn by Lauren Bacall. Clothes worn in this studio by a fashion model who was all over *Vogue* that year before going off to Europe, never to return.

"That's not my face," the model said, looking at the painting. "It's not even close." He promised to do a separate drawing of the model, a portrait. "But who is *she?*" she said in an irritated way. Cormac smiled and said, "A woman I used to know."

He sits down at the end of the couch, leans back, and looks up. The rain-streaked skylight is made of one hundred and twenty-six panes, nine across and fourteen down, often repaired and strengthened or replaced, but the grid as it was when Bill Tweed gave him the building. The skylight faces south, and he can see the green shimmering lights of the Woolworth Building to the left and the icy towers of the World Trade Center to the right. They give off a light that pulses through all of downtown, every night of the week. Down there, up there, over there, men and women are moving in a thousand offices, speaking eighty languages, working the markets from Tokyo to Geneva, making sales, making bets, creating the light. Capitalism in the midnight hour of its long triumph.

On this night, Cormac can't see the tops of the towers. They're shrouded in spring fog.

He thinks: I miss the sound of foghorns.

Remembering their mournful baritone voices as the great liners arrived before daylight from Europe. The way they crowded the harbor for the first sixty years of the last century and how they moved so majestically up the North River to the Midtown piers. And the next day the *Daily News* centerfold would show photographs of the Duke and Duchess of Windsor or Clara Bow or Douglas Fairbanks, all posing on deck, the actresses propped up on piled steamer trunks, showing their legs. And how he sometimes went to the river when the great liners were sailing, the decks crowded with people waving toward the piers as they went off to somewhere else, and how he wished he could go with them, make his escape from Tir-na-Nog, and waved farewell himself, although he did not know a soul.

"What about you?" said Delfina Cintron.

Can he tell her about the foghorns in the morning dark?

"What about you?"

He wishes he could tell her the whole long tale.

* * *

Once he understood that he would live for many years, Cormac had worked hard at placing his nostalgias in a mental jail. This was an act of will and a means of self-defense. For a long time, New York (which is to say, the world) was as people thought it always would be, and then suddenly it changed, and the present was shoved forever into the past. There was never a sense of cataclysmic collapse, no shared admission that Rome was now finished. New Yorkers took for granted that nothing would ever remain the same, and nostalgia was their permanent protest. And because most of them were immigrants, they had begun their New York lives with aching memories of the places left behind. The habit never went away. Even now, in this latest city, they prefaced many remarks in the same way. "In the old days . . ." Or, "When I was a kid . . ." Or, "This place has gone into the crapper. . . ." Russians said such things, and Chinese, and Dominicans, and Palestinians. You lived in the present, but that present always contained a past, some image of a ruined paradise.

Cormac noticed as the years passed that New Yorkers shared a sense that whatever had changed, they could do nothing about it. A kind of optimistic fatalism. Reformers arrived with golden promises and left office in disgrace and impotence. Bill Tweed's line was a kind of municipal motto: *"What are you gonna do about it?"* Some of the big changes were welcome. He never met anyone who yearned for the city before the arrival of the Croton water, the city that smelled of shit. Nor did anyone protest the triumph of electricity, except those Uptown women who longed for the softening glow of gaslight. If the past had been reasonably happy, as New York had been before the collapse of 1893, the new present was drowned in permanent mourning, a lot of it dishonest, driven by a longing to return to the lost past. Cormac had gone through all that too many times. He had seen reputations blaze and then end up as burnt offerings. Heroes too often turned into scoundrels. Banks and corporations and newspapers ruled the city, and ended up as a handful of dust. Even language had term limits. In long separate eras, Cormac heard people use words like "fiddlesticks" or "groovy," and then one morning, as if a secret referendum had been passed, the words vanished. Nobody, of course, ever ran a referendum against the word "bullshit." That was a word and an emotion as permanent as the rivers. But the past had tremendous power here for the very simple reason that it was an American city that actually had a past. In his strange way (Cormac thinks now, swallowing cold Evian water) he is its custodian, he had been there, had smelled it, touched it, argued in it, fucked in it, killed in it; but he knew the treacheries and dangers of nostalgia. He was, after all, Irish. And he had too much past in his life. His defense against it was will. But even then, as in Madison Square only an hour earlier, will was never enough.

"To hell with the past," he says out loud in the darkened Studio, gazing at the misty towers before him. And thinks of Simone Signoret, great blowsy actress whose memoir was called *Nostalgia Isn't What It Used to Be.*

And yet . . . And yet, there were moments, here in the loft, when he longed to see the lost city of chimney pots and slate roofs, all blue after rain. He wanted to stand in woods where wolves still howled. He wanted to sit in the Polo Grounds and look at Willie Mays. At such moments, here, or in Madison Square, or at other odd moments in banal places, it was as if the bars of the mental cage had turned elastic and the past had forced its way out. Anything could set it off: the fragment of a tune, a glimpse of sun on cobblestones in a forgotten street, an accidental encounter with a building where he once knew a woman and loved her, even if she did not love him back.

He watches a flock of tiny birds emerge from between the Twin Towers to fly past the upper stories of the Woolworth Building, heading east. They know where they're going. He envies them for their freedom and their certainty, and lights a cigarette and sits there smoking in the dark.

86.

Cormac picks up his mail from the box he keeps in the post office on Vesey and Church. Big, ugly, solid stone post office, carrying the chiseled names of Robert Moses, master builder, and Fiorello La Guardia, master mayor, and the year of its unveiling, 1935. He riffles a sheaf of mail from his box. Bills. Time Warner cable service. Con Ed. The telephone company. A tax notice. And a plump brown envelope from the Argosy Clipping Service. He slips them into a cloth shopping bag, steps outside, smokes a cigarette. A Jamaican man is selling fruit from a cart. Messengers pedal by on bicycles. Men and women enter and leave the Jean Louis hair salon across Church Street. The sky is bright and traffic moves slowly from the Brooklyn Battery Tunnel, heading north. Bells toll in St. Peter's on Barclay Street and are answered by the bells of St. Paul's. Over everything, melding the sounds, he hears the murmuring, ceaseless drone of the city.

He crosses the street into the Borders bookstore, glances at the new books in paperback and the displays of bestsellers. On each visit, he hopes to be surprised. He seldom is. Today is Saint Patrick's Day and so one table is stacked with Books of Irish Interest: Joyce, the McCourts, Seamus Heaney, Yeats. Along with cookbooks and guidebooks and songbooks. He moves past them, browsing, touching, his hands caressing covers, allowing images to flash into him: Mayan temples, Brazilian prostitutes, bombed-out London. He chooses a new translation of Dostoyevsky's *Demons,* which he has always known as *The Possessed*. Paperback. Seventeen dollars. A week's pay in the year the post office opened. Three times what he earned in a week in 1840. When he first read the novel a century earlier, he was reminded of his friends in the Fenian Brotherhood and its endless, sometimes hilarious debates about the use of terror against the English enemy. What if someone innocent dies? What do you mean by innocent? And suppose the fella is not in a state of grace? Will you follow him to Hell? One of their offices was on Cortlandt Street, up above a man who made barrels, the building plowed away in

1969 to make way for the Trade Center. He wrote for their newspaper. Or one of their newspapers. And wondered which of them worked for the police. There were good people among the Fenians, along with a few lunatic true believers. Thinking about them years later, he realized that certain Irish exiles were pure Dostoyevsky.

He pays for the book, adds it to his shopping bag, then goes down the escalator from Borders and out into the endless concourse until he finds an ATM. He has no personal credit cards, but he does have a bank card in the name of ABCDuane Real Estate and he takes two hundred dollars from the company checking account. People in personalized green bunting are hurrying in every direction, buying sandwiches and sushi, cold drinks and coffee. Green ties, green shirts, green slacks, green dresses. Buttons that say, "Kiss me, I'm Irish." Many move down the escalators to the PATH trains, and Cormac wonders why anybody is going to New Jersey at one-thirty in the afternoon. Then thinks: Who am I to judge? I've never been there myself.

He heads south for the exit on Liberty Street, avoiding a hundred possible collisions in the frantic rush of the mall. One window of Sam Goody's is filled with Irish music. The Chieftains. The Clancy Brothers. Luke Kelly. De Danann. U2. He goes in, wondering for a moment whether it's time to buy a DVD player, to add one more piece of technology to his life. Come to my house, Delfina, and I'll explain the journey from a blacksmith's forge to the DVD version of *The French Connection*. Thinking: My life is absurd.

He buys a CD of the old music. Celtic music older than Saint Patrick. Along with Mozart's *The Magic Flute.* The Berlin Philharmonic conducted by von Karajan. All about the Otherworld and the dark powers of the Queen of Night.

In the Liberty Street vestibule, four homeless men huddle near the doors. Filthy. Eyeless in Gaza. In the 1890s, there were Bed Lines, for men ruined by the collapse, and when the post office was built, there were breadlines. Now there are homeless shelters where nobody wants to sleep. These four men must sleep here, where Cortlandt Street used to be. One of them, his white beard sprouting from dark brown skin, wears a plastic shamrock.

He has lunch in a sushi place, his eyes wandering from laminated views of Kyoto to the swift hands of the chef. He sits at the bar, those hands in front of him, clipping, trimming, carving. Like a great swordsman.

He doesn't look at the bills or the envelope full of press clippings. They can wait. He opens the Dostoyevsky. By the time he finishes his platter, he's laughing.

87.

He spreads the clippings on the dining table on the lower floor. Cindy Adams. Liz Smith. Mitchell Fink. Some scraps from Page Six. Others from Rush & Malloy. There's a spread in *Town & Country,* with handsome photography and views of a Hamptons beach, and a talk with William Hancock Warren across three pages in *Editor & Publisher*. Most of the stories he has read in the local newspapers, but there are odd clippings from the *Rocky Mountain News* (about a charity event in Aspen) and a sarcastic column from the *Guardian,* about Willie Warren's most recent trip to London, where he met with his tailor, the editor of the *Times,* and Tony Blair, in that order.

Cormac pushes them around on the polished mahogany table, as if trying to make a collage that will reveal their meaning. He sighs. There is no meaning beyond the one that brought him to New York across the ocean sea. The ancient vow. The oldest contract. He feels sludge congealing inside his skull.

He turns away from the clippings, imagines himself telling Bill Tweed the story. "What?" Tweed says. "You made a promise two hundred and sixty fucking years ago — and you're going to keep it?" His belly rolls and heaves. "You are a lunatic, Cormac.

You're living some insane dream. Forget this nonsense and jump on a woman, or order a steak!"

Cormac laughs too. And then he sees his father's body in the doorway and his mother in the mud. And the words come back, the words that have never left him. His father: *They must be brought to the end of the line.* And Mary Morrigan on the people who are barred from the Otherworld: *Those who fail to avenge injustice. For want of courage. For want of passion. If an unjust act is done in the family of a man or woman, it must be avenged.*

Such words have shaped his life, he thinks, and he can't roll them back. He gazes out through the windows, then takes a deep breath and returns to the clippings. There, smiling and a bit suety in excellent reproduction, is William Hancock Warren. He is not the last of the Warren line, perhaps, but he's the most recent Warren to come to New York. He will have to stand for all the rest, scattered as they are around the world. *He appears, he's here, I must act, or . . .* Warren has an eighty-one-foot yacht in the North River, a Fifth Avenue apartment, an eight-bedroom mansion in Southampton, designed (so they say) on the back of an envelope by Stanford White, and a thirty-one-room compound in Palm Beach. The chalet in Aspen is a minor property, and the place in Klosters is merely leased. Willie Warren: newspaper publisher supreme. Now courted, always photographed in public places. A fresh young prince of New York. Cormac smiles and thinks: How can I think of killing a man called Willie?

In many of the pictures, and most of the texts, there is also Elizabeth. The standard British trophy wife, with a vague genealogy and an untested claim to bloodlines going back to the Battle of Hastings. A model for a few years, adored by French and Italian photographers for her high cheekbones, long neck, elegant shoulders, and sleek black hair. She was on seven *Vogue* covers in two years and featured in spreads in Majorca and Rio, Cancun and Istanbul, all of them now in a separate folder in the file cabinet in the cubicle at the rear of the upstairs Studio.

The modeling is over, a phase, she explained to one interviewer, exciting and rewarding and educational, but a phase. She has not modeled for anyone since meeting Willie Warren. The stories imply that she has one responsibility now: to be lean and perfect. To be perfect at dinner and (Cormac supposes) perfect in bed. To be perfect when doing her charity work, campaigning against land mines, visiting the poor, the crack babies, the homeless in Thanksgiving Day shelters, where she exudes a luminous perfection that keeps everyone at bay, except, of course, the paparazzi. She visits the maimed, injured, luckless casualties of life, the flashbulbs flutter, and she's gone.

Cormac slides the clips around one final time, then assembles them like cards and gets up, thinking: They have no children. Why? Don't they have the usual dynastic ambitions of the rich? Are they free of the need to pass on their things and their houses to another generation, to be sure there will be no end to this branch of the line? Or are they merely waiting, like yuppies, until all is secure in life and business? Cormac walks to the spiral staircase and winds around the steps to the upper Studio. He flicks on lights, opens the door to the small office he calls the Archive, and goes in. The wall to the right is completely covered with corkboard, most of it occupied by the Warren family tree. He drops the fresh clips into a wire basket, to be filed later, then pauses.

"The other curse of my twice-cursed life," he says, and laughs, gazing at the family tree. "Jesus Christ . . ."

For more than a century, he has been gathering the documents in the Archive, the whole long saga of the Warrens who were the descendants and other relatives of the Earl of Warren. Certificates of births and deaths; newspaper clippings; obscure memoirs; yellowing hand-scrawled letters, real estate transactions, accounts printed in private; regimental histories. They have been retrieved through correspondence or through serendipity (in auction rooms, on the shelves of antiquarian booksellers) and in a flood these past ten years through the Internet. My hobby, Cormac often tells himself. My demented obsession. What I collect instead of stamps or coins.

On the far wall, the known faces of the Warrens exist in drawings and old engravings, crude woodcuts and reproductions of paintings, along with one photograph of a Warren made in the

1930s by Horst. On a map of the world, Cormac has placed flags in all the places they are known to have gone: India and Afghanistan and Nepal, Syria and Palestine, places where they preached the Christian virtues of British civilization to Muslims and Hindus and Buddhists, raising holy British rifles against heathen scimitars, dividing one religion against another, one province, one tribe, one family: dividing and dividing, while helping themselves to plunder.

The Warrens didn't invent that world, Cormac knew, but they did not struggle very hard against it. They went to Shanghai and Hong Kong, where some of their ships carried opium from the British fields of Burma to the Chinese. "We are surely doing God's work," one Warren wrote home. "They cannot be permitted to resist us, or they will be resisting Christ." This one joined the patriotic killing spree called the Opium Wars to force their drugs on an endless supply of heathen customers. Beijing, where a mad Warren missionary, his head full of God and sin and the redemption of the poor pagans (as well as of himself), walked out bravely to face the Boxers in 1900 with only a cross and a Bible. His head ended up on a pike, and the rebels wiped their asses with his Bible.

Here on the wall is the American branch, budding and tentative in Philadelphia after the Revolution, flowering in the coal mines of Pennsylvania, where years later its members employed Pinkertons against Molly McGuires, using gunshot and ambush to keep the anthracitic cash flowing, eventually giving way to the harder, more modern, more ruthless will of the Rockefellers. One of the Warrens entered steamboat manufacture along the Mississippi after the Louisiana Purchase, building a grand mansion in the Garden District of New Orleans, investing in cotton and helping finance the Confederacy. Another burrowed mines in Colorado and then, as thousands of factories opened across the Northeast and the first automobiles from Detroit rattled comically on lumpy American streets, his children discovered the black liquid pleasures of oil. Out there, in the lands stolen from Mexico, was the true El Dorado, filled with black gold. More lucrative than the slave trade and free of any moral qualms.

Not all of them were parasites or predators. Two died at Gettysburg, and one at Antietam, fighting for the Union, helping free the ancestors of men and women brought to America by the earl and his friends. One of the remaining British Warrens, Richard Benoit Warren, died trying to save an Irish enlisted man in the second Battle of the Somme (and his great-grandfather had fed the starving Irish during the Famine, without asking them to become soupers). A young man whose legs were broken in a barroom brawl — his name was Charles Asquith Warren — became a Communist, worked in the slums of the New England mill towns (in spite of his limping gait), joined the Lincoln Brigade to fight in Spain in 1936, and was killed in the Battle of the Jarama. One Warren was killed at Anzio. One died on Iwo Jima.

Some simply vanished, of course, to die in failure or brawls or forgotten wars in strange places. But the known ones are here on the wall, and their tales are here in the Archive. There is very little about the earl and nothing about the son who died during the American Revolution. None of the narratives mention Cormac Samuel O'Connor.

Cormac couldn't kill them all, of course, and didn't want to. Even if he'd had the desire, as a prisoner of the blessing of Africa he couldn't leave Manhattan to track them down. Very early, he decided that the Warrens would only matter to him if they invaded this place, this granite island, this Manhattan. If they entered these turreted castle grounds (he said, mocking himself as the Irish Edmund Dantes), he would send them off to join the sea-scoured bones of the earl.

But after Cormac killed the earl's son, the Warrens did not try again to establish themselves in New York. It was as if they believed that some invincible curse hovered in the New York streets, mysterious, spooky, fatal. And besides, America was big enough. None of them tried to drive roots here until the arrival of William Hancock Warren. Who is here now, defying family superstition and ancient history. The first Warren in more than two centuries to take up residence in Manhattan. There are seven photographs of the man here, including one as a boy and one taken at his wedding. The man smiles. The man's eyes twinkle. In one image, dressed in a tuxedo, he is juggling three balls. Cormac thinks: He doesn't know I exist. He doesn't know he is my quarry.

88.

*Cormac dials Delfina's number, but there is no answer. Her answer*ing machine gives only a number, no name, but it's her voice, hoarse and whispery. He leaves his name and number. He walks around the Studio in the gray afternoon light and begins to sing. *Each time I see a crowd of people . . . just like a fool I stop and stare . . .* He loves to sing. He sits at the piano and sings. He walks the streets and sings. Thousands of songs are parked in memory, from Bowery theaters to Prohibition speakeasies, from vaudeville to Rodgers and Hart, many of them fragments, some of them complete, and when he plays Sinatra or Tony Bennett, Johnny Hartman or Lady Day, they are all duets. *I know it's not the proper thing to do . . .* He sings to Miles Davis CDs too, and to Ben Webster. He sings French with Piaf and Becaud and in Spanish with Tito Rodriguez . . . but he never dances. He can't dance. Or he won't risk it. Never in public, seldom when alone. Long ago, in the time when Master Juba and John Diamond were inventing tap-dancing in the Five Points, in an exuberant collision of Africa and Ireland, he decided that white people had no gift for dancing. At least not for American dancing. The waltz, perhaps. The minuet. But it was better when the rhythms moved more quickly, when drums and bass came in a rush, to sit this one out. And perhaps it wasn't white people, for after all, there were Fred Astaire and Gene Kelly and Bob Fosse. It wasn't white people, it was Cormac Samuel O'Connor. He could not dance. It was as simple as that. He yearned to dance, but had been taught by life that every man has his limitations. Dancing was as far from him as basketball.

Now he goes downstairs to the living area, to the book-lined walls, the dark bedroom. He is bound for his daily nap. Since the 1890s, this has been his indulgence, his pleasure, his necessity. The siesta (he always insists to his friends) is the most civilized of all institutions sent to us from the Mediterranean. The gift of Spain and Italy, and perhaps of Islam. The siesta gives him two mornings. The siesta allows his worries to marinate in his brain, where solutions can be found for riddles, and always grants him on awaking a refreshed clarity. In the back bedroom, thick drapes seal off light and muffle sound. The daily routine is almost always the same: lunch, then a siesta, and then down to the streets for his walk, which he calls his Wordsworth.

He traces this ambulatory habit to reading the great poet when he was young. One variation on the Wordsworth were the years in the 1890s that he spent trying to photograph every building on the island. The years he spent trying to freeze a city that could not be frozen. Now most of those buildings exist only as photographs, and almost every leafy glade in Manhattan has been paved, but he continues walking. Sometimes he takes the subway to some distant stop and does the Wordsworth all the way home. On weekends, when trucks are gone from the streets, along with thousands of suburban cars, he takes his bicycle to the streets and pedals for miles. He never walks fewer than twenty blocks and never pedals less than sixty. In the 1970s, he began riding the bicycle late on summer nights, when the asphalt had cooled, and there he would see mysterious black riders, each a solitary, each on a ten-speed, each with shorts and helmet and backpack, all, like him, indulging the loneliness of the long-distance rider. One night, pedaling into Central Park after midnight, he saw one of these riders and was certain it was Quaco. They glanced at each other. He saw Quaco's eyes, his nose and mouth and line of jaw, and Cormac said hello in Yoruba, hello and nice night, and the man said yes in Ashanti, yes, a nice night. They pedaled away, and he never saw the man again.

He can't go more than three days without the Wordsworth. He needs the regular flushing of blood and lungs, particularly in the years when he smokes. But he also wants the multiple layered visions of the changing city and the provocations of memory. A bar called Grogan's becomes Farrelly's and then Mangan's, and then the Flowing Tide, and then Chapo's, and then the Quisqueya Lounge, and never stops being a bar. One spring, an entire block vanishes from Chelsea to be replaced by white-brick humming apartment houses. A factory is turned into lofts. He needs to see it all, to be in the city as it is and not a prisoner of the city as it was. To watch the change as it happens helps him combat the sludge.

He never gets tired, even during the years when he smokes. The trick he has learned is a simple one: focus only on the twenty feet directly in front of him. Move with willed looseness through that closed space (eating time along with space), and avoid looking at any point in the distance. That imposing hill will exhaust you, he says to himself. You will never get past that dense warren of factories. Twenty feet: That's the immediate goal. The habits of the Wordsworth mirror the habits of his life.

Now he removes his clothes and takes an old cotton nightshirt from a wall peg. He lies on the bed, but sleep does not come easily on this afternoon.

The quarry rises in his mind.

89.

Twelve years earlier, nobody in New York knew the name of William Hancock Warren. Now Cormac is thinking about him each day and seeing him in dreams. He must have been known, of course, by bankers and brokers, by a few well-tipped headwaiters, by the manager of the Plaza or the Pierre, the Stanhope or the Sherry-Netherland. But he didn't live here and was not yet a public figure. His name was buried in the middle of the *Forbes* and *Fortune* lists, among the largely anonymous people who had more money than they could ever spend but not so much that they faced curiosity and scrutiny. Those who knew him well enough to call him Willie lived in Houston and London and the endless Arab emirates. He was as comfortable in the desert cities of Saudi Arabia as he was in the deserts near Palm Springs. Some of his older friends, including those from the House of Saud, had known his father, a man who'd risen from the oil fields of Oklahoma during the Great Depression and hammered together his own security and wealth with judicious bribes to politicians of both parties and a passion for anonymity. For the first thirty-two years of his life, William Hancock Warren was true to his father's style.

Nine months after his father died in Texas, aged eighty-one, and buried discreetly, with two of his pallbearers retired officers of the Central Intelligence Agency, the son moved to Manhattan with his wife. They bought a seven-bedroom triplex one block north of the Frick, but this caused no sensation. Such men arrive periodically in New York, tarry awhile, and then leave. William Hancock Warren was among those who stayed, who found life and purpose in Manhattan. But he was here for a year before Cormac saw his name in a gossip column and another three years before the public became aware of his presence. He bought real estate in deals that attracted little attention. A Chelsea warehouse here, some West Side apartment houses there, an ancient office building on William Street, which he quietly closed for rehab. He avoided the fashionable restaurants, the charity ball circuit, the seasonal cycle of opera and theater openings. He stayed away from politicians and so eluded those prying journalists who inspected campaign contributions. He wasn't part of anyone's A list for dinner parties. He invested in Internet companies, to be sure, but in those years such companies were not covered by the general press. Occasionally he lunched with a business acquaintance at the Century Association, but he did not become a member. His name did not appear in the columns of Liz Smith, Cindy Adams, or Rush & Malloy, and Page Six did not seem to know of his existence. In the style of his father, William Hancock Warren preferred to be a member of the anonymous rich.

Then, only nine years ago, he emerged as a public figure as if visiting from the planet Krypton. That was when Cormac first saw his photograph. The occasion was an acquisition that he must have known would put him in the public eye. No baseball team was for sale that year and the football teams were prisoners of long leases in New Jersey. So William Hancock Warren did what so many other rich young American men do when they want more than money: He bought a newspaper.

The *New York Light* was not, to be sure, a thriving enterprise. It was a large dull broadsheet, full of Wall Street news and stories from the police blotter. It was the last afternoon newspaper in New York, with a loyal, aging readership that bought it at Grand Central and Penn Station for the long ride to the suburbs or had it delivered to their apartment buildings on the East Side. A few serious gamblers read it for news from West Coast racetracks, and businessmen trusted its closing stock prices and analyses of earnings reports. But its gray pages repelled many other New Yorkers, and reporters from the morning newspapers said that it bridged the generation gap between the living and the dead.

For eighteen years the *Light* had been owned by a foundation, whose members stated that they felt a civic obligation to subsidize the second-oldest newspaper in the United States. The staff was small, the advertising thin, the losses substantial, but after all the paper went back to 1835, the year that James Gordon Bennett started modern journalism with the *New York Herald*. Among the survivors, only the *New York Post* could trace its lineage back to an earlier time, the year 1801, when Alexander Hamilton assembled a group of New Yorkers to serve his interests and those of the Bank of New York. But as time passed, the clubby old-guard members of the Light Foundation began dying off, carrying what was left of *noblesse oblige* into their marble crypts, and their children preferred yachts and airplanes and houses in Southampton or Positano to civic duty in New York. One June morning in 1991, on page one of the *Light*, the board announced that if a new buyer was not found within two weeks, they would fold the paper. Other newspapers wrote mournful editorials, but their owners were rooting for the *Light* to die. It was a hindrance, another competitor for space on newsstands, and in the privacy of their offices they dismissed any hope for its survival as mere sentimentality. Several semi-insane owners of parking lots and grocery chains offered to buy the *Light* for a dollar and operate it for at least a year. Each got a few minutes on local television; but sane men knew that it was doubtful that even a one-dollar check from such men would clear at the bank. The surviving members of the foundation didn't want to be remembered for selling the *Light* to a lunatic. In stepped William Hancock Warren.

"New York without the *Light*," he said in a press release, "would be like New York without the Statue of Liberty."

On the Fourth of July that year, Warren handed the foundation a check for one million dollars, which the surviving members promised would be used to study threats to the First Amendment. The fireworks on the Hudson seemed like acts of celebration for the newspaper. "Re-born on the 4th of July!" their page-one headline said the following day. And when the holiday ended, William Hancock Warren walked into the rat-infested building on West Street where the *Light* had been published since 1947, its fourth location since its foundation in a three-story building on Beaver Street. He uttered only one sentence to the assembled television cameras, and as Cormac watched that evening on channel 4, the words jolted his heart: "I'm a descendant of people who lived in New York before the *Light* was born! I hope to see it flourish and live to an even riper old age!"

Cormac thought that night: This cannot be. His most natural reflex, taught to him by living a very long life, was doubt. A wise old editor had said to him once, "If you want it to be true, it probably isn't." But then he saw Warren's eyes and the familiar features (only marginally altered by the work of generations) and once more resumed a search that had lasted in some ways all his years. He read everything he could find about the man who, in print, was now being called Willie Warren. This wasn't much, but he subscribed to the Argosy service anyway. Thinking: I don't want it to be true, so it probably is. If this was the last of one branch of the Warren line, the old vows required him to act. He wished he had the sword. His father's sword. He wished the sword were there to connect him to the younger man he once was, full of certainties. And there was something else pressing upon him now.

He wanted more than ever to find the dark lady marked by spirals. She had nothing to do with the Warrens and the curse of Ireland. She was part of a separate story. And yet her story and the story of the Warrens were coming together, forced into union by the pressure of time. He had found a dark lady. Delfina Cintron. But he did not yet know if she bore the markings, if she was *the* dark lady. Caution kept him from making the discovery. Caution, and a kind of fear. If she did not bear the markings, he would go on and on and on, like the North River. If she did, he could be entering his final days. At last. And he could not go to that ending without completing the unfinished business of the other story, the demand for completion imposed on him by family and tribe. My father first, he thought, and then, with any luck, Delfina Cintron, and finally release and a swift passage into the emerald light.

The newspapers told Cormac that on the day Willie Warren moved into the publisher's office, he took calls of congratulation from the mayor, the governor, and the president of the United States. That day, he also hired Howard Rubenstein to handle his press relations, and his secretary referred all other calls to the Rubenstein office. The trade press cobbled together stories, using words and phrases like "quixotic" and "deep pockets" and "amateur," while predicting that no matter what Warren did, the *Light* was doomed. The losses would be immense. The rich boy would eventually turn his attention to other toys. Prepare the obits now. In Cormac's solitude, he agreed.

Everybody was wrong.

In the months that followed the purchase, Cormac's old newspaperman's heart quickened as he saw Warren make a series of superb moves. He hired an excellent editor and left him alone on all matters involving the news. He gave the editor a budget that allowed him to expand the tiny staff with a mixture of seasoned professionals and passionate youngsters. He hired Milton Glaser to give the paper a new look, and one Monday morning it became a broadsheet with the graphic energy of a tabloid. Bold and bright, without being loud. He started building a new color-printing plant in Brooklyn, which would get the newspaper around Brooklyn, Queens, and Long Island, delivered to doorsteps. His trucks could enter Manhattan when incoming traffic was light and copies of the paper were soon stacked on the newsstands at Penn Station and Grand Central when commuters headed home. He hired away a few star columnists from the *News* and the *Post* to add some personality to the *Light*'s sober news pages, paying them twice the money they were getting at the papers they left behind. He tripled the space in the sports section and encouraged huge action shots from his photographers. He sent handwritten notes to reporters when they did solid stories, gave bonuses to those whose stories were picked up by television, made certain that notes were sent to staff members on their birthdays and wedding anniversaries or when death took place in a family. He advertised heavily in the subways and in the foreign-language press. The editorial pages, which he controlled, became a model of judiciousness, and the op-ed pages were intelligent and well-written without ever talking down to the readers. He added no fuel to any municipal fire. He endorsed Bill Clinton and Rudy Giuliani and even had nice things to say about Al Sharpton. For the first time in decades, Cormac began to see people reading the *Light* on the subways.

William Hancock Warren was also lucky. He bought the newspaper at almost the precise moment when the boom started. His own holdings boomed. But so did the city of New York. Crime was down. Money was flowing. People began going out again at night. New businesses opened every day of the week. Warren expanded his business pages and insisted on covering both the Internet and the media. The young dot-commers began reading the paper and then advertising in it. The *Light* became the newspaper of the boom. But his editors knew that they needed more than the brash kids to read their paper. Warren read a biography of Joseph Pulitzer and decided to follow the old man's example by covering the huge immigration wave. The *Light* became the immigrants' newspaper, defending them, telling stories of their progress, running a column about green cards and visas and the process of naturalization. The word got around. Those immigrants who were learning English began reading it, and more important, so did their children. Then, about two years ago, he made a move that drove a tormented ambiguity into Cormac's heart.

He announced that the *Light* was moving into a building on Park Row. Across the street from City Hall. Up the block from J&R Music World. He could do it now, the Rubenstein office explained, because the computer had freed newspapers from the plants in which they were printed. You could write a story on a high floor in Park Row and it would be printed miles away in Brooklyn. The other newspapers were all produced that way. Now it was the turn of the *Light*. And the city room would be located on Park Row.

Cormac wanted to weep. Once upon a time, he had worked on thirteen different newspapers on Park Row. As a reporter, a rewrite man, a copy editor, a typesetter. He had watched Walt Whitman sleep on the floor of one of those papers and had shown young Sam Clemens how they set type in New York. After the Civil War, Cormac had seen Father Dongan organize the orphaned newsboys and force the publishers to buy them shoes and get them doctors (the largest donations came from Bill Tweed). He'd walked past Hearst and Pulitzer in the lobbies and drunk with Brisbane in the whorehouses of Chapel Street. In those days, Park Row wasn't just a distinct neighborhood; it was a kind of civilization, peopled by gaudy men of rapacious ambitions and appetites, great talent, enormous weaknesses, and much fun. Too much fun to last. Cormac had seen the Park Row papers die or move away, until all of them were gone by 1931. And here came a man who said that the past was now the future.

In spite of himself, in spite of a terrible ancient vow, in spite of history and memory, part of him began to root for William Hancock Warren.

For eight years, he watched and compiled his files and secretly applauded Warren's growing triumph. For those eight years, he gazed at dark-skinned women on his walks through the city and turned away from them. After so many years of too much time, he wanted more time now, to see where Warren's project would go, to postpone fate, to wait until he found the true dark lady. The century was winding down. The Wall Street boom rolled on.

Then, on a sweaty day in August, he saw Delfina Cintron.

She calls after he returns from his walk. She is cool but not distant. They make a date for the theater. Next week. Under the marquee. Then she says good-bye, and he stands there, holding the cordless phone. I must move more quickly, he thinks. I must move closer to her, and soon, to find out if I can love her. I who have loved no woman for so many years. He gazes out toward Church Street, thinking: It's much more difficult to love than to kill.

90.

At ten after eight in the morning, Cormac is in Mary's Café on the corner of Chambers Street and Broadway. He's gone past the cakes on baroque display, and the counters where lone men crunched well-done English muffins and read the *New York Post,* past the booths on the right with their view of rain-swept Chambers Street. He wishes he could bring Delfina here and try to explain who Miss Subways was, as seen in all the posters hung like historical artifacts upon the coffee shop walls. But he is here to meet Healey, his friend, his last friend, who knows all about Miss Subways (and even dated one for three marvelous weeks in 1959), and so he has picked a table as far back in the large rear room as he can go, pushed up against fake leather banquettes. The choice of Mary's was not entirely up to Cormac. The waitresses here know Healey, and that makes things much easier. And this is Tuesday, the day when Cormac and Healey have their weekly breakfast and the waitresses are prepared for whatever comes their way.

Cormac is always happy here and not simply because Mary's is a few blocks from where he lives. The corner of Broadway and Chambers has been part of his life from the beginning. Across the street to the right is the corner of the old Common, where the Africans and Irish were burned or hanged in 1741. To the left stands the building where he once worked as a clerk for Alexander T. Stewart. Forgotten now, but once one of the three richest men in America. And that building (now covered with rigging as part of a rehab) was Stewart's masterpiece. The Marble Palace, it was called after it opened in 1848, and it was the first department store in New York. With that concept, and fixed prices (no bargaining, but no giving goods to your relatives for half price either), Stewart changed the city. He was a tough, reticent, decent man from Lisburn in Northern Ireland (he sent food and clothes and money to Ireland during the Famine). He started in his twenties, importing linen from the mills of the North, and then gambled everything on the Marble Palace. Everyone predicted disaster: It was on the wrong side of the street, with the Five Points at its back. A department store? In the era of specialized shops? When you visited a button shop for buttons and a lace shop for frills and a haberdasher for hats? The notion was too radical, too . . . common. But Stewart made it work. Cormac wonders what A. T. Stewart would have made of his friend Healey. He knows what Healey would have made of Bill Tweed, whose twelve-million-dollar courthouse is halfway down the block. He'd have asked the Boss for a list of the places where he wanted him to vote.

Like some of his other friends over the years, Cormac enjoys Healey's company too much to tell him the story of his life, even part of it. The rule behind most New York friendships is "don't ask, don't tell." If Healey doesn't ask, Cormac will not tell. Healey never asks. He's the last of the old-style bohemians, the author of three good plays that had long runs off Broadway in the early 1960s, which meant he was shaped by the 1950s, when the worst sin of all was to name names. He's a reformed drunk who now walks twenty-seven blocks, in rain, snow, or summer heat, to meet Cormac for their weekly breakfast. He's also very loud, which is why the waitresses place them near the coffee shop's outfield wall. Healey is loud because in the battle for the Chosin Reservoir in 1951, he lost half his hearing when a Chinese mortar exploded fifteen feet away from his left eardrum. "I've got a good ear for dialogue," he used to say. "I just wish I had two." He doesn't write anymore, but he lives decently on royalties, since one of his plays is always being performed somewhere. He retired from writing when his stupendous young second wife ran off with a bass player. He now claims that he wrote all of his plays for her and after she left, whenever he tried to write, her face always appeared over his desk. The result was fury and sorrow, followed by paralysis and too much drinking. He stopped writing first, and then stopped drinking. The writing did not come back. He and Cormac have been friends for eleven years, and Healey has never mentioned anything about Cormac's unchanged features, the absence of marks of age. It's as if the playwright listens to Cormac but doesn't see him. He has never been to Cormac's house, nor has Cormac been to his. They sometimes meet in bars, where Healey drinks great quantities of Diet Pepsi, or here at Mary's for breakfast.

Now Healey is making his entrance again, huge and wide-eyed, dressed in a plaid Irish hat, his anorak dripping with the morning rain. His shoes make a squishing sound as he passes alarmed customers. When he reaches the table, smiling with his mouthful of yellow teeth, he heaves his soaked shoulder bag to Cormac's side of the banquette. He rips off the anorak and hangs it on a wall hook and leaves the hat on top of his head.

"Jesus Christ, what a filthy morning!" he bellows. "And there's nothing left to look forward to now when you wake up! Kathie Lee is gone! No more slave labor in Thailand to worry about! Jesus Christ, no more infernos on cruise ships! What will we do without her, man? What will keep the pulse of the metropolis pulsing after breakfast? We're doomed, man! Kathie Lee is history!"

Cormac suggests (as Healey sits down heavily, making the banquette wheeze) that maybe there'd be some Kathie Lee videos he could buy. Kathie Lee's Greatest Hits. The Golden Age of Kathie Lee.

"No, no. No, they can't do that, man! What made her so great — what made her an artist, man — is it was LIVE! No script! It was happening right there in front of your fucking eyes, man. That's why she's such a great artist, you dig?"

A waitress named Millie comes over. Everybody named Dotty, Penny, Ginger, and Bridget has passed into history, and here must be the last Millie left in Manhattan. Mary's Café is that kind of place; nobody is ever named Heather and everybody knows about Miss Subways. Millie is fifty, heavy, with a wicked mouth on her when she wants to be wicked. Cormac cherishes her.

"What's yours, hon?" she says, meaning both of them.

"The usual," Healey says.

"Let's see: scramble three, crisp bacon, whole wheat toast, coffee, no milk, fake sugar."

"As always, you got it perfect, Millie."

"You the same?"

"Why not?" Cormac says.

"He actually likes oatmeal," Healey says. "It's an Irish thing."

"Our oatmeal tastes like cement," Millie says.

"That's why he likes it."

"I'll take the egg," Cormac says. "Four minutes, rye toast."

"You got it, sweetheart," Millie says, and hurries away.

"I love waitresses who call me 'sweetheart,'" Cormac says.

"So marry her."

"Why ruin a romance?"

Healey takes the *News* and the *Post* from his bag, the headlines filled with RUDY and DONNA, the latest chapter in the pathetic saga of the mayor in love.

"You read the papers yet? I mean, watching Rudy manage women is like watching an ostrich shit."

Cormac laughs. Millie comes back with a basket of rolls, Danish, butter and marmalade, and a tall white plastic pot of coffee.

Healey and Cormac start eating out of the basket. Healey taps the tabloids.

"I gotta terrible confession to make," he says. "I'm starting to feel sorry for that Giuliani. I mean, his whole life story changed in the last year. Cancer! His wife splits! A new broad shows up! He drops out of the Senate race! He goes walking with the new broad, along with a bunch of photographers, and he doesn't even realize he looks like a fucking idiot. Then they make his father for a hoodlum in the thirties! Doing time. Breaking heads. Stuff from sixty fucking years ago! Fact is, you weren't doing time in the thirties, you were some kind of pussy, man. I want to go across the street to City Hall, see Giuliani, put an arm around him, and say, Come on, Rudy, LET'S GO GET A BLOW JOB!!"

At that point, Millie arrives with the eggs and bacon.

"Whad you say?" she says, pulling the plates closer to her ample breasts, as if holding them hostage.

"Aw, gee, Millie, sorry, pardon my French, man."

"Don't call me 'man,' Healey. I'm a girl."

"Of course, man."

She puts down the plates and wrinkles her brow, staring at Healey.

"What were you talking about, anyway?"

"The mayor, of course. I'm telling this Irish hoople I'm feeling sorry for the mayor these days —"

"Careful, he'll have ya indicted."

"And I was saying how I'd like to just put my arms around him, I swear . . ." Here his voice cracks into a counterfeit sob. "And just say to him, RUDY, LET'S GO GET A BLOW JOB!"

The coffee shop goes dead silent. Millie looks at Healey for a second and then laughs out loud and whacks Healey's hat with her hand, sending it flying toward the kitchen.

"You're RIGHT!" she says. "You're absolutely RIGHT! That's what he NEEDS!"

"I mean, can't you see it?"

"I don't wanna see it."

"I mean —"

"Good-bye, Healey!"

She walks briskly away. Two other waitresses are giggling, and when Millie reaches them, she starts telling the story. The coffee shop is again filled with the sound of murmuring voices and clattering china. Cormac sees the waitresses in dumbshow.

"You ever notice," Healey says, "that Millie's got a beautiful ass?"

"A BLOW JOB!"

Millie's voice.

Reaching the punch line.

Healey's eyes widen.

"PUT IT ON MY CHECK!" he instantly bellows down the full length of the coffee shop.

Shouts. Applause. Fists pounding on counters.

Cormac doesn't care if Healey ever writes another word.

91.

The telephone keeps her present in his life as he waits for their night at the theater. Sometimes they speak twice in a day, at noon and at night. She talks about how she hates working at the drugstore, and he says she must find another job where she can use her brains, just look in the *Times* and go for the interviews and fill out the forms. She says she has no references, except Rite Aid. He says just be straight. Tell them you were raising a baby. Silence for a beat. Then more talk about where she'd want to work and how she could use Spanish and how bilingual secretaries are in demand. Then she tells him she is taking a day off from Rite Aid to apply for three jobs. One in a bank on Forty-eighth Street. Another at a dot-com outfit on Greene Street. Another in a law firm in the World Trade Center. He wishes her luck but says she should be careful about the dot-commers, there is a collapse under way.

"Hey," she says, "are you what they call a mentor?"

On Saturday morning, she calls and her voice is bubbling and high-pitched.

"I got it," she says. "I got the job! The one at the World Trade Center! An outfit named Reynoso and Ryan — they hired me. I got home last night and the message was on my machine and . . . I start Monday, can you believe it? Can you fucking believe it?"

She comes downtown and they celebrate in Chinatown at a place called Oriental Gardens on Elizabeth Street. They order leek soup and dim sum and rice with vegetables and separate mounds of cool shrimp and hot chicken. Her mood shifts from girlish excitement to nervousness to determination, each shift reflected in the way she uses her chopsticks. When Cormac can eat no more, she continues. Her eyes sparkle. Her breasts move under her black T-shirt. She is like a prisoner released from jail.

"Thank you, Cormac," she says, and reaches across the table and squeezes his right hand. "If it wasn't for you . . ."

"Stop," he says. "This is all you. You did it. I didn't."

She sips green tea. He wants to ask her to come home with him, to plunge with him into the dark nest of Duane Street. To begin. She senses this too. But then glances at her wristwatch.

"I'd better run," she says. "I've got to buy some clothes. Or at least clothes for Monday morning."

She asks the waiter to wrap what is left of the food. He pays the bill with cash. They go out together into bright sunshine. They walk together toward Canal Street, passing the old police station marked 1881. The year of the gunfight at the OK Corral and the year Henry James published *Portrait of a Lady*. He thinks: What a marvelous country.

"I'll see you at the theater," she says, getting into a taxi. "And Cormac? Thanks again."

92.

Cormac waits for Delfina under the marquee of the Royale Theater on West Forty-fifth Street, searching the crowds for her face. The wind off the river is raw for May, and there are gusts of rain driving most people into the shallow lobby or directly to their seats.

Cormac wonders how many times he has walked under this marquee since the theater opened on New Year's Day in 1927. He was at the opening, sent there by a features editor from the *Daily News*. The architect's name was Krapp. Herbert J. Krapp. "I got a real crappy assignment for you," the editor said. "Irresistible." And off Cormac went. He remembers the name of the architect but can't retrieve the name of the play. The theater was handsome and the street was busy all night with theater people and whiskey joints, and if you stayed up late enough and watched the entrances to the speakeasies, you might even get to see Babe Ruth.

For three months that year of Ruth's sixty glorious home runs, Cormac had a secret affair with a glorious dancer named Ginger Everett. She was in an Earl Carroll show up the block toward Times Square, and he met her under this marquee where she was sheltering from a rainstorm. She had the Jean Harlow white-blond look before anyone ever heard of Jean Harlow, and like most dancers in those days she was short and a bit chubby, with a bosom that moved when she did, which was most of the time. Ginger Everett seemed to move when she was sitting down. Or sleeping.

She had come to New York on a train from Lorain, Ohio, in 1926, seventeen years old, brown-haired and zaftig and desperate to be a star, and somehow found her way to the arms of a bootlegger named Sonny Rivington. He made her a blonde and found her a gig in a chorus line and a suite at the Dixie Hotel. His suite. Cormac had seen him around the speakeasies: a small dapper man with shiny black hair combed straight back in the Valentino style. His face was so closely shaved that it glistened. He had eyes like a rattlesnake's.

Sonny Rivington was only about twenty-five but seemed older than the other bootleggers, except when he was dancing. He loved to dance. And watching him from the bar or a corner table, Cormac was always envious. Sonny could do the Charleston without looking ridiculous. He was the best tango dancer in town until George Raft showed up. And every night after the show, he and Ginger Everett bounced from speak to speak. Dancing and drinking and dancing some more, until she could barely move. In the Rivington suite at the Dixie Hotel, she would usually go right to sleep. Poor Sonny: Though his eyes were as old as the lairs of rattlesnakes, he was still too young to know that dancers work so hard at night they can only make love in the morning. This annoyed him, because he never woke up until noon and therefore had no mornings. So he threw her out. She came back. He gave up on her a week later. They got back together. But Cormac's mornings were always free, and sometimes before noon, she would slip away for a late breakfast in his studio, racing downtown on the subway, and make love to him as if working out in a gym. He was certain that the thing about him she most admired was that he could not dance. One other thing was absolutely clear: She was never in love with Cormac Samuel O'Connor. She was mad for Sonny Rivington.

Finally, one night in 1928 (around the time Mae West was doing *Diamond Lil* at the Royale, a show he does not remember), Cormac was sitting at the bar in Billy LaHiff's saloon when Sonny and Ginger came in together. She glanced at Cormac in a nervous way, but then Sonny Rivington started hauling her around the dance floor. She left after two lindy hops to go to the ladies' room, probably to steal five minutes' sleep standing up. Then two gunsels walked in wearing gray hats and black overcoats, went straight to Sonny's table, shot him twelve times, and walked out. In the uproar, Cormac went to the ladies' room and told Ginger Everett to get the hell out of there, and she dashed out the back door, while he called in the details to the *Daily News* city desk without mentioning her. She showed up at his studio three hours later, cried for five minutes for poor Sonny Rivington, and then slept for eighteen hours. Two days later she left by train for Hollywood, where she got two small parts in Harold Lloyd movies, married a real estate operator, and disappeared forever.

Now on this street where Cormac met Ginger Everett on a rainy night while Sonny was out of town, here comes Delfina Cintron. Head down, raincoat collar high, cheeks rouged by the wind. She sees him, whispers a hello, takes his arm, and they go in to see *Copenhagen*. A few men turn to look at her. She removes her coat as they find the seats. She's wearing a low-cut black sheath and a string of fake pearls and matching fake-pearl earrings and she glows with golden beauty. The houselights dim. She folds her coat over her knees with the *Playbill* on top. She takes Cormac's rain-chilled hand. Her own hand is very warm.

"I'm so *excited,*" she says. "A *play!* A Broadway *play.*"

As they watch the first act, he hears her make several gasping sounds. Her hand gets wet and she removes it in an embarrassed way and tamps it dry on her coat. He glances at her. Her face is totally concentrated on this drama about the physicists Niels Bohr and Werner Heisenberg and the morality of using their science to build an atomic bomb. The writing, by Michael Frayn, is excellent, but Cormac can't follow the technical language and imagines Mae West walking in from stage right and causing a riot. At the interval, the lights come up and Delfina's eyes are welling with tears.

"Are you okay?"

"Yes. No. Oh, I don't know." They stand to let others pass to the aisle. "I'll explain later. Do we have time for a smoke?"

The area in front of the theater is packed. Delfina is composed now, coat draped over her shoulders, and they each smoke Marlboro Lights.

"You see, at Hunter, I had this physics class, and —"

Lights begin blinking, ordering them to return to the seats. She stamps out the cigarette.

"We'll talk later."

In the dark, she disappears into the play, or into memory, or both. The rest of the audience seems as absorbed as Delfina Cintron. In the last days of the giddy boom, they are actually paying attention to a moral dilemma. At the end, he and Delfina join in the standing ovation and then move slowly back up the aisle toward the street.

"Thank you so much, Cormac," she says. "That was — it meant a lot to me."

He tries not to sound like a stiff but does anyway: "I'm just glad you could come with me."

The lame sentence goes past her. She says: "I could feel things popping in my brain. You know? Like tiny little dead things suddenly coming to life. It was like — if you didn't use certain muscles for a long time? Then you do, and *pop-pop-pop*."

They walk out into the cool street. The rain has stopped. They hurry toward Frankie & Johnny's on Forty-fourth Street off Eighth Avenue. One flight up. Delfina has never been here before, but Cormac remembers a night when Owney Madden threw a police lieutenant down the stairs for trying to double the payoffs. He and Delfina go up the same flight of stairs, and he's at eye level with her golden thighs, and now he remembers Madden's enraged gangster face. The restaurant is filling up with the New Jersey people coming out of the theaters. They check their coats. Men look up when Delfina walks in her street swagger behind a waiter to a table against the wall, with Cormac behind her. She sits down, scraping the chair as she pulls it forward. She wants a glass of wine and Cormac orders a glass of the house red and a large bottle of sparkling water. She lifts the menu.

"Steak," she says, grinding her jaws in an exaggerated way. "Steak, steak, steak."

"I guess you want steak."

"With cottage fries and tomatoes and onions and then some amazing dessert."

"I'll have the same," Cormac says. "I can walk it off tomorrow."

She looks at him in an amused way, as if she has other ideas about working off the calories. The waiter arrives with the wine. Cormac orders. Every table is now full and there are people standing near the door.

"What a great place this is," she says.

"Used to be a speakeasy."

"A what?"

He has forgotten how young she is, and explains about Prohibition and what speakeasies were and how the modern Mob was invented in places like this. She finds the notion of Prohibition hard to understand.

"You mean they banned all drinking? Like with drugs today?"

"Yes, and with the same kind of success."

"Holy shit."

"That's what New York said too."

They touch glasses, and she sips, then twirls the glass by the stem.

"That's *good.*" Her tongue passing over her upper lip. "Here's to the end of Prohibition."

She glances around, her brow furrowing. A chill washes over her.

"Listen," she says, "I'm sorry I got so upset back there in the theater."

"What was that all about?"

"Oh, I don't know."

"Sure you do."

"Yeah. I do."

A pause. The diners are murmuring, laughing, leafing through *Playbills* for the names of actors.

"It just, I mean, the whole thing, the play, the subject, it just reminded me of what I threw away," she says. "At Hunter, I was a whiz at physics. I don't know why. It sure didn't come from genes. I just got it from the beginning, it was a kind of center of things for me. And the professor knew I got it. He paid me a lot of attention. Too much attention. I was just a kid, eighteen. But I guess he never had a Latina in his class who got it the way I got it. Physics was for Jewish kids or Chinese kids or Korean kids. Not for kids from the D.R. But I got it. And I thought, Hey, maybe I'll *major* in this, keep learning, keep growing, go to graduate school, MIT or Cal-Tech, discover some new principle, the way Bohr did and Heisenberg did. I knew about these guys, from my teacher. Shit, I had a photograph of Einstein on the wall of my room in Queens. You know, the one where he's sticking out his tongue? You know that one?"

"Sure."

"Well, I guess you knew this was coming, right? I got involved with the professor. It's such a cliché. Student Falls for Professor. Puh-leeze. But, anyway, I did. By then I was nineteen. He was forty-two. And married. Hey: Are *you* married?"

"No."

"But you've been married?"

"Yes."

"So you know it's never easy, I guess. Not for anybody." A pause. "Anyway, I came on to him just before the end of the term. I didn't have a plan or anything. I just felt, hey, I've got to have him. The details don't matter. We saw each other all that summer. He rented a house on the Jersey shore for his wife and two kids and went down after class on Friday and came back Sunday night. Sometimes he had to take his boy to Yankee Stadium, or the Planetarium, or something, but the rest of the time we were together. He kept teaching me about physics, making my head explode, and he did his best in bed. Until finally his wife caught on. She made him choose. And he chose her, okay?" She sips the rest of her wine. "Oh, well, fuck it. Fuck him. Too."

"Did he kill physics for you?"

The salads arrive. She eats and talks.

"No. I went back in the fall and took courses with another professor. One that my guy recommended, a nice old Austrian. And in a way, the Austrian helped me get over my guy, just by challenging me to be better, to go deeper and deeper. I finished my course with him. He told me in that Austrian accent that I had a great future. And then I threw it away."

Another pause. Cormac waits.

"I just felt, this is all wrong. I'm in a world where I don't belong. It's only gonna hurt me. I've gotta get out. What did I think I was, anyway? That's what they always ask in the street. What did I think I was, *white?* Ghetto bullshit always wins. I walked away. I found my man, had my baby, all that sad song I already told you." She looks up and smiles in a wounded way. "When I met you, I was the only cashier in the history of Rite Aid who understood quantum theory."

"Can you use it in the new job?"

"No, it's a law firm, import-export, NAFTA, all that. My Spanish helps with calls to Monterrey." She grins. "But the guys there are pretty good guys. Reynoso is a Mexican who came here in 1968, after all his friends were shot in some massacre. He went to Columbia, gave up Marx, became a business major, then took a law degree. He can be very funny."

"What about Ryan?"

"I don't even know if he exists," she says. "He's always off in Europe or someplace, making deals. Or that's what Reynoso says."

She smiles in a pleased way, all regret about physics now vanished. The salad plates are carried away by a Mexican busboy ("Mil gracias, joven," she says); the steak arrives. She seems grateful for the interruption and begins slicing meat.

"Oh, wow — this is *good.*"

She glances around the room, and then giggles.

"Why do I feel like I'm in New Jersey?"

"Because New Jersey is here at all these other tables?"

"What do you think their lives are like?" she says. Cormac can't tell her that since the night he washed up on its shores after killing the Earl of Warren, he has never been in New Jersey.

"Nasty, brutish, and long."

She smiles, chews, swallows. He realizes she hasn't used "fuck" all evening long. The noise of the diners is rising.

"So, anyway, that's why I was upset."

"You don't look upset now."

"I'm not."

She looks directly at Cormac, her eyes lustrous and black in the restaurant's yellow light.

"You're a nice man."

"You're a good woman."

"Not so good."

"And I'm not so nice."

Her face darkens in an embarrassed way and she twirls the glass toward the waiter. He comes and takes it away. The steak is gone. She looks sated. Then starts to get up, murmuring about the ladies' room.

"Go to the front door," Cormac explains. "Make a left, then down the short flight of stairs."

"All that to get to the ladies' room?"

"It used to be a speakeasy, Delfina. They never changed the layout."

She gets up and walks through the crowded dining room. Older women look at older men who are looking at Delfina.

Then turn to look at her themselves. Cormac remembers Ginger Everett turning heads in this room and singing "Bluebird of Happiness" for the crowd in a thin little voice; but Ginger never came close to weeping over quantum physics. When Delfina makes her return (the table cleared of plates, a fresh wine waiting), a lot of eyes fall upon Cormac too. His eyes are on Delfina's belly, under the black sheath. He rises and makes an effort at moving her chair, but she's too quick.

"You were staring at my belly," she says, leaning forward with elbows on the table.

"I want to see what's there."

She glances behind her to see if she can be heard. She can't. "First I want some chocolate cake."

The waiter comes over. Cormac orders two coffees, one chocolate cake, and two forks. The waiter glides away. Then, on the far side of the room, a woman starts shouting at a man. She's about fifty, with blue-rinsed hair and real pearl earrings. She's a little drunk, and at first her words are indistinct in the general din of the restaurant. Then the room hushes, and they can hear what she's shouting at the large white-haired man across the table from her. He starts patiently wiping his eyeglasses with a handkerchief.

"Go over and talk to her, Harry, why don't yuh?" the woman shouts. "Just go over and tell her you want to fuck her, Harry, why don't yuh?"

Delfina's face shifts. There's a flicker of a smile and then a tense freezing of her features as she realizes the woman is talking about her. Other diners look at the woman, then at Delfina.

"Go over, Harry, offer her money. Isn't that what you ushally do? How much to look at a tit, Harry? Five hundred? Is that your ushual rate? And her snatch? How much for that, Harry? Five grand? Go ahead, ask her."

Three waiters surround the table, blocking the woman and her man, Harry.

"Jesus Christ . . ." Delfina says darkly. "It's always the same old shit."

They hear the high-pitched voice from behind the fence of waiters. Cormac glimpses Harry fumbling for cash. "Go ahead, Harry, she'd prob'ly love it, you old fool."

"Hey," a beefy man shouts. "Pipe *down,* willya? I'm tryin' ta *eat!*"

A dozen other diners applaud.

"Eat shit!" the woman yells at all of them. "Eat shit and die!"

Harry gets up now. He's very large, very old, and very embarrassed. The waiters are trying to move the woman gently toward the door. She now looks about seventy.

"What is this?" she yells. "The bum's rush? When Meyer was alive, you wooden dare pull this shit."

Other diners now try to look normal. Then Harry moves through the diners to the table where Delfina seems to be shrinking and Cormac is preparing for an assault. The old man bows in a stiff, old-hoodlum way. Cormac relaxes.

"Folks," Harry says, "I'd like to apologize to yiz, bot' of yiz. My wife is def'nitely out of order. She's a little cuckoo."

He turns and moves toward the door, where the waiters are draping a coat on his wife's shoulders. The murmur of the room returns in a relieved way.

"Just another romantic dinner in the Big Apple," Cormac says.

"Yeah." Delfina chews the inside of her mouth. "Let's skip the cake and coffee."

She still seems mortified. Other diners continue glancing at her, as much to see her reaction as to judge the provocation for another woman's rage. She squirms in her seat. Cormac realizes that the only other Latinos in the room are the busboys.

"There was a time," Delfina whispers, "when I used to wish I was flat-assed and flat-chested. Just so I wouldn't be bothered so much. Then I realized T and A gave me some kind of power over men. Then it became a bother again. Like tonight. Sometimes I wish I was a hundred years old and everything like that was behind me."

Suddenly the waiter is there with the cake and the coffee, and a half smile on his face.

"Sorry about all that," he says. "She gets stewed on two highballs, that one. She doesn't want to know Meyer is dead, and she's old. Dessert is on the house."

He hurries away. Delfina looks at the cake, then at Cormac, smiles, and lifts a fork.

"What the hell, Cormac! We earned it."

They attack the cake in a fever of release, and Cormac struggles to imagine her at Hunter, lost in the abstractions of physics, a place where she didn't have to think about being thinner or smaller or less beautiful. She makes "um" sounds now as she eats the cake. Um. Um-um. Um. Women ate this way after escaping from the Five Points too.

"By the way," she says, "who is Meyer?"

"His last name was Lansky and he was the smartest gangster who ever lived. I'll tell you all about him one of these days."

"Not tonight?" she says, the tip of her tongue flicking chocolate off her upper lip.

"No," Cormac says. "Not tonight."

93.

She steps into the bright darkness of the Studio and gazes at the skylight. She makes the same small gasping sound he heard in the theater. She moves forward and stands very still. Looking through the panes of the skylight.

"Up there," she says. "Way up there? The eighty-fourth floor? That's my office."

She looks amazed.

"I can see you from there," she says, and turns to him. Her teeth are very white, her skin receding into the obscure light. "Anyway, I can see your roof."

She looks up at him, and he puts a hand on her waist, and she eases into him like a partner in a slow dance. Slowly, he kisses her brow, her cheek, her lips. Her breasts are hard against his chest. He can feel her belly pressing against his own. He inhales the soapy smell of her wiry African hair.

In the dark bedroom, a floor below the Studio, they lie together for a long while, her body pressed against his, her head on his chest. Her breathing slows into comfort, and his follows. She is wordless, and he feels that speaking would be an intrusion. He hears the ticking of a clock that sounds like the drip of a water tap. Away off, the city murmurs through the thick drapes. Finally she rises on one elbow and gazes at him, holding the sheet to her body.

"Who are you, anyway?" she says.

"I was thinking the same thing about you."

She giggles, then sits up, Cormac thinking: Don't go, not yet.

"Where's the john?" she says.

She demands the tour and he gives it to her, the two of them barefoot in terry-cloth bathrobes, Cormac flicking on lamps as they pad across scattered rugs and polished plank. She looks smaller now, without shoes, engulfed by the robe. She examines the first floor as if it were a museum, her eyes moving over the long rows of tall bookshelves, the paintings, the African masks, the yellow vellum lampshades and Moroccan rugs. He hopes she doesn't say *Have you read all these books?* She doesn't. Her feet splay on the hardwood floors as she touches the polished top of the dining table, the brocaded Mexican fabrics of the chairs, the silver candelabra. They can both hear rain now spattering the four windows on the Duane Street end, the second stage of an early storm, coming in hard off the harbor. She stops to examine herself in a large white-and-gold mirror, a hand going to her rain-exploded hair, which now looks like a black wiry halo. He stands behind her, his own flesh pale beside her. He wraps his arms around her and then fumbles with the knot of the robe until it opens.

He sees his own pale hand gently holding a dark-skinned breast, and her head leaning back into him, lips parted, and his hand moving down to her belly.

To the twin spirals.

They are there. Traced lightly, delicately on her skin, facing each other like enraptured sea serpents.

His heart bumps and bumps and he is sure she must hear it and feel it. They are here: She is the dark lady with the spirals.

His fingertips trace their outlines, their wide bottoms vanishing into the thick black vee of her pubic hair. She pushes back into him, and must feel his hardening.

"Are they disgusting to you?" she says.

"They're beautiful," he says.

"Hold me tight," she says.

Later, rising from the floor, she tightens the robe and walks to the kitchen. He is relieved: She doesn't review her own performance. Or his. She opens the refrigerator, which holds a bowl of fresh green grapes and some oranges, picks a crisp grape, munches it, grabs a handful, then takes a bottle of water and closes the door. She finishes the grapes, takes an amused swig from the bottle, sloshes the water in her mouth, swallows. Then she moves slightly to her left, peering down the corridor like a cat who has arrived in a new place: alert, poised, wary of danger.

"This is beautiful," she says.

"It's comfortable," Cormac says, sounding to himself like a real estate salesman. "I like being here."

She looks directly at him, her eyes liquid. "Me too."

He leads her up the stairs again to the Studio, to the view of the Woolworth Building and the Twin Towers, all misty in rain. He opens the small refrigerator and she takes an icy bottle of Evian and hands it to him. Now she sees the desk, the computer, the television set, the CD player. The door to the Archive is closed. As is the door to the bathroom and the jacuzzi. Cormac thinks: I could paint you just like this, in that terry-cloth robe.

"I never met anyone rich before," she says, and giggles.

"I'm not rich."

"Come on: A place like this costs a mint."

"Not when I got it," he says. "It was just a dump then."

Hoping she doesn't ask what year. Hoping she doesn't ask where he got the money. She doesn't. She leans back against a bookcase full of large volumes on Mexico and Italy and other places he has never seen. She takes another gulp of water. For a long silent moment, he can feel her staring at him, can feel shapeless questions traveling in the air between them. Cormac thinks: If she asks, I might even answer.

And then to himself, and to her, he says, "I'm alive."

That night he dreams of swimming in a vast sea, his body making wide spirals in the water, curving, turning, the forms remaining in his wake. When he finishes cutting spirals with his body, they glow against the dark waters. Something comes from beneath him, bumping, pushing him.

He awakes in sweat and tears.

The clock tells him that it's 8:48. She's gone into the gray morning. He is not surprised. He is, in fact, relieved. There is nothing more clumsy than the talk on the morning after the first night before. He turns in the bed, inhaling the mixed scents of her body. He pulls a pillow close to his chest. He hears church bells ringing beyond the drapes.

He walks south on Broadway in the Sunday-morning quiet, passing shuttered stores and tourists with unfolded maps and white shoes. At the Battery, he goes to the final iron railing, where he can hear the languid slapping of the sea. Images of Delfina move through him. A warm breeze brings him the salt of the harbor. He watches a Nigerian tanker heading for the open sea. A squadron of gulls wheels above the tanker, completes a swift reconnaissance, and angles away toward Governor's Island.

They are there, Cormac thinks. The spirals are there. I've traced them with my tongue.

His heart quickens and he turns from the harbor and walks toward South Street, where he can sit at a breakfast table and see the masts of a sailing ship.

94.

She calls him about six. She is shy at first, holding back, uttering banalities, talking around what happened between them. Then he hears her inhaling a cigarette. She is abruptly more direct.

"My tattoos didn't disgust you?" she says.

"Not at all. They're kind of beautiful."

She laughs. "Kind of."

"Like sea serpents. Or snakes in a Hindu temple."

"I've never seen a sea serpent. Or a Hindu temple."

"Neither have I. But I've got a book down the hall —"

"I want you to show it to me. Soon."

"Soon."

She pauses, and her voice flattens.

"I got them to make myself disgusting."

Cormac says nothing.

"I wanted to scare men away," she says, taking a deep drag, exhaling slowly. "I'd fucked too many of them and didn't want to fuck another. And I thought, Shit, even if I *want* to give in, you know, some night with too much to drink, or too filled up with loneliness, or anger, or hatred, I thought, If I can scare them with something, their cocks will die." She likes using the hard, blunt Anglo-Saxon words, talking "street," letting Cormac know which version of Delfina Cintron is now talking. "It was like wearing a sign that said, 'Beware of the cunt.'"

Cormac wants to laugh, but doesn't. In her way, she's letting him know that she will take sex when she chooses to have it, but she will not be hurt. He listens to the words beyond the hardness.

"Who did them for you?" he asks.

"Some guy uptown," she says. "Way uptown. Like on the top of the island. I can't even remember his name. Black dude. Blacker than any black man I ever saw, talks in some African accent? Like the guys peddle incense around Bloomingdale's? One of those guys. Maybe sixty years old. Maybe older."

Cormac imagines the face of the tattoo artist. The face of Kongo. His skin tingles.

"Did he have a set of designs?"

"Yeah, the usual stuff. You know, Malcolm X, and words in Chinese, crosses, stars, skulls, the stuff these goddamned basketball players wear all over themselves like graffiti."

"And yours?"

"He just sketched it on paper," she says. He knows her hand is moving in air, making a sketch. "It looked simple and scary at the same time. It was me that told him to make it go all the way down to my bush." She chuckles sadly. "I had to go to him four times, he called them four *treatments,* like he was a doctor, a million little needles. He did half of one, you know, looped around my belly button, and it hurt so much I wanted to give up, and then thought, Shit, this will look ridiculous all by itself, like shaving half your head. So I had him finish the job. To get the bottoms where I wanted them, I had to shave. In a way, that turned me on, but it didn't do anything for the old man. Between the tattoo and the shave, I itched for a month."

She laughs.

"They sure didn't work with you," she says, almost solemnly. "I mean, didn't scare you off." A pause. "I'm glad." A longer pause. "Until last night, I hadn't fucked anyone in almost two years."

95.

At dusk, he takes the bike for his Wordsworth. He pedals up the West Side and turns right into Soho, heading for Crosby Street to avoid the Sunday tourists on Broadway. He will see Delfina on Wednesday. He will cook. She will pose for his charcoaled hand. He does not try to imagine that night. He pedals across the immediate space in front of him. It's dark when he reaches Houston Street, and he wonders where all the black bicycle riders went. One summer, they were all gone, never to be seen again. He did not again see the man who answered his Yoruba with Ashanti.

But he knows that other figures and things and odors are gone too. The shopping-bag ladies were everywhere for six years, pushing their packed supermarket wagons into frozen doorways, talking steadily in streams of scrambled nouns, sorting through tiny bags of socks or knitting needles or empty envelopes; and then they were gone. To shelters or asylums or the Potter's Field on Hart Island. There were jugglers on certain corners, drawing crowds on summer nights, their faces familiar for a dozen years, and then they were gone too. One year, there were no more cooking odors from the tenements of the Lower East Side, and no more clotheslines on the rooftops or in the backyards. The familiar city vanished; the new city emerged; and in each new city, Cormac was new too.

He moves now into what he once knew as Kleindeutschland, where Germans were everywhere, and he worked for a year setting type at a German newspaper. Most of the older Germans were the children of those who left in 1848 and the relatives who kept coming after the first wave settled: socialists and engineers and mechanics and doctors, all of them creating their own version of America, making deals with Tammany, using the system that they didn't invent while trying to make it more orderly. They too had started in the Five Points, but kept moving north and east until they had forged a neighborhood that most were certain would last forever. Little Germany.

Right there on Stanton Street, where the Quisqueya la Bella bodega now offers fresh mango and papaya, was the saloon of Peter Reuter. All the newspapermen went in the evening to drink there after the edition was locked up. Writers, reporters, men still smelling of melted lead from the composing room; and here too came the poets and painters and mad architects, the inflamed or disillusioned socialists, the anarchists and syndicalists, to drink lager or ale, to consume great barrels of sausage, and to sing the old songs at midnight. That's where he went on the night in 1904 after writing his story for the *Sun* about the burning of the *General Slocum*. Nobody remembered it anymore, but the sinking of the *General Slocum* in the East River was the worst disaster in New York history. Everybody on board was heading for an annual excursion to Long Island. All Germans, most out of St. Mark's Lutheran Church, many of them children. A fire started, then exploded, then the ship was burning and moving, the fire hoses rotted, the women and children diving away from the fire into the June waters, unable to swim, and then the ship sank in the violent waters of Hell Gate. More than a thousand died, and the funerals went on for a week and when it was over the Germans all left Kleindeutschland. They went to Yorkville and tried to forget, and the Jews from Central Europe moved in and started the legend of the Lower East Side. That night in Peter Reuter's saloon, with death throbbing in the streets around him, Cormac couldn't wipe the horror from his mind, not even when he slept with a blowsy red-haired woman from Bavaria.

Now Cormac pauses on the corner. In Tompkins Square Park, there's a monument to the victims of the *General Slocum,* but nobody in the neighborhood knows what it's commemorating. Now merengue music plays from an unseen radio. Now, on stoops and on sidewalks, kids strut and pose and curse. He hears Delfina's voice: Same old ghetto bullshit.

The telephone rings around midnight. Cormac picks it up, drops his voice, thinking it's Delfina, whispers hello.

"How seductive . . . ARE YOU AWAKE?"

Healey.

"I am now."

"I just opened the MAIL ten days late. And there's an INVITE to the Metropolitan Museum. Tomorrow night. Some kind of a NEW YORK ART SHOW! And all the biggies, the MIGHTY ASSHOLES OF THE PLANET, will be there. Go with me. It should be a million LAUGHS."

"What time?"

"Seven-THIRTY!"

"I'll see you on the steps."

96.

*Cormac comes up out of the Lexington Avenue subway at Eighty-*sixth Street and walks west toward the park into a dazzle of silver light. The sidewalk is like pewter, tarnished only by the shadows of men and women whose faces are obscured and formless. The sun is behind them. There are silvery reflections on windows, and the upper stories of apartment houses are drained of color by the light. He came here one afternoon long ago in a carriage drawn by two horses, sitting beside Bill Tweed. There were a few rutted dirt roads then and some stands of trees and much scrub. In his wheezy baritone Bill Tweed spoke with excitement about what was coming: streets and apartment houses and a great green park and perhaps even a museum for the city of New York. "It will change before we're buried," he said, and laughed. "There won't be a live rabbit left on the island." As on so many other things, the Boss was right. He just didn't live to see it happen.

There's a milling crowd on the steps of the Metropolitan, made of tourists and visitors from New Jersey and a slew of photographers dressed in formal wear. A huge banner proclaims the name of the show: *Art and the Empire City: New York, 1825–1861*, and Cormac smiles. Thinking: I'm the only person here who actually lived in that lost city. The photographers stand in a tuxedoed pack at the foot of the stairs, waiting for the heavy doors of arriving limousines to open and for their inhabitants to emerge into the sheet lightning of electronic flash. As he climbs the broad stairs on the far right, dressed in his twenty-seven-year-old tuxedo and wearing his fake plain-glass spectacles, his patent-leather shoes glistening and his hair brushed straight back, Cormac can see Madonna getting out of a stretch limo as if she had arrived at the Academy Awards. Ordinary singer, fair dancer, but a marvelous act. Ahead of him, Healey is standing with some tourists just short of the top step. His tuxedo looks thirty-two years old. He hands Cormac a ticket.

"You see, failure is a fucking COMFORT, pal," Healey says, waving a huge hand at the crowd and gesturing toward poor Madonna and the engulfing photographers. A few people back away from Healey's bulky loudness. In the excited din, Cormac hears scraps of French and German. "You're a certified failure, nobody blinds you with those goddamned FLASHBULBS! Nobody asks you to spell your fucking NAME! Nobody asks you whether you like the show, even if you haven't SEEN IT! They don't give a shit. You're a *nobody.* They don't care if you LIVE OR DIE."

More photographers are inside the main hall, and a few reporters scribbling notes, and several hundred people in what used to be called evening wear. There's another eruption of flashbulbs as Madonna comes into the museum, smiling broadly, dressed modestly, moving past Cormac and Healey in the direction of the galleries, and then behind her comes Lauren Bacall. She looks at them through hooded eyes and smiles.

"Healey, you big ape," she says with a growl. "Where's that play you promised me twenty years ago?"

"It's coming, Betty, it's ALMOST DONE! I swear to Yahweh!"

She laughs and gives him a shove and keeps moving. At these rituals, celebrities have one basic tactic: smile and keep moving. A young woman photographer confronts Healey with a notebook in hand.

"Excuse me, sir," she says. "Can you tell me your name?"

"I don't HAVE a name! I'm *a nobody.*"

"Come on, man —"

Then more white lights explode and the photographer turns away and the rumbling crowd sounds grow louder, with several hundred voices bouncing off glazed marble. Walking in the door are the people Cormac has come to see: William Hancock Warren and his wife, Elizabeth. Warren's tuxedo is rumpled and he needs a haircut and keeps brushing at his hair while chatting amiably with the reporters. As he listens to a question, the mouth moves into an amused smile. From where Cormac is standing on the fringe of the crowd, he can't hear a word. But Warren seems relaxed, holding Elizabeth's hand lightly, and when he says something, the reporters smile too. He is charming them. His wife says nothing to anyone.

"This is hard to BELIEVE," Healey says. "I mean, this isn't Vladimir Putin, or Seamus Heaney, or PUFFY FUCKING COMBS! This is a *real estate* guy that owns a paper!"

"That's why they like him," Cormac says. "Especially the freelancers. He could put them all on the payroll and never miss a meal."

Then Warren turns toward another shower of flash and sees the mayor come in, police bodyguards behind him wearing dark blue suits and buttons in their ears. The mayor looks hunched and tired. But the mayor's brain tells the mayor to smile. He smiles. His brain tells him to embrace Warren. He embraces Warren. The embrace is digitally immortalized by the photographers, though only Warren's newspaper will ever consider running the picture. Elizabeth slips her hand out of her husband's grip and backs away, a smile fixed on her face. A look of melancholy passes across her face, as if she has long ago grown weary of photographs.

"Shit, look who's here," Healey says, gesturing toward a small ruddy man with thinning white hair who has come in with a fat woman, right behind the mayor. "This butterball owes me MONEY!" The fat man is a literary agent named Brookner. Sometimes known as Legs, for the speed of his movements in the William Morris mailroom in the 1950s. He had enriched himself with 10 percent of some fabulous paydays, but now in the years of his wealth and respectability, when he even has a foundation named after himself and the wing of a medium-sized hospital in Sarasota, Legs Brookner insists on being called Irving.

"LEGS!" Healey bellows, and goes off in big-shouldered pursuit. Cormac watches Elizabeth Warren, who is chatting with an elderly woman while her husband and the mayor turn to embrace the arriving governor.

Cormac moves around casually, drawing Elizabeth Warren in his mind. She's indeed a beauty of a classic English type. Smooth cream-colored skin. Lean, athletic body sheathed in a black Valentino frock. Oval head, with a well-defined jaw. Her dark burnt-sienna hair is pulled back tightly off the clean plane of her brow, and she wears a silver stud in the lobe of each small, slightly protruding ear. There's a hint of blush on her high cheekbones. She has heavy eyebrows, widely spaced hazel eyes deepened by makeup, and her mouth is wide when she smiles. As Cormac drifts closer, he notices one crooked bicuspid among the otherwise perfect white teeth. All of this rests on a long regal neck, rising off narrow shoulders and emphasized by a silver necklace holding a single lustrous opal. Sargent might have used her as "Madame X."

Then Warren and the mayor and the governor move forward, the mayor pointing at nothing to give the photographers a bit of fraudulent action, and Elizabeth moves too, smiling and shaking hands with the wife of the governor. Cormac hangs behind; the eyes of two sets of political bodyguards are now scanning him, along with other visitors. He sees the Warrens and the politicians merge with the crowd of several hundred people and tries to move in casually behind them, but they vanish into the blur of black tuxedos.

The glorious high-ceilinged room now smells of perfume, cologne, and money. They all move with practiced ease, shaking hands, embracing, the men smiling, the women offering cheeks to be kissed. Most of them are indifferent to the show-business celebrities among them. They won't cross the room to meet Madonna. They won't tell Steve Martin they admire his work. After all, a few of them own the companies that employ the performers. If the mayor says hello and remembers a name, they will chat with him. If he utters a mere hello, they will nod in a restrained way. He is now a lame duck, forced to leave office at the end of the year because of a law on term limits that he supported. His marriage is a public mess. His popularity ratings are dropping like a stone. He is on his way out, to be rewarded with the customary farewell present of all reasonably well known politicians: a Book Deal. The mayor is important but not *that* important.

The older guests know this event is just another New York ritual. The celebrities are there to draw the media, which in turn will draw paying customers to the museum. But most of them have contempt for the media too. Cormac has heard that contempt expressed for more than a century. In their view, the reporters and photographers know nothing about how things really work in New York. Fame isn't the goal; power is. And power is forged over Armagnac and cigars. If any of these men employ public relations counsel, the flacks' primary task is to keep names out of the newspapers.

Cormac sees some people he knows casually but edges away from them, the habit of a long life. Gazing with lust at the mayor, the governor, and Warren is a once-famous sixties hippie, friend of Jerry and Abbie and the Democratic Republic of the Lower East Side. Cormac used to see him at love-ins and be-ins and fund-raisers for the Weather Underground. Now his face is clean-shaven and pasty and he's considered a genius at the deals that have driven the NASDAQ over the moon. "Concept," he told Charlie Rose one night on channel 13. "Concept is everything." Cormac thought at the time: Okay, give me five thousand dollars' worth of symbolic logic. The man would almost certainly have answered, "Is that a derivative?" That was two years ago. On this night, as tech stocks keep tanking, the ex-hippie's face looks ashen. Cormac wonders if he knows the dot-commer on the second floor at Duane Street, the fast-talking young man who this morning gave a month's notice, due, he said, to the decline in the market. Cormac has seen the doomed, ashen look of the ex-hippie before, in 1893, in 1929. One morning, as the bad news becomes a flood, the blessed genius of money starts looking at the faces of strangers as if his brain has turned into an abacus. How much can you invest? How much can you loan me? How can you keep me from suicide?

Over on the side, looking like an enormous soft rock in his tuxedo, is a Cuban exile who burned with a mad fanaticism in the early 1960s. He took CIA money until 1971 and used it to fight Fidel Castro by buying lots in Bergen County while helping clumsy agents from Cali and Medellín peddle the marvelous white-powder exports of Colombia. Now he owns banks in New Jersey, Dade County, and Puerto Rico; controls a Spanish-language television network; has developed more than seven hundred acres along the Hudson below the Palisades; and recently turned down the American ambassadorship to Spain. Cormac has read in *Art News* that he owns four Frida Kahlos, six Wilfredo Lams, three Picassos, and sixteen Boteros. Two directors of the museum hover near him as if expecting his collection to come to them in a massive bequest in the event of a massive coronary. The Cuban's large gorged face pulses so vividly that the process could begin at any moment.

Some guests have planted their feet and refuse to move, waiting to be approached by potential partners, political fundraisers, or aspiring acolytes now available after the dot-com collapse. Others work the room in a restrained way, trying to avoid the unforgivable New York sin of vulgarity, clearly envious of the faded Wasps who have been trained for ten generations to avoid sweating, belching, and farting. Some wear expensive rugs. Some tamp with handkerchiefs at sweaty upper lips. Others perform affection toward their wives, touching their hands as if petting cats. Cormac has lost sight of Healey but assumes he's all right, gleefully impaling Legs Brookner on a lance in the medieval armor room.

The sound of the event grows louder, amplified by more marble and stone, nouns and verbs caroming off the walls, the stony rumble of blunt consonants punctuated by trills of female laughter. Searching for the Warrens, Cormac sees a few middle-aged men, recent transplants from Kabul or Karachi, who have the feral eyes of those distant ancestors who perched with rifles in mountain passes, awaiting human prey. There are a number of black couples, looking delighted to be here, and a larger number of Asians than is usual at such affairs. The diplomats are present too, invited from the consulates and the United Nations, a few up from Washington for the evening, several of them alone, others clutching wives twenty years their juniors, acquired on some distant posting: a Norwegian with a Mexican wife, a Mexican with a French wife, a Frenchman with an Israeli wife, and none with American wives. Their eyes shift, dart, stare, drift, trying to read the room and its crowd; they look at everything but the art.

Coolest of all are the people of semi-old money, those hard, intelligent men who shoved the old-moneyed Wasps out of real estate and banks and brokerage houses. These are children of the old immigrants, the Jews and Irish and Italians, men shaped by the Depression and the infantry, veterans of the Hürtgen Forest or Anzio or Iwo Jima, finally freed from the receding European past of their parents by combat and the G.I. Bill. They spent twenty years outworking, outthinking the Old Money, vowing in some private way that nobody in their family line would ever be poor again. Cormac likes them very much. They have gone through life without kissing a single ass. They are old now, tennis fit and golf tan, discreet and restrained, and tougher than steel. Their sons and grandsons try playing tough. They shout at waiters. They rail at employees. They sneer at politicians. They curse the business journalists. But (Cormac thinks) all of the children combined are not as tough as one of these men who came home in 1946 with bupkis in their pockets and changed New York forever.

Cormac can't see Warren, or the mayor or the governor. They must be chatting in a private room. He separates himself from the crowd and drifts into the galleries to look at the remnants of the world where he once lived. There are only six or seven people walking quietly in the first room, glancing at an old print here, a varnished portrait of some stern Protestant there, a crude map. They bow to squint at the explanatory captions. An African-American couple, perfectly groomed, living well-defended lives, gaze together at one lithograph that includes black street musicians and white revelers. Cormac hopes they know the true history. His hope is wan. Not many people know anything about their own past, he thinks, and New Yorkers are most amnesiac of all.

He passes a portrait of De Witt Clinton, remembering his delusions of Roman grandeur, his arrogance and gift for respectable larceny, and he nods in salute. Clinton was, when all was carved upon his tomb, still the man who rammed through the Erie Canal and changed New York from a village to a metropolis. If I had time, Cormac thinks, I would write a book about the man and how his immense ambition led to Fernando Wood and then to Bill Tweed and established forever the long, unbreakable tradition of our corruption.

Another painting shows a group of nine men in respectable clothes, painted tightly and painfully, every detail, every object displayed as proof of successful human existence. They are in an anteroom somewhere, with high ceilings and French furniture, presenting to the viewer a framed and lifeless painting of the Hudson River Valley. Beside Cormac now, a man with the long white hair of an aged bohemian removes his glasses to examine the cramped details and says, "I wonder what they'd have thought of Franz Kline?"

Cormac smiles and says, "They might have loved him." Which they surely would have, had they lived to know that sweet man with his plain worker's face. The old bohemian turns to Cormac and says, "Yeah, or they might have burned him in City Hall Park."

They both laugh, and Cormac feels an exuberant conversation about to begin. But then he sees a piece of sculpture against the wall to the right and he is drawn away.

Cormac's heart thrums as he stands before a marble version of Venus, with both arms mercifully intact, executed in the style of Canova. He knew the sculptor. He knew the model. Her name was Catherine Underwood, and for four years in the mid-1860s, she was Cormac's wife. His only wife. Catherine something Underwood. He met her at Niblo's Opera House, three weeks after she arrived with her widowed mother from England, penniless, hopeful, and beautiful. Her mother died of consumption within a year, but by then Cormac and Catherine had married. The mother, of course, disapproved. She wanted a rich husband. Catherine wanted love. Catherine won. Cormac was driven to marriage by loneliness, by the need for a warm human dailiness, by his desire for the permanent presence of her astonishing beauty.

He gazes at her marble face now, in the year 2001, and remembers how they lived in a small, comfortable flat in Horatio Street, financed by his work at newspapers and the sale of an occasional still life or cityscape. She uttered banalities in an exquisite accent. Her manners were excellent too, and she dined with a languid grace, and posed for his brush with a languid grace, and made love in the same vaguely beautiful, languid way. He was bored with her after nine months, and in his solitude often longed for the silky pleasures of the Countess de Chardon. He was certain that she was bored too.

She was. Cormac doesn't need to bend close to squint at the caption. The sculpture was done by his closest friend, a dashing and drunken genius named Trevor Morris Parker, who stole Catherine from Cormac and took her and his chisels off to Rome. The date on the sculpture is wrong. The piece must have been done in 1868. After she left him. The cold polished marble can't convey the color of her flesh, of course, the silkiness of her pubic hair, the soapy smell of her neck. But in his Roman studio, Trevor got the firm plumpness of her breasts right and the contours of her belly and buttocks. He got the languor of the pose. He got the emptiness of the eyes.

Cormac walks around the statue twice, the glistening stone as cold as death, remembering her beside him, so warm on winter nights, and remembering the evening when he discovered she was gone: the card propped against the candle in the kitchen, the keys beside it, the armoire emptied of her clothes. And how he picked up the card, his eyes welling with tears, and read the banal words, about how she was sorry to hurt him, but time healed all wounds, and how then he began to laugh. That night he was filled with an enormous surge of freedom. By morning, he was thinking of her as a character in an opera that somebody else had written.

He turns away from Catherine Underwood, his lost languid Venus, and then another picture catches his eye. He crosses the gallery to look at a carefully painted view of dark buildings and a sky lit up by furious orange flames. Engulfed by the flames are chimneys, useless ladders, roofless walls. Crowds are assembled to watch, herded by leather-capped constables on horseback, while firemen work in impotent anger with their frozen, waterless pumps. In the lower corner of the picture, two men stand safely on a stone balcony, one of them wearing a swirling cape. The caption explains that this is the Great Fire of 1835 and the painter is Anonymous. Cormac knows better. It once hung on the wall of Bill Tweed's suite in the Ludlow Street jail. The painter was Cormac Samuel O'Connor.

Then he senses an odor of perfume. A woman leans in beside him to read the caption.

Elizabeth Warren.

"I didn't know that New York had a great fire too," she says in a cool way. "London did, of course. . . ."

"This was an amazing fire too," Cormac says. "It destroyed more than seven hundred buildings, a third of the city."

"Good God."

She straightens up, her head rising on her long neck, and she looks at Cormac with those wide-spaced hazel eyes.

"Well, how did it start?"

"Arson."

"You're kidding me."

She has one of those Atlantic accents that are acquired by Brits who spend years in America and Americans who spend parts of their youth in Britain. Precise use of words. Hard consonants. Cormac flashes, absurdly, on Pat Moynihan and George Plimpton. Away off, someone begins playing a piano. "Dancing in the Dark" . . .

"It was a form of urban renewal," Cormac says. "The old Dutch houses were too small for profit, and someone — almost certainly a landlord — torched one of them, and then another. Just to get rid of them and rebuild with larger buildings and higher rents." *I have you, love, and we can face the music, togeth-er. . . .* "Then a huge wind came off the harbor, and the thing went out of control. There was no water either. See, in here? It was bitter cold, just before Christmas, and even the river was frozen. Down there? Those are firemen whose pumps are useless."

"Are you a historian?"

"Well, I've read a lot of the city's history."

He can't tell her that he is in the painting too, there in the distance, tiny and furtive in the purple shadows under the orange flames. Making notes and sketches. The piano pushes through the murmur of marbleized voices. The sound of the old tunes pushes in from the other room. *"Looking for the light of a new love . . ."*

"New York *does* have a history, doesn't it?" she says. "So many American cities have a past but no history."

Cormac looks at her and smiles.

"That's true," he says.

And feels that a last act is beginning.

97.

In the morning, there are five messages on the answering machine. Healey cancels breakfast, promising an explanation later in the day, then explaining he's got a live one on the line from Hollywood. Delfina says she's just checking in. The other calls are from the mysterious Area Code 800, the vast hidden limbo of American life, selling services for high-speed telephone lines or newspaper delivery or real estate. Cormac calls Delfina and gets her machine. He leaves a message. In the shower, he feels a jittery nervousness, as if various unseen filaments were trying to form a web.

After the shower, dried, shaved, dressed, he sees the message light blinking again on the answering machine. He plays it.

"Hello, this is Elizabeth Warren. We met last night at the museum. My husband and I are having a dinner party on Friday night and I'd love it if you could come. We could talk more about great fires and such. I think you'd find it amusing. . . ."

He calls back and gets a social secretary with a French accent and writes down the details. He thinks: The rivers are converging.

98.

In the foreground is Delfina, but now, back near the tree line in an imagined landscape, Elizabeth Warren makes her appearance too. In small ways, Delfina is revealing herself, and so is Cormac. They speak by telephone. They send e-mails. On one of his walks, he throws away his cigarettes, and when he tells her this, she says perhaps she'll do the same. "The smell is disgusting," she says. "I can't stand it sometimes. . . . And I can't stand going all the way down to the street to smoke with the other addicts. It's a long way to go in my building. . . ."

He takes her to lunch at Windows on the World, high above the city, and she's excited by the views, which are even more spectacular than the views from her office, Cormac, in a smaller way, is also impressed. He can see the Bronx and much of New Jersey and the slopes of Brooklyn. Pieces of the undiscovered country. He can see the greensward of Central Park and the roof of the Metropolitan Museum and the mesas of apartment houses, one of which contains the Warrens. He can look down at the pinnacle of the Woolworth Building, where he worked humping steel in 1912 and watched Cass Gilbert gazing from Broadway in troubled acceptance of his own masterpiece. He can see human beings down on Church Street, the size of commas. In Delfina's presence, he fights off the past: It is gone, finished, unrecoverable (he tells himself), and yet might indeed be parked in what was called a century earlier the Fourth Dimension. Another phrase now lost.

Delfina begins to relax with him. To make bad jokes. To drop the street language. To be at once younger and older. She makes no moves at all toward permanence. Time is provisional. Perhaps they will meet tomorrow. Perhaps after work she will come to his bed. Perhaps she will not. She loves the bookshelves in his loft and borrows a book about Rafael Leónidas Trujillo, the Benefactor, who tortured and killed some of her relatives in the Dominican Republic. Then she talks about the mayor's long year of tabloid agony, and how if Donna, the mayor's wife, were

Dominican, she'd have cut off his thing and thrown herself on the mercy of the court.

She avoids asking now about his past. And she never mentions the future. She has a new job and wants to do well, but the job, like Cormac, is part of the present tense. Along with food, drink, and bed.

When he's alone, he realizes that she is living one narrative and he is living another. He doesn't mention Elizabeth Warren. And he is not certain what Delfina's hidden narrative contains. His own contains too many secrets.

99.

The butler is tall, dark-haired, about forty. He nods at Cormac's name, takes a drink order, and says, "They're all out on the terrace, Mister O'Connor." A *landsman,* the accent pure Belfast. No sentence from the North is ever declarative; every statement contains the possibility of some other way of seeing the same set of facts. Like Yiddish, a language that contains escape. In his nod, and the slight smile, Cormac senses an acknowledgment of old conspiracies. Across a long, quietly lit room he sees glass doors with silhouettes moving behind them against the darkening sky. Then Elizabeth Warren is coming to greet him.

"Oh, Cormac, welcome, welcome."

Dressed in a black Armani frock, knee-length with a scoop neck, short sleeves. Her lean, flawless arms. A sudden glitter of diamonds from her earrings. Cartier, of course. And those shoes Cormac saw in a story in the *Times*. Manolo something. Her tan darker in the muted light.

"Did Patrick take your drink order?"

"He did."

She grasps each of his hands in greeting, her own hands cool, then leads him toward the balcony. They're on the top floor of a triplex, high above Fifth Avenue, a few blocks north of the Frick.

A story on the Internet told him that the Warrens occupy sixteen rooms here, but the place has a sense of planned, cultivated intimacy. He glances in passing around this wide sitting room that opens to the deep terrace and wonders if the terrace counts as a room. Off to the right: a huge silvery Sargent portrait of a red-haired woman in a full silk gown; Sargent, as always, makes the silk whisper. Luscious paint, buttery skin. Two Corots. Real ones. A Degas view of a racecourse. A wall of leathery books, tooled morocco, complete works and matching sets. Cormac remembers a party forty years earlier, a few blocks from this place, where the ex-chorus-girl wife of a real estate operator gazed at a similar wall of collected works and argued with a friend: "That can't be Thackeray. Thackeray is *green*."

Then Willie Warren himself comes forward and Elizabeth introduces them. He smiles in a tentative way, lifts a tumbler of scotch in salute, brushes at his untended hair with the other hand. Dark business suit. Violet tie. His face is fleshy, sweaty, but not yet fat. He has a pleasant smile.

"Ah, yes, Mister O'Connor. You're a kind of historian, I take it. I've heard so much about you from Elizabeth. Welcome."

A small tuxedoed Latino man arrives with Cormac's cut-glass tumbler of ice water, the cold base wrapped in a cloth napkin.

"Thanks for having me," Cormac says to Warren. "And by the way, this morning's paper was terrific."

"Well, *that's* refreshing to hear. Usually people come to me with some kind of complaint, bitch, bitch, bitch, the usual New York thing — and I have to keep saying, 'I'm just the *publisher!*'" He laughs. "But please, tell my editor, will you? Oh, Mister James, here's a *fan.*"

And then it's like an anthology of a thousand other New York dinner parties: drinks, remarks, and rehearsed wit, mixed with testing, auditioning, seducing. Warren introduces Cormac to Max James, his small, intense editor. Thinning gray hair. A bitter slash of mouth. Cormac says he was a copy boy at the *Post* in the three months before Dolly Schiff sold it to Rupert Murdoch (a lie, of course), and James says it's much more fun running a paper for Warren — a tabloid in a broadsheet dress — than hanging around the bowels of the *New York Times,* where he worked for twenty-three years. Nobody mentions the story in *New York* magazine the year before, the article that said Max James left the *Times* for Warren's rowdier broadsheet because he'd been told he was completely out of the running for the top editor's job. "He's too much of a prick," said one anonymous source. "Even for the *Times*." They chat now about Punch and Mort and Rupert and the problems that all of them are having and how the papers would be in a lot better shape if the Mets would start playing the way they did the year before, since nobody likes reading about losers. But Cormac can see the editor's eyes wandering, longing to talk to the other guests, to Someone Important, instead of wasting time (at Warren's command) with this unknown. Cormac wishes Healey could appear at his side, with his genius for disruption. And then Elizabeth is there to take him away.

"Come, you must meet the others," she says.

She introduces Cormac to a few guests. Casually, smiling, then slipping away. Cormac exchanges polite nods, pleased-to-meet-yous. Men sipping. Ice clinking. He hears Billie Holiday singing from the inside room: "He's Funny That Way." Across the park, the tall broad-shouldered buildings of Central Park West are forming a black wall pierced with diamonds. The plump Dakota. Rosemary's terrible baby. John Lennon lying in his blood. *"Just glad I'm living . . ."* The sky over New Jersey is orange streaked with purple. An airliner heads north before the right turn to LaGuardia, using the black line of the river as a guide. Much lower, helicopters beat toward Thirtieth Street. Cormac can see the Twin Towers in the distance, flashes on Delfina, *the spirals,* turns back into the party, remembering when all of this was fields and sky.

He shakes hands with a small pinched investment banker who reminds him of John Jay when he came back to New York after the signing of the peace treaty in Paris. The treaty that brought independence from the British. Jay in turn reminded him of the little dance teacher who used to come to Hughson's to marvel at the Africans. Jay and his dreadful wife, her large pointed bosom always at attention . . . The investment banker's name is Ridley. He has no interest in Cormac, of course, and why should he? He shakes hands and keeps talking. He's saying that anybody with a tenth of a brain could have foreseen the death of the dot-coms. "But nobody wanted to face it," he says. "They thought they could have capitalism without profits."

"They were putting money in the NASDAQ without even knowing what the initials stood for," says a tall, smiling man whose teeth are very white against his tanned skin. His name is Farragut and Cormac knows from the *Post* business pages that he's in real estate. "By the way, what *do* they stand for?"

They all laugh.

"Everybody made mistakes," says a balding, heavyset man named Sterman. He works for some vague foundation. The National Institute of Some Kind of Policy. A major fund-raiser for the Democratic party. "Even Clinton. He should have blocked that goddamned suit against Bill Gates. Microsoft was the El Dorado, the real thing, a technology outfit with real profits. It made a thousand other people think they could hit the same jackpot. When that asshole judge found Microsoft guilty, the gold rush ended."

"That was part of it," says Ridley. "I agree. The illusion was crucial to the thing. But Clinton's dick didn't help."

"Yeah, Frank, but this dickhead in the White House isn't helping either."

On the edge of the terrace, flicking ashes into a planter, a former ambassador to Prague is talking to a television reader named Brownlee. Cormac reaches for his pack of cigarettes, but he has none on his person. He knows that if he borrows only one he'll be smoking again at midnight. A lean, tanned woman named Peggy Ashley, the operator of a Soho gallery, her beige dress accentuating her deep early-season Saint Martin tan, listens to the talking men, her brow furrowing in concentration, while behind her back a film director named Johnson chats with a black banker and a pitching coach for the Yankees. They are people who resemble the subject matter of a newspaper. Emblems of the new century: eclectic and democratic, delegates from the meritocracy.

All remain true to certain New York traditions, which Cormac first saw in the Brownstone Republic in the 1840s. That tradition still insists, among many other things, that it's bad form at social gatherings to ask a stranger what he or she does for a living. As he's introduced, Cormac is not asked what he does. Hangover from the 1840s, when no rich New Yorker under fifty had ever done anything at all. In those refined precincts, the children of the rich were trained to be useless. The second wave, after the Civil War, avoided all queries because each of them was a secret gangster. Now they all let you know what they do, to avoid being asked. Cormac notices that they show their identity cards now with hints, angular references, declarations of hard-earned knowledge. Don't ask, I'll tell. The blond wife of the pitching coach, with the sun-crinkled, glowing face of a retired airline stewardess, doesn't know the rules. She asks Cormac what he does. He smiles (wanting to protect her too) and tells her he's a kind of historian.

"How wonderful," she says. "Of what?"

"New York City."

"Cool," she says. "I must tell Mike. He loves history, 'specially the Civil War and World War Two. He has every book Stephen Ambrose ever wrote. And he must have fifty books at home about the Civil War. He talks about Grant and Lee like he pitched against them. . . ."

The sky is mauve now. When she mentions the Civil War, he sees Bill Tweed shouting for calm. He is in bed in Tweed's mansion, his thigh taped, his head in bandages, and Tweed says, "What sword?" He mumbles to the former stewardess about the Civil War in New York, and the Irish Legion marching bravely off to die, and General Meagher with his mad courage, and the way the town boomed, selling uniforms and blankets. And all the cripples later. She smiles in a fixed way. She wants Scarlett O'Hara and Rhett Butler. Not this bore, with his dark visions. She turns in relief to a new tray of drinks.

Proper nouns ricochet around the terrace: Rudy and Donna, Dubya and Clinton, Piazza and Clemens, Gates and Rupert. The verbs don't matter. What matters is to be current, to speak intimately about public figures. Cormac drifts to the edge of the balcony. The former ambassador to Prague and Peggy from the Soho gallery are discussing Kokoschka. Cormac could mention that he talked one long afternoon in 1909 with Gustav Mahler on a park bench across from the Majestic. The composer loved the sound of Klaxons and bicycle bells, and mumbled about his goddamned wife, Alma. Here, among the guests of the Warrens, Cormac chooses the silence of a lifetime and says nothing. After all, how could he have known Mahler when he looks as if he were born around the time of the Kennedy assassination? All these decades later, he looks about forty.

The Metropolitan is still brightly lit, its roof washed coppery green, and lights mark the paths cut into the blackness of the park. Away off to the right, on the northern rim, is the rosy sky over Harlem. Cormac flashes again on Stanford White: his ruddy face and twinkling eyes as he describes his plans for the Harlem block later called Striver's Row. Our Bernini, creating the vision of New York the way Bernini invented modern Rome. All of that in a forgotten year before Harlem turned black; before the great exodus from Thirtieth Street and Hudson began (down there where the helicopters land); before Minton's and Monroe's Uptown and Frank's restaurant and Duke Ellington. And then, absurdly, Cormac again sees Washington in his bloodstained shirt, sword in hand, standing straight up, nostrils flaring, shouting to his men to fight these bastards, fight them and they'll *run*. . . . And right up there, Bantu died. And Carlito and Big Michael, Silver and Aaron, and from here it all looks so small and bare when it was once huge and dense with woods.

Then Warren is beside him. He hears Vivaldi playing from the inside room.

"Every time I see this view," Warren says, "at this time of the evening, I feel like I've died and gone to Heaven."

"It sure is beautiful."

"So what kind of history are you writing?"

"It'll be about New York. I guess I'll write it to find out what it is."

"I wish we had some history in the paper."

"Good idea. Although someone once said that journalism was history in a hurry. So, in a way, the paper is filled with history."

"Yes, but there's no goddamned context in *any* of our papers. They write as if everything is happening for the first time."

"Even if it's the first time that week," Cormac says.

"Or that morning."

He laughs, sips his scotch, and lays a foot on the rim of a flowerpot.

"Hey, what about you taking a crack at doing — I don't know — a history column for us? You know, giving us some of that goddamned *context*. If the mayor and his wife have a battle over Gracie Mansion, tell us who Gracie was and where he got his money and how the mansion got there and how the mayor of New York came to live in it. *That* kind of thing."

"Good idea," Cormac hears himself saying. "But I'd better finish what I'm doing first."

"I mean, who the hell was Major *Deegan*, anyway?" He smiles broadly. "One of Rupert's Aussies once looked up from his desk down on South Street, gazed at the FDR Drive, and asked, Who is this *F.D.R.?*" He switches to a British accent, very plummy. "Who *is* this F.D.R., anyway?"

Cormac laughs, encouraging Warren.

"Well, at least I know who Washington Heights is named for, even if I don't really know where the hell it is."

"It's right up there," Cormac says, pointing up toward the George Washington Bridge. He wants to say, You have an ancestor who lived there once, his bones long scoured by the river and the sea. Instead, he says, "Irving Place, in Gramercy Park, is named for Washington Irving, our first great New York writer, and Irving was named for George Washington too. Everything's connected."

"God damn it," Warren says with enthusiasm, "we could have a weekly feature just on the names of streets! Explain who Irving was, and Beekman, and Bayard, and Mott, all those streets downtown . . . Of course, we'd get some letters asking who the first Mister Broadway was."

"Joe Namath, I think."

"Exactly," he says. "A great figure of the distant 1960s . . ."

The former ambassador to Prague puts a cigarette out in a flowerpot, thus licensing the owner of the Soho art gallery to do the same. Brownlee the anchorman doesn't smoke. Anchormen never smoke. Patrick arrives on the terrace.

"Ladies and gentlemen, dinner is served. . . ."

He bows, sweeps an arm toward the interior, and Elizabeth leads the way. Cormac now realizes that the Sargent must be a portrait of a descendant of Bridget Riley. Taller, grander, more at ease. But the same color of hair. Same neck. Same audacious defiance in the eyes. A daughter of Tony Warren, perhaps. He had three children, according to the charts in the Archive, at least one of them a son, before he came to New York to die in the American Revolution. To die, that is, thinks Cormac, at my hands. Had to be late Sargent, just before he left London, sick of painting *paugh-traits,* as he said, around the time he began subverting his subjects instead of serving them. Painting them as they were instead of as they wished to be. Like Velázquez. Cormac thinks: It's her, all right. Some kind of Riley. A granddaughter, perhaps. Or great-granddaughter. Of course.

They go down a flight of carpeted stairs to the next level, filing along a cream-colored banister, finished in matte enamel like all the other woodwork; moving past two Bonnards and a Vuillard. Remembering the ghastly Meissoniers in the homes of the rich a century ago, all those heroic Frenchmen dying in the fields of the empire, facing the naked Egyptian maidens of Alta-Tadema across the room, poised to be seduced by Islam. At the foot of the stairs, a Matisse from the Fauve period. Green shadows, yellow cheekbones. The guests now all chatting, glancing at the paintings. Cormac glimpses a corridor with many enameled doors, some surely leading to still other doors. And here are more paintings. Cormac feels like a burglar casing a target. Raffles without the mask. Peggy from the art gallery tugs the sleeve of the retired diplomat and nods at a Kokoschka self-portrait, rippling with muscular impasto.

They pass the closed doors and into another large living room, designed as a refuge from winter, filled now by people whose chatter anticipates the coming summer. Tonight must be the last dinner party until after Labor Day. He notes the Persian rugs on oak floors that are perfectly tongued and grooved. Tall, deep fireplace, leather chairs, orderly bookcases (including bindings designed by Stanford White, whose presence never leaves New York), art books piled on tables, muted lamps, three original wash drawings by Delacroix, a Hopper evocation of a desolate beach, and on one wall, a portrait of Elizabeth Warren, ivory-skinned in Madame X gown and lighting, by one of those painters who still aspire to be Sargent. No Jeff Koons. No Schnabel. Not even the usual Marilyn or Mao from Warhol. Conservative taste everywhere, but confident, sure of quality.

On a grand Steinway, original sheet music awaits someone's loving gaze, as the keys await caressing fingers. The paper is browning and slightly ragged. Gershwin. "Someone to Watch Over Me." Images of the Brill Building: seven pianos on each floor; Joe Liebling's telephone booth Indians working the golden lobby. On top of the piano, laid upon doilies, are family photographs in Tiffany frames. The new Tiffany. Cormac pauses as the other guests back up before entering the dining room, while others search for place cards. Cormac sees Elizabeth and her husband in Positano. In the Yucatán. On the Riviera, and on a market street in what appears to be Bangkok. On yachts. On matched motorcycles. On horseback. There they are with both Bushes, Clinton, Reagan, Princess Di. In the city room of a newspaper. In a secret garden.

Into the wood-paneled dining room now. Chased mirrors. A single perfectly lit drawing by Rubens. All of them bending, leaning, examining place cards. The gleam of plates and yellow roses in a fluted silver bowl.

Delfina.

Where are you at this very moment?

Warren is at one end of the long polished table, Elizabeth at the other, facing him with all the others between them, as in a thousand *New Yorker* cartoons. Cormac is to her left. The black wife of a black banker is to Cormac's left. Ochre-skinned, plump, bejeweled, and nervous. A woman in her fifties. She and Cormac exchange hellos and a handshake. She wonders why Donna doesn't just pack up and leave Gracie Mansion. And is it true that the mayor has moved in with two gay guys? She read that in the *Post,* so she isn't sure it's true. She has a marvelous smile. Her husband is down at the far end beside Warren. His name is Criswell, white-haired, slight trace of Jamaican accent when he was introduced to Cormac. To Elizabeth's right is Max James, and he flatters her with questions about her opinions on the economy and who might win the election for mayor. To the right of James are Peggy from Soho, Brownlee the anchorman, a woman whose name Cormac didn't get but surely the wife of one of the men, wearing the blank look that comes from the double slumber of the marriage bed. Then Ridley, the John Jay double, and a single woman with streaked blond hair, same age as Elizabeth. Probably the same gym. Wearing a just-divorced look and a tan from two weeks at Canyon Ranch. Boy, girl, boy, girl.

Waiters arrive now with salad, with succulent tomatoes, cheese crisp or runny, while a steward expertly offers wine. There's a thin clinking of glass, the touching of forks to plates. Cormac doesn't need to turn over a blue-patterned plate to know that it's delft, most of it from the early nineteenth century, passed down to this table from some outpost of the Warren diaspora. Rills of laughter from the far end, in the same tone as the pinging of glass. The voice of a man who sounds as if he has swallowed a banjo. Warren brushing his hair with his fingers. Max asking Elizabeth about dot-commers. Silverware from Tiffany. Heavy and confident. The *old* Tiffany. Napkins folded into bishops' miters. And here's the food. The culinary neutrality of veal.

Warren addresses them all: "Can somebody please tell me what this whole globalization thing is all about? I see them in Seattle. I see them in Genoa. At war against Starbucks, it looks to me. But I just don't know what the hell they *want.*"

"They want to spread poverty and pestilence to every corner of the earth, starting with us," says the former ambassador to Prague. "They want to democratize misery."

"Oh, that's pretty drastic, don't you think, Larry?" says Elizabeth. "Most of them seem fairly decent sorts."

"Yes, and they want a hippie paradise," says the former ambassador to Prague. "You know, small is beautiful, everybody eating roots on five square feet of land in some malarial forest. Everybody wearing a Che Guevara T-shirt and begging God, of course, to provide. It's pure sentimental rot. And as the Nazis taught us, sentimentality can kill millions."

"But they *do* have a certain nostalgic charm," says Peggy from Soho. "It's right out of Haight-Ashbury."

"We know what they're against, Peggy," Warren says. "But what are they *for?*"

At tables like these, generation after generation, Cormac has heard variations on the same question. What did the Africans want? What did the South want? What did the Irish want and the Italians and the Jews? And, of course, what did women want? He glances back toward the living room and is startled by a gigantic Lucian Freud painting of an immobilized man and a fat naked woman. He missed it coming in to find his place card. The only painting that is not by a traditional painter. Raw and brutal. Cormac flashes on the year when he focused all of his own painting on ugliness. To destroy all bullshit notions of beauty. Is the painted man knitting? Is the man a man? What does Lucian Freud want?

And as the courses arrive, and plates are exchanged, and silverware removed, all under the watchful eye of Patrick, he remembers those great groaning boards of the nineteenth century and the men and women whose motto was: We eat, therefore we are. The era of the 25,000-calorie meal. Tonight, Cormac thinks, the guests of the Warrens are unwittingly doing what their obscene social ancestors did: behaving like the people who provoked the French Revolution. The style is low-key, and Elizabeth seems relaxed, casual, understated, confident. After all, Renay the florist comes each week to fill the house with delicious aromas, and Patrick assures a perfect flow of movement at the table. Light, fresh calamari salad. Veal roast. Potatoes. Frozen soufflé. Cormac thinks: We're in the era of cholesterol, blood sugar, and coronary heart disease. But they still use newspapers to provide conversation at dinner. They don't argue about what Horace Greeley said anymore, of course; he is a statue in City Hall Park, keeping a bilious eye on J&R Music; they discuss Tom

Friedman's column in the *Times,* or Safire, or Maureen Dowd. They laugh at some dreadful bulletin in Page Six of the *Post,* about people they know, or a column by Stanley Crouch in the *News,* about people they will never know. Once Dana or Bennett, Pulitzer or Hearst inflamed these dining tables, igniting the flames of outraged invective. They rasped about Walter Lippmann or Dorothy Thompson and wanted to abolish the First Amendment. In their presence, Cormac acquired the habit that he maintains here tonight: saying nothing memorable. He doesn't want attention. He wants to be a blur. An observing blur. In the past, he didn't want to be remembered by such people. He wanted to remember. Still does.

And so the talk goes back and forth, sometimes joined by all the guests, sometimes breaking down to knots of two or three. Globalization and the Middle East and Alaskan oil drilling and stem cell research. Or, in several ways, What do the Palestinians want? Elizabeth is cool and distracted, ushering in each new course with the tinkle of a golden bell, providing paragraph breaks for the chatter. She says little. She does not flirt. Not with Cormac. Not with anyone. Beyond reproach, they'd have said in the corseted gloom of Gramercy Park. He hears someone say, without irony, "Only the strong survive." And turns his gaze on the Rubens drawing. A muscled man with a warrior's shield, an imagining of a scene Rubens surely never saw. Cormac thinks: The truth is that the strong don't always survive. Usually the weak survive and the cowardly and the mediocre. They gather their forces to destroy the strong, because the strong are at the core of their fear. They burned strong Africans at the stake and reduced others to tortured rubble. Cormac used to think of them as the League of Frightened White Men. Some of them are here at this table. Frightened of change. Frightened of the new. Frightened of losing secret powers, privileges, and control. Imagining apocalypse. The kind of people who destroyed Bill Tweed.

Criswell, the black banker, rises to offer a toast. "I'd like to salute our host and his lovely wife," he says. "They have brought a measure of grace and glamour to our city. They have begun to make it more just, to use what they have to help the process of healing. I don't want to embarrass them by reciting their accomplishments. Everyone at this table knows them." Pause. An image of Tomora brushes through Cormac. "But all of us have benefited from their presence, and we thank them for their friendship." He raises his glass. Max James shouts, "Hear! Hear!" All sip, including Cormac. Then all sit. Warren remains standing.

"If I have one more glass of wine, I'm likely to start believing such kind words, Mister Criswell," he says. "But I do want to thank all of you for your presence, for your kindness to us these past few years, for your support in what we're doing at the newspaper — and for what I hope shall be long and enduring friendships. I toast all of you."

"Hear, hear," shouts James. Cormac notices Patrick hovering in the adjoining room, hands at his side. In his chilly eyes, the deepest kind of skepticism. Elizabeth tinkles a bell.

"Now," she says, "some brandy and cigars."

Cohibas, of course.

Cormac longs for a cigarette.

They all rise and begin to drift and scatter. A few slip away home, their minds already on breakfast meetings. Cormac pauses to look more carefully at the Rubens, at the extraordinary confidence of his hand as it laid down charcoal and washes. Then he strolls down one of the corridors. Some doors are open. He glimpses a mahogany four-poster covered with a handmade quilt. Then Elizabeth is behind him, with Brownlee the anchorman.

"It's the fourth door on the right," she says. "If you need the little-boys' room, Cormac."

He bows and thanks her. Into the men's room. A lithograph by Francisco Toledo above the toilet. The master of Oaxaca. Individual Brazilian napkins for drying hands. The Internet story about the Warrens said they had six bathrooms in addition to sixteen rooms. Cormac thinks: I have lived in quarters smaller than this bathroom. Outside again, he faces a drawing by Pascin, delicate and erotic. Another door is open. Elizabeth waves him in. She's explaining the decor to the anchorman. Each room has a kind of theme, she says, tracing the history of the United States through furniture, art, interior decoration. "My husband's idea," she says. "The Warrens have been here a long time." Yes. Since 1741. Here, for example, are the 1930s, with first editions of Hemingway, Fitzgerald, Dos Passos, Sherwood Anderson. Framed sheet music by Rodgers and Hart. Photographs made in Sacramento of Warren's father and grandfather. All standing by automobiles whose license plates provide the year.

In the next room, through a connecting door, World War One, and a doughboy helmet, and photographs from the AEF, and a framed 78 rpm recording of Enrico Caruso's version of "Over There." Cormac thinks of Jack London dying of pills and booze, Carnegie and Frick dying in the same year, while Wilson blathered about war and peace and civilization above the rumble of parades, drums, funerals, and memorials. The anchorman seems touched.

"My grandfather died over there," he says.

Elizabeth says, "So did mine."

They pass from the Gold Rush to the Mauve Decade (or the Gilded Age, Elizabeth says, or the Gay Nineties) to Prohibition, a room for each. San Francisco newspaper headlines. Photos of costume parties. Ostrich feathers and a battered hip flask. Flappers by John Held Jr. In each room, a bed, or a couch, or a desk. The anchorman excuses himself, and now Elizabeth directs him to the boys' room.

Cormac and Elizabeth enter another room. Photographs of Elizabeth at a girls' boarding school in Switzerland. With parents, slightly dowdy, in Folkestone. Standing beside Warren on the worn steps of an Anglican church. Some framed letters of thanks from various New York charity organizations. A desk and a Mark Cross blotter upon which sits a leather book of the sort used by hostesses a century ago to arrange seating plans and menus. Books of New York history on six shelves, one shelf devoted to Astors and Vanderbilts and Carnegie. A couch. A smaller desk with a computer and a chair for a secretary.

"This is my study," she says. "It has no decor at all."

Then, to the side of the bookcase, Cormac sees a Georgia O'Keeffe painting of a lily, and to the side of the O'Keeffe a graphite drawing he made many years ago. The paper has darkened over time, making it resemble a silverpoint. It shows the secret place of the Countess de Chardon.

"Where did you get this?" he says.

She smiles. Gently tips the door closed. "That? You like that, I suppose? I'm almost sure it's from Christie's. They told me it was probably done around 1861 or '62. In there somewhere."

Wrong by almost thirty years.

"I already had the Georgia O'Keeffe," she says. "And when I saw this" — stepping closer — "I thought she might have made the drawing too. She was certainly the greatest twentieth-century painter of cunts."

She likes saying the word, although when she says "cunt" it sounds shaved. Still, she enjoys it the way Delfina likes saying "motherfucker." She turns, eases her buttocks onto the corner of her desk. Pressing against wood. Staring at Cormac.

"I see what you mean," Cormac says. "Particularly if you turn the O'Keeffe upside down."

She smiles in a neutral way.

In the hall, Cormac hears murmuring from the far end, men and women laughing in the buzzed upper register of alcohol. He can now pick out Warren's loud guffaw.

"One more thing," she says, glancing toward the laughter and opening another door. She flicks a switch.

Inside, in indirect light, he sees frayed medieval battle flags behind glass, lithographed views of Jerusalem and Acre, dead Crusaders, men holding crosses.

"My husband's other museum," she says. "All pretty ghastly, and very interesting."

Cormac's heart stops. On the wall to the right, hanging from hooks by leather thongs, some jammed into cracked leather scabbards, are five weapons.

In the center, longer than the others, its corroded face marked by spirals, is his father's sword.

100.

He leaves the party in a state of fevered blur and icy clarity. At the door all mumble the buttery words of social banality: good night see you soon pleasure to meet you we had a fine time. Warren tells Cormac they must lunch at the Century, or right here again at the apartment, once he returns from a ten-day trip to Europe and Israel. No long summer doldrums for a newspaper publisher, are there? Elizabeth gazes at Cormac in a cool way and shakes his hand at the elevator door. On the sidewalk, under the awning, Ripley offers him a ride. The pitching coach suggests drinks at Elaine's. Cormac smiles and says he'd better walk off the sumptuous meal. He starts down Fifth Avenue.

His heart is beating hard.

His father's sword.

Hanging like a trophy on a rich man's wall. And not any rich man: this rich man, descendant of his father's murderer.

For years he searched for the sword among collectors and antiquarians, in junk shops and auction rooms. He carried with him sketches of the sword, drawn from memory, showing the spirals. Twice he met with men who tried to sell him clever counterfeits. He held them in his hand, felt their deadness, and knew they were fakes. Once a month, he scrolled through the auction sites of the Internet, saw swords of the same rough design, from the same period in time. All lacked the spirals. Now he has found the sword, through chance or fate. He thinks: I must have it.

Must devise a plan to go back to that triplex on Fifth Avenue and once more hold my father's sword.

And then, for the final time, I must wield it.

As he walks downtown on Fifth Avenue, he knows this will not be easy. A frontal assault is impossible. There's a doorman and an elevator operator. And almost certainly a second elevator for deliveries and freight. With another operator. Video cameras. Security alarms, in the building and in the apartment. Hidden buttons and buzzers, at least one connected to the local precinct. The rich live well-defended lives.

No (he thinks): I must return as an invited guest. And then stops.

What about Delfina?

And answers himself: Timing is all.

101.

His dreams are turbulent now. Most take place in the first hour after sleep, but they seem to last for years. He is in them, with time stretched, expanded, slowed, the images more vivid than life, and then he wakes up, trembling.

He sees Delfina in an endless tenement corridor, fleeing a fireball. She wears a terry-cloth robe. The fire is at the far end of the block-long corridor, orange and angry, and she is running toward Cormac. She has an infant bundled in her arms. He extends his arms, unable to move his legs, and can't reach her, and her face contorts in a scream.

There is the Earl of Warren, rising from the water near the Battery, his clothes and flesh in shreds, his skull devoid of skin.

There is Delfina on the ramparts of the Woolworth Building, smiling and barefoot in a gauzy yellow gown riffled by the high wind. She is unaware of the edge of the copper roof. She whirls in delight, calling his name, Cormac, Cormac, come here, Cormac — and goes off the edge. He is calling to her, leaping for her into the air above the city . . . and wakes up with his heart hammering.

He sees a horde of men in scarlet, mounted on ten thousand white horses, rising on the rim of the hills around the Sacred Grove, many of them holding machine guns. There is a bellowed command and then they come pounding, the earth shaking, the air filled with explosions, the forest burning, and his mother holds a pike to await their charge, and his father is slashing at them with his sword, and still they come, and one of them waves on his spear the head of Mary Morrigan, and he laughs and sneers.

He is in a cemetery and facing him are all the women he once loved, for a week or a month or a year, and in the center is the Countess de Chardon. They are dancing in morning fog. Some hold lyres. Music comes from beyond the tombstones. They hold hands. He walks forward to join them in the dance, and coming to him is the countess, smiling in welcome, and behind her with her body naked is Delfina.

Then they are gone. He stands in mournful fog. The music still plays. A flute. The pipes. He tries to dance alone and cannot move. He hears a dog barking and knows it is Bran. Here I am, Bran, he shouts. Come to me. But Bran does not come. Nobody comes. Cormac is alone, mourning his dead.

102.

Elizabeth Warren calls and asks Cormac to breakfast on Sunday morning. A wash of betrayal passes through him, as if he were cheating on Delfina, but he agrees to meet Elizabeth in a hotel restaurant just north of Washington Square. On Saturday night, after much splashing in the jacuzzi, and after she had lounged for him on a couch as he traced her body on a charcoal sheet, after he was empty, after she had dozed and purred and said little, he walks to Church Street with Delfina, kisses her goodnight, and sends her uptown in a taxi. The following morning, with the fog-thick streets still empty of most human beings, he walks north.

When he sees a brightening ahead, he knows he is almost at Washington Square. And remembers the small ceremony when they opened this land as a park, and how the politicians and clergymen acted as if everything beneath their feet had been cleansed. All of the others in the small crowd knew they were wrong and that this ground would never be cleansed. For this was the execution ground across five decades, going back to the British. There stood the gallows, down to the left of what they all called the Fifth Avenue. Slaves were hanged from that gallows, and patriots, and Jesuits, and deviates, and even, before 1741, three witches. They were buried in shrouds in the swampy earth, where blackberries grew all the way to Bleecker Street, and wild partridge raced through thickets, and fox held their ground against humans until they finally joined the animal exodus to the north. For a year before fencing off the park, the authorities disinterred the bodies, of course, and drained the marsh. But they did not find all of the dead.

And when the mansions started rising on the north side of the square, constructed with Holland brick that had come to America as ballast, and when people named Rhinelander and Minturn and Parish began to shape their mannered lives within the walls (preparing the way for Henry James), the disturbed dead rose on foggy nights.

Cormac knew the dead were there because he had seen them, as he had seen the dead (or the undead, as the Irishman Bram Stoker called them) move through old houses and along those few streets at the tip of the island that still were cobbled. Murderers and Catholics, deviates and freaks, soldiers, seamen, and teamsters driven mad by the city: and then three pale women, the color of ivory, their dresses ragged as fog, walking in the yellow light of gas lamps.

He had last seen the three pale women in Washington Square on a fog-shrouded night in 1971, after a demonstration in the square had railed against the war, against the bombing in Cambodia, against Richard Nixon. He sat on a bench that night for hours after the protestors had gone home, leaving only the litter of their slogans, and then saw the women rise from the waters of the fountain, singing a lament. Every language seemed to have been mixed into the words, which mourned the death of the young. He understood them in English and Irish and Yoruba, in Italian and German and Yiddish. The young must not die, the three pale women sang. Old men must not bury their children. Weep for all the young dead.

After that, he had not seen them again, but he knew they must still be there. Must still inhabit the earth beneath the fountain and the meth dealers, the dog walkers and the Frisbee flingers and the students of semiotics. Preparing fresh laments.

Cormac crosses the square, past the caged Washington arch, separated for years now by a wire fence from citizens who might actually use it, and remembered Stanford White again, on the day it opened, talking a streak, red-haired, laughing, proud that he had designed the arch, chatting with reporters (including Cormac) as if he and the arch would live forever. That day, a young woman brushed against him, eyes wide. He paused, blinked, stared, whispered, and she went off smiling.

The hotel dining room is cozy with dark wood and tinted steel engravings of Little Old New York. Elizabeth Warren isn't there, but a half-dozen people are already working on breakfast: an older couple, some young people. Cormac hears a fragmented conversation in German about the Statue of Liberty and Windows on the World: destinations of the day. He walks to the reception desk, buys the Sunday *Daily News,* throws away the special sections and the advertising junk, and, back at the table, glances at the sports pages. He's reading Mike Lupica's column when he sees her coming in the door.

She's wearing one of those expensive pink jogging suits, and dark violet glasses, and a white cotton beret under which she has bundled her hair. She walks in her lean, ratcheting way on thick white running shoes, looking like Monica Vitti leaving the set of a 1960s movie to go to a gym. She sees Cormac, smiles, and he stands as she reaches the table. She brushes his cheek with a kiss, and he can smell a fragrance — apples? — rising from her skin.

"A ghastly morning," she says. "It's like London out there."

"The sun will burn it off in an hour."

"One hopes." She gazes around. "How cozy. And I'm famished."

A waiter brings menus. She takes off the sunglasses to read, folding them and tucking them into a pocket of the jogging suit. Her makeup is so subtly applied that she seems to be wearing none at all. There's a restrained gloss of pale lipstick on her wide mouth.

"I want one of those gigantic American breakfasts," she says. "Mounds of pancakes and bacon and sausage. The whole lot. And an OJ. And a steaming mug of coffee. Everything."

"Sounds good to me."

"I'm still trying to get over last night," she says. "We saw this movie about Pearl Harbor, and I exhausted myself laughing. Have you seen it?"

"I'd rather go to jail."

"Oh, you *must* see it. It's so ghastly that you can't help yourself. My husband, as usual, thought I was crazy. But —"

"How is he?"

The waiter returns with a coffee pot, pours two cups, takes their orders, moves silently away.

"How is he? Oh, he's what he is. A perfectly kind and loving man. Full of mad idealism."

She says this like one of those Brits who believe that most Americans are botched Brits.

"He's doing a good job with the newspaper," Cormac says.

"Isn't he, though? Excellent. Even *I've* begun to read it."

"That would make a good commercial."

"Yes, wouldn't it, though. But in that case, *I'd* rather go to jail."

The food arrives. She eats with the greedy carelessness of someone who believes she'll always be thin. And Cormac thinks: Delfina eats as if she will die tomorrow. Elizabeth finishes before Cormac. Talking all the while about the president, and missile defense ("Who exactly are the Americans planning to defend themselves from?"). Then, glancing at the engravings, she goes on about New York, and her discoveries, and the energy of the city, and the good manners of its citizens. "It's come a long way since Mrs. Trollope was here," she says. "Have you ever read her book?"

"Yes," Cormac says (remembering the woman's pinched, nervous face). "She had an unforgiving eye for human weakness."

"Exactly. I should do a sequel. 'Domestic Manners of the New Americans.'"

Cormac finishes breakfast. A Mexican busboy takes their plates. Cormac yearns for a cigarette and wonders if nicotine withdrawal has been giving him bad dreams.

"I so wish I could belch," Elizabeth says. "But the ghost of Mrs. Trollope is intimidating."

"If anyone notices, I'll explain you're an Arab. New Yorkers believe anything you tell them about Arabs. They've become what the Irish were in the nineteenth century."

Her eyes bright with schoolgirlish conspiracy, she covers her mouth with a napkin and smothers a gassy belch. Then laughs.

"I did it, I did it!"

"Excuse me. I have to call Page Six."

"No, no, not *that!*"

She talks then about Page Six and the gossip columns in the *Daily News* and what wicked fun all of them are, unless you are the subject of their wicked scrutiny. The waiter pours fresh coffee. Then Elizabeth Warren seems to wind down, poking a spoon into the coffee, her elbows on the table. She looks up, her face serious.

"Let me ask you something," she says.

"Sure."

She seems embarrassed.

"Are you a free man?"

"I suppose."

"Don't suppose. You're not married, I take it. But do you have a woman?"

A moment of hesitation. "I'm seeing a lot of a woman."

She smiles in a rueful way.

"God damn it."

Cormac says nothing.

"Before we moved here," she says, "one of my friends warned me. All the attractive men, she said, are married, or drunks, or gay."

She sips her coffee.

"But I'd like to see more of you. You look like a man who can keep a secret. And there's something you can help me do."

Cormac does not ask her to define that something.

"And you're cautious too," she says. "That always helps." Now there's a hint of hardness in her voice and she glances at her watch. "I have to see my husband, alas."

She gets up, forces a smile, and shakes Cormac's hand.

"I'd better go," she says. "The agents of Page Six are everywhere."

She leans close, kisses him on the mouth. Then she turns and walks across the restaurant, hips ratcheting, and goes out to the city.

103.

Before leaving the hotel, he buys a pack of Vantage cigarettes. Outside, the fog has lifted and he uses book matches to light his first cigarette in nine days. He feels a mixture of failure and relief. Then, walking east along the edge of the park, with children now playing in the grass with their fathers or mothers (the nannies all off for the day), and a few stray homeless men scouting benches, he inhales deeply and thinks about Elizabeth Warren. Nicotine, after all, is a clarifying drug. He is groping for clarity.

There's something about Elizabeth Warren, he thinks (dropping his cigarette butt down a sewer opening), that is not Elizabeth Warren. She faces left when she should be facing right. In one way, she's the woman she presents to the world: cool and smooth and intelligent. But the woman at breakfast was a flopped tracing of that original, the reverse of what she seems to be, while remaining the same woman. The cool Elizabeth at breakfast revealed someone hotter and darker. Clearly, she's pulling me, a total stranger, into something that she wants me to do. The lure is familiar: the hidden pleasures between her lean thighs. But she hints at something else. Something about her husband. As if her need has detected my need.

As if she wants help in a killing.

104.

He reaches the Astor Place station and then he sees a man coming up the stairs. His name is Bobby Simmons, and he has skin the color of tea with milk, hair almost white, a hunched stance. He's carrying a worn saxophone case covered with hotel decals and old clearances from customs. Cormac blocks his way. The old man looks at his face as if he's being challenged, and then smiles.

"Gahdamn," Simmons says. "It's you for sure, ain't it? Cormac O'Connor himself."

They embrace as Simmons reaches the street. People move around them, glancing at fresh newspapers, taking Metrocards from their wallets.

"Hello, Bobby," Cormac says.

"Gahdamn, such a long time."

Simmons is breathless from climbing the subway stairs and from the seventy-six years he carries on his spare frame.

"I didn't know you were back from Europe," Cormac says.

"Six weeks now, and damn, the dirty ol' Apple looks good. Never seen so many good-lookin' women all at one time." He grins and starts walking west, Cormac beside him. "I was gone fourteen months, ya know. Paris — mostly Paris — but Copenhagen too, and London, and Prague, and hey, even Dublin, man. With *your* people. Crazy motherfuckers, your people. They got music comin' outta they asses. Hey — where you going?"

"Home."

"No, you ain't. You comin' with me. I gotta gig down here on Eleven Street, in . . ." He glances at his wristwatch. "In three minutes. And I need a piano player." He pronounces it "pianner," in the old New York style, and grins when he says the word. "Who says they ain't a god? You come out of the subway, and there's the pianner player."

"Hell, Bobby, I can't play with you guys, no rehearsal, no —"

"Come on. It's just you, me, and a bass player. Some kid from Juilliard. We'll play the old stuff. Nothin' fancy."

He grabs Cormac's arm, leaning on him for support.

The place is called the Riff Club and fills an old dining room off the lobby of a small hotel. The operators of the club are experimenting with afternoon concerts on weekends, Simmons says, and about forty people are waiting when they arrive. At the back of the room there's a bar and a dozen people with cigarettes sending a blue nicotine haze to the ceiling. Cormac smiles. The place is like five hundred other joints where he's done time since the nights and days of Prohibition. The crowd is mixed. About half white, half black, half young, half old: a 200 percent saloon crowd. Cormac sees a few graying faces from vanished nights at the Vanguard and the Five Spot. Everybody is drinking.

They go into a small room to the side of the bar. The bass player looks at his watch as they enter. He's dressed in a Brooks Brothers blazer, gray slacks, red tie; Cormac thinks he could easily pass for a banker.

"Cormac, this is Justin Gilbert, great bass player, outta Juilliard, just like Miles," Simmons says. "Justin, this is Cormac O'Connor, our pianner player for today."

"Where's Artie?" the young bass player says.

"Called in wrecked," Simmons says.

"Fuck," Justin says, his annoyed face annoying Cormac. He's twenty-two years old, Cormac thinks, and he acts like he's Milt Hinton.

"Cormac played with me before," Simmons says. "Before you were born, Justin. So relax, man." He grins. "Jazz is the art of improvisation. Don't they teach you that at Juilliard?"

The bass player sighs. "So what are we gonna play?"

"Duke."

That's the rehearsal. They walk out on stage, where Justin's bass is already leaning against a stool and a boxy grand waits for Cormac. For a moment, Cormac is nervous. He doesn't care about failing in front of the audience; he just doesn't want to fail Bobby Simmons. He flexes his fingers. He gazes out at the smoky room and sits down. Then, very slowly, in a blues tempo, he plays an introduction to "Take the 'A' Train." *Baaah. Ba, bop, bim, baa bah . . .* Justin waits; Simmons watches and listens. And then the release. Justin's bass is deep and powerful, as steady as a heartbeat, and here comes Bobby Simmons, attacking the old melody, driving it hard, the notes flying over the piano and the bass, playing the Ellington tune as if nobody has ever played it before, while honoring it as an old New York anthem. The crowd erupts. They yell and stomp feet on the old hotel floor and cheer through the final ride.

Without a break, Cormac moves into "Sophisticated Lady," slowing the mood into a smoky midnight sound, leaving space for Julian to bow his bass for a long solo, and then drives hard into "C Jam Blues." Cormac feels released, sweat pouring from him, the past vanished, the morning gone from his brain, his fingers filled with joy.

Then, from the side, a tall black man, even older than Bobby Simmons, comes on stage, his fingers running over a Selmer tenor sax. A few voices shout in recognition from the crowd, and Cormac knows him too: Horse Campbell, an old Texas honker who played with Basie and Jay McShann, old whiskey prince, old lover of all the wrong women. Someone shouts from the dark, "Horse, let's ride!"

"I heerd you was back," he shouts to Bobby Simmons, "so I figured I'd come play!"

Simmons grins, Julian looks uneasy, and then Horse starts talking with his horn, challenging Simmons, waiting for the alto man's reply. Like two men younger than Julian. And the crowd roars as the exchange goes back and forth, call and response, attack and counterattack, Cormac's left hand synchronizing with Julian's pounding bass. There's a huge roar and people standing and even Julian smiles. Then, as if to prove he is no mere Texas honker, Horse starts a hurting, grieving version of "Mood Indigo," and Bobby Simmons follows, as if saying, That ain't all, my man, that ain't all, I been hurtin' too, a long gah-damned time. The hushed crowd doesn't clink a glass. They stand again at the end.

Then Cormac plays the first bars of "Perdido" and Horse grins at him, and Simmons grins at Horse, and they go at each other, making fun of old Illinois Jacquet riffs and Flip Phillips riffs, taking the basic riff from twelve different angles, the exhilaration building, the crowd standing, the two old men now younger than anyone in the room.

And then the set is over. Bobby Simmons holds his horn out flat, one hand on the neck, the other on the bell, like a knight presenting a sword to a prince, and he bows to Horse Campbell, who returns the gesture, and then the two men hug. Simmons goes to the microphone.

"Folks, I want to introduce the band," he says. "On pianner, Cormac O'Connor. Nice to meet you, Cormac. Cormac, this is Horse Campbell; Horse, this is Justin Gilbert. I'm Bobby Simmons. . . . Oh man, it's good to be home in New Yawk."

At the break between sets, Cormac hurries to the telephone and calls Delfina.

"You might want to come down here," he says. "I'm playing piano in a band."

"Are you drinking or something?"

"No, I mean it. We play again in twenty minutes."

He tells her about meeting Bobby Simmons, gives her the address of the Riff Club, hangs up, turns away. He lights a cigarette. Justin Gilbert comes over to him.

"Listen, I'm sorry for acting like an asshole before," he says. "You got some chops."

"Thanks," Cormac says. "I understand. It's hard, a new guy, doesn't know the book. I felt bad. . . ."

"How come I never heard of you?"

"Nobody has," Cormac says.

"Where'd you go to school?"

"Saloons."

"Same as them," Justin says, nodding at Simmons and Horse, who are up on stools at the bar, talking to fans, flirting with women.

"There's worse places to learn things in," Cormac says.

"I guess."

They start the second set with "A Night in Tunisia," and now Simmons and Horse exchange quotes from Bird and Diz, and the two of them step aside to give Justin a solo, which includes an homage to Charlie Mingus, the young man thanking his elders. Horse is soloing on "Gone with the Wind" when Delfina comes in.

Cormac sees her easing around the side of the large room. She's wearing a black sweater and black slacks, and her skin glows. A few men and women turn to look at her, but only Cormac can see the spirals. He smiles as she sits at a table beside a pole, and her smile looks dazzling in return.

And then Bobby Simmons nods at Cormac to take his solo. He plunges into it, hugging the melody but playing changes on it too, and folding in a quote from "Manhattan" and then from "Oye Como Va" with his eyes on Delfina. She grins. A few people in the audience smile. And then he's done, and the whole band now moves in a languid, bluesy manner to the end. There is one final tune: "Flying Home," roaring and honking and blazing, and then the set is over. The room roars for more. The men bow and then hug. Even Justin Gilbert looks happy.

Cormac hurries to Delfina. She rises from her chair and throws her arms around him.

"*Oye, como va* yourself," she says.

They go to Duane Street and make love at dusk and then order Chinese food, and eat, and talk, and make love again. She asks him to play for her. He presents her with a nocturne, as if it were a gift, and then, without singing, he plays the melody of the Fight Song, filling it with small variations on the tune, inserting the years before minstrel shows and ragtime and the twentieth century. She listens intently, curled like a cat in a chair. Finally he gives her his own version of "Oye Como Va," mixing Tito Puente with Scott Joplin. She gets out of the chair and presses her breasts against his back.

105.

That night, he enters the Delfina Summer. She is the essential element, humid and loamy, with her long thin legs in odd contrast to the thick pliancy of her flesh. They meet without plans, without agendas. If he speaks about architecture, she counters with the language of flowers. Surely, she says, roses must whisper in words that are different from those of chrysanthemums. But trees, he says, are like buildings, rooted in earth, rising against blank skies. Trees provide shelter, the way buildings do. Some trees are brilliant with colors, he says, and others stark with abandonment and old age.

Yes, she says, I see what you mean. And stares for a beat at the abandonment in his face.

They keep a cool, respectful distance from each other too, which makes the moments of intimacy even more fevered. In between, it's as if each were wary of domesticating the time they share. They have no compact, no agreement about rules. If they meet on Monday, they will not meet on Tuesday or Wednesday, unless some urgency grips her and she must see him. He has his friends, like Healey; she has hers, whose names and faces he does not know. What matters is what happens when they are together. The music of the present tense. They make love in the Studio, on the couch, on the bed, on the old model's stand, in the jacuzzi, and once on top of the piano, giggling all the way. They make love in full morning light or in the luminous glow of towers; and once, in a rush, in the dusky woods near Grant's Tomb. On some weekday nights, she sleeps with him, fresh clothes packed for an early-morning meeting at her job in the North Tower. She sleeps deeply, breathes shallowly, has a whisper of a sated snore; she is without need then for companion or accomplice, only warmth. In the morning, she never says goodbye. They speak little about the flesh and not at all about love, which Cormac thinks is why she is with him. After the first tentative weeks, they stop performing and shift into being. They dine together in restaurants, visit museums, go to see shows or movies, as he shows her a New York she has seldom seen. She comes to listen when he sits in with Bobby Simmons. He takes her to one breakfast with Healey, who approves of her in capital letters, while she says later that Healey should be committed. Eventually, on every day that they are together, and without concern for clocks, they make love. Life's small dessert. Always in his place, never in hers. She makes clear without saying a word that she is entering his life but that he is not yet entering hers.

She reads the *New York Times* each morning now and has added the *Wall Street Journal* because of her new job, but she doesn't dice up the newspapers for subject matter at dinner. The saga of the missing intern in Washington does interest her, with its script of younger woman and older man, and she wonders why the police don't deal with the suspect congressman the way they would deal with a bodega owner in the Bronx. "He'd be in a cell long ago," she says. "But hey, this is America, man. . . ." She says she can't look at the president on television because he reminds her of snotty rich kids she'd see in restaurants when she was at Hunter, sending back the wine. She wonders whether stem cell research can cure the woman in her building uptown who shakes with Parkinson's. She wishes the navy would stop using Vieques for target practice, but the Middle East, where bombs are now exploding in pizza parlors, could be in a different solar system. "I just don't get it," she says. "It's gotta be me." Some people, she adds, are just driven crazy by God and there's nothing that can be done. The election in Peru is good news for Reynoso & Ryan because they have some business in Lima, but in general politics, domestic or foreign, she finds an emptiness, a series of speeches and explosions. "How many of these goddamned politicians ever heard 'Oye Como Va'?"

Sometimes she speaks of her job as if she's witnessing a daily soap opera. She describes Reynoso, the flamboyant partner, and his vice president, Sarita, a Colombian who is twenty years older and thirty pounds heavier than Reynoso, and mad for the man. At least twice a day, she gives Delfina dirty looks, as if her blouse is too frail or her sweater too tight. "She'd like me better," Delfina says, "if I dressed like a nun." There are sixteen people working in the office and all of them wonder about

Ryan, the permanently absent partner who is always calling in from distant hotel rooms. Reynoso jokes about deliveries from Bogotá or schemes for paying off union leaders in Yucatán. Delfina punctuates her accounts by saying that capitalism is a bitch. Then glides away into other realms.

"Do you believe in God?" Cormac asks her at a show of religious tapestries at the Metropolitan.

"I believe in gods," she answers. "Plural."

And that draws him closer to her, as a dozen gods move through him from the Irish mist, and he wonders if they could ever merge with the sun-soaked gods of the Caribbean. There could be a tapestry of gods as profuse as flowers.

They talk about monotheism, and how it has led to so many slaughters. He wonders out loud why that single God is always so cruel.

"Because he wants love, man," she says, "and he can't get it. Look at all the commandments. They all say, Love me or die. What a weird message! God insists that you love him. He says, If you don't love me, I'll punish you with boils and plagues and locusts. I will burn you in Hell. His vanity is endless. Love me, he says, love me, love me, love me. He's supposed to be the most powerful dude in the universe, El Señor, the Father of us all, and he comes across as a huge pain in the ass."

She laughs when she says these things, which means she is serious.

"Hey, why can't he be *indifferent?*" she goes on. "Why does he give such a big rat's ass about getting people to love him? He's like some kind of rapper. You know, Love me, baby, or I'll throw you under a truck."

Cormac smiles.

"I mean, the *real* gods are not so jealous, man, not so vain," she says. "They have weaknesses, like everybody else. And they have real jobs. They have to take care of water and fire and the sky and the stars. Some of them have powers, but not *all* powers. Not everything wrapped up in one vain dude. I mean, they're too busy, man, to demand love from each and every person on the planet. . . . They got the whole damn universe to take care of."

And then she smiles in a secret way.

She can change the subject so effortlessly that he often doesn't notice until later that she has moved on. She's like a musician, hearing some riff and then doing variations on the theme, or introducing some completely new idea, while never going out of tempo, out of time. The macho vanity of God can lead to a discussion of the New Testament as poetry, an epic poem about a young man who thinks he is God too, and then ends up on a cross and discovers that he's just a man, that he's not God at all, that he will die for his delusion (and his vanity); which is why he says, God, why hast thou forsaken me?

And then she goes on to discuss poets, to talk about Rubén Darío and Octavio Paz, Pablo Neruda and César Vallejo, all of whom she has read in Spanish, some of whom she has memorized. Such talk comes like a river that has been blocked for too many years, halted when she left Hunter, halted by marriage, a child, death, anguish; and he is thrilled when she speaks Spanish, when she drops a bucket into deep waters and draws a dozen lines of poetry from her bottomless well of vowels.

She is sometimes baffled by him. One sweltering Saturday, she wants to show him Orchard Beach, along the shores of the Bronx, where conga players drum into the night. "You gotta hear these guys, Cormac," she says. "They'll shake up your gonads." He can't go, and can't explain why. She wants to see a show at the Brooklyn Museum. He's busy, and she goes alone. She arrives one evening with CDs from J&R Music by Benny More and Tito Rodriguez. She plays them and begins to dance while he sits and watches, shouting, "Come on, man, you can't hear this music and *sit.*"

And he gets up, clumpy, stiff, awkward, and she laughs and says, "Man, you're gonna be a project! We gotta go to Jimmy's, up in the Bronx! Right now, Cormac! Get dressed!"

And he says, "Uh, no, well, I, why don't we try that some other time?"

And plays piano along with the Latin CDs. While Delfina dances alone.

But she is revealing herself in fragments, and so is he. They are like two archaeologists, examining unearthed shards and trying to make them whole through imagination. When he's alone, longing for her abundant presence, he speaks to her in the emptiness: "To tell the truth, Delfina, my life has no shape at all. There are no straight lines. I have this strange life, but it's not, in the end, strange at all. There is no plot. There is only luck and chance."

106.

The Delfina Summer was not a neat sequence of day following night following day. Her part of the summer was condensed, edited together in his mind by his need for a story. But he still took his naps and went for his walks. He made entries in his notebooks. He listened to Ben Webster and Sinatra, Coltrane and Miles. He felt a need to read again the books that had enriched his life, and so he took down *Don Quixote* and read it in three days, and was filled with sadness. "Don't listen to them, old knight," he said to the emptiness. "They are not windmills. They are dragons." And wondered what Quixote would make of the Woolworth Building and the Twin Towers. He laughed through Dante's *Inferno,* imagining John Gotti leaning over the poet's shoulder in his northern exile, saying, *Da lawyizz. Put in about da lawyizz!* He wanted to stand in applause for the shamelessness of *Bleak House,* the sight of Dickens demanding from his audience what Fosse used to call a Big Mitt Number. At one point Dickens has a man die of spontaneous combustion, exploding into fragments, into ash and dust. *Sinvergüenza,* he said. Shameless. And as delicious as a great extravagant meal.

And through the Delfina Summer, he still sat each Tuesday morning with Healey in Mary's marvelous coffee shop, the city gilded with July or August, and heard his tale of a possible Hollywood miracle, and how the fabulous goniff Legs Brookner, for reasons of guilt or avarice, was offering him a twenty-thousand-dollar advance to turn his second play into a screenplay. "He's gonna make me SOMEBODY again! Can you imagine?" Cormac could imagine, and they talked about ways to update the old play, or whether it should be done as a period piece, and what Healey would do with the immense fortune that might be coming his way. "Maybe I'll move to Kabul and watch the Taliban shoot statues!"

One Tuesday morning, Healey walked in waving the *Daily News*. "Did you see THIS? The FBI just discovered that someone robbed four hundred and forty-nine guns from FBI headquarters, and one hundred and eighty-four laptops! One of the laptops has CLASSIFIED information on it! Is this the GREATEST? I mean, I LOVE this country! If you gotta have the secret police, then make sure they are INCOMPETENT!"

Cormac also saw Elizabeth Warren.

They meet twice for lunch, each time in a hotel. Each time she is in town from Southampton on a shopping trip, or to see friends from Europe. The first meeting is in the Grand in Soho, sandwiches in the restaurant, where she nods at acquaintances, and talks about politics and Africa and the forgiveness of debt. That day she sounds like a one-woman seminar and never once mentions what she really wants from him. Three weeks later, it's room service at the Millennium, facing the World Trade Center across Church Street. She talks about Downtown as if it were another country, and he tells her some of its history, and who lived where, and how Matthew Brady had two separate studios on Broadway where he photographed everybody from Walt Whitman to Abraham Lincoln. He talks to delay; she listens but doesn't listen. He hopes he is boring. And feels as if he is doing an audition.

She needs him in some way that she has not spelled out. He needs her to get to his father's sword, and to the places that the sword will take him. In a room on a high floor of the Millennium, they make love. She is awkward, in the way that some models are permanently awkward, as if thrown back to the gawky, breastless girls they once were, when no boys could see beyond the braces glittering in their mouths. She wears her passion as if it were rouge.

"You're what I thought you'd be," she says when they are done. "Just marvelous."

He thinks of Delfina, who never gives him a review. She is out there beyond the window of the hotel, across the plaza, on the eighty-fourth floor of the North Tower. He wishes he could enter the air, do some marvelous dance high above the city, as light and graceful as Fred Astaire. Dance for Delfina. Dance to her. And let the harbor winds cleanse his shame.

In the neutral space of the hotel room, Elizabeth Warren talks about schedules and assignments and duties, about a trip to Angola and Rwanda with a land mine committee, and how she needs shots for malaria. She talks about some fund-raising events in the Hamptons, talking as if she has endless time before she gets around to telling Cormac what she wants. Her summer is a schedule, rigorously shaped, not a life. He doesn't say anything about what he wants from her: the sword. She smiles in a cool way, assembles her few things, checks her hair, and then goes. Cormac lights a cigarette and gazes off at the towers. *"Mea culpa,"* he says out loud. *"Mea maxima culpa."*

Delfina calls before daylight on a morning in the third week of August. Her voice is quick, almost abrupt, and thin with tension.

"I'm on my way to the D.R.," she says. "My father's dying."

She has seldom mentioned him in their time together. He was, she said once, handsome. At least in her small-girl's memory. He played piano in various bands around Santo Domingo. "He's not as good as you are," she said, and smiled. He was married at least twice after her mother left him for the healing snows of New York.

"I don't even know him," she says. "That's why I have to go. To ask him some questions."

Something dark and uneasy is in her voice, and she knows it.

"My aunt Lourdes called around midnight," she says, forcing herself out of the darkness. "I didn't want to wake you."

"Where are you now?"

"Kennedy. I wish you were with me."

"Me too." He pauses. "Call me when you get time," Cormac says. "Call collect. But only if you can."

"I will."

The hardness seeps out of her voice now. He can hear the blur of public announcements in the background.

"I hope all goes well. For you. For him too."

"I hope so too. For him. You always think you have all the time in the world to find out the things that really matter to you. Then you get a phone call in the middle of the night, and you're talking about days or hours. Life is weird, sometimes."

"It sure is."

"And Cormac? We'll have dinner in my place as soon as I get back. For the first time . . ."

"Of course. Just do what you've got to do down there."

"Okay."

"Vaya con Dios."

Then she's gone. He lies on the couch for a while and then picks up the remote control and clicks on New York 1 for the time and weather. Temperatures in the high eighties. No wind. He needs to go out into the city. In August, he thinks, I can even wear shorts.

She doesn't call that night, or the day after. And on the following morning, he walks down Broadway with Healey, who is unhappy in a new way. Without warning, Mary's coffee shop has closed. The building is being rehabbed, with money obviously raised before the dot-com collapse. The pipes and planks of rigging climb three stories above the sidewalk, throwing the front of the coffee shop into darkness, and a team of Mexicans is adding one new floor of rigging to another. The interior of the coffee shop is dark. The Miss Subways posters are still there, but gone are all those waitresses who called them sweetheart in the New York mornings.

"They're gonna take everything we love right out of the world, Cormac," says Healey, his walk slower, his face rippling with emotion. "They'll put a fucking Starbucks in here, wait and see. With waitresses right out of Area Code 800. Women from NOWHERE. Wactresses, waiting for the BIG BREAK, not *waitresses."*

Their legs take them south, as if there were concentric rings of time and eventually they'll find their way to 1947, when Mary's opened, selling eggs and jelly doughnuts to politicians from City Hall. But it's all Duane Reade and Staples and Gap, flying the flags of globalization. Stockbrokers move in urgent waves from the subways and PATH trains in the World Trade Center, crossing Church Street, heading for Wall, right up past Brooks Brothers, all of them carrying the *Times* or the *Wall Street Journal,* and briefcases full of anxiety. Healey and Cormac watch them as if they are part of a movie, and then wander toward the Twin Towers.

"If all these business guys are going to their offices," Healey says, "there must be some room for US." They turn at a sign marked Cortlandt Street, which is no longer a street but only a marker erected at the plaza. "I mean, there's gotta be a COFFEE shop, where you can sit down, and make remarks." Cormac thinks: I lived on this street once, and then they shoveled it into landfill. They find a door and descend on an escalator into the vast concourse of the underground mall, looking at the strained faces on the packed stairs of the up escalator.

Then, in the concourse, Cormac sees a woman he is certain is Delfina. Coming up out of the N&R trains. There are hundreds of people moving around one another, and he has only a glimpse. It's her hair. Her skin color. His stomach flips. She's here, not in the Dominican Republic. She made up a lie. He excuses himself to Healey, then hurries after the woman, calls, *"Delfina."* The woman turns. It's not Delfina.

He goes back to find Healey in the swirling morning crowds, standing in front of a Florsheim's shoe store.

"What's with YOU?"

"I thought she was someone else."

"That Latin chick?" Healey says.

He looks at Cormac, who mumbles, and then he shakes his head and says, "Fucked up, man. Fucked up."

107.

Now Cormac feels time expanding, contracting, then expanding once again. His narrative has stalled. Through the pages of the *Light,* he keeps track of the separate journeys of the Warrens, while Delfina is off on her own journey, about which nobody writes. Elizabeth is photographed in an African village, and then meeting with a U.N. investigator, and then at a hospital. Adopting a "letter to the reader" format not seen since the Hearsts abandoned New York in the 1960s, Warren writes his impressions of Tony Blair and Jacques Chirac and Silvio Berlusconi, their concerns about the missile defense shield, about the threats of terrorism spreading from the streets of Tel Aviv to all of Europe, the problems of immigrants, or the need to create a humane form of globalization. Warren writes, or dictates, articles on peace in Northern Ireland and how it could be a model for peace in the Middle East, each article running with a photograph of Warren shaking hands with the leading politicians. The pieces are tedious, written in the flat prose of a ghostwriter, but from them Cormac knows where Willie Warren has been, if not where he is. He feels like a burglar from the 1950s, studying the society columns to find out whose apartments were empty on Park Avenue.

Delfina calls collect late in the evening of the second day after she leaves. The connection is bad, with gaps in words, and blurred by a parallel nonstop conversation in Spanish that he can hear from a separate line.

"I've been trying every which way to get a number for you," he says, trying to be cheerful. "I even called Reynoso and Ryan, but Reynoso is out of town too."

"I'm okay," she says. "My aunt picked me up at the airport and got me here. It's out in the boonies. I'm calling from a neighbor's house." Static and interference. Then: "My father's still alive. But *quién sabes, mi amor.* Hey, I'll try to find a better phone and call you tomorrow. . . ."

She doesn't call.

Elizabeth does. She's back in town. Can he come to dinner?

108.

It's the eve of the first weekend in September. On his Thursday walk, taken around noon, he sees the streets emptying, as the city evacuates for Labor Day. Buses groan uptown on Church Street, loaded with passengers for Staten Island and New Jersey. Taxis push their way to Penn Station, Grand Central, or the Port Authority bus terminal, and he sees men and women waiting on corners with black wheeled suitcases, waving frantically for someone, anyone, to stop and take them away.

Above him, the sky is tossing, the clouds scudding and turbulent before the power of an emptying wind. Down at the Battery clouds assemble into a white horse, complete with rider. He thinks: New York 1 should add an Omen Report. With a Portent Index. And a Death Chill Factor. He stares for a long while as the clouds unravel and blow to the east.

He naps and dreams great shuddering dreams that he can't remember when he comes awake. Through the skylight, out past the towers, the clouds are now arranged like a stallion. The Black Horseman of famine. And then a shift of wind, and the dying sun colors the horseman red. The Red Horseman of war. Which then bleaches into the Pale Horseman of pestilence and death. Joined to the White Horseman of the afternoon, they warn of strange births and terrible deaths, ruinous storms, conflict and rage, the season of Apocalypse. Are they forming over New York for the first time, or were they drawn by Albrecht Dürer half a millennium ago? Yeats would have read those clouds.

"And what rough beast, its hour come round at last, slouches towards Bethlehem to be born?"

Which Bill Tweed would answer with another question: What are you gonna do about it?

He sees a light blinking on the answering machine. He plays the lone message.

"It's me," Delfina says, her voice wavering across the miles. "I had a terrible time getting through to you. Sorry, mi vida. Everything's okay with me, but they don't think my father can last the night. I'll let you know as soon as I can come home. Check the e-mail too. Love ya."

That's all. The crisp message of someone using someone else's telephone, at long-distance rates. A voice that's at once concrete and vague, but alive.

And then he feels a green worm move in his heart. Suppose this is a game? Suppose she is lying? Suppose she never left New York? Just because the woman in the Trade Center concourse was not Delfina, that doesn't mean she's not somewhere else in the city. He calls her number. In English and Spanish, she says she has gone on a short trip out of town, on family business, and should be home by Labor Day, please leave a message. Cormac relaxes and curses himself for an adolescent fool. But the worm still gnaws. He glances at the clock. Almost six. He calls her office and asks for Mr. Reynoso. "Sorry, he's out of town until after Labor Day. Would you like to leave a message?" No, he says, I'll call after the holiday.

He checks e-mail, but there are no messages from Delfina, and he thinks: I'd better read Stendhal tonight. I'm too old for this shit.

109.

The doorman looks at Cormac as if he's a jewel thief. Standing in the vestibule, the doorman is like a remnant of the Hapsburg Empire, all gold braid and buttons on a field of royal blue, and in the great tradition of doormen, he has adopted the haughty manners of his masters. He fixes his hooded eyes on Cormac while he calls the penthouse. The clock behind him says 8:15. Back turned, he murmurs into the house phone, then hangs up.

"Penthouse," he says. "Take a right to the elevator."

"Thanks."

Cormac is carrying a draftsman's case, purchased from Pearl's Paint on Lispenard Street, and the man in the elevator looks at the case first, then at Cormac. If he suspects the case hides a shotgun, he says nothing. He punches PH. Up they go in silence. Cormac flashes on Delfina, in a Caribbean town he will never see. He hears the disappointment in her recorded voice, and the sound of hard rain. Now he feels for a quick beat that he's once more betraying her. He tells himself, I imagine her betrayal while I enact my own.

The elevator stops, the door opens and Elizabeth Warren is smiling at him.

"Come in, come in," she says, full of practiced brightness and formality, played for the elevator operator. The door clicks shut behind him and he stands the draftsman's case against a small table, which also holds a bowl of keys.

"Is there a rifle in that thing?" she says, smiling.

"Not even a round of ammunition. I promised a friend I'd loan it to him. He's an artist, lives over on Second Avenue."

"Is he any good?"

"Not bad."

They walk down the hall, past the many cream-colored doors, including the room where the swords hang together on a wall.

"Patrick arranged some soup for us, and sandwiches," she says. "We almost never eat heavy in the evenings, except when William is entertaining. He'll be gone a few more days in Israel, getting a tour of the terrorist outposts." She says this with a certain sarcasm. "Patrick has tickets to a baseball game — and the maids are off tonight."

Ground rules established firmly and casually, she gestures at a small table in the corner: soup bowls, silverware, a silver tureen for the soup. Sandwiches neatly piled on a plate, the crusts pared from the bread.

"I told you we'd have to rough it," she says. She's wearing a loose, flowing Mexican skirt, white peasant blouse, low shoes: a Frida Kahlo sketch for someone other than Frida Kahlo.

"It looks perfect," Cormac says.

"Let's sit before the soup goes cold."

She talks about Israel, and how Willie actually admires Ariel Sharon and hopes to urge him to meet with Arafat; and how depressed she was about the scattered killings in Northern Ireland; and quotes the old line about how peace comes dropping slow. The land mine problem is urgent. "There are children dying all over the world," she says. "In Afghanistan there are two million buried mines, and the Russians have been gone for twelve years." The problem, she says, is the idiots from the Taliban. Has he seen the footage of the way they destroyed the two immense statues of Buddha? Dreadful, dreadful. Then she switches to national politics and the economy, the president and his men, the ripple effect of the economic collapse on Mexico and England, and eventually the world. Speaking with intelligence and a certain journalistic precision. Cormac feels sludge seeping into his brain.

The soup is a variation on *sopa de tortilla,* without the avocados or the *chicharrón*. At least one of the cooks must be Mexican. The sandwiches are tomato and mozzarella, almost certainly the reduced-fat variation of the cheese. Elizabeth places herself so that the lamplight emphasizes her cheekbones and the elegant column of her neck.

"I told my husband you were coming here tonight," she says. "Just so you don't feel strange when you see him next."

"Any objections?"

"No. He said to tell you that they could use Major Deegan in Tel Aviv."

She smiles, and they are into the dance. Cormac knows all the patterns, far better than Elizabeth does, but the steps are always slightly different. Here Yo-Yo Ma plays cello on a CD full of the tango. He sees what she doesn't: Valentino and George Raft and the hoarse cigarette voice of Agustín Lara at an upright piano. His eyes roam over the paintings. He loosens his tie. She holds his hand. The CD ends. A moment of silence.

"Come," she says.

Later, in a small dim room behind her office, she falls limp and soft and silent for a long while.

"Were you thinking of someone else?" she says.

"Yes," he says, telling her the truth.

"Poor woman," she says, with a hint of bitterness. "To have missed this."

"Who were you thinking about?"

"My husband."

This is a new step in the ancient dance.

"I love him," she says. "I want to be with him the rest of my life."

"Tell me the 'but.'"

She smiles and turns her head to the wallpaper.

"I'd rather not."

He sits up. She follows, back against a bare wall, knees drawn up. Her face now is exhausted and drained, her hair blowsy.

"I have a question," he says.

"Ask it."

"What do you want from me?"

She's quiet for a long moment, sorting out words, staring at her long fingers as they form a little steeple. There's a twitch in her cheeks.

"Intimacy, I suppose."

The word breaks something in her. She starts to weep. Her hands fall hopelessly to the bed, her knees move toward Cormac, her porcelain shell cracks. He feels pity make its treacherous entrance. He holds her tight for a long time, and she dozes, as he eases away from her, and then she falls into sleep. He lets her thin body relax into the pillow. He covers her with a down comforter and lifts hair from her brow. Intimacy. Another one of those big words that James Joyce said always get us in so much trouble.

The night man is on the door when Cormac comes down at twenty minutes after twelve and says good night in a firm voice. The night man nods in an uncertain way, and Cormac keeps walking with the draftsman's case in his hand, heavier now than when he arrived. He strolls into the chilly blue air.

He crosses to the park side, walking south, once more in possession of the sword but robbed of elation by what he did to get it. He thinks: I should be rushing home, to examine this old weapon in all of its details, to feels its old power. But I don't want to go home. Not yet. I want to walk off the details of this night. The mixture of shame, pity, and treachery. To shove them, as I've shoved so many other things, into the past. Then he tells himself that such matters must recede before the demands of the old vows. "Now I have the sword," he says out loud. And then, to himself, Delfina exists for me, as vivid as dawn. If I can join those narratives, I'll be free. May all gods grant me benediction.

A cold wind blows from the west, and he wishes Delfina were waiting for him on Duane Street instead of brooding on death and fathers under the forest rains of the Dominican Republic. Wind-dried leaves rattle down from the trees of the park, the autumnal sound denser in the darkness that lies beyond the low stone walls. Taxis move downtown on Fifth Avenue. The cased sword feels heavier, his body more weary. He goes to the curb, hails a taxi, and gets in. He names his destination for the Pakistani driver. Then sits back, the sword in its case on his lap. The window to his left is open to the night air.

He watches pedestrians walking in couples along Fifth Avenue, and the glittering blur up ahead, and the lights very bright on the Empire State Building.

The taxi stops for a light at Fifty-ninth Street, with the Sherry-Netherland to his left. Then a figure draws up beside the taxi. A black bicycle rider. His head bare, gazing off to the left. The head turns. The black man smiles.

"Hello, Cor-mac," he says.

It's Kongo.

"See you soon," he says in Yoruba. And then turns the ten-speed against west-bound traffic into a side street where the taxi cannot follow.

"Kongo!" Cormac calls after him. "Stop, Kongo! Wait!"

He starts to thrust money at the taxi driver, to open the door. But Kongo has vanished into the night.

110.

Across the day, Cormac polishes the sword. He uses sandpaper and emery cloth and a burin to pry time's corrosion out of the etched spirals. He oils the steel. He sands again. On the CD player, he listens to Ben Webster and Duke Ellington, trying to bring their love and polish to his task. The phone call he wants to receive does not come. He takes a break, laying the sword on a towel, and goes out into the emptied streets.

He spends an hour at J&R Music World, buying a cell phone, asking a surly clerk to explain its workings. Later, he can add its number to the message on the answering machine, so that Delfina can find him if he's out. He sits for a shoe shine in the almost empty concourse under the towers, glancing at the tabloids, speaking Spanish with the bootblack, all about how the Yankees are sure to win, then wondering to himself how many pairs of shoes he has worn across the years. Six hundred pairs? A thousand? He remembers the time when all shoes had the same shape, blunt, rough, all-purpose boots, until some ingenious cobbler changed everything by designing shoes for the left and the right foot. And how many pairs of new socks has he pulled over his wide Irish feet and then thrown out as rags?

He walks north on Church Street, and at Chambers Street turns right to a barbershop. Two barbers. No customers. He asks for a trim, and the questions come again in his head: How many pounds of hair have been trimmed from my head? Thousands? More? The barber is seventy-two years old and from Cuba. His name is Albor, and he has been cutting hair, he says, since he was seventeen. Cormac asks how many tons of hair he has chopped off human heads and chins. He laughs out loud. "I star' thinkin' abou' things like that, *'mano,*" he says, "I go nuts."

In the afternoon, Cormac plays piano for an hour, noodling Ellington, playing a jokey piece of Satie. His fingers feel oiled from use. Then he works again on the sword, smoothing pitted steel, using steel wool now, digging gently, running fingertips over the blade. On the day he took the sword, he saw Kongo. All streams converge in one river. Now he traces the spirals, thinking of Delfina. With her spirals, she is never nude. Two paintings of her are upstairs in the studio, one with spirals, one without; she asked for the painting without the tattooed markings. "I want to see what I used to look like," she said. He has the paintings, but she remains somewhere in the Dominican Republic. Call me, *mujer.* Call now. Call tonight. Call soon. Call.

He carries the sword to the Studio, lays it on the low table beside the couch. He gazes at the two portraits of Delfina, thinking: If I have time, I can fix the eyelashes. I can make her painted flesh seem to breathe. I can make a viewer hear her voice.

He thinks about Kongo, out there in the city. Visiting from the eighteenth century. He sleeps. And dreams of Willie Mays, racing in the outfield grass of the Polo Grounds, his back to Cormac, his back to Jimmy Walker, home from European exile, sitting beside Cormac in a box, the three of them blended in the timelessness of dream. Willie's back is to the world, running and running and running. The centerfield wall keeps receding. And Willie Mays runs toward eternity.

When he awakes, the Studio is dark. The towers glitter against a mauve sky. He lies there for a long moment, and then sees the room fill with versions of himself: shadowy figures, faces barely visible but all looking like his own. He is bearded and he is clean-shaven, he wears waxed mustaches or long sideburns, his hair is down to his shoulders, or cut to a balding pate: the disguises of a shadowy man. He wears the suit made for him on the *Fury* by Mr. Partridge, and the rough clothes he wore laying cobblestones or digging the subway or catching rivets high on the Woolworth Building. There he is in the worsted suit he wore for two decades while working at the *Herald*. There he is in a suit and vest he wore to so many other newspapers. There he is in a blacksmith's leather apron and a painter's smock. One of him wears a Five Points derby and another a hoodlum's stovepipe hat, a plain cloth cap or a thirties gray fedora. All the

Cormac O'Connors stare at him, and at the object gleaming on the low table.

The sword.

The sword glows now in the dimness, as if soaking up all the free-floating illumination of the city. It points north.

He reaches for the sword. Grips it. And all the versions of himself vanish.

He steps into the dark open space, plants his feet, then thrusts with the sword. Then cuts back with the sword. Then slashes with the sword. And then does it again, faster. And then faster. Feeling the power surging through his arm. Surging to his shoulder. Surging through his heart and guts.

On his evening walk, he searches the blank streets for Kongo but does not find him. He feels observed, as if the windows with their closed shades are watching him and tracking his movements. Did Wordsworth feel observed by trees and meadows? He pauses for a stoplight and laughs. Is anyone else in this city thinking at this moment of William Wordsworth? Maybe. Up near Columbia, in housing provided to faculty by the university. Somewhere in the city, almost every subject is being pondered by someone.

He sees a young Muslim woman in black, her head covered and her handsome face bared, crossing Astor Place, passing the liquor store, heading west toward NYU. How did she find her way here? Where is her family? What language does she dream in?

Cormac dreams sometimes in Irish, and in Yoruba, and in German or Yiddish. He thinks: Dead languages live in my head at all hours. He walks north on Fourth Avenue, remembering vanished bookstores, and the many volumes he discovered in their dusty bins, books that are now on the shelves of Duane Street. He flashes on Cicero's *Murder Trials,* describing the stuff of tabloids in elegant Latin. And then thinking: I must make a will.

He passes a synagogue and remembers the way he has memorialized his mother's death every fifty years. On January 17, 1737, the day she fell into Irish mud under the black coach. Across his American years, he has visited synagogues to bond himself forever to her and to Noah's lost daughters. In all those years, he was a man without faith in a single God, blind to the Torah, filled with Celtic mists and Celtic goddesses. But still he retreated to those ever-larger rooms, to the places of her secret faith, in which he whispered kaddish. In 1787, and in 1837, and in 1887, and in 1937, and in 1987. Every fifty years. Not world enough, but with more time than most other men. Whispered her name in Hebrew, learned slowly from one old Brazilian rabbi. Whispered prayers in bookish Yiddish, absorbed from the exiled socialists of Kleindeutschland. Yiddish was one of the secret rivers of blood and history. And each time he prayed, he yearned for a cloak of many colors.

Here where Kongo has arrived at last to be his Virgil, to lead him to the secret city of emerald light.

For the first time in many years, he doesn't want to go.

111.

O*n the morning of Labor Day, he uses the cell phone to call Healey.*

"Where ARE you?" Healey shouts. "In Central Booking?"

Cormac explains that he's on a bench in City Hall Park, facing the Woolworth Building. That accounts for the background noise.

"You mean you GOT one? You got one of those goddamned YELL phones?"

"Guilty with an explanation," Cormac says. "As with everything in this life. A Labor Day sale at J and R . . ."

"I don't want to HEAR it! What about lunch, comrade?"

They meet in a coffee shop on Twenty-third Street off Seventh Avenue and sit in a booth in the back, engulfed by orange plastic. The Greek owners and waiters all know Healey, and laugh with him as his voice booms around the place.

"They like me 'cause I speak Greek with them," he says. "In the second year at my high school, the Jesuits offered me a choice: Greek or German. Along with four years of Latin. I took Greek instead of German because I hated the fucking NAZIS, little knowing that I'd end up working with them in the theater."

But he's happy about other things. The check from Legs Brookner actually cleared at the bank. The producer is off in the south of France, and they will meet again in two weeks.

"It's a SCORE. Any Hollywood score is a good score. Just as long as they never make the MOVIE!"

The word "movie" makes heads turn in three booths jammed with unemployed dot-commers. For years, most young people told you they were working on movie scripts. Then they talked about start-ups. Now they are back to movie scripts.

"Don't think about it!" Healey yells at the young people. "Movies are the worst work in the world. I mean, there's a movie playing down the block that's all about FARTS! Learn honest trades. Be carpenters. Repair plumbing. Take the FIREMAN'S test! Be HAPPY!"

The three booths break into applause. Healey gives Cormac a look that says: Am I nuts or are they?

The e-mail is waiting when Cormac gets home. From Delfina. Across the miles.

> Cormac, querido: I'm writing this in a cyber cafe. I've been upset since talking to you — upset with myself, not with you — and now I want to talk some truth. About me. And about us. I felt in your voice that you were jealous somehow, maybe about Mr. Reynoso.
>
> The truth is that my father was really dying, and is now dead. But the truth gets more complicated. When I went to see Mr. Reynoso to get some time off, he was very understanding. Not only did he give me the time I needed, he paid for the round-trip ticket to Santo Domingo. I wanted you to come but somehow I knew you couldn't. I mean, you can't

even go to Brooklyn. So I went to the airport alone, in a car service from East Harlem.

When I got there, who's in first class? Mr. Reynoso. When I see him, I'm irritated. This was, like, too neat, too easy. He said he had some business in Santo Domingo, that this was a real coincidence, etc. I thought, Man, you're so full of shit. But once we got there, he was a model citizen. A car was waiting, and after he got off at his hotel, he sent the car off to the hills with me in it, to go to my aunt Lourdes's house.

A day passed, then another, as I meet all my endless relatives and my father is lying there in the hospital. On the third night, I come to the hospital, and Mr. Reynoso is there. He's checking up on the nurses, the doctors, the care, making sure money isn't the problem. He was doing this very low-key, not playing a big shot. I was touched. When he asked me to go to dinner, I said yes.

That was a mistake. You know how it goes. One thing led to another. I slept with him in his suite at the hotel, and cried all the way home in the limo. I cried over my own weakness. I cried for you. Or to say it more clearly, I cried for us.

Until coming here, I had this idea in my head, you know, not spelled out, not anything I could say to you, but there — that we might be together for a long time. And yet that night I knew I couldn't tell you the truth about what happened with Mr. Reynoso. You might never trust me again. You might think of me as a weak and trivial person. You might throw up your hands and take a walk.

But I also knew something else. There are things about me you don't know. Some of them are very important. I keep them hidden, because I don't know how you would react to them. I'm not ashamed of them. I just don't know if you — if anyone — could understand them. This trip has reminded me that the two of us just might not be a true fit. I don't know, even now, sitting in this fucking cyber cafe at 10:30 on a Saturday night.

I do want to be with you. Forever. When I get home, I'll try to explain everything. All about who I really am. And maybe for once, you'll tell me about yourself. Then we can decide. If it's good-bye, I understand. With all my love, Delfina

Cormac prints out the letter, reads it again, full of a deep, aching sadness. He walks around the rooms, looking at the places where she has been with him, at tables, in bed, on the model's stand, along the packed shelves of books, in the kitchen. He sees her peering into the refrigerator that first night, trying to read his character from juice and water and fruit. And then thinks: Jesus Christ, I love her.

He sits down and writes a reply to her e-mail address, hoping she'll open it somehow and somewhere.

Delfina, mi amor. Received your letter and want you more than ever. Let me know when you are coming back. Bring clothes and appetite, and we'll talk for as long as we need. Much love, C

He speaks out loud in a voice full of amazement and sorrow. "I love her," he says. "I love her."

112.

Tuesday, and a sense of imminence in the air. The sky is gray and bleak. In the streets, there are a few lonesome joggers and dog walkers, engulfed in solitude. Cormac walks to the Battery and back, nodding at the firemen in their ancient house on Liberty Street, passing the old *New York Post* building on West Street where he worked his last shifts on night rewrite. It's a condo now, filled with young businesspeople and students from NYU.

At the Battery, whitecaps rise on the surly harbor. A freighter plods toward the Atlantic. Seagulls move in widening arcs. The sky is a smear, vacant of horsemen. He hears the voice of Mary Morrigan: *Something bad is coming.*

He writes a will. He types a long detailed note to Delfina explaining which books and paintings are valuable. He gives her the name of his lawyer. He explains how to sell what she doesn't want. The note becomes a letter of thirty-six pages. On Tuesday, he goes to the lawyer's office near Foley Square, signs the will, and has the letter attached and sealed, as a kind of codicil.

While copies are being made, Cormac gazes out the window of the lawyer's office. Down on the sidewalk, dressed in black, his arms folded across his chest, is Kongo. He doesn't even try to open the window.

Delfina calls from the airport around eight o'clock on Wednesday night. She sounds drained.

"I want to come to your house," she says. "But it's been a long day. I'm tired and dirty and —"

"Tomorrow night is fine."

"You sure?"

"Absolutely."

"Then come to my house tomorrow night," she says. "I brought some things from the D.R."

"Great."

"And Cormac? Thanks for that e-mail. I know I'm a goddamned fool for telling you anything, but it made me feel better."

He hears his voice lower. "It's great to hear your voice."

A pause. "Yours too."

Twenty minutes later, there's another call. Elizabeth Warren. Cool, but not cold. She tells him she's in Ottawa at a three-day conference.

"But that's not why I called," she says, her voice rising into anger. "I called to tell you what you already know. You're a goddamned thief."

"Let me explain —"

"What can you explain? You're a thief, Cormac. My husband comes home this weekend and I want that sword back on its hook!"

"I'll bring it to Willie myself."

"That's no good."

A wire of hysteria enters her voice.

"My husband owns that sword!"

He lowers his own voice, thinking: Don't argue.

"Elizabeth, those spirals were cut into that blade by my own flesh and blood, back in Ireland," Cormac says. "More than two hundred and fifty years ago. I've been looking for it a long time now. . . ."

"Please, no fairy tales."

"I've been cleaning it, polishing it."

"It's not your property. It's Willie's."

"I know, and I'll return it to him when —"

He hears a sob.

"How could you have done that to me the other night?" A pause. "I trusted you." A longer pause. "I — I said things I would never say to —"

"I know."

"I wanted one simple thing from you. Intimacy. Just that, just simple intimacy, some hope that for an hour or a minute, we —" She stops. "And all you had in mind was theft."

She's right, of course, but he can't explain. He thinks: I can't explain almost anything.

"I'll call you when I get back," she says. "If you don't bring the sword, I'll call the police."

"And the police will call Page Six."

"You're a terrible man," she says.

"I probably am."

* * *

Hunger eats at him now. He feels some remorse for what he has done to Elizabeth Warren, imagines her alone in a hotel room in Canada, imagines her own hunger. He wonders too about Delfina, and whether she was truly so exhausted that she needed a night alone, or whether she has gone somehow to Reynoso's apartment, wherever it is, to perform a proper farewell. The green worm will not leave. In the morning, she will be back at her office on the eighty-fourth floor, performing distance and neutrality. And Cormac thinks: Doubt, once felt, never goes away.

He decides to go out to eat, to escape the house. He brings a copy of *The Decameron* with him, to read at a restaurant table, and breathes deeply of the cool September wind. He walks uptown on Church Street, then cuts over to Varick. The night is damp and warm. SUVs are pulling up to the converted factories of Tribeca, depositing children, dogs, tennis rackets, and worried young couples on the sidewalks. The end of the prolonged Labor Day weekend, two days added to the usual three, or two free days that come with unemployment. The restaurants are filling up, their interiors warm with yellow light. He crosses to Murphy's at North Moore. Away to the south, the Twin Towers are blazing with light, the offices busy with all those people from Japan and England and Canada and India who don't add extra days to the Labor Day weekend. He can't pick out the eighty-fourth floor.

In the bar side of Murphy's, just inside the front door, a Yankee game plays on the television set over the long polished bar, and the Met game is on the set beside the men's room. Cormac likes the place, with its mixture of teamsters, telephone workers, defense attorneys, and artists. Every high-backed stool is full, and at the tables people are talking, laughing, yelling into cell phones. All of them are smoking. He wants to smoke too, and decides to wait at the bar until a table is free; two groups are already drinking coffee. The bar is all dark wood and mirrors and a tiled floor out of the twenties, like a painting by John Sloan. Guinness and Harp flow from copper taps. On each table there's a red carnation in a cut-glass vase. Cormac enjoys the place after the lunch hour, when most people have returned to work and he can read a newspaper in the emptiness and doodle with a crayon on the white paper table coverings. He lights a cigarette, then reaches between two men on stools and orders a Diet Coke. The bartender gives him change from a five-dollar bill. A heavyset man in a denim shirt turns a flushed face to Cormac.

"That shit rots your teeth," he says, a curl of belligerence in his voice.

"Only if you drink more than one a day."

"That right?"

"I read it in the *Post*. It must be true."

"Are you puttin' me on?"

"Why would I do that?"

"You got the kind of face, you like puttin' people on."

Ah, Christ, one of these people. Looking for trouble. One of the ten thousand others Cormac has met across the years.

"I never realized that about my face," he says. Saying to himself: Stop. Watch the ball game. He glances at himself in the mirror. "Looks just like another face to me."

"Yeah — and I'd like to smash it in for you."

The bartender, sad and somber, leans in.

"Cool it, Frankie."

"Guy says he read in the *Post*, your teeth only rot if you drink more than one Diet Coke a day."

"So?"

"It's the way he said it."

"And?"

"I want to smash his face in."

"Cool it, Frankie."

Frankie looks at Cormac again. He has a mean, dead look in his eyes, and purses his lips as if savoring the moment.

"Fuckin' wiseass."

"Sorry," Cormac says, sipping the Diet Coke. Now the owner comes over, a stocky Irish American in his forties. A few people at the tables are looking at them, ignoring the ball games and the jokes. Cormac can hear Tim McCarver's voice analyzing the Yankee game.

"Frankie," the owner says, "maybe you should walk around the block a couple a times. Go over the firehouse and bullshit awhile."

"Yeah, after I cream this cocksucker."

The owner turns to Cormac. "You sure set this idiot off, whatever the fuck you said."

"All I said was —"

Frankie stands up, scraping his stool on the floor, puts his glass on the bar, and whirls. Cormac steps to the side, astonished that it's come to this, and Frankie goes past him, landing on a table with a crash of glasses, ashtrays, plates, and a vase. A woman screams. Blood pumps from Frankie's forehead. People look at Cormac, and he shrugs, raising his eyebrows in a stage version of bafflement. He thinks: This kind of trouble is all I need. Two waiters and the owner heave and haul, trying to get Frankie to his feet. Cormac steps into the small men's room. When he returns, Frankie is holding a towel to his head, while the waiters walk him out the door.

"Jesus, what'd you hit him wit'?" says a plump dark-haired woman, her voice filled with awe. She's wedged into a stool.

"Nothing," Cormac says. "He swung and he missed."

His hand trembles as he lights another cigarette. He realizes that he hasn't had a fight in a saloon in almost sixty years. That is, since the week after Pearl Harbor. Fights in saloons end up in police stations, places he can't afford to visit. He inhales deeply. The smoke is delicious. The bar turns noisy again, the broken glass swept up, the blood mopped away. The customers resume their noise. A cell phone rings, but it isn't Cormac's. The owner comes over.

"Sorry about that," he says. "He's usually pretty harmless, Frankie, as big as he is. Works for Verizon, loves the Mets. But he lost his wife, maybe six weeks now? Two months? Whatever. Anyways, he hasn't been right in the head. They had no kids, except Frankie, and now he's another lost soul. One of the guys is driving him to Saint Vincent's."

"Ah, shit," Cormac says. "I'm sorry."

"Not your fault," the owner says. "You didn't kill his wife. Life did. Hey, have one on me."

"Thanks," Cormac says, and gazes out the window.

Kongo is across the street. He nods, and Cormac leaves his change and hurries to the door.

113.

They embrace on the corner and start walking together toward the river. Kongo is wearing a zipper jacket and jeans, like a million other men in the autumnlike city. Silver is scratched into his hair, and there's a melancholy look in his eyes. His grave voice is deeper, his accent more refined and English. They talk about how much the city has changed since they were young, how their small shared village became the metropolis. Cormac tells Kongo of the image he sometimes sees from the top of a skyscraper: a huge sculpture, thirteen miles long, two miles wide, the island of Manhattan being shaped by a restless unknown hand, a godlike artist who is never satisfied, forever adding elements here, erasing them there, lusting for perfection.

"On the final day," Cormac says, "after due warning to the citizens, the god of New York will lift his creation into the sky. It will be thirteen miles high, its base in the harbor, the ultimate skyscraper."

Kongo laughs.

"You could see *that* New York from Africa, Kongo."

"I've never stopped seeing New York, Cor-mac."

He doesn't explain where he has been, nor does he ask Cormac about his own long life. Kongo inhales the odor of the unseen river, and mentions a river in Gabon that has the same mixture of river and ocean salt. "If you are wounded on its banks," he says, "the salt will heal you." Cormac talks about how he has read his way into Africa through a hundred books, absorbing the narrative of slavery and colonization and the bloody struggle of the twentieth century to be free at last; and how he used to listen to the memories of Africans in New York, and lived to see all memory, African, Irish, Italian, Jewish, German, Polish, English, all memory of injury and insult, all nostalgia for lost places and smashed families, all yearning for the past: saw all of it merge into New York.

"I see it every day," Kongo says.

"It's harder to see if you live it one year at a time," Cormac says. "There's too much of it. Too many faces, too many people, too many deaths and losses."

Kongo looks at him. "I'm an old man too," Kongo says. "Just like you. But one thing I've learned, after all the bloodshed and disease and horror: Forgetting is more important than remembering."

"Yes," Cormac says. "But memory goes on, Kongo. In the end, all men and women say the same thing: I was, therefore I am."

They are at the river now, on a new path cut along the waterfront for joggers and bicycle riders. A pair of lovers huddle on a bench. A wino sleeps on another. There's a bicycle chained to a tree. The river is a glossy ebony bar. Lights twinkle on the distant Jersey shore, close enough to touch, yet beyond distance.

"Your frontier," Kongo says, and chuckles.

"Yes," Cormac says. "The border."

A small yacht moves south toward the harbor, lit up like a child's toy.

"Well, you know why I'm here," Kongo says.

"I think I do."

Kongo leans on a rail, gazing at the darkness.

"You have the sword," he says. "That allows you to settle the affair of your father, to bring it to an end."

"Yes."

"And you've found the woman at last."

"A wonderful woman."

Kongo glances at him, as if trying to decode the sentence. And then goes on.

"When you're finished with the affair of your family," he says, "you must take her to the cave. To the cave where you were given your . . . gift." He speaks like a commander issuing orders, glances at a clock on an old industrial building, then turns back to the river. "You will make love to her in the cave." A pause. "And then you can cross over."

His words are at once a promise and a sentence.

"I'll help get you there," he says. "You've got one week."

They stand in silence for a long time. Then Kongo turns and walks toward the bicycle that is chained to a tree trunk. He turns a key in the lock.

"Wait, Kongo, don't go yet."

"I'm not going. I'll be here in New York."

"There are a hundred things I want to talk about with you," Cormac says.

Kongo shrugs and exhales, as if there's nothing at all he wants to discuss.

"How do I find you?" Cormac says.

"I'll be around," Kongo says in Yoruba. "Don't worry."

He smiles and swings onto the bicycle and pedals away to the north. From the blackness of the unceasing river, Cormac hears a foghorn.

I was, he thinks, therefore I am.

114.

There's an e-mail waiting when he opens the computer the next morning. In this latest edition of the world, e-mail evades the overheard whisper, the visible evidence of flirtation, the eye of the private investigator. Combined with the cell phone, it makes cheating easier, and life more dangerous.

> Cormac: I'm at work, and still have a job. Que sorpresa! Can I come by around 12:15? Can't wait for anything formal. Gotta see you. Love, D

He sends an e-mail back, saying twelve-fifteen is fine, and he'll order sushi. He lights a cigarette, using a saucer for an ashtray.

She arrives at twelve-ten, breathless after walking from the office to Duane Street, a fine film of sweat on her skin. She's smartly dressed in a navy blue business suit, smiling and radiant. Her skin is darker from the sun, and tinged with red. She kisses his cheeks and lips and neck, pushes her belly into his, grasping for buttons and belt. He lifts her out of her shoes. Her skirt falls, her jacket, blouse, and bra. They make writhing, gnashing love on the table. And then fall back into panting languor. They laugh, as if they've gotten away with something.

Then he turns, slides to the floor, goes to the kitchen, and takes the sushi and sashimi from the refrigerator.

Delfina vanishes into the bathroom with her clothes, washes quickly, combs her hair, dresses, returns to sit down to the platter of food, glancing at the clock. No review. No accounting either.

"Buenas tardes, mi amor," she says, and smiles.

"Buenas tardes," he says. Then adds, "How was it?"

Her gaze falls on him, tentative, choosing what she will tell him.

"All right," she says. "Considering."

A smile plays on her face. Away off, he can hear a siren from NYU Downtown pushing through lunchtime traffic.

"I knew it was cancer," she says. "They told me that before I left. But that wasn't why he died. It was everything else. Cigarettes and rum and heroin and cocaine. Like every poor fucked-up musician who ever lived. But it was women too. Always women." A pause. A hesitant smile. "I went to the hospital, and the room looked like a beauty parlor. He was dying, all gray and shrunken up, and all the women came to say good-bye. Fat, skinny, young, old." She chews a piece of maki. "If the cancer didn't kill him, the perfume would've done the job. You'd have thought he was Warren Beatty." She sips green tea and smiles. "I just slipped into the room, stood with my back to a wall. I counted three former wives. And yeah, four young guys came in and out, his sons by different women, but mostly it was women, all staring at him, with the tubes in his arms, and the Virgen de Altagracia above his head."

She has told Cormac about this Virgen, the divine Madonna who intercedes for all Dominicans. Now she is moving into street rhythms, into that language that she dons like a shield. "But it's not just the wives, who are whispering and praying and crying all around the room. It's the whores too. They're showing up from everywhere, and in comes a fat shiny *mulata* chick with four gold teeth and la Virgen tattooed over her left boob, and she's bawling. The nurse — skinny, eyeglasses, white uniform — she goes, 'You gotta leave, *m'hija!*' and the *mulata* chick goes, 'How can I leave? *I'm the only one he ever loved!*'

"The nurse busts out laughing. I mean, every fucking whore in Moca is in the room or out in the hall. And I can't help myself, I start laughing too. My father's dying, but, Jesus . . . The nurse grabs the end of the bed to hold herself up, she's shaking with fucking laughter, and I grab the door frame, and we're both pissing in our pants."

She starts to laugh now, remembering.

"But the whore with the gold teeth looks at us like we're totally insane. She goes, 'What's so funny, you *hijas de putas?* What's so fucking funny?' The sons look at each other, and so do the ex-wives, and I'm waiting for the knife to come out of the whore's panties, and then she looks at my father, as if asking his permission to kill us, and now his eyes are open, and she screams: '*He's alive!* This motherfucker is *alive!*'"

She bends toward Cormac and grips his wrist.

"I mean, he was alive *all along,* but this crazy whore must've thought he was dead, because she spreads her legs and goes down on her knees and starts giving thanks to God. She's got no panties on, so I was wrong about the knife, and now the four sons are looking at her box, which must terrify them — and she goes, '*Oh, thank you, God, you are a great fucking man!*'

"Now the nurse bounces back, screaming in laughter, and knocks me into the wall! I see my father's eyes get wider, and now all the other whores are crowding in from the hall to see what all the hollering is about, and it's like the six train at rush hour. Now a little security guard comes in, gray mustache, big wide eyes, wearing some kind of old UPS uniform — and he starts shouting, 'Out, out! Everybody out!' The fat whore with the gold teeth is still on the floor, surrounded by a wall of boobs and miniskirts, and she goes, 'No, you get out, *pendejo!* This is a fucking *miracle!*'"

Cormac joins her in slamming the table and laughing. Delfina struggles now to breathe, then calms herself.

"And then he sees me."

A pause. She daubs at her eyes with a napkin, wiping away the evidence of laughter.

"He sees me, and he stares at me, and for the first time all of them — the fat whore on the floor, the sons, the nurse, the whole team of other whores and the security guard — they all turn to look at me. Everybody shuts up.

"'Delfina?' my father says. It's the first time since I got there that he said a word.

"I go, 'Sí, Papi.'

"Tears come into his eyes. His fingers curl, long piano-player fingers, calling me to him. I go to his side and take his hand, which is very cold. I lean down close to his ear and say, 'I love you, Papi.'

"His lips move — they're blue in the light — but nothing comes out. I massage his hand with both of mine, trying to make his hand and fingers warm. I put my head next to his mouth. And then I hear the words. The words I came to Moca to hear.

"'*Lo siento,*' he says. I'm sorry."

She chews at her lip and shrugs.

"Then he dies. He takes two more breaths and then nothing. He doesn't look scared, or even relieved. He just stops."

She stops now too for a moment. Her forefinger is curled in the tiny handle of a teacup. Wiggling it.

"The whores scream and wail. The fat whore tries to get up, to rush to my father, but she can't do it, she's too fat. She grabs the leg of a skinny whore like it's a small tree and tries to pull herself up, but the skinny whore gives her a shove back on her knees. Two of the young men go over to help her, each grabbing a foot, so they can peer at the holy of holies, and they roll her over, so she can get some traction. They lift her like she's a manatee they found on a beach. The security guard gives up and walks out, leaving the nurse to control the crowd, and I wish you were with me."

Cormac touches her hand. She turns away, shaking her head slowly.

"The dumb son of a bitch."

A muscle ripples bitterly in her jaw.

"Everybody loved him, but he couldn't love anybody back. Not my mother. Not me. Not himself."

She exhales, gestures with the cup.

"I gotta go back to my job."

Cormac glances at the clock. She has ten minutes to walk to the Trade Center, and mumbles about calling later and picking a time to go to her place. He goes with her to the door. She looks at him.

"It was enough," she says. "*Lo siento* . . . It wasn't 'I love you.' It wasn't even about me. It was about him, and how *he* felt. But what the hell."

115.

That's all there is to the great return. Hair, wetness, food, laughter. Most of all, laughter. And then departure. Staring at the door, Cormac notes that she never once mentioned Reynoso and uttered no words of regret, no request for forgiveness. Cormac smokes a cigarette and wraps the garbage and rinses the plates before stacking them in the dishwasher. He thinks that perhaps this is the style of her generation, common to all who grew pubic hair in the age of AIDS. Don't risk true intimacy (so desired by Elizabeth Warren). Don't delude yourself about love. Death could come at any time, and love would only add to the pain.

The computer might be part of it too, he thinks, allowing them to create little folders inside their brains. Each marked with an icon separate from all others, easy to call up or erase. Even if sometimes they cut and paste. After all, the high-speed printing press changed New Yorkers, adding urgency, fear, envy, even solidarity to their daily lives. It gave them Wordsworth and Homer and the *Evening Graphic,* Buffalo Bill and *Moby-Dick* and Jackie Robinson, gangsters and gun molls and the Death House at Sing Sing. Around 1840, New Yorkers started thinking in words on paper, visible or invisible, and acquired the habit of telling stories, and recycling them, and letting them marinate into myth. Human beings weren't like that before the printing press and the penny paper. Cormac thinks: The computer must be making a similar alteration. Another grand mutation. With any luck, I will not live to see the results.

And yet, for all their differences, and in spite of her silences, he was charged with happiness when Delfina arrived, when he saw her smile, embraced her flesh, ran tip of tongue along the path of her spirals. Making love on a table was comical; but in most cases, in all places, no matter what the position, making love was always comical, in large ways or small. He was sure if she knew the truth about him she would dismiss him as another laughing Irishman with a splinter of ice in his heart.

And on some levels, she'd be right. Cormac hasn't truly loved a woman in many years. He's slept with plenty of women, and had deep affection for some of them. To be exact, nine of them, just like his number. But all of them died. That was the curse attached to the gift: You buried everyone you loved.

And after a while, around the middle of Prohibition, he could no longer feel that sense of deep connection, wordless need, and abundant ease that he thought was love. The armature of love seemed to have worn out. And now, astonishingly, it had returned with Delfina Cintron.

That was surely why he'd said nothing about Reynoso. He didn't want to provoke words that he didn't want to hear. He didn't want to prosecute her for an offense he had committed himself. What he had done with Elizabeth was surely worse than what she had done with Reynoso, and after all, they had no contract, had made no vows to each other. He felt shame about Elizabeth; in her e-mail, Delfina expressed rage at her own weakness. That might be all two human beings can do, after the spasm called *el muertito,* the little death. The cliché is true (Cormac thinks), as clichés are usually true: The flesh is weak; each of us falls to its urgent tyranny. He hopes now that she took at least some small pleasure in the suite in Santo Domingo, was released for a minute or an hour from past and present, felt for ten seconds as one can feel after a sumptuous meal. In the end, what happened down there didn't truly matter. Cormac thinks: I need this young woman. I want her. I love her.

Innocent, with an explanation.

They exchange e-mails. He tells her that on Sunday he celebrates his birthday. She replies that they must celebrate together, at her house. He agrees. She says they will dance. He says he will try.

The sense of imminence returns, a blurry feeling of the end of days. The cleaning woman arrives. Her name is Soledad, and she's from Colombia, from the region of Macondo. She's about fifty and lives in Queens and has been in New York for fourteen years. They talk in Spanish. *Qué tal, señor? Muy bien, Soledad, y usted?* She plays the Spanish station with the old boleros and sings along with them in a plaintive voice. While she vacuums and dusts, Cormac places five thousand dollars in an envelope for her. To be delivered later. He does not know what will happen in the coming days, but if he is truly leaving, he does not want to leave behind some dreadful mess. He would say one kind of farewell the way Bill Tweed did: to help someone else live.

Healey calls.

"Believe this? In ten minutes, I'm heading for the fucking HAMPTONS with this mark! In a limo! He asked me if I played TENNIS and I told him I had a bad back caused by the lack of FUCKING. He laughed, the runt, unable to listen to the truth. He says we can SPITBALL the script out there. . . . For the money he's paying me, I could spitball *KING LEAR!*"

Cormac wishes him luck, urges upon him the slogan of Fiorello La Guardia — patience and fortitude — and asks him to call when he returns.

"We can spend some of this BLOOD money!" Healey says, and hangs up.

Forty minutes later, Elizabeth calls.

"Willie will see you on Monday night," she says. "I told him you were bringing the thing to some expert, for cleaning, that you had some ideas for the newspaper. It's all set. I'll be in Boston, Patrick at some ball game, Willie awaits you. About seven-thirty."

"I'll be there," Cormac says.

"You are a prick," she says, and hangs up.

Cormac glances at the sword, wrapped in a towel. Soledad is upstairs in her own tight and noisy solitude. Cormac wanders to the bookcase and takes down a volume of Dürer drawings. There are the horsemen, the four of them, wielding a pitchfork, a measuring scale, a bow with arrow, and a sword. The man with the sword wears the pointed cap of the fool.

Cormac thinks: Have I seen my last snowfall? My last spring? And have I walked for the final time through a summer afternoon?

Nine

Ever After

I dream'd in a dream, I saw a city invincible to the attacks of
the whole of the rest of the earth;
I dream'd that was the new City of Friends.

— Walt Whitman, "Leaves of Grass," 1891–92

116.

A chill wind blows north on Sunday evening. Cormac leaves the 6 train at 110th Street and walks east. The streets are emptied by the cold. Police cruisers move slowly along the avenue, suburban eyes studying the city profiles. They peer at Cormac too, a white man probably searching for a connection. Before him are tenements, bodegas, a shuttered church. But other images rise from the pavements. He sees the African faces of old comrades. He sees hills that were scraped away. He sees the subway tunnels being chopped out of earth and granite. He thinks: I'm making a long circle home.

He sees an old brown-skinned man staring from the top of a stoop. He doesn't see Cormac. He is staring into the past. A man who was an infant when Cormac was already old. Does the brown-skinned man dream of palm fronds rattling on a tranquil shore? No: Cormac is sure he dreams of a lovely woman who is now long gone.

This morning, as on every ninth of September, he walked to the river to drop a rose into the flowing waters. A rose for his mother. He wonders now if any of his flowers have ever reached the dark Atlantic, where they might catch a current bound for the Irish Sea. No matter, perhaps: With any luck he will see them all soon, in the place of emerald light. He imagines Kongo somewhere in the city, wonders where he sleeps, or if he sleeps at all, wonders where Kongo has been while he has lived his own long life in Manhattan. In this neighborhood, in this East Harlem, here in El Barrio, many people would understand the existence of a babalawo.

Now Cormac arrives in a dark street of darker tenements. The iron calligraphy of fire escapes. Lights glowing beyond curtains. New lampposts with hard bright burning light. Cars jam the curbs. Two men work on a double-parked Chevy, each wearing woolen gloves. A few kids run past hills of stuffed trash bags (where did all the garbage cans go?), darting from one tenement doorway to the next.

Here is the building. Number 378. No stoop. Just a door on street level, with clear glass to reveal anybody waiting in ambush, and then a second door with stairs beyond. Cormac enters the vestibule and sees rows of mailboxes and bells. He rings 4-A. Top floor. A buzz comes back, and he enters with a click. The stairs resemble those of a hundred other tenements that were old the year they were built. A banister scabby with layers of paint, the pentimento of the poor. Walls chipped and painted and dirtied and painted and battered and painted. Up one flight. The joined odors of meals, of sauces and roasts and chicken, seeping through closed doors (as they no longer drift into the streets), along with soundtracks from sit-coms and telenovelas and baseball, and the flooding vowels of Spanish warring with the consonants of English. The word PUTO spray-painted on a wall, and a reply, in a different hand, with an arrow pointing, saying SU NOMBRE.

Another flight. On each landing a sealed door where once a dumbwaiter hung from ropes. Now *dumbwaiter* floats in the Sea of Lost Words. The last flight. A closed green door, with 4-A neatly lettered on its face.

He knocks.

The door opens. He sees no face, no light: a darkness.

And then the sound of a fat wooden stick hitting a block of wood.

Klok-klok, klok-klok-klok.

And the lights explode, and Delfina is standing there, all golden and shining, with her wide white grin, and behind her there's a band, and they smash into the music, four musicians jammed into the kitchen, a man on timbales, an old man with a gourd, a kid bent over a tall conga drum, a bearded young man playing flute, the music loud and full of joy. And from other rooms come smiling men and laughing women, and Cormac sees a table against a wall, heaped with food, and a bucket full of ice and canned beer, and the music drives and now more people are coming in the door with more platters of food, neighbors celebrating a stranger, and Delfina grabs each of his hands and says: "Oye, como va?"

For that's what they're playing; that's the tune the musicians sing, the words full of flirtation and bravado, all of them beaming at the success of the surprise, at Cormac's astonished face, at the many fine women, at the children who start dancing, at the great exuberant release of the music.

And now Delfina takes Cormac and she begins to dance with him. To move him with her hands: a touch, a nudge, a shift of the wrist. And then she adds the staccato of her shoes against the floor, the abrupt bump of a hip. And he surrenders to the music and surrenders to her. His hands come up, and he feels the music in his hips and his waist and his legs, in his shoulders and hands, he feels the music pushing him, driving him, he feels it invade him, he feels himself taking small precise steps in the narrow space of the kitchen, crowded with dancers, feels the music in his bones and in his flesh: he cuts left, then right; he laughs and whirls; and gazes at Delfina, at this golden woman, at her fathomless eyes, at her urgent grin, at her body showing him the way, her body telling him how and where to move, her body telling him when to pause and when to explode, her body setting all the moves.

And then the band finishes and shifts into a bolero and she pulls him close and puts her hands on the back of his neck.

"Happy birthday, *mi amor.*"

He pushes his face through her hair to kiss her skull. He feels her breasts and belly against him, as someone dims the lights, and then Delfina, still dancing, is introducing him to her friends and her neighbors. This is Elba. Mariano. Rosa. Gerson. Meet Cormac. Hey, glad you're here, happy birthday, man. This is José. Marisol. Pancho, a crazy Mexican from the second floor. *Hola, cómo está* . . . This is my friend Cormac. Chucho. María Elena. Doris. Ramona. You better be nice to this girl, man. Yes, Cormac says. *Claro que sí.*

They are dancing in every room of the railroad flat, and Delfina gives him a tour, still dancing with him, leading him, moving him. Hey, meet Miguelito. This is Cormac. My lonesome gringo. The rooms are laid out like those of every other railroad flat in history: first the kitchen, with its table, refrigerator, shelves, and sink, the furniture pushed against walls to make room for the band, the windows open to the night, and a door leading to the bathroom; then two tiny bedrooms, which give way to a living room that overlooks the street, a room filled with a large bed, an armchair, a television set. Four couples are dancing in the open space beside the bed. To the right of the bed is the only room in the flat with a door. The door is closed. Delfina pauses, kisses Cormac on the cheek, but says nothing under the force of the driving merengue that follows the bolero. She makes more introductions, while he puts a map of the flat into his head. The first bedroom holds a desk, computer, and printer, with five or six small Mexican mirrors, a map of Hispaniola, a wall of books. The second bedroom is all books. On the walls above the bookcases there are rows of primitive masks; small tin hands with eyes painted on the palms; framed browning nineteenth-century photographs of bejeweled women and mustached men squinting in the harsh Caribbean light; a poster from the Museo del Barrio for a show of Taíno art. It's a smaller version of Cormac's own eclectic piece of New York. He tells her it's beautiful.

"Hey, it's not much, but it's mine," she says.

More than half the books are in Spanish: histories, treatises, reference books, novels, and poetry.

"I had a friend," she says, leaning close so he can hear over the music, "an old Dominican man who lived on a top floor on 116th Street. He was a schoolteacher back home and an exile for forty-five years. When he died, his grandchildren wanted to throw his books in the garbage. So I rescued them. . . . You know what I really mean: I stole them."

She laughs.

One shelf is packed with books on physics, the legacy of Hunter. Another is jammed with histories of the Dominican Republic, including a few oversize volumes from the nineteenth century, and she points at them in an excited way, tells him how rare they are and how the first editions were lucky to reach three hundred copies, and her excitement reminds Cormac of talks they've had across the summer, scattered over dinners and long evenings together. Then she turns away from the books and pulls him again into the dancing, into the music, into the rising heat of the rooms, into the bumping collisions of bodies, into the drum breaks, and the scratching of gourds, and the sound of vowels: and he is for a moment back in Stone Street, in Hughson's when the Africans played for themselves, when they took Africa into New York to stay; when they joined the Irish in filling their laments with defiant joy.

He takes Delfina Cintron by the hand and dances to the music of her time. And his.

Food becomes feast. A deep covered dish of steamed stringbeans cut lengthwise in a vinaigrette of olive oil and lemon juice. Bowls of moros, black beans, or red beans, to spread wetly on a field of white rice. "Blacks, Indians, and white guys," she says. "Mix 'em all together and you've got me. *Una trigueña.*" Then two kinds of chicken, roasted and boiled, and slices of pork, and *pescado en coco,* red snapper with a coconut milk sauce, reddened with annatto (she explains) and laced with cilantro. On the side, platters of sliced avocado and limes. The band breaks, descends upon the food, and everybody pauses while Benny More sings from the grave on the CD player. Hello. Welcome. Happy birthday. How old are you? Too old. Yeah, like everybody. I hope you're not married, man, or Delfina gonna put you in a river.

Cormac feels pleasured by the small perfections of spice, of taste and texture, the flow of vowels, the humid warmth. Thinking: How many meals have I consumed on this passage? How many as good as this one? And then remembers the Cuban barber: *I star' thinkin' abou' things like that, 'mano, I go nuts.*

Music again from the CD player in the first room off the kitchen: Juan Luis Guerra (Delfina says). Fragments of grief and anger behind the smooth vowels; here, timbales serve as consonants. Then the front door opens, and three kids come in with a birthday cake on a platter, huge and creamy and bearing a single candle. A large beaming brown-skinned woman is behind the kids and the platter, and Delfina directs her to a space on the table and then lights the candle, and then Pancho, the Mexican from the second floor, pushes in with a steel guitar, plays a few notes, and starts to sing "Las Mañanitas," a song as sad as Donegal, a song about all the little mornings of life, and then everyone is singing.

Estas son las mañanitas
Que cantaba el rey David . . .

The emotion fills the room, one woman sobbing, not for Cormac, and not for herself, but for loss itself, for vanished mornings, for years that won't come back. At the end, cheers, and shouts of *vaya!* Cormac bows to Pancho from the second floor and the Mexican smiles and bows back, holding the guitar as if it were the weapon of a glad warrior, the way Bobby Simmons held his alto in homage to Horse Campbell. Then here comes the coffee, the aroma permeating the entire flat, the taste rich and sweet, brewed in a *greca,* sipped from demitasse cups. *Dos cafecitos, corazón*. She tells him it's Café Santo Domingo, but if he wants American coffee, they have that too. Then an immense plate of guava paste and *queso blanco*. And the band playing again, after shots of dark Barcelo rum. Cormac lights a cigarette and Delfina points at an ashtray, where three cigars are smoldering while their smokers dance. He tamps out his own cigarette after a few drags, grabs her, and they dance, Cormac leading her now, moving her body with his, leaving behind his past for this present, for this room, for this woman before him, for all the other joyous dancers. *Cuidado,* man: Don't mistake this for a Happy Nigger scene. No, he answers himself: I know better. His head then fills with images of verandas, tropical foliage, the bougainvillea on a wall in Sargent's watercolors, the wind in Winslow Homer. *Que tropical, señorita.* And white men in white suits unleashing machetes with a nod and a grunt upon the brown necks of Dominicans. Upon the bodies of slaves and

Indians and rebels. The world that sent Delfina here, as remote now as the arctic Irish wind that sent him on his own long voyage to Manhattan's granite shores.

She reaches for his face.

"Why are you crying?" she says.

The band leaves first, bound for another gig, all smiles and carrying away pieces of cake wrapped in napkins, refusing money. Cormac tries to help with the dishes, but Elba and Rosa and Marisol and Doris and María Elena and Ramona push him aside. "It's your birthday, man," says Elba (bony and a bit worn around the eyes). "You just be nice to Delfina, you hear me?"

Delfina comes in from the other rooms with glasses and plates and one of the women (Marisol? Doris?) takes them and washes them and stacks them on a drainer (for there is no dishwasher), while someone else (María Elena?) scours pots and pans and another wraps unfinished dishes with Saran Wrap. "You can eat here for a month," says the woman named Rosa. "Maybe more!"

In the bathroom off the kitchen, the door closed and the guests all gone, Cormac sees lotions and vials and soap, towels and facecloths, all arranged on shelves as neatly as her books. Over the toilet, there's a portrait of Trujillo, the old dictator, with his white pancake makeup and killer's eyes. When Cormac comes out, the women are gone, as if on command, and Delfina is leaning against the opening to the rest of the flat. She has changed into a long high-collared yellow gown. Cotton. A kimono. Her feet in red thong slippers. Nails painted yellow too.

"Thank you," he says in a soft voice.

"You danced."

"I did. Thanks for that too. Maybe most of all."

She says nothing, then flicks off the kitchen lights. The flat is now dark. She takes his hand, and her palm is damp. She leads him through the dark book-lined rooms to the place where she has pitched her bed. In the darkness, he hears her kick off slippers, and he sits on the edge of the bed and unlaces his shoes.

"I want to pray first," she says. "Do you mind?'

"Of course not."

She opens the door to the small room. Slowly. As if revealing something about herself that she fears might frighten him. But he has been here before, at the bottom of an Atlantic slaver, in the vanished streets around the Battery, in the small house of Quaco, in sealed rooms in the Five Points. He has been here with Kongo. He has been here with men and women now dead. For he knows he is in a chapel of the old religion of Africa. Which is like the Old Religion of Ireland, with different names and similar verbs. Here in Tir-na-Nog.

Before them stands a long table made of a door set upon wooden sawhorses. A dark green cloth covers its top, and set upon the cloth are sixteen burning votive candles. In their flickering, ancient light, Cormac sees other things: glasses of water, unlit cigars in ashtrays, a plate of broken chocolate, crackers, a slice of coconut. He counts nine brass bells of different sizes. On the table there are two fetishes. To the left stands a double-edged ax adorned with silvery beads, for Chango, god of fire and thunder, iron and male power. It is set at an angle facing the goddess Oshun. Cormac knows her too: the goddess of water, of rivers and streams and wells. A cool, liquid deity. Tender, healing, yielding, cleansing, free of jealousy and avarice. She is cradled in a yellow wooden boat and adorned with fans, amber beads, cowrie shells like tiny vulvas. She is flanked by a mound of parrot feathers and a wooden mortar and pestle containing smooth black stones, shaped by the lightning. Above Oshun on the wall hangs a machete with a red handle. Oshun wears spiral earrings.

"*Moyuba,*" Delfina says in a supplicant's voice, a Yoruba word that Cormac knows means "I salute you." She lifts one of the bells.

Then she kneels on a straw mat spread before the altar, stretches in her yellow gown, facedown, and rings the bell. Oshun, Cormac thinks. Like Oisin. Or Usheen. Kongo gave me his gods, those words, with his blood; as I gave him mine from the Sacred Grove of Ireland. Delfina rings the bell sixteen times. Then chants:

Olokun, Olokun
Baba Baba, Olokun
Moyuba — Baba Olokun . . .

A submission to the God of Gods, the Owner of the Ocean, the Owner of all Destinies, the god above Chango and Oshun. Above Yahweh and Jesus and Allah, and all the other gods. She must be thanking her god for food and drink and music and dance, and perhaps even the gift of love. When she rises, she turns to Cormac and reaches for him with her hand.

"Don't step on the mat," she says.

"I know."

Then she leads him out of the small chapel and lights a votive candle on a small table beside the bed. He sees a bowl, beads, a jar. She tells him to undress and then she touches a switch. From the far end of the flat, he hears music from the CD player. All drums. A sharp bata drum, and then counterpoint from smaller drums, the toques, like altos playing into and against the baritone of the bata. The rhythm is insistent, caressing, suddenly explosive, then returning to a steady texture, and he surrenders to it.

Delfina opens the buttons of the yellow kimono. There's a slight, ironical smile on her face. She wears a high *collar de mazo* on her neck, like the many-layered necklaces of sculpture from Benin. Cormac knows that there's a bead for each ancestor, and nine strings sewn into a single piece. On each wrist and ankle she wears an *ide* made of amber beads, the color of Oshun. Her *orisha*. Her Santeria guardian angel. The drums are joined by the sounds of shaking gourds filled with gravel or nuts. She climbs on the bed and leans toward Cormac and kisses him.

"I don't want you to cry," she says.

They lie together for a long time, the flesh of her body cooling against his in the dark. They hear a siren somewhere in the night. And from the street, a muted shout, a bottle breaking. Candles still flicker from the chapel of Oshun. She reaches behind her neck and unclips the *collar de mazo*. He kisses her naked neck.

"I have a couple of things to tell you," she says.

"Tell me."

"First? I'm not twenty-eight. I'm thirty-two." Her voice is remote. "I left out four years when I told you the story of my life. The four years I lived in Puerto Rico, in a town called Loiza Aldea. A black town up in the mountains, with jungle all around it, and Oshun living in the rivers. In the old days, *cimarrónes* hid there, escaped slaves, the wild men. I went there with a priest. One of *our* priests. He gave me the tattoos, not some man in the Bronx. I didn't know one day from another, one month from the next." A pause. "But I saw the gods there."

"Why did you come back?"

"He told me to come back. He said he had read my shells, and they said I should go back. He didn't say why. Maybe he didn't know. But when I saw you that first time, I knew why. I could smell the blood of a babalawo from you."

The smell of Kongo.

"Mi Chango," she whispers with affection, and a hint of irony, and then chuckles.

Their breathing merges in the darkness.

"You said there were two things you had to tell me. What's the other one?"

She's silent for a long moment, then exhales softly.

"I'm pregnant," she says.

117.

In the morning, leaving her to dress for her downtown job, he goes to the street, his head swirling. He lights a cigarette, trying to steady himself, to focus. He sees kids playing, and traffic thickening, as cars peel off the FDR drive into the streets, coming in from the Bronx and Long Island, pushing for passage. A boy of ten or eleven pitches a pink rubber spaldeen hard against a box painted on a factory wall. He uses a complete windup, mixing Roger Clemens with El Duque Hernandez. He throws one strike after another. A thickset woman in a yellow dress turns a corner pushing a child in a stroller, her eyes puffy with morning or the loss of sleep. She has a blue sweater over her shoulders and pulls it tighter with a free hand. Autumn is coming now.

Cormac feels a heaviness rising in him. It's as if too many events are pushing for his attention and combining to block all focus: the party, the musicians, the women, the food, the dancing, and his yearning to live in a crowded, intimate world. The heaviest presence of all is Delfina. And the creature she says she is carrying. Could this be true? They talked and talked, and she is certain that the boy — she knows it is a boy — could not be from Reynoso, she made certain, and there has been nobody else except Cormac. He did not ask her any of these questions. She raised the subject, blurting it out to him, her voice trembling with emotion, swearing on Oshun. The words coming in a rush: *I lied about my age, yes, but every woman lies about her age. This I can't lie about.* She saw a doctor in the Dominican, just to be sure, but never thought for ten seconds of staying for an abortion. *I want this child because I've already lost one, do you understand me?* Yes, he said to her, I understand, I do understand. I do. And she said, fiercely: *I want this boy.*

He walks now toward the Lexington Avenue subway and tries to remember Delfina's words and what he said to her in reply and what he thought and didn't say. A lifetime of caution still caged him; he promised her nothing, neither marriage nor money nor the best doctors. He could speak none of the oily clichés, none of the plastic language of paternal joy. Five thousand movies and a hundred thousand television commercials have robbed those words of meaning. He knew he would take care of her, would make her richer than she could imagine, but he couldn't say that, couldn't bring those words to her like a gift, and she wasn't demanding them. She asked him for nothing. Not even love.

Which made him love her more. He loved her toughness. He loved the way she faced the world.

And as he reaches the subway, he asks himself again: How can this be? He feels in his bones that it is true. Everything is now altered by the arrival of a life. All plans. All old vows. The end of the Warren line. The journey to the cave and the passing into the Otherworld. The sense of time too. All changed. His blood will live on, no matter what happens in the next forty-eight hours. *How can this be?*

Kongo will know. Of course. When Kongo returned to the city, Cormac thinks, something must have changed. He must have seen something in me. Or in Delfina. Or in this big scary heartbreaking piece of the world. He must be here as a messenger.

Yes: Kongo will know.

He hears a woman's voice, sibilant and tough, speaking under the roll of music: *You better be nice to this girl, man.*

118.

At 7:30 on Monday evening Cormac left Duane Street for the home of William Hancock Warren. There was no passion in his movements, no tingling anticipation, no feeling that he was rising out of a trench to confront the enemy. He was going uptown to fulfill an ancient contract, its terms set many years before and remembered now in the voices of Mary Morrigan and his father. He had an appointment to keep, the day and hour set by Elizabeth, but an appointment that could fulfill an old vow. In the morning Warren had called to confirm. We'll have to rough it, he said on the phone, his voice waxy with the effort at good cheer. Everybody will be gone, he explained. Even Elizabeth, who's off somewhere for a few days.

"We can send out for pizza," Warren said, and laughed. "And by the way, bring me back my bloody sword."

* * *

The rest of Monday morning had been spent on final things. The news from Delfina moved in and out of him, swinging back and forth. *A child. Absurd. Too strange.* He cleaned the loft while listening to Prokofiev's Fifth Symphony and the CD of Charlie Parker with strings, and an album of Spanish monks singing Gregorian chant. The music of farewell. *I won't even see this child.* He dusted the bookshelves. He tied up all the newspapers, his eyes weary of the shrapnel of the world beyond New York. Killings on the West Bank. Assaults in Belfast. The endless violence of believers. *Won't hear him squalling.* He carried two roped bundles down to the bin at the back of the ground floor. *Where is Kongo? What will he tell me about the child?* For lunch, he ate a bowl of yogurt filled with grapes, sliced papaya, and mango, and then emptied the refrigerator.

Safe in Delfina's womb, right down there, seven blocks south, at a desk on the eighty-fourth floor. Listen, son. Pay close attention. I made a vow to my father, and I must keep it, or live in damnation. *Everything truly serious is absurd.* He called Delfina. Just to hear her voice. And got her recorded voice, with its curl of a Spanish accent, explaining she was away from her desk, please leave a message. "It's me," Cormac said. "I love you."

Around four, he walked down to Chambers Street under an iron-colored sky. Can I look at this world from the Otherworld? Can I see the boy learn to walk? Three Africans were emptying a truck outside a Big Sale shop named Great Expectations (how Dickens would have embraced them), talking in the percussive rhythms of Ashanti. Cormac couldn't make out all the words and wished they were speaking in Yoruba, but the subject seemed to be soccer. *I won't see him run.*

He bought some things he needed from an Indian shopkeeper, and then went into a Korean deli on the corner of Church Street. He bought a black coffee and then stepped outside and stood beside a pay phone, using its back wall to shield him from the river wind. He lit a cigarette. The view down Church Street was as always: the post office, the towers in gray fog, all lights burning. He wanted to be in Mary's with Healey, hearing his booming voice, but Mary's was closed now forever, and he hadn't been able to find Healey since his expedition to the Hamptons. He might still be there. He might be lashed to a bed in a hospital, lost on Long Island, cursing fate and Hollywood. Cormac thought: Where are the morning sirens who called us sweetheart? Healey's my last friend. The only friend in the great dense city. I couldn't bear to bury another.

Time was racing in him now, the way it did when he would meet deadlines on the newspapers. Decade after decade. One deadline tonight, at Warren's house. Another deadline tomorrow night, in a cave in Inwood. He might never see Healey again. He would never see the waitresses again. Nor would he see faces like these, passing him on the street: the high cheekbones and flared nose of this elegant high-hipped black woman hurrying downtown toward the post office or the World Trade Center; the gullied skin of the Puerto Rican man with the worried face and gray mustache, angling through traffic to the coffee shop across the street; the slack jaw of the teenage hip-hopper shambling along in his suit of polyester armor. *Never see the boy become a man.* He tried sketching the faces in his mind, drawing on old habit, using his eyelids like the shutter of a camera, freezing a moment: the Asian woman wrapped in solitary thought as she came out of a watch shop; the panicky glance of a heavy black woman whose three-year-old had jerked free of her grip. *Never hear him talk about the Count of Monte Cristo.*

And here's a white rummy in filthy clothes spewing a personal jumble of words as if looking for directions to a mission that no longer exists. Take a left, Cormac instructs him from the side of the phone booth. Go up past Broadway and make another left. You'll be in the Five Points then, old man. You'll be in the Bloody Ould Sixth. They'll know you there. Someone will give you succor.

There is harm in the world, son. There's evil. There's whiskey. There's smack and crack and too much heartbreak. There's violence. Listen to me, son.

And then he thought: If I do what I need to do tonight, I'll see her on Tuesday evening. Then I'll try to explain why I've killed a man named Warren. I'll tell her that he's the man in all the morning newspapers, on television, on radio. That man.

William Hancock Warren. Then I'll take her to the north, to my farewell in the cave that gave me too much life, and tell her all of the truth. The least I can do: the truth. About who I am. All of it. While swearing to her that Usheen and Oshun will bring us once more together, forever.

He imagined her at this very moment, coming back from lunch, smiling, radiant, possessing her secret, walking between desks in her new suit from Century 21, women pleased with her, or envious, and men watching her with hungry eyes. *But you can deal with it, son. You can deal with anything the world throws at you.*

He stepped into the booth and called Healey.

"This is Healey," the recorded voice said. "I am out of TOWN. With any luck, I will rob a BANK before I come home. If you leave a MESSAGE, I will call you BACK from the penitentiary!"

Cormac laughed and left a message: "Make sure it's a big bank."

He dropped the empty coffee cup in a trash bin and started walking home. Rain was predicted on New York 1, and they were never wrong. In a corner store, he bought a small bag of jellybeans, tiny, glistening, and delicious, one of the marvels of a long life. His sweet tooth had cost him many hours in a dentist's chair, but he'd never gotten fat. Too much walking with Wordsworth in his head. Or (he thought) one more eerie mutation of my metabolism. A pregnant woman walked into the candy store as he was walking out. She was ochre-colored, with tired eyes above high cheekbones. He thought: Will her daughter ever know my son? *You're free to wander the whole wide world, son. Do it. See Paris and Rome and Florence. See Tokyo and Samarkand. Roam deserts and jungles. Sleep in an Irish meadow. Climb the Matterhorn. Go. Do what I could never do. Your mother will keep you safe.*

He turned on Duane Street. Kongo was waiting in front of his building.

He wore a dark green corduroy jacket, a black turtleneck, and jeans. His brown boots were polished to a high sheen. His hands were jammed into his pockets. When he smiled, Cormac realized how much he looked like Michael Jordan. The true messenger of Chango.

"Good afternoon," he said, as they embraced. "I just wanted to make certain all was ready."

"All is ready."

They talked about the coming night and where they would meet after Cormac's appointment with Warren.

"It will be a cold night," Kongo said.

"With rain, says the weather report."

"Yes, with rain."

They stood for a long moment without speaking, while cars and taxis honked for passage, the street blocked by a wide truck holding a construction crane. Kongo smiled.

"The woman is pregnant," Cormac said. "With my child."

Kongo looked at him in a severe way.

"I know," he said.

"It's unfair."

"Think of it as another gift."

"But why *now?* Why after all the other women . . ."

"The time was right."

Cormac thought: God damn you.

"You made it happen, didn't you?"

"No, you made it happen and she made it happen." He looked toward the river. "It was a sign that I must come and help you cross."

"And leave the child behind me?"

He touched Cormac's arm.

"Don't worry about the child," he said. "The gods will watch over him."

He smiled, raised an open palm, then walked away toward the waterfront. To the flowing waters. To the abode of Oshun.

When Cormac entered the loft, there was a recorded message from Healey:

"Brother O'Connor, it's me. I'm in the city of Lost Angels. My idiot producer was so excited over our spitballing, he ordered a private jet. He says it's perfect for REDFORD, and this kid named DiCAPRIO, and some young blond chick with a belly button. He's gonna pay me a SHITPOT of money to turn it into a movie. Believe this? I'm in some hotel, the Tarantula Arms with room service, and I got some insane real estate lady in the lobby, looks like Carol Channing; shit, maybe she IS Carol Channing. She's taking me to see some apartment she says is PERFECT. Probably in a nursing home. Sorry I missed you, amigo. I'll call when I know where the FUCK I am!"

He was always Healey, and Cormac was relieved, knowing he was safe. He sat down and wrote him a letter. He would ask Delfina to mail it on Wednesday.

He went to the bedroom and took a long nap, full of poisonous dreams. And then he dressed for his appointment with William Hancock Warren. One final uptown ride on the Lexington Avenue subway. One final trip back home. The sword was inside a long black Chambers Street backpack, the kind made for camping.

119.

In the lobby of Warren's building, the sour doorman looks at Cormac, takes his name, calls the Warren apartment. Then he grunts his dubious approval. Cormac feels his heart and blood racing. When he reaches the penthouse, Patrick is standing in the open door. Cormac thinks: Shit, he isn't supposed to be here.

"Evening, Mister O'Connor," he says.

"Hello, Patrick."

"Would you like to leave your — the pack, sir?"

"No, I have something in it for Mister Warren."

"Very well. A drink?"

"Just water."

Warren is standing near the fireplace when Cormac enters the downstairs living room. A large chunky log burns in the hearth. Cormac thinks: When I'm finished here, I'll leave by the Western door, as in Ireland long ago. The door reserved for the dead. With me, I'll take the fire out of the hearth. Warren reaches out a sweaty hand and Cormac shakes it. He wears a long-sleeved Brooks Brothers dress shirt, pale blue, the cuffs folded up, stains in the armpits. He glances at the backpack.

"You going camping?" he says.

"No, I've brought you something that would look strange on the subway."

He opens the zippers and takes out the sword, which is wrapped in a blue towel. Cormac removes the towel in a ceremonial way and shows Warren the sword. His eyes widen and he leans forward.

"My God," he says. "It's beautiful."

"'Tis."

Cormac offers him the handle and Warren grips it, turns the sword to examine the blade and tip, and then squints at the etched spirals. Holding the sword, he stares at Cormac for a beat.

"Your fellow did a fine job."

Cormac thinks: The fine job was done by the man who made it.

"He says it was almost certainly made in Ireland in the eighteenth century. By a blacksmith, not an armorer. It could be worth almost anything, depending upon the desire of the buyer. The spirals are Celtic. They're symbols of immortality."

With a kind of reverence, Warren lays the sword on the polished top of a captain's table and sits down in an armchair. Cormac sits facing him. The sword points north.

"Thank you, Cormac, for seeing what I didn't see," he says. "I bought it, oh, ten years ago, in a junk shop in Rhinebeck. Hanging in a mess of cobwebs. The owner had no — what is the word? No *provenance*. No history of the sword. He thought it was made around the time of the Revolution but didn't really know. I had been collecting other swords, in England, in France, thinking someday I might have time to become an expert, and the size of this one — well, it just seemed to fit with the others."

Warren sees a piece of decoration or a hobby for old age. Cormac sees the sweat on his father's brow as he worked at the forge.

"It was good of you to do this, Cormac." A small smile. "Of course, you could have just *asked* me for it. You didn't need to steal it while my wife was asleep."

So she told him everything, Cormac thinks. And here he is, still mad for her. Or so it seems.

Patrick comes in with a tumbler of water on a tray, ice in a cup on the side. Cormac glances at the fake Sargent portrait of Elizabeth Warren and hears her say the word "intimacy," the name of a place as far from her as Jupiter.

"Would you like the food now, sir, or —"

"Now, Patrick. That would be fine."

Patrick bows and goes out. *If I kill Warren first, Patrick might hear, might call the police, or race to the street . . .* Now it's Warren's turn to glance at the portrait of his wife, as if he has noticed where Cormac's eyes had drifted. He takes a deep breath, then exhales. Cormac feels shame seeping from him.

"The sword is one thing, Cormac," Warren says. "But I want to discuss something personal with you. Personal, and painful."

"And I with you."

For a second, Warren looks as if they are thinking of the same subject. Then he smiles in an uncertain way. His hands find each other, the fingers opening and closing. The sword is within Cormac's reach.

"In that case, I'll go first," he says. "It's about my wife."

"Yes?"

He exhales. "First, a confession. Many weeks ago, I put a private detective on your trail." He shrugs as if this were a ludicrous decision. Then smiles. "I simply wanted to know who you were. Elizabeth was very impressed with you, with your interests, your way of speaking, your good looks. From the moment she met you at the Met, and more so after our dinner party . . . So I wanted to know more. Were you married? Or gay? Were you some kind of con man, the sort of predator that always hangs around museum openings with a slick line of bullshit? I wanted to know. I don't ever want Elizabeth to be hurt. Emotionally or physically."

He does love her, Cormac thinks. That he does.

"The private detective did discover something very interesting: You don't exist. You don't have a driver's license. You don't use credit cards. You don't pay taxes, at least not under the name of Cormac O'Connor. You don't vote, or subscribe to magazines. You live in a building downtown. He followed you there one night, but your name is not on the bell, or on a lease. And you do have a girlfriend. A beautiful young Latin woman who lives in East Harlem. Otherwise, nothing, nada, zilch."

"Sorry to have been such an inconvenience."

"But here you are, sitting in my living room."

Cormac stares at him. "And why were you *really* on my trail?"

Warren inhales deeply, then exhales slowly, and says, as if uttering a confession, "Because I want you to become my wife's lover."

Cormac smothers a smile. It's absurd. A moment from a daytime soap opera. On cue, Patrick enters with a tray: a small pizza sliced in quarters, plates and silverware and napkins, salt and pepper. Cormac moves the sword to his side of the captain's table. Patrick places the tray on the table. Bows slightly.

"That will be all, Patrick," Warren says. "You're going out, am I right? Well, we can clean up. See you in the morning."

"Good night, sir. Good night, Mister O'Connor."

He leaves, the door clicking shut behind him. Warren's hands knead each other. He stares at Cormac, then looks at the pizza.

"Are you shocked that I'd want you to make love to my wife? Or that I suspect you already have? Or that I still want you to take up with her?"

Too many words. The daytime audience would now go to the refrigerator. But Cormac can feel anguish in those words. His hand trembles as he lifts a slice and lays it on his plate.

"No, I'm not shocked," Cormac says. "The heart has its reasons. . . ."

Warren smiles in a knowing way. He trims the point off the triangle of pizza. Spears it with a fork. Cormac does the same.

"So you see, your blank résumé doesn't bother me," he says. "It's actually a plus." A pause. "If I can't find you, can't prove you exist, then how can Page Six?" He chuckles, and then his face goes grayer and more troubled. "You see, I have a problem. I can't, uh — well, let's say, I can't . . ."

He doesn't finish and starts chewing his small wedge of pizza. Not looking at Cormac. Not looking at anything.

"I have a problem," he goes on, the voice waxier now. "I love my wife. I think she loves me. But we can't give each other what we need. I need other women. Don't ask me why, because I don't know. I do know that I must have her in my life, even if we have no children, even if we have to create a public image, a double mask, that's different from our private lives. The fact is, I need her. And she needs a man who can give her what I can't. If I had to name that thing, it would be intimacy."

Her word fills the air as Warren shrugs his shoulders hopelessly, and Cormac feels pity again make its treacherous move, as it did with the man's wife. For Warren, this conversation might be worse punishment than any swipe with a sword.

"So I want you to know that I don't mind if you, if she — if she takes a lover and that lover is you. I don't really mean lover. That's the euphemism. I mean if she has me for love and you for sex. I told her this. Told her that all I would ask is discretion, which I would guarantee in my own life with her. She could find a small apartment, in a building without a snoopy doorman or nosy neighbors. You could still love your girlfriend as I love Elizabeth. There would be certain, uh, material compensations for you. At the newspaper, where I'm known as a generous boss. But with my wife, it could be . . ."

Cormac thinks: The rich are all like this, God damn them. Even the best of them. From the end of the Revolution until now, they've been certain that money can provide the solution to every human imperfection. The men have whores or mistresses. The women find other cocks. I know: Across the years, I've provided my own share of these services.

Now sweat is blistering Warren's brow and he tamps at it with a napkin. His voice trails off. He chews a second portion of pizza, looking defeated and sad. He stares at the portrait.

"She's a beautiful woman," Cormac says.

"And a beautiful person."

"I'm sure," Cormac says.

Warren chews another bite of pizza while Cormac now uses his hand to lift a full slice. It's very good pizza.

"I do have my fears," Warren said. "I just don't know you, can't find a line in your life that makes sense. You understand?"

"I do understand," he said. "And I'm afraid I can't do it, Mister Warren."

Warren stares at Cormac, looking as if he realizes he has blundered.

"I'm sorry if I offended you."

Fuck you, pal.

Cormac says, "I'm leaving on a long trip."

Warren struggles to control the anger of a man accustomed to buying what he wants.

"I wish you would reconsider."

"It's a wonderful offer, Mister Warren. To take your money and fuck your wife. But I have other things to do."

Warren stands up angrily. Cormac remains seated and lays a pizza crust on the plate.

"You can leave now," Warren says, jerking a thumb at the door. "And you can take the pizza, if you like."

Cormac reaches for the pizza but picks up the sword.

"Sit down," he says, tapping the tip of the sword on the table. For the first time, Warren looks afraid.

"I want to tell you a little story," Cormac says.

Warren sits down heavily, his eyes moving to the door, to Cormac, to the sword. A nerve twitches in his cheek.

"Once upon a time, almost three centuries ago in the north of Ireland, there was a boy who lived with his parents, their horse, and their dog," Cormac begins. "The mother was dark-eyed and beautiful, a descendant of the daughters of Noah, a secret Jew among masked Christians. The boy's father wore a mask too. He was Irish, not Christian, and his allegiance was to the old gods. He made this sword."

Cormac raises the sword, admiring its beauty. Warren's eyes don't blink.

"But in this part of Ireland there lived a man named the Earl of Warren. . . ."

Warren squints now.

"There also lived a woman named Rebecca Carson, whose real name was Rebecca O'Connor," Cormac says. "She was killed by a coach belonging to the earl. She was crushed by its wheels and died in the mud of Ireland. Her son was raised by his father, a man called John Carson, whose real name was Fergus O'Connor. The false names were necessary because they were Irish, and suspected of being Catholics, which they were not. The boy loved his father more than life itself."

"The earl was my ancestor?" Warren said quietly.

"Yes. He made money in the slave trade and entertained his friends by juggling. Smiling, laughing, proud of his skill. And one day, on a frozen road in Ireland, he confronted the boy's father over a horse. He wanted the horse, whose name was Thunder, and the boy's father resisted. One of the earl's men shot him dead."

Warren's brow creased. He had obviously never heard this part of the Warren family saga.

"And what happened to the boy?"

"The boy escaped."

"And then . . . ?"

"And then followed the earl to America."

"Where he killed him?"

"With this sword."

Warren listens intently, elbows on knees, chin supported by thumbs. There's a long silence. They hear distant thunder, a whisper of rain.

"I know some of that story," Warren says in a sober voice. "Family legend and all that. Nobody ever found the earl's body."

"It's out there," Cormac says, pointing the sword west. "In the river."

"An obvious question," Warren says. "How do you know?"

"I'm the boy."

* * *

Warren's eyes blink. Then he laughs.

"What a marvelous story," he says.

"It's not just a story," Cormac says. "It's history."

Warren stares at Cormac as if he were a madman. His eyes move from Cormac's face to the sword.

"But that was almost three *centuries* ago."

"I know. I know better than you do."

Warren stands, and so does Cormac, who holds the sword at his side. Warren jams his hands in his pockets.

"Would you like a brandy? The bloody pizza is cold."

"No, thanks."

He eyes the sword again. Now he squints, his eyes cold and clear.

"You came here to kill me, didn't you?"

"Yes."

"That would be truly stupid."

"But necessary. At least to me."

At the small wheeled bar Warren pours a brandy for himself, his hands trembling.

"Well, if you're going to do it, can we go out to the terrace? Elizabeth would be very upset if there was blood all over the rug."

Cormac thinks: God damn it, Warren. Stop making this harder than it will be. Warren drains the brandy, pours another. Then walks to the door opening out on the lower terrace. Cormac follows, holding the sword at the present-arms position. There's a spray of rain, a rising wind. The shrubs flutter in their pots. All is dark in the west.

"You know," Warren says, gazing out at the rain-lashed city, "when I invited you here tonight, I thought part of me would die. The part that involved pride. I knew that when I asked you to . . . to give Elizabeth what she needs, that I would be stripping myself naked. So be it. Life is strange." He lets the rain spray his face and shoulders. "It never occurred to me that I could end up a corpse." He laughs. "Over some ancient relative." He turns to Cormac. "Or that I would meet a man who thinks he has lived since the eighteenth century. Jesus Christ . . . But now, right here, right now, part of me thinks, Well, fuck it, why not? Why not just die *now,* instead of crumbling into some fleshy ruin. Besides, we'd sell a ton of newspapers, wouldn't we? PUBLISHER SLAIN IN PENTHOUSE MYSTERY. No, that's too many words. How about BOSS DEAD, with an exclamation point?"

He drains the brandy and drops the glass among the potted plants.

"I don't have a clue about you, old sport," he says. "You're just another New York demento, as far as I can tell. . . ."

He sighs. "So go ahead," he says. "Just do it."

Cormac is facing him, seeing his head and shoulders silhouetted against the rain-smeared glow of distant lights. The sword feels heavy. He spreads his feet, prepared to strike.

"Just do me one favor," Warren says. "When the deed is done, please tell Elizabeth that I loved her. Somewhere out there, beside the telephone, you'll find the number of her hotel. . . ."

And Cormac feels something dissipating in his heart: the hard knot of the past. The fingers of his free hand open and close and he longs to sit at a piano. I can't do this. To hell with the past.

"You can call her yourself," Cormac says.

The tension seeps out of William Hancock Warren. He leans on the rail. Cormac turns and goes back inside, with Warren behind him.

"That's it?" Warren says.

"I'll be going now," Cormac says. "Please don't call the police."

"And have what: a tabloid scandal?"

Cormac smiles. Warren stands there looking at him, his hair and shirt wet from the rain. The fire is guttering in the hearth. The smoke rises slowly, as if it contained all the hatred, all the old vows of revenge, all the unburied dead that Cormac has carried across the decades. They walk to the door and Cormac lifts his black bag.

"Take the sword with you," Warren says. "I don't want it around here."

"I never thought about leaving it," Cormac says. "My father made it in his forge."

120.

He comes out on Fifth Avenue and feels that he is rising into the air. The bag is slung on his back. His feet are moving on the sidewalk. Taxis move south, their wheels making a tearing sound on the wet pavement. But he feels lifted, weightless, floating. He has failed to keep his vow but now feels released from its long burden. There is no blood on the sword. There is no corpse on a living room floor. On this rainy Monday night, there is no need for flight.

And now he hears drums. He looks for Kongo but does not see him, and yet the drums pull him north. He crosses to the park side, under the dripping black trees. Ahead are the bright lights of the Metropolitan Museum. He hears the bata. He hears the toques. Somewhere, a dog is barking.

Then he sees them high on the steps: three musicians. Two on drums, one playing flute. They are together out of the rain, playing for the empty world. He floats up the stairs. The musicians are young but seem older than the city. The bata player has bandages on three of his fingers, the sleeves of his jacket rolled up, his black forearms laced with muscle. The man supplying the toques is short and squat, like a fire hydrant. The flute player is tall, lean, with a hawk nose and jet-black beard. His gleaming skin is the color of coffee. The drummers are singing in Yoruba, slyly invoking Chango. Asking for his intercession. Smiling. Celebrating. Asking Chango to bless them with women, to bless this great city, to bless this cold world.

The drummers play without pause. The flutist rises high above the drums, telling five thousand stories at once, filling the night with lost women, with laughing children, with the sigh of tropical winds.

Cormac puts down the backpack with its hidden sword. He steps forward, feeling the rain on his face, letting the drums enter his body, his arms and legs and belly and balls, and a drummer shouts, "*Vaya!*" and Cormac Samuel O'Connor begins to dance.

121.

In the morning, Duane Street glows with the rising sun. At ten after eight, Cormac goes out for the tabloids, passing volunteers on Broadway handing out leaflets for the primary election. He has never voted in an election because that would have left a trail, an identity, proof of his presence in the world, but he loves the intense faces of the few people heading for the polls. They care about this process, which took so long to turn from promise into fact. He remembers the ward heelers reporting to Bill Tweed's office, and the way Hugh Mulligan's shoulder hitters roamed the streets near here, bumping people away from the polls or delivering others to vote for the third time in an hour. If he had registered under some name, any name, and used his address on Duane Street, voting year after year, decade after decade, Willie Warren's private detective would have found him on some computer weeks ago, and warned off Warren, who would have closed the door against him (too mysterious, too uncertain), and he would never have faced that baffled man with a sword in his hand.

He wonders now what happened after he left Warren the night before. Did he open another bottle? Did he consult some family history where the earl still lived in a line engraving? He probably did call Elizabeth. He probably did tell her that he loved her. Cormac feels that none of the aftermath matters. He only needs this day, this evening, this night.

There's a long line at the Korean deli for bagels and coffee, as courthouse guards and a few stray policemen carry away their breakfasts. The tabloids are full of politics. Cormac glances without interest at the headlines and walks back home under a sky scrubbed blue by the night's rain. On the corner of Worth Street, parents and kids wait for a school bus. He wonders if Delfina will wait some morning on this corner too, gripping a boy's hand. He calls her with the cell phone, but there is no answer at home, and her own cell phone is shut down. He leaves a message on her voice mail at Reynoso & Ryan. He's certain that she's in the subway, heading for work.

At home, he sips coffee, chews the bagel, and scans the newspapers. His mind shifts from release to weariness. He glances at the sword and then whispers a few words asking his father to forgive him. He was to pursue the Warrens to the end of the line, and instead had chosen mercy over vengeance. Please, he says to his unseen father, understand that I am sick of killing. I'm sick of revenge. If that should bar me from the Otherworld, so be it. I can't kill again. I can't kill a man I actually like. Forgive me, he says, I hope I will see you very soon.

Tonight I'll meet Delfina and travel north, driven by another script from the eighteenth century. I have failed to keep one eighteenth-century vow, but perhaps it will not matter. Perhaps pity and mercy will count in any verdict about entrance to the Otherworld. With any luck, tonight I might be released.

He glances through the skylight and decides to finish his coffee under the cobalt sky. The day is glittering and lovely. With any luck, he can inhale the sky itself. He climbs the stairs and opens the door that leads to the roof.

He stands there for a long time, breathing the clean morning air. The fresh sparkling air of the world. The wind that is blowing from the north and making dazzling horizontals of the flags. The air of a city built on rivers and the sea.

Then he hears the sound of an engine. He turns right, smothering a yawn, and sees a jetliner moving south above the river. Coming very fast toward the North Tower. An airplane that looks black against the brightness of morning. Moving on Delfina. And their unborn son. Roaring straight at the tower. Small and black and flying with purpose.

"You fucking idiot!" Cormac shouts into the wind. "Turn! *Turn!*"

As it smashes brutally into the north face of the tower.

He runs down Church Street, punching buttons on the cell phone, shouting into its deadness, gazing up at the streaming black smoke. The smoke is billowing violently now, trailing south in the hard wind, a long dark diagonal that throws immense black faces against the sky, and gigantic black horses. At Park Place, he can see orange flames erupting from a high floor. What floor? The eighty-fourth floor? He can't tell, can't pause to count. If the tower is one hundred and ten stories, it would be easier to count from the top down. How many stories? Can't tell. Some kind of facade is in the way. A steel grille he's never noticed. And what if the plane crashed below the eighty-fourth floor? Could she get down? Can she reach the roof? Can helicopters lift people to safety?

The television antenna on the roof now looks like a standard without a flag. The stream of smoke is moving to the Narrows, over the Verrazano, moving remorselessly south. Sirens split the air. The sounds of Mayday. The soundtrack of emergency. Police cruisers, fire engines, ambulances. Hundreds of coatless people are running north, waved on by policemen, their faces stunned and blank, while others run east and south. High above the street, sheets of paper move gently in the blackening air, like snowflakes. Again, Cormac dials Delfina's cell phone. Gets a whining sound. Dials again. Gets nothing. Dials his own number on Duane Street. Nothing.

At the corner of Vesey Street the giant wheel of an airliner lies on its side, four feet high, its housing ripped and torn and scorched. Beside it is the body of a heavy black woman, blood flowing from a hole in her head, and an ambulance crew works frantically to save her. Newspaper photographers are leaping from cars, green press cards flapping from chains, looking down at the black woman, up at the burning North Tower, shooting and shooting and shooting. The smoke is streaming, while atomized glass rains down from the smoke. Cops bark orders. Dozens of firemen trudge into the lobby of the North Tower. A cop shoves Cormac back, shouting: "Get the fuck *out* of here. *Now!*"

And then he hears the sound of another airliner, roaring from the south, unseen behind the North Tower. Everyone around him looks up too: cops, firemen, ambulance drivers, newspaper photographers, civilians rushing out of the North Tower. Sirens screaming. They sense that the second airliner is following the streaming smoke as if it were a beacon. Then, for a fraction of a second, they glimpse it: small, black, looking puny as a wasp as it aims itself at the South Tower.

Lower than the first. A woman screams. Then another. Then a black man beside Cormac says, "Oh, shit, man."

The world freezes.

Cormac feels all of time leave him.

And then the second airliner smashes into the South Tower with a ferocious orange explosion. Cormac can't move. Burning fuel erupts from three sides of the tower, a third of the way down from the roof. In a kind of erupting orange counterpoint to the streaming black smoke of the North Tower. As if this pilot were trumping the first. And Cormac knows, along with everyone else, that this is no accident. Knows it's not some spectacular replay of the plane that crashed through fog into the Empire State Building in 1945. Knows that both planes have been aimed at the towers like missiles. Knows that the madmen are here. Knows without thinking that they've come from across the planet, from blasted deserts, from the ruins of Acre, from the road to Medina, from Saladin. He can hear the death calls. Death to crusaders. Death to infidels. He can hear the orgasmic scream of *Allah Akhbar!*

There's a moment of absolute silence, and then the street is loud with screaming shouting running. Cormac rushes toward the lobby of the North Tower, but the same cop grabs his arm and turns him. *"How many fuckin' times I gotta tell you, pal? Get the fuck out of here. This ain't over!"* He heaves Cormac toward the giant wheel, he bounces off its hard rubber, and another cop hurls him into Vesey Street. To face the burning towers. On Cormac's left is St. Paul's Chapel, with its ancient graveyard, its tombstones smoothed blank by weather and years. The place where Washington prayed after his inauguration, and Cormac stood on Broadway, watching him leave. Behind him, next to a coffee shop masked by the rigging of rehabbers, is 20 Vesey Street, where he worked for nine years as a reporter for the *Evening Post.* On what he then thought was a high floor. The fifth.

Now he gazes at the coal-colored plumes of smoke rising into the wind from the North Tower, and he tries again to count floors. *Delfina, please come down from there, go down the stairwells, follow the firemen out.* One ten, one nine, one eight . . . Then, above the orange flames, he sees people. Moving dots behind the steel grille. Above the orange flames. Waving shirts and hands as signs of life. Surely gasping for air. Surely feeling as if condemned to ovens. Not the ovens of the twentieth century. Not Auschwitz. No barked commands of *Arbeit macht frei.* New ovens, created without blueprints. Here in New York. Where fire attacks steel and oxygen at a few thousand degrees above zero. And he sees that the people are being pushed by the heat of the ovens to the edge of that high floor. Is it eighty-four? Above eighty-four? Below? *One hundred, ninety-nine, ninety-eight* . . . There they are: tiny figures: men indistinguishable from women: voiceless at this distance: beyond help: beyond helicopters: without parachutes: beyond salvation.

He tries the cell phone again.

"Forget it, buddy," a uniformed cop says. "They're all out of order."

Cormac knows he's right. He lights a cigarette with a trembling hand.

And then sees the first man jump. From a floor above the flames of the North Tower. Shirtless. Faceless at that height. White skin. Tumbling and tumbling and tumbling through the indifferent air. Then vanishing behind the building where Cormac used to buy books at Borders. Gone. Like that.

And here comes another. And another. And then a couple. A man and a woman. Holding hands. Her skirt billowing above her pale thighs.

Then gone.

"I make that fourteen," the cop says.

More cops arrive, walking backward, all of them young, gazing wide-eyed at the burning towers. "They just hit the fucking Pentagon," one of them says. "I swear. The Pentagon!" They look at Cormac, who has been joined by an older reporter, a Japanese woman, a young photographer, and they gesture to them to move back. *Are you people outta your minds?* They spread yellow crime scene tape across the aluminum poles of the rigging. *Get back! Get the fuck back!* Under the rigging, a coffee shop. Two Mexicans inside, stoic, unmoving. In the gutter, Cormac sees a puddle of coagulating blood, thickening with purple ridges. Along with an unopened bottle of V-8 Splash and a cheese Danish still wrapped in cellophane, and a single high-heeled woman's shoe. *Come down, Delfina. Go to the street. Run.* And there, in the middle of Vesey Street: a smaller wheel from the first airplane. The wheel that must have hit the woman whose shoe lay next to the blood. She must have died before breakfast. *Come down.*

And then his eyes catch movement at the top of the South Tower, above the glossy orange flames. It's pitching forward. A cracking sound. *Oh.* It's tipping at an angle, aimed for Church Street, for Century 21, for Brooks Brothers. *Oh oh oh.* He hears a scream, another, a chorus of screams, and then the tower begins to come down.

But it does not topple. The high floors, above the crack, above the flames, right themselves, and then they all come down in a straight line. Floor hitting floor hitting floor, like pancakes from a machine. There's a sound of an avalanche. A glass and steel avalanche. With some high-pitched sound that must be the meshed screams of a thousand human beings. The sound of impact is so loud it shuts down Cormac's hearing. And in that sudden silence he sees the Cloud begin to rise from the empty space.

He knows that the Cloud is made of pulverized carpet, desks, computers, artwork, paper, flowers, breakfasts, shoes, umbrellas, briefcases, mirrors, doors, counters, toilets, tons and tons and tons of concrete, and thousands of human beings. He knows this: The nouns skitter through his mind; but he can't absorb it. He glances at the North Tower, still burning, still sending smoke into the sky, while a helicopter lurches through the sky behind it. *Delfina. Oh, baby.*

The Cloud is now rising like some angry genie. So opaque it looks like a solid. Like some new creature. Some devouring god released from the ruptured earth. Animated by those who have just died. By those who flew that airplane. And by those who lived here when Cormac was young. Up out of Cortlandt Street, up out of the rotting timbers of the house where he once lived. Writhing with power and dirtiness. Coming at them. Coming to take them too.

Cops ram into them, into Cormac and the others, cops running from the Cloud, cops looking for foxholes. One grabs the Japanese woman and hurls her toward Broadway. *"Run,"* he shouts, *"run run run run."* Others push into the lobby of 20 Vesey Street. Cormac starts to run toward Broadway too, trips over something in the street, falls. And like a whirlwind the Cloud comes down upon him.

The world vanishes. There's no horizon. No floor. No sky. No limits. No exit. He hears voices within the Cloud. Men screaming. *Noooooooooooooo.* Women screaming. *Nooooooooo.* Names called. *Nancy. Mary. Freddie. Harold. Enrique.* And then a mixture, male and female: *Nooooooooooooooooo.* A high-pitched chorus of the dead. Calling to husbands and wives and lovers. Shouting farewells to children. Reduced to powder. Then, rising above them all, in the dense dry powdery heart of the Cloud, he can hear the meshed voices of weeping women. Dead of smallpox and typhus and cholera. Dead of gunshots and knife wounds. Dead in childbirth. Dead of shame and loneliness. Calling from the unburied past, from the injured earth, from landfill and ruined wooden houses and splintered ships, from vanished decades and lost centuries. A chorus. Symphonic and soaring, the voices of the New York Götterdämmerung.

Then receding echoes.

Then silence.

* * *

When the Cloud settles, the world has turned white. The color of death to the Africans who once lived here. A fine white dust covers the graveyard of St. Paul's and the steeple of the chapel. It covers the street and sidewalks of Vesey Street. It covers the police cars. It covers the small wheel of the first doomed airliner and the blood of the woman who must have been killed by it. Up toward Broadway he can see the building on Park Row where J&R Music has its stores. It's white. So are the buildings on Ann Street. The Cloud has coated them all.

He looks at the emerging stump of the South Tower, black and jagged through the wind-tossed dust. Smoke still pours from the high floors of the North Tower. He knows that it soon will come down too. Carrying all with it. No sound drifts through the white air. Not a sob, a whimper, or a prayer. And then, away off, he hears sirens. He moves east.

Broadway is white and City Hall Park is white and City Hall itself is white, and then he sees people moving lumpily through the white landscape, and they're white too. Black men and black women are white. Mexicans and Dominicans and Chinese: all white. They move like stragglers from a defeated army. Like refugees. Coated with white powder. All heading north. Alive.

Cormac joins them. If Delfina escaped, if she's alive, coated white, she'll head for Duane Street. She would believe that Cormac must be there. Broadway is covered with the powder, which is fine and slippery, like the powder used on babies. He sees hundreds of women's shoes, kicked off so that women could run faster on bare feet. Two school buses, coated with dust, are at the curb near Park Place, with nurses offering water and help. He looks inside for Delfina. She's not in either bus, although some children are huddled together in each of them, while a policewoman tries to calm them and get them moving. He sees movement in the interiors of shops and hurries over to peer inside, but Delfina isn't in any of them. That's when he first glimpses himself in a mirror: completely white. His tongue is dusty, his nostrils clogged. He tries the cell phone again. No sound at all. At Chambers Street, dozens of people are lined up to use a pay phone. Delfina isn't one of them. He waits for a few minutes on the northeast corner, not far from the Tweed Courthouse, hoping she will come along in the stunned line of survivors. She doesn't.

Then he hears the roar of the North Tower coming down. Above the building where Mary's once served laughter and breakfast, he glimpses the upper floors and the television antenna vanishing, feels the ground shudder from the impact of a million tons of pancaking floors, all of it coming down beyond the view from Chambers Street, carrying with it Windows on the World, and uncountable stockbrokers, and the offices of Reynoso & Ryan. All vanished. And then, after a few seconds, he sees the second cloud.

This one is wilder, denser, angrier than the first cloud. It rises over the buildings, extending a thousand arms, rumbling up Murray Street and Warren Street toward City Hall, recombining on Broadway, engulfing every puny human before it, rising high when it hits an obstacle, a parked police car, a hot dog vendor's cart, a park bench, then, filled with the screams of dead souls, rolls on its furious path until it settles on the southern border of the Five Points. At the vanished ridge of the Collect. At the hanging ground. On the graves of the Irish and the Africans.

In the shocked stillness, a flock of birds, confused and stunned, races across the sky from Park Row toward the Hudson, then turns back toward Brooklyn. Away from the whiteness. Away from doom.

And now people are running again, dozens of them, then hundreds. They abandon the pay phones. They burst out of the shops where they've found shelter. They run in a chaotic wave up Broadway past the federal buildings, past the police cars and the ambulances, racing toward Canal Street and the city beyond. There's no emotion on their whitened faces. Cormac sees no blood. But they run. Everything else can wait.

He hurries down Duane Street, hoping Delfina will be waiting at his door.

She isn't.

Even here, seven blocks from the North Tower, the walls are white with dust and ash and death.

* * *

There are five calls on the answering machine. The first is from Delfina. "Hey, it's me. Call me back at work." Cheer in her voice. A call made before the airplanes. Before the horror. He skips past the voices of Healey and Elizabeth. Each has called twice. There is no other call from Delfina.

He peels off his clothes and steps into the shower, rinsing his eyes, scrubbing away the white powder, shampooing his hair. He can hear the screams now, but his ears feel stuffed and muffled. He dries himself and pulls on a bathrobe that smells vaguely of Delfina. He plays the answering machine again.

Delfina's last tape. Then Healey (grave and straight): "Hey, you got the TV set on? Put it on, man." Then Elizabeth. "Call me." Followed by a click. Then Healey, very gently: "Hey, man, you okay? Call me at 310-265-1000." Then Elizabeth, hysterical: *"Cormac, he was there, in the goddamned tower, in that Windows on the World place. Willie was there! And the fire was below him, and the building just went down! Oh, my God."*

Cormac turns on CNN, which is full of pictures of the burning towers, and running people, and the collapse. He switches back and forth, from network to network, to New York 1. While reports flood in, he calls Healey, gets a machine in his hotel room, leaves a message that he's okay. He doesn't call Elizabeth. But he feels a surge of pity for Willie Warren. Cormac thinks: The world is truly nuts. Last night, I wanted to murder him and didn't. I walked away from his house thinking he would live for decades. Long after any possible crossing into the Otherworld. And here on a bright Tuesday morning in September, a dozen hours later, he's probably dead. There is no family vow that can now be fulfilled on this island.

He tries Delfina. The machine at home. Nothing on the cell phone.

A grave television reporter is saying that nobody yet knows the numbers of the dead but they could be in the many thousands. Talking heads take turns offering theories, while the screen splits, showing the towers falling, showing people in the streets. He studies each image, looking for Delfina, while the talking heads talk. Surely it was terrorists. Surely it was Osama bin Laden. A terrible day for America. More casualties than Pearl

Harbor, more than D Day, more than the *Titanic*. Now on the screen: the mayor, with his commissioners, their faces masked by inhalators, all of them grave and restrained. Cormac switches to MSNBC and then New York 1 again, to each of the networks. The same. More and more of the same. Talk of survivors. Talk of the loss of hundreds of firemen. And details about the Pentagon being hit, with hundreds dead, and another plane down in the fields of Pennsylvania, after a possible fight by passengers against hijackers. A canned piece on Bin Laden. Much about terrorists and the attack on the Trade Center in 1993, and the embassies in Africa, and the U.S.S. *Cole,* and the trails that lead to Afghanistan. Clearly it's terrorists. Clearly it's an act of war. All played against the astonishing images: the black planes, the tendrils of smoke, the collapse of each tower, and the Cloud that followed each, as if hunting down the survivors. He studies the crowd scenes. Looking for one face.

He leaves the volume on, very loud, while he dresses in jeans and denim shirt and boots. He keeps flexing his jaw, trying to open his cottony ears. Then an announcer gets excited, as another building goes down. Live. Just behind the post office. Number 7 World Trade, where the mayor had his crisis center. A smaller building this time, and a smaller cloud, like chamber music pitted against a symphony. More shots of people running from the Cloud, this time up Greenwich Street. Cormac squints at the new images, looking for Delfina. She's not there either.

Then the TV goes abruptly black, the sound ends in midsentence. The lights go off. Power gone. He pockets the cell phone, slips a portable radio into his shirt pocket, tuned to an all-news station, takes a thousand dollars in fifties and twenties from a wall safe, locks up, and goes down to the street.

She's out here somewhere. He's sure of that. He has to find her.

122.

In his search for her, Cormac tries to be methodical and careful. If she is under the twisted steel and rubble, there is no hope. But before the power failed, the television news was encouraging. The airliner had crashed into the ninety-first floor, destroying the stairwells (or so the anchormen theorized), setting off the fire, almost certainly dooming everybody above the flames. From those floors, Cormac had seen men and women jumping into eternity. But several thousand people below the flames in the North Tower had made it down the many flights of stairs to the street. Delfina's office was on the eighty-fourth floor. There was footage of these people bursting out of the building, gasping for air, and of police and firemen urging them to run. Cormac saw some of them. He knows now that he must act on faith: She ran out with them.

As he moves through emptied streets, starting as close to the burning stumps as possible, moving first east, then west, combing the grid for signs of her, he assaults himself with questions. *If that boy lives in her, would she have accepted easy death? Never.* She'd have killed to live. How would he have behaved if he'd been on that eighty-fourth floor? Would he have chosen death from roaring flames or the emptiness of the air? Perhaps, for the jumpers, the final leap wasn't even a choice. It was driven by the flames. And for Cormac? For decades, death has been his goal. Not death by his own hand. Not death through the violence of others. The sweet, consoling death that completes life. If there had been time, how would he have chosen?

He walks the white darkness of John Street, smelling the river on whose shore he arrived long ago, plus a new odor, rising from the ruined towers: burning steel and desks and carpets and paint and food and files and human flesh. Sheets of paper still drift through the sky like giant snowflakes. He sees the orange glow and remembers Diamond screaming as he was charred on the Common. The odor of Diamond's roasted flesh was a stench he never smelled again, not even during the fires that came later. Now it has returned, multiplied by many thousands.

He imagines himself now in the North Tower above the flames, holding Delfina's hand. She wants to dive into the sky. And she calls on Oshun, goddess of river waters. "Save us," she calls to the emptiness. "Save us both and save the boy." They jump. And the river goddess sends zephyrs of cool air, lifting them together above the fire, beyond the smoke, beyond the circling helicopters, beyond all harm. Why could that not have happened? After all, I am a man once saved by the river gods. Bumped through a black night while the tides took the Earl of Warren. In the grainy black air above the burning city, Delfina might have found confirmation of all she believed. Or learned a terrible lesson about the whimsy of the gods. Thinking this, imagining it, he hears a cynical New York ensemble from the streets below, a piano tinkling in a slow honky-tonk style, Bill Tweed leading the chorus:

He flies through the air
Wit' da greatest of ease . . .

And laughs grimly at himself.

He is, after all, here on the ground, alive on his own streets, not performing on the perilous stages of the Bowery Theater. At Murray Street, where all is white from powder, he sees a lone Chinese teenager pedaling a bicycle, a kid in a Stuyvesant High School jacket. He waves him down and buys the bike for three hundred dollars, including the chain and padlock. The kid takes the money and runs, as they used to say, like a thief. Cormac needs the bike if he is to make any time. *Delfina, show me your face. Show me your golden skin. Protect that boy who is not yet here.* The subways are shut down. There are no buses running below Fourteenth Street. Blue police barriers are being erected everywhere against cars and taxis. The tunnels are sealed. On the transistor, CBS reports hundreds of survivors walking across bridges to Brooklyn and Queens or trudging many miles uptown. Like refugees walking away from napalm in Vietnam, from killers in

Armenia and Macedonia, from bombs in Kosovo and Cambodia and a thousand other places Cormac has never seen.

The boy will live in safety. He will read ten thousand books. He will play basketball in playgrounds. He will live in this city, in its plural streets, in its magic. He will gaze at the Woolworth Building. He will dance with many women. He will never trudge to a refugee camp. He will not shoot guns at strangers.

Cormac moves more quickly on the bicycle, slowed only by the slippery fine powder on the streets. A policeman, grungy with ash, tells him that NYU Downtown is closed. "They're taking the hurt people to Stuyvesant, or Saint Vincent's. You know where they are?" Yes, Cormac says, I know where they are, and thanks, man. "Be careful," the cop says. "Who knows what's next?"

He makes it across the pedestrian bridge at Chambers Street to the new building of Stuyvesant High School. *This place will still be new when the boy is fourteen.* Looking downtown, he sees flames rising angrily from the Marriott Hotel, and an immense column of smoke blowing now toward Brooklyn. Ambulances scream down the West Side Highway in one lane, and north again in another. The entire eastern side of the highway is starting to fill with heavy trucks, with emergency generators and lamps, with earthmovers, all aimed at the burning site, which the radio is now calling Ground Zero. Cormac locks the bicycle to a fence and hurries into Stuyvesant. The students are all gone, of course, the lobby now filling with doctors and nurses. Volunteers are unfolding cots. Technicians set up rigs for blood transfusions. But so far, a nurse says, the only patients are firemen with damaged eyes or blistered hands. Not a single civilian is there. She says these words in a mournful voice. She is saying that there are no survivors.

"If they come, we're ready," the nurse says. "But they're not coming."

Delfina isn't at St. Vincent's either. "Hey, man, she could be anywhere," a black EMS driver tells Cormac. "'East Side, West Side, all around the town . . .'" Then Cormac wheels back downtown, in and out of streets. Delfina's nowhere that he looks.

Cormac circles home, and she isn't on his doorstep either. God damn it: I should have given her a key. She should have moved in with me when she returned from the Dominican Republic. I should have loved her more. God damn it all to Hell.

Now he has two bicycles but no lights. *I'll save one for the boy.* The radio tells him that power is out from Worth Street to the Battery, from Broadway to the Hudson. Battery Park City is being evacuated. *The boy will read all this in a history book, but I must tell Delfina to save all the newspapers.* He was short of breath. *I must tell Delfina how much I love her.* Police are knocking on doors all over Downtown, afraid of fires, afraid of exploding gas mains. Come here, Delfina. Join me here, bring your inhabited body here as I close these drapes against the dust and the sirens and burn these logs in the fireplace. As we did in Ireland one terrible winter. The hearth will give us light and heat, and even food. As each hearth did before electricity surged in these streets.

Every muscle in his body now feels pulled and extended beyond all limit. He sleeps for two dreamless hours, and then goes out again. This time with a backpack slung on his shoulders, filled with a towel, a roll of bandages, a flashlight, a bottle of Evian water, and the box containing his mother's earrings. They are for you, Delfina. When I find you, you will wear them. You will wear them when I'm gone.

This time too he takes his own bicycle, pedaling all the way to East Harlem. He locks the bicycle to a fence and buzzes his way into Delfina's building. *Look who's here. El irlandés. El amigo de Delfina from the four' floor . . .* Here are Elba and Rosa and Marisol. All out in the hall, their doors open, their faces blank with shock and horror and the repeated images of towers flaming, smoking, collapsing. Here is Pancho the Mexican from the second floor. No, nobody had seen La Guapa Dominicana, La Soltera, from the fourth floor, the one that threw the party the other night. Cormac explains that she worked in the North Tower. There are sobs, tears, wailing. *Que pesadilla . . .* Elba from the third floor starts praying at the kitchen table, facing the Virgen de Altagracia, others come in and pray too, while the news from channel 41 plays in another room, the voices of announcers filled with urgency. Cormac glimpses images of the burning towers. A shot of one of the airplanes, black and small and low, aiming at the South Tower. They try to get Cormac to eat chicken and rice and then accept his refusal, spoken in his clumsy Spanish. *A time like this who can eat?* They give him a beer. *They say it's crazy Arabs, they say they hijack four planes, one of them hit the Pentagon.* Pancho offers him a Pall Mall, which he smokes. Then Elba puts her arms around Cormac and begins to weep. They go with him in a procession to the fourth floor and he scribbles a note and slips it under Delfina's door. *Come to my house. I love you. C.*

He pedals downtown along Lexington Avenue, whispering the lyrics of "Give My Regards to Broadway" as if the old tune were a dirge. He thinks that if Delfina tried to walk home and then fell, because she was somehow hurt and didn't know it, stunned, in shock, if she fell like that, then she might be here in some doorway. Anywhere. Even up here. She wasn't. The radio is now loud with the cause of the calamity. Islamic terrorists. Four different hijacked airplanes. Teams of hijackers armed with box cutters. A brilliantly simple plan, flawlessly executed. He tries to imagine those final seconds, tries to imagine himself at the controls as he soars toward the tower at six hundred miles an hour, tries to imagine himself shouting "Allah Akhbar," and understands that the moment of obliteration might also have been a moment of consuming ecstasy.

"Tell all the gang at Forty-second Street that I will soon be there." Nothing approaches ecstasy in P.J. Clarke's on Third Avenue. Four men, each in a pool of solitude, stare at Peter Jennings on the TV set. The bartender seems to know that Jennings understands the Middle East better than most because he spent years there as a reporter, and so he does not flick from channel to channel. Jennings talks about a nation at war. On the jukebox Sinatra sings about Nancy with the laughing face and how summer could take some lessons from her. Cormac remembers when the song was first played on the radio, during another kind of war. Jennings is smooth and effortless as he moves from

one piece of the story to another, but anger is very close to his urbane surface. On tape, the towers fall once more. On tape, the Cloud once more comes rushing between buildings or over their rooftops. On tape, men and women run north. The firemen run into the smoke. Over and over and over again. He peers at televised faces. He does not see Delfina.

Cormac orders a hamburger at the bar, remembering glad nights here in the 1950s, with Lady Day and Sinatra on the juke, and sometimes Sinatra himself at a table in the back room with Jimmy Cannon or Jilly Rizzo or William B. Williams, and dancers and stars coming in after the shows and the night stretching out forever. Fragments of songs move through him, and now on the juke Billie Holiday is singing "I'm a Fool to Want You." The voice ruined, her ravaged face before him in a flash, alongside her beautiful face when she first arrived in 1936. None of the music sounds sharp, and he realizes that his ears are still plugged from the roar of the collapse. Cormac finishes the burger. Delfina is more beautiful than all those beautiful women of the 1950s. Summer could take some lessons from her, all right. And still the television tells the story of death and horror. Cormac forces himself to remember the Great Fire and the seven hundred ruined buildings and how a year later all were replaced. But that was when houses were three stories high and there were no airplanes, no gasoline, no God-sick lunatics prepared to kill thousands, including themselves. This is disaster nostalgia, he tells himself, a new category among all the New York nostalgias. He smokes a cigarette. Sinatra dead, Jilly dead, Cannon dead, Billie dead, William B. dead. The dancers are grandmothers. I'm alive, he thinks. Delfina is alive too. And so is the boy. I can feel it in my bones.

He pays the check and goes past the out-of-order cigarette machine through the side door into Fifty-fifth Street. The bike is where he left it. Even the thieves are home watching the calamity on television. And all the way up here, so many miles from Ground Zero, the air is dirty with the odor.

* * *

Back at home, he lights three candles. He wishes he could wrap himself in a coat of many colors. He tries the cell phone again and hears only the void. Where is Kongo? he thinks. Where the fuck is Kongo? And where are you, Delfina?

In the morning, his ears are unplugged, but his body aches. Lying there, nothing about Tuesday seems real. Was this another act of New York theater, a working of the mad imagination? He hears the roof door banging, left unlocked when he ran to the street to find Delfina. He goes upstairs in a bathrobe. The skylight is sprayed with ash. Ash and powder have entered the loft from the open door, to gather in drifts an inch deep, and when he gazes out across the rooftop, his heart trips. The towers are gone. He saw them falling, but now he sees how completely they have disappeared. From the place they once occupied, a long black pennant of smoke drifts toward Brooklyn. And the air is heavy with the odor.

There are no birds in the Wednesday sky. Not even a raven. He remembers seeing the first airplane, the simplicity of its path, and then glimpsing the second. Each pilot heading for a city he did not know. Each heading for this dense and layered, most human of all places. Each heading here to kill thousands and find Paradise. Heading for Delfina, and all those others they did not know.

Then he sobs. He whispers, *"You lousy fuckers."* He holds a chimney to steady himself, and his body is wracked with tears for the ruined world.

He thinks: I want to go. More than ever before, I want to flee the world.

Except for this: I cannot go until I find Delfina.

Routine is created as he makes his rounds. There is still nothing to discover at Stuyvesant or St. Vincent's, no civilians, no wounded. He has added the sword to the backpack, the blade at an angle, the handle rising out of the top and covered with a towel. He thinks he might need it, since the cops are all dealing with the emergency and the bad guys will soon be back on the streets. He sees no bad guys, only crowds cheering as fire trucks go by, and accuses himself of paranoia. He has breakfast in Healey's new favorite coffee shop on Twenty-third Street, his arms full of newspapers. The unemployed dot-commers are packed into booths. He uses the pay phone to call various casualty hotlines. Sorry, nobody by that name. He calls Delfina's number too. No answer. He calls Elba from the third floor, and Delfina is not yet home (but the whole building is praying for her). Now Cormac knows what everyone else must know, what the mayor meant when he said about the numbers that they would be more than anyone could bear. Nobody who was in those towers when they came down would be found alive.

In every newspaper, starting on page eight of the tabloids, he sees Warren's face. He was one of the best-known people at breakfast in Windows on the World on Tuesday morning. A businessmen's alliance breakfast, a clean-up-the-city breakfast. The stories don't say he's dead. He is just among the missing. But even his own newspaper writes about him in the past tense. The *New York Times* uses a handsome portrait by Richard Avedon, from a profile in *The New Yorker*. There are pictures taken at openings, including one from the show at the Metropolitan. Most of them include Elizabeth. The *Daily News* runs two photographs of her taken on Tuesday afternoon, one leaving the apartment house on Fifth Avenue, the other, her back to the camera, peering south from the Chambers Street Bridge at the burning ruins. The second was at dusk on Tuesday. The *Post* was also on the bridge, and their photo shows her with a scarf covering the lower part of her face, as if wearing a *burka*. The scarf turned into a filter against the ash and the odor. As always, she looks beautiful. And in the *Post* photograph, stricken. And to Cormac, detached. She has nothing to say to reporters except, "I'm so sorry for everybody."

* * *

After his long day's journey, and an evening patrol, Cormac comes home in the dark. There are still no lights. Duane Street is black and empty, although Church Street is now full of hard, bright imported lights and out-of-state police cars and a holding pen for the media and a long line of heavy vehicles pointed south. He thinks: They are already organized, they know what they are doing, they are doing it better than any other city could have done it. He enters Duane Street from the Broadway side and finds himself whistling the Coleman Hawkins version of "Body and Soul." The last whistler on Duane Street. The only man in all of the wounded city who is whistling. *"I long for you, for you, dear, only . . ."* He gets off the bicycle and fumbles for keys, his eyes sore from the poisoned air. He wants to be rid of the weight of the sword. He wants bed. Some drops of soft rain begin to fall. He thinks: Rain will help. Rain will clean the air. Rain will cool the molten steel. Rain will chill the burning bodies.

Then he sees Kongo.

He's squatting low in the doorway, a cape turning him into a dense black triangle. He stands up slowly.

"Do you still want to go?" he says.

Cormac knows what he means. He pauses, weary, exhausted, without much residue of hope.

"Yes."

"You don't sound as certain as you did."

"How can I go without finding the woman? I need to find her. I can't go without that."

He looks toward Church Street, hearing the unseen muffled voices, the grinding of gears. Kongo sighs. A siren wails.

"You couldn't kill this fellow Warren."

"True."

"That was the sign of a merciful man," he says, and smiles. "And after all, his death was your duty, not ours."

"They were always together in my mind, like the East River and the Hudson, coming out in the harbor," Cormac says. "But you're right, of course. You're right. And now it doesn't matter. The man, Warren, was in one of the towers, above the fires. It's in all the newspapers. He's surely dead."

Kongo looks at him.

"You can leave this world tonight."

"Not without seeing Delfina."

"I know where she is," he says.

123.

They use both bicycles and pedal north. They pull over at the corner of Fifty-eighth Street, a half block from Roosevelt Hospital, and chain the bicycles to a lamppost. Cormac knows the hospital. When the third Madison Square Garden was still on Eighth Avenue and Fiftieth Street, battered prizefighters were taken here to be stitched up or to die. Now, Kongo says, Delfina Cintron is in a bed on the sixth floor.

"I can heal her," Kongo says. "The way I once healed you."

He shows Cormac how he entered in his own search of the city. The route goes from a loading dock in the rear to a freight elevator. Most ambulances are downtown, along with many of the nurses and doctors, and there is an atmosphere of abandonment around the back entrance.

"I'll wait for you there," he says, pointing a few blocks toward Central Park. "Just inside the entrance, in the darkest trees."

He gives Cormac the cape and takes the backpack that holds the sword, the towels, the earrings. Its weight makes Kongo smile. Then he walks away in a loping, long-legged stride, and Cormac slips into the hospital. He finds an elevator, pushes six.

With the cape on his shoulders, he walks past an empty nurse's station and into a large room with six beds, each filled with a sleeping woman. Delfina is in the bed nearest the window. Her face is swollen and she's deeply sedated. But there are no tubes in her nose, no IV dripping into her veins. Her right hand is raw, her nails cracked, and her breath is shallow. She looks like an injured child. *Boy, nothing can be harder than the road that you took to get here.*

"Hey, who are you? The Phantom of the Opera? What are you *doing* here?"

A heavy black nurse with a tough face stands in the doorway, hands on her hips.

"This is my wife," Cormac says. "I've been looking for her for two days."

"You can't —"

"She was in the North Tower."

The nurse picks up a clipboard from the foot of the bed. She still looks professionally angry.

"She's pregnant too," Cormac says. "Or she was."

The nurse squints at the case file.

"She still is," she says. "Some kind of miracle."

"I want to take her home."

She looks at him more carefully now. "Sorry for your trouble," she said. "But I'm sure that ain't possible. It sure ain't advisable. Let me go find a supervisor. You can wait right here."

When she leaves, Cormac wraps Delfina in the cape, lifts her heavy body, feeling its warmth, and carries her down the deserted hallways to the stairwell. *Easy, boy, don't make a move, just take a ride now.* All the way down to the loading area, Delfina makes small whimpering sounds, tiny protests, but says no words, not even when Cormac moves with her into the rain.

Columbus Circle is slick with rain and Cormac can see lights downtown in Times Square and nothing at all in the far distance. Traffic is light. A dozen yellow cabs. A few buses. No police cars at all. When the street is empty, he hurries into the park, straining against the weight of Delfina. As promised, Kongo is waiting in a grove of dripping maples.

With Thunder.

He is here again, as he was on the night when Cormac and Kongo rode him north, blood merging, language merging, gods merging. Thunder: back from the place where he has been waiting.

The great horse paws the earth, stretches in pleasure and renewal, shudders, but makes no other sound. The sword is slung from the saddle horn, the black bag beneath it. Kongo hands Cormac the reins and holds Delfina in his own arms, her face masked by the cape against the rain. Cormac strokes the great horse and whispers in Irish. *We go now to see Da.* Then he swings into the saddle. Kongo passes Delfina to him. Her eyes are closed, her face bleary. She faces Cormac, her body against his, her legs spread in the saddle, burrowed against him. He pulls the cape tight around her body, steadying her with his elbows, gripping the reins.

"I'll see you there," Kongo says, and slaps Thunder's haunch.

124.

*They move north through the park to the place of farewell, to the hid*den cave. Delfina is pressed against him and he can feel her breath against his chest. A woman dressed like an Eskimo in a fur-trimmed coat comes toward them on the path, holding seven dogs on seven leashes. All are docile, heads pressed to the ground, anxious to be taken to dry rooms. Neither the Eskimo nor her dogs seem surprised by the presence of a horse in the rain, holding two riders.

They make good time. Away in the distance to the east, he sees the bright lights of the Metropolitan Museum, and suddenly imagines an airliner packed with fuel smashing into it and destroying the finest works of man. They could do it. They want to do it. Here, and everywhere. He turns Thunder to the west, away from the revealing lights of the Metropolitan. He hopes the musicians are back on its steps. He wishes he could take Delfina there and dance. *You will dance on marble terraces, boy. You will feel candle wax dripping on your shoulders from the chandeliers. You will waltz. You will mambo. Vaya.* Raindrops now look like a shower of atoms in the more distant lights of the park lamps. The rain fills the world with a steady drumming sound, without accents from bata or toques, without congas or bongo, just steady drumming, erasing the sounds of the city, mashing time, cleansing the filthy air. Delfina murmurs through unconsciousness. *Oh, shit . . . oh, shit . . .* Her head stirs, her nose sounds clogged. He holds her closer with a free hand, her head flat against his chest.

He can see the turrets and battlements of Belvedere Castle as they move across the Great Lawn into the North Meadow, empty now of people, of children, of ballplayers. He loves this place. A place created long ago by the sweat and muscle of Irishmen and Africans and Germans who came here from the Bloody Ould Sixth when Cormac was already old, who loved one another, who married one another, who huddled together in the shacks of Seneca Village. All these eight hundred and forty-three acres were then a wilderness of rock and scrub and shanties, where men and women and children shared the land with the last of the free animals and five hundred thousand birds. They were the same people who changed the place, who moved the earth and drained the swamps and cut the roads from a master plan, knowing that when they were finished they could not come back to live, only to visit. Cormac thinks: They left us this tamed sylvan man-shaped place, and all of them are dead and buried, and I am still here. The only man left alive who ever saw them work. Now, on a wet, moonless night in the wounded city, the lawns drink the rain, the last birds huddle in nests, and even the ghosts are silent.

Thunder carries them out of the park at 106th Street, following the smell of earth westward into the strip of Riverside Park. Man, woman, and horse are joined now, like a single creature, pelted by the rain. They pass the gloomy monument they visited together in the summer, and Cormac remembers Delfina saying, "I want to be buried in Grant's Tomb." You will be buried nowhere, he says now. Not for a long, long time. Thinking: You will see Rome, you will stroll in the piazzas of Florence, you will see our child walk and read and dance. I will not. But you and the boy will swim in the azure waters of the Mediterranean, off the point named for Palinurus. You will read *The Aeneid* at a table where lemons await you in a white ceramic bowl. You will teach the child to be strong and kind.

Through the rain, he sees a rusting freighter plowing toward Albany. He glimpses it between buildings, and then the ship is gone. The rain is now washing away the city's cargo of fine ash. The great swooping arc of the George Washington Bridge is dotted with the red taillights of stalled commuters heading for New Jersey. No cars are coming into Manhattan. Cormac feels Harlem's presence from the heights to the right, here where Washington fled to the killing plains of New Jersey. *He was not a face on a dollar bill, boy, he was a great big tough son-of-a-bitch who made a country.* Cormac sees Washington as he always sees him: slashing the air with his own swift sword. And sees Bantu and the others, sees them fighting for the liberty that Washington did not deliver. All of that in a year when he was still too young to know that most great hopes end with a broken heart.

Then Washington disappears, and now Cormac feels Duke Ellington beckoning him to a table at Frank's, in a year when he was writing about music for the *New York Sun,* and there too is Charlie Parker raising his alto to the night and Lady Day whispering through the rain. What was the name of the hotel on 118th Street where Minton's Playhouse opened the stage to the true geniuses of the wretched twentieth century? Cormac can no longer remember, but there was Max behind the drums and here came Birks and there was Bird and in from the coast one night came Art Tatum. That was the night, hearing Tatum shower the room with music, when he knew his own work on a piano was a pathetic counterfeit. His hand drops to Delfina's belly.

You will hear them all, son, the greatest artists of the century; you will hear their music smile, or protest, or console, and you will hear in them what the Africans made of America, all of them in you, as I am in you, and Ireland is in you, and the Jews are in you, and the Caribbean is in you, from me, from your mother, even in the blood I carry still from Kongo, and always, in all years, no matter where you go, son, you will be of New York.

His hand is above what he is sure is the boy's beating heart, although he cannot feel it. If only the musicians all could have seen the towers fall, seen the Cloud, reached for their horns or the black and white keys. Make it into art, man, he once heard Miles tell Coltrane. For they all knew one immense New York secret: no pain, no art. Here in these streets the alloy of Irish and Africans invented the new world. Here is where Master Juba's spirit floated in the wings, dancing beside his Irish friend John Diamond, the two of them inventing tap-dancing. Harlem was the true northern border of the Five Points, after all the Know-Nothing race bullshit broke the Irish away from the children of Africans. Except for those who loved one another. Except for the Africans who took Irish wives and the Irishmen who took African wives and loved them until death did them part. Here on the right. Up there. In this place. This Harlem. Far from the North Tower. Far from Ground Zero.

Oh, how I want music now, Cormac thinks, high on this great muscled horse, this immortal stallion, moving north with my last woman. Moving north with my unborn son. Moving north to die. I want to hear music as I ride through cleansing rain, with my back turned to the great downtown necropolis. Music to redeem the murderous spectacle that now dwarfs all other New York deaths, starting with my own.

They pass under the bridge, gradually rising on wooded slopes into Fort Tryon Park, passing the Cloisters, still moving north, where he will keep his appointment.

The woods are denser now, the trees taller, more majestic and primeval, the rain harder, and Thunder moves cautiously, avoiding small escarpments of rock. They are deep inside Inwood Hill Park. Cormac can see tiny waterfalls, where rivers of rain are rushing over cliffs and pouring down in swift, glassy sheets. Some trees rise more than a hundred feet above them, trees that have been here since he arrived in the lost village on the southern tip of the island. Then Thunder stops. They are before a vaguely familiar wall of jagged rock. Delfina murmurs and Cormac pulls back and sees that her eyes flicker, blink open, close again.

And Cormac thinks: This is madness. I'm going to kill her, and the boy too, bouncing through rain to the chill of a cave. I should have left her in the hospital, where there were nurses and doctors and medicines. A place of warmth and food. He considers going back. Or veering off to the right and the emergency room of Columbia-Presbyterian. And knows that he can't, that he has moved beyond choice.

"Delfina," he murmurs. "It's me."

She does not answer.

Thunder stops. *Don't die on me,* mujer. *After I'm gone, you must bring this boy into the world.*

They arrive at the foot of the cliff that is sliced by the entrance to the cave. Her face remains swollen and shut. He lifts her down and lays her upon the cape and then turns the cape into a sling, using ropes from the backpack. He buckles on the sword in its scabbard, a tool now for digging instead of killing, and whispers good-bye in Irish to Thunder. Delfina moans. He slings her dead weight over his left shoulder, his knees buckling, pulls the ends of the sling as tight as he can, using the backpack as a cushion, and then starts up the rock face.

Some dim memory guides him to a rough path, hidden by the zigzagged markers of rain-slick boulders and mossy stones. *I'm coming; I'll be there soon . . .* At one angled ledge, he slips backward, totters, then uses Delfina's weight as an anchor, leaning her against the rock face, gripping her. She babbles words he does not understand and then goes silent again. They climb another three feet, and then Cormac wobbles, his balance lost, and is about to fall more than twenty feet when he grabs the gnarled root of a tree. He trembles, his strength gone, and struggles for a long minute to steady himself. His heart is beating fiercely. He wants nothing to happen to her, or to their child, and he inhales deeply from the wet air. He must go on. And wonders: *Are you there too, Mary Morrigan?*

Then they are on the narrow ledge and Cormac can see above them the blocked mouth of the cave. Another path moves right and turns abruptly to the higher ground. To a passing pilgrim, some Sunday hiker in pursuit of wildflowers or butterflies, this would be another blank outcrop of schist and granite, lost in a dark forest. But now he has found the path. The city is gone now, dissolved in the falling rain, screened by the primeval trees. He will see no more trembling eastern dawns, no more scarlet western dusks, no sun rising in Brooklyn to set in New Jersey. This is the end of it. The city itself is as erased from sight as the towers. Every man and woman, all those thousands who have just died, all the countless millions who preceded them, reduced now to us, to me, to you, Delfina, to the child, here at the sealed entrance to this last hidden cave. Up ahead are all the others I have loved, in the place where I will wait for you. *I will see you soon, Da. I will tell you all that has happened.*

Gathering strength, hugging Delfina to him, Cormac remembers his image of the city as gigantic horizontal sculpture, and now sees the gods, all of them, speaking Greek and Latin and Yoruba and Irish, looking down upon this last dreadful alteration, this atrocious mauling of life, and they decide that there should be no more time for the invisible sculptor. They will give all the puny humans twenty-four hours to evacuate, and then they will lift the island from its northern end, and raise it into the sky, thrust it thirteen miles above the harbor, and leave it there forever, as monument to human folly, as warning against all forms of hubris. Cormac sees it being lifted, hears the sucking sound as it rises from its mooring, sees the dangling roots of trees, the bones of humans long dead, the tangled web of ruptured sewers and water pipes and subway tunnels, all buses and automobiles and cranes and trucks falling loosely through the streets to the bottom, while the merging waters of the North River and the East River and the vast Atlantic rush in, to cover the jagged remains of what once was an island called Manhattan. And he sees himself: clinging to the side of the Woolworth Building, the last man left alive, the man who can't evacuate, the man who must tell the story.

He looks down and Thunder has galloped once more into mist. A rich dark aroma of soaked earth and rotting vegetation rises through the rain to enter both of them. The water of Oshun. The sea of Usheen.

Then, carrying Delfina, he goes up the twisting path until he is at the sealed entrance of the cave that gave him too much life.

He holds her very tight, breathing into her ears and face, kissing her cracked nails and raw hands. The wind is rising.

I must do this, woman, for you, for the boy. He turns from her, and moves her out of the rain, and unsheathes the sword, and begins to chop furiously into the sealed entrance. A kind of cement has formed, made of stones and pebbles and sand, tufts of grass, the enameling power of rain. *God damn you, God damn you, open, open to us.* He smothers the rage, then makes controlled slices in the surface, wiggles the sword to widen them, then stabs with purpose at the next layer. He keeps thrusting until he feels an emptiness on the other side. He has breached the outer shell, and then the entrance crumbles into porous dust and rubble. He uses his weight and bulk and the sword to keep widening the hole, and then at last the mouth opens. He takes a flashlight from the backpack and peers down its rocky throat.

The cave.

The place where he will find the entrance to the Otherworld. His hidden *shee* in the American earth.

He pushes into the slit, turns, and gently drags Delfina behind him. She doesn't stir. *I know the child is safe, I know your body shields him, I know that he will live.* He wraps the two of them inside the cape, gripping the bag, using it to cushion her body, and they slide gently down a slope, Cormac using his heels as brakes. Then they stop in the blackness. *You will not lose him, you will not . . .* He plays the flashlight against the walls. The cave has not changed since last he saw it: dry and high-roofed and deep. He sees the waxy stumps of old candles, made by men long dead, their wicks like tiny black fingers. He needs matches.

The lighter. Where's the lighter? He lifts Delfina and carries her to the place where he awoke long ago and saw Tomora, and felt her healing caress, and heard from Kongo about his gift of life, and its limiting terms, and its possibilities of escape. He lays Delfina on the cape and she moans in a chilly, helpless way.

Her feet are sliced and scabbed. Her face is swollen and distorted on one side, as if she had been punched. Her damaged hand seems thicker now. Her eyes are closed. Her breathing is slowing and then she moans and a hand goes to her stomach, to her spiraled belly, to the place where the child lives, to the place where the child might now be dying. Now Cormac lashes himself. *She is broken and hurt and you brought her here because you need her for your own good-bye. You selfish idiot. She will die. The child will die. For you.*

He touches her face. She begins to shake from the cold. Her teeth clack. Death has entered her.

He shouts at the emptiness: "Kongo! Where are you, Kongo?"

He arrives from the dark rear of the cave, not the entrance. He is dressed now entirely in white, including a white shawl over his shoulders. He looks at Cormac in the light of the upraised flashlight, says nothing, lights two of the candles with matches and then kneels over Delfina. Cormac switches the flashlight off as Kongo begins to chant in a language that is neither Yoruba nor Ashanti. His head is bowed. As he chants, he moves his own hands above her hands, and above her damaged face, and then takes each scabbed foot and runs his tongue over her wounds. His voice is pitched higher than her moaning. Then he places both hands a few inches above her stomach. He is more intense now, his voice rising from chant into plaintive song. His hands move horizontally above her stomach, then caress her belly, as his singing begins to float, to echo, to fill the cave.

The scabs on her feet fall away. The swelling leaves her face and her injured hand. Her moaning stops. Her eyes remain closed, but now she is radiant.

Kongo ends with a small song of supplication and then rises. He turns to the rear of the cave. To the darkness.

"The place you are searching for is back there," he says, pointing into blackness.

He removes the white shawl from his shoulders and lays it over Delfina's breasts and shoulders. He nods at Cormac, and then walks abruptly to the entrance, to climb the slope and go out into the wet New York night.

She sits up and faces Cormac, flexing her fingers, turning her feet as if they were adorned in spangles. She smiles in a shy way, she stretches, she rubs her hands on her belly. Her eyes move around the cave, wide in surprise and alarm.

"Where are we?" she says.

"In a cave in Inwood."

"How did I get here?"

"I carried you."

He holds her face in his hands and kisses her very lightly on the lips.

"I can feel him," she whispers. "He's there. He's moving. He wants to meet you."

He hugs Delfina, her golden warmth streaming into his own body, and he feels his own surging emotion, his need, his fear. They are quiet for a long time. And then she stares around her at the walls of the cave.

"I was in a staircase, packed with people, with lots of smoke," she says, a kind of wonder in her voice. "There was thick smoke everywhere. I looked down and there were hands on banisters going down and down and down, all the way down." She pauses. "There was a man in a wheelchair being carried by three men. Doors opened and the smoke was thicker, and we kept going down, and then there were firemen, lots of firemen, all going up, and we were reduced to one lane, and then we weren't moving at all. Everybody was quiet. Nobody was crying. And I tried my cell phone, and it didn't work, and I thought: I might die here. I might die here, carrying this baby, I might die here without . . . without ever saying good-bye to you."

She begins to weep now, her body shaking with great wracking sobs.

"I was trying to find you too," he says. "The cell phones didn't work anywhere. . . ."

Her weeping slows.

"After that, I don't remember much of anything," she says. "Just running and falling. Like a dream you have when you're six."

He tells her what happened, and how both towers fell, how many thousands are dead, how Islamic hijackers took four different airliners and smashed them into the World Trade Center, the Pentagon, a field in Pennsylvania, how everybody is talking of war. She listens and doesn't listen; she hears but does not hear. She stares straight ahead. Cormac says nothing for almost a minute, as her lips move silently and she absorbs what he has said. She clears her throat.

"They've ruined the world," she whispers. "They've ruined the world where this boy will walk. They've ruined it, haven't they? God damn them all."

Candlelight suffuses the part of the cave in which they sit upon the cape. He gazes at her, feeling seconds becoming minutes, and then rises to one knee and turns to face her. He takes her hand. She looks at him with wariness in her eyes.

"I have to tell you a story," he says. "One that I've never told you, or anyone else, and one you never asked to hear."

"So tell it, man."

He takes a deep breath, then exhales slowly.

"I was born in 1723, in the north of Ireland," he begins. She smiles up at him as if expecting a joke, but his serious face keeps her from saying anything. "When I was sixteen, my father was killed over a horse. . . ."

And so he tells her about the Earl of Warren and how he crossed the Atlantic in pursuit of the man, intending to kill him. He tells her about the indentured Irish and the slaves in the hold of the *Fury* and how he helped give the Africans food and water. He explains about the revolt, and how he saved Kongo's life, and how his blood merged with the African's blood as they rode north to this cave.

"He was a babalawo," Cormac says.

"A babalawo."

"And in this cave, he gave me a gift."

"Eternal life," she says.

Cormac is surprised. "How did you know that?"

"A babalawo can do that," she says. "The babalawo in Puerto Rico, the man who made my tattoos? Some people say that he's been there since before the Spaniards arrived. That another babalawo gave him the gift . . . He was here just now, wasn't he? I can smell him. I know that smell. And he healed me, didn't he?"

"Yes."

She stands now too, pulling the white shawl tightly over her shoulders, bending her head to inhale its odor, gazing around the visible part of the cave.

"You really are a little old for me, man," she says, and laughs.

"I'm a little old for everybody."

She turns with a wistful smile on her face.

"What's the rest of it about?" she says. "There's got to be more."

"There is."

"You're gonna leave me, right?"

He doesn't answer directly.

"There were terms to the gift," he says. "I couldn't leave Manhattan. If I did, I would die. And I'd be barred from the Otherworld. It would be a form of suicide, and suicide was forbidden. . . . That's why I couldn't go to Brooklyn with you, or Orchard Beach. I was told by the babalawo that I would meet a dark-skinned woman adorned with spirals and that I would make love to her in this cave and then I could pass over. . . . I looked for the woman for many years and never found her. Until the day I saw you on Fourteenth Street. This might all sound preposterous, but it's true. I've lived it. My life is the proof."

He thinks: There is no time to tell her how he had lived through all the history of the city, how he absorbed its life, its menace, its cruelties, its toughness, its joys and sorrows and beauties. He could tell her about the women he knew and the friends he made and how Bill Tweed gave him the house on Duane Street, and how everybody he loved had died. But there's no time. There is no time to tell her of the men he killed. No time to explain how his enemies had died, how houses had died, and neighborhoods had died, and how he kept going: through words and art and time.

She walks around him, looking at him. She pinches the flesh of his arm as if to verify his presence. Then she laughs in a bitter way.

"This is such a bitch," she says. "I loved you so I could live. And you loved me so you could die."

She leans down and lifts the cape, angrily shaking away its dust, and slips it over her shoulders with the white shawl beneath it. She picks up a candle.

"I'll see you, Cormac," she says, and begins to walk toward the deep part of the cave, the dark unknown place that Kongo pointed to for Cormac.

"Delfina —"

"If you want to die, go ahead," she says, tossing the words over her shoulder. "I'm just not gonna help."

Her candle bobs as he goes after her.

"Don't go there," he says, his voice echoing now. "That's the wrong way out. That's not for you."

He reaches for her, finds her hand. In the light of the candle, her skin is the color of cinnamon, her eyes liquid with fear and hurt.

"Don't go there," he says.

She begins to bawl. A great hopeless weeping, filling the cave. The candle falls and goes out. He holds her, running hands through her hair, caressing her skin, kissing her eyes and ears and mouth, until they fall to the ground, fall upon the cape, fall together, and begin to make love.

"Go," she whispers, "go. Just go. Please go. Go."

They rise into each other, joining as one, writhing and weeping and gnashing, obliterating life in the little death. And then breathe as one. And lie silent.

Off in the distance, in the far reaches of the cave, Cormac can see a sliver of emerald light.

* * *

He snaps on the flashlight. Her head is turned away from him. He takes the spiral earrings from a pocket. He clips them to her ears.

"Wear these," he says. "Wear them always."

"I will," she says, sitting up and leaning her head to one side and then the other. The earrings dangle in the light, changing shape with each movement of her head. "I'll always wear them."

He feels empty now, and free: the story told, the secret revealed. If she has questions, she can ask them now. She asks no questions.

He stands up now, finds the fallen candle, lights it with his lighter. He gazes at her face, its toughness and humor and the way the flicker of candlelight keeps altering her beauty and the way the yellow light glistens on the earrings. Without a word, he takes a breath, picks up the flashlight, and hands it to her. Then he takes the candle and moves into the darkness.

Up there, somewhere, is the entrance. Beyond the jagged stone and the dripping walls. All of them are waiting for him in the emerald light. Some have been waiting for a very long time. His father and his mother, Mr. Partridge and Bill Tweed, Bantu and the black patrol, women and friends, even Bran. He raises the candle and plays the light on the walls. He sees the ceiling lower. He sees a crack that in the distance seems to be an inch wide. He can hear a flute. A damp gust of wind blows out the candle. He moves closer. They are all there, beyond the shimmer of emerald light. All the people he has ever loved.

Except one.

He turns and walks back to Delfina. He reaches down and takes her hand.

"Let's go, *mi amor,*" he says.

"Where?"

"Dancing," he says. "Let's go dancing."

He feels her smooth, pliant hand pulsing with life.

"All right," she says.

"We can try to find a cab."

"That would be nice."

"I love you, *mi vida,*" he says.

"But for how long, señor?"

"Forever," he says, and they start to climb together toward the rain-drowned city.

By way of thanks

This is a work of fiction, an imagined journey through times past and present. But it was stimulated by my own many decades as a New Yorker, by my reporting during four of those decades on the events and people of my native city, and by a lifetime of reading into the extraordinary history of the city itself.

Among the books I cherish, and which helped directly or indirectly in the imagining of this narrative, are the amazing six volumes of *The Iconography of Manhattan Island: 1498–1909* by I. N. Phelps Stokes. These were given to me in his last year of life by my friend Edward Robb Ellis, author of *The Epic of New York City,* which itself remains a fine introduction to our dense, layered history. More than a decade ago, Eddie Ellis urged me to write this novel; I wish I could have handed him his own copy. I will miss him all my days.

I also learned much from *Gotham: A History of New York City to 1898,* by Edwin G. Burrows and Mike Wallace. This is the first of two volumes, and it is a majestic piece of work. Its dense pages contain the raw material for hundreds of novels and will continue to inspire scholars and writers long after all of us are gone. It's a book that every New Yorker should read, along with all others who want to understand this very American city.

In addition, *The Encyclopedia of New York City,* brilliantly edited by Kenneth T. Jackson, is an invaluable resource for all of us who still marvel at the endless complexity of this metropolis.

For many years, the diaries of Philip Hone and George Templeton Strong have helped put me into the New York that has vanished but is still not gone. The novels of Louis Auchincloss and Edith Wharton have helped bring that world to vivid life, elaborating the many generations that were built upon the original templates cut by Strong and Hone. I've absorbed all of them in different ways.

My own vision of William M. Tweed was deepened by Oliver E. Allen's *The Tiger: The Rise and Fall of Tammany Hall,* Alfred Connable and Edward Silberfarb's *Tigers of Tammany,* Leo Hershkowitz's *Tweed's New York: Another Look,* and Denis Tilden Lynch's *"Boss" Tweed: The Story of a Grim Generation,* a 1927 biography with a fierce tabloid energy. The last book was passed to me by my old *New York Post* editor, Paul Sann, who originally drove me to understand the history of New York while educating me as a reporter.

On the "Great Negro Plot" of 1741, Thomas J. Davis's *A Rumor of Revolt: The "Great Negro Plot" in Colonial New York* is indispensable, as is the contemporary report by Daniel Horsmanden called *Journal of the Proceedings in the Detection of the Conspiracy Formed by Some White People in Conjunction with Negro and Other Slaves Burning the City of New-York in America and Murdering the Inhabitants.* I read the abridged version, edited in 1851 by William B. Wedgwood. Michael G. Kammen's *Colonial New York: A History* is a fine work of reconstruction of the years before the American Revolution and helped me with the wider context of 1741.

Many other books fill my New York shelves, from Herbert Asbury's classic *The Gangs of New York* to Sean Wilentz's *Chants Democratic.* Most recently, I've learned from Gerard T. Koeppel's *Water for Gotham,* M. H. Dunlop's *Gilded City,* and Richard B. Stott's *Workers in the Metropolis.* I have hundreds of volumes too on Irish history, too many to list, but some of which provided details of the arctic winter of 1740 and the famine that was forgotten after the much larger horrors of the Great Famine of the 1840s, which changed Ireland and New York for a century.

History is not everything, of course. The poetry and journalism of Walt Whitman are essential for any writer about New York, as are the works of Edgar Allen Poe, Herman Melville, Stephen Crane, and Theodore Dreiser, and, of course, Henry James. But much is to be learned from the pulp fiction produced for more than a century in New York, from the dime novels of the dreadful Ned Buntline and his more respectable contemporaries to the works of the Black Mask school of detective fiction. I admire too the works of Caleb Carr, Jack Finney, and above all, the splendid New York fictions of E. L. Doctorow, who has turned so much of our narrative into high art.

My writer friends Julie Baumgold and Carolina Gonzalez helped with details I could not know. But this novel the process of imagining and writing was almost constantly a process of reimagining and rewriting, of finding fresh connections and unexpected patterns, and making decisions about what could be eliminated and what must be kept. That process was driven by the high standards and respect for craft of my editor, Bill Phillips. His contribution to this work was absolutely essential. He goaded me, pushed me, cajoled me, encouraged me, made me laugh, and gave me the time to do what had to be done, regardless of deadlines. It was a marvelous experience; our e-mails alone would make a small book, and I'll be grateful to Bill Phillips, well, forever.

I was accompanied on this journey by my wife, to whom this book properly belongs. But I was also in the company of Charlie Parker, John Coltrane, Erik Satie, Scott Joplin, Benny More, Miles Davis, J. S. Bach, the unknown masters of Gregorian chant, and Duke Ellington, and by a marvelous creature named Gabo, who was what John Cheever once called "a former dog." Gabo didn't live to see me finish, but he's in these pages too.

About the Author

Pete Hamill has been editor in chief of both the *New York Post* and the *New York Daily News,* for which he currently writes a regular column. In his writing for these publications as well as the *New York Times, The New Yorker,* and *Newsday,* he has brought the city to life for millions of readers. He is the author of previous bestselling books, including, most recently, the memoir *A Drinking Life* and the novel *Snow in August*. He lives in New York City.

Forever

a novel

PETE HAMILL

A READING GROUP GUIDE

On writing *Forever*

Pete Hamill talks with Mark Miller of *Time Out New York*

If you're one of those New Yorkers who believe that the world begins and ends at the city's borders, then you have a lot in common with Cormac O'Connor, the protagonist of *Forever*. The story begins in the 1740s, when O'Connor, fresh off the boat from Ireland, saves an African slave from certain death. The slave turns out to be a shaman, who returns O'Connor's goodwill with the gift of immortality. There is, of course, one catch: O'Connor's life will last only as long as he stays on the isle of Manhattan. Thankfully, New York isn't such a dull place to spend an eternity. And as O'Connor experiences the city's tumultuous transformation from a little village to a towering metropolis, we get to come along for the ride.

As authors go, Hamill, a Brooklyn native and the son of Irish immigrants, is uniquely qualified to guide us through this story. A decorated general of NYC journalism, the sixty-seven-year-old author served briefly as the editor of both the *New York Post* (in 1993) and the *Daily News* (in 1997), where he remains a contributor. He's also written nine novels, including 1997's best-selling *Snow in August,* about the friendship of an Irish Catholic boy and a rabbi in working-class Brooklyn; four books of nonfiction, including a biography of painter Diego Rivera; two short-story collections; and the best-selling 1994 memoir *A*

Drinking Life, about his battles with the bottle, which came to an end on New Year's Day almost thirty years ago.

Before landing a job as a reporter at the *New York Post* in 1960, Hamill studied painting at Mexico City College and Pratt. He still splits his time between New York and Cuernavaca, Mexico, where he and his wife, the journalist Fukiko Aoki, rent a house. TONY caught up with Hamill at his local pad, a warmly lit Tribeca floor-through stocked with art books and a painting easel, to chat about *Forever.*

Time Out New York: Did you ever consider setting the book in any place other than New York?

Pete Hamill: It had to be Manhattan. If you had to live through more than 200 years in one place, it better be in a place that changes a lot. You start with the idea of wishing to live forever. What would you do? Read everything you ever wanted, learn different languages. . . . There's no end to it. With Manhattan, you'd want to know it block by block, understand the people that live on each block and why it is the way it is. Another thing I wanted to do was show how New York style and character were shaped, starting off with the African influence. I always think of this city as kind of an alloy, not a melting pot. I wrote somewhere, "Who the hell wants to be a fondue?" We're an alloy; we take all these metals and forge a character.

TONY: Brooklyn is so much a part of that character. Does it still hold allure for you as a subject?

PH: The Brooklyn I knew was the Brooklyn before television. That Brooklyn disappeared more or less when the Dodgers left. I don't have any memories of watching Sandy Koufax with the Dodgers. His great moments happened in L.A. And by then I was so pissed off [at the Dodgers] that I never watched baseball. I didn't go to another ball game till 1969.

TONY: You still hate the Yankees, though, right?

PH: There's still some residual adolescent part of me that can't stand the Yankees, but it's hard to dislike this group. It's hard to dislike Joe Torre. One thing I was fascinated with while covering the Subway Series is that the vehemence is gone. The fans still tease one another, but it's good-natured. It's not life or death. And now you've got all these people wandering around with Yankees caps who've never even heard of the Brooklyn Dodgers. The real mystery is whatever happened to the Giants fans? There's no nostalgia for the Giants. They just went away.

TONY: You must have been pretty deep into writing *Forever* on September 11. Did that change the process at all?

PH: On September 10, 2001, I finished the book. My plan for the next day was to go to Balthazar and celebrate. But then everything changed. It was nine straight days of work for the *Daily News*. There was no electricity for four or five days below Worth Street, so at night, walking home, it looked like the nineteenth century. It was kind of beautiful. On my first day off from the *News*, I told my book editor, "I need to write more." I couldn't have a New York novel that had the 1835 fire and the cholera and smallpox epidemics, and not include September 11. It wasn't too hard, though. I already had O'Connor living on Duane Street with his apartment looking out on the World Trade Center, where his girlfriend works. It's weird; I finished the book again on September 9.

TONY: Other than your love of the city, what was the initial inspiration for *Forever?*

PH: Part of the inspiration was a mural [called *Dream of a Sunday Afternoon in Alameda Park* in Mexico City] by Diego Rivera. In it, Rivera puts himself right in the middle, surrounded by heroes and villains, his aunts — everyone is in it. When I first saw it, I thought it was amazing how he simultaneously captured different times.

TONY: What's your fascination with Diego Rivera?

PH: I went to school in Mexico on the GI Bill in 1956. I was twenty-one. I didn't know Spanish, but I loved some of the Mexican painters. I was there when Diego died; there was a huge outpouring of eulogies. I didn't think much about him then, though. The late Diego was kind of cold — his hand was painting but not his guts. And the mural form itself had died; once movies came along, there was no need for it. But later, I saw some of his earlier work, and it was much better than I remembered. I decided to do a book. It was a way for me to write about Mexican artists and learn more. And I wanted to write about art in a relaxed way. Art writing doesn't have to be so filled with jargon.

TONY: What did you think of [the movie] *Frida?*

PH: It was better than I thought it would be. The guy who played Rivera, Alfred Molina, was great. He understood Diego — that he was a liar, a cheat.

TONY: I notice the easel. Do you still paint?

PH: Every once in a while. With *Forever,* I looked at a lot of artwork from different periods. I looked at the detail around people's eyes and asked myself, "What's happening there?" Then I hand-copied some of that artwork. When you draw it, it gets into your hands, and that helps you when you're writing fiction.

TONY: What's the longest stretch of time you've spent in Manhattan without leaving?

PH: I don't know. I've started working on a book about New York, and I made a list of all the places I've lived in Manhattan since 1957. There have been fourteen. I want to go back to each one and see what's happened since I left. But I've always been, for some reason, someone who also went away. I've lived in Barcelona, Mexico, Dublin. It's probably my version of a grand tour of education.

TONY: Do you think you'll ever move off Manhattan? Maybe try Brooklyn again?

PH: Probably when my plot is ready at the Green-Wood Cemetery.

The complete text of this interview with Pete Hamill was originally published in issue 378 of *Time Out New York,* dated December 26, 2002–January 2, 2003. Reprinted with permission.

Reading Group Questions and Topics for Discussion

1. Cormac O'Connor is given the opportunity of a lifetime — to live forever. Before he's actually granted immortality, Kongo insists that Cormac "must truly live," not "simply exist." Does Cormac fulfill this mandate? Given Cormac's experience, would *you* choose to live forever?

2. With Cormac's arrival in Manhattan, we see that ethnic diversity is a predominant feature in eighteenth-century New York. The city is a cultural meeting place for British colonists, African slaves, and Irish immigrants, to name a few groups. In what ways do these groups come into conflict with one another? In what ways do they live side by side harmoniously?

3. Cormac participates in some of the key events in the forging of the American republic. Yet after centuries in Manhattan, Cormac still does "not exactly think of himself as an American, but he was definitely a New Yorker" (page 404). What does he mean by that?

4. New York City is as much a character in the novel as any of the people Cormac meets, and he has the opportunity to see the city change through the centuries. How does New York grow alongside Cormac? What are your impressions of New York City after reading the book?

5. The relationship between Cormac O'Connor and Mary Morrigan begins in the summers when Cormac is learning the Celtic traditions. Describe this unique relationship. How does it color Cormac's future interactions with women?

6. When Cormac's mother is killed, Cormac's father begins to forge a sword. After his father's death, Cormac vows to seek revenge according to the Celtic code. What do you think of the acts of violence Cormac commits in the name of this vow? How do you account for the choice he makes when he meets the last of the Warren heirs? Is it possible to maintain honor while seeking vengeance?

7. Cormac and Kongo meet under horrific circumstances and initially have no common language. Yet they forge an unusually strong bond. What is the basis of their mutual understanding? What role does each play in the life of the other?

8. Over the years, many women pass through Cormac's life, yet he becomes emotionally involved with only a few. Who are the women Cormac loves? What impact does his relationship with each of them have on him?

9. Cormac comes in contact with people from many different religious backgrounds — from pagans and mystics to Jews, Catholics, and Protestants — throughout his epic journey. Describe the ways in which adherents of various faiths affect Cormac's life. How does religious belief in general influence his actions? Does his view of religion change over the course of the book?

10. After three centuries, Cormac finally faces the choice of entering the Otherworld and being reunited with his family or staying with Delfina and his unborn child. Do you think Cormac makes the right decision? Why? What decision would you have made in his place?

More bestselling fiction by Pete Hamill

Snow in August

A novel

"Wonderful. . . . This page-turner of a fable has universal appeal."
— *New York Times Book Review*

"A tender novel. . . . When it comes to evoking the sights and sounds of postwar Brooklyn streets Pete Hamill has no peer. . . . When you finish that roller-coaster last chapter you'll wonder if the shade of Isaac Bashevis Singer whispered in his ear."
— Frank McCourt, author of *Angela's Ashes*

"A beautiful tale of pain, evil, retribution, and hope."
— *Fort Worth Star-Telegram*

"Hamill delivers with his sharp prose. . . . You can hear the sounds of kids playing stickball, taste the Communion wafers, and see Jackie Robinson stealing home."
— *Associated Press*

"A great American novel. . . . Hamill blends fiction and fantasy to produce a masterpiece."
— *Winston-Salem Journal*

"Lovely yet heartbreaking. . . . A moving story of a boy confronting mortality. . . . In Michael Devlin, Hamill has created one of the most endearing characters in recent adult fiction. . . . *Snow in August* is a minor miracle in itself."
— *Hartford Courant*

Look for these other bestsellers by
Pete Hamill

A Drinking Life

"A remarkable memoir. . . . Energetic, compelling, very funny, and remarkably — indeed, often brutally — candid, Hamill's tale won't soon be forgotten." — *Entertainment Weekly*

"Magnificent. . . . *A Drinking Life* is about growing up and growing old, working and trying to work, within the culture of drink." — *Boston Globe*

"Tough-minded, brimming with energy, and unflinchingly honest." — *New York Times*

Why Sinatra Matters

"As succinct and laconically classy as its title." — *Seattle Times*

"The most intimate and thoughtful eulogy yet for 'the Voice.' . . . It leaves you wanting to listen again to Sinatra's best songs." — *Entertainment Weekly*

"A brief but eloquent homage. . . . Hamill succeeds — convincingly, with natty aplomb — in explaining why Sinatra, even now, matters." — *LA Weekly*